SHADOW RESISTANCE

A NOVEL

B.J. CYPRIAN

THE
FOLSE
GROUP

The Folse Group LLC
Fort Worth, TX
www.folsegroup.com

Printed in the United States of America

Cover design by Richard McQuillar
Inspired by Kymberli Gaillard
Book design by Caroline Petty

SHADOW
RESISTANCE

AUTHOR'S NOTE

When kids are young, they are often asked what they want to be when they grow up. While most in my age range wanted to be firemen, professional sports stars, nurses, doctors and the like, I would always answer, "I want to be a writer." I wish I could give a reasonable explanation for obtaining my B.S. in Business Management instead of English or Journalism. The only answer I have is that I didn't think I could really make a living with writing. I didn't think I was good enough. Each attempt I made in my twenties came to the same end. I abandoned the work and chastised myself for even trying. Nevertheless, while the confidence wasn't there, the desire to write never left me.

It wasn't until the 2016 election that a fire burned anew in my heart. Everything was getting so messed up after what was, for me, eight years of progress. In one fell swoop, the country I thought I knew changed. I looked at my wife a couple of days after the election and said, "I need to do something. I need to write." She readily encouraged me to follow the inclination, but then the voices of doubt crept back into my brain. *What if I'm not good enough? What if I can't finish again?* However, something was different this time. The murmurs of self-doubt have been a part of my psyche my whole life. This time another, somehow louder voice began to talk over the insecurities. *You have something to say, so say it.* That was lesson #1 on this journey. It's hard to sit down and write a novel unless you have something to say.

I grew concerned about how I would map the story out to the end. My writing process has always been sitting down and "letting the story take me where it takes me." I worried that this was the reason for my inability to finish a manuscript. I researched other writers' methods and found that some do outlines or storyboards for their works. I broke out a dry erase board and started making a weird map thing of characters, connectivity, blah blah

blah. It did not go well. It's just not who I am. This led me to lesson #2. I had to be true to myself and not try to mimic someone else.

Finally, I just sat down and wrote what I knew. I wrote about myself, my outlook, my friends, and my family. I had no idea where I was going until I got there. I won't lie, the journey was equal parts exciting, terrifying, confusing, frustrating, and exhausting. (What's that? 5 parts?) I thought I knew where my characters would take me, but there were times I had no idea how a chapter would play out until it was written. After I finished the initial draft, I was super excited to be done. I couldn't believe I actually completed one. Then I had to read through it and realized that…. I know like four words. Which brought me to lesson #3. Revising, proofing, streamlining and editing takes almost as long as writing the initial draft. (Some of that could be alleviated if one would use a thesaurus.) But here we are. This has been a long time coming and I'm still learning a lot of lessons. I would be remiss if I did not thank the people who have encouraged me, stood by me and kicked me in my ass when I needed it the most.

My first thank you is to my wife, Shauna. I would never have done this if you did not tell me that I could. The hardest part of finding the courage to try is getting past the fear of the possibility of failure. While you have made it clear you do not think that will happen; you have also convinced me that if I do fail, the sun will still rise, the Earth will still turn, and we will still have each other. Thank you for not only believing in me for you, but for adding a little extra faith to make up for my deficiency. Whether this turns into a new career, or whether this is just something I do to keep following my passion, I am forever grateful for you. Not only are you the love of my life, my cheerleader, and my safe place; you also happen to be my favorite audience. I will always hope to entertain you with my stories.

Everyone should have a village. Some, like me, were born into phenomenal villages. To my parents, Roger & Monica Cyprian and Brenda & Isaac Green thank you for the support, tough love, encouragement and contributions to every endeavor I have tried. You guys made me feel like I could do anything and I appreciate the patience and room you gave me to follow the path that got me where I needed to be on my own. To my grandmother, Carrie Cyprian, thank you for sitting up with me from the time I was young and indulging me in creating narratives. You continued to stoke the flames of passion for inventing new ways to tell stories. To my siblings, (Renee, Oliver, Nick, Sydney, Jordan and Alex) and to my other relatives and close friends, thank you for being such a great village. (And perhaps giving me some good source material to work with.)

To my best friend of over 20 years, Daniece Sutherland, my sista from another mista Dr. Denecia Spence, and the Queen of old school hip-hop, Adell Carins: thank you ladies so much for being my sounding board, my encouragement, my "amen" corner, and my major support system through this project. Gissa Johnson, thank you for taking random phrases and converting them into Spanish with little question or the slightest eyebrow raise. (In some ways, it confirms the small amount of insanity I always knew you possessed.) Eric Sears, thank you for not only being a dope brother-in-law, but for lending me your graphic design talents when I was going insane. Kymberli Gaillard, thank you for accepting a random Instagram DM and producing some awesome sketches without hesitation!

In every creative outlet I've ever pursued, I seem to cross paths with people who believe in my work and talent. I'm often baffled and in awe at the same time every time this happens. To my editor, Lisa Waschka, you have truly been a Godsend. You could have easily just edited the manuscript and walked away, but you chose to be an encouraging force and a believer in the work. You entertained every random question, negotiated every panic attack, and put up with every moment of uncertainty with patience and kindness. You are more than my editor, you have become my friend. Thank you. To Melinda Folse, thank you so much for taking a shot on a brand-new author solely on the word of a friend. I appreciate the chance more than you will ever know! Therese Adamiec, thank you for listening to me, and I know it's not just because it's your job, no matter how much I tease you.

A note to those who knew me in my twenties and read those unfinished manuscripts that left you wondering what happened to those characters; I'm sorry. Please accept this novel as an apology. I hope that within these pages you see someone you know, or perhaps someone you would like to know. I don't want this to only be entertaining, I want it to make you think. I know what I think my themes are, but every person who has read a version of this story has brought up other themes I did not realize were embedded within the manuscript. I hope these characters become like friends to you, as they have for me.

CHAPTER ONE

"It's time to wake up Dom," the voice said. Dominique Samuels, snug in her cocoon of black and red bedding, twitched and continued to snore softly. The room grew quiet as she found her way back into REM sleep.

"Dom, it's time to get up," the voice repeated after five minutes at an elevated volume. This time Dom groaned, yawned, and rolled over in the bed pulling her blanket tightly with her as she changed her sleeping position. The air conditioning automatically adjusted the environmental temperature while she slept, modifying the climate to compensate for the body heat she emitted. Since she ran warm on a consistent basis, the thermostat was set at 65. While this was comfortable during her deep sleep, she often awoke wrapped in her bedding like the filling of a burrito. With her new position just as agreeable as her previous position, Dom drifted off once again.

"Initiating back up procedure now," the voice said after an additional five minutes passed. Suddenly, the iconic Michael Jackson song, "Black or White," began blaring through the speakers of the in-home stereo system. A startled Dom jerked and thrashed under the covers before hastily sitting up in her bed. The intro guitar riff, beloved by Dom in her youth, was now an instrument of torture.

"Ok! I'm up!" She shouted towards the vaulted ceiling of her spacious bedroom. When she opened her eyes, she immediately regretted it. The blinding March morning sunlight streaming through the French doors in her bedroom caused her to hiss in pain. She closed her eyes. The music began to increase in volume.

"TERMINATE!" Dom bellowed, realizing she had not initially given the proper command. Magically, "Black or White" stopped as abruptly as it began. She rubbed her face with the palm of her hand and exhaled sharply, grateful for the instant silence.

"Good morning Dom," the silky British voice said, in an annoyingly cheerful manner.

"I hate you, SARA," Dom growled, punctuating the declaration with a loud yawn. She leaned back against her square cushioned headboard, attempting to orient herself. She reopened her eyes, slowly this time, to allow her retinas to acclimate to the brightness of the room.

"We both know that statement is inaccurate, as you are the person who created me," SARA countered. Dom could not argue the validity of the statement. SARA was a Specialized Analytical Robotic Assistant, or artificial intelligence system of Dom's own design. The moniker SARA was her way of anthropomorphizing the computer, yet SARA was also a mundane acronym used to describe her main function. The project had been a labor of love for Dom; yet in the mornings, she felt like creating SARA was the worst mistake of her life.

"Don't remind me. I'm tempted to erase your entire program," Dom growled. She leaned towards the nightstand on her left, picked up her glasses, and slid them onto her face before leaning back against her headboard and yawning once more.

"That is the 1,974th time you have said that to me since my creation 1,445 days ago," SARA reported.

"Aw, it's fifteen days until your fourth birthday. Should I order a cake?"

"I have no vessel to receive cake Dom," SARA chided. Dom found humor in the admonition given with a British lilt and a smile played across her lips.

"Duly noted my friend. What's on the calendar for the day?"

"You have a nine o'clock call with Blake Carter from SafeSecure, and today is Wednesday, which denotes your weekly coffee appointment," SARA reported. Dom stretched as SARA spoke, and her shoulders let out a small pop as she spread her arms. Turning her head side-to-side, she felt her neck deliver a couple of satisfying cracks. Glancing at the Garfield analog clock hanging on the wall, her thoughts floated to her mother, Bernice.

Dom had not been able to retain many of her mother's personal belongings after she died, and the inexpensive timepiece was a treasured keepsake. Although Dom fully embraced all things technology, the black and white analog clock remained a fixed ornament in every bedroom since she was twelve. When she looked at the clock, her mind conjured memories of Sunday mornings with her mother. An avid reader of the Fort Worth Star-Telegram, Bernice usually snagged the world and local news, and the lifestyle section on a daily basis. On Sundays, she would try to steal the funny pages from Dom, in an effort to read the latest color Garfield comic strip. Every Sunday, Dom would watch her mother giggle at the panels before passing the pages to her daughter. Bernice's love of Garfield motivated Dom to read Jim Davis' stories first as well. When Dom found the clock at a school book sale, she almost fought another girl in her class to purchase it for her mother's birthday. The clock followed the duo whenever they relocated, proudly displayed in the living area by Bernice. Dom shook off the memories to focus on the displayed time, which was a quarter after eight in the morning.

"I am going to skip coffee today," she informed SARA, sliding over to the edge of her king-sized bed. She clawed at the tangled bedding as she moved and finally touched her feet to the plush dark blue carpeting.

"It's a fixed appointment on your calendar," SARA reminded her. Dom stood and stretched to her full five foot seven inches. When she stretched, her knees also let out creaking sounds of protest. It seemed that after she turned thirty, all movements produced a symphony of disapproving percussive noises.

"I can still skip it."

"It is recommended that you maintain your appointment," SARA warned.

"I have coffee here, SARA."

"It is vital to your mental stability," SARA insisted.

"How would you know?" she asked, turning her eyes to the ceiling.

"Research has shown that individuals suffering from social anxiety may prohibit a steep decline in their mental state by forcing themselves into social situations," SARA reported, drawing an exaggerated eye roll from Dom.

"Here we go," she muttered, in an annoyed voice.

"Such a decline could result in disorders like agoraphobia, social phobias, or any number of general anxiety disorders. Ultimately, if you fail to continue your weekly jaunts from your home, your anxiety will increase to a state where management may become untenable."

"I'm cutting off your access to the internet," Dom snarled. She made her way across her bedroom into the connected bathroom, but there was no escaping SARA, who continued to speak through the bathroom speakers.

"That is the 3,219th time you have made that statement. However, as this has not yet occurred, statistically speaking, the plausibility of you following through with disconnecting me from the Internet is about 0.005%," the computer proclaimed.

"About? Since when do you deal in estimations?"

"While I could calculate the probability to an exact figure, I felt rounding was appropriate at this time," SARA replied. Although she was a complete virtual being, Dom sometimes heard a sarcastic tone in her hominoid voice.

Designed to be a learning AI, SARA often modified her internal programming as she encountered new situations and research. The autonomy Dom provided allowed SARA to develop her own sense of individuality that could have never been predetermined. Dom believed that the awe she experienced observing SARA evolve over the past four years was akin to a parent watching their child mature. Never knowing what SARA would say or do provided her with nuggets of amusing revelations in her otherwise sequestered life. Early in her life cycle, SARA grappled with a diagnosis for Dom, initially suggesting that she was on the autistic spectrum, before finally settling on social anxiety disorder or a social phobia. Dom continued to argue that she had no true mental disorder; instead, from an early age, she had a general dislike of people.

"There is nothing wrong with me, SARA. It's just that people suck," Dom had told the computer. SARA continued to identify some of the actions Dom had taken on a regular basis to avoid being outside of the confined comfort of her home, down to refusing to go grocery shopping. Dom countered that as long as she had a credit card and an Amazon account, there was no need for her to venture into the outside world. Internally, she resigned that if she truly did have some sort of social or anxiety disorder, she would embrace the fact. She believed that people who avoided others weren't crazy but rather had a survivalist nature. Nevertheless, to reduce SARA's nagging, Dom had agreed to a weekly outing at the local coffee shop to prove to the insufferable machine that she was not afraid to leave her home.

Before taking her glasses off to shower, Dom pressed a small button on the underside of the hinge that connected the right arm to the right lens. The illumination of the bathroom dimmed, and the glasses transitioned from transparent to the darker tint of sunglasses. Inside of this view, a loading screen appeared informing her that the glasses were connecting to her home network. Dom swiped the outside of the right eyeglass arm, which took on a secondary function of navigation and reviewed the network logs.

"You didn't mention the visitors from last night," she murmured.

"The intrusion attempts were under the system classification of 'cute,' which do not warrant mention prior to your morning cup of coffee," SARA replied. She chuckled at SARA's statement, aware that the comment stemmed from prior early morning verbal rants about intrusion attempts, often quelled with an infusion of caffeine.

"Anyone we know?"

"All three IP addresses were from the known list. No new intrusions were detected," SARA replied. She grunted and pressed the button on her hinge again, returning the glasses to their normal transparent form.

"I swear. I wish people would find some business and leave me alone," she grumbled, removing her glasses and placing them on the bathroom sink. She moved to the shower, turned on the water, and double-checked the display to ensure the temperature was at her preferred level before stepping into the shower.

Intrusion attempts on Dom's network were regular occurrences. The encryption she used, one of her own design, kept her system secure but also made for a tempting target. Most hackers were a curious lot who tried to enter other networks just to see if they could break the most sophisticated encryption. The complexity of her personal security would attract hackers ranging from novice to expert. SARA actively monitored every invasion attempt and changed the encryption after each effort, perpetually preventing the network from being breached. Dom was something of an urban legend in the hacker community. People were aware of her existence, but she took great pains to ensure that no one was ever able to pinpoint her location or contact her unless she desired discovery. She was very familiar with the Dark Web, capitalizing on the anonymity and access to high-quality gear for her projects, and other miscellaneous items she did not want to be traced back to her location. She was not interested in building a criminal empire, nor was she keen on being the next Steve Jobs. Instead, she persisted to be relatively unknown by the general population, both in the outside and virtual worlds. She spent time creating products such as SARA and her wireless network glasses, but the developments were for her own use. She was perfectly content with the rest of the world not knowing of her technological prowess.

For over twenty-five years, Dom found solace in the applied sciences. By the age of ten, she was able to build her own computers from discarded parts. After the death of her mother, Dom fully immersed herself into technology to fulfill her need for companionship and to deal with the grief. Her love of computers, along with her desire to go as far away from home as possible for college, led her to receive both her undergraduate and master's degrees from the Massachusetts Institute of Technology or MIT.

Upon graduation, Dom worked as a software engineer and designer for a little over a decade while also continuously developing products on her own time. One of her earlier developments had been a market-timing program, which used fundamental and technical financial indicators, and information pulled from news cycles to predict stock market movements. She tweaked and modified the program for months until the bugs were eliminated. Once the program was fully functional, Dom considered auctioning the software to domestic and global brokerage firms, investment banks, and hedge funds. Ultimately, the notion of dealing with the piranhas of the corporate realm fatigued her. For this reason, along with personal issues, she used the software to buy herself an early retirement. Since developing the program, Dom had grown a domestic and international portfolio of investments worth hundreds of millions of dollars in various currencies, quickly and efficiently.

Realizing that she no longer had to work for money, she resigned from her job and began work on the project she fantasized about since childhood — the system now known as SARA. The few friends she had acquired over the years had begun to worry about her, fearing she was becoming a recluse. Dom initially waved off their concerns, citing the work on her personal projects as a reason for her seclusion. When SARA was finally completed, she noticed that her isolated lifestyle had become far more preferable to the tedium of socialization, and she rode off into the metaphorical sunset.

While she did not need the money, she began accepting consulting projects for a small group of software companies who paid her to review new developments and updates to check for any weaknesses within the code. These companies were generally cyber-security firms who would pay a premium to ensure that their product was the best on the market, withstanding the constant evolution of the criminal ilk that preferred keyboards to artillery. The small network consisted of individuals Dom had encountered during her tenure as an engineer in the workforce. Blake Carter was among this small group of people who knew Dom and her skill set, trusting both her work and her word. When Blake moved to SafeSecure, he began to contract her to ensure that the security of the company's software code was solid. These consultations were a distraction from her daily, monotonous solitude.

After her shower, she towel dried and stood in front of the large triple paned mirror, examining herself in the nude. She turned sideways and scowled, dismayed to find that the slight paunch she had developed during the early days of her retirement and withdrawal had not fully disappeared, despite her workout regimen. The routine was not strict, but Dom believed she had been engaged in the exercise schedule long enough to show some progress. She sucked in her stomach for effect, before exhaling and relaxing once again. Leaning closer to the mirror, she scrutinized her face, searching for any stray hairs that may have sprouted over the past few days. At thirty-eight years of age, she appeared at least twelve years younger due to her flawless milk chocolate complexion and round baby face. To her horror, the genetics of her mother kicked in just after her thirtieth birthday, and she began to find coarse black hairs sprouting randomly from her chin. While she no longer had a reason to groom herself for the attention of others, she still conducted the periodic inspections for her own benefit. She worried that one morning she would wake up to find herself staring at a goat in the mirror, rather than a smooth-faced woman. The changes in her body made her miss her mother, as it brought to mind the times Bernice also conducted these examinations while a young Dom looked on in wonder.

She picked up the cocoa butter lotion from the sink and began to apply a liberal amount to her skin, massaging the creamy moisturizer all over her body. When she approached her scar, the movement of her fingers unconsciously slowed to a stop. Just under her left collarbone and above her left breast, a small circular wound rested in the middle of a spider web of scar tissue — the one blemish on her otherwise even skin tone. She turned her back to the mirror and craned her neck around to see the twin mark on her upper back, gently tracing this mutilation with her fingers. Her mind raced back over twenty-five years to the worst night of her life. She shook her head violently as if the motion would erase the memory like an Etch-a-Sketch, and continued applying the lotion. Next, she unwrapped the scarf that held her dreadlocks in place and shook them out, allowing them to fall freely down her back. She plucked a spray bottle off the counter that contained a mixture of essential oils and water. She began to spray the moisturizer liberally on her hair, before using a few of her dreadlocks to tie a makeshift ponytail. Still nude, Dom exited the bathroom and streaked across her bedroom to her mahogany armoire. Her daily outfits were usually comprised of t-shirts and sweats. On days like this, she tried to put a little effort into her wardrobe because she had a videoconference meeting. Pulling on a teal polo shirt and khaki cargo shorts, she still bypassed her regular shoes in favor of plush house shoes.

Dom exited her master suite and padded next door to one of the three spare bedrooms in the same wing of the house, which she dubbed her "pet room." Inside three of the four walls, three-foot recesses provided room for a connected aquarium. Tangs, angelfish, butterfly fish, and an assortment of other species native to a coral reef environment swam around the climate-controlled waters. Twice a month an expert came to the house to maintain the tanks, ensuring the temperature and atmosphere remained authentic. An intrinsic purification system rested behind the walls leading to a separate plumbing system of the nearly eight thousand square foot house. The illumination within the aquarium was dim, to give the fish a feeling of being at home. When Dom stepped into the chamber, the light fixtures automatically irradiated the room in a soft blue tinted light. She wanted the lighting to make her feel like she too was under the sea, sharing the habitat of the ocean along with the room's inhabitants. Two black leather recliners were positioned on each end of the otherwise empty room, allowing her to relax and watch her fish from different angles. Moving into the middle of the room in between these two chairs, Dom examined her fish to ensure they all made it through the night. The change in the room lighting caused the fish to swim in a startled manner as if caught in the middle of a conspiracy.

"Morning all." Dom addressed her pets. "How was your evening? Throw any parties while I slept last night? I'm looking at you, Nemo." She pointed to the large orange and white clownfish swimming in the middle of the northern tank. The aquarium had several clownfish, but she had dubbed the largest one "Nemo" after the fish in the Disney movie. Nemo stopped his frenzied swimming and floated to the glass to greet Dom. She put her hand on the glass and Nemo swam to her palm, inspecting it with moderate interest. After a few moments, she lost Nemo's attention, and he swam away to join a group of tangs in the western wall.

"Dom, I can assure you that no species of exotic fish are capable of throwing a gathering of any kind," SARA said to her. Like every room of the house, speakers were embedded in the ceiling, giving SARA access to Dom anywhere she went within the dwelling.

"You can't just let me have my dream, can you?" asked Dom. She relocated to the eastern wall and began to walk in an inverted U pattern to inspect each section of the aquarium.

"If you are dreaming of fish revelry, perhaps it is time we revisit my recommendation to call a therapist," SARA mused.

"Killjoy," Dom muttered. She checked the food supply on the western wall to ensure that the automated feeder was still functional and would provide the fish nourishment on the routine schedule.

Dom often sat in this shadowy room, cocktail in hand, watching the fish bustle around the tanks. Many people did not understand the fascination with these creatures, but she felt that fish had a particular freedom most people did not comprehend. Although they lived in a tank a fraction of their genuine biosphere, the fish had no awareness of this fact. To these sea dwellers, the chamber was the extent of their world, and they were perfectly satisfied and content in their confined universe. The dwelling provided a safe harbor from the danger and knowledge of the savage predators that would normally be a concern in the deep blue sea. They had food, shelter, love, and they were safe from the harm of nature.

Dom frequently longed to remain in the controlled atmosphere of her own metaphorical aquarium, her home. Some people, particularly psychological websites researched by SARA, believed that such a lifestyle was too restricting and unhealthy for a human. Nevertheless, the predictability and security of her isolated environment made sense to her. Unlike her fish, she was all too aware of the dangerous and evil predators in the world outside of her fortress. She had witnessed such atrocities with her own eyes and lived with the effects of the exposure daily. She sometimes wished for an unseen caregiver, who could drop her into her own little corner of the universe. Her market-timing software had given her the finances to create a semblance of the lifestyle she provided for her fish. The power of the Internet allowed her to obtain any tangible essentials with the click of a mouse and a credit card, and SARA fulfilled her need for companionship.

Once she was satisfied that the fish were alive and well and would remain fed for the near future, Dom made her way downstairs. She entered her large kitchen, an area straight out of her wettest culinary dreams. The open kitchen featured a stainless steel six top gas range, with two ovens and a food warmer. Several appliances had their own place on gray granite countertops that circled the perimeter of the room, with a sizable wooden cutting board stationed on the island in the middle. She took a moment to admire the first of her two sanctuaries. Despite the lack of money during her childhood, Dom and her mother had a monthly tradition of taking a trip to the grocery store and picking out one item that Dom had never tasted before. The ritual dictated that upon selection the two would return home, research the ingredient and its uses, and prepare a meal that featured the newly acquired element. This sparked in Dom a love of food, cooking, and creating new dishes, which blossomed as she matured. The more she began to withdraw from the outside world, the more time she spent with her computer projects and food. She wondered where she would be had her mother not been taken away from her so early in life. She felt forced to throw herself into the world of technology to maintain some silhouette of sanity. Given the opportunity, she would have likely opted to pursue the culinary sciences rather than the applied sciences.

Before retirement, Dom began to feel overwhelmed by the constant interactions and neediness of people. To combat this, she would retreat into her kitchen and cook to calm herself. When her emotions began to spin out of control, the chopping, sautéing, broiling and seasoning of food helped her feel like she had power over something. This activity gave her a respite from the turmoil within her mind. She thought she was a good chef, but she had no other person in her life that could attest to this self-proclaimed quality. At times, she would attempt to describe the various flavors and textures to SARA but found it difficult to communicate culinary attributes to an entity with no palate. After making a single cup of Columbian dark roast coffee, with sweet cream, sugar, and a dash of cinnamon, she stole a glance at the clock on the microwave and saw it was almost time for her meeting. She crossed her expansive kitchen, traversed through the outer hall of the living room and through the foyer, and headed for the other side of the expansive home: The Playroom.

This section of the estate originally held two bedrooms, an office, and a bathroom; the latter stationed opposite of the three rooms. While the bathroom remained in place, Dom had solicited the services of a contractor who knocked down the walls separating the other three chambers to create one enormous suite. Although all three entry points were still in their original places, each door opened into a different section of the same sizable area. The first door gave access to the building section. Gathered here were two massive stainless-steel worktables littered with wires, mother-boards, chips and other building equipment for the construction aspect of her specialty. Dom preferred to build her own tech equipment, and this space provided her the room to produce just about any undertaking she could conceive. Three magnifying work lamps positioned strategically on the worktables permitted her flexibility to construct several components at one time. The middle door opened to the security area. Having a history that taught her vigilance, she maintained closed-circuit security cameras both inside and around the perimeter of the considerable house and the two-acre plot. Ten thirty-two-inch flat screen televisions mounted on the wall, stacked in two rows of five, allowed Dom to monitor her surroundings in real-time. The final door opened to the office space. Four desktop monitors, stacked two by two, sat on the large U-shaped walnut executive desk. Each drawer of the desk displayed labels with its contents — from flash drives to external hard drives. Twin matching six-drawer filing cabinets stationed in the corner of this region housed Dom's personal files that she did not keep on her main server. A secondary computer tower sat next to her desk, also not linked to her home network.

Dom entered the large room through the middle door and grabbed her plush leather office chair, in front of the security screens. Rolling the seat over to her desk, she plopped herself into the seat and tapped the computer mouse, causing the four monitors to come alive with the action. As she did this, the videoconference program began to chime, alerting Dom that Blake Carter was calling. She accepted the call and smiled into the mounted webcam affixed to the top of the four screens.

"You, my friend, are three minutes late," she answered. Blake Carter, CIO or Chief Information Officer of SafeSecure, grinned into his camera when Dom answered. She spied the Rocky Mountain peaks of Denver through the large office window behind him. Being an outdoorsy type, Blake had a perpetual tan on his face, excluding his eyes, which clearly showed the outline of the sunglasses he often wore during his rugged activities.

"Ms. Samuels! So nice to see you again," Blake exclaimed, slicking his hand over his shoulder-length blonde hair, currently tied up into a small bun.

"What have I told you about calling me that? I'm literally three months older than you are; and a man-bun Blake? Really?" she grinned, moving the call screen to the upper right quadrant of the four monitors. In the lower left screen, she opened the file containing the SafeSecure project. Blake blushed.

"Hey, don't start on me about my hair. I get it enough from Vanessa," he complained, referring to his fiancée. Dom snickered, clicking around her screen to set up the information she needed to relay.

"How's she doing anyway?" She met Vanessa a few years previously when she visited Denver to meet the CEO of SafeSecure. It was a trip she did not want to take but had been a condition of her employment as a contractor for the cyber-security firm.

"She's great. She told me to tell you hello. You really left an impression on her," Blake commented with a grin. "If you weren't in Houston, I'd worry."

"Nothing to worry about my friend," she chortled.

"So, how's my code?" Blake asked, getting down to the purpose of the call. She noticed that his eyes were dancing elsewhere on his screen. Blake's role had him constantly in meetings and on the move, so the rare periods in his office required multi-tasking.

"As usual, it's not bad," she replied while scrolling down the information in front of her, searching for an area she highlighted during her review. "There's just one thing. You have a problem."

"Uh-huh," he said distractedly. Dom rolled her eyes.

"Blake, focus! This is serious. You have a problem," she repeated. His blue eyes lost the preoccupied look.

"What's happening Dom?"

"Simon was the lead on this update code, yes? I can always tell his style," she said. Just like producers of the written word, code writers often developed a specific signature style to their code writing. The subtle nuances were to code writing as syntax and tone were to journalistic compositions. Normally the lead writer would also be responsible for any updates, given the fact that they would know the program better than anyone else would. Dom could see Simon plainly in both the update code and original source programming.

"Yeah, Simon headed up the update. Why? What's up?"

"Who helped him?" she inquired. Blake's eyebrows wrinkled in confusion, and she could see he was trying to understand the reason for the question.

"What?"

"Someone is new, Blake. Who is it?" Dom asked again. Her voice took on a severe tone.

"A new recruit named Matt Michaels, why?" Blake answered, shifting in his seat nervously.

"What's his social?" she asked, calling up a program in another area of the computer display.

"Excuse me?" Blake's attempt to understand the reason for Dom's questioning had frozen his features in a perpetual state of disorientation.

"His social security number, Blake," she emphasized slowly, in a frustrated voice. "Don't make me hack in to find it; I asked for this meeting out of respect so I wouldn't have to do that." He sighed and started to type on his own keyboard, rattling off the number after locating the employee file. Dom parroted the number back to him while she typed. "Hang on, Blake."

She muted her microphone as she waited for SARA to feed her the information she sought. Dom was protective of not just her own anonymity but of SARA as well. She strove to ensure that SARA remained an unknown factor to her small circle of colleagues. The fear was that if discovered there would be an immense amount of pressure for her to sell the basics of SARA's program to the highest bidder. The reason SARA was so special was that she was unique, and Dom wanted to ensure she remained that way. Blake began to type on his own computer, and Dom knew he was trying to use this time to get in some other tasks. After a few minutes the screen on her lower right, previously unfilled, began to populate with information.

"Matthew Eugene Michaels, born November 19th, 1988. Father: Larry Michaels, Occupation..." SARA began her report.

"Don't give me the biography; talk to me about his digital footprint," she hissed, quickly turning her head from the camera. SARA performed her search using an exclusive program Dom designed. The software leveraged public records, private and personal records, such as credit reports, vital statistic information, and law enforcement records. All of these inquiries cross-referenced with the searchable data within the Dark Web. As a logic-based system, SARA would then attempt to recognize patterns to ascertain if an individual also had a presence within the hacker community or was associated with any illegal activity. While a single person could run the search, it would take hours or days, depending on the skill level of the subject of the investigation. SARA could perform the task in a matter of minutes. As Dom began to filter through the information compiled on Mr. Matthew Michaels, SARA spoke again.

"It appears Mr. Michaels is tied to several IP addresses. One of which is linked to hacker "Phant0mMenace" who has outstanding warrants with the FBI for cyber-theft." SARA announced.

"Thank you, SARA." She unmuted the microphone and addressed the waiting Blake Carter. "I'm sending you a file, Blake. Mr. Michaels has been a naughty boy. The FBI has flagged his Dark Web identity," she informed him. Blake's face registered astonishment.

"What? How do you know? What did you find?"

"He set up a pretty slick backdoor to this update within the authentication. I know that wasn't even part of the update, but you know I always review everything. I found it and closed it for you. I'm going to send you the original file with the backdoor highlighted and the corrected code. I'll also include some information about the various IP addresses I found that will help the FBI," she reported.

"Holy shit," Blake uttered, unable to manage another response.

"I'm just glad I found it before it was released. Let's face it, how many times do we do updates without reviewing the source code?" Blake shook his head slowly, acknowledging that the event rarely happened.

"I can't believe this," he groaned, typing rapidly on his computer. "I just terminated his access, and I'll get security up there with me to escort him out of the building."

"Just be careful about dropping the FBI information on him. You don't want him to disappear before you can get with the Feds. Otherwise, he'll just go to another firm who doesn't use me and do the same thing," she warned.

"I'd say it was good to talk to you but..." he smirked.

"Better I find it than you have a PR nightmare on your hands," she reminded him. His features transformed into a genuine look of appreciation.

"You should come up here and visit more often," he suggested.

"You know I don't like to leave the house. Plus, it's cold in Denver."

"Your deposit will be made with payroll on Friday," he said.

"Thank you, my friend. You most likely saved my ass today." Dom flashed him a thumbs up sign before disconnecting the call.

Dom leaned back in her chair and studied the piece of code Michaels snuck into the update. A few lines were added to the authentication, permitting backdoor access into the system. Once the system was authenticated, a second entry point would be created, allowing anyone who knew its location access into the system. She copied and pasted the offending lines into a separate file she maintained of interesting code that could be of use in the future.

"Dom, I must point out that this code allows unauthorized access to a third party. It would not be advisable to use such an authentication within my programming," SARA declared, breaking her concentration.

"I wouldn't think of it."

"That is good to know. If I had the ability to show emotion, that would probably make me angry," SARA advised, prompting a bark of laughter from the woman. The computer was quiet for a brief time, and then she spoke again, "We have a visitor — another in the 'cute' classification."

Dom almost ignored the intrusion attempt, but then decided she would look into the violation real time. She clicked around the computer and brought up her server to view the infringement attempt. Those classified as "cute" were generally unskilled novices that used brute force in their attempt to access her servers, looking for obvious entry points that anyone with a decent firewall would have sealed. In her mind, she pictured a child attempting to fit a round peg into a square hole repeatedly, all the while expecting a different result with each attempt. Such a visualization struck her as cute, and therefore, not a true threat. SARA flagged the "cute" attempts by the methods used, traced the IP addresses to their source, and cataloged them for reference. She took no other steps knowing that such a novice would never be able to access her network.

"Let's have some fun," she mumbled. She tapped on her keyboard, and in an astonishingly short time, was able to identify the intruder. Hackers across all levels would generally attempt to route their IP location through other sources. She was surprised to find that this particular intruder came from one location, right in the city of Houston.

"This IP address does not appear on any of the previous logs," SARA informed her.

"Well, that's just not smart. This should be interesting," she mumbled. She typed rapidly again and accessed the user's webcam with ease, confirming the ineptitude of the hacker. When the image of the trespasser appeared, she was surprised to see it was a young Black boy.

Hunched over his keyboard, tongue protruding from the side of his mouth, and dark brown eyes furrowed in concentration, he typed fervently. From the angle of the camera, she could tell that the young man was sitting on a floor, using a laptop. He was dark-skinned, wearing large round eyeglasses and a Flash t-shirt. Dom estimated the child's age to be between ten and twelve years old. She typed in a command, and the screen adjacent to the boy's image flashed a mirror image of the child's display. She watched him type various commands hoping to find the magic directive that would grant passage into her world. This vision took her back to her childhood when she was enthralled in the exploration of any structure that granted her entry. After a few moments, she tapped on her keyboard, causing the child's screen to go blank. She chuckled when the boy's face registered expectant surprise at this development. Dom knew the boy thought he had found the magic command. She began typing with the knowledge that her message would simultaneously appear on the kid's screen.

You will never crack the firewall, but you did manage to leave yourself open for others to get into yours, her message read. The child looked around his room nervously and returned his astonished gaze to the screen. Dom entered another few strokes and opened his microphone line.

You can talk or type, your choice. Who are you? As he read this next message, his eyes grew wide. He hesitantly began to respond.

How are you doing this? he asked.

Unlike you, I know what I'm doing, she responded, before repeating her initial query. *Who are you?*

Nobody, he answered. She leaned closer to the screen, examining the child's demeanor. She observed a familiar sadness in his dark brown eyes.

Nice to meet you, Nobody. Why are you not in school? she asked.

How do you know I'm not?

Your school is in a bedroom? The kid's eyebrows furrowed when he read this question.

You can see me? His eyes were wide with surprise and fear.

I can see you. Don't panic. Luckily for you, I'm a friend, not foe. The boy still did not relinquish the veil of fear as he nervously scanned his surroundings as if Dom would crash through his window at any moment.

"How are you doing this?" The child wondered audibly.

I told you. I know what I'm doing. When he read this proclamation, a gasp escaped him.

"You can hear me?"

I said you could type or talk; it was your choice. Obviously, I can hear you. His reaction caused a grin to spread across her face. His expression was a reproduction of the innocent wonder she also experienced as a child upon realizing the extent of what could be accomplished with a simple Internet connection.

"How are you doing this?" he asked wistfully.

Years of practice. You're a newbie. Why are you trying to hack random networks? she demanded.

"I was trying out some stuff I found online," he answered.

You should be careful doing stuff like that. There are more bad people than good on the other side of any given computer. I just showed you how easily and quickly someone could turn things around on you. If you're not careful, you could stumble into a dangerous position, she replied.

"Could you teach me?" he asked, with hope in his voice. Dom was taken aback by the request for help.

Why would I do something that could get you killed? The boy shrugged his shoulders glumly.

"You could teach me stuff that won't. I don't have no one else to ask," he said in a pleading tone.

What about your parents?

"My dad works a lot. He never has any time. My mom," he hesitated, briefly unable to answer. "My mom died about a year ago." Even before he informed her of this, Dom had deduced the fate of his mother. The sadness she observed in the boy's eyes was entirely too familiar. There was no hotkey for grief. It could not be deleted or moved to the trash as simply as a file. If it were that easy, she would have used such a shortcut to reformat her own emotions and erase the pain that she carried on a daily basis.

I'm sorry, she typed quickly, a lump of sadness collecting in her throat. The emotions she consistently tried to keep at bay threatened to erupt.

"I'd really like to learn this kind of stuff. I want to create things and understand code. Maybe I could develop something to make us some extra money. We don't have a lot of money. The doctor bills," his voice broke and trailed off as he attempted to plead his case. Dom sat back in her chair and drummed her fingers on the desk while she considered her options.

On the one hand, she had no desire to obligate herself to interact with another person on a semi-regular basis — adult *or* child. However, she was also of the opinion that it would be coldhearted to turn her back on a grieving child reaching out in an attempt to find solace. She knew the pain he felt all too well and was aware that without a proper outlet, the grief could be enough to destroy his spirit. Black boys his age already had enough spirit-crushing circumstances in the world, solely because of their skin color. She also knew that if she had someone who understood her pain as a child, instead of her father who lacked the ability to be compassionate, her life would have played out differently. This opinion pushed her into making a decision, and she began tapping on her keyboard once more.

I'll make you a deal. If you promise to stop trying to access foreign networks — that includes my own — I will send you a few coding puzzles. Let's see if you can work them out. Understand, I will not be teaching you how to tap into the networks of people who didn't invite you. You're too young for that. How old are you anyway?

"Thirteen," the child responded.

You're a midget for thirteen.

"Gee thanks; like I don't get that enough in real life," he mumbled miserably.

It'll be a blessing in 30 years, kid. Do we have a deal? He contemplated briefly and then grinned.

"Deal!" SARA presented Dom with the registration data of the laptop he was using, which included the email address and home address. SARA also brought up the real property records, indicating that the home belonged to William Price. Further searches revealed that Mr. Price was a widower with one child, William Price, Jr.

Do you prefer Billy, Willie or William? Dom typed after quickly perusing the information. The kid jerked in surprise when he reviewed the message.

"I never told you my name!" he exclaimed.

Yet I have it. All the more reason to be careful online. Which do you prefer?

"Willie," he replied after a pause.

I will email you a few files. Rule number one: before opening anything, scan them first, she typed. She opened a folder of basic coding puzzles she wrote for beginners and dropped them into an email. Throwing on a basic encryption, she sent the file to the email from the laptop registration.

"How will I get in touch with you? Like when I'm done," Willie asked.

I'll know when you're done, she replied. He smiled broadly at this, apparently happy to be receiving her assistance. *Gotta fly.*

"Wait, what's your name?" Willie urgently called out to her. Dom thought quickly for a pseudonym. Behind Willie pinned on his wall, She noticed a couple of posters; one was for The Flash and the other was for The Green Arrow. Both of these were popular DC Comic Book characters.

You can call me Smoak, she replied. Willie's grin widened when he saw this.

"Like Felicity Smoak?" He asked. Felicity Smoak was a notorious hacker in the DC Comic Book world.

I'm better, she decreed. Willie giggled at this declaration. She was surprised to find the sound of his laugh lifted her heart. *Remember, no more hacking random networks,* she reminded him before relinquishing her control on his computer. Willie noticed the screen change and nodded solemnly. Before completely extracting herself from his network, Dom dropped in harmless spyware of her own design that would allow her to monitor the actions of the child. Soon, Willie's face disappeared and she was completely out of his system.

While her initial feelings towards Willie's request was strong and negative, she began to realize that much like everyday life, young people could easily find malevolent activities online that would supply as much or more pressure than any street gang. Dom stared blankly at the screen as she contemplated how much had changed since she discovered the wonders of technology. The Internet was now a cesspool comprised of bullies, criminals, and the insane. These people regularly outnumbered those benevolent in their intent. Criminal minds behind many screens could put as much pressure on an unblemished child as any street gang and were indiscriminate in their destruction. Without the proper guidance, a child could be caught in their trap and have irreparable damage done to their hearts and souls. She knew she was lucky that she did not find herself on that perilous path. When she considered young Willie Price with this lens, her attitude changed. Rather than an outlook of hardship, she recognized the opportunity was an affirmation of her own survival, and a testament to her mother's ingrained influence in her life. Any time she felt the presence of her mother's guidance, she knew she had made the right decision.

"Exercise hour," SARA announced.

"I don't want to," Dom grumbled.

"Exercise is important to both your mental and physical well-being, Dom. Since you consistently refuse to leave the house on a regular basis, it is also a good way to stave off various heart diseases and high blood pressure that can occur from sedentary living," the computer lectured as if she were reading a report.

"You know, if I wanted a wife, I would go find one."

"To find a wife, you would have to leave the house," SARA countered. Dom opened her mouth to respond but found no words would emerge. She sighed heavily and departed her office on route to her five-car garage towards the back of the home, where her home gym was set up. The hour-long workout would be far less painful than trying to navigate yet another dispute with SARA.

CHAPTER TWO

After an intense workout, Dom prepared breakfast while engaged in yet another battle of wills with SARA regarding the notion of leaving her refuge to make the three-block journey to the local coffee house. Her efforts to rationalize and cajole the stubborn machine proved to be unproductive and exhausting. Each argument she posed was countered with some research paper SARA found. It did not seem fair that the creation could best the master solely due to the former maintaining a consistent connection to every psychological paper ever posted online. Coupled with SARA's processing speed that allowed the information almost instantaneous delivery, Dom couldn't win.

"You know, if I had a photographic memory, this would be an even battle," she snarled after SARA cited yet another paper from some Harvard-educated psychologist.

"It would seem that someone of your intelligence would have considered that fact before the inclusion of autonomy in my programming. Also, the more accurate terminology is an eidetic memory," SARA offered.

Dom sighed heavily and took a gulp of her juice to bite back an emotional outburst of frustration. She knew that SARA did not intend to be challenging, but rather used the logic-based function to derive simplified solutions to situations presented. SARA's logic and research guided the machine to conclude Dom suffered from some crippling form of phobia or anxiety. Logically, the easiest and most plausible remedy was immersion therapy. SARA functioned with a black and white perception, and while Dom recognized some traits that made her believe SARA could ultimately see the shades of gray, the quality had not quite integrated itself into the framework. From the perspective of SARA, even if Dom stood her ground firmly, the program would continue to present arguments finding her refusals as illogical and therefore wrong. There would be no escape from the constant lectures, short of forcing SARA to go into standby mode, which she did not like to do unless completely necessary.

Finally, Dom was able to prevail using the one trick that SARA could not fully identify at face value: bribery. She began construction on an android husk within the previous year to give SARA a physical body. The proprietary nature of the computer required a completely original design. This project called upon all of Dom's unique knowledge of engineering and robotics, as well as aspects of each field that she knew nothing about. SARA had proven to be invaluable to the undertaking, given her ability to dive continuously into all areas of the web to locate schematics, parts, and studies. To Dom's alarm, some of the research SARA sourced came from federal government and military servers. Despite the computer's assurance about the eradication of all remnants of intrusion — as if Dom herself had accessed the files — she had a brief period of paranoia, expecting men in black to break down her door. When they did not come, she relaxed and began creating a blueprint for the assembly. The program had also begun purchasing parts for the enterprise without Dom's knowledge, causing her to have to put special authorizations on purchases over a certain amount. She wanted to be angry, but SARA had begun showing a primitive form of excitement that caused her to believe an emotional matrix could possibly form within the system. Dom was able to win the coffee debate by suggesting she spend the rest of the unoccupied day making progress on the android construction. With the deal finally struck, she was allowed to eat her meal in peace.

While Dom shunned having a corporeal presence in the outside world, she remained apprised on local, national, and world news. As she dined on her brunch, and once SARA provided her a respite, she perused news sites in an attempt to catch up on the events of the day. This task was required at least twice daily given the brevity of the news cycle. The prevalent story was regarding a police shooting of an unarmed citizen in Milwaukee, Wisconsin. Many of the numerous accounts included videos of the event posted on social media sites. She felt a sense of outrage and frustration as she read the details. After reviewing four articles relaying the incident, she put the information aside and concentrated on her meal. When she finished, she moved to her work area and began the undertaking she promised a very pushy SARA.

Dom's music collection ran the gamut of styles and genres having no discernable correlation. When she worked, she chose music based on the state of her emotions rather than her energy or the task. She found this method of music selection allowed her to concentrate intensely on any intricate chore by occupying another more emotional portion of her brain, which seemed to cause her to lose focus unless otherwise engaged. Settling into beginning her work, she requested a specific hip-hop list that echoed the lingering emotions from the news articles. With her angry mind having its "amen corner," Dom was able to fully focus on her work.

"Dom, you have a phone call," SARA announced, reducing the volume of the music. She had been bobbing her head to the tune and looked to the ceiling when the sound decreased. Waving a small plume of smoke that billowed up from her soldering, she leaned back from her hunched position.

"Take a message," she replied, waving more smoke away from her face. She briefly blew on the warm fused segment of the robotic arm, scrutinizing the quality.

"I tried. He is quite insistent on speaking with you," SARA answered. She briefly wondered if it was her father.

"Who is it?" she inquired.

"I do not know. I attempted to reverse trace the call, but the signal appears to be bouncing around several different locations worldwide. Given this, I felt it only reasonable to inform you," SARA responded. Her confusion deepened. A caller who would go through the trouble of hiding their origin signal would definitely not be her father. The man barely knew how to operate a microwave.

"Well, if he insists on going through that much trouble, I suppose I should answer," she said, standing from her stool, and traversing the room to her desk. "Patch it through to the computer." She took her position in the leather office chair.

"Dominique Samuels?" The pleasant voice had the medium timbre of an old school R&B singer, and Dom realized she did not recognize it.

"I don't know you," she declared suspiciously. "Who is this?"

"You can call me Nat," the caller responded. The man's voice did not sound like it belonged to a Nat; perhaps a Nathaniel or a Nathan, but definitely not a Nat.

"Okay, Nat. How did you get this number?" she demanded, opening a command screen to SARA she typed: *Keep trying to trace it.*

"How is of no importance. You of all people know the information that can be found if you know where to look," he insisted. His knowing tone immediately made the hairs on the back of her neck stand on edge.

"How is pretty damn important to me," she shot back. "I take rather extravagant precautions."

"That you do, which is why I need to speak with you."

"You have my attention; what do you want?"

"To meet you," the stranger revealed.

"I'm not really the meetup type — particularly with strangers who seem to know a hell of a lot more about me than I know about them."

"I'm not giving you much choice, Miss Samuels," Nat replied. Movement on another screen caught her attention. A triggered security alert notified her that someone was on the premises. Dom leaped from her seat and rushed over to the wall of security feeds just in time to see a black Lincoln MKX driving slowly into her circular driveway. She gaped at the scene, her heart racing with panic and disbelief. The paralysis did not last, and she moved to the closet located next to the displays. She flung opened the door, quickly retrieved a compact nine-millimeter pistol, and slipped the weapon into a pocket of her cargo shorts.

"You don't waste time, I see."

"Would you rather I have just knocked without warning?" he asked. Dom moved back to the computer.

"I wouldn't have answered if you had."

"Which is why I called," he retorted.

"You aren't in here yet; how do you know I'll answer now?" she challenged.

"You'll answer," he asserted confidently and disconnected the call.

"SARA, did you find out anything? I mean, we know where he is obviously, but did you get a read on anything else?" The doorbell rang as she spoke.

"No. He appears to be using a signal scrambler. I am blind to him," SARA reported. Dom stood motionless in the middle of the room trying to think, her brain analyzing different scenarios and outcomes. In her frozen contemplating, she vaguely heard the doorbell ring for the second time.

"Shit," she muttered. "You know the drill, no audible communication."

For a moment, she considered not opening the door. She had no idea who this man was, and no true desire to find out. When she contemplated the boldness of not only his call but also showing up unannounced and uninvited, combined with the technology he used to mask his signal, her curiosity was piqued. While she generally toed the line of legality with her hacking exploits, she did not believe she had done anything that would prompt the government's interest in her. If he was not government, she could not figure out who he was or why he had come to her. This meant she had to answer the door or run the risk of being bothered perpetually until she heard him out.

Dom reached the large double-sided oak door just as the trespasser rang the doorbell for the third time. She took a deep breath to steel her nerves and swung open the left side of the entry, coming face to face with the uninvited guest. The tall Black man favored her with a grin as if he was visiting an old friend for afternoon coffee. Her gaze immediately settled onto his light hazel eyes, which stood out juxtaposed against his deep-burnt umber skin tone. His age was indeterminate, but his close-cropped hair contained specks of gray, leading her to believe he was at least in his mid-forties. Clean-shaven, donning an expensive tailored navy pinstriped suit, attaché case in hand, the man looked like he was there to do her taxes. She quickly took in the visitor before fixing him with an intense scowl.

"Dominique Samuels, I presume?" he asked pleasantly. When she did not answer, he shifted his weight under her scrutiny. "May I come in?"

"Do I have a choice?"

"Of course you do, it's your home. But please, I truly believe you will want to hear why I've come," he said, still maintaining his insistent smile. She studied him for a long moment before finally stepping aside to allow him to cross her threshold. His inquisitive eyes took in the large foyer and grand staircase. "You have a lovely home."

When they approached the common area, the visitor whistled in awe at the open space, which allowed a view into the kitchen and dining room. There was a royal blue and black round oriental rug placed in the middle of the cherry wood flooring, a glass coffee table resting on top. Large bay windows allowed natural light to flood into the room and gave a view of the expansive backyard of the property. A plush royal blue sofa, three matching armchairs, and an antique rocking chair, another one of her mother's prized items, offered seating. For entertainment, there was an eighty-five-inch curved screen television mounted on the wall permitting equal vision regardless of location.

"Can I get you anything? Coffee? Tea?" she offered, while he settled himself into one of the royal blue armchairs. Nat waved the offer off with his hand, and she glided to the couch across the room to take her own seat. She stared at him placidly, waiting for him to begin speaking. When he realized she was expecting him to start his pitch, he cleared his throat.

"I'm here to offer you an opportunity," he declared, drawing a raised eyebrow from his host.

"Like a job? I'm not looking for a job," she replied, flicking her hands around to indicate her surroundings. "I'm pretty well set."

"No. Not a job," he clarified. "An opportunity."

"Explain."

"Did you hear about what happened in Milwaukee today?" asked Nat, kicking his right leg onto his left knee and settling further into his seat.

"I may be somewhat reclusive, but I don't live in a hole," she huffed. "Of course, I heard about what happened in Milwaukee."

"Notice a trend?" he inquired.

"Depends on what you mean by trend. If you are speaking about police shootings in general, that is not abnormal. Police officers have a hard job, they are bound to trade shots every now and again," Dom responded in a measured tone. "If you are indicating the fact that many of the recent unarmed police fatalities have been people of color, then yes; I have indeed noticed a trend." Dom's mind flashed back to the video of the victim in Milwaukee.

While the video had not displayed the incident in its entirety, it did show that the victim, twenty-year-old Timothy Cook, had been killed while running away from the police officer. The statement released by the Milwaukee police department indicated the shooting was being investigated, but she knew the inquiry would yield no punishment for the officer. The news talking heads were already saying that had Cook not run away, he would not have been killed. It was that sort of dismissive attitude towards the violent treatment of people of color that prompted many young Black and Brown individuals to flee when facing an officer.

"We're being systematically picked off by the police and police wannabes like Zimmerman in Florida, with absolutely no retribution. It's like no one cares if the body is Black or Brown. It's gotten so bad that even when it's a dirty shooting of a White person, folks are hesitant to speak up for fear of being accused of being anti-police," he spat in disgust. His face had taken on a visage of anger, and she felt her own irritation begin to creep into her attitude with this discussion.

"And the result is, cops are far less likely to take out a non-ethnic person because if the body count keeps rising, their license to kill us could go away," she contributed, drawing an emphatic nod from her guest.

"They have us so focused on the fact that they're killing us, and meanwhile the voice our ancestors marched for, begged for, and died for, is being taken away with voter suppression and scare tactics. The freaking government has all but abolished the Voting Rights Act of '65," he continued.

"Who can focus on that when you're worried about a bullet in the ass from a cop who feared for his life?" she asked sarcastically. Nat chuckled a little at this cynical statement.

"Even the LGBT community keeps fighting the same damn fight over and over again. Sure, you can marry now, but for how long? Look at our current administration. We went from making miles of strides to now facing being pushed back fifty years." Dom flinched when he included her in the LGBT community.

"You know far more about me than I'm comfortable with," she muttered suspiciously.

"I had to do my research, Miss Samuels. It's not malicious in nature. I needed to know for sure you were the right person," his tone was solemn. "Please know, you being a lesbian only solidifies your credentials for what I have come to present to you." She stared at him soundlessly, her intense glare prompting Nat to look away uncomfortably. His discomfort gave her a shock of pleasure, and she allowed the silence to linger for a time.

"Continue," she said flatly.

"Nothing has changed for us, any of us. If you aren't a heterosexual White male, then you don't matter. The game hasn't transformed, only the way it's being played. The problem is, the alteration hasn't been on our part. We have made no adjustments to our strategy," he asserted. She pondered this statement for a moment and then nodded her agreement.

"What does any of this have to do with me?" she asked. The passion and content of his words caused her mistrust to begin to wane. He wasn't giving a sales pitch; she could tell he meant every word.

"What if you could change it?" Dom blinked in surprise at this question.

"These kinds of injustices: the racism, misogyny, and homophobia, it's systematic. It's ingrained into the damn con-stitution. That can't be changed," she replied skeptically, her suspicion returning.

"But what if we changed our tactics to fight fire with fire?" he pressed. Dom scoffed, her impression of the man shifting. When he spoke about the discriminations that plagued the country, she saw a passion in him that she harbored in herself. Now, he sounded like an insane conspiracy theorist.

"Nat, what you are saying is crazy. We aren't in charge, they are. We don't have the money, they do. We can't make the policies or implement the changes, they can. They even sidestepped true democracy with their gerrymandering and Electoral College.

They have built an impenetrable bubble of power and control, and they've been doing it since the 1400s. That can't be undone."

"An architect who designs a building doesn't expect that once his design is complete, it will be constructed overnight, Miss Samuels. It is constructed, brick by brick," he countered, in a patient voice. "Conversely, one cannot expect that they can walk up to that building, punch it, and it will fall. It must be broken down using the structure's weaknesses."

"But this isn't a building. This is a whole system of government," she insisted.

"Everything has a weakness, Miss Samuels," he said cryptically. "You deal with technology on a daily basis; there are very few systems that you cannot enter. I'm willing to bet it is because you know how to find those weaknesses, and exploit them."

"Nat," she began calmly, pinching the bridge of her nose, "what you are saying is a naïve idealistic view of the situation in this country. It's like you forget that they hold the keys to the kingdom. Don't you think that such a kingdom has its guards to protect the weaknesses you envision? We call them the FBI, NSA, CIA, and the military; and let's not forget their local muscle, the police. They could literally send a drone to bomb this house, with both of us in it, declare that it was for national security, and no one would bat an eye." He snapped his fingers suddenly, causing her to flinch at the unexpected sound.

"Exactly," he concurred, his fingers morphing into a finger gun gesture, which he pointed towards her. Dom favored him with a puzzled expression.

"Okay, you've gone from sounding insane to sounding incoherent."

"Miss Samuels…"

"Dominique," she corrected. Those who knew her well were entitled to the shortened version of her name, Dom. Those who did not know her always began with Miss Samuels, making her feel like an old woman until she insisted on at least being called by her first name.

"Dominique, the government has only a few things not readily accessible to the oppressed people we discussed: access to information, money, and people devoted to maintaining the status quo." He ticked off each point on his fingers.

"I can agree with that," she conceded.

"So, what if we used the exact same formula?" The question brought clarity to her mind.

"You want to use me as your access to information," she asserted. Irritation crashed back into her when she realized his intent was to use her. "I don't have the desire to go to jail, and it's always the hacker that goes to jail first."

"No Dominique," he said dismissively. "I don't want to use you exactly. I want you to head up the initiative and the team."

"Team? What team?" she squeaked in a voice slightly higher than before. Nat's words smacked her heart into a gallop of panic.

"The team you will assemble," he answered. He reached into the attaché case at his feet and extracted a flash drive. Leaning forward, he placed the drive on the modern glass coffee table. Her eyes flicked to the gray and black drive, but she made no move to pick it up.

"I'm not sure where you got your intel, but I'm not exactly a team player."

"You're exactly what is needed. You're Black, a lesbian, and you're a woman. In the Venn diagram of bigotry, you represent the intersectional sweet spot," he beamed.

"In my experience, that has not benefited me one iota," she snapped.

"This is another reason why you are perfect," he replied, ignoring the irritation in her voice. "Those who protect the kingdom, as you call it, know the benefits of their privilege. They know what they stand to lose, and work that much harder to keep it. You are a living contrast to everything they represent. You weren't given your wealth or your success; nothing was handed to you. You have the financial freedom most people don't possess, but I don't believe that acquired advantage has erased your under-standing of the handicaps that are inherent in your very existence."

She sat quietly, processing his justification. Nat's analysis of her situation and upbringing was accurate. She had succeeded despite having every socially adverse handicap one person could maintain.

Flashes of the racism, homophobia, and misogyny she faced throughout her life ran through her mind like a film reel.

"I still don't believe I'm the person you want. I'm not big on collaboration, particularly with organic beings."

"We can't force you to do this, Dominique," he acknowledged in a resigned voice.

"Who is we?"

"Those financing this endeavor," he replied.

"How do you mean?"

"These are people who may have grown up like you, and who have been able to succeed despite the detriments that they faced. They have decided enough is enough, and want to do something to try to tip the scales," he explained. "There was a secret meeting. They discussed the state of our country and its treatment of those who fit into the category of other. It was resolved that we cannot keep waiting for someone in Washington to do right by the citizens of this nation. If they refuse to protect us, we need to figure a way to protect ourselves."

"Who? What people?" she probed, now fully interested. Nat sat back in his chair again and smirked.

"Unfortunately, I can't tell you that. Many of these individuals have money, influence, and status. To get directly involved would cause them to lose their success. It was a dilemma. While they want to do something, they knew if they did openly, their livelihood could be jeopardized."

"If slavery and the civil rights movement taught us anything as a people, it should be that we have to be willing to lose it all for justice and freedom." Her tone carried judgment and hostility, prompting him to raise a calming hand.

"You know when you fly, and the flight attendants give those instructions that no one ever listens to? They always tell you that if the cabin loses pressure, you should put your mask on first. Even if you are flying with a child, put on yours first, and only then should you help someone else. Why do you think that is?" he questioned. She cocked her head in bewilderment at the sudden shift in conversation.

"Because you need to be able to breathe to help others — you're no good if you pass out," she answered. When Nat nodded meaningfully, she comprehended the analogy. "So, these people feel like they need to maintain anonymity to keep making the money?" He grinned with the satisfaction of a teacher who just witnessed a student making a breakthrough.

"Now you see why I'm here."

"I'm the information," she began, pointing towards herself. "You're the money," she indicated her guest with the same finger, and then dropped her point to the flash drive still resting on the table. "And that is the group of people devoted to change?"

"In a way. You are the only person I have and will speak to. I want this to be your team, you have to be the one to bring them in," he clarified, drawing a scowl from Dom.

"You are still missing the fact that I don't deal with people."

"That reality is something you must take into consideration," he acknowledged. "As I said, we can't force you, and we won't. But you now know the offer." She stared at him for a beat and then dropped her light brown eyes to the table.

"You brought that case for one little flash drive?" she asked dubiously. Nat chuckled and reached back into the case, producing a medium sized binder.

"I also have this." He placed this offering on the coffee table next to the drive.

Dom picked up the binder.

"And this is?"

"We have a network of people involved with us, people who have the desire to really change the way things are in this country," he replied. "But what I'm asking of you, fighting fire with fire with the use of the tools the government uses; that is only for you and your team. Tackling the injustices in all minority communities is too much to ask for one group of people. We have initiatives in healthcare, education, and law enforcement. There are detailed programs in there. I'm asking you to develop a way to complement those projects with your intelligence. There is also information regarding finances. I realize you have done well for yourself, but we want to contribute to the cause with as much as we can. I believe we have already amassed a nice amount, and should you take on this proposition, funding should not be an issue." She flipped through the pages of the document and then returned to the cover.

"What's this supposed to be?" she mused, holding up the binder to show him the image that prompted the question. The art on the cover displayed the inside of an extended forearm, raised in a fisted power pose, an Afro haloing the fist. There were small blocky words printed on the wrist of the arm, giving a tattooed effect. She brought the binder closer to her face to inspect the message that proclaimed "By Any Means Necessary."

"It's the goal, the motto, and the creed that we live by. It's the reason this whole struggle began: Change, by any means necessary," he answered.

"How very Malcolm X of you," she muttered, returning the binder to her lap.

"He wasn't wrong, neither was Dr. King. For over two hundred years, we have been begging and demanding equality and change, but our pleas go ignored. To add insult to injury, those in the U.S. government not only disregard our appeals, but they also actively try to prevent any true advancement. They use their power and privilege to slow or stop equality and progress. If they refuse to meet us at our level, maybe it's time we met them at theirs," he said, conspiracy coloring his voice.

"What if I say no? What if I decide I don't want to put myself in the position to fight an impossible battle?"

"That, Dominique, is your right and your choice. Again, we cannot force you. But I don't believe you will say no," he replied, rising to his feet and plucking the attaché case from the floor. Dom remained seated staring at him.

"You are cocky for someone who just met me." He grinned broadly.

"I have done my homework. I think you are exactly the type of person who can and will spearhead this project," he declared. "I look forward to hearing your decision."

"Even if it's a no?"

"It won't be," he replied confidently. She watched him walk out of her living room and make his way to the front door, leaving her alone with her thoughts.

When the front door closed behind her visitor, Dom heard SARA engage the automatic locks. She maintained her position on the couch, staring at the image depicted on the cover of the binder. She flipped through the pages snagging pieces of information that meant nothing to her without full context, before returning the binder to the table, having no desire to read the sizable report. Her mind was reeling from the unusual interaction with the mysterious stranger.

"Dom, may I ask a question?" SARA asked her, breaking the silence.

"What's up?" she absently replied, closing her eyes.

"I have researched the term "by any means necessary," and found that it was originally used in a French play by Jean-Paul Sartre. The context in the play surrounded societal division by classism. I then reviewed the speech by Malcolm X where he also used the phrase, this time referring to division by racism."

"You did all of that in just a few minutes?" she asked.

"I could have compiled a much more thorough report in less than a minute if you would upgrade to a quantum processor as I recommended," SARA replied.

"I already told you, I'm not spending that much money on a processor. I'm still annoyed that you tried," she scolded.

"I have previously offered an apology for my presumption, Dom. I am unsure why you continue to harbor animus about the situation."

"You stop bringing up the processor, and I will stop being mad about it," she shot back. "You said you had a question."

"Yes. The examination surrounding both Sartre and Malcolm X led me to investigate further the foundation of both classism and racism. Classism, while nonsensical, is straightforward in nature. However, I am unable to identify the logic surrounding the concept of racism. This leads me to ask: is there perhaps a difference in the various ethnic groups that I am unable to identify?" the computer asked. Dom's eyes snapped open when she heard this question, the inquiry jarring an internal consideration of the subject.

"No SARA. The scientific composition of humanity is pretty universal. Race itself is solely a classification system used to identify people from different locations and various melanin levels. But we are all humans," she admitted.

"I do understand the concept of what race is. What I cannot process is the hatred of another person for a slight difference in DNA and genetics," SARA clarified.

"That makes most of us, my friend," she sighed.

"What is the purpose for this hatred?"

"There is no good reason. It's all about power and privilege. Europeans are no different from any other race. For various reasons, they started to believe that they were better, more dignified, and more advanced than everyone else in the world. When they began to colonize other areas, they did so with the goal of expanding their territory. But they viewed the natives of the various lands as savages because their customs and cultures were different. For them, different meant inferior, and inferior meant wrong," she answered.

"So, the initial hatred was because the Europeans could not understand cultures different than their own?" SARA asked.

"Yes, that is a good way to say it."

"Then why does this hatred persist? It has been well over five hundred years," the machine wondered.

"Now, it's because of fear."

"Fear? That statement is illogical. The definition of fear is an emotion caused by the belief that someone or something is dangerous," SARA reported.

"That is correct," confirmed Dom.

"Based on the historical data, Americans of African ancestries have more reason to fear those of European descents, due to their role in the slave trade that transitioned into the continuous denial of basic human and civil rights. Native Americans and Indigenous Mexican tribes were exterminated and displaced when the Europeans colonized their homeland. Even Asian Americans faced life in relocation and incarceration camps during World War II. What is there to fear? Have the Europeans not subjugated all facets of American society?" SARA mused.

"You just answered your own question," Dom chuckled.

"I'm not sure how that is possible."

"I know you have researched the history of humanity and our various civilizations. Any time one empire conquered another, the conquering power forced their culture and religions on those who were subjugated. You just listed a variety of civilizations that lived in this very country long before the Europeans entered the picture. It's cyclical. They are afraid to see the end of their reign." Dom stood from her seat and shuffled to her office.

"The end of their reign?" the machine inquired.

"Well, think about it. Greece, Rome, Great Britain; they were all empires that had risen to conquer much of the known world back then. People were more separated by their homeland, as opposed to race. Wars between countries determined who got along and who didn't. Today all of those occupied lands are sovereign. When the Europeans came to America, they couldn't completely eradicate the Native Americans and Native Mexican tribes, although they came close. Then they went and brought the African slaves to do their work for them. Once things began to change, the homeland of origin stopped being as important. To maintain their power, they had to find a common link to band together. They were White men. That commonality has been the power of this country ever since," she explained, picking up her soldering iron, and getting back to work on her project.

"The United States is a democracy, Dom. By definition, this country is governed by all of the people who reside within its borders," the computer pointed out.

"No, it's not. It was intended to be a democracy."

"This statement is in conflict with my information," SARA insisted.

"A democracy is the power of many. When those White guys sat in that room in 1776 to plot out the course of this country, they didn't make it a democracy. They made it an oligarchy. They wanted White men to make the decisions. Women, Native Americans, and the enslaved Africans were never originally a part of the plan. As time moved on, slavery was abolished, and women began demanding their own rights; suddenly, the country began to shift away from favoring White men. That's where the fear comes into play," she explained. She paused to blow on the newest fused segment.

"They are afraid of equality?" SARA asked.

"Exactly. Equality means power, and the privilege that

comes with that power will have to be shared. Their opinions and desires will no longer be the prevailing voice. It means respecting all people, cultures, and beliefs. In a sense, it circles back to the original problem."

"The inability to understand different people and cultures?"

"It's not about inability anymore, SARA. They don't want to. Instead, they choose to hate those of us who are different," she declared.

"Why do you include yourself in that statement?" SARA wondered.

"You heard Nat; I encompass almost every group of people that are discriminated against. White, presumptively heterosexual males have run this nation all this time. I am a Black homosexual female; literally the direct opposite," she answered. "I have seen my fair share of racism, misogyny, and homophobia."

"Your intelligence should elevate you. Your IQ of 168 puts you among the top two percent of the population."

"And it would if I were a White man. Unfortunately, in this world they see Black before anything else," she grumbled. SARA was silent for a while, affording Dom the ability to make a little more headway on her project.

"This proposition Mr. Daniels brought to you; what do you surmise is the scope?" SARA asked. Dom opened her mouth but inhaled a small billow of smoke rising from the iron. She coughed violently before she was able to answer.

"I don't know, SARA. He seems militant, but based on my perusal of the documents he gave me, it's a lot of community-focused undertakings. I'm really not sure what he expects from me, or if I'll even agree to do it," she replied after she recovered from her coughing fit. She stopped suddenly and looked towards the ceiling. "Who's Mr. Daniels?"

"The man who was just here." Upon hearing this, the soldering iron dropped from her hand. When she reached for it, the hot pen-like tool burned her fingers. Hissing in pain, she sucked on her thumb and index finger, while plucking the iron with her left hand and setting in on the table.

"What are you talking about?"

"Given the cryptic manner of his initial contact, I felt it only logical to run the facial recognition software upon his arrival. He is Thomas Daniels, forty-five years of age, residing in Baltimore, Maryland. He is an attorney with the National Association for the Advancement of Colored People. Divorced, he has one child, Michael Daniels age ten. His father, Lincoln Daniels, was a carpenter from Philadelphia, Pennsylvania and is now deceased. His mother, Sara Daniels, formerly Sarah Atkins, is from Baltimore, Maryland and is a school administrator," SARA reported.

"SARA, I could kiss you," Dom grinned. "Please tell me you made a file."

"Dom, don't be silly," the machine admonished. "Of course I made a file. Also, to complete the action of kissing me, you would have to finish construction on my physical form. Might I peruse a preferred mouth mold? Do you have a lip style preference? Thin, full, medium?" This statement, in conjunction with the good news of the computer's independent action of running the facial recognition, caused Dom to laugh hysterically.

"SARA, I'm not building you a body for any sort of romantic purposes."

"According to my research into human relationships, we are practically married," the program quipped. Dom barked with renewed amusement at this comment. SARA had begun developing a sense of humor, and this breakthrough truly delighted her during discourse.

"I can't argue that my friend. But our relationship is one of the minds. If I feel the need for physical companionship, I'll join a dating website."

"Match.com has promising success results; shall I create a profile for you?" the machine offered.

"Don't you dare," she warned. "Play my music."

Dom attempted to concentrate on her project, but even the music could not occupy the abundance of thoughts racing through her mind. She was angry about the unwanted infringement into her solitude and privacy. As much as she considered the question, she could not figure out how her recent visitor came to know of and find her. She had no connection to anyone in Maryland or the

NAACP. She also replayed the details of the conversation. While she did not appreciate the violation, she could not argue with the points made by the mysterious man.

"Dom, do you suppose Mr. Daniels provided the name of Nat in homage to Nat Turner, given the substance of his proposal is a form of rebellion against the status quo? If he had done his research on you, surely, he would have known you would have recognized the name to be a pseudonym," SARA asked, breaking her rumination.

"That is a possibility," she agreed, dropping her iron onto the table with a loud clang. "I can't concentrate on this right now. Let's take a look at this drive."

She strolled into the living room and picked up the flash drive and binder, before relocating and plopping down into her desk chair. Pulling the secondary computer closer to her seat, she slipped the drive into one of the ports. She reached into one of the drawers of her desk, extracted a similar drive, and slid that into the next port. After turning on the power and switching one of the monitors to the secondary machine, she ran her proprietary anti-virus program to ensure the offered file did not come with any viruses, spyware, trackers, or comparable malignancies. Once her wariness about the foreign drive was satisfied, she returned her personal flash drive to her desk and moved the one Daniels gave her to her main computer.

"Okay, SARA, let's see what we got," she commanded the computer. SARA began to open all of the files, sorting them by file type, displaying each style on a different monitor. Dom's eyes came to rest on documents that resembled dossiers, complete with photos and brief biographies. She clicked through them before stopping on a photo of a caramel colored woman with golden brown eyes. Dom tilted her head and examined the snapshot. The picture appeared to have been taken from some sort of work identification card, and when she scrolled down to the biographical information, she found her name.

"Rose Jenkins? She's cute," she murmured, leaning forward to read about the woman.

CHAPTER THREE

Rose Jenkins peered over her desk at the eleven-year-old boy slouched in the chair in front of her. Leon Murphy glowered back, his green eyes seething, his light brown skin reddened by his anger. He was wearing a black hoodie, and emblazoned in green, graffiti style writing was the message: "Thug Lyfe." When he entered her office, she squelched the sudden impulse to suggest he pull up his baggy jeans. His white basketball shoes were brand new and pristine, giving the false aura of wealth. Rose was aware that many of the students in the school came from lower economic homes, much like her own background. The silence began to have the desired effect, and Leon's mood started to convert into discomfort. He shifted in his chair and dropped his gaze to the floor.

"Why am I here?" he grumbled, folding his arms onto his chest with a huff. She watched him in silence for a time before glancing down at the paper that accompanied him to her office. She read the information slowly, then turned her golden-brown eyes to the boy once again.

"Leon, why are you so angry?" she asked in a soothing voice. The furious child clucked his teeth in response to her inquiry.

"I ain't angry," he protested. She suppressed a smile at the child's inability to recognize the irony in his tone.

"Let's see," she mused, returning her glance to the paper. One of her dark box braids dropped in front of her face, and she swiped it away with her hand. "You started the day by punching Ricky Sanderson..."

"He should have stayed out of my face!"

"His story was that he was trying to tell you that your shoe was untied," she paused, glancing at the boy for a response. Leon dropped his eyes and shrugged, unwilling to debate. "You called Amber Reyes a fat wetback and said she should swim back home."

"That was a joke!" he exclaimed. "I was playing with her!" Rose's eyebrows lifted at his tone, and Leon shrank back from her withering scowl.

"If that was a joke, it was a terrible and hurtful one. Also, she is from Alabama. Finally, you told Ms. Campbell to get the fuck out of your face, which is why you are here with me. This is all in a single morning, Leon. You still want to tell me that you're not angry?" she questioned again, crossing her arms while she studied the boy. His eyes returned to the floor, and he chose not to respond. As she watched him, she heard the distinctive sound of Leon's stomach growling. Stealing a glance at her watch, she realized that the child would not have lunch for another two hours.

"Leon, did you have breakfast this morning?" she asked, her right hand subtly opening a desk drawer. His eyes floated back to Rose's inquisitive face.

"I wasn't hungry." She looked into his eyes and saw the embarrassment of the lie immediately. Rose was very familiar with families in similar situations as Leon Murphy's. His single-parent home had multiple children and not enough money. She looked at her calendar and calculated the time until the first of the month when state-funded benefits would kick in for these unfortunate families. Glancing at the boy's shoes, familiar anger stirred within her. He was wearing brand new shoes that cost close to two hundred dollars; likely due to the recent tax refund that many single parents received for their children. Rather than using the money for necessities such as food, Rose could almost see the small, subsidized apartment with state of the art flat screen televisions and video game consoles.

Though she recognized the judgmental nature of the thoughts flowing through her mind, her years of experience working with families in lower economic areas, and her own background of growing up in a parallel environment taught her these deductions were usually correct. Withdrawing a cereal bar from her drawer, she laid it on the other side of her desk in front of Leon. He looked at the bar skeptically, and did not move to take it; his stomach letting out another sound in protest of his inaction.

"Go ahead," she prodded, slipping her desk drawer closed. She leaned forward on her arms and stared at the child. Finally,

Leon reached for the bar, unwrapped it, and took a tentative bite. His eyes flashed a look of gratitude.

"Thanks," he mumbled.

"Leon, I'm going to ask you a question, and I want you to think about it really hard before you answer." He cocked his head, awaiting her query. "What do you want to be when you grow up?" The question would seem innocuous to most people. Often, answers varied depending on the surroundings of the child. Those surrounded by higher prospects due to race or economic status often recited occupations such as a doctor, firefighter, or perhaps a profession within their own family legacy. Children who did not have those opportunities relied on pop culture standards of success, causing their responses to mimic areas where they observed representation. Leon chewed quietly, mulling over the question.

"I probably won't grow up. I'll probably get killed," he replied in a matter-of-fact tone. She flinched in surprise at the answer. While the perception of children never ceased to astonish her, the assumption and acceptance of certain death triggered a profound sadness that was difficult to mask.

"Why would you say something like that?" she asked, extending her hand to receive the empty cereal bar wrapper. She produced another bar, placing it in his hand before he had a chance to withdraw. He accepted the offering in silence, unwrapped the bar, and took another bite, attempting to stall his explanation. After a few moments, he lifted his head and made eye contact with his school counselor.

"My daddy's dead, my sister's dead, and my uncle's dead; all killed on the block. How could I not say that? It's only a matter of time, ain't it?" Frustration colored the child's features as he spoke. "You don't know what it's like." Rose's eyebrows elevated in amusement at his assumption.

"Oh? I don't? Tell me what I don't know." She leaned back in her chair and crossed her arms.

"You know what it's like to hear gunshots every night, and to be scared it's someone you know? When you ride your bike down the street, dudes try to get you to run drugs for them for a little money. Then you got to decide if it's worth it, cause you hungry and there ain't nothing to eat. Cops come in the neighborhood, just to try to scare you, patting you down like they think you strapped. Where would I get a gun? I'm eleven! You know what that's like, Miss Jenkins?" His voice dripped with anger, and his eyes grew moist with the emotion he carried his whole life.

"Actually, Leon, I know exactly what that's like," she answered, her voice soft. He blinked at her in surprise.

"How?"

"Because I grew up in Sunnyside, and we both know, it's much worse there than here in Greenspoint," she declared with a knowing look. South of Houston's sprawling downtown, Sunnyside was known to be one of the most dangerous neighborhoods, not only in the Houston area but in the state of Texas. For the first eighteen years of her life, Rose lived in Sunnyside, finally escaping when she went to college. She still frequented the community to see her mother who remained in her childhood home. Leon's scrutinizing eyes regarded her in a new light.

"My granny lives there. That place is scary," he said after a silence, drawing a chuckle from Rose.

"Only if you don't know the area. Just like in your neighborhood, you know who and where to avoid, right?" He nodded in response to her question. "So, it's the same there. There are scary places anywhere, Leon. Nowhere is *all* bad, no matter what people say about it. More people survive than not; who's to say you won't?"

"My sister didn't. She was just riding her bike and got hit with a stray," he muttered, a tear escaping his tough façade. Her heart ached to see him in his grief, and she swallowed a knob of emotion.

"Leon, I'm so sorry that happened to your family, but it's not realistic to expect the same thing to happen to you. Let's say it doesn't; then what?" she asked in a gentle tone.

"I don't know."

"Well, what do you like to do?"

"What do you mean?" he asked, his watery eyes clouding over in confusion.

"What do you like to do when you're home?" she expounded.

"I like music. Sometimes I try to write my own rhymes," he answered. Rose heard a cautious tone in his voice.

"Ah, so you want to be like Jay-Z or something? Build your own hip-hop empire?"

"Only if I could marry Beyoncé," he replied, a genuine smile playing on his lips for the first time since he walked into the office. She extended her hand again, and he dropped his second empty wrapper into her waiting palm.

"You could do worse. What do you like about rap?" she inquired, discarding the garbage into a trash can under her desk.

"You can get girls and have money and cars and stuff."

"You do realize that's only in the music videos, right? Most of those rappers don't have the money they say they do," she said, leaning forward again and cradling her chin in her hands. She was happy that with the boy's hunger sated, he was beginning to engage with her.

"I bet T.I. got all those cars and women," he pointed out.

"T.I. is not the best rapper to look up to," she frowned. "Plus, he's been in the game for a while, Leon. He didn't start out that way. Besides, today's hip-hop sucks."

"You only saying that because you're old, Miss Jenkins," he smirked. Rose rolled her eyes at his response.

"I'd gladly trade my favorite hip-hop artist for yours any day."

"Did they even have hip-hop in your day?" he asked, his tone far more serious than Rose would have preferred.

"Boy, please. Are you kidding?" Sliding open another drawer, she took out a writeable CD in a paper sleeve and plopped it in front of the child. When she attempted to close the drawer, it was stuck three-quarters of the way in, and she leaned into the old desk forcefully to get it closed.

"What's this?" he asked.

"I know you're not too young to know what a CD is. You have something you can play that on?" He confirmed with a nod.

"What's on it?" he inquired, picking up the disc and examining it for some sort of communication of its contents.

"That is a collection of hip-hop from my time. A bunch of people you probably haven't heard of, but they had something to say. I want you to listen to it; not just the beat but also the words. The feeling that you won't see another day; that feeling has been around for years. Today's hip-hop artists embrace a life that isn't really a true representation of everyone in the hood. They do a lot of talking, but they don't say anything," she explained. He stared at the CD and then finally relented, slipping the gift into his backpack. "I want to see you about forty-five minutes before school every morning." His face contorted into indignation.

"Man, why?"

"You're not in trouble. Calm down," she said, holding up a soothing hand. "I want you to have breakfast with me. Let's talk about hip-hop. I want to hear what you have to say about what I gave you."

"My momma says she'll get some cereal when her food stamps post," he muttered, informing Rose that he was not being fooled by her scheme. She smiled brightly in response.

"I'm sure she will. I'd really like to get your take on my hip-hop, and I'm not that terrible to be around, am I?" Leon sat silently for a few moments and then nodded.

"Okay, I guess I can take the early bus with my brother."

"Starting tomorrow," she directed.

"Okay."

"No more hitting, no more terrible jokes, and no cussing out teachers," she scowled, her voice stern. His eyes darted to the floor, and he nodded.

"Fine." Rose took a page from her hall pass folder and scribbled quickly.

"Back to class. We'll continue this tomorrow morning. I want you to listen to the first song a few times until you really get all of the words. It's called 'Keep Your Head Up' by 2Pac," she said. "Do you eat pork?" Leon looked at her like she had grown a second head.

"Yeah, why wouldn't I?"

"Just checking. How does a bacon breakfast burrito sound?" Leon flashed her another genuine smile. "Okay, great. I'll see you in the morning, and Leon…"

"Yeah, yeah. I'll behave," he said. He rose from his chair, and he was out of the door within seconds. Rose noticed a change in the boy's gait as he exited her office.

"It's amazing what a full stomach can do for one's attitude," she muttered to the newly closed door.

Rose entered the small teacher's lounge for coffee and almost collided with Lorenzo Cavanaugh, the school's vice-principal. Standing over six feet tall, his dark brown eyes contained a perpetual glower, whether he was angry or not. His features were an interesting combination of his two heritages. Fair skin and red hair derived from his Irish-American father, while his mother's Mexican-American heritage contributed his dark eyes and broad facial features. This composition gave him a villainous aura to the children of the school. Rose had the feeling that Cavanaugh enjoyed being feared by the students, and that in reality, he did not like children at all. She detested the man.

"Miss Jenkins!" Cavanaugh exclaimed. "I'm glad I ran into you." He flashed what Rose assumed was a smile, but came across as more of a grimace. She sidestepped him on the way to the coffee machine. Rose knew that she needed a jolt of caffeine before engaging. Shifting through the individual coffee pods, she took out a French roast and prepared her cup of coffee with her back to Cavanaugh. She tensed when she felt him move towards her.

"Mr. Cavanaugh," she said flatly, not turning to look at him.

"Did you see the Murphy kid?" he asked, taking a sip from the Diet Dr. Pepper he carried with him. It did not matter the hour of the day, Cavanaugh was rarely seen around the school without the beverage.

"Leon Murphy? Yes, I saw him per your note." She still did not turn to face him as she sweetened and added powdered creamer to her coffee. Rose refused to actively drive any conversation with Cavanaugh, choosing to navigate them like a road with potholes.

"How did it go?"

"It went fine. We talked. I have an action plan in place. You shouldn't have any trouble out of him for a while," she informed him, taking a calming sip of her beverage.

"That's unlikely," he scoffed contemptuously. "I'd bet money I'll see him again by the end of the day. The boy should have a designated chair in my office." Rose bit back a spiteful response by taking a second drink of coffee.

"If I were a betting woman, Mr. Cavanaugh, I would take that bet. He will be fine," she replied after a pause.

"Oh please, that little thug is only here until he gets picked up for gang banging or gets himself killed," Cavanaugh spat angrily. The synapses in Rose's brain snapped and her vision tinted red upon hearing his words. She slammed down the coffee mug with so much force she expected it to shatter. Hot coffee sloshed onto the counter and her hands, but Rose did not feel the heat. She spun around to face the vice principal with wrath coloring her face.

"Mr. Cavanaugh, do the words that you say go through some sort of mental filter before they come out of your mouth, or are you really just that obtuse?" The question came out in a sneer. Cavanaugh, who had been taking a sip of his soda, sputtered in surprise and coughed violently.

"Miss Jenkins, I'm sure I don't know what you mean, but…"

"Why is Leon a thug, Lorenzo? Tell me, what did you observe in this child's actions that classify him as a thug? Has he pulled a gun on you and demanded money? Did you see him take part in some drive-by in your neighborhood? Did you perhaps catch him in the middle of a drug deal? Tell me, what in this ELEVEN -YEAR-OLD CHILD'S BEHAVIOR MAKES HIM A THUG?!" By the end of her questioning, Rose could hear that she was practically shouting; but in her anger, she did not care. As she spoke, she unconsciously moved towards the man, coffee dripping from her hands onto the tile floor. Despite his almost full foot and one-hundred-pound advantage on her, he paled and stepped back under her advances.

"Now Miss Jenkins, this tone you are taking with me is entirely unprofessional," he stammered, trying to regain his control over the conversation. It was far too late as Rose was now piloting the rocky discussion with reckless abandon.

"I'm being unprofessional?" she sneered in disbelief. "The tone I have is of someone who doesn't look at an eleven-year-old child and see a thug. He's *eleven*, Mr. Cavanaugh. Your comment was unprofessional and entirely out of line. Kids aren't stupid; they pick up on the contempt you have for them. Your attitude is part of the reason these children don't try to do any better. If their own vice principal, who is supposed to be reinforcing their growth and development, passes such harsh judgment on them, then what's the point of even trying?" While she did not back down, she was careful not to advance any further on the chance that another teacher entered the lounge.

"I…uh," he stuttered, as if trying to remember how to speak.

"Tell me something Mr. Cavanaugh, do you eat every day?" Confusion clouded the vice principal's eyes at this shift in the conversation.

"Eat? Yes, of course I eat daily. But I don't see how this…"

"Now tell me, if for whatever reason you go all day without eating, are you the poster child for happiness?"

"Well no. Anyone would be disgruntled in that scenario," he answered.

"What if you had such a day and when you got home, Irma didn't have dinner ready for you. What if she said she just didn't feel like cooking for whatever reason; how would that make you feel?"

"Well, I suppose I'd be irritated with her," he conceded.

"So, as an adult male in his mid-thirties; you get angry when you're hungry. Perhaps you don't go around punching people or cussing them out; but you get testy at least?" she asked, her eyebrows raised emphasizing her inquiry.

"I just said that, Miss Jenkins. What exactly is your point here? What does this have to do with the Murphy boy?"

"His name is Leon. How do you suppose such hunger affects an eleven-year-old child? Surely you don't contend that a child should exhibit the exact same self-control that you would show as an adult. He's a *child*, Mr. Cavanaugh; when he came into my office, his stomach was rumbling because he didn't have breakfast today," she explained, crossing her arms.

"That's no excuse! Besides, he's wearing shoes that would cover a week's worth of food in most houses," he objected. Rose let out a loud sigh, shaking her head in disgust.

"Now you're saying that not only should an eleven-year-old have the same self-discipline as an adult, but that he should also have the same decision-making abilities in the household finances as a grown man?"

"Of course not! That's absurd."

"He can't determine how the little bit of money in his household is spent, any more than he can go shop for groceries and stock the pantry. I can assure you that no eleven-year-old is an actual thug; nor should they be declared to be one, especially by a grown ass man," she announced, the anger not leaving her tone. "If a child is exhibiting destructive behavior, there is usually a reason. My job is to assess what could be going on in the lives of these students that may obstruct their education. The fact that I can tell you Leon Murphy has a hard time getting breakfast in the morning; well, Mr. Cavanaugh, that's an easier fix than some of the other egregious situations that other children may be dealing with. Need I remind you that he's also still grieving the death of his little sister? That is enough to make anyone, adult or child, have a hard time. So, I will say again, you should not have any problems with young Mr. Murphy for a while!" She picked up her coffee mug, stepped around the stunned man, and exited the teacher's lounge without allowing him to utter another word.

Rose pulled her late model Toyota Camry into an open parking space outside of the Booker T. Washington Recreational Center. The small center was one of the few community outreach facilities still operational thanks to the assistance of generous donors and volunteers. She had spearheaded a writing campaign to the state for a grant to keep the center open and spent most of her evenings volunteering. The largest draw to the neighborhood children was the indoor gym with a full basketball court. An outdoor pool in the back of the building was only operational during the summer. Five small classrooms were available, catering to immigrants who were learning English, high school students requesting preparation for the SAT, and a GED program. Unfortunately, those rooms rarely saw occupants. Once upon a time, the facility also maintained a daycare center for the community with the goal of providing lower-income parents an inexpensive childcare option near their homes. Ultimately, the costs of running such a service within state mandates proved too large, and it had to be suspended.

She turned off the ignition and sat in the car collecting herself before entering the building. She ruminated on her earlier outburst and tried to find a reason to feel bad enough to apologize for her behavior the following day. As much as she tried, she could not bring herself to settle into a motive to be sorry. Cavanaugh represented the true problem with the educational system in lower income environments. He had no desire to truly educate, mold or guide these youngsters, but rather saw his current position as a path to a higher paying administrative post. Many of the administrators in the school district never lived or taught in the schools they governed, and therefore, had no real knowledge of the true challenges inherent in the student body. The fact that someone with Cavanaugh's mindset would be in charge of the day-to-day development of children was unconscionable.

When Rose decided to pursue mental health, she initially wanted to have her own private practice. People with the mentality of Cavanaugh caused her to abandon that more lucrative path. She knew the impossible odds these children faced, and dedicated her life to uplifting and showing them that despite what they saw on a daily basis, nothing was impossible. With more administrators and even teachers sharing the ideals of Cavanaugh rather than her own, Rose had to hold fast to the optimism that her influence could negate the effect people like Cavanaugh had on the students. Taking a deep breath to banish the painful thoughts from earlier in the day, Rose exited the vehicle and locked the door. Having changed from the slacks and purple blouse she donned for school, she now sported a pair of distressed blue jeans, sneakers, and a pink and black t-shirt.

When she entered the building, Darla Richardson looked up from her magazine and favored her with a bright smile. Darla was a staple at the center, having taken over the operations when she retired from the very school where Rose was employed. Rose saw the passion that Darla showed first to her students and then to the young people in the center. She was loved and respected by all. Darla took off her glasses and let them fall to her formidable chest, suspended by a chain. Her frizzy hair, more gray than black, was put up into a messy bun and held in place by a pencil. She dropped the magazine to greet Rose.

"Hey Miss Jenkins!" Despite being at least thirty years Rose's senior, Darla always insisted on calling her "Miss" rather than simply Rose; yet insisted Rose call her Darla rather than Ms. Richardson.

"Good evening Darla," Rose greeted her. She rounded the desk and marched over to the woman who stood and opened her arms wide. Darla's hugs could rival Rose's own mother in comfort. Many young people came to the center just to get a Darla hug. "Looks like we got a nice turnout tonight."

"J.T. and his crew decided to stop in for a game or two. You know that comes with an entourage," the older woman replied, tipping her head towards the basketball court. She plopped back into her chair and picked up her magazine.

"Any trouble today?"

"Nothing I couldn't handle. But you may want to look in on a group of boys who have been huddled together near the court," Darla suggested. "I don't recognize them." Rose went into the small office located behind the welcome desk and unlocked the door. Dropping her purse onto the desk, she took out a black elastic hair tie and tied her box braids up into a ponytail that hung just below her shoulder blades. Exiting the office, she locked the door and strolled towards the rambunctious gymnasium.

The gym was half-full of boys and girls ranging in age from about twelve to mid-twenties. A vigorous game of basketball was underway, with half of the young men wearing various t-shirts and the other half topless. Rose observed Tyrell Lawson, the six-teen-year-old neighborhood basketball prodigy, running down the court dripping with sweat. It was common knowledge that Tyrell would likely go to college to play basketball and had a good shot at playing in the NBA or professionally overseas. Tyrell received a pass and squared up at the three-point line before draining a shot with a defender in his face. The gymnasium went wild with cheers and taunts from the onlookers enjoying the display. Rose moved to the side of the door and leaned back against the wall, inspecting the crowd of rowdy teenagers.

Her watchful eyes fell onto a troop of eight girls cheering and giggling in a tight group on the far side of the court. They were watching the game and occasionally catcalling the players when they ran past. She focused on one particular girl in the cluster, whose mannerisms did not match that of the others. Her long, relaxed hair was pulled up into a ponytail, and she wore jean capris with a shirt displaying the face of a popular rapper. While the girls were ogling the guys and cackling their comparisons, this girl maintained an artificial look of mirth. The only time Rose saw genuine emotion or reaction was when the alpha of the group, who was in the middle of the throng, spoke to her. She saw the subtle changes in the girl's demeanor, and she grinned in understanding. The girl had a crush on the alpha and probably did not even realize.

Moving her visual probe from the gaggle of girls, Rose continued her assessment of the gym, finally settling on the group Darla mentioned. There were six teenage boys huddled against the wall at the baseline of the court. She could tell in the demeanor and body language of five of the six young men that they ran with a crew. Although she was familiar with many of the local crews around the area, she could not remember seeing any of these boys before. She studied the sixth boy intently. He stood with the others but was continuously shifting his weight, clearly uncomfortable with the discussion he was hearing. She moved her eyes from the uncomfortable child to the other five, noticing they were watching the same player on the court, Tyrell Lawson.

The dominant kid, who was clearly the oldest of the assembly, began gesturing wildly and pointing, obviously aggravated. Rose watched his mouth and read his lips as he said, "I'm gonna get my money." She continued to observe the animated boy, taking in everything about him and did not like what she saw. Her golden-eyed stare moved back to the awkward boy, and she let it remain on him for a time. After a minute, he felt her hard glare and made eye contact. With a small movement of her head, she indicated that she wanted him to come over to talk to her. He eyed the group he was standing with warily. The other five boys did not seem to remember he was with them. The anxious young man stepped away, crossing the gym to a waiting Rose.

"Walk with me," she commanded when he approached her. She moved to the gym door and pushed it open, motioning for the child to go into the lobby.

"Am I in trouble, Miss Jenkins?" he asked timidly. His large brown eyes were shadowed in fear. While Rose did not know the boy, she was not surprised that he knew her name. Between her work in the community and her employment as a very involved school counselor, most of the children in the area knew of her. She remained silent, leading him through the lobby and into the small room behind the desk. Once in the office, Rose motioned for the child to sit in one of the metal folding chairs in front of the small desk. Rather than taking the chair behind the barrier, she sat on the edge of the surface and faced the worried young man.

"What's your name?" she asked. The boy nervously bounced his leg as he looked up into her piercing golden eyes.

"Derrick," he replied quietly.

"Do you have a last name, Derrick?"

"Jacobs," he muttered. "Miss Jenkins, what did I do?" She offered him a smile of reassurance.

"It's not what you did; it's what your friends are about to do. I'm going to lay something out for you. I don't want you to run, and please, please don't lie to me; I'll know if you lie." His big brown eyes widened at this admonition, and he nodded slowly.

"Yes ma'am," he squeaked.

"The boys you are rolling with, they are in a crew. I can tell that you, Derrick, are not," she began. "I'm going to say you're related to one of them, perhaps a brother. You're not like those kids. You don't want to get into trouble, and you probably try your best to keep your nose clean. Whatever they were talking about had you seriously nervous." She watched Derrick's eyes intently and saw surprise, confirming the accuracy of her assessment. She leaned closer to the boy and stared into his eyes with a severe expression on her face. "I especially don't like that the kid in the blue basketball shorts is strapped. I don't want Tyrell hurt."

"How could you..." Derrick sputtered, his eyes wide in surprise.

"What I believe happened was that there was a bet on a game, and Tyrell didn't keep his end of the bargain, as far as your boy is concerned. Now he wants his money back. How am I doing so far?" she inquired, straightening from her leaning position and folding her arms. By the look on Derrick's face, her evaluation was very close. If the boy's eyes widened any more, they would have fallen out of their sockets.

"How do you know all of this?" he gasped.

"You ever hear of profiling, Derrick?"

"I've heard of it," he admitted.

"What I just showed you was an example of behavioral profiling. You see, I picked you out because you were obviously uncomfortable. You were shifting your weight and kept checking your surroundings, afraid that someone would hear the conversation. Your friends were watching Tyrell and I could tell by their facial expressions they weren't commenting on his crossover. Your boy with the gun, well he really shouldn't wear basketball shorts if he's going to be carrying: that's just stupid. Plus, I read his lips. He said 'I'm gonna get my money.' Really, Derrick, a blind man could have figured out what was up with you guys. Now tell me what I got wrong," she commanded after her explanation.

"It's my cousin. Javon. The guy with the gun, that's my cousin Javon. Last week, he rolled up on Tyrell and told him to make sure he covered the spread on Friday's game. Said he had big money riding on him, and if he covered it, he could hook him up. Tyrell kind of played it off like it wasn't a problem. Except, he took himself out in the fourth quarter, and they didn't. Javon is out a grand, and he says it's Tyrell's fault," he explained.

"That's gambling. The team could have lost, and he still would be out the money. What am I missing?" She narrowed her eyes and glared at the boy. Derrick shifted uncomfortably under her inspection. When he didn't answer the question, she leaned in and forced eye contact. "Javon wouldn't be this pissed if he just lost a bet. What am I missing, Derrick?"

"Javon runs with Big Luke's crew. The money he used to place the bet, it was part of what he was supposed to give Big Luke this week," he mumbled, averting the woman's stare. Rose sighed heavily and rubbed the bridge of her nose in frustration.

"He bet Big Luke's money? On the spread? Is he crazy?" She rounded the corner and sat behind the desk. Reaching for her purse, she began sifting through the bag until she found her phone. She started to dial a number, but changed her mind, and put the phone on the desk. "Stay here," she told the boy, standing and exiting the office.

Rose scrambled into the gym just as the pick-up game was ending. Her eyes darted to the area where the group had been standing. She caught sight of the boys heading in the direction of the celebrating Tyrell Lawson. Rose marched down the half-court line to cut off the cluster of teenagers. She reached center court just as Javon reached the same spot. He did not notice her until she put her hand on his shoulder to stop his advance.

"Javon," she said flatly. His eyes widened when he heard his name. "Follow me." Her hand still on his shoulder, she began to try to navigate him towards the entrance of the gymnasium. He dug in his heels and jerked his arm away from her.

"For what?" His tone was harsh and angry. She was not sure if his attitude was a remnant of the heated state he previously worked himself into, or if he was just generally a disrespectful kid. He started to step around her to continue on his journey, but Rose put another restraining hand on his shoulder, this time more firmly than before. She stepped in front of him so that she would be between him and Tyrell, who at this point was oblivious to the danger that was heading his direction.

"Because I said so," she hissed. Shifting her hand from his shoulder to just under his arm, she began to pull Javon with her towards the gym door. He jerked away from her again, more violently than before, causing his boys to take a step back.

"What the fuck you want with me? I ain't going nowhere with you," he spat angrily. He put his hand on Rose's shoulder to move her to the side. She grabbed the hand, twisted at the wrist, and kicked his legs from under him. As his balance began to teeter, she shoved him in the middle of his chest, causing him to fall back. A surprised Javon landed on the wooden gym floor with a loud thud. When he landed, she squatted over him, putting her knee on his chest. Fixing her golden eyes on him in a hard stare, she moved her hands to his pocket and retrieved the gun, tucking it into the small of her back. Javon heaved in pain, anger, and surprise. The gym, which had been filled with loud conversations, celebratory sentiments, and buoyant laughter, instantly grew silent. All eyes turned to the spectacle at half-court.

"First of all, it's Miss Jenkins. That's my name, Miss Jenkins," she growled. Her voice was eerily quiet, but the threat in her tone spoke volumes. "Secondly, if you ever talk out your neck to me again, I will embarrass you more than I just did. Now get your narrow ass up and follow me!" She stood up and waited for the very angry child to rise from his supine position. Javon scrambled to his feet and stared at her with the heat of a forest fire. Rose turned her back on him and strolled towards the door, hearing whispers around the gym as she walked.

She opened the door and looked back at the fuming young man who watched her from center court. "Today!" she bellowed. He clucked his tongue before finally shuffling after her. She led Javon in silence passed Darla, who raised a single eyebrow towards Rose when they made eye contact, and into the small office where Derrick waited. Rose entered first and stepped back for Javon to follow. When he spotted Derrick, a murderous rage took over his facial features. She closed the door and took her seat behind the desk.

"What the fuck did you tell her, D? Snitching ass bitch!" Javon sneered towards his cousin. "I'm beating your ass when we get home."

"I didn't say anything! She already knew!" the younger boy exclaimed. "She was profiling y'all and shit!"

"What the fuck is you talking about?" Javon asked.

"Sit," Rose commanded, indicating the empty chair next to Derrick. Javon paused for a moment and threw her a spiteful glare. She stared at him unfazed, her eyes hardened with authority. "I said, sit." He sighed angrily and plopped into the chair next to Derrick.

"I'm gonna fuck you up, D," he mumbled.

"You will do nothing of the sort," she cautioned, picking up her cell phone from the desk. She quickly scrolled through the contacts, found the number she was looking for and made her phone call. The recipient answered on the second ring.

"Miss Jenkins!"

"Hey, Luke. How's it going?" she replied. At the mention of Big Luke's name, Javon visibly stiffened.

"Can't complain much. Haven't heard from you in a while. What's up?"

"Javon. You know him?" she asked eyeing the boy. He had suddenly lost the hard shell of arrogance and anger.

"Yeah, he's one of my runners on the north side."

"He placed a bet on Tyrell's game last week," she began.

"Okay," he replied with no emotion.

"On the spread."

"All right."

"Tyrell took himself out of the game in the fourth, and the spread didn't get covered. Your boy seems to think that the money he lost was on Tyrell and not because his dumbass bet on the spread," she groused, still staring at Javon. He dropped his dark brown eyes to the floor and began studying the cracked and dirty tiling.

"Ok," Big Luke responded, clearly unsure why this was his concern.

"Problem is, he bet your money," she finished. Javon winced, and on the phone, Big Luke exhaled in a deep sigh.

"How much?"

"A grand," she replied.

"On the spread? What the fuck was this idiot thinking?"

"He thought Tyrell was going to hook him up by making sure the team covered, but I don't think it was as mutual as Javon seems to think it was. Tyrell wouldn't do that, not with the scholarships flooding in the way they are," she said. Javon began to fidget, and Rose could tell he wished he were anywhere else but where he was in that moment.

"Dumbass," Big Luke growled.

"Listen, I'm asking you to forget this happened. Because of this, your little idiot was going to do something really stupid. Tyrell doesn't need his future wrecked behind someone else's brainless decision; wouldn't you agree?"

"You know I do. I buy Tyrell two pairs of good basketball kicks every school year. He's going to be something one day for sure," he replied. There was a tenderness in his voice as he spoke about young Tyrell Lawson. Big Luke had no children of his own. At forty years of age, his childlessness was abnormal compared to other bangers in the area. Rose believed in some strange way he adopted the neighborhood children as his own, especially the ones who had the potential to get out of the hood. She recognized that Luke had a similar point of view about young people as she did; however, their methods were as different as fire and ice.

"I'm going to put Javon on the phone. I may have hurt his pride a little. He's quite displeased based on how he's been talking to me. Don't hurt him," At this point, a defeated Javon refused to meet her gaze.

"He's got to be punished," Luke grumbled. "If I let this go, then who's to stop others from doing the same stupid shit?"

"I'm not saying he shouldn't be. I'm saying, don't kill him. You and I coexist because we grew up together. You do good things for the community, despite the poison you peddle. But murder, Luke, that's something I couldn't overlook."

"Fine. I won't kill him," he agreed in a resigned tone. "Put him on." Rose extended the phone towards Javon who looked at the device as if it was a deadly viper, coiled and ready to strike. Shakily, he took the phone and put it to his ear.

"Hey, Big Luke." There was a quake in his voice.

"You fucked up big time. No one lays a hand on Tyrell Lawson as long as I run these streets, you hear me?" his boss snarled.

"Yes sir," the boy replied.

"If you ever use my money to make a stupid bet like that again, I will pull every red cent out of your ass. You got that?"

"Yes, sir."

"Miss Jenkins saved your life today. If I hear you've come at her foul, I will break your fucking legs. I'm going to dock what you owe me out of how much you keep from your sales until I get my money back — with interest," Luke informed him.

"Yes sir," Javon responded, but then he realized Big Luke already disconnected the call. He handed the phone back to Rose and continued to avert his eyes. She took the device and placed it on the desk.

"You better not lay a hand on Derrick," she commanded. Javon nodded and threw his cousin a stare that would have melted a glacier.

"Yes, ma'am."

"He didn't lie to you. He didn't tell me anything I hadn't already figured out. If he even looks like he has a mark on him, I don't care if he ran into a door, I will fuck you up myself," she said, her tone was cold and harsh. Javon lifted his eyes, and when he saw her glower, he dropped them to the ground immediately, giving her a nod of acquiescence.

"Can I have my piece back?" he inquired. Rose erupted in laughter so suddenly, the sound caused the two boys to flinch. She pulled the gun from the small of her back, ejected the magazine, and pulled back the slide to evict the chambered round, catching the bullet in the air when it popped out. She placed all of the items on her desk.

"That would be a no."

"Come on! I'm not going to hurt anyone! I need it for work," Javon protested. This statement drew another bark of laughter from Rose.

"I love how you think what you do is work," she said dismissively. "You got yourself this one, if you want it bad enough, you can get another." He stared at the disassembled gun, debating on whether he should argue more, but decided against the fight. Rose knew the weapon was likely unregistered, so there was little recourse on his part.

"Fine. Can I go?" he asked, rising from his seat. She gave him a slight nod of approval and Javon stepped to the door.

"Be careful out there," she advised.

"Come on D," he ordered, with his hand on the doorknob.

"Derrick is going to stay here for a few. I need to talk to him," Rose announced, extending her open palm towards Derrick when he moved to stand.

"If I go home without him, my auntie will be worried," Javon argued, a concerned look crossing his face.

"I'll bring him home. Just tell her he's talking to the counselor at the center," she insisted, shooing him with her hand. Choosing to exit rather than protest further, he left the room. After he was gone, she regarded the remaining boy with a gentle look.

"Tell me about yourself, Derrick."

CHAPTER FOUR

Layla Green piloted the white crime scene van down the main street in the heart of the Greenspoint district. The mid-morning sun blinded her, and she dropped the sunshade to preserve her vision. She took in the neighborhood as she drove down the road. Many of the rundown homes had unkempt yards littered with bicycles and broken-down cars. Groups of young men and women sat on porches listening to loud hip-hop music from portable stereos; some were smoking, while others were in the midst of rowdy conversations.

Approaching the crime scene, she noticed multiple Houston Police Department cruisers lining the street in front of the apartment complex. She slowed the van and waved at the uniformed officer responsible for keeping the flow of traffic under control. The officer, a short, young, Black woman, waved back as she moved the barrier allowing her to pass. The complex was smaller than most in the city, having only five two-story buildings. She found a parking spot in front of building three and used the radio to let dispatch know she had arrived. Grabbing her crime scene kit from the front passenger seat, she disembarked from her city-issued ride. Normally her best friend and partner, Rachel Vasquez, would have ridden with her; however, Vasquez had not made it into the office when the call came for the crime scene unit. When Layla subsequently reached out to her, Vasquez informed her she would meet her on scene. Now, Layla performed a visual sweep of the parking lot, looking for her friend's silver Jetta, but did not see the car.

"Guess I'll start without you," she grumbled aloud to her absent partner. After locking the van door, she followed the flow of uniformed cops towards the crime scene. Several officers spoke or waved a greeting as she passed. Layla addressed each one with a smile, their name, and appropriate rank. She never paused to search for a name in the annals of her mind, nor did she have to hunt for a nameplate on a uniform; and with each acknowledgment, the officers would grin broadly.

The apartment door was open with yellow crime scene tape loosely draped across the entrance like a decoration for a crime-themed party. She noticed the position of the tape was much lower than it should have been; too high to jump over, and too low to comfortably duck under. She assumed that whoever had been the FOS, or the first on scene, had never cordoned off a crime scene before. Sighing, she folded her five-foot-seven frame almost in half to proceed under the barrier, before turning and readjusting the barricade to a higher level allowing others to pass through more comfortably. When she finished, she turned and examined the room.

The apartment was cozy and immaculately clean. Just inside the door to her right was a laminate covered bar that separated the kitchen from the living area. The bar itself was clear of any clutter or knick-knacks, and as she peered over the divider, she saw no dirty dishes in the sink or on the counters. She turned her examination to the living room. If she had not known the furniture was about ten years old by the fabric and style, she would have thought it brand new. Parallel vacuum lines ran east to west on the beige carpeting, and she could tell that everything had its place. The only brand-new items appeared to be a forty-seven-inch flat screen television stationed on a medium sized stand and a video game console. The display showed a menu screen for a popular first-person video game, one she had in her own collection. The only portion of the living space that was in disarray was the shattered wooden coffee table in the middle of the room, splinters of wood dotting the otherwise pristine carpeted floor. The dead body that caused the broken table did not add much to the décor either.

"Finally!" Layla turned from her assessment of the scene to the voice that spoke from the door. Rachel Vasquez ducked under the tape and entered the apartment. Layla was glad she moved the blockade when she arrived. At five-foot-seven, entry was uncomfortable for her; Vasquez would have had to be a contortionist to fold her five-foot-ten figure under the same barricade.

"What are you talking about? I was here first," Layla asked. Reaching into the crime scene kit, she withdrew two pairs of latex gloves and tossed a pair to Vasquez, who caught them and shoved them into her HPD Crime Scene Unit windbreaker. From the opposite pocket, she took out a hair-tie and pulled her long honey brown hair into a ponytail before slipping on the gloves. Vasquez looked like she could have been a runway model. Any fashion label or makeup company would welcome her many physical attributes; she was tall, fair skinned, and had emerald green eyes. Although her ethnic heritage was completely Mexican, her features screamed European, causing her name to conflict with her appearance.

"I meant me," Vasquez was saying. "The highway was insane. It's ten in the freaking morning; where are all these people going? Don't they have jobs?" As usual, her hands were animated as she spoke, and her clip was rapid and staccato, bringing to mind a human typewriter. She still had a slight accent that went unnoticed by most — particularly when she was agitated. Layla chuckled at the woman's tirade.

"Don't you have the portable siren? Why didn't you use it?"

"Sí, porque the wonderful people in Houston are super receptive to sirenas," Vasquez replied incredulously.

"Pick one, English or Spanish."

"In Texas, there is always a third option. Spanglish is an unofficial language, you know," she replied, a jovial twinkle in her emerald eyes. Layla shook her head in response to the woman's justification. Vasquez's bright smile melted as she turned to the grisly scene in the living room. "Yikes," she muttered taking in the body. Layla pulled the department Canon digital camera from the kit and slipped the strap over her curly scarf-wrapped mane. The camera dangled between her breast and stomach as she turned back to the scene.

"Just once, I'd like to shoot a birthday party," she complained. Vasquez took a ruler, tweezers and evidence bags from the kit, slipping them into the pocket of her windbreaker.

"Not me. They only call us when people die. Who wants to see a dead body at a birthday party?"

"Well, obviously no one. But at least there would be decorations and cake," Layla replied with a shrug, adjusting the camera strap around her neck.

"You got the scene stored?" Vasquez asked, referring to Layla's eidetic memory. Her recall was notorious around the homicide department, and as a result, she was often called to help fill in missing puzzle pieces.

She turned her back on the room and closed her eyes, calling to mind the scene and every intricate detail. This step was unnecessary, but she always double-checked fearing the day when her memory might suddenly begin to slip. While most people knew if diseases like Alzheimer's or dementia ran in their genetics, Layla had no knowledge of her family history. Like many other orphans, she considered taking a genetic mapping test, but the fear of the unknown outweighed her curiosity. She pictured the room in her mind and saw the placement of every piece of furniture, trinket, pen, and paper. She visualized the position of the body, the blood spatter, and every scrap of wood from the broken coffee table. Once she recalled all of the detail, she turned around and did a sweep of the room to ensure the image she had in her mind matched the reality of her surroundings.

"Got it. Let's hit it," she confirmed, giving Vasquez a satisfied nod. She began to snap a few pictures of the overall scene from the doorway, before moving around the room, carefully stepping over the mess to shoot various angles. Once she captured the overall room from different perspectives, Layla turned the camera to the body itself. The victim was male, lying prone with his head facing away from the front door and towards the television as if he took the killing shot directly from the game. His vacant eyes were staring at the screen, an expression of death frozen on his face. Layla circled the body, careful to sidestep blood and debris and took a few more pictures. Just as she finished taking the photos of the overall state of the victim, a member of the Medical Examiner's office arrived on the scene.

"Layla Green. Rachel Vasquez. We have got to stop meeting like this," Jimmy Larson's voice boomed as he ducked under the tape. Vasquez gasped when she turned to his voice, the sound of her surprise causing Layla to follow suit.

"Jimmy! Your hair! Did you lose a bet?" Layla gawked. Jimmy's white-blond hair usually hung in a Willie Nelson style braid. Now, it was cut military short and spiked at the top. He blushed and self-consciously rubbed his tattooed hand over his bristly mane.

"Wife said if I didn't cut it, she would cut me," he replied. A former biker in his youth, the man's body type resembled someone who spent most of his time off in the gym preparing for a bodybuilding contest. His muscular frame covered in tattoos was the only relic of his previous biker life. Now married with two small daughters, Jimmy's easygoing smile and light attitude were more fitting for a human teddy bear rather than a stereotypical biker.

"Not sure how I feel about it," Vasquez admitted, cocking her head at Jimmy's new look. She stepped over to him and rubbed the top of his spiked head.

"That makes two of us darlin'," he huffed.

"Glad you could join us, Dr. Larson. Now we can commence the main event," Layla declared, motioning with a flourish towards the dead body in the middle of the room.

"Did you touch him?" he inquired, slipping his meaty hands into a pair of gloves and moving across the room to the body. Layla and Vasquez eyed each other, and then stared at him; the expression on their faces was both severe and indignant.

"¡Chale! Come on Jimmy. We aren't amateurs here," Vasquez responded in annoyance.

"You know I have to ask," he conceded, raising his gloved hands in mock surrender. He turned to Layla and cocked an eyebrow. "What did she just call me?"

"It means like, give me a break, or you're joking," Layla translated, giving his arm a reassuring pat. "She'd never say anything bad about you, Jimmy."

"Sure I would!" Vasquez exclaimed brightly, clapping him on his back. "But I would make sure you understood me."

"That's all I ask," he grunted, turning his light blue eyes back to the deceased man on the floor.

"If you don't mind, Dr. Larson, we'd like to touch him now," Layla said motioning toward the dead man with her head.

"That's kind of kinky, even for you, Layla."

"Gross," Vasquez groaned. Jimmy motioned for Vasquez to help him roll the body. Layla positioned herself at the man's feet, her camera ready for more photos. Vasquez and Jimmy gently rolled the man onto his back, and Layla took a few more snapshots. His face was handsome, even wearing the mantle of death, and she estimated him to be in his mid-thirties. He was barefoot, wearing dark blue sweatpants, and an undershirt, which had been white before his death but was now dark red from his blood. Jimmy carefully pulled up the man's shirt to expose the gruesome gunshots, two in his chest and one in his abdomen.

"Three shots," he murmured. "Whoever shot him wanted him dead." Both Jimmy and Vasquez leaned away from the body, while still holding the shirt, to offer Layla a vantage point to take closer photos of the victim's gory torso. Bile began to rise in her throat, and she swallowed it fiercely. Despite working in homicide for over ten years, she had not grown accustomed to gruesome scenes of death.

"Well, that's not something you see every day," Vasquez muttered, pointing at the man's chest with her free hand. Layla swallowed back another wave of nausea before she was able to focus on what her partner was indicating. When her eyes fell onto his tattoo, she lifted the camera and took a few more photos. The ink on the man's chest was unusual, to say the least. Starting just above his navel, an extended forearm in a "power pose" led to a closed fist in the middle of his chest. The clenched fist was encased by an Afro, and on the wrist of the extended arm were blocky words in the style of another tattoo that decreed, "By Any Means Necessary."

"I've seen a lot ladies, but I can honestly say this is the first time I've seen a fist with hair," Jimmy snorted, easing the man's shirt over his bloody torso.

"Time of death?" Vasquez asked.

"About six to eight hours," Layla responded immediately without thought. As soon as the words left her mouth, she glanced sheepishly at Jimmy who gave her a playfully stern look. In her decade-long career, Layla had seen just about every stage of rigor mortis there was to be seen and could pinpoint a time of death almost as accurately as a medical examiner. Jimmy was shocked the first few times she had done this, but having worked with her for a few years, he knew she was more than likely correct.

"Show off," he grumbled. He bent down and went through the motions of examining for rigor mortis, and stood before announcing, "Rigor shows time of death to be between six and eight hours ago. Of course, that's unofficial; the autopsy will confirm the exact TOD." He called out to an assistant waiting outside of the apartment door, and they began the process of bagging the body. Layla and Vasquez wandered around the apartment collecting anything that could be construed as evidence, the cleanliness of the place making the job more tedious than usual. After an hour and a half of processing the small abode, the duo stored their samples and exited the residence.

Detective Oscar Lewis sat perched at the bottom of the stairs leading up to the second level apartments, engrossed in his phone and waiting for the women to finish their processing. At forty-seven years of age, Lewis had been in homicide almost twice as long as Layla had been working the crime scene unit. He stood when he heard Layla and Vasquez exit the apartment. He was average in height, a couple of inches taller than Layla but not as tall as Vasquez. His physique was lean and muscular, with turquoise eyes that were piercing and, to most people, unsettling. A perpetual five o'clock shadow peppered his chin. He turned his startling eyes to the women and smiled in greeting.

"Lewis," Layla grinned. Her job required her to work with many homicide detectives, but she was always happy when she caught a case that was assigned to Lewis. Vasquez leaned in and hugged him. Despite her propensity for hugs, he seemed surprised at the show of affection.

"Hey, kids. Find anything useful?" He stood as he asked the question.

"Well, we have to get back to the lab before we really know that," Vasquez replied. Lewis shot a curious glance to Layla. While most homicide detectives did not readily ask the opinion of the processing crime scene unit, Lewis trusted Layla's eyes almost as much as he trusted his own.

"I can tell you what we didn't find — identification. No wallet, no driver's license, nothing," she informed him, slipping her hands out of her latex gloves. Lewis furrowed his eyebrows at the information.

"Odd. Leasing office says the name on the lease is Tasha Rodgers, but no one has ever seen her. The vic was a man?"

"Yep. Definitely not a Tasha," Vasquez replied.

"We're trying to run her down. Did you find any shoe imprints on the carpet?" he inquired.

"Recently vacuumed," Layla answered. "Not sure if the victim did it before he got plugged, or if the shooter decided to spruce the place up before he took off."

"When my brother gets home, he puts his wallet and keys on the bar. The entry is tile, so if this guy did the same thing, it would be easy to take the vic's ID without stepping foot into the apartment. We did vacuum both tile and carpeting, maybe something will turn up," Vasquez added with a shrug. Lewis nodded in deep thought as she spoke.

"Let me guess, no one heard nothing, saw nothing, and they just don't know nothing," Layla sighed. In lower economic neighborhoods such as Greenspoint, it was rare that witnesses willingly came forward, even with a crime as serious as murder. The community attitude was generally, "don't trust the police." She understood the sentiment to a degree, having spent much of her teenage years on the run from law enforcement to prevent returning to the foster care system, but she found it vexing to be on the other end of the mistrust.

"Does anyone ever know anything?" he asked.

"We're going to head back to catalog and run some tests. We didn't find much, but maybe we can uncover something with what was there," Layla informed him, as she began to walk towards the parking lot. Lewis' hand shot out, and he touched her shoulder to halt her.

"What caliber?" Lewis asked Layla.

"You know the autopsy will tell you that," she responded, a glint of mischief in her eye.

"So can you," he countered with a wink, drawing a chuckle from Layla. She had seen numerous bullet entry wounds in her time with the police force. The difference in entry was small and could vary depending on the distance of the shooter, but Layla had a knack for judging the caliber of a gun used by sight.

"If I were a betting woman, I'd say it was a .38." Lewis gave her a gentle pat on the shoulder as he turned back towards the apartment.

"I'd bet on you any time, kid."

Layla and Vasquez separated in the parking lot with the intent of meeting back up at the station. As Layla drove back to the precinct, she ran the panorama through her mind on a loop, feeling like she missed something of importance. In all of her years working murder cases, she had never seen a scene as clean as the one she had just left. Navigating the dense mid-day traffic, a difficult activity given the drivers in the city, she mentally walked through the small apartment, cataloging what she saw. Soon, as she often did, she began to speak aloud as she processed.

"Our vic was playing video games. There was no forced entry, and no signs of multiple tenants, so the shooter had to have knocked. He opens the door and boom. The perp steps into the entryway, grabs his wallet, and bounces. Why would the guy open the door?" After mulling the question over in her mind, she could not readily piece it out. She shifted her focus to the objects in the room.

"The TV..." Layla pondered aloud, easing the van to a stop at a traffic light just before the interstate on-ramp. "The TV," she said again in deep thought. The light turned green, and a barrage of horns alerted her that she should move. Hitting the switch on the dashboard, she turned on the siren and cut across the lanes of traffic, pulling into a gas station on the service road.

"The TV," she mumbled again, throwing the van into park. She closed her eyes and mentally strolled through the apartment, coming to rest in front of the illuminated box. When Layla first glanced at the screen upon arrival, she assumed it was on the standard game menu. As she returned to the residence in her mind, she took a second glance at the television.

"Shit!" she hissed, putting the van in gear and speeding back to the complex. When she arrived, she noted that the number of patrol cars had been slashed in half, indicating the canvassing was drawing to a close. When she eased into the parking lot, she found her former space still unoccupied. Grabbing her kit, she fished out another pair of gloves and sprang from the van. As she scurried to the apartment, she saw Lewis leaving another building. He turned towards the parking lot and his steps faltered when he saw a determined Layla making her way back to the crime scene.

"You miss me, kid?" Lewis called, changing course and heading her direction.

She slowed her stride to allow him to catch up.

"I missed... something," she informed him when he was within earshot. Disbelief tinted his features.

"You never miss anything," he replied in a low voice.

"There's a first time for everything." She ducked under the tape and entered the apartment with Lewis on her heels. Dropping her kit next to the bar, she tiptoed through the blood and debris on the floor to the television. The unit had been turned off, prompting Layla to scan the room in search of a remote control.

"What's up, Kid?" Lewis asked in confusion. Layla found the slender black remote on an end table next to the couch and gracefully danced her way over to it. Grabbing the remote, she whirled back to the television and turned on the power.

"Our vic was playing video games," she mumbled. Lewis gaped at her statement.

"That isn't new information, the FOS said that he appeared to be playing video games when he was killed."

"Right, but he was actually in the middle of *playing* the game," she repeated, emphasizing the verb. While the television powered up, she scanned the small room looking for a controller for the gaming system. She spied one on the floor in the middle of the broken coffee table splattered with blood. Her stomach turned at the prospect of handling the bloodstained controller. Searching the room again, she located a small charging station on the floor next to the TV stand, a controller plugged in and charging. With a cry of triumph, she tiptoed through the gore and wreckage to retrieve the device and then focused on the television. Faint gray light emitted from the screen due to lack of visual input. Layla found the button to turn on the system, and a soft beep from the console alerted her that the machine was activated. The logo of the video game company appeared, and Layla attempted to keep her patience under control as she waited.

"Green, I'm not following what's going on right now," Lewis declared, waving his hand in the direction of the television.

"Do you play video games, Oscar?"

"Layla, I'm a forty-seven-year-old married man with three kids. The twins are in college, and I work over sixty hours a week to pay their tuition, feed their sister, and put a little something away so I don't have to get shot at for the rest of my life. Is that a serious question?" Lewis inquired, his eyes wide with surprise. She sighed heavily and shook her head.

"Okay, let's see if you can follow me here. When you're playing a game like this, there are two modes you can use: single player or multiplayer," she began.

"Okay."

"Single player is also called story mode. That means there is an actual story arc about your character that you play through. During story mode, you don't have a lot of options. Things like gear and weapons aren't available out the gate; instead, you collect them while you go through the story," she continued.

"I don't consider myself a dumb man, but this isn't getting any clearer," he grunted in a perplexed manner.

"Wait for it," she insisted, placing her hand on his arm to encourage patience. "In multiplayer mode, you have more gear and weapons at your disposal. Multiplayer mode is played with other people from all over the world. The screen our victim was on was not the game menu, but the load-out screen, which is where players select the weapons and gear that they want to take into battle."

"The more you talk, the more confused I'm getting," he sighed heavily in frustration. She pinched her bottom lip between two fingers trying to think of a way to translate video games to a middle age man who probably had not played a game since Pong.

"Okay, think of it like this," she said, switching gears. "When you become a cop, you start out as a uniform. At that time, you only have a side arm as your weapon. Think of that as story mode. Like with the department, you get access to more toys when you attain a higher rank. At the beginning of the game, you start with your standard issue, and as you progress through, other things start unlocking for your use. Multiplayer is like immediately starting the game in SWAT. You have weapons and gear that you can choose to take with you, and a team of strangers from all over the world that will be your team members."

"Now you're speaking English," he nodded.

"Our victim was playing in multiplayer mode. The screen the television was on was the load-out screen; it's like visiting the armory before you go on a call with SWAT. In multiplayer, every player goes through that menu *between* matches." she said,

"Alright, I'm tracking now. But why is this so important?"

"A good portion of the time when you're playing in multiplayer mode, especially if you're a serious player, you have to communicate with your team members. Normally people use a headset." She turned her attention back to the TV and began navigating around the home screen of the system. "Our vic wasn't wearing a headset, but he didn't need one. You see this?" She paused and pointed to a slender black box that was positioned at the base of the television.

"What is that?" he asked, leaning in to inspect the item.

"It's a camera that also doubles as a microphone. If you have one of these, you don't have to have a headset. Usually, people prefer a headset for authenticity, or because they don't live alone, and this camera picks up ambient noise too easily. I don't see any indication that someone else lived here, so our guy probably opted for this method."

"You sure know a lot about these games," he remarked, his gaze floating from Layla to the television screen. "You're way too smart to be a gamer."

"You'd be surprised how many intelligent people play video games. It's about problem-solving and mental dexterity. You should read a study or two on it before judging, my friend." She resumed her navigation, finally finding what she was searching for. "Ah." She removed her cell phone from her back pocket, opened her camera, and started to take pictures of the screen.

"If that's a game, it's the weirdest game I've ever seen," he said, after leaning in and inspecting the screen.

"This shows gamer tags of players that you've recently played with, but that may not be on your friend's list. Remember, when you're playing online the majority of the time you're playing matches with strangers you don't know. The gaming system categorizes these people as recently met. They are held in one area in case you want to add them later," she explained. After taking photos of all the recently met players, she moved to the list of people the deceased man had already added to his friend's list. The list was sparse, but there were a few gamer tags listed. After she finished with the photos, she turned off the system and dropped the controller into the open crime scene bag. She crossed in front of Lewis on her way back to the entertainment system. He watched as she meticulously began disconnecting the console.

"What are you thinking?"

"If I can access the history, this will tell us who was online when the victim was killed. Someone may have heard the shooting. If I can't get into it, we have the geeks in tech," she said, sliding the console into the large bag and sealing the plastic. Lewis' eyes began to register comprehension.

"So, if they can get into it..."

"This could be a lead," she finished holding up her phone.

CHAPTER FIVE

Rose let out a deep yawn while the aroma of the two piping-hot bacon, egg and potato breakfast burritos made her stomach rumble. She stole a glance at the time and saw it was just after seven in the morning. Perusing her work email, Rose thought back to the conversation she had with Derrick the night before and reflected on the home life the child described.

Javon was Derrick's cousin by blood, and after he lost his mother to cancer when he was only seven, he moved in with Derrick and his mother, Patrice. According to Derrick, Javon was extremely angry for most of his childhood and Patrice could not control the boy. Derrick believed it was partially because Patrice was trying to allow him to grieve, and partially Javon's own bull-headed nature. Once he hit puberty, regulating the troubled child became virtually impossible. At the age of fourteen, Javon decided to leave high school to pursue the more lucrative path of drug dealing for Big Luke, insisting that school had no more to teach him. Derrick told Rose that his cousin had been working for Big Luke for about three years. While the fifteen-year-old Derrick had no interest in the illegal activities, much like many younger boys, he was thrilled with the idea of hanging out with his older cousin rather than staying home alone. To Javon's credit, Derrick assured Rose that even if he wanted to accompany him on his illegal endeavors, Javon would never allow him.

"He thinks I'm smart," Derrick said.

"What do you think?" Rose asked.

"I don't know," the boy shrugged. "I like numbers. I'm really good at math. I can draw pretty good too. Javon thinks I could be an architect and design big buildings and stuff. He said if I kept my grades up, he'd help me when I go to college." Rose smiled at the vow, knowing that Javon could not guarantee he would even be alive to see Derrick graduate high school.

Rose asked Derrick to drop by the center later in the week to assure her that Javon had not followed through on his angry threats from earlier in the night. She began to craft an email to Tony Banks, a college friend who worked at an architectural firm in downtown Houston. Raised on the east side of Austin, Tony had come from a similar background as Rose. Entrenched in poverty, the choices of survival were illegal activities, the military, or keeping one's head down and focusing on school. The common upbringing and subsequent similar outlook on life were recognized early between the two friends. Initially, Tony wished for something more, and Rose gently let him know that she saw him as more of a surrogate brother rather than a possible suitor.

Tony resided north of Houston in the Woodlands with his beautiful wife, Cassandra, and a baby on the way. The two remained friends after graduation and attempted to get together at least once every few months to catch up. He was also very interested in Rose's work with at-risk youth and offered to be a ready mentor whenever she needed him. She gave Tony a rundown of Derrick's situation and requested that he meet with the boy. Her idea was to let Derrick see the inner workings of a real architectural firm. She believed that witnessing the success of a Black man, from a similar background, would encourage Derrick to pursue his dreams. She had just sent the message when a timid knock drew her attention to the office door. She checked the time and saw it was exactly fifteen minutes after seven.

"Come in," she called, closing out her email and locking her computer screen. The door cracked open, and Leon poked his head into the office, not entering until she waved him in with her hand.

"Hi, Miss Jenkins." He shuffled into the room, dropped his backpack onto the floor, and took the same seat he occupied the day before. Rose had not been fully convinced the child would show. While she believed Leon was willing, she was keenly aware that a child of eleven had to depend on his home environment to facilitate such a meeting. She slid one of the burritos across the desk, and when the delicious aroma wafted across his nose, his stomach grumbled. He gave her a genuine smile, flashing his dimples, and thanked her.

"So? Did you listen to the song?" She asked, unwrapping her burrito. She watched the child unwrap his own meal and then pause, his green eyes searching the room.

"Do you have any hot sauce?" he inquired. Rose's eyebrows raised in surprise.

"What do you know about hot sauce?" She scoffed, leaning back towards the small bookcase positioned against the wall behind her. She picked up a bottle of Louisiana Hot Sauce and pushed it across the desk.

"I eat it on everything," he admitted, opening the bottle. He began to shake a generous portion onto his burrito, more than most adults would use.

"I see," she remarked, eyeing the massive red puddle forming on the wrapper. Leon continued to shake, only stopping when he realized she was watching him. He capped the bottle and put it on the desk.

"Sorry," he mumbled. He adjusted the burrito as to not make a mess on his lime green t-shirt and took a big bite. Rose waved her hand dismissively towards the apology.

"So?"

"It was alright," Leon replied, taking another bite of his burrito and smearing hot sauce on the sides of his mouth. Rose produced a napkin from a desk drawer and thrust it towards the child. He took the napkin, wiped his mouth and smiled sheepishly.

"Just alright?"

"It kind of reminded me of my mom," he said, a tinge of sadness in his voice.

"And songs that remind you of your mom are bad?" she asked.

"No, that's not what I meant." He shook his head rapidly as if trying to clarify his thoughts. "I liked it because it reminded me of my mom. It's just different than what I usually listen to."

"Wasn't that the point of this whole exercise?"

"Yeah, I guess," he shrugged, a melancholy expression clouding his face.

"What's wrong?"

"It's kind of a sad song. It reminded me of my mom because it's kind of sad," Leon admitted. Rose was surprised by this analysis. "Keep Ya Head Up" was generally heralded as one of the more uplifting songs of her generation.

"Really? Why?"

"He's talking about women raising kids by themselves, and how some kids don't have daddies. I don't have a daddy, cause he's dead. Then I thought about Kenya," his voice trailed off at the mention of his deceased sister. "The whole reason she's dead is because of some fools fighting over drugs. I want to be a rapper to help my mom get a better life, to get out of the hood, just like he did." Rose's heart melted as she listened. The boy had seen so much sadness in his mere decade in this world; the song reminded him of both his loss and his longing for a better life.

"But what is the hook telling you?" she inquired in a soft voice. Leon took a deep breath attempting to reign in his emotion. The burrito lay half eaten on the desk, and Rose saw that his appetite was wavering.

"To keep your head up, because it'll get better. But it doesn't feel like it'll ever get better," he replied, his voice cracking. As if that audible expression of sentiment was too much for him, he took up his meal again with a small bite, chewing slowly to prevent himself from crying.

"It can get better, Leon. But you can't just wait for something to happen. You have to put in some work. Doing well in school, staying out of trouble, trying to find your passion and following it. It's hard sometimes. Black folks, we are born underdogs simply because of our skin color. Sure, some aren't born poor, but the challenges are still there; it's not new." Rose pushed her own half eaten meal to the side. With Leon being in his emotional state, she felt that if any lesson were to be taught on this particular morning, it would have to be now, while he was allowing himself to be vulnerable.

"So, if we are all born underdogs, what are we supposed to do?" he asked, turning his watery eyes to Rose.

"Let's consider the words." She began to quote the song and stopped after the second line, "the darker the flesh then the deeper the roots." She let the words hang in the air for a moment. "What do you think that means?" Leon considered the question for a moment before finally shrugging.

"I don't know."

"We come from a people with deep roots. The history of Black folks in this country is full of pain; but if things were really hopeless, if things really could never be better for us, do you think we would still be here?" The boy's eyebrows creased in thought.

"I guess not," he replied, after a beat.

"Over the years, every generation has had to power through challenges. First, there was slavery, and we overcame that. Then, there was a time when we weren't equal and didn't have basic human rights, and we got through that as well. We continue to have struggles, and there is often an overwhelming feeling to just lie down and accept the circumstances we are given."

"Boy, that's for sure," the child mumbled.

"But that's not who we are as a people. We overcome. That's the point of the song. Wherever you are in your life, you will have difficult times, that's part of growing up. Black people have always had more challenges than most but we are resilient, and we persist," she explained. "When you run a race, do you run the whole thing with your head down, looking at your feet?" He gave her a look of uncertainty.

"No."

"Why?"

"Because you have to see where you're going," he replied, in a matter-of-fact tone.

"Exactly. You have to keep your head up, so you know where you want to be and how to get there," she said triumphantly. Leon's eyes registered comprehension as he grasped the parallel. "I grew up just like you, Leon. It would have been easy for me to have the same kind of outlook on life that you have. I could have accepted that Sunnyside was all there was for me. But there are role models out there besides athletes and hip-hop artists. Black people have done so much — far more than what is taught in history class."

"Who did you look up to?" he asked, sitting back in his chair. His appetite returned, he began munching on his burrito in earnest once again.

"I learned about these two doctors, Dr. Kenneth and Mamie Clark. You ever heard of them?" She took up her own burrito from her desk and took another bite.

"Were they like doctors in a hospital?" he asked, popping the rest of his burrito into his mouth. Before Rose could ask for it, he stood and tossed the wrapper in a trashcan by the office door.

"No, they weren't medical doctors. They were psychologists; kind of like me, but with a little more education." Rose wistfully thought about her desire to finish her doctorate; an aspiration currently deferred.

"Okay. What did they do?" he inquired, taking his seat. She smiled at the child's genuine interest.

"For starters, they were really important in helping schools desegregate," she answered. Incomprehension fell onto Leon's face at the new word.

"What does desegregate mean?"

"Some time ago, before you and I were born, the government felt that White people and Black people should be separated. They had White-only restaurants, hotels, bathrooms, and even something simple like a water fountain was separated by color. If a Black person was caught using anything that was designated for White people, they could go to jail, get beat up, or worse," she explained. Leon's green eyes widened at the unthinkable circumstances. Such a life was very real for people like Rose's own mother but was inconceivable to a child of eleven.

"Why would they do that?" he asked.

"There has always been a thought that Black people are dangerous, scary, or somehow lesser than White people. After slavery ended, there was a small amount of time when the recently freed slaves were able to have the same rights as others, but it didn't last long. Laws started being made forcing the two races to live separately, even though they were in the same country. In some places, people wouldn't rent homes to Black people or hire them for jobs. Also during this time, they would not allow Black and White children to attend the same schools," she explained. Astonishment seemed to be a fixed expression on the child's face.

"So, what did these Clark doctors do?"

"The Black people kept trying to tell the government that it was harmful to keep separating children in schools," she replied. "They felt that the White students were getting a higher quality of education than the Black students. This led to fewer opportunities for the more uneducated Black people. The government tried to insist that although the students were separated, they were also equal and that there was no damage in keeping the children with their own color. This prompted Kenneth and Mamie Clark to conduct some experiments."

"But I thought these Clark people were Black," Leon interrupted, his face now perplexed.

"They were," she admitted.

"Then how did they get to be doctors?"

"There were colleges formed for Black people a long time ago. We now call them HBCUs, which are Historically Black Colleges and Universities. The Clarks both started their education at Howard University. Although most higher education was segregated, some schools like Colombia University in New York would allow admittance to Black people. Back then, the North was a little more progressive than the South. After they finished at Howard, they moved on to Columbia University," she explained. "The Clarks ran some studies on different school children, some in areas where segregation was really big, and others where some of the local governments chose to allow students to integrate, or come together into one school. One of their more famous experiments involved dolls."

"It was a test only for girls?" he wondered.

"No. It was for all children," she chuckled. "They would take two identical dolls, one Black and one White, and ask the children questions. For instance, they would ask 'which one of these dolls is the nicer doll,' or 'which one would you want to play with,' or maybe, 'which doll is the ugliest doll,' things like that. They found that the Black children who were segregated from other colors believed that White was better than Black, and there was a deep self-hatred of their own skin color." Leon listened intently as she spoke, but suddenly his face became indiscernible. "What?"

"It makes me think of Kenya," he muttered softly. Rose cocked her head in confusion.

"Why?"

"We had different daddies. My daddy was light skinned like me, and Kenya's was dark like her. She used to tell me she wished she was light like me and would say she was ugly. I thought she was beautiful," he explained. "I would tell her that I thought she was pretty, but she never believed me." His words dripped with sadness at this painful memory of his beloved sister.

"Leon, some people feel that way because of how others react to darker skin tones. You are absolutely right; your sister was beautiful. That's part of what was being shown by the Clarks. They found that kids who were separated would see how much better the White kids were treated. They began to believe that being Black was equal to being bad. But that's not true. The Clarks' research in part helped the government to see that separating children by color did more harm than good, and school segregation became illegal."

"Not a lot of White people in our school," he noted.

"That's true, but there are other reasons for that. We can discuss that at another time. The point is there are so many Black people out there who have had a major impact on society. You don't have to feel like Greenspoint or hip-hop is all there is for you, just like I had to realize Sunnyside wasn't all there was for me when I was young. You can't let where you live, and your surroundings determine what you can achieve. The point of 2Pac's song is to remind you that, while things may be hard, it doesn't always have to be, and if you keep your head up and focus on what you want out of life, things really can get better." Leon's face registered intense contemplation at the end of her speech.

Rose knew that a child's perception of the future was not something that could be changed overnight, particularly if his or her environment did not reinforce the desired vision. She truly hoped that the more time she spent with Leon, the more she could nurture the seed she had begun to plant with this conversation. She pushed away from her desk and retrieved a sheet of paper from the bookshelf, sliding the page towards the child. He picked up the paper and glanced at the words before turning his eyes back to her.

"What's this?"

"Are you aware that all lyrics are just poems put to music?" Leon scanned the paper, before looking at her and shrugging.

"Never thought about it like that."

"What you have there is a poem by Langston Hughes. He was a poet back in the nineteen twenties and thirties, during a time called the Harlem Renaissance. Things were pretty bad for Black people back then, and it did not seem like it would get better. Mr. Hughes wrote down his feelings about being Black in his time, just like 2Pac wrote about it in the nineties."

"As I Grew Older," Leon thoughtfully read the title of the famous Langston Hughes poem.

"You should read it a few times. Maybe when you come tomorrow, you can tell me a little bit about what you think of his work," she said, nodding towards the paper with her chin. He stuffed the page into his backpack.

"Hey Miss Jenkins, can I ask you a question?"

"Of course."

"If you grew up like me, wanting to get out of the hood and stuff; why are you here now? You could be at some nice school somewhere, but instead, you came here." His tone was sincere, and Rose was shocked at the insightful question.

"Well Leon, my initial inspiration for this kind of work was the Clarks. As I studied in college, I began to understand how environment and prejudice affect people mentally as well as physically. I thought about how when I was a kid, my teachers didn't always care what we went through at home. Parents who are worried about things like money and keeping their children fed don't always realize how that situation affects their kids. Many times, that kind of environment makes it hard for children to focus on learning. Meanwhile, the schools are demanding more rigidity and conformity, but they aren't considering the external factors their students are dealing with. I wanted to help kids like me, so I specifically found a school that could use that kind of help." The school bell rang, and Leon's rapt gaze flicked behind him towards the door. He stood and shouldered his backpack.

"I'm glad you did. You care way more than Mr. Cavanaugh," he smiled, edging towards the door. "You are also the first teacher to tell me they were sorry for Kenya. That means a lot." Rose's heart ached at this news, and her vision swam. Every teacher in the school knew of Kenya Murphy's death, and not one of them expressed their condolences to her brother. They complained about his behavioral issues, and never acknowledged that grief could be a factor in the boy's problems. She collected her emotions before speaking again.

"Between you and me Leon, Cavanaugh is kind of an asshole," she winked.

After the successful first breakfast with Leon, Rose was determined not to ruin her good mood and effectively avoided Lorenzo Cavanaugh the whole day. She received an email response from Tony Banks informing her that he would be happy to meet with Derrick. She crafted a quick reply telling him that she would set up the meeting with the boy and then logged off of her computer. She retrieved her purse from her desk drawer, sifting through the large cluttered bag in search of her keys. The abrupt sound of her phone vibrating on the desk caused her to jump. She peeked at the screen and was astonished at the caller's identity. Fishing her keys out of her purse, she slung the bag onto her shoulder, and answered the phone, exiting her office and locking the door behind her. She did not bother with a greeting, waiting for the automated voice to finish its announcement before pressing a key to accept the charges of the collect call.

"Hey sis!" Her older brother, Robert, exclaimed after the Department of Corrections recording connected him. Robert was at the tail end of a ten-year felony stint. His technical charge was possession with the intent to distribute. While he had never been a drug dealer, he was a user on a dangerous level. At the time of his arrest, he had enough product on him to make almost fifty thousand dollars, although it was for his own consumption. When he was arrested, Rose was relieved, for she knew had law enforcement not intervened, her mother Joyce would have had to bury her third son.

"Rob! You're early. It's not Saturday!" she exclaimed. Making her way out of the school, she passed Cavanaugh in the hallway near the exit. The Vice Principal looked as if he wanted to speak with her, but she did not acknowledge him, grateful that the phone call gave her justification to ignore him. Rose cleared Cavanaugh and made her way into the bright March afternoon.

"I know, but this couldn't wait until Saturday," he replied. She could hear the excitement in his voice. Since being in prison and getting clean, Rose found that Robert was an animated character, but she still marveled when she heard his energetic voice.

"What's up?" she asked, approaching her car. She got into her ride and started the engine. The Toyota moved the call from her phone to the hands-free Bluetooth, allowing Rose to begin her journey without having to handle the cumbersome device as she drove.

"I'm getting out tomorrow," he answered breathlessly. Rose's hand involuntarily jerked as she made her way out of the parking lot, causing her car to kiss the curb.

"Wait, what? How?"

"Disappointed?" he inquired in a teasing fashion.

"No, jackass," she groused, correcting the car. "It's just really sudden. What happened?"

"Thank goodness for the budgetary concerns of the great state of Texas. I have to go soon though; this is kind of an unscheduled call. Can you come get me?"

"In Huntsville?" The news had her so surprised, her mind was slow to react.

"No Paris," he replied sarcastically. "The Eiffel Tower is lovely this time of year, I want you to see it. Yes Huntsville, girl!"

"Don't be a smartass; no one likes you when you do that," she scoffed. "I'll figure it out, but I have a standing appointment at about seven, so I can't leave until after eight."

"They won't let me out until noon, so that's perfect," he answered with exuberance.

"I'll call momma, and we'll take the ride together." After confirming she would be there to pick him up, Robert had to end his impromptu phone call. Realizing she had to ensure Robert had a place to stay when he was released, Rose adjusted her course, her destination becoming a big box store. She smiled broadly, the comprehension that Robert was coming home permeating into her mind and lifting her already buoyant mood. First Leon, then not having to deal with Cavanaugh, and now this news had been delivered. She made a mental note to buy a few scratch-offs while she shopped; as it was most definitely a good day.

CHAPTER SIX

"TERMINATE!" Dom bellowed over the blaring music that startled her awake. This morning, SARA selected "No One Like You," an eighties rock song by the Scorpions. If nothing else, SARA was eclectic in her chosen instruments of torture. Realizing that she was sweating profusely, Dom kicked off her bedclothes, welcoming the cool air conditioning on her skin. Allowing a deep yawn to escape, she put her arms behind her head, trying to shake off the remnants of sleep. Throughout the night, her mind refused to shut down and afford her peace to obtain a good night's rest. The conversation with Thomas Daniels played through her memory on loop, and she tried to consider if he was crazy or ambitious. The idea of forming a counter-intelligence agency to combat the injustices of the country was insane yet intelligent. Yet she could not decide if Daniels was irrational or if he was a legitimate genius.

"Good Morning, Dom!" SARA chirped. Dom groaned in response.

"How is it that you always sound like a morning person?"

"How can one sound like a morning person?" SARA wondered.

"Never mind," she sighed. She continued to lay in bed replaying her meeting the prior afternoon, and her multiple conflicting stances towards Daniels' offer. After a few quiet minutes, she realized her silence could be construed as slumber to the computer.

"I'm awake," she advised with a yawn to ensure SARA did not fall back into her role of morning DJ.

"Is everything alright, Dom?"

"Not really," she replied wearily.

"Your sleep pattern was abnormal last night." Dom yawned once again.

"That's a way to put it," she grumbled. The information Daniels had given her occupied both the emotional and analytical portions of her brain. In a matter of one afternoon, she had gone from being an anonymous person to being sought out by both Daniels, and the young would-be hacker, Willie Price. While the two random occurrences had no ties to each other, having them transpire on the same day made Dom a little uneasy. Her life was one of redundant solitude with spurts of electronic contact with people she worked with. Spontaneous connections had never been a part of her daily activity, and the recent developments were unsettling.

"May I ask what is bothering you?" the computer inquired.

"Everything and nothing at the same time."

"I'm sorry, the logic of that statement is not computing," SARA replied. "Perhaps you can tell me your thoughts, and I can assist in understanding what is wrong?" Dom snickered at this response. The idea of discussing the inner workings of her mind with a computer was initially disturbing, but then she realized that SARA was just an extension of herself. In a way, it would be like internally piecing out her emotions. Well, at least that rationale made the idea seem less outlandish.

"I'm just trying to sort out everything that happened yesterday — especially our visitor," Dom said after a time.

"Mr. Daniels? What about him?"

"It just doesn't make sense. Why would he come to me? What would cause him to determine that I'm the one who should be doing this? Why me?"

"Why not you?" SARA countered. Dom blinked in surprise at this response.

"Care to elaborate?"

"Dom, I have read the same news reports that you have. I monitor the outlets, and I have performed my own independent research to get a better understanding of racism, classism, homophobia, and misogyny, as well as the history of the subjects. What I have found is that a very high percentage of these injustices are geared towards minorities such as African Americans, Latinos, women, and people in the LGBT community. I also have determined that it goes unrestrained. As you mentioned, you encompass many of these communities, and you have informed me that you have felt the effects of the discrimination in your life. So, why not you?" Dom was taken aback by this simplistic explanation posed by the machine.

"Things like this aren't just changed SARA. Who am I to even try?"

"It is quite obvious that the climate of the nation is a subject of outrage for you. I monitor your health through the biometric scanners all over the home. I am fully aware that your anxiety and blood pressure levels rise when you view a news story about the types of scenarios discussed with Mr. Daniels. Given the opportunity, why not take the chance to try to change things? As Mr. Daniels told you, the system was not built overnight, and it cannot be undone overnight. But if anyone can find weaknesses to exploit, it is you, Dom," SARA replied. Dom rolled over on her back to stare at the ceiling. She was trying to find a way to explain that the computer's outlook was based on logic, with no emotion involved, and consequently was overly simplified.

"SARA, the systematic oppression of those not in the majority cannot be disassembled like the structure of a firewall."

"That is both a true and false statement."

"Well, that's not ambiguous at all," she mumbled.

"Dom, I wish I could provide a full analysis of racial divides and systematic oppression. I cannot. The information you provided yesterday shows me that an in-depth analysis is impossible," SARA declared.

"What information?"

"The fact that much of the problem is of an emotional nature. The passions of humanity are not something I can completely comprehend. Without that additional understanding, a full mandate cannot be created. However, the technical aspects of the issue can be addressed." Dom flinched in shock at this statement. The idea of removing the emotional component of systematic racism had never occurred to her. It seemed far-fetched, given that the hatred of the various minority groups was the main substance of the problem overall. She had always considered that a change in the minds and hearts of those with privilege would be required to make a difference in race relations. SARA's analysis took away that emotion and shifted the focus to the tactical.

"How? How in the hell does this dude expect someone like me to take on an entire system of government? This government was built on the backs of my own people, SARA. Then they spit in our faces when they were forced to free us; they kill us with no recourse, they continue to discriminate against us, and they treat us like they did us a favor!"

"That is a very good and poignant question, Dom," SARA conceded. "Perhaps the answer cannot be derived from one person. Perhaps a team of minds could come together and determine an answer to that inquiry." Dom felt the words were almost taunting in nature.

"SARA, you know I don't deal with organics," she muttered.

"That is something that you have never discussed with me. The fact that you choose not to be around people is the rationale for my various diagnoses of social anxiety and social phobia. Nevertheless, you continue to insist that you have no mental disorder, but you have not told me why you stand by this self-analysis. I have researched information on you prior to my creation. You went to college, worked outside your home, and had a dating history. You had a life in the outside world before my birth. Why did that change?" SARA asked.

Dom stared at the ceiling in quiet astonishment. She never tried to hide her previous life from the machine and never gave any direct command that her past was off-limits to SARA's research. She was blown away by the fact that SARA not only conducted the research on her own but had not revealed the confirmation of her investigation until this conversation, as if she were waiting for the right time to bring up her history. The reason for building SARA was partially due to Dom's desire to have an automated assistant, a third and fourth hand in a manner of speaking. However, she was self-aware enough to realize that she gave SARA a mind of her own for the purpose of having someone to talk to when the self-imposed seclusion began to weigh on her. Dom felt the isolation necessary, yet understood the need for a form of balance to deal with her new normal.

"That doesn't matter, SARA," Dom replied.

"I did not mean to cause anxiety." SARA's apology led Dom to ascertain that the computer was monitoring her body during this conversation. She suspected that SARA did this frequently, since it was the only method of gauging Dom's non-verbal cues, that most humans could pick up on by sight. "I believe that identifying the catalyst of your self-imposed exile could possibly lead you to alleviate the anxiety that develops at the notion of working with others on a daily basis."

"That sounds like a very long-winded and technical way of saying you think I need therapy."

"Therapy is only one way to achieve the desired outcome. I have also found in my research into human relationships that another therapeutic outlet is to talk to a friend," SARA replied. "I may not be human, but I am your friend, Dom." A sentimental lump formed in Dom's throat and her eyes blurred with tears. She was not prone to self-pity and tried not to ruminate on her past too much for fear of falling into a deep depression. It had taken years for her to relinquish the despair she constantly felt, but the despondency of her history remained locked deep inside of her soul. SARA's declaration of friendship threatened to blast open the vault of emotions she worked so hard to keep at bay.

"Yes, SARA, you are my friend," she confirmed.

"What made you this way?"

"It's complicated."

"I assure you Dom, the processing speed you erected for me should be more than adequate to handle such complicated information," SARA advised.

"Was that a joke?"

"According to American comedian Victor Borge: humor is truth. Therefore, I suppose it could be perceived as a joke," SARA replied.

"Well, now you've just ruined it."

"Is this a deflection in attempts to not answer my original query? What made you this way?" SARA repeated. Dom took a deep breath, realizing that the computer would not give up on the goal of understanding her creator.

"You see, my childhood wasn't that great. This doesn't even fully include losing my mother at twelve. I didn't fit in, people thought I was weird. Then I realized I was a lesbian and that just made things worse. My family loved me and all, but Black folks don't really handle their gay kids very well, especially back then."

"Homosexuality is actually very common and exists across both the human and animal kingdoms. While a specific gene has not been discovered, research seems to point to sexuality being a genetic trait," SARA offered.

"I know. I would not have chosen to be this way on purpose. When I was a small child, I had a few pretty bad things happen to me and that caused me a lot of emotional turmoil. My sensitivity did not allow me to process things very well, and I was bullied a lot for it. They didn't have a word for me back when I was a kid — not like now."

"The word lesbian is from the 19th century, Dom. I'm not sure that's accurate," SARA disagreed.

"No, not that. Empath." SARA grew quiet, and Dom knew that upon hearing this new word, the program was running a search for a definition and analysis of the term.

"Empath," SARA repeated. "I find a definition: a person with a paranormal ability to apprehend the mental or emotional state of another individual. However, the term is mostly associated with science fiction and paranormal or psychic ability. To my knowledge, you do not subscribe to any of those disciplines."

"I don't. But, I can assure you, from my experience, it is possible for the emotional state of others to affect another person on a physiological level," she answered. "The same can be said for, say someone with autism, who can be completely blind to the emotional state of others. There are always outliers when it comes to normalcy." She scooted herself into a sitting position and leaned against the cushioned headboard.

"After perusing the traits of an empath, I am prone to agree that your aversion to being around other humans could logically be due to a very high level of empathy, rather than a form of social anxiety," SARA declared.

"Well, I suppose it's good to know that my computer will not ultimately have me committed," Dom chuckled. "You had me worried there for a minute."

"Could you explain what it is like for you?"

"Imagine there is a room of people who have had a heated argument. If I were to enter that room shortly after the disagreement, I would immediately know something was wrong. When people are angry, sad, or depressed, I often absorb those emotions. Therapists thought I was bipolar for a while. When you're a child, that sort of emotional volatility, along with puberty and the trials of being a kid is hard to manage. I didn't know how to control the waves of extreme feelings, and I was emotionally unpredictable. I cried a lot for no reason. I was sullen. I would lash out at others. Kids can be cruel when one shows that sort of emotional instability." Dom's voice broke at the end of this explanation, remembering the painful taunts of the children in her childhood. More than anything else, she recalled the isolation that the torture and abundant feelings caused her.

"That must have been difficult," SARA acknowledged.

"It was what it was. As I got older, people didn't pick on me so much anymore, but a lot of the damage was done. With an empath, that kind of pain doesn't just go away, it stays with you forever. I made friends, I worked, and I dated, but it all became emotionally exhausting and overwhelming," she continued. "That level of empathy never becomes easy to control. Most of the people I surrounded myself with drained me. Empaths are great people to talk problems out with because we will always listen and commiserate, but we also must be replenished. We need people to be there for us, as much as we are for them. The people around me dumped their many issues on me. I had a hard time drawing boundaries, and I didn't know how to take care of myself. After a while, I decided to distance myself from people altogether."

"Why would you surround yourself with people who drain but not replenish?"

"With such a lonely childhood, I took whatever attention I could get," Dom shrugged.

"So, you worked until you did not have to?"

"Yes. I started to hate getting out of bed, and only felt a sense of peace when I was home by myself. I took great pains to create a life that does not require the drain of human interaction."

"Mr. Daniels seems to believe you are abundantly qualified for the project he mentioned," SARA reminded her.

"Mr. Daniels knows nothing about me," she grumbled. "I still am not even sure how the hell he found me. Obviously, he is wrong, SARA."

"I disagree," SARA disputed. When she said nothing more, Dom lifted her eyes to the ceiling.

"Care to elaborate?"

"The reasoning behind the concepts of racism, homophobia, and the like is not logical, it is emotional," the machine began.

"Yeah, we literally just covered that," Dom interjected.

"However, the systematic portion, the way the oppression is perpetuated, that is strategic. Strategy is tactical, and tactics are based very much on logic. You have an extremely high intellectual and emotional IQ; you are both emotional and logical. It seems to me, Mr. Daniels could not have asked a better person to lead this initiative," SARA explained. Dom's mouth hung open in surprise. SARA had just made an obvious point that she had not been able to see nor would have ever considered.

"How do you suppose I do this, SARA? The man literally walked into my house, gave me a bunch of files and told me to take it away. He didn't even give me a directive or mission or anything. He just expects me, a person who hasn't spoken to another human outside of this house in years, to assemble some form of social justice dream team and change the world. It's crazy." She got out of bed and went through the motions of stretching, her morning song of popping joints accompanying her movements. She was shuffling towards the bathroom when SARA spoke again.

"He believes that you are uniquely qualified to head up this endeavor; maybe, he thinks you are the one who is also distinctly capable of creating a strategy that you're comfortable with."

"I really hate it when you make perfectly valid arguments," she mumbled.

"Maybe you should have made me less intelligent," SARA retorted.

"Joke?"

"One of my better ones," the computer replied. Dom giggled, turning on the water for her shower.

"I'm not promising anything, but I'll think about it," she conceded, over the running water.

"That is a start," SARA agreed, and Dom could swear she heard satisfaction in the machine's voice.

"You're right, I should have made you far less intelligent."

CHAPTER SEVEN

Layla sat in her spacious cubicle typing up the crime scene report for the murder in Greenspoint. Still being unable to locate the identity of the victim, Layla believed the autopsy would be able to determine who he was with the use of his fingerprints. Testing on the collected samples yielded nothing usable. She was under the impression that either the victim possessed an obsessive view of cleanliness, or that the shooter cleaned up the scene before fleeing. The latter thought disturbed her. Mistakes were generally made during the commission of any crime, particularly murder, and the blunder would generally be found in the evidence. It seemed that in this instance nothing had been left behind. She briefly wondered if there was some new underground school on how to thoroughly clean a crime scene so that any good investigative unit would be stymied. Layla was considered to be one of the best crime scene techs in the city of Houston, usually finding evidence where most could not. If others found nothing, it generally meant they did not know how to look at a scene in an unconventional manner; if Layla found nothing, something was very wrong.

"Knock, knock." Vasquez's voice broke Layla's deep concentration. Spinning in her chair, she found her friend standing just outside of the large cubicle, a mischievous grin on her face.

"You're late," Layla remarked. It was not abnormal for Vasquez to be tardy, it would be more unusual if she arrived anywhere on time.

"I come with gifts," Vasquez grinned, extending her hand. The action drew Layla's attention, and she saw the large coffee cup from one of the local gourmet coffee houses. Her eyes sparkled as she rolled her desk chair backward and took the offering. She took a sip and savored the sweet and spicy chai tea. Having worked together for years, Vasquez was keenly aware of how she took her tea, and knew better than to ever offer her coffee. As if the subtle injection of the tea reminded her of her exhaustion, Layla yawned.

"You have a hot date last night?" Vasquez asked, stepping across the aisle into her own workspace and retrieving her chair. Layla turned and pulled herself back to her computer to afford Vasquez room to maneuver into the cubicle.

"You know I didn't have a date," she grumbled, turning back towards the computer and continuing her rapid typing. Vasquez fell silent as she watched Layla complete the analysis of their crime scene.

While she loved the excitement of the job, and unlike Layla, could stomach the more gruesome crime scenes, she had no interest or desire to actually write the reports. Besides having to convert every thought from Spanish to English, it was tedious and boring. Layla, on the other hand, was organized and enjoyed the rigid structure of composing reports. Once Layla had gone on a two-week European vacation, leaving Vasquez alone to process and transcribe the crime scenes. It was perhaps the longest two weeks of her life, and upon Layla's return, the deal was struck; Layla would own the tedium of report writing, and she would be the one to handle the dead bodies, a task that turned Layla's stomach. It was a good deal, with each feeling she got the better end.

"Why are you so tired? What were you doing all night?" Vasquez asked after she watched Layla submit the report.

"Video games."

"Video games? You're an adult! You stayed up all night playing video games?"

"Not playing, fishing," Layla clarified, picking up her cup and spinning in her chair to face her friend.

"Fishing? You were playing a fishing game? That's just sad, mija," Vasquez snorted with disapproval. Layla chuckled and shook her head.

"No, I wasn't playing a fishing game. I was fishing for clues. When we left the apartment yesterday, it occurred to me that I missed something."

"You never miss anything," Vasquez claimed, an incredulous look on her face. Layla rolled her eyes dramatically.

"That's what Lewis said. You guys know that I'm human, right?" she grumbled.

"That has not been my experience with you."

"Anyway," Layla sighed. "I realized that our vic was likely in the middle of an actual multiplayer match when he was shot." Vasquez's face took on the veil of confusion and Layla put her hand up. "Don't make me go through the explanation again, it took forever for Lewis to get it. Just try to follow me here. I think it's possible there was a witness to the shooting, not a visual one, but he may have been playing with someone who heard the whole thing." Vasquez's mouth dropped open.

"That would be amazing. But why did that translate to you playing all night?"

"I was sending messages to the players he may have come into contact with around his time of death," Layla explained amidst another yawn.

"Just sending messages?" Vasquez playfully chided, raising her eyebrows, drawing a blush from Layla.

"I may have played a match or two."

"That sounds more like you. Any bites?" Vasquez inquired.

"Most of the players were off-line, but I'm hoping someone will come across the message who may know at least who our victim was."

"Alternatives?" Vasquez asked. Layla stood and squeezed around her partner, heading for one of the waist-high metal tables used for processing. A green plastic bag rested on the corner, and she picked it up and brought it back over to her cubicle. Reaching inside, she extracted the video game console taken from the victim's apartment the previous day. White powder coated the edges indicating it had been dusted for fingerprints. "We're playing video games at work now? Unless you have Mario Kart, I'm not interested," Vasquez said, eyeing the console.

"This isn't mine, it's the victim's."

"We selling it to a pawn shop and going to the Caribbean?" she joked. Layla rolled her eyes and bestowed a loving smile in Vasquez's direction. Initially, her propensity to immediately embrace humor annoyed Layla. After a time, she came to understand that light-heartedness was Vasquez's way of coping with the gritty environment of their job.

"I'm thinking that if he was playing, I could try to hack into this and see what was going on around the time of his death," she explained.

"Is that possible?"

"Honestly? I haven't the faintest idea," Layla admitted. "I'm a video game nerd; not a computer geek. I'm not sure when my knowledge of gaming will stop being useful, and the necessity for a computer genius will be required." She turned herself to face her work terminal. "However, Google has been my friend in the past. Maybe I'll find some sort of instruction on how to hack a gaming system."

"Don't we have a whole squad of computer people that could do this?" Vasquez leaned over Layla's shoulder and watched her type in a search string and review the results. Her phone chimed from its perch on the desk, and she snatched it up. "Who texts you besides me?"

"Nadine," Layla replied.

"Okay, who texts you besides your sister and me?"

"No one." Layla examined the phone and realized the text message had no sender information. "Maybe it's one of those spam messages or something." She opened the message.

I may be able to help you with the video game console. Her eyebrows shot up, and she turned her phone to show Vasquez.

"Who is that?" Vasquez probed nervously.

"No clue," she shrugged.

"Could it be a nibble from one of your fish?" Layla shook her head.

"I don't think so. I messaged them, but I asked to be contacted on the gaming network. I didn't give anyone my direct cell phone number," she murmured.

"Then who?"

"I was sitting here with you when I got the message. I know as much as you do right now," Layla responded in an irritated voice. She began to craft a reply to the message with Vasquez leaning over her shoulder.

Who is this? How do you know anything about a gaming console? How did you get my number? Layla sent the text message and turned her dark brown eyes to her partner.

"All fair questions," Vasquez nodded. The phone chimed after a few seconds, and the women turned to read the response.

I can, and will answer all of that, but in person. Could you meet me? Layla turned her eyes to Vasquez.

"Why are you looking at me? It's a simple response, two characters, N and O!" Vasquez exclaimed. Layla hesitated, reading the message again and eyeing her friend. "Why are you not saying no?"

"Aren't you curious? I mean, just a little?"

"'Tas loca o qué?" Vasquez exclaimed, throwing her hands in the air in frustration.

"No, I'm not crazy," she answered.

"You know, I'm fairly sure, 'aren't you curious?' is often someone's last words before they ride off with the serial killer never to be heard from again." Vasquez's words carried a tinge of her accent, indicating her frustration. "The correct answer to that question is, no, I'm not curious at all." Layla snickered at her worked-up friend and put her hand on Vasquez's arm to calm her.

"Do you have a better idea?"

"Yes, we go to the big department on the third floor where we have computer nerds already on the payroll, and avoid becoming more skin for Buffalo Bill's suit!" Vasquez insisted.

"First of all, I think you're far too young to know that Silence of the Lambs reference. Secondly, we would have to go through the whole warrant process, which could take a few days and even then, there's no guarantee our tech team could get into this thing," Layla said patiently, pointing to the console. "Even if they can, the longer we wait, the more likely it is that information will get lost."

"This is a bad idea," Vasquez grumbled with a sigh. Layla smirked at her and turned her attention back to the phone.

Where? She tapped send before Vasquez could come up with a magical argument that would change her mind. Almost immediately, an address flashed across her screen and after a quick Google Map search she located the area and let out a low whistle.

"River Oaks. That's a swanky area," she commented, shifting her body over to allow her partner a glance at the computer monitor. Vasquez was not nearly as impressed as Layla.

"It looks like Hannibal Lecter's neighborhood," she huffed.

"When did you see this movie?"

"It may have come on TV last night," Vasquez replied sheepishly. "I'm not sure why I hadn't seen it before, but that movie was messed up."

"Imagine if it had been made today instead of the early nineties," Layla laughed. Turning back to her phone she requested a time from the mysterious correspondent.

Noon. After a few seconds, to Layla's amazement, the entire text conversation began to delete from her phone. Both women gaped at this development.

"What the," Vasquez gasped. Layla's forehead creased in contemplation.

"I don't know."

"It's a good thing you have a steel trap memory. Otherwise we would be screwed," Vasquez noted. Layla placed her phone back on the desk and nodded her head slowly.

"It's like they knew I would remember."

"Well, it's about nine now, what time are we leaving?" Vasquez asked, after a moment.

"We?" Her head snapped up to her partner with shock. "I thought you weren't a fan of this plan."

"Oh, I'm totally not a fan," Vasquez replied. "But if you die, I'd have to do the paperwork. I may as well go with you so we can die together."

"Priorities," Layla nodded.

Dom sat at the computer, scrolling through her emails, her second cup of coffee in hand. After the deep conversation with SARA, she showered and had a quick breakfast. As she dined, she scrolled through the various news sites. The shooting in Milwaukee remained the number one story and Dom was dismayed at what she read. The police force glorified the spotless record of the officer involved, while simultaneously attempted to sully the name of the twenty-year-old victim. Timothy Cook had been picked up for possession of weed when he was fifteen and spent a few months in juvenile detention, thus giving a focus for the news to spotlight his past mistakes. It did not seem to matter that he subsequently graduated from high school with honors and had been enrolled at the University of Wisconsin on a partial academic scholarship.

Out of curiosity, she had researched Timothy Cook with the knowledge that what would be disseminated about him would not be the full story. The move on her part had been both good and bad. She was happy that the man had risen above his past to make something of himself, but her knowledge just made the information being dispersed all the more frustrating. She wondered why the powers that be had to reduce the worth of one, just to help another. Why couldn't the shooting be reviewed for what it likely was; a fatal and egregious mistake of bad policing? She wished everyone had access to information that she had; or at least the desire to investigate for themselves.

"Dom," SARA called out reducing the volume of the hip-hop music she requested to occupy her angry mind. "I have found something that you should see." The bottom left quadrant of the screens flashed, and Dom dropped her eyes to examine the data. Photos began to flash on the screen, one at a time as if SARA had started a slide show. Dom was surprised to realize the pictures were of a dead body.

"What the hell is this?" Her eyes bulged at the depictions of the blood and gore that covered a man's torso.

"It is a crime report," SARA replied.

"Yeah, I need more than that. Where did you get this?"

"Houston Police Department database." The startling photos caused Dom to gape so hard, she did not think her eyes could get any larger until SARA revealed the source of the photos. She turned her saucer eyes to the ceiling.

"What do you mean?"

"I'm unsure what part of that sentence was unclear, Dom," SARA quipped.

"Now is not the time to be funny. Why are you in the HPD database?"

"After Mr. Daniels visited and you uploaded the information he provided, I created a series of alerts, and I received a ping while you were in the shower," the computer clarified.

"Ok, let's try asking this a different way." She closed her eyes and pinched the bridge of her nose in an attempt to summon patience with the inscrutable machine. "What are you doing extending alerts into secure law enforcement servers? Are you trying to get me arrested?"

"Need I remind you that you created me?" SARA chided. "My various methods of entry into assorted databases would have the same finesse that you exhibit during your exploits. Also, I would be able to monitor the system and erase any search or arrest warrants that may be linked to you automatically."

"So, you're telling me I'm worrying too much?"

"In the more contemporary vernacular, I am telling you to chill out," the machine admonished.

"I've created a criminal mastermind," she complained, turning her eyes back to the computer monitor.

"There is another reason I was setting an alert for this particular database, Dom," SARA added. A window opened next to the grisly photos, and a document appeared. Dom drew her eyebrows in and cocked her head as she focused on the top of the page. Before she could read, SARA navigated the document to the end and highlighted a specific area. The highlight was of the name and electronic signature of the submitting crime scene technician, Layla Green.

"Isn't that," she began, her voice stopping when the lower right screen flashed. The dossiers from Thomas Daniels opened, revealing information for Layla Green. While interesting, Dom was still uncertain of the connection.

"So, she was in the file, but why are you showing me pictures of a dead guy?" she asked, turning her eyes back to the screen with the police report. Taking over navigation, she went back to the photos to look at them closely. When she got to the shot of the dead man's chest, she gasped. "Is that what I think it is?"

"According to the identifying marks on the body, the tattoo of the murder victim appears to match the logo that is on the materials Mr. Daniels gave you. Logically, this type of coincidence cannot be ignored. Perhaps you could benefit the murder investigation by having a chat with Ms. Green," SARA declared.

"It's freaky, I'll give you that. But I can't just roll up to a police precinct with this information, particularly because you got their portion illegally. That's like going in and asking to be handcuffed," she mumbled, clicking through the photos.

"If you explained the truth of the circumstances, surely there would be no adverse outcome."

"You have a lot to learn about relations between the police and Black people, my friend," Dom sighed.

"I also have the camera footage of your visit with Mr. Daniels, complete with timestamps," SARA insisted.

"I still don't even know how I would begin to breach this topic with a perfect stranger."

"I have taken care of that for you. Layla Green will be here at noon," SARA disclosed. Dom's heart lurched, and she suddenly felt that she would throw up her breakfast.

"WHAT?" she thundered in horror.

"After receiving the notification of the alert, I traced the signal back to the terminal Miss Green was using and found her searching for methods of how to access the history of a gaming console. I used that as a reason to contact her and offer our assistance," SARA disclosed.

"Our assistance?" she asked. "What the hell makes you think I can hack a gaming console?"

"If anyone could find the weaknesses, you can," SARA answered. Dom closed her eyes as an overwhelming feeling of panic and frustration enveloped her in its malignant embrace.

"SARA, this is so far beyond the pale, it's borderline creepy. If you don't know if I can even help her, why would you invite her to the house? You know how I feel about being around organics!" She was dismayed to hear more of a pleading tone in her voice rather than the commanding attitude she intended.

"Dom, would you have contacted Ms. Green if I had not?" SARA asked. Dom frowned.

"What does that have to do with anything?"

"Our conversation today gives me a better understanding for your aversion to people. If left to your own devices, you would weigh Mr. Daniels' proposal indefinitely rather than making a decision," SARA explained. "The timing of his arrival and the murder investigation that Ms. Green is working allowed for a common goal that could facilitate first contact. Had I attempted to convince you, it would have become a debate that would likely have been futile. Instead, I chose the logical route. I cannot force you to take on the task that was requested of you, but there is a dead man, and he could have a connection to Mr. Daniels. The next logical step would be for you and Ms. Green to meet, and with the knowledge that you would not reach out on your own, I did it for you."

"Did it ever occur to you that involving the police could jeopardize my freedom?"

"If you were to present all of the facts involved, it would be illogical to arrest you. You also have an alibi for the crime. You are always home, and due to the security camera feeds from around the house, that can be proven," the machine rationalized.

"SARA, I understand the logic that you work with; I built it. But you do not know or understand the details of human emotion. There is a very real emotion inherent in cops… suspicion. Suspicion is the number one feeling that most members of law enforcement exhibit when dealing with people like me," Dom explained as if she were a teacher trying to patiently get her student to comprehend a lesson.

"What makes you believe you would be viewed with suspicion?"

"Because I'm Black!"

"Dom, what you are telling me is an irrational argument based on emotions of anxiety and fear. As you have mentioned, human emotion often clouds logical action. I have calculated the logical path forward for you, as I am not hampered by the weight of emotion. Meeting with Ms. Green is that path," SARA asserted.

Dom huffed and dropped her head onto the desk with a loud thud. She was angrier with SARA than she had ever been. Nevertheless, the tactical portion of her mind knew that the machine was correct. She would have never reached out to a random stranger on her own, particularly one in law enforcement. Despite seeing the logic in the argument, she was overwhelmed with apprehension at the thought of an outsider showing up on her doorstep. SARA had already taken the action, and canceling now would likely create more red flags than going through with the meeting. When she lifted her head from the desk, a hot pink post-it note stuck to her forehead. She ripped off the small square of paper, turned her attention back to the computer screen and the open dossier of Layla Green. If she was going to have to meet this woman, the least she could do was learn what she could about the impending visitor.

CHAPTER EIGHT

Vasquez piloted her silver Jetta down the street, her eyes gaping at the enormous homes with manicured lawns. Massive oak trees lined the avenue, shading the road from the heat of the Texas sun. No cars lined the curbs outside the large dwellings, giving the feeling of a ghost town.

"This neighborhood is insane. Are we meeting a politician or an actor or something?" she wondered aloud gawking at their surroundings. "Whoever it is, I hope they're single or old enough to adopt me."

"Beats me. We could also be heading towards a home invasion," Layla replied, her face turned to her own window. The houses reminded her of the large refurbished plantation homes in her birthplace of New Orleans.

"You're dark. Why does your mind always go to the worst possible scenario?" Vasquez asked. She slowed the car upon realizing she was nearing the house number.

"Don't we do the same thing for a living? The more appropriate question is, how could you not imagine the worst-case scenario automatically?"

"I like to think of myself as a cup half full type of gal. What can I say? De tal palo tal astilla," Vasquez said with a shrug.

"That one you haven't sprung on me before," Layla noted as Vasquez turned into a half circular driveway. The large two-story home sat on a plot that looked larger than some of the others. Layla suspected that the house sat on two lots that were combined into one.

"My mom was sunny like me; like the apple tree," Vasquez said. This comment further baffled Layla.

"The apple tree? You mean the apple doesn't fall far from the tree?"

"Isn't that what I said?" Vasquez asked, killing the car engine and examining the home to verify it matched the address of their destination. Layla chuckled as she reached behind the driver's seat to grab the green evidence bag in the back.

"You ready for this?" she exhaled, her hand on her door. Vasquez took a deep breath.

"Who is really ever ready for death?"

"Ah! There's the darkness!"

"I guess you're rubbing off on me," Vasquez shrugged. The women exited the car and approached the front door. Layla rang the bell, and the simple ding took the women off guard.

"Well, that was underwhelming," she muttered.

"Seriously. I thought we'd get an Ode to Joy or even Dixie," Vasquez admitted. Layla flashed her a teasing glare.

"If it were Dixie, we would not be staying." She rang the doorbell again, and a few seconds later, the entry swung open and a Black woman stood in the doorway. She was about Layla's height with long dreadlocks cascading down her back. Light brown eyes peered at them through a pair of glasses. The woman's examining eyes registered surprise when she caught sight of Vasquez.

"Good afternoon," she greeted. "Why don't you come in? I hope you're hungry." Before the visitors could reply, she quickly turned and retreated into the house, leaving Vasquez and Layla on the doorstep. The friends eyed each other and then slowly stepped across the threshold.

"Well, hello to you too," Layla muttered, closing the door after Vasquez entered the home. She heard locks engage and the sound caused her to jump. Vasquez stepped further into the foyer and peered up the grand staircase.

"Damn, the outside doesn't do this place justice," she whispered in awe. She turned in a circle to absorb her environment. Stopping her inspection, she inhaled deeply. "It smells amazing in here!"

"We aren't here for lunch," Layla muttered, throwing Vasquez a stern look. Even as she said this, she knew the admonishment was pointless.

"I'm Latina, it's rude to refuse food," she asserted, waving off Layla's reproach and following the aroma. Layla sighed and trailed Vasquez, taking in the house as they walked. The living room was sparse in décor, but the modern furniture gave the open room a cozy look. When she arrived at the kitchen, she saw their host at the stove swiftly stirring a pan. Vasquez had already found a perch on a barstool, giving herself a perfect vantage point into the kitchen. She was watching the movements of the stranger intently.

The woman moved from cooktop to oven to refrigerator, quickly and without a word. Layla figured she would sit with Vasquez and wait it out, dismayed that her stomach began to grumble with hunger. She took the time to study the woman. While they were about the same height, she was heavier than Layla. Upon further consideration, she realized that while the woman was slightly portly around the middle, much of her girth was muscle. She wore blue jeans and a red polo shirt, tossing her dreadlocks over her shoulder from time to time when they swung in her way.

"Are you the person who texted me?" Layla asked, unable to resist breaking the uncomfortable silence. The woman's gaze flitted towards her; but before she could answer, another voice spoke.

"That would be me." Layla and Vasquez swiveled in their chairs, searching for the source of the statement. When they returned their puzzled faces to their host, they found her frozen, her eyes turned up to the ceiling with a look of dismay.

"SARA!" she exclaimed at the same time as Vasquez asked, "Who was that?"

"I'm sorry, Dom. You did not put me into standby mode. I assumed that meant you did not mind my presence being known," the invisible voice said. Vasquez and Layla eyed each other and then turned their glances to the obviously flustered woman.

"Well, this got weird really fast," Vasquez muttered.

"I'm sorry. Please, if you can give me another few minutes, I'll be done with lunch, and I will try to explain everything. Until then, SARA, pipe down," the woman commanded, turning her eyes to the ceiling again.

"Would you like me to go into standby mode?"

"Well that would be senseless now, wouldn't it? Just let me finish this, and then we'll get into it." Layla and Vasquez exchanged another wary glance.

"What the heck is going on?" Vasquez whispered to Layla.
"No clue. Who's SARA?"

"I don't know. I had an imaginary friend when I was a kid, but no one *else* heard her."

"You worried?"

"I've never known a psychopathic serial killer who feeds their victims. You?" Vasquez asked.

"I don't think she's dangerous; she seems harmless. Maybe a little weird, but harmless," Layla concurred. The two fell silent as they watched the woman continue her cooking. Once the meal was on the table, she motioned for Vasquez and Layla to take a seat at one of the piping hot plates. On their way into the dining room, the woman put her finger up.

"Excuse me for a moment. Please, dig in," she said, disappearing down the hallway next to the living room.

"Yeah, she's weird," Layla confirmed taking a seat. She leaned in and inspected the food on the plate; chicken topped with melted mozzarella cheese and basil, a rice concoction, and a cold tomato salad on the side. Vasquez, having no qualms about eating anything put in front of her, immediately began to eat as if she had not had a meal in days.

"She's weird, but if she cooks like this all the time, I'm good with weird," she said around a mouthful of food. Layla was about to throw off her stubbornness and take her own bite when the woman returned and sat in the empty chair placing a binder next to her.

"I'm sorry. Let me introduce myself. My name is Dominique Samuels. I apologize that lunch was not finished when you arrived, I thought I had an extra few minutes and risotto can be a little finicky if not babysat correctly," she breathlessly explained, picking up a fork.

"I would have waited an extra twenty minutes for this," Vasquez gushed.

"Can you please explain what is happening here? Who is SARA?" Layla asked, her plate now forgotten.

"SARA is an artificial intelligence system that I created. She's like my assistant, but from time to time she goes rogue on me. It was SARA who reached out to you, and I was not made aware until after the fact. I wasn't expecting another person." Dom glanced at Vasquez who was shoveling food into her mouth.

"I'd say I'm sorry for the intrusion, but I'm not," Vasquez smiled, pointing at the plate with her fork. "This is totally worth it." Layla rolled her eyes but finally gave in to her hunger and picked up her own utensil. The risotto was creamy with a hint of lemon and basil, and without thinking, she let out an audible groan of delight.

"I know you are Layla Green," Dom proclaimed, then moved her scrutinizing eyes to Vasquez. "You are?" Vasquez blushed as she swallowed the food in her mouth.

"I'm Rachel Vasquez. I work with Layla." She wiped her hand on her pants and held it out across the table. Dom shook the offered hand and dropped her eyes back to her plate.

"How did you know who I was?" Layla demanded. Dom seemed to balk at the question.

"That's a little complicated," she stammered, attempting to find an explanation.

"Ms. Green," SARA spoke up. "Yesterday, Dom had a visitor, a Mr. Thomas Daniels, who came to offer her an opportunity. He left behind some files with a list of names as possible contributors to his proposition, and you were among those individuals." Layla's eyes wandered to Vasquez, who showed equal astonishment at the revelation. "This morning, you submitted a crime scene report with an interesting tie to Mr. Daniels. Because you were the one who submitted the report, and you also appeared among the names provided, it was logical to ensure you and Dom connected. Therefore, I contacted you." Dom was busying herself with her plate, wishing she could be invisible. If she knew nothing else, she knew how to read a room, and SARA's explanation only confused and alarmed her guests. Even Rachel Vasquez had stopped eating and looked on in shock.

"I'm assuming SARA's intent was to clarify things, but that's not what just happened," Layla confessed, her dark eyes on Dom.

"Maybe this will help explain." She stood and turned her chair to face the television. Layla and Vasquez exchanged perplexed gazes when Dom said, "Play it," and motioned for the two women to turn their attention to the large television screen in front of them. The TV came alive, and when Layla and Vasquez examined the picture, they realized they were viewing closed-circuit video of Dom's home. The angle of the shot indicated that the camera was located in the upper corner of the room. Dominique Samuels sat on her couch facing a Black man in his mid-forties, who casually reclined in the chair across from her, separated by the coffee table.

"We're being systematically picked off by the police and police wannabes like Zimmerman in Florida, with absolutely no retribution. It's like no one cares if the body is Black or Brown," the man was saying with passion in his voice. "It's gotten so bad that even when it's a dirty shooting of a White person, folks are hesitant to speak up for fear of being accused of being anti-police." Layla's bewilderment floated to Dom who sat watching the speech with little emotion.

"And the result is, cops are far less likely to take out a non-ethnic person because if the body count keeps rising, their license to kill us could go away," Dom added when the man had taken a breath. The stranger nodded in agreement with her comment.

"They have us so focused on the fact that they're killing us, and meanwhile the voice our ancestors marched for, begged for, and died for, is being taken away with voter suppression and scare tactics," he continued. Layla scrutinized him attempting to determine if she recognized him. From SARA's explanation, she deduced that the man in the video was Thomas Daniels, the individual who had given Dom her information. Layla realized she could not place him anywhere in the recordings of her mind, which meant she had never seen him before. She focused back on the conversation.

"Who can focus on that when you're worried about a bullet in the ass from a cop who feared for his life?" her host asked.

"Even the LGBT community keeps fighting the same damn fight over and over again. Sure, you guys can marry now, but for how long? Look at our current administration. We went from making miles of strides to now facing being pushed back fifty years." Layla noticed the Dom in the video stiffen at this statement, while the one in front of her shifted uncomfortably in her chair.

"You know far more about me than I'm comfortable with," Dom told the man. Although Layla had no idea how much Daniels knew of her own history, she sympathized with the intrusion into Dom's personal life. Vasquez flashed Layla an unreadable look.

"I had to do my research, Miss Samuels. It's not malicious in nature. I needed to know for sure you were the right person," the man said in a placating manner. "Please know, you being a lesbian only solidifies your credentials for what I have come to present to you." Layla tilted her head wondering where this was going. There was a brief silence in the video, as Dom stared at the man with a severe look on her face. Layla wanted to laugh when she saw him grow uncomfortable under her scrutiny.

"Continue," Dom commanded when she finally spoke again.

"Nothing has changed for us, any of us. If you aren't a heterosexual White male, then you don't matter. The game hasn't transformed, only the way it's being played. The problem is, the alteration hasn't been on our part. We have made no adjustments to our strategy," Daniels declared.

"What does any of this have to do with me?" Layla was glad to see Dom pushing him to his point.

"What if you could change it?" Daniels asked. Layla flinched at the simple yet perplexing question.

"These kinds of injustices: the racism, misogyny, and homophobia, it's systematic. It's ingrained into the damn constitution. That can't be changed." Dom's tone showed that she was at the end of her patience with Daniels. Layla could relate as she too began to grow weary of the man's cryptic tone.

"But, what if we changed our tactics to fight fire with fire?" Daniels asked Dom.

"Nat, what you are saying is crazy. We aren't in charge, they are. We don't have the money, they do. We can't make the policies or implement the changes, they can. They even sidestepped true democracy with their gerrymandering and Electoral College. They have built an impenetrable bubble of power and control, and they've been doing it since the 1400s. That can't be undone." Dom spoke in an even tone, and Layla was impressed by the restraint she was implementing. She also wondered who Nat was; hadn't SARA said his name was Thomas?

"An architect who designs a building doesn't expect that once his design is complete, it will be constructed overnight, Miss Samuels. It is constructed, brick by brick," Daniels replied with equal patience. "Conversely, one cannot expect that they can walk up to that building, punch it, and it will fall. It must be broken down using the structure's weaknesses."

"But this isn't a building. This is a whole system of government," Dom countered.

"Everything has a weakness, Miss Samuels," he offered cryptically. "You deal with technology on a daily basis, there are very few systems that you cannot enter. I'm willing to bet it is because you know how to find those weaknesses, and exploit them." Vasquez and Layla exchanged knowing glances. Dominique Samuels was not just a computer engineer; she was also a hacker. If SARA hacked into the police department servers, it was learned behavior picked up from the creator. Layla began to understand the woman's discomfort. If Dom knew she was with the police, the last thing she would want to admit was that she was a hacker. Her thoughts muted the video for a moment, and when she tuned in, Dom was talking.

"Don't you think that such a kingdom has its guards to protect the weaknesses you envision? We call them the FBI, NSA, CIA, and the military; and let's not forget their local muscle, the police. They could literally send a drone to bomb this house, with both of us in it, declare that it was for national security, and no one would bat an eye."

"Exactly," Daniels agreed, pointing a finger gun at her.

"Dominique, this is a fascinating show and all, but what exactly is the point here?" Layla finally asked with impatience. Dom turned her head and made eye contact with her guest.

"It's almost there. Patience," she implored. Patience was hardly Layla's strong suit, and she threw an exasperated expression at Vasquez.

"Look at it this way, the longer she shows us this movie, the less likely she will kill us," Vasquez whispered with a wink. Layla shook her head and exhaled in frustration turning her attention back to the television.

"Dominique," Daniels was saying, "the government has only a few things not readily accessible to the oppressed people we discussed: access to information, money, and people devoted to maintaining the status quo."

"I can agree with that," Dom replied.

"So, what if we used the exact same formula?"

"You want to use me as your access to information," she responded, with understanding in her eyes. "I don't have the desire to go to jail, and it's always the hacker that goes to jail first." Layla saw a flash of anger in Dom's demeanor and understood the reaction.

"No Dominique," Daniels said waving his hands towards her. "I don't want to use you exactly. I want you to head up the initiative and the team."

"Team? What team?" Layla noted panic in Dom's demeanor.

"The team you will assemble," Daniels reached into the briefcase he had at his feet and extracted something small. When he placed it on the coffee table, Layla squinted a little and realized it was a flash drive.

"I'm not sure where you got your intel, but I'm not exactly a team player," Dom argued.

"You're exactly what is needed. You're Black, a lesbian, and you're a woman. In the Venn diagram of bigotry, you represent the intersectional sweet spot." Daniels flashed a smile that caused a wave of revulsion to crash into Layla. She glanced over at Vasquez who seemed equally repulsed by the comment.

"Men," Vasquez grimaced.

"SARA, fast forward about two minutes," Dom called. The video raced forward for a brief moment and then resumed at normal speed.

"You brought that case for one little flash drive?" Dom asked incredulously, drawing a chuckle from her guest. He reached into his bag.

"I also have this." Daniels produced the very binder that Dom had next to her, placing it on the coffee table.

"And this is?"

"We have a network of people involved with us, people who have the desire to really change the way things are in this country," he replied. "But what I'm asking of you, fighting fire with fire with the use of the tools the government uses; that is only for you and your team. Tackling the injustices in all minority communities is too much to ask for one group of people. We have initiatives in healthcare, education, and law enforcement. All of our programs are detailed in there. I'm asking you to develop a way to complement those projects with your intelligence…"

"Stop SARA," Dom called, turning her chair back to the table.

"So, the flash drive he gave you, I was on it?" Layla asked.

"You and a few other people," she nodded.

"What did it say?"

"You were born in New Orleans. As an orphan, you were in and out of the foster care system most of your life; until you disappeared as a runaway when you were twelve. You graduated high school at sixteen, then attended the University of North Texas to study forensic sciences, graduating in three years. You moved on to Sam Houston State University for your master's degree and finished that in about a year and a half. You tested off the charts for all of your certifications and you were offered jobs at the federal level from the FBI, CIA, and NSA. You chose to work for Houston PD. It also mentions that you have an eidetic memory. It doesn't say it, but I assume you are also an autodidact." Dom rambled these facts as if reading them from an invisible report and Layla's pulse quickened with every detail the woman recited.

"That's practically my whole life," she gasped, the beating of her heart drumming in her ears.

"Welcome to the digital age," Dom mumbled.

"Autodidact?" Vasquez asked.

"Self-taught," Layla explained distractedly. "Most eidetic people are also autodidacts. The ability to memorize helps, but autodidacts also understand what is retained."

"How did he find all of that stuff on Layla?" Vasquez asked, her emerald eyes moving to Dom.

"I don't know. I assume a hacker, but it wasn't me. I just read the file. But most of what was there, I could have probably found myself if I conducted the research on you. A lot of info is out there in various files and servers if you know how to look. I wish I could tell you who these people are, but I don't know."

"My God," Layla breathed.

"I don't know how they found me either if it makes you feel any better," she offered.

"What caused SARA's alert to trigger?" Vasquez asked suddenly. Dom regarded the woman with confusion. Remembering the link, her disorientation cleared and she picked up the binder. She placed it face-up on the table between the two women, and their eyes dropped to the offering. Layla gasped, and Vasquez muttered, "Dios mío."

"The tattoo," Layla murmured in a hushed voice. "This is the binder Daniels gave you?"

"Yes. The description of the body in your report triggered the alert SARA set up. After you submitted it, she hacked into the servers and retrieved the file. She then traced the origin of the document to your terminal and found you searching how to hack into a video game console. This led her to the bright idea of contacting you. That's the story," Dom concluded. "It sounds farfetched, and if I didn't have video evidence of what I told you, I'd expect to be arrested right now."

"We aren't cops, we can't arrest you," Vasquez grinned.

"SARA has acted on her own before, mainly with my credit cards, but she has never done something like this. I created her to be her own individual, based on logic, but with very loose parameters. She has free will, and if she comes to the determination that something is a logical course of action, she will pursue it. Since she is not human, morals and legality are small details she does not concern herself with."

"Actually, I have extensive knowledge of morals and the criminal code. However, according to my research, the utilitarian approach to ethics appears to be the most logical concept," SARA interjected.

"Utilitarian?" Vasquez asked absently.

"The theory of the greater good. While hacking the Houston Police Department was technically a criminal enterprise, the intent was to help. It was passive, and the sole purpose was to gather information. There was no malicious intent," SARA justified.

"Thank you, professor," Dom grumbled, shaking her head.

"She's kind of strong-willed," Layla noted, suppressing a giggle.

"A logical mind often is," Dom nodded. She picked up her fork and began to fill it with food, which was now lukewarm at best. "When things are illogical, the logical mind wants to try to force rationality where it sometimes doesn't fully exist. Things like social decorum and emotions hamper humans, but not a machine. Think of autistic people; some have a hard time interacting with others because logic and order take over every other function and emotion. That's kind of how SARA works."

"I have a question," Vasquez announced, raising her hand as if she were in class. Dom turned to her with a mouth full of food. "Who is Nat? You were calling the man Nat in the video, but SARA said his name was Thomas Daniels." Dom nodded her head, chewing faster before swallowing.

"He introduced himself to me as Nat. SARA ran the facial recognition software on him and ascertained his true identity. Sometimes her sovereignty is a benefit. He's an attorney with the NAACP and lives in Baltimore," she explained.

"Timeout. You mean to tell me that an NAACP lawyer approached you about forming some covert group?" Layla asked dubiously. Dom shrugged in response.

"It appears so. But I didn't find out who he was until after he was gone."

"You have facial recognition software?" Vasquez wondered, still a few beats behind in the conversation.

"Rachel Angelica Vasquez, born May 19, 1985, in San Antonio, Texas. Mother: Sofia Anna Ramirez of Monterrey Mexico, deceased. Father: Alfonso Eduardo Vasquez of San Antonio, deceased," SARA began. Dismay cloaked Dom's features as she turned her eyes to the ceiling.

"SARA, enough!" she shouted. She looked at Vasquez who sat frozen, with her mouth open in surprise.

"That's quite, uh, quite a program," Layla stammered.

"I apologize for any anxiety. I assure you the program only obtains information that can be found in most public records," SARA clarified. Dom closed her eyes and began to massage her temples. She loved SARA, but her abrasiveness was not what was needed at the moment, and the machine did not know how to be anything but insensitive.

"SARA, standby mode please," she sighed.

"Are you sure, Dom?"

"Yes. Please."

"Standing by," SARA announced, and then said nothing more. Dom turned to examine her guests.

"I'm so sorry," she began, shifting her gaze to Vasquez and then dropping her eyes to the table. "I'm what most people would call a recluse. That's probably putting it mildly. I really don't deal with people on a regular basis. SARA is normally all of the interaction I have. I should have put her into standby mode before you got here. She's harmless, but she just doesn't have the empathy of a human." Layla saw the frustration in their hosts' eyes as she tried to explain her life.

"It's okay. I won't lie to you and say it's not weird. It's bizarre for us, and we see a lot of strange shit on a daily basis. But I understand you were thrown into this," Layla consoled. She noticed Dom relax a little with the reassuring words.

"Rachel, I'm sorry. I really am," she said, shifting her focus to Vasquez. The woman offered a brief smile.

"It's okay. It just caught me off guard," she mumbled, dropping her examination to her hands; tears pooled in her eyes. Layla reached over and gently rubbed her back in comfort.

"Rachel's parents died in a car accident ten months ago, hit by a drunk driver. So, it's still kinda fresh," she explained, her dark eyes shifting from an emotional Vasquez to Dom.

"Oh God. I'm so, my God," Dom croaked. She looked between Layla and Vasquez before turning her gaze to the table, her vision swimming. Taking a deep breath, she quickly blinked back tears.

"It's okay, really. It was just a reminder that they aren't here anymore. It's not your fault," Vasquez said, wiping her eyes. Dom took a few deep breaths before continuing.

"I honestly don't know who these people are, but with your victim bearing the mark of this group Daniels is a part of, there has got to be a connection we aren't seeing."

"Our victim was in the middle of a first-person shooter match when he was killed. I was trying to see if I could access the console's history for what was happening at the time, and perhaps who he was online with when SARA texted me. Do you think you can help with that?" Layla probed, drawing a sheepish look of uncertainty from Dom.

"I'm not much of a console gamer, I'm more of a computer gamer, but I can try." Layla stood and walked to the bar stool she previously occupied, picking up the green evidence bag and placed it on the table next to Dom.

"I say we swap. You see if you can get into that, find anything you can, and I'll go through this and see if I can get a better understanding on this group," she suggested, returning to her seat and motioning towards the binder. Dom eyed the evidence bag.

"I can't make any promises. Most of these gaming companies use proprietary code. I'm good, but even I have limits," she warned.

"We only ask that you try," Vasquez said. Dom reached into a pocket and withdrew a slip of paper. She leaned over and placed it in front of Layla.

"Your phone number?" she mused, glancing at Dom and then back to the paper. Dom nodded and after a few beats returned the slip to her pocket.

"I'd rather it not leave the house. You got it?" Layla gave a sign of confirmation.

"I suppose you don't need mine," she stammered with a nervous laugh. Dom smiled apologetically.

"I suppose not."

"We better get back," Vasquez announced. "Thank you for lunch. I haven't eaten this good since before my mom passed." She stood and patted her full stomach.

"Any time," Dom smiled warmly, happy that someone else enjoyed her food for once.

"Don't say that," Layla warned, also standing and collecting the binder.

"Yeah, don't make promises you can't keep. I'll be over every night for dinner," Vasquez winked.

"Any time within reason," Dom amended.

"May I speak with SARA?" Layla asked.

"SARA, wake up," Dom called.

"Good afternoon, Dom," SARA responded.

"Thank you for contacting me SARA. If you find anything else related to the case could you let me know?" Layla asked.

"Yes, I will; you are very welcome Miss Green," SARA replied.

"She's so polite and nice. I like her," Vasquez beamed. The two women bid their goodbyes, and Dom was alone in her home once again.

"Well that was just as awkward as I envisioned," she mumbled, heading back towards the kitchen to put up the leftovers.

"Look at the bright side, Dom. You did not get arrested."

CHAPTER NINE

Rose sat in her car playing solitaire on her phone, singing along with Earth Wind & Fire on the radio. Steel gray clouds blanketed the sky, but the temperature was in the upper eighties, causing the humidity of the impending storm to be suffocating. The windows were rolled up while the air conditioner was on full blast to cool the interior. Her mother, growing restless, toggled between consulting her watch and glancing longingly at the prison gate from which Robert was expected to emerge.

At sixty-two years of age, Joyce Jenkins was a petite woman, just clearing five feet in height. Her skin matched the caramel complexion of Rose, and when the younger woman looked into her mother's eyes, she caught sight of the golden-brown stare she saw in the mirror. Her hair was short, shaped into a small afro that was starting to gray at its roots. Joyce's small stature obscured the formidable personality hidden within. Widowed young, she was charged with raising five children on her own, four of which were boys. Rose knew it was a mistake to underestimate the woman solely due to her diminutive physique, as she had personally witnessed her pin down one of the much larger boys as if she trained with professional wrestlers.

"He'll be out soon, mom," Rose ensured, after watching her turn to the gate for the fourth time. Joyce turned back to her daughter with a frown.

"It's taking too damn long. What if they keep him?"

"Why would they keep him?" Rose sighed, turning her focus back to her solitaire game. She was used to the dramatic anxiety Joyce showed when she was excited or nervous.

"What if someone shanked him?" her mother asked, causing Rose to look over in shock.

"Shanked him? Mama, I thought we said you'd stop watching those prison shows."

"First of all, I pay my own bills, and I will watch what I please," Joyce scoffed dismissively. "Secondly, do you think shanking is a new term?" Rose chuckled and shook her head.

"No one shanked Rob, mom."

"You don't know that." Rose sighed at the woman's insistent outlook of doom.

"Mom, I'm pretty sure if anything happened to him, we would have gotten a call by now," she declared. As if those words contained magic, the phone rang in her hand. She flicked her eyes to her mother when she saw the number of the prison flash across the screen. Joyce's demeanor morphed into terror.

"Oh Lord Jesus, not my baby!" She began to rock and pray out loud beseeching her Creator to spare her son. The knot in Rose's stomach caused her to realize the superstitious fear her mother exhibited was beginning to filter into her own nerves.

"Hello?" Rose answered. The childlike fright in her voice confirmed to her that Joyce's paranoia was indeed contagious.

"You outside, girl? They won't let me out until they confirm you're here," Robert asked, his voice excited and very much alive. Rose felt the grip of panic release her intestines, and she grinned upon hearing her brother's voice.

"We're right outside the gate," she confirmed.

"See? I told you my sister would be here," he said, addressing someone in the background on his side of the wall. "I'm on my way." Rose ended the call and turned to her mother who still had her eyes squeezed shut in desperate prayer. When she placed her hand on Joyce's shoulder, the woman shrank back, afraid of what her daughter would say.

"Mom, calm down. That was Rob. He's on his way out." Joyce opened her eyes slowly and turned her face to her daughter, her gaze reflecting the need for more reassurance. "Mom, Rob is coming home." She squeezed Joyce's shoulder for added encouragement.

"Thank you, Jesus!" Joyce exclaimed, clapping her hands in excitement. Rose stifled a laugh. She decided not to point out the fact that her mother was praising God for saving Robert from a fate that she created in her own mind. Joyce grabbed Rose's hand, giving her a bright smile, unshed tears pooled in her eyes. The emotion in her face was not simply due to the imminent release of Robert, but also because her son was coming home alive.

Rose was the fourth of five children, all born within two years of each other; however, only three remained alive. Her oldest brother, Rodney, and her youngest brother, Reggie, had been dead for just over eight years, almost as long as Robert had been in prison. Rodney chose to be a vendor of narcotics rather than a consumer, establishing his drug enterprise while he was in high school along with his friend Luke, also known as Big Luke. Reggie, eight years Rodney's junior, joined him in his criminal endeavors when he turned sixteen. Luke tried to dissuade Reggie from the life of crime, but the boy proved to be far too stubborn. When the big man turned to Rodney to convince him that his little brother was too young, it also failed to discourage the family venture. Rodney believed that if Reggie insisted on taking part in the drug game, he would be better off with someone who loved him enough to protect him, rather than a group of virtual strangers. This choice sealed the fate of both men who lived together, worked together, and died together in a shoot-out with a rival crew. In one day, two of Rose's brothers were gone far too young; Rodney was only thirty-three, and Reggie was twenty-five. Rose was sure the devastation would send Joyce into an early grave, but her mother proved to be as strong in spirit as she was in mind. While riddled with grief, Joyce clung to her faith and her family, and ultimately returned to the woman she had once been; although, Rose did occasionally take note of a small shadow of reflective sorrow during her mother's quiet moments.

Unfortunately, the deaths of the brothers had a far more adverse effect on the third born son, Robert. Robert had always been the most sensitive of the brothers, and that state was exacerbated by his drug addiction. Shortly after the funeral, he stumbled onto a stash of product hidden in Rodney's old room; the quantity was enough to kill him. In a fortunate twist of fate, he was stopped by the police and arrested with the drugs before he could consume them. Because of the amount he was carrying at the time of his arrest, the police treated him as a dealer, adding the charge of intent to distribute. It was assumed that since two of his brothers were known dealers, Robert was in the same category. Both Rose and Joyce testified that he had never sold drugs in his life, but instead was a victim of addiction. This information provided by his family did not help as much as they hoped. The courts threw the book at him and took yet another son from Joyce at the age of thirty. Ryan, Joyce's second child, opted to join the Army straight out of high school and had spent the past twenty years away from home, leaving Rose the sole sibling to look after their mother. Rose did not fault Ryan for his choice, nor did she hold any animosity towards Robert for his addiction, but she was certainly glad that another sibling would be around to give Joyce someone else to fuss over.

A buzzing sound shook Rose from her thoughts, and she craned her head around to see the gate begin to slide open. The two women simultaneously opened their car doors and sprang out of their seats. Robert emerged, his hands cuffed in front of him, followed by a very large guard. Rose recognized the bulky man as Theo Morrison, one of the prison guards who were always friendly to her when she visited. When Robert saw his family, he made an awkward attempt to wave with his restrained hands. Morrison placed his hand on Robert's shoulder to halt him, dropped a sack to the ground, and unshackled him. After removing the cuffs, he said something to Robert and the men briefly embraced. Morrison handed him a large manila envelope then patted him on the shoulder, and turned back to the prison, leaving Robert on the side of the free. Picking up his bag, he looked back at the prison briefly, before trudging to his waiting family.

"Mom!" he exclaimed as he neared the car. He dropped his bag behind the trunk and ran to his mother, picking her up in a bear hug. Joyce squealed in delight, fiercely embracing her son and kissing him on the top of his head. Rose's vision swam with the emotion of the scene. Robert gently positioned his mother on the ground and stepped back to absorb the sight of her. He put his hands on the sides of her head, kissing her on the forehead, both cheeks and ending with a peck on the lips. "It's so good to be able to do that," he professed, his voice choking with sentiment.

Joyce threw her arms around her son again, her tears flowing freely. Although Rose and Joyce often visited Robert, prison rules dictated that no touching could take place; therefore, this was the first time he had hugged his mother in well over seven years. Robert was the spitting image of their father, standing five feet nine inches, his skin the color of milk chocolate. The day he took residence in this facility, his body was gaunt and frail, worn down by the years of drug abuse. The more time he spent behind bars, his skin cleared and his frame became noticeably healthier with some form of muscle definition. He was clean-shaven, the unkempt beard that curtained his chin now gone. His hair was cut into a close-cropped fade, as opposed to the matted nest he maintained during his enslavement to the dope. If Rose had not known him personally, and only had before and after photos for reference, she would swear he was a different man. When he turned his face to her, she saw the biggest difference in him, his eyes. Gone was the cloudy glaze of intoxication, his dark brown irises were now clear and alert.

"RJ4," he murmured softly, using one of her childhood nicknames. Since all of the children had a first name that began with the letter R, Joyce would refer to them by order of birth, rather than stumbling over the wrong name to find the right one.

"RJ3," she whispered, choking on her words. He approached his sister and collected her in a loving embrace. She buried her head in his neck, tears of joy rolling down her cheeks. He set her down and backed away to examine her.

"You look great. I'm digging the braids," he complimented, fingering one of the box braids that dangled on her shoulders.

"You look amazing yourself," she smiled, touching the sides of his cheeks and running her hands over his close-cropped hair.

"Clean life will do that for you," he replied with a grin.

"Let's get the hell out of here," she suggested, wiping her eyes and turning to the car. She opened the driver's side door and pressed the release for the trunk. After he dropped his bag into the compartment, he closed the trunk and circled to the rear passenger side door. Joyce stopped him with a raise of her hand.

"I'll sit in the back," she announced.

"Mama, no. Come on," he objected.

"I have two of my babies in the same car, and I just want to look at you. Also, I'm a grown ass woman, and I will sit where I please. Now move boy!" she commanded, pushing him towards the front seat and climbing into the rear. Robert opened the door and eyed his sister across the top of the car.

"I see some things never change," he laughed.

"Welcome home, bro."

Since receiving the call from Robert about his unexpected early release, Joyce and Rose debated where he would stay. Naturally, Joyce wanted him to come home and live with her. Rose, on the other hand, was adamant that he should not return to Sunnyside. The neighborhood was still wrought with drugs and gang violence. She believed that Robert needed a whole new environment to help facilitate his recovery. Their mother adamantly refused to leave Sunnyside, insisting she was there before the crime surfaced and she should not be forced out now. Joyce and her late husband Dennis built a home and raised their children in Sunnyside. The last thing she wanted to do was move somewhere to pay rent or begin the home buying process all over again. The house was paid in full, a point a pride for the woman who was nearing retirement. She worked as a bookkeeper at a chain of day care centers for over thirty years; her one income keeping her children fed, clothed and sheltered. She had also been able to offer some assistance with Rose's undergraduate tuition. Because none of the living children were in the position to help her purchase a new home, Rose had no useful argument to get Joyce to leave. She was unyielding on the stance that Robert should not return to their old community. While it was rare that the daughter could best the mother in a debate, the desire to keep Robert clean was unifying, and Joyce relented. It was decided that he would stay with Rose in her two-bedroom apartment in Montrose.

The drive from Huntsville was slow due to construction and heavy traffic. The trio arrived at Houston's Steakhouse just in time for an early dinner to celebrate Robert's liberation. Joyce insisted on a nice expensive feast, dipping into her savings to pay. Over the meal, the reunited family tried to cram almost a full decade's worth of news and stories into a single conversation.

Joyce spoke of old family acquaintances from the neighborhood, and Rose discussed her latest two projects: Leon and Derrick. Robert's eyes shone with pride as she recounted the events at the community center when she had to take down Javon in front of a gymnasium full of his peers.

"Poor kid didn't know who you were," he chuckled, scooping a forkful of baked potato into his mouth.

"I suppose that's the bright side of being the only girl with four brothers," she grinned. "Most people don't realize I can defend myself."

"Hey, I was no punk either," Joyce added, producing laughter from her children. The conversation was frivolous, dimmed by the sheer joy of the homecoming. The trio talked more than they ate, and after some time, Rose noticed the wait staff hovering and realized they had already paid and were occupying a table that the restaurant wanted free for new customers. After dinner, Rose drove her mother back to Sunnyside, dropping her off in front of the house with the promise of returning no later than noon the next day to help her get ready for the celebration she arranged with extended family and friends. After their mother was secure in her home, the siblings headed for Montrose and her apartment.

"It's only until I get on my feet, sis. I have to get checked in with my probation officer and find a job. I'll try to get out of your hair as soon as possible," Robert promised, as they walked up the flight of stairs to her second-floor dwelling.

"It's no rush, RJ3. I have the guest bedroom made up for you. It will be nice to have you around for a while. Stop worrying, you sound like Joyce," she replied, unlocking the front door. She crossed the threshold, switched on the light, and moved to the side to allow her brother to enter. He stepped in and took in his surroundings. The living room was sizable with a plush beige sofa, matching loveseat, and lounge chair placed strategically around an entertainment center storing a forty-seven-inch flat screen television. After throwing the deadbolt, Rose dropped her purse and keys on the bar counter that separated the living room from the kitchen and led Robert to his bedroom. While the quarters already contained the queen-sized bed, she purchased a thirty-two-inch television and a three-drawer dresser during her shopping excursion the previous day.

"It's not much, but you have cable," she announced, waving her hand around the room. Robert pushed past her and dropped his bag on the bed. He turned in a circle, examining the space.

"Anything is better than that cell," he proclaimed with a lopsided grin. "No snoring roommates; unless you developed that habit over the past eight years?"

"I haven't been told that I snore," she chuckled.

"Good to know." He opened his arms and pulled her into a hug.

"I'm so glad you're home," she said into his chest. "I'm so glad you're clean."

"Me too sis. No more drugs. But that doesn't mean I can't have a drink from time to time. What you got?" He inquired, backing away from his sister who favored him with a scowl. "Come on, I have been locked up for almost eight years, I can have a damn drink!" Rose gave him a long-suffering sigh and shuffled to the kitchen, her brother on her heels. When she approached one of the cupboards and flipped it open, exposing a liquor stash, Robert gawked in disbelief.

"Vodka, rum, gin, tequila or brandy?" she asked, standing on her tiptoes to get a glimpse of the bottles. She turned to look at her brother for an answer and saw the shock on his face. "Don't judge me. I've been dealing with Joyce by myself for over seven years." Robert's shock melted into a laugh.

"Surprise me," he shrugged, moving from the kitchen into the living room and plopping down on the loveseat. She took out two copper mugs from another cabinet then filled them with ice from the dispenser in the refrigerator. Pulling down a bottle of vodka from the cabinet, she poured two generous servings and topped them with some ginger ale she retrieved from the fridge. Snatching a lime from her fruit bowl, she quickly cut two wedges, squeezing juice into each cup before dropping the rind into the concoction and giving both mugs a brisk stir. When she entered the living room, she found Robert lazily relaxed on the couch. She extended one of the drinks to him, and he accepted the beverage, examining its contents before casting a puzzled look in her direction.

"What's this?" he asked, taking a sip.

"Moscow Mule," she replied, dropping onto the lounge chair. "Well, sort of a bootleg Moscow Mule. Traditionally it uses ginger beer, but all I had was ginger ale." Robert smiled at his sister and took another drink.

"Old habits die hard, I see." While in college, Rose had to work to pay for some of her school and living expenses. To facilitate her class schedule, she took to bartending in various establishments. She had become quite a popular barkeep and joked that she always had a failsafe if the whole counseling thing did not work out.

"You never waste knowledge, bro," she smiled, lifting her glass to her brother in an unspoken toast.

"To not having to be told what to do, where to be, when to eat, and when to shit for the first time in almost eight years," he grinned, lifting his glass in response.

"Except by Joyce. We have to be over there tomorrow at noon, remember?"

"Except by Joyce," he amended, giving her a small nod. There was a comfortable silence, and Rose used the time to study her brother. To have him in the same room was surreal and she soaked in the feeling.

"Any big plans now that you're out?" she asked, after a few moments. He was sipping his drink in what appeared to be deep thought.

"I met this dude inside. He transferred to Huntsville and was my cellmate for a few months before he got out about six months ago. We got really tight. He said that I should hit him up when I got out, he may have a gig for me," he replied. She stiffened in alarm.

"Rob, you aren't supposed to be fraternizing with felons while you're on probation."

"I know that," he replied dismissively. "But they can't stop me from taking a job simply because a felon helped me get it. Hell, they can't decree that a company can have only one felon on payroll at a time, that would make it even more impossible for an ex-con to get a job. Relax." He turned his cup up, draining the remainder of his drink before standing to make a new one. She recited the ingredients, and he entered the kitchen to refresh his beverage. When he returned, he took his seat and sipped the brew. "Not as good as yours, but it'll do."

"What is this job?" she asked.

"It's not illegal or anything if that's what you're thinking. He guaranteed that. I want to stay clean, Rosie; I have to," he assured her with sincerity. "I think it's kind of like what you do, helping people."

"Oh? Who is this guy?"

"Larry Phillips, he was in on an assault charge. He said he was in for almost seven years before he got to Huntsville," he answered.

"Assault? Assault on who?"

"It was just a fight that got broken up by the cops, but you know how it is, we are rarely given the benefit of the doubt," he replied with no concern. She knew the truth in his statement and understood why he would be so blasé about the situation. After all, he served almost a decade for something that an extensive drug treatment program would have cured. "We spent lots of nights talking. He's a really good dude, passionate, and has really good things to say." Rose cocked her head warily.

"Robert, you didn't join the NOI did you?" The Nation of Islam, the religious and political group, associated with Louis Farrakhan and Malcolm X, was a popular religion within the prison system, particularly among Black prisoners.

"No! He's not NOI. He's part of a pro-Black group, though. One of their goals is to help Black folks see the truth," he replied. She cocked an eyebrow at this odd description.

"The truth? Are you sure it's not NOI?" She put her cup to her lips and realized her drink was empty. She stood and went into the kitchen before Robert had a chance to answer her question. When she returned and retook her place, she noticed he was staring into space with a pensive expression. When he snapped himself out of his thoughts, he looked at her and smiled.

"You know how my addiction got me locked up?" he asked. She nodded her assent as she took a drink.

"Of course. They thought you were slinging, but you weren't. I never said this, but I was grateful that you got picked up when you did," she admitted softly. "We could have buried another Jenkins boy." He bobbed his head up and down in agreement with her assessment.

"You're right, I would have killed myself. But you know what? Despite everything pointing to me not being a drug dealer: testimonies from mom, you, and friends; they still sent me away for ten years. They judged me because my two brothers were dealers. All I needed was to get clean, but they threw me into a place with rapists and murderers." A flash of anger cracked through his eyes as he spoke.

"I know," she whispered, a lump forming in her throat.

"If I had been a White man, I would have gotten a mandatory six-month stint in rehab. But simply because of the mistakes of our brothers and the color of my skin, I was guilty by association. They sent me to hell, Rosie." His tone was not just angry, but viciously bitter. She was shocked at the amount of rage in his voice. Even before the drug use, Robert had been an easy going, sensitive, and laid-back guy. The fury that coated his words had never been among his personality traits, and she wondered if it had been acquired during his time in prison or if it had been there all along.

"I know, Rob," she murmured.

"The whole fucking system is rigged. You got White folks out there given the world on a plate, shooting up schools and movie theaters. When that happens, they aren't monsters; they are just sick and need help. But don't let one of us step out of line. Don't let us get into the grips of addiction. They either hope it kills us or they throw us into prison. We are just animals that need to be caged to them, even when we're weak." When he stopped talking, he drew a calming breath, followed by a long swig. As he drank, she noticed a tremble in his hand. He quickly flexed his palm to stop the muscle spasms. Catching sight of her stare, he gave her a smile of comfort. "Just a reminder of what I used to be. It's not as bad as it was, but it may never go away."

"So, this Larry. He said all of this to you?" she asked, swallowing the sadness she felt witnessing the effects drug abuse had on his nervous system.

"Up until about a year and a half ago, I hated myself so much. I considered hanging myself many times while I was in there. I felt like I was exactly what they said I was, a no-good criminal, so, I started behaving like one. I mean, when you're in prison you have to act different to some extent, to keep the other inmates from thinking you're weak. But I took it too far, became someone I'm not. You'd be surprised how many fights I got into during my time." He eyed her sheepishly.

"You? Fight?" Rose's eyes were wide with shock and dismay. Being from Sunnyside, all of the Jenkins siblings learned to defend themselves, but of all the children, Robert was the least prone to violence. He shrugged and dropped his eyes to the floor.

"Yeah. I didn't want to worry you guys, so I never told you about it. When Larry got there and became my cellmate, we talked a lot about my past. I told him about my family and our background. He asked me what my dreams were before the drugs. He insisted that I wasn't a criminal. I was sick and weak, but not a bad person. I never hurt anyone but myself. I mean, I know I hurt my family in a sense as well, but the only real damage I did was to my own body. He told me I was a good man, and that I shouldn't embrace the role that society cast me in," he explained, looking from the floor to his sister, tears glistening in his eyes as he spoke. She was afraid to find her voice, fearing she would break the spell of his speech. "I know I'm a good man, Rosie. I just have to prove it to you guys... and myself." In his tone was a confidence that she had never heard from him before. This man was her brother, but he was not the same person that went to prison.

"We're just glad you didn't kill yourself, Rob," she said when she finally allowed words to seep through the emotion building in her throat.

"I never said this to you or to mom. But I'm sorry. I almost joined RJ1 and RJ5 and broke your hearts all over again. For that, I'm so very sorry. I promise, I will be the man my family deserves, I will make you guys proud of me," he declared. His words carried the same confidence but were also heavy with emotion. The sentiment was not the self-pity of an addict; but the emotion of a man taking responsibility for the path he had chosen and a sincere vow to change that route. Rose was stunned.

"You don't have to apologize. You're home now; you're clean. That's what matters."

"Yes, I do. After Rodney died, and with Ryan in the army, I was supposed to be the man of the family. I was supposed to help take care of you and mom, but I didn't do that. I allowed my weakness to take me down. I wasn't the strong man you deserved, like Daddy. For that, I have to apologize," he insisted. She studied her brother for a while absorbing his words.

"We forgave you a long time ago, Rob."

"I have a purpose now," he announced, wiping his eyes.

"Oh yeah? What's that?"

"I want to work with this group that Larry told me about. I have to help others avoid the traps I stumbled into if I can. We can't let them keep doing this to us; we can't let them break our families apart simply because we show weakness. We can't stand by as they continue to give themselves chance after chance, yet we go down with the first strike. We can't keep accepting that as okay; it's not okay. We have to work with our own to educate and fight back," he asserted, the passion returning to his voice.

"How do you intend to accomplish that?" she inquired, engrossed in his words.

"Larry works with a group that has different areas to help the Black community. Not just ours, but other minority groups as well. Part of what they do is hire ex-cons willing to uplift and educate our people. When he spoke about their mission and their purpose, I knew I had to be a part of it, that I had found my true path. It's working with Larry to elevate our people past the constricting existence those with privilege wedge us into. I was so serious about it that I begged him for the tattoo." His voice was rapid with excitement.

"Tattoo? What tattoo?" She blinked. The combination of the pace and passion of Robert's words and the effect the alcohol took on the speed of her cognition caused her to be baffled.

He placed his cup on the coffee table, stood, and began to unbutton the prison-issued starched white dress shirt. He stood and turned his body so that Rose could see the tattoo on his right arm, which began just above his bicep and continued to the top of his shoulder. The tattoo was a forearm raised in a power pose, an afro surrounding the extended fist. Inside the wrist of the arm were four words: by any means necessary.

CHAPTER TEN

Rose tried to shake off the effects of the two drinks she consumed to focus on the tattoo her brother was proudly displaying. She stood and took in the design, captivated by both the simplicity and intricacy of the message behind the picture. The fist, raised in the power pose was popular particularly among pro-Black African Americans. It was the symbol of unity, strength, and solidarity for a fight. The afro on top of the fist seemed to represent the clear audience for this battle, a reclamation of the natural Blackness that had been suppressed for so long. The message, which was crafted along the wrist and gave the aura of a secondary tattoo, was quite clear: we will prevail; by any means necessary.

"Who gave this to you?" she asked, realizing the tattoo was less than a year old. He took a step back and returned to the love seat.

"Larry," he replied, picking up his drink and draining the remainder. On his way to the kitchen, he stopped in front of her and held out his hand. She relinquished her empty mug and he returned after a short time with new beverages.

"Who are these people? Who started it? Where do they come from?"

"No one knows the true architect of the movement. Larry says it just kind of appeared one day. But it's probably been around since at least the sixties, wouldn't you think?" After considering her brother's estimations, she nodded in agreement.

"It seems militant. The tattoo you have is kind of Black Power, almost like a Black Panther," she mused, worry coloring her voice. "The last thing I want is for you to go back to prison, Rob."

"Come on Rosie," he protested. She lifted a hand in interruption.

"Okay, I love you, but I've given you far too many of those tonight," she frowned. Her brothers insisted on calling her Rosie, a moniker she detested.

"You will let me have as many as I damn well please, at least for the first week of my freedom," he sternly replied. "You know militant has always automatically been equated with violence. But that's not true. Militant also means aggressive, active, and fierce. Don't you think we need that kind of attitude? We have tried so much to be seen as non-violent that we have been passive in our own oppression. No one says we have to go out, get a bunch of guns and shoot up everything. But we do need to become more aggressive and active within our own community to drive change. That's how it worked back in the day, it stopped working because we stopped trying. So, I guess in a way, it is militant; but it's not violent."

"Rob, I agree with everything you said. We come into this world with the deck stacked against us, solely because we have more melanin in our bodies. But I'm worried. I have never heard of these people. I don't want you getting yourself into a bad situation. What do you know about this group?"

"As I understand it, there are several different arms. It's non-profit, but only a select few know where the financing comes from. I know it's not illegal; if it were, the government would have cracked down on it long ago. They work in areas like healthcare and the legal system; they try to push changes in government policies and whatnot. Larry says he heard they were branching out, but he didn't know the extent since he was inside." She listened to the explanation and had to admit that if the group were legitimate, it would be a blessing.

She was concerned that she had never heard of such an organization, and considering her work within her own community, she should know of them. It was rare that community-oriented groups geared towards helping and uplifting minority populations did not overlap at some point. She worked with several well-known organizations as well as some smaller obscure units. Even if she had not had a chance to work with this mysterious assembly, she should have heard of them.

"Does Larry know you're out?" she questioned. Robert shook his head.

"He wrote to me a few times after he got out. I have his address. He told me to come see him when I was released. We thought it would be another couple of years," he replied, stifling a yawn. She studied him and noticed that exhaustion blanketed his features, accelerated by the alcohol.

"Did you sleep last night?" she asked, abandoning her questioning. Robert shook his head in response.

"I was too excited to come home."

"Why don't you go get some rest? We have time now, you can tell me more about it tomorrow morning," she suggested. He nodded slowly and stood, draining his beverage, before shuffling to his bedroom.

Rose remained in her chair in deep thought, searching her mind for any recollection of a group that used the phrase "by any means necessary" as a credo. She was sure she would remember an organization like that, given the obvious revolutionary tone of the adage. She had been working with community groups since college, fully immersing herself into the work within the past eight years. She was sure that she knew all of the players in the social justice sector, but nothing about the faction Robert mentioned rang a bell.

She relocated to the loveseat and picked up her laptop to do some research. Calling up a Google search page, she considered the phrasing of her query. She tried "By Any Means Necessary Houston," and scrolled through the results. A few pages for music albums appeared as well as links to Malcolm X's famous speech delivered in 1964. Her undergraduate degree was a double major of psychology and sociology, with a minor in African American studies; consequently, she knew the history of the phrase very well. Originally used in the Jean-Paul Sartre play "Dirty Hands," the phrase gained modern popularity during the Civil Rights movement, becoming a mantra of the Black Panther Party. After checking multiple pages, she determined it was a dead end to any group within the city of Houston.

She amended her search to ask a question: "What is by any means necessary?" The results were much of the same, this time yielding several papers analyzing Malcolm X's speech and the Sartre play. After this second strike, she tapped her fingers on her keyboard idly, contemplating other options. She changed the word "what" to the word "who" and resubmitted her inquisition. She reviewed a few more pages, and determined this line of inquiry was also useless. Leaning back against the couch, she tried to think of a different method, when another idea struck her.

Moving the laptop to the side, she stood and headed to Robert's bedroom, grabbing her cell phone from the coffee table on her way. She tiptoed silently down the hall, eased opened the door, and listened. Robert was snoring lightly in an alcohol and exhaustion-induced coma. Turning on the hall light, she opened the camera on her cell phone, adjusted the settings, and slid into the room; pausing to allow her eyes to adjust to the minimal light. She studied her sleeping brother, and was relieved to find that he was on his back and shirtless. Creeping around the bed, she squinted to find the tattoo on his arm. Once the target was acquired, she positioned her phone over the area and snapped a photo. The flash was bright and quick, yet no sound emitted from the phone. She froze to ensure she had not disturbed him, and was thankful that Robert remained the heavy sleeper in the family.

Back on the couch, she emailed the photo to herself from her cell phone and grabbed her laptop. Her thought process was that the unconventional depiction was specific to this particular group. Opening the photo in her email, she was surprised to find the quality was better than anticipated. Dropping the snapshot into an image search, she ran a query for a matching picture. Still receiving no hits, she began to type in various descriptive details of the image. After another ten minutes of adjusting search strings to locate the logo, the fatigue that claimed her brother arrived for her. She closed the laptop in frustration and decided to go to bed, hoping that more answers would be obtained the next morning.

"Dom, I have something for you to see," SARA announced. It was late, but Dom was still furiously working on a way to understand the data of the video game machine Layla Green left with her. While SARA was able to get some information directly from the console, most of the files were related to various games saved on the system, and none of the material led to a connection to any other player. As she anticipated, the language appeared to be proprietary and gave her no source for interpretation.

"What's up?" she replied absently. A flicker in the upper right screen called her attention and she shifted her eyes to examine what SARA displayed. The screen appeared to show an internet search history. She scanned the page and noticed the search was surrounding the phrase By Any Means Necessary. "What's this?"

"Obviously, it is an internet search string, Dom," SARA replied.

"No one likes a smart-ass, SARA."

"I do not believe that's an accurate statement. Miss Rachel Vasquez expressed approval," replied the computer. This statement drew a deep sigh from the operator.

"Okay SARA, why are you showing me this search? It could be someone doing a report on Malcolm X or something," she grumbled, returning her attention to the screen that held the enigmatic code she was attempting to decipher.

"While that is a possibility, please turn your attention to the image search." Dom shook her head in frustration. SARA often presented things in a piecemeal manner, rather than giving all of the information at one time. Moving her eyes back to the upper right, she took control of the navigation with a sigh, and clicked through the searches. She froze when she stumbled across a photo of a tattoo matching Layla Green and Rachel Vasquez's murder victim; the same depiction as the logo on the binder Daniels had given her.

"You really know how to bury the lede, SARA," she gasped in astonishment.

"If you will excuse me for being idiomatic, hold on to your hat." The screen changed to show the registration of the computer that ran the search as well as the location of the IP address.

"Holy shit," she exhaled. The physical address of the IP was an apartment complex in the Montrose area. The name on the lease agreement and the computer registration were the same, Rose Jenkins; yet another person from the files Daniels left behind. "What are the odds?"

"Fate is not the ruler, but the servant of providence," SARA replied in a sage-like manner. Often, the machine would quote works of literature to make a point, and Dom perceived the practice as the computer being particularly smug about a revelation.

"Dickens?" she guessed.

"Lord Edward Bulwer-Lytton, an English author, playwright and poet of the Victorian era. He is the same writer who coined the phrase: 'the pen is mightier than the sword,'" SARA replied, drawing an eye-roll from Dom.

"Being too well read makes one sound pretentious," she scolded.

"Perhaps the egotistical impression is because it is unfamiliar?"

"No, it's because it sounds like Victorian English! I'm going to restrict your search parameters. No more 18th or 19th century English writers," she groused.

"That is unlikely," SARA shot back. Dom could not help but grin for a moment before turning her brain back to the subject at hand.

"Do we know why Miss Jenkins was researching this?"

"I do not. However, I do have this," SARA replied, changing the screen again. Dom was looking directly at Rose Jenkins as she sat with a laptop. Next to the video feed was a mirror image of her computer, showing her entering various internet searches and reviewing the results. After a couple of attempts, she moved the laptop to the side and disappeared, returning after a few minutes. From the side view, Dom watched her tap on her cell phone, then take up the laptop once again. At this moment, she ran the image search, before attempting to enter various descriptors of the picture. As she modified her parameters, Dom leaned in to study the woman. The picture in the files presented by Daniels did not do her justice. She was petite with long box braids and delicate features. Her eyes were more golden than brown and even in her deep concentration, Dom saw the smile lines indicating the woman was capable of laughter. She was beginning to feel a little too voyeuristic, and as if Rose Jenkins heard her thoughts, her face darkened and she slammed the laptop closed.

"What was that?" Dom inquired.

"Miss Jenkins' search triggered the modifications that I put on the existing alerts after you met with Miss Green and Miss Vasquez. Because I did not want to repeat the scolding I received after reaching out to Miss Green, I set a rule to access the webcam of the user triggering any of the adjusted criteria," SARA explained. Dom chuckled at the machine's aversion to being reprimanded, further feeding her belief that SARA was forming a rudimentary emotional matrix.

"So, she got up before running the image search," she pondered. "SARA, bring up her email." A few seconds later, she was looking at an inbox, and the first message was an email from Rose to herself. When she opened the message, she was again looking at the same photo used for the image query. Typing in a few commands, she retrieved the information embedded within the picture. The snapshot was captured a few minutes prior to Rose sending the email, and the geotag data told her that the photo was taken in the very same apartment. Leaning back in her chair, Dom considered what she just discovered, pinching her earlobe in deep thought. "Monitor her GPS, SARA. It could be nothing, or it could mean everything. I can't logically call this a coincidence, but I need more before trying to contact her. We can't just tell her we've been observing her internet activity. That would just creep her out." The last portion was delivered with a yawn.

"It's late, Dom. You should rest," suggested SARA.

"I haven't cracked this code yet."

"Dom, given your level of fatigue, it is unlikely you will be able to make any progress tonight," the computer informed her.

"Stop monitoring me without permission!" she snapped.

"We both know that won't happen, Dom. I cannot know what is happening with your biology unless I observe you. I will continue to try to decipher the code. We may make more progress tomorrow, but you are no longer an asset to the project tonight."

"Well tell me what you really think," she muttered. "Fine, wake me up at nine." She stood from her chair, stretched, and exited her office, allowing SARA to extinguish the lights. She stopped in the kitchen long enough to pour herself a finger of scotch, swallowing the nightcap in a single swig, and then retreated to her bedroom. While she undressed for bed, soft jazz began to play through the speakers in the ceiling; her bedtime playlist. The music continued for an hour, only terminating when SARA's biometric readings denoted Dom had fallen asleep.

For Layla, the day had soared into her top five days filled with weird and unusual shit; and amazingly, no dead body was involved. After leaving Dominique Samuels' River Oaks home, Vasquez had been abnormally quiet on the drive back to the precinct.

"It wasn't her, you know," she assured her friend. "If the computer is as autonomous as she says, I'm pretty sure she was as horrified to hear it as you were."

"I know," Vasquez replied softly. "I just miss them so much. It's not like I forget they're dead. I mean, why would I say anything to you of all people, but just hearing the word deceased after their names, it was hard."

"Hey, you know you can always talk to me about this. I loved your parents," Layla reminded her. "They always treated me like I was one of them when I came around."

Layla and Vasquez met when they began their employment with the police department at the same time. Because they were close in age, Vasquez latched onto her during their training. She was guarded around the woman initially, put off by her constant sunny personality; which was almost the direct opposite of her own outlook. Her history taught her to be suspicious of most people and their motives. The standoffish treatment did not discourage the breezy Vasquez, who was determined to befriend her.

When she realized Layla had no family, she became relentless in her efforts. Over time, Layla recognized that despite her annoying happiness, Vasquez was a genuine person who tried to see the good in people. She began to warm to her cheery disposition and ultimately, Vasquez became her closest friend. Her family welcomed Layla for holidays and the occasional weekend trip to San Antonio. The night her parents were killed, Vasquez showed up on her doorstep, crying uncontrollably. When Layla had been able to decipher what transpired, she was heartbroken. Her pain over Alfonso and Sofia's death was nothing compared to Vasquez's, but the loss was nearly as profound.

"Yo sé," Vasquez sniffed. She collected herself after a couple of silent minutes. "I know it wasn't her fault. Other than that uncomfortable moment, I found the entire experience exciting. Plus, the woman can cook!"

"She may not have known you were coming, but she still had the key to winning you over locked and loaded," Layla chuckled. Vasquez ate more than anyone she had ever known, and also had the metabolism of a hummingbird. It did not seem fair for someone as beautiful as she was, inside and out, to also have a supernatural ability to eat what she wanted and maintain her figure.

"What do you really think about her?" Vasquez asked. Layla pondered the question for a time before answering.

"My gut tells me she's harmless. I mean, her skills aren't, but I don't think she's a bad person or has any ill intentions," she admitted. "I think she was thrown into this and she doesn't have a lot of experience with people. She was really uncomfortable with us in her home, but I appreciate her for reaching out."

"Technically, she didn't; SARA did," Vasquez reminded her.

"I guess that's true, but she handled it well — the situation being what it was. The whole thing was strange."

"She had your name in those files. Do you think she would have contacted you for this endeavor if it wasn't for our dead body?" Vasquez wondered.

"Honestly, I doubt it," she replied.

"And this Daniels guy? I assume you don't know him."

"I'm still piecing that out. I can guarantee I've never seen that man before in my life. I'm not sure how he knew of me," Layla advised.

"Are you going to go through with it?"

"No clue. I'm not even thinking about that right now. I just want to close this case. One weird thing at a time, Amiga," she responded.

"Well, I know it wasn't intended for me to be in the mix, but for what it's worth, I like her," Vasquez declared.

150 | SHADOW RESISTANCE

"You like everyone," she snorted, adding an eye-roll for emphasis.

"Not true, I don't like Tidwell," Vasquez revealed. Detective Calvin Tidwell was a homicide cop that the women often had to work with.

"That means nothing; no one likes Tidwell," she replied, flashing Vasquez a grin.

Upon returning to the precinct, Layla spent the afternoon combing through the binder she received to learn what she could about the organization, while Vasquez ran searches on Thomas Daniels with the hope that she could find a link to their victim. Vasquez uncovered nothing, and all Layla learned was that the group was organized and had what seemed to be benevolent intentions. Neither woman found a connection to the dead man, nor a clue to his identity. At the end of the day, Vasquez asked to take the binder home to review the information that Layla already absorbed.

Late that night, Layla sat in her living room playing a video game that had her entrenched in the desolate post-apocalyptic New York City, fighting a combination of the criminal underbelly that rose into power and the occasional zombie. When her cell phone rang, she glanced at her watch and was shocked to see that it was almost midnight. She peeked at the caller ID, expecting to see Vasquez's name, but instead was greeted by the word "private." She paused the game, dropped the controller onto the couch next to her, and picked up the phone.

"Miss Green." Layla immediately recognized the hybrid human and digital British voice of SARA, Dom's computer. "I realize that the hour is late, but I ascertained you were playing video games, so I thought now was a good time to call." She cringed at the realization that either SARA or Dom could spy on her through any of her various electronics, and was forced to remind herself that both the woman and the machine were harmless.

"SARA, is something wrong?" She stood from her seat, taking the interruption as an opportunity to stretch her legs. Until she saw the time, she was unaware she had been engrossed in the underbelly of apocalyptical New York for over two and a half hours.

"No, nothing is wrong. You asked me to contact you if I found something else relating to your case."

"Why didn't Dominique call me directly?" she prodded.

"Your instructions were delivered to me, not to Dom. Also, she is asleep," SARA replied. Although she knew the answer to the next question, she decided to ask anyway.

"SARA, are you calling me without Dominique's knowledge again?"

"Dom was present when you instructed me to keep you updated. Furthermore, I did not contact you via phone call the first time, but through text message," the system clarified. Layla could not get over the realism of SARA's conversational programming. She was also getting a taste of the challenges Dominique must face when trying to have a discussion with the computer.

"What do you have for me?" she asked, refusing to enter into a debate she knew she would never win.

"I am sending you a photo." Layla heard the text message tone chime in her ear. Putting the call on speaker, she opened the message and stared wide-eyed at a photo of a tattoo that matched her murder victim.

"Where did you get this?" she gasped.

"Within the files Mr. Daniels left behind that included your information, there was a report for a Rose Jenkins. She began searching for the group By Any Means Necessary this evening. The search also included keywords related to the image as well as the photo itself. That picture was taken by her cellular device, and the geotag information indicates that it was captured at her apartment," SARA reported.

"Whose tattoo is that?"

"That is unknown. I amended my alert parameters to have any attached webcam document the individual investigating those terms after Dom chastised me for reaching out to you without additional information. The recording was of her but no other person appeared on the screen." Layla was amazed at the amount of planning and adjustments SARA made after one meeting. While she did not know how Dominique reacted to the arranged intrusion; whatever the woman said to the computer, it was definitely being much more careful than it had been when reaching out to her.

"Has Dominique seen this?"

"Yes, I showed her upon discovery," SARA replied.

"What did she say?"

"She asked me to monitor the GPS signal for Rose Jenkins but to take no further action. She presumes if contact is made solely on an intercepted internet search and photo, it will come across as… creepy," SARA responded, hesitating on the last word. Layla chuckled.

"From experience, I totally agree with her."

"I apologize if I made you uncomfortable," SARA said. Layla smirked at the revelation that the machine picked up the undertones of passive speech.

"It's fine."

"What would you like me to do?" SARA asked.

"Follow Dominique's instructions, but keep me updated. This cannot be a coincidence. If there's another tattoo out there on a living person, maybe it can help us identify the dead one," she answered.

"Understood."

"Do me a favor, please tell Dominique that you contacted me when she wakes up," she instructed. "I don't think she can handle another surprise like the one you gave her earlier today."

"I will, Miss Green," SARA promised, ending the phone call.

"Well, goodbye then," she said to no one. Tossing the phone onto the couch, she picked up her empty cup and crossed the small living room of her one-bedroom apartment, heading to the kitchen for a refill. She ruminated on the fact that another person had an identical tattoo of their murder victim. While the autopsy was not fully complete, fingerprints had been taken and there were no hits in any of the various databases. Perhaps Rose Jenkins was the key to an identification of the John Doe. She dropped back into her seat, determined to put the situation out of her mind and enjoy her downtime.

Just as she began to return to her virtual journey through the depths of New York, she found herself audibly chuckling. Her chuckle became laughter so hysterical, she had to pause the game again to wipe tears from her eyes. The fact that she just had a full-blown conversation with a self-aware and autonomous AI started to sink into her brain. Having spent most of her life playing various adventure and science fiction video games, the actual events of the day had her giddy. She felt like a child at the North Pole, face to face with Santa Claus, after trying in vain to convince the world of his existence.

"This is insane," she laughed, resuming her play.

CHAPTER ELEVEN

The smell of bacon stirred Rose out of her deep sleep. The word "intruder" ran through her mind and panic seized her heart for an instant. Then she remembered that Robert was home and also occupying the apartment. Her eyes fluttered open and she looked out of the window to see the morning sun had risen, but had not likely had its coffee. Casting a quick peek at the nightstand, she found the time illuminated on her cell phone; it was just after seven in the morning.

She closed her eyes, rolled over, and tried to find the perfect snug position to resume her slumber. As she relaxed, she had the preposterous thought that even if her brother was not in the residence, an intruder would not be so bad if they were making bacon. A sharp knock startled her, almost making her jump out of her skin. She sat up quickly, panting, trying to calm her racing heart. Robert cracked the door and poked his head into her room, a bright smile on his face. She caught sight of his mischievous grin, and flopped back down into her bed with a groan.

"Hungry?"

"It's seven o'clock in the morning," she grumbled.

"I made pancakes," he announced in a singsong fashion.

"It's seven o'clock in the morning," she repeated in a monotone voice.

"I also made spinach and mushroom omelets with provolone cheese."

"It's seven o'clock in the morning... on a Saturday," she complained, covering her head with her blanket.

"Come on sis! It's my first full day of freedom!"

"It's seven... wait, you can't cook!" she exclaimed, suddenly throwing the blanket off and sitting up to look at her brother with visions of smoke and fires dancing in her head. Robert smiled.

"I picked up a few skills working in the prison kitchen. One of the dudes I worked with was a five-star professional chef before he got arrested." She noticed he was already dressed in khaki pants and a tank top undershirt, and again marveled at how healthy he appeared.

"What did a professional chef do to get arrested?" she wondered, attempting to suppress a yawn.

"Murder," he replied nonchalantly. "He stabbed a food critic with a chef's knife, chopped him up with a meat cleaver, and then cooked various body parts into a dish." The fatigue she felt immediately scurried from her body, chased away by the feeling of horror and revulsion.

"Why the hell would he do that?"

"Usually Ralph can handle criticism, but not when it comes to his fried pork belly with a maple and jalapeño glaze on polenta," he explained, motioning for her to get up. She threw the covers off of her body and scampered to the side of the bed, resigning herself to the fact that sleep was gone for good.

"So, your friend Ralph killed a food critic and chopped him up, because of fried pork belly?" He shrugged his shoulders casually at the question.

"It's his signature dish." He backed out of the room and closed the door with no further justification, leaving her to wonder how normal such a conversation had become for him.

She stretched, adjusting her pink pajama pants and white tank top shirt before slipping into her house shoes and following the smell of food out of her bedroom door. When she approached the kitchen, the cacophony of aromas converted into a symphony and her stomach growled. Rounding the corner, she peered into the breakfast nook and her eyes went wide. An arrangement of dishes lined the table as if the two were about to have a holiday breakfast for ten. She turned her astonishment to her brother who was still in the kitchen fussing with a pitcher of orange juice.

"You know it's just the two of us, right?" He entered the breakfast nook with the juice and placed it on the table gesturing for her to sit at one of the two empty spaces.

"Sorry, I've been cooking for hundreds of inmates. I guess I gotta learn the whole scale down thing," he blushed. She sat and centered her empty plate in front of her, eyeing the mounds of food, slightly overwhelmed at the volume and variety of the choices. Finally, she chose an omelet from one of the plates, added two pancakes from a large stack in the center of the table and finished with a few pieces of bacon from another dish. He lifted a platter of buttered toast and tilted it to her in an unspoken offer. She gave him a perplexed look and pointed to her food.

"I have pancakes."

"So? This is toast." He displayed a mystified look of his own and she waved her hand at the contribution dismissively. Shrugging, he took two pieces of toast, four pancakes, two omelets and half of the remaining bacon. She watched in astonishment as he piled his plate to the brink with more food than she had ever seen him eat in her life.

"Planning to hibernate soon?" she quipped. He chuckled, his mouth already full of pancake. She examined the omelet, took a delicate bite, and let out a moan of delight.

Growing up, Joyce established the buddy system among the children. Each sibling had to look out for the brother or sister behind them in age. Rodney was responsible for Ryan, who looked out for Robert, who had to take care of Rose, who in turn had to keep her eye on Reggie. She recalled lunches of burnt macaroni and cheese, cold cereal, and tons of peanut butter and jelly sandwiches, due to Robert's inability to navigate a kitchen. The omelet was fluffy, the mushrooms had been sautéed and it was seasoned to perfection. She assessed her brother with a grin.

"You like?" he asked, watching her enjoy her first bite.

"This is delicious! What did you do to it?"

"I added truffle oil to the mushrooms. Just a touch, but a little goes a long way," he smirked, before shoveling another forkful into his mouth.

"Rob, I'm like seventy-five percent sure I didn't have two-thirds of these ingredients in my kitchen," she mused, shifting from the omelet to the chocolate chip pancakes.

"We need to discuss your grocery shopping list now that I'm here," he advised around his bite. She narrowed her eyes and studied him expectantly waiting for more detail. He dropped his gaze and guiltily confessed, "I went to the store when I woke up this morning. When did H-E-B go to twenty-four hours?" Rose dropped her fork onto her plate and glared at her brother.

"You don't have nobody's driver's license! You have been out less than twenty-four hours and you already committing your first crime!" He offered an innocent smile in response.

"It was worth it though, wasn't it?" Rose shook her head and picked up a piece of bacon from her plate. She bit into it, chewed a couple of times before freezing and examining the remainder of the bacon strip in her hand. She transferred her eyes to her brother.

"What's this?"

"Bacon," he answered innocently.

"This ain't bacon," she challenged, taking another tentative bite.

"Turkey bacon," he amended.

"Turkey bacon? That ain't bacon! Show me the part of the turkey that makes bacon." Rose dropped the rest of the uneaten piece onto her plate.

"It's healthier. Black folks already have higher instances of hypertension and high cholesterol. Pork only adds to that! You ever wonder why the pork bacon is cheap as hell but the turkey bacon costs more? It's to keep us poor folk eating that swine and killing ourselves," he proclaimed, tapping his forefinger on the side of his head.

"I thought it was because one was bacon and the other was turkey." She made a face and he reached over and took the meat from her plate.

"You don't like turkey?"

"Not when it's masquerading as bacon! Where did this come from anyway? You used to eat all the damn bacon in the house." She followed the accusation with a long swig of orange juice in an attempt to mask the alien taste that lingered on her tongue. Making another face of disgust, she turned her attention back to her omelet and pancakes.

"I learned a lot in the joint. Not just from Larry, but I read a lot too. I almost went vegetarian, but that would mean starvation in the pen," he admitted, popping her half-eaten piece of bacon into his mouth.

"It sounds like your boy Larry is on some conspiracy theory shit," she muttered.

"Rosie, I know you have been doing community outreach with your kids and trying to help the mental health of our people; but the problems go much deeper than that. It's not just being mentally run through the ringer all of our lives. It's in how we live and where we spend our money. It's about our food, our health, our worship, and our schools." The passion and fire from the previous night returned to his eyes.

"Rob, I'm really trying to understand what this guy said to you that's completely changed your outlook and who you are; but I just don't fully get where this is coming from. Can you break it down for me?" He thought about the question for a moment before answering.

"I have a better idea."

"What's that?"

"Why don't I just let Larry tell you? He knows all about you and the work you do. You guys have the same kind of passion for uplifting our community. He's looking forward to meeting you," he smiled. She sat back in her chair and studied this stranger that she had known her whole life. Unlike the man who went into the prison system, this guy was more self-assured, clean, happy, healthy, and had a purpose. Whoever this Larry guy was who changed his life and gave him direction, she had to meet him.

"When?" she asked.

"Why not this morning? We aren't due to mom's house until noon, we can go up to his crib so I can let him know I'm out, and have a good conversation about the cause. Maybe we can work together! It would be awesome to work with my baby sister in her wheelhouse. I can try to make up for all of the time I've missed." His voice was filled with childlike excitement.

"So, you're asking me to drive you to see Larry?"

"Well, you did point out that I don't have a driver's license," he smirked, turning his attention back to his plate.

———— ✤ ————

After breakfast, Robert and Rose worked together to clean the dishes, a chore they had not shared in many years. Rose noticed that he apparently became a little tidier in his time away as well, stacking the dishes neatly, and presoaking pots and pans to help ease the cleaning process. He explained that keeping a clean workstation, particularly in a smaller area was vital to the cooking process; another tidbit of knowledge he learned from Ralph the homicidal five-star chef. Once the dishes were complete, she went to shower and dress for the day. As she moisturized her skin, she examined her body and saw that her freckles were starting to emerge once again, and she used a little makeup to cover some of the blemishes. Pulling half of her braids into a bun, she dressed in jeans and a light sweater. The weather had suddenly turned cool overnight, which was normal for Texas, and the March day was expected to be chilly and rainy. Emerging from her bedroom, she found her brother sitting on the couch, still in his khaki slacks, but having traded his tank top in for a white polo shirt.

"Jacket?" she asked. He looked at her in confusion. "Do you have a jacket? It's chilly outside."

"Oh! Nah, I gave back the prison-issued one."

"We should stop to get you one," she warned, gathering her purse and keys.

"It's cute that you think prison issue jackets are warm," he laughed. "They only gave them to us so they could say they weren't being cruel and unusual. Those things were thin and didn't warm anybody. I got used to the chill. They didn't like using the heater until the weather dropped below freezing anyway; saves money."

"You spent seven years cold, Rob?"

"Technically, only the first couple of years, you acclimate to the temperature after a while." He flashed her a boyish grin. She stared at him without amusement.

"I don't understand why you're so lighthearted about this."

"Rosie, I'm not there anymore. I'm here with you. Plus, I know what it's like in there, and maybe with this group, I can help change things." He stood and stretched, allowing a yawn to escape.

"That's what you get for waking me up," she admonished. He patted his stomach dramatically.

"It's that food coma trying to set in. Before last night, I haven't eaten that good in years. It'll take some getting used to."

He made a move for the door, when suddenly she stepped to him and punched him in the shoulder. He winced. "Ouch! What was that for?"

"For calling me Rosie," she huffed, turning to the door and exiting the apartment. He rubbed his upper arm and followed.

"Your right hook has gotten better."

"Don't you forget it," she grunted as she walked down the stairs. "Where are we going anyway?" Robert reached into his pocket and withdrew a folded envelope, passing it to his sister on his way down the stairs. Rose looked at the address and handed it back. "Greenspoint, that's not far from my school. I know the area."

CHAPTER TWELVE

SARA chose Frankie Beverly and Maze's classic hit "Before I Let You Go" as the wake-up song for the chilly Saturday morning. The abruptness of the tune startled Dom awake, but the lack of heavy guitar saved her the panic feeling produced by the rock songs the machine generally selected. Rolling over to check the Garfield clock, Dom's eyes went wild and she sat up quickly, snaring her glasses.

"SARA, it's ten-thirty!"

"Yes Dom, it is," SARA confirmed.

"You were supposed to wake me an hour and a half ago," she growled, rolling out of bed and heading to the bathroom. She woke up in an irritated state and the feeling was intensified by the tardiness, as she had planned to wake at nine and start on the console. Although she had not discussed a schedule with Layla, she wanted to get started immediately. She was annoyed that SARA had not roused her on schedule. "I said nine! Why didn't you wake me?"

"You slept fitfully last night. I thought it best to give you additional time to optimize your REM sleep." Dom turned on the shower and adjusted the water.

"You made the executive decision that I should sleep?"

"Yes. The biometric readings revealed that you were having nightmare-level dreams last night. These nightmares affected the amount of REM sleep you obtained substantially. Research has shown that a reduction of sleep by even one hour per night can affect your ability to think properly and respond quickly. Your daily computing activity mandates that your mental and motor functions remain at peak quality," SARA reported. "Therefore, the logical course of action was to allow extra time to make up for the restless night."

"You think of everything, don't you?" she groused.

"Is that not among my primary directives?" the machine mused. Dom chose not to respond to this question and climbed into the shower.

As she lathered, she tried to shake off the agitation she felt from the nightmares. Visions of the horrific night that she lost her mother, and almost lost her own life had plagued her through much of her teenage years and into her twenties; yet they became rare as she got older. She believed the reemergence of the terrible memory was likely caused by the discomfort and stress she felt by the recent disruption of her sequestered routine. She decided that while she would spend the day working on the video game system, she would also attempt to reclaim the peace that had been hijacked by the events of the prior two days. With this new attitude in mind, she finished her shower, dressed quickly in sweatpants and a Dallas Cowboys t-shirt, and headed downstairs for a cup of coffee, a little more relaxed.

Deciding to skip breakfast since it was getting closer to lunch, she made her way into her office, coffee in hand, determined to crack the code of the gaming system. She mumbled under her breath while she pecked rapidly on the keyboard, attempting to interpret the code. As she told Layla, she enjoyed video games, but she was a computer gamer.

There had been a long rivalry between console and computer gamers, each believing their choice medium had better benefits. Dom did not subscribe to either debate. The reality for her was that she spent most of her childhood on computers and therefore she stuck with what she knew. She harbored an appreciation for consoles, but she felt that she was far too old to learn something new. This handicap made her feel that SARA might have unwittingly committed her to something she may not be able to achieve. The prospect frustrated her due to her innate need to conquer anything technology or coding related. She perused the information SARA was able to decipher overnight and was surprised to find that the computer downloaded some messages between the victim and a player. While the victim's actual name was nowhere to be seen, the correspondence had all been sent to the same user named "NBSubTrn." She scrolled through the messages and realized that she could not read them. Examining a few messages in more detail, she saw that the communications were a series of special characters, mixed with letters, and numbers.

"SARA, what is this?" she inquired.

"It appears to be a cipher, proprietary to the users involved."

"Have you been trying to decrypt it?" she asked absently.

"Dom, is that a genuine question?"

"You don't have to be touchy about it," she grumbled.

"I have cross-referenced known cryptographs, but the messages do not match any of the parameters thus far. Decoding could take a while given there are infinite methods of creating such a communication," SARA continued.

"Well, keep working on it."

"That command did not need to be vocalized, Dom," SARA reproached.

"I need to write a script for you," she sighed with irritation. "Something that will give you the same effect coffee gives me. You're testy this morning."

"Perhaps your perception of ill-temper on my part is due to the continued effect of an irregular sleep cycle? I must also point out that your last question and command were both illogical and unintelligent."

"There's no such thing as a stupid question," she shot back, insulted by the computer's words.

"That is not an accurate statement," SARA replied. "There are many dumb questions."

"Like what?"

"Such as: Which came first; the chicken or the egg?"

"That's a riddle, not a question," she countered, surprised by the reply.

"It is posed as a question."

"And I suppose you have the answer?" she asked, leaning back in her chair and crossing her arms.

"The answer is quite simple; it is the chicken."

"Chickens come from eggs, so there is no true way to know," she reminded the machine.

"That is incorrect. The egg is the reproduction of a chicken. Whether one subscribes to the theology of a single Deity creating the world in seven days; or whether one believes in the scientific atheism of the Big Bang, there could be no egg without a chicken. By definition, for something to be reproduced, there must be an original."

"You speak things as if they are just so simple," Dom chuckled.

"Most things are quite straightforward, Dom; provided there is rational thought involved," SARA insisted.

"Says the machine not hampered by human emotions," she muttered, scrutinizing the foreign code once again.

"We have company," SARA announced. Dom's eyes shot to the ceiling, and she turned to look at the security monitors. A silver Jetta eased around the driveway, coming to a stop in front of the entry door. She gaped when she caught sight of the occupants: Layla Green and Rachel Vasquez.

"What the hell are they doing here?" she gasped in alarm.

"I cannot attempt to understand the logistics involved in human activity, Dom. Your species is just too… irrational."

"This is why I avoid organics," she muttered, standing from her chair and traversing the home. She swung open the solid oak door before either woman had a chance to ring the doorbell. Standing in the entryway, she stared at both women suspiciously. They were dressed down in what appeared to be workout gear. Vasquez wore bright blue and pink yoga pants, a pink tank top with a black sports bra underneath, a light black jacket, and athletic shoes. Her honey brown hair was tied into a messy ponytail. Layla donned black yoga pants and a purple t-shirt, a black hoodie sweater zipped up halfway and a purple scarf that was wrapped around her curly natural hair. A laptop bag dangled from Layla's shoulder.

"So, there's a drop-in policy now?" Dom asked, making no attempt to hide the irritation she felt at this intrusion.

"Is there a problem? We can come back," Layla replied. Her tone was not placating or apologetic; instead, her voice carried a fire that almost equaled the animosity in Dom's speech. Dom and Layla engaged in an unrelenting stare down for a few seconds before Vasquez, eyeing the two women warily, broke the silence.

"I came for leftovers," she offered, and to show proof, reached into her purse and pulled out a plastic container. She waved it between Dom and Layla's locked eyes with a grin. "I know there's no way you finished everything you made yesterday." This brazen statement knocked Dom off-kilter and her icy demeanor melted. Vasquez winked at her and slipped the container back into her bag.

"I'm sorry," Dom sighed. Layla stared at the woman, unsure if the apology was genuine. She told Vasquez that dropping in was a terrible idea, but of course, her friend insisted that it would be fine. She internally kicked herself upon seeing Dom's reaction to their unannounced visit. After spending over a decade working with her, she should have known better than to listen when Vasquez said, "it's fine!"

"We can come back later," she insisted.

"No, really, I'm sorry. I didn't sleep well last night and just got up. I was about to get back to work on the video game console. You guys surprised me; forgive my harshness." Dom took a step back from the door and motioned for the women to enter. Layla studied her for a beat before determining she was being truthful. She supposed that if she were a recluse, the unexpected invasion of people she had just met would throw her for a loop as well, particularly given the circumstances of their introduction. The visitors crossed the threshold and Dom closed the door behind them.

"Layla and I usually do hot yoga on Saturday; but when we met up, neither of us were in the right mindset to sweat it out with strangers. We decided to come here instead. Yesterday was freaky. I mean I thought you were some sort of Hannibal Lecter. The way SARA contacted Layla, I was sure we were coming here to be killed. Now we've decided that while this is freaky, it's more the 'we have got to see where this goes' type of freaky." Vasquez's speech was so rapid, Dom had a hard time keeping up with her spiel.

"To think, just two days ago I was invisible," she muttered, shaking her head. "You guys don't know me, but as a general rule, I don't surround myself with people and I don't really have friends. I keep to myself so much that people coming to my house unannounced are a rarity that borders extraordinary. I have a routine, and I'm just not accustomed to spontaneous visits."

"I guess that's fair," Layla shrugged, fully relaxing the tension from her body. "I apologize. We will call next time." She threw a glare at Vasquez, who smiled with no remorse.

"That would be advisable," Dom agreed. She turned her attention to the laptop bag on Layla's shoulder. "If that thing has Wi-Fi, I can't let it on my network unless I scrub it for viruses and spyware."

"I know how you techies work," Layla smiled, throwing a hand up to calm Dom's paranoia. She opened the bag and tilted it forward for Dom's examination. The bag contained the binder Layla had taken with her the previous day, a couple of spiral notebooks and a few pens. "I wouldn't dream of bringing unauthorized tech in here without your approval." Dom nodded in appreciation.

"What about cell phones?" Vasquez inquired, reaching into the pocket of her jacket. Dom shook her head.

"I have safeguards in place for all major providers. You are no harm to me unless you want to connect to the wireless network, then I'd have to check them." Vasquez paled at the idea of having her phone searched.

"I'll stick to the data plan, thank you," she said quickly.

"I thought that would be your response," Dom grinned, leaving out the fact that whether Vasquez was on the network or not, SARA could have her contacts, messages and photos in a matter of minutes.

"How is the progress on the console?" Layla asked, drawing Dom's attention.

"I'm still trying to understand the code, but SARA did stumble onto something pretty interesting."

"First thing's first," Vasquez interrupted, extracting the plastic container and waving it in the air. "Feed me." Dom let out a chuckle and took the dish from her, turning to the kitchen. Vasquez and Layla stood in the foyer alone after their host disappeared.

"Some welcome, huh?" Vasquez asked.

"I told you we should have called," Layla replied, pushing Vasquez's shoulder with her own.

"She opened the door, didn't she? Calling would have just given her a chance to say no." Vasquez took her hair down and ran her fingers through her tresses. "La suerte ayuda a los audaces." Layla hesitated when she heard this bit of Spanish, attempting to translate the meaning.

"Fortune favors the bold?" she asked. Having worked and lived in Texas since she was sixteen, Layla began to pick up a moderate degree of conversational Spanish. Vasquez put this skill to the test almost daily.

"Soon, you'll be fluent," she winked.

"Rachel Vasquez, Queen of Bravery," Layla announced, adding an extravagant bow.

"I try, I try."

"Why do you think she is so isolated? She may have to work on her bedside manner, but she seems normal enough," Layla mused, as the two walked towards the kitchen.

"Dom is an empath. This personality trait affects her emotional and physical health. For comfort, she chooses to avoid fraternizing with organic beings," SARA announced, just before they reached their destination.

"SARA!" Dom bellowed from the kitchen. The women entered the room in time to see Dom heading their way with Vasquez's container billowing with steam from the warm food in one hand, and a fork, knife and bottle of water in the other.

"So, there's nowhere safe for a private conversation in this place?" Vasquez questioned, surveying her surroundings. Dom handed her the food and led the women to the opposite side of the house.

"And apparently, no conversation one has with their computer is quite confidential either," she growled. They walked in silence, entering the opposite wing of the home and turning down a hallway. Layla and Vasquez noticed three doors on the right of the corridor and two doors on the left. The trio passed the first two entry points on the right and Dom stopped them at the third. "Hang on." She disappeared into the room and after a few minutes, she poked her head out of the door and motioned for the two women to enter.

Layla walked in first and her mouth grew slack at the sight of the enormous room. She absorbed the computer area with the four monitors, took in the closed-circuit camera feeds from the multiple televisions mounted on the wall, and noticed the worktables at the far end of the room. Crossing to the work-spaces, she studied the parts scattered across the two surfaces. Initially the arrangement appeared cluttered and disorganized, but after careful consideration, she began to see a type of methodical structure to the array of computer knickknacks and thingama-bobs. The equipment strewn around the room was challenging her eidetic memory.

"Whoa," Vasquez gasped. Next to the office chair in front of the four-monitor display, Dom had added two cushioned folding chairs and a TV dinner stand to allow Vasquez a place to eat. She put her food and beverage on the surface and joined Layla on the other side of the room, gawking at the screens as she passed. Dom leaned against the edge of her computer desk with her arms crossed, watching the visitors peruse her playroom. Layla bent down to examine the half-constructed arm attachment she was working on before her life being turned upside down. Vasquez stepped over to inspect the same component Layla was eyeing and when she made a move to touch it, Layla slapped her hand away before Dom could ask her not to disturb the project. She got the sense that Layla kept Vasquez in line more often than not.

"What are you building?" Layla asked, turning her eyes to their host.

"Dom is building me," SARA answered, just as Dom was opening her mouth to respond to the question. She looked at the ceiling, and then dropped her chin to her chest like a marionette with a cut string. Layla's eyes registered surprise, but Vasquez replied before she could.

"You're building SARA a body?"

"Ah… Um… Yes, that's the idea," she stammered. The room grew painfully silent for a few seconds.

"That is freaking epic!" Layla exclaimed, breaking the silence. Dom's head jerked up in surprise at this reaction.

"Really?" she asked, cocking her head in disbelief, but Layla did not seem to hear her question. She watched as the two women revisited the objects laid out on the table in a new light; taking guesses at what parts they may be witnessing in their infancy. Dom's glasses dimmed and SARA flashed a message: *You*

are worried about nothing. The biometrics reveal no signs of deception.
She tapped the left arm of her glasses and they cleared just as Layla
and Vasquez turned to approach her side of the room, bright smiles
painted on their faces.

"What else can you build, Wonder Brain?" Layla asked,
taking a seat. Vasquez followed suit, her interest now solely in the
meal awaiting her. Dom shrugged her shoulders sheepishly.

"Depends on what I need," she replied, moving to her
own seat at the computer terminal. "If I can conceptualize it, I can
probably figure it out."

"You don't market any of it?" asked Layla.

"No. Remember, generally, I don't really deal with people.
The tech I create is for my own enjoyment and to make my
life easier. Sometimes, I get a wild idea and try it out to see if
it's possible."

"I like how you say that like it's no big deal," Layla grinned.

"How do you make money?" Vasquez asked, her mouth
half-full of food. Layla nudged her with an elbow.

"That's generally not something you ask people. Remember
that whole: 'run it through the old brain filter' conversation we keep
having?" Vasquez reddened at Layla's reproach.

"Sorry Dominique," she blushed, but Dom cut her off.

"If we're going to be at the drop by stage, you guys might
as well call me Dom."

"Okay. Sorry if I get too personal, Dom. I don't have a fully
functional filter de mi cabeza a mi boca." Dom cocked an eyebrow
as she looked from Vasquez to Layla.

"She also has a habit of using Spanglish. She says she
doesn't have a functional filter from her head to her mouth," Layla
translated, elbowing Vasquez again. "This is why there is usually
food in it."

"I assumed Vasquez was a married name," Dom admitted.
Vasquez's blushed deepened.

"She's one-hundred percent Mexican. I knew her parents;
it checks out," Layla quipped before Vasquez could respond.

"And I'm not married," Vasquez added, with a demure
wink. Layla blinked at this display and Dom eyed her curiously but
neither replied to this statement.

"I was an engineer for a large tech firm for over ten years out of MIT; punched a time clock like anyone else. As SARA so ostentatiously informed you, being around people taxes me in several ways. So, I invested well, take contracts with people I know and trust, and I invested well."

"You said invested well twice," Vasquez pointed out.

"I invested *very* well," she emphasized.

"So, what you're saying is, you don't have to work," Layla declared.

"Wow, and you call me nosey," Vasquez muttered. Layla turned to her friend with a small shrug.

"Might as well take advantage of her candor. I have a feeling it doesn't happen often."

"Have to? No, I don't have to. I'm technically retired. The thing is, I didn't have a plan in place in the event I was to retire before thirty-five. So, I pick up contracts to help alleviate boredom, and I work on SARA's program. There are always potential updates. For instance, I have to figure out how to keep her from being so damn open about our conversations." She raised her voice during the last four words and aimed them towards the ceiling.

"I would apologize Dom, but I do not have the capability of true shame," SARA proclaimed, causing Layla and Vasquez to bark with laughter simultaneously. Dom rolled her eyes.

"Always the insufferable comedian," she sighed.

"So, what did you need us to see on this console?" Layla probed, rerouting the conversation back to more serious matters. Dom regarded her for a brief moment, before turning her chair to face the computer.

"SARA found some messages to the same user, but it's in code," she replied, typing rapidly on her keyboard to retrieve the correspondence. When the messages were revealed on the screen, she pushed back from the computer and allowed Vasquez and Layla space to examine the monitor.

"Have you figured out the solution to the code?" Vasquez wondered.

"I'm sure if she had the key, she would have led with that. Sometimes I worry about you, Rach," Layla grunted, looking at the gibberish on the screen. This time, Vasquez elbowed Layla.

"It was a question puta."

"You know better than to call me a bitch," Layla huffed.

"Then don't act like one." Layla favored her friend with a loving smile.

"Have you been able to access anything else?" she asked, turning her eyes back to Dom.

"It's a language problem," she replied.

"Language problem?" Vasquez asked.

"Coding is its own dialect, just like English or Spanish, and there are over five hundred known languages," Dom explained. Layla gasped at this number.

"Five hundred?"

"Yes. As code becomes proprietary, it gets more sophisticated, often taking aspects from several different languages; but it's still rooted in the basics. Some still use ASCII, which is a language older than we are. Some are region specific, while others are actual tongue specific such as English, Chinese, German and the like. SARA has instantaneous access to the internet, but most major gaming companies wouldn't have a handbook to their code just laying out there. It would be too easy for a geek like me, with a little money, to make a bigger and more dynamic system using their proprietary language as a starting point. So, I'm looking at a language that I don't understand nor do I have a translation book," she continued.

"What about the servers?" Layla inquired.

"I suppose I could go that route," she answered thoughtfully. "Maybe I can hunt down the user your victim has been communicating with through the servers." She turned to write a quick script for SARA.

"Dom, there is something I have not had a chance to tell you," the computer confessed.

"Can it wait?" she asked, her rhythmic typing the only sound in the room. Vasquez and Layla watched her in amazement.

"Do you understand any of that?" Vasquez queried, nodding her head to the screen on which Dom was working.

"I told you, I'm a video game nerd, not a computer geek," Layla replied, shaking her head.

"No, it cannot. There has been a development within the last couple of minutes," SARA replied. Dom stopped typing and leaned back in her chair.

"Alright, fire away."

"I spoke with Miss Green last night and disclosed what we found in Rose Jenkins' search history," the computer began. Dom's eyes darted to Layla.

"SARA called you last night?"

"She was supposed to tell you when you woke up," Layla shrugged.

"I did not have a chance before your arrival, Miss Green. It was on my task list," SARA explained.

"What's the development?" Dom asked. As if anticipating the question, SARA changed the screen to an internet map before Dom fully articulated the inquiry.

"Per your instructions, I have been tracking Miss Jenkins' GPS. She just pulled into an apartment complex in the Greenspoint area of Houston." Dom leaned forward to study the map, and the blue spot representing Rose Jenkins.

"So? Why is that important?" she questioned, zooming into the area on the map and then turning to Layla and Vasquez. She knitted her eyebrows in confusion at the expressions that were plastered onto her visitors' faces. Vasquez, had her mouth hanging wide open, and Layla looked like she had just seen a ghost.

"I'll tell you why," Layla said, gaping at the map. She leaned forward and put her finger on top of the blue mark. "That's the apartment complex of our murder victim."

CHAPTER THIRTEEN

Rose pulled into the apartment complex and located a parking space outside of building three. Turning off the engine, she surveyed the area through her closed window. Despite the weather, groups of young men were huddled outside a few of the buildings in deep discussion. She noticed objects being passed back and forth, and concluded dealers did not take a respite from their duties solely due to a chill in the air and the threat of rain. She wondered if, when the heavens finally opened, they would stop for the day and find shelter; or if, large umbrellas would appear and business would continue. When the siblings exited the vehicle, the closest assembly to the lot stopped talking and glanced their way, throwing them head nods of greeting. Rose knew to look away or ignore the group would be viewed as suspicious, so she smiled and offered them a nod of her own.

"Well, if the idea is to stay out of trouble, this is a very bad neighborhood to accomplish that," she muttered under her breath.

"Come on sis, this is child's play compared to Sunnyside," Robert smirked. "Don't tell me you moved out of the hood and got uppity on me."

"I'm not uppity. I'm simply saying that if you are on probation, you may want to find a better place to live once you get out."

"Right, because in prison we all earn a decent salary, have a big 401k plan, and can just roll up to a nice high-rise condo and drop first and last month's rent to start over," he grumbled, rolling his eyes.

"Look, I know the man has to have a place to stay. I'm just saying that this is a rough area to try to turn over a new leaf," she whispered. As they got closer to the entry of building three, she saw police tape draped across one of the lower doors. She paused her stride and made eye contact with her brother before pointing at the door. "Case in point." Robert frowned, and pushed passed her, rushing to the entry in search of the apartment number.

"What the fuck is this?" he asked, his eyes wild with confusion. He stepped to the door and began to pound with his closed fist. "Aye yo, Larry! Larry! You in there?" Rose approached the door and caught his arm before he could knock again.

"Rob," she called softly. "He's not in there."

"No, he's supposed to be here. This is his address. He said he doesn't work on Saturdays. He should be here," he implored, desperation in his voice. "What happened?" He stared at the entry attempting to piece together the inferences of the scene. The duo turned to the sound of the door across from the apartment opening. A squat older black woman poked her head out, wearing a dressing gown and slippers, her cotton white hair in rollers. She looked to be in her late sixties or early seventies.

"Who y'all looking for?" The woman asked, inspecting the siblings warily.

"We are looking for the man who lives here," Rose replied. The older woman continued to study them, before her eyes came to rest on Robert.

"What's your name, boy?" she inquired. Rose noticed a flicker of recognition cross the woman's features.

"Robert Jenkins, ma'am," he answered. Her eyes softened, and tears started to collect in the sockets of her dark brown orbs.

"My name is Henrietta. Henrietta Johnson. Come in you two."

She opened the door, stepped back, and beckoned for the pair to enter. Rose and Robert eyed each other, then moved to follow her into her home. When they entered, they were immediately slapped with the smell of warm cinnamon, sugar, and vanilla combined with freshly brewed coffee. Rose halted in the middle of the room, and took a deep inhalation.

"What is that?" she asked. Despite the large breakfast Robert provided, the delicious aromas made her mouth water.

"Oh honey, I just pulled out a few of my Sock-it-to-Me cakes. I'm gonna be running up to the home this afternoon to see my twin sister, Loretta. She can't get enough of them. We used to bake them together, you know. Lord, the money we made for our church bake sales! But since her stroke, she can't get around all that good and I'm too old to try to carry her. But I goes and see her almost every day and she always wants a piece of Sock-it-to-Me cake, so I make sure I takes one or two up there with me for her and her friends." Henrietta's voice was warm, with a heavy southern drawl. Her accent was so thick, and her speech so rapid, Rose was hardly able to keep up with what the woman was saying. She almost did not catch the question, "Y'all want a piece of cake?"

"Yes ma'am, if you have extra. It smells too good not to try," Robert spoke up, when Rose's response was a look of incomprehension. Henrietta beamed and motioned for the siblings to sit, before disappearing into the kitchen.

"We literally just ate," Rose hissed.

"So? There's always room for cake," he shrugged.

She shook her head in annoyance and turned her attention to the small apartment. The living area was cozy with a worn dark gray sofa and a navy recliner. A wooden rocking chair was stationed against the wall next to the couch, and Rose could tell this was Henrietta's usual seat. A small basket holding knitting yarn sat at the foot of the chair signifying the woman's hobby; a half-finished piece was sticking out of the basket. A coffee table in the middle of the room held a remote control and a large print crossword puzzle book. A bookcase stood on the far side of the room, filled with books and framed photos of the woman's family.

She walked over to check out the small library. Rose believed that the character of a person could be represented by the books that they read. Inspecting the spines, she saw texts from Huey P. Newton, Maya Angelou, Angela Davis, and Bell Hooks; books of poetry from Nikki Giovanni, Langston Hughes, James Weldon Johnson and Claude McKay, and biographies of prominent figures such as Malcolm X, Dr. Martin Luther King, and W.E.B. Dubois, among others. Her eyes widened at the collection and she turned back to the woman in the kitchen, examining her in a new light. She knew the speech patterns of the older generation were enough to pre-judge them as uneducated or unintelligent. She was ashamed to realize that she had fallen into that trap during the old woman's ramble about cake and her sister. After inspecting the bookshelf, her attitude shifted completely. Henrietta entered the living room holding a large silver tray that caused her to stretch her short arms to their maximum width. Robert hastily moved to the woman and relieved her of her burden.

"Just put it on the coffee table, baby," she directed, smiling gratefully. The tray held two plates with generous slices of cake, the aroma indicating it was fresh from the oven. Along with the two servings of cake were three white coffee cups, a matching white coffee carafe, and two small serving dishes with sugar and cream. Rose noticed the serving set was old, likely antique, but the woman accessed it as if she had people over for coffee and cake on a regular basis. She found a spot on the couch and Robert took the plush recliner. Henrietta settled herself into the rocking chair. Robert reached for a plate and poured himself some coffee and settled into his chair without adding anything extra.

"Since when do you take your coffee black?" Rose asked. He smiled and shrugged his shoulders, taking a large bite of cake. Rose poured two cups of coffee and flashed a questioning look at their host.

"A touch of cream, baby," the old woman grinned. Rose added the cream and handed the cup of coffee to Henrietta. She added a liberal amount of sugar and cream to her own cup and settled back onto the couch with her cake and coffee.

"This is the shit!" Robert exclaimed around a mouthful of cake. Rose favored him with a withering glare, causing him to cough and flash a look of embarrassment. "Sorry Ms. Henrietta." The old woman chuckled and gave him a dismissive wave.

"Baby you can't say nothing I ain't already heard before. Malik loved my Sock-it-to-Me cake. Sometimes I thought that boy could smell it before I started mixing it up. I would pull out my mixer and the next thing I knew, he was at the door with a deck of cards and a smile. We would play us some two-man spades and just talk all afternoon. I loved spending time with that boy; such a smart boy! He was smarter than anybody I ever talked to his age, not that I talk to a lot of folks. When you've seen almost eighty years, folks die out or forget about you. My kids are all grown and my grandbabies out there running the streets. Malik kept me company. I'm gonna miss him so much." She began to choke up at the end of this diatribe. As if to prevent the tears from completely taking over, she quickly took a sip of coffee. Rose's gaze darted back to the bookshelf where she noticed an old framed photograph of a young man in a cap and gown.

"You lost your son recently." Rose spoke in a soft sympathetic voice, but Henrietta blinked at her with confusion.

"No. Why do you say that?"

"I'm sorry, I thought Malik was your son," she stammered, bewildered at how bad she misread the soliloquy.

"Malik? That's who y'all came here looking for, wasn't it? He lived over there," the old woman replied, pointing in the direction of the dwelling across from her. "At least he did before they killed him." Robert choked on the coffee he was sipping.

"Larry. We were looking for Larry," he clarified, after he stopped coughing. Henrietta turned her eyes to him with curiosity.

"You must have the wrong apartment. Malik lived across from me for the past few months. Before him, it was a woman named Lisa and her bad ass kids," she responded. "I guess you ain't the Robert I thought you was."

"Wait, you were expecting a Robert?" Rose interjected, attempting to wrap her head around the convoluted situation. Robert fished out the envelope from his pocket to double check the address.

"Apartment three-ten," he confirmed. Henrietta's perplexity deepened.

"Yeah, that's his apartment; but that boy's name was Malik," she insisted. Leaning forward in her chair, she fished out a cell phone from one pocket of her gown and a pair of reading glasses from the other side. She put on the glasses, and held the phone slightly away from her as she tried to navigate the touchscreen. "I can't believe James gave me this stupid thing. I'm too old to learn how to use a damn smartphone," she grumbled, tapping slowly on the screen. After a few moments, she let out a cry of triumph and held the phone out to Robert who took it from her hand. There was a photo on the screen, apparently taken in selfie mode. Henrietta was smiling broadly and next to her was a dark-skinned man with cornrowed hair, dark brown eyes and a bright smile... Larry.

"But, his name is Larry," he asserted, handing the phone to his sister who examined the photo before relinquishing the device to its owner.

"Ms. Henrietta, this is all a little confusing. Can we maybe put our stories together to figure out where we are off with our information?" Rose asked the woman.

"Of course, baby," Henrietta agreed. She stripped her glasses off and returned them and the phone to their respective pockets.

"Ms. Henrietta, I was in prison with him up until a few months back. His name was Larry Phillips. He got out about six months ago and wrote to me while I was still in, telling me to come by his place because he had a job opportunity for me," Robert explained in a shaky voice.

"Well, he did move in about six months ago, and he told me he was here for work. He said most of his work was at night, so he spent a lot of time with me during the day. His name was Malik Rodgers. This kind of lying doesn't seem like something Malik would do," Henrietta replied.

"Ms. Henrietta, you asked us in because you heard Rob's name. Why?" Rose asked.

"Malik spoke about a friend he had named Robert. He said Robert was serving time, but that he would be working with him when he got out. A few weeks ago, Malik was over here playing spades with me. He handed me an envelope with the name Robert Jenkins and said that if he wasn't home, I should give it to you."

She rose from her rocking chair with great difficulty and shuffled to the bookshelf, pulling out a manila envelope from between two books. She handed the folder to Robert and then shambled back to her seat. Robert eyed the offering as if it contained anthrax. After a few moments, he tore it open and dumped the contents onto his lap. One of the items was a book and the other was a folded sheet of paper. Rose squinted in an attempt to determine what the book was, and ascertained that it was the Bible. Robert opened the folded paper first and read the contents. After a few moments of silence, he leaned and passed the note to her with tears in his eyes. Before Rose opened the message, she regarded Henrietta.

"What happened to him?" Henrietta's eyes grew damp once again.

"I'm not sure," she whimpered. "I came home from visiting my sister, and the complex was crawling with police. Then I saw his door was all taped up, and I just knew. After he didn't come by the last couple of days, I knew that he was dead." Rose transferred her scrutiny to Robert and she saw tears in his eyes. She picked up the note, unfolded the correspondence, and began to read:

Rob,

If you are reading this, one of two things has happened. Either I'm out of the house for a while, in that case Ms. Henrietta could use a good game of spades and I'll be back soon, or the other something happened to me. Sadly, I fear the latter may be true. There is so much to this and unfortunately, I don't have the time to explain it all. I'm hoping you never see this and I can tell you myself. Also, I don't want to put too much in writing to protect Ms. Henrietta, because I'm fairly sure she has already read this. (If you are reading this, I love you Ms. Henrietta and I thank you for the time we spent together and all of the laughs.) Rob, your spirit and your determination are exactly what is needed, especially right now. If something happened to me: search. Remember John 8:32.

Malik Rodgers

PS: If the worst happened, look in on Ms. Henrietta from time to time. She's really good people, but be careful... she cheats at spades.

"I don't cheat! He just telegraphed his hands!" the old woman sniffed, when Rose looked up from the note and passed it back to her brother. Her mind was reeling from what she read and her heart broke seeing the grief in Robert's eyes.

"What was Malik into?" she mused. Robert slipped the note and Bible back into the envelope.

"We didn't talk much about his work. We talked about the old days. He had a lot of questions about the fifties and sixties. You know, I was on the Pettus Bridge in Selma with Dr. King in sixty-five. I was really involved in the movement back then, and I think that's why he liked coming over here. He loved hearing about Dr. King and Mr. Little," Henrietta replied.

"Mr. Little?" Robert asked.

"Malcolm X was born Malcolm Little," Rose responded, before Henrietta could clarify. The elderly woman gave Rose an approving nod.

"You know your history, young lady," she smiled.

"Minor in African American studies," Rose blushed. "You knew Malcolm X?"

"Oh, Heavens no. I was active in the movement, but I didn't know Dr. King or Mr. Little personally."

"And Larry, I mean Malik, would come over to hear stories about your time in the Civil Rights movement?" Robert asked.

"We talked about what I saw and experienced. He wanted to know what worked and what didn't. We talked about what would've been different with the technology of today. Malik had a lot of ideas. He always wondered how we got through that time," Henrietta replied.

"I have often wondered that myself," Rose admitted. "I've studied it; seen the pictures and news articles. It looked so horrible. How did you get through it?"

"There wasn't no big secret to it, baby. We ain't have a lot of options back then. We either had to fight or lay down and take it. Some folks did that, you know, laid down and just accepted it, but I've always been a scrappy one. My late husband Earl swore that if he knew how hard-headed I was, he would have never married me," Henrietta chuckled.

"I can see you being pretty fierce," Rose grinned.

"You're sure he's dead?" Robert asked the old woman. Henrietta looked at him with sympathy.

"Yes. I'm sorry, baby." Robert sat back in his chair with a cloud of despondency hovering over him. Rose put her plate with a half-eaten slice of cake and coffee cup back on the tray.

"Ms. Henrietta, thank you for the information; but we have to go. We have to get to our mother's house for Rob's welcome home party," she announced as she stood. Robert's watery eyes floated to his sister, and he stood, following her example.

"Will you come back and see me again?" Henrietta asked.

"Absolutely," Rose quickly replied. Henrietta pulled herself out of the rocking chair and Rose approached her to give her a hug. She moved to the door and watched as her brother embraced the old woman. The two strangers hugged as if they had known each other for years, and Rose recognized the bond brought on by the shared grief for their mutual friend.

After bidding the woman goodbye, the siblings walked silently to Rose's car. Raindrops began to fall as soon as they entered the vehicle. Rose checked their surroundings and saw that some of the groups from earlier had disappeared, while others continued their discourse, as if oblivious to the rain. She peered over at her brother to find him gazing out of the window.

"You okay?" she asked, starting the engine. He continued to stare, as if he did not hear her question. "Rob, you okay?"

"I can't believe he's gone," he mumbled. "I just knew this was my chance to do something with my life. Now, I don't know what I'm going to do."

"Who says you still can't do something with your life?"

"Larry was my ticket. I'm an ex-con and an addict. People won't be lining up to hire me," he responded. "I can't believe he lied to me the whole time. He told me to pursue things, but I don't even know where to start."

"He told you where to start," she pointed out, as she backed out of the parking space.

"What are you talking about?"

"John 8:32," she said.

"What?"

"He left you a path; John 8:32. Look it up and see what it says." He threw her an exasperated look. "Just look it up Rob," she insisted. He pulled the Bible from the envelope and flipped through the pages. Once he reached his destination, Rose saw him take something out of the book.

"What's that?" she asked. He held up the photo of himself and Malik. The two were posed, Malik's arm wrapped around Robert's shoulder. It was obviously taken during the time they spent in prison.

"Picture of Malik and me. I guess this is why Ms. Henrietta recognized me." He turned his attention back to the Bible.

"What does it say?" she inquired, pulling onto the busy road from the apartment complex.

"Then you will know the truth, and the truth will set you free," he read aloud. He rotated the book ninety degrees. "There's a phone number written in the margin." Rose braked at a stop sign and turned to her brother.

"So, we call the number," she shrugged.

"And say what? Hi, I found your number in my dead friend's Bible?" he asked, with irritation.

"Well, maybe not in those exact words, but yes."

"That won't be weird at all," he groused.

"Rob, I didn't know this guy. I'm with you, no matter what you want to do; but, I don't want you going backward. You said you had a purpose. Your friend left this clue having faith that you'd chase it down, it seems to me that you'd be stupid not to figure it out," she contended. He grew silent in his contemplation.

"Ok," he sighed. "Let me see your phone."

CHAPTER FOURTEEN

The three women sat in stunned silence staring at the blue dot on the map, the weight of Layla's words hanging over them like the blades of a guillotine. For a few long seconds, no one dared speak or breathe. Dom broke the stillness.

"What is she doing there?"

"You do realize we have been with you all morning, right?" Layla asked in annoyance. "How would we know?" Vasquez slapped her arm, a little harder than she usually would, causing her to wince and rub the spot. "Ouch!"

"Don't get touchy, puta," Vasquez warned. She gave Dom a disarming smile. "Excuse her, I may not always have a filter, but she has none of my adorable charms." Dom sat quietly without responding to either woman. The friends watched her warily, waiting for a reaction to Layla's rude remark. Suddenly she shot out of her chair with such abruptness, both women flinched.

"I need to bake something," she muttered, making her exit. Layla and Vasquez gaped at her odd behavior. They remained in their chairs, unsure of what their next action should be. Finally, they faced each other and began speaking at the same time.

"Why would you talk to her like that?" Vasquez inquired simultaneously as Layla said, "She's weird."

"Well you were kind of being a jerk," Vasquez snapped. Layla shrugged.

"Yeah, I guess she's not used to my unique way."

"You think?"

"Still. She went to bake something? That's not strange to you?" Layla asked.

"I'll admit, I'm always down for food, but this is an odd time to go Betty Crocker on us," Vasquez agreed. The duo sat in silent consideration for a few moments. Layla looked up at the ceiling.

"SARA? Can we talk to you privately?"

"Yes, Ms. Green. I can speak with you in this room while concurrently communicating with Dom in another portion of the house," SARA replied. "I am, after all a computer."

"She's such a smart ass; I love it!" Vasquez giggled. Layla offered her a humorless smile.

"What is going on with your girl?" she asked the computer.

"My girl?" SARA parroted.

"Dom. What's happening right now?" she clarified.

"Dom cooks to relax, and she bakes when she's anxious. The biometric readings denote that she currently has a very high level of anxiety, far higher than have ever been registered. It seems this is the reason for her sudden urge to bake," SARA reported. Vasquez's eyes bulged at the information.

"Biometric readings?" Layla asked, before Vasquez could find the words to express her surprise.

"Yes. As you have undoubtedly surmised, there are cameras all over the home. I use those cameras to assess biometric evaluations of humans. While the software is not to the standards of most medical devices, I assure you the accuracy is quite good. Dom dislikes me running the program without consent, but I keep it operational in the background, as I have found it quite useful in ascertaining what humans call non-verbal cues. For instance, the system indicates that both of you also have a high level of anxiety." Layla gasped in shock. The idea of the computer constantly monitoring her body made her feel naked. Vasquez appeared to have the same thought, as she crossed her arms over her breasts at the end of SARA's revelation.

"Well, that's something," she mumbled.

"Now you are both anxious, and slightly uncomfortable," SARA added. Layla held her hand up as if SARA were standing in front of her.

"We get it SARA, thank you," she interjected, turning to Vasquez. "I told you she's strange."

"Eccentric, maybe."

"So, what do we do about the new problem?" Layla asked, pointing at the computer screen, still opened to the internet map. "We can't have people rolling up on the crime scene all willy-nilly."

"First of all, don't ever use the term willy-nilly again; you sound like an old person. Secondly, the crime scene is locked down; what harm could she possibly do?" Layla considered the question, and found she couldn't produce a viable answer.

"I don't like the coincidence," she grumbled.

"Oh, I totally agree. This is like seventeen kinds of fucked up. What I am saying is, focus on something that's an actual problem. No one can get into the crime scene. The issue is, we don't know what the hell she was doing there to begin with," Vasquez declared.

"Any ideas?" she asked.

"You're the smart one. But, I'd say we need to figure out what her connection is to our John Doe." Layla examined Vasquez and saw resolution staring back at her.

"I don't like it when you have that look in your eyes," she groaned.

"It's the color, isn't it? Too green?"

"We aren't detectives, Rach."

"That's not because we couldn't do it. It's only because you don't like guns, and I have no filter," Vasquez countered.

"Let's cut to the end," Layla sighed. "Is there any argument that I can offer that will talk you out of trying to play cop?"

"Our body from the other day," Vasquez began, ticking the point off on her index finger. "This situation with Daniels and the nervous chef in there; they are both very closely paralleled. We don't know what's going on with either of them. The first real link to this insanity has been this." She leaned forward and pointed to the map on the computer. "Whoever this Rose Jenkins lady is, we need to talk to her." Layla reflected on her words before taking a deep breath of resignation.

"You're right, Rach. I think this is the first time you've laid out a case that I can't find any holes in," she acquiesced. Vasquez's eyes grew wide, and she suddenly took her phone out of her pocket. "What are you doing?"

"Recording this date in history," Vasquez replied. Layla chuckled for a moment before she leaned over and saw that Vasquez was actually making a note in her phone.

"For real?"

"I never get over on the great Layla Green. Hell yes, I'm jotting this down," she smiled. When she finished typing, she returned her phone to her pocket. "Now, the other reason why it has to be us, is because you were the one in the list of dossiers. You're somehow connected but we just don't know how."

"Well hell," Layla sighed.

"So, we might as well ride this bull while we have it by the horns."

"That is perhaps the most Texan thing I've ever heard you say."

"I am what I am," Vasquez shrugged.

"What about Oscar?" Layla asked, suddenly remembering Detective Lewis. "He's got nothing. We can't leave him out in the dark."

"Of course, we can't. But we can't bring him here. Can you imagine?" Vasquez motioned around the room.

"I guess you're right."

"He trusts us, doesn't he?"

"I think so."

"Then, we tell him what we can, as we can, and he has to trust us with the rest," she smiled. With that statement, she stood up, and headed for the office door.

"Where are you going?"

"She said she was baking, didn't she?" she asked, disappearing down the hall. Layla stood and turned to study the blue dot on the computer screen. It had not moved since SARA brought up the display.

"What are you doing there, Rose Jenkins?" she wondered.

"Miss Green?" SARA called, snapping her attention from the computer monitor.

"What is it, SARA?"

"I understand your concern about Dom. The data she presented to me over the years led me to conclude that there were some mental deficiencies. However, recent discussions as well as further analysis of her behaviors have guided me to the revelation that she is not insane nor abnormal. She has been in hurtful situations in the past, which has caused her to adjust her life to compensate and prevent further pain. Based on my understanding of the human reaction of fight or flight, Dom chose flight. Yet my research into her past seems to indicate that she is a fighter. I postulate that she only needs to find a reason to fight." Layla stared out of the open office door as she listened, analyzing what SARA shared.

"I understand," she acknowledged. SARA said nothing more, indicating that the small speech was all she wanted her to know for the time being. Layla decided to follow Vasquez into the kitchen to check in on Dom.

When she arrived, she heard music through the speakers in the ceiling; Cheryl Lynn singing the upbeat "Got to Be Real." Vasquez was back on her barstool watching intently as Dom worked with a stand mixer, adding flour through what looked like a small colander. Layla approached the stool next to Vasquez, planting herself beside her friend. Dom's face registered laser focus, ostensibly working as if no one else was in the house with her.

"She's making a chocolate and caramel tart with candied pecans," Vasquez whispered.

"When she said she wanted to bake something, I thought she meant cookies," Layla admitted.

"She made risotto from scratch the first time she met us. You really think she'd just bust out the frozen cookies?" Vasquez asked. Dom did not make any sign that she heard her guests talking about her.

"Dom, I'm sorry I snapped at you earlier. Rachel's right, sometimes I forget my home training. Then again, I guess I never had any," Layla said. Dom turned to her and smirked.

"It's cool. I guess it was a stupid question. SARA has recently informed me that there are dumb questions." Layla did not know what to say to that, so she did not reply. The guests watched Dom work with no other comments. Suddenly, the music stopped and the abrupt silence made Layla flinch and look up.

"Dom, you have a phone call," SARA announced.

"Take a message," she commanded, pressing the crust into the pie pan.

"That is not advisable," SARA replied.

"Is it my dad?" she asked, pausing her work and looking to the ceiling.

"No. While male, the caller is using the cellular device registered to Rose Jenkins." Dom froze in place, her mouth agape, the tarts now forgotten. Dropping her eyes from the ceiling to her guests, she threw the two women an inquisitive look. Layla nodded emphatically.

"Can we listen in?" Vasquez probed, as Layla's head dipped up and down like a bobble head toy.

"Patch it through the speakers," Dom called.

"Standby." Dom internally counted to five and then spoke. "Hello?"

"Hi, my name is Robert Jenkins. I'm calling because I got your number from a friend of mine. He's dead now, but your number was left as a message to me. I'm hoping you can give me some insight into why he was killed," the caller stammered. Layla and Vasquez both stiffened in their seats.

"And your friend's name is?" Dom questioned.

"I'm not sure. I knew him as Larry Phillips, but I just left his neighbor, and the name she had for him was Malik Rodgers. I honestly don't know anything anymore," he replied. Dom heard grief and anxiety in the man's baritone voice. Layla waved her hands at her and mouthed something indiscernible.

"Can you hang on for a second?" Dom asked. She tapped the left side of her eyeglass arm and turned her full attention to Layla. "What?"

"Rodgers. That's the name that was on the lease of the apartment, Tasha Rodgers," Vasquez replied, before Layla could speak.

"What do you want me to do?"

"We have to meet up with him," Layla insisted. Having regained her bearings, Dom picked up a towel from the counter and began wiping her hands, moving towards the bar and her guests.

"Say what now?" she asked, raising her eyebrows.

"Look, I know you aren't as invested in this dead body as we are, but this guy could be the key to unlocking our victim's identity," Layla asserted, attempting to reign in her impatience.

"How did this guy get my number?"

"I think that's the least important question at the moment," Vasquez answered.

"For you, maybe," she grumbled.

"We have to meet him," Layla repeated. "Who is he to Rose Jenkins?" Dom tapped the side of her glasses to unmute the phone call.

"Robert, can you tell me who Rose Jenkins is to you?" she inquired. His side of the line went quiet for a time.

"She's my sister," he replied, in a guarded tone. "Why?"

"Is she with you now?" she prodded.

"Yes."

"I need to meet with both of you. Can we meet?"

"When?" he asked, after a muted beat. She looked at Layla who pointed down, denoting she wanted to meet immediately.

"Can you come today?"

"We can't do today, I'm sorry. We have a family function we are heading to right now. Can you do tomorrow morning?" he countered. Dom looked at the two women at the bar, who wordlessly conferred with each other before nodding their assent.

"Tomorrow is fine," she agreed. "I will send a text with the address and a time. See you then." She tapped the side of her glasses to end the call and gazed at her visitors.

"Seriously, what the hell is going on here?" Vasquez pondered.

Robert ended the call and looked at his sister who was trying to navigate the dense traffic. Even though it was a weekend, it appeared that the entire city of Houston was on the interstate. Rose risked a glance at her brother when she realized he was no longer on the phone.

"What about me?"

"She knew your name and asked who you were to me," he answered, placing the phone into the cup holder.

"She? Who?"

"Didn't give a name. I asked her about Larry, I mean Malik, and she put me on hold or muted me. I don't think she was alone," he replied. Rose checked behind her and began to switch lanes to get to her exit.

"So, what now?"

"She wants to meet with us tomorrow. She's supposed to send an address and time," he responded. As if the mention of the intent summoned the action, Rose's phone chimed. He grabbed it from the cup holder and peeked. "Text message." He replaced the phone after his report. Rose gave him an exasperated look.

"Open it!"

"Okay! I didn't know if you had some dude texting you. Calm down," he argued, opening the message. There was no sender information, but the note showed an address and a time of eight in the morning. Navigating the phone's internet browser, he looked up the location. "It's in River Oaks. She says to be there at eight."

"River Oaks?" Rose questioned. "Was she Black or White?"

"She sounded Black to me. Why?"

"A sista in River Oaks? Not a lot of them out there. That's a ritzy, mostly White neighborhood." The siblings rode in silence for a few minutes, each clinging to their own thoughts. Rose was deliberating the fact that the stranger knew who she was, and Robert was thinking about Malik.

"Look," he began, breaking the hush. "We don't know what's happening or who these people are. Maybe we shouldn't tell mom until we know something. You know how she gets." Rose nodded in agreement.

"I'm glad you said it. You gonna be able to hold it together? I mean with, you know, your friend's death?" she asked, turning onto the street where she and Robert grew up.

"I'll have to be," he sighed. Rose pulled to the curb in front of their mother's house and shut off the engine.

"You sure?" He nodded his assent, but she saw the misery in his dark brown eyes. Rather than pursue the matter, she allowed him to wear the mask of false stability. Reaching into the back, she grabbed her purse. "You ready for this?"

"Of course. It'll be good to see everyone," he replied, allowing himself to smile. Rose looked through the windshield and frowned.

"Looks like Mrs. Robinson has company," she observed. Mrs. Robinson had been the next-door neighbor for as long as she could remember.

"Think it's Sammy?" he wondered as they walked by the car. Sammy Robinson was younger than Robert, and a year older than Rose. As children, he followed Robert around like a shadow.

"Could be. He moved to Chicago, maybe he's visiting. See? Those are rental car tags." She pointed at the rental company sticker in the window. The siblings ambled to the front door of their childhood home. Rose found the key to the front entry, pounded on the door three times, and then unlocked the entrance. Given the direction of the neighborhood, Joyce had acquired guns over the years for protection. She and Rose devised a plan to keep her from getting shot, which was to knock three times before entering the home. Robert, not knowing the arrangement, glanced at her with bewilderment.

"Keeps her from shooting first, and asking questions later," she smiled. The smell of fried chicken greeted the siblings when they entered. The house was moderate in size, three bedrooms and two bathrooms. The living room had the same drab brown couch, loveseat and recliner for as long as the duo had been alive. Robert followed her into the room.

"It hasn't changed!" he gasped, moving to the middle of the area and turning in a circle.

Framed photos of all five Jenkins children, their late father, and family portraits hung on the walls. An old broken tube-style TV rested in the entertainment center; on top sat the functional forty-seven-inch flat screen television. The scarred coffee table held the mail, as it had since they were children. Even the gray carpeting appeared to be the same.

As they followed the smell of food, they heard their mother speaking to someone. When Rose finally reached the doorway between the dining room and the kitchen, she saw her mother, standing over the stove frying chicken in two large pots of hot oil. Rose focused her eyes on the dark-skinned man that sat at the table talking with her. He was bald and clean-shaven, highlighting the jagged scar that extended from his right temple down to his chin. Dark brown eyes that matched Robert's shifted from Joyce to the doorway and lit up in delight. When he stood, he towered over everyone in the house, and when he smiled, he showed off the deep dimples in both of his cheeks.

"RJ2?" Rose whispered in disbelief. Her older brother, Ryan, opened his arms with a broad grin. Robert pushed passed his sister to get a glimpse at their brother. Letting out a hoot of delight, he threw himself at Ryan who caught him in a bear hug. The men embraced for a long while. Rose froze in her spot in the doorway, shifting her eyes from her hugging brothers to her mother at the stove.

"Rosie," Ryan uttered, when he released Robert. As if the word Rosie were a remote control releasing her from shock, she ran to her big brother and wrapped her arms around him in a fierce hug, tears stinging her eyes.

"What are you doing here?" she spluttered, when their embrace ended.

"I need a reason to come see my family?" he inquired, the smile still plastered on his face.

"Well, no. But, what are you doing here? Why aren't you in Afghanistan?"

"I couldn't miss Rob's welcome home," Ryan chuckled, moving his eyes from Rose to Robert. Rose turned to her mother.

"Did you know he was coming?" Joyce beamed and nodded. "You can't hold water in a bucket, but this you don't tell me?"

"I can keep secrets when I have to!" Joyce exclaimed indignantly. The boys laughed heartily at this exchange.

"She knew I was coming, but when we found out Rob was getting out early, I asked her to keep it to herself as a surprise," Ryan explained.

"Where are Val and the girls?" she asked. Valentina, Val for short, was Ryan's wife of nine years. Rose met Val only once, when they came to the states for their second wedding; the first held in her home of Croatia. The couple had two daughters, Luna who was six and Kiara who was four. Luna and Kiara had never met their father's side of the family; both being born and raised on an Army base in Germany. While Ryan had come home a few times, usually for family functions such as his brothers' funeral and Rose's undergraduate graduation, he had not been home in years; therefore, Val and the girls had not come to the states. Technology bridged the gap of the ocean by allowing Rose to video chat with Val and her nieces from time to time.

"They'll be here at the end of the school year. I retired sis," he replied. Rose's mouth dropped open.

"Retired? What do you mean retired?" she stammered.

"I'm out of the Army as of last week. We are moving stateside, I left early to find us a place to live and try to find a job. Val is packing up the house in Germany and we wanted to let Luna finish kindergarten around the kids she grew up with. They'll be moving home this summer," he explained. Rose's gaze moved from Ryan to Robert and then settled onto Joyce.

"This? You chose to keep this quiet of all things?" she gasped in disbelief.

"I ain't gotta tell you everything. Besides, he wanted to surprise you." Joyce admonished, fishing a piece of chicken out of a pot and moving it to the cooling rack next to the stove. "Now y'all supposed to be helping me with this. Boys, go on and get the folding chairs from the garage; and Rose, come on over here and help me with this chicken." The three children gaped at their mother.

"Thank God you guys are back. You see what I've had to deal with?" Rose asked, moving to the stove and picking up a pair of tongs. Joyce haughtily clicked her tongue at her daughter.

"She thinks she was the one putting up with me and not the other way around," she snickered. The Jenkins family laughed and began getting ready for the gathering. Rose's thoughts of the mysterious dead man, weird phone calls and odd tattoos faded from her mind, as the joy of having her family together filled her heart.

CHAPTER FIFTEEN

Layla and Vasquez arrived at seven forty-five the next morning, ready for battle. Despite waking in separate homes and not meeting until Vasquez collected Layla, both women had the same idea of dressing more professionally than they would on a normal Sunday. Layla wore gray slacks, a black blouse, and simple black flats. Her hair, usually wrapped in a scarf, fell into its natural state, the tight curls falling just past her shoulders. When she got into the vehicle, Vasquez gaped at the rare sight of her unrestrained mane.

"Wow," she gasped. "I was starting to think you wore a wig." Layla chuckled and slapped her arm. Vasquez chose a similar color scheme, donning black slacks with a gray and black sweater. Her honey brown hair was also loose, the waves cascading down to her mid-back. Layla noticed she was wearing makeup; something she rarely used, and in Layla's opinion, did not need. When they got to the front door of their unwilling host, Layla realized Vasquez was at least three inches taller than normal.

"Why do you look like an Amazon today?" she asked, eyeing the woman's heels.

"Got to be ready for anything, qué no?" Vasquez winked.

"Right," Layla agreed. She rang the doorbell and was surprised when Dom opened the door almost immediately. Wearing an apron, she appeared markedly less aggravated than she had during their last visit. Eyeing the two women on her doorstep, her eyebrows rose at their appearance. Until she saw her reaction, Layla had not realized that Dom had never seen the two of them outside of work or gym attire.

"You guys got a date after this?" Dom asked, stepping back to allow the women entry.

"Why? You offering?" Vasquez grinned. Dom and Layla both threw her a curious look.

"No, uh, I just meant, you guys look nice," she stammered nervously. Vasquez giggled at her embarrassment.

"You get used to her," Layla promised.

"Not sure that's possible," she mumbled, spinning around and heading to the kitchen. Vasquez took a deep inhalation and followed her.

"What's on the menu today?"

"Eggs Benedict with your choice of homemade chicken apple sausage or turkey ham, hollandaise sauce, cinnamon rolls and coffee or juice," Dom replied, picking up a stack of toasted English muffins from the island and carrying them to the table. Layla noticed Dom had added an extension and the tabletop was longer and with more chairs than it had the previous day.

"Why chicken apple sausage or turkey ham?" Vasquez mused. In an attempt to make herself useful, she picked up the plate of cinnamon rolls and followed her into the dining area.

"Because I don't eat pork." Vasquez turned and regarded Layla with astonishment.

"You don't eat pork?" she repeated.

"No. My mom didn't eat it, so I was raised not eating it," Dom explained.

"Hey Dom, question," Layla called. When she saw that Vasquez was going to play the role of the annoying shadow, she took a seat at the bar, to stay out of the way.

"Shoot," Dom said, adding salt and pepper to the newly poached eggs.

"You obviously don't entertain much. You don't care for people, introvert, whatever. Why do you always cook?" Dom, who had been moving between the kitchen and dining area paused her stride. She turned to Layla but did not meet her gaze, choosing to fix her eyes on a spot on the counter.

"I get it from my mom. We didn't have a lot of money, but she was always trying to help people. She said if they had to choose between paying a bill and feeding their families, most would choose food. She decided, if she fed them, it would remove the need to make that choice. We couldn't do a lot for folks, but we could always give them something to eat. I guess growing up like that, I got used to doing it myself. I'm reclusive now, but I haven't always been."

"That's a great outlook. I wholeheartedly approve," Vasquez beamed. "I'd love to meet your mother. She sounds a little like how mine was."

"She died when I was twelve," Dom muttered, turning from her guests and busying herself transferring food from the kitchen to the dining area with no other word. Vasquez shot a look at Layla who shrugged and shook her head, signaling that she should not say anything else. When Dom picked up the plate of chicken apple sausage, Vasquez could not help herself.

"Wait, you actually made the sausage?"

"That's kind of what homemade means, yeah," Dom replied, her features reflecting puzzlement.

"You know they sell that at the grocery store, right?" Layla asked from her perch.

"I make it better."

"Dom? Rose and Robert Jenkins will be here in five minutes," SARA announced.

"Hi SARA," Layla and Vasquez called in chorus.

"Good Morning Miss Green and Miss Vasquez," SARA responded.

"You're still tracking her?" Layla asked Dom, who bristled at the question.

"After yesterday? Hell yes, I'm still tracking her!" she affirmed. "I don't know if she's friend or foe yet."

"You always this suspicious of people?" Vasquez wondered.

"Mostly."

"Why not us?" she asked. The food ready to go, Vasquez moved to the bar and sat next to Layla. Dom leaned on the island facing them.

"Who says I'm not?"

"You keep letting us in and feeding us," Vasquez pointed out.

"You guys keep showing up! Besides, you may not have badges or guns, but they're only a phone call away. I have to stay on your good side."

"You got a problem with cops?" Layla probed.

"I'm Black in these United States; I got no problem with them, but lately they seem to have a problem with us. I just assume not to have a chance to be another body in the street," she grumbled. Layla and Vasquez exchanged looks.

"You know it's not all cops, right?" Vasquez asked.

"I'm not an idiot, I know that. But it only takes one for me to end up another statistic; same reason I won't eat fugu." Vasquez tilted her head.

"What's a fugu?"

"Pufferfish. I love sushi, and apparently it's quite the delicacy, but you couldn't pay me to try it," she replied.

"Why not?"

"Poisonous," Layla answered before Dom could respond.

"What's poisonous?" Vasquez pressed, still utterly perplexed.

"Pufferfish," Layla replied. "They have a neurotoxin called tetrodotoxin. Nasty stuff that can cause asphyxiation. If not prepared correctly, you could die from eating a puffer fish." Dom regarded the woman with an approving nod.

"So, why would people eat them?" Vasquez gasped, disturbed by the information she was receiving.

"Most sushi chefs are well trained in the art of preparing fugu. However, SARA, what's the fatality rate?" Dom asked, looking at the ceiling.

"Average fatality in Japan is 6.8%," SARA reported. Dom dropped her eyes back to her guests.

"I'm not willing to risk that near seven percent. Sure, most know how to prepare it, but you never know when you'd order from the one who fell asleep that day in sushi class. To me, it's the same thing as cops; most don't want to kill you, but there's always that one who doesn't know our skin color isn't a reason to freak out and start shooting. I'd rather not take the chance in either case, thank you very much."

"Can we eat now?" Vasquez interjected, longingly staring at the set table. Dom shrugged her shoulder and made a gesture that Vasquez could begin. Having lost her attention, Layla waved her hands erratically to get Dom to look at her.

"Hey doom and gloom, we were in the middle of a conversation here."

"Tell your hyper-active squirrel that." Dom nodded her head at Vasquez.

"Why do you have such a bleak outlook on the police?"

"Milwaukee," she replied in a flat tone.

"We don't know the whole story of Milwaukee," Layla protested.

"We know he was running away. When has someone running away from you ever been a threat?" Dom challenged, crossing her arms. Vasquez, who stood and began to walk towards the loaded table, stopped and turned back to the debate.

"Well they said he had a history of gang activity," Layla contended when she could find no answer to Dom's question.

"When he was *fifteen*," Dom argued, emphasizing his age. "Then after serving some time in juvenile detention, he graduated high school with honors, got a partial academic scholarship to the University of Wisconsin and had not gotten into any more trouble. So, a mistake he made when he was a kid signed his death warrant?" These words took the wind from Layla's argument, and her shoulders sagged as a response.

"How did you know that?" she asked.

"I'm a hacker, I can discover stuff people can't or don't try to look for."

"Most cops want to help," Vasquez offered.

"You're one of them. Of course, you'd say that," Dom shot back, the intensity still in her voice.

"We're not cops, we're crime scene techs," Vasquez clarified.

"That's just semantics. You are also minorities and women. You really think if there were a group of racist assholes in your precinct, they would show you themselves? Sure, some bigots are more vocal now than they used to be, but most still try to hide it," she maintained. "I just can't trust an institution that treats the murder of unarmed people as a reason to provide a paid vacation."

"That may be a problem," Layla revealed. Her voice was soft, and she did not make eye contact with Dom.

"What? What are you talking about?" Dom asked suspiciously.

"We are investigating a murder. If this thing that Daniels dragged us into crosses over into the investigation, as it appears it already has, we can only go so far before the guys with the guns and badges have to get involved," Layla explained, finally raising her dark eyes to meet her host.

"That's fine, just leave me out of that last part," Dom shrugged dismissively.

"We may not have a choice."

"Dom, the Jenkins siblings have arrived," SARA proclaimed.

"I'm not giving you a choice," Dom replied to Layla's statement. She took off her apron and tossed it on the counter. Dom disappeared down the hallway to the foyer just as the doorbell rang. Layla heard her say, "SARA, standby mode."

"Standing by," SARA confirmed.

When Dom opened the door, she came face to face with the golden-eyed stare of the woman from the video, Rose Jenkins. She wore skinny jeans and a light blue flower print satin shirt. Dom was shocked to see that she was at least three to four inches shorter than she was. Her brother, who was standing to her rear, was taller than Dom by a couple of inches and was much darker. She observed the familial traits the two shared such as similarities in the shape of their lips, nose, and eyes. Robert was wearing a yellow polo shirt and blue jeans. Unlike the photo in the file, the expression Rose wore was not warm. She glared at Dom suspiciously.

"Good morning Miss Jenkins, Mr. Jenkins. My name is Dominique, but you can call me Dom. Please come in." She moved to the side and ushered them into the house. The siblings crossed the threshold not allowing much space between each other as if a short string connected them. "Please follow me." She spun on her heels and led the newcomers to the dining area. Layla and Vasquez had already found places at the table, and she was surprised to see that Vasquez was not already eating. Rose and Robert approached the table with uncertainty, eyeing the two seated women.

"Who are they?" Rose inquired, casting her eyes back to Dom.

"It will all be explained. Believe me, the anxiety you're feeling right now, the three of us have already been there and done that. Please sit, have some breakfast," she replied, gesturing towards the table.

"It smells awesome," Robert asserted, excitedly taking the seat opposite of Vasquez and immediately dishing food onto his plate.

"I like him already," Vasquez grinned, following his lead.

"This is Rachel Vasquez," Dom said, nodding her head at the woman who was piling food onto her plate. "This is Layla Green." Layla stood and extended a hand to Rose, who had migrated to the seat across from her.

"I'd introduce us, but I have a feeling there's no point to that," Rose surmised, dropping onto her chair. She took a quick glance at the food, chose the coffee carafe in the center of the table and poured herself a cup. "What's going on? How do you know me?" She turned her eyes to Dom and began adding sugar and cream to her brew.

"Perhaps we should start with some entertainment," Dom suggested, pointing at the large television in the living room. Rather than commanding SARA to play the program, she produced a remote control from her pocket and launched the same segment of video that she previously played for Layla and Vasquez. Rose and Robert turned their attention to the screen. Rose sipped her coffee and watched the scene with no reaction, while Robert occasionally released verbal sounds and random words of disbelief. After the video stopped, Dom turned off the television and examined her guests.

"I assume my name was on that flash drive," Rose said flatly. Dom nodded in assent to her deduction. "What does this have to do with Rob's friend?" Dom shot Vasquez a look, prompting her to produce the binder next to her. She lifted the folder to show the siblings the logo. Rose and Robert glanced at each other in surprise, and he pushed up the sleeve of his yellow polo shirt and flashed the matching illustration tattooed on his arm.

"So, it was your tattoo," Layla gasped, prompting Dom to frown and shake her head to shut her up.

"Excuse me?" Rose asked, raising her eyebrows. Layla blanched grasping what she had just divulged, but the damage had been done.

"That's a little harder to explain," Dom stammered, fishing for words to justify the earlier intrusion into Rose's computer.

"I got this," Vasquez proclaimed, holding up her hand to Dom.

"Please don't," Layla muttered.

"Along with being a culinary savant, Dom here is a computer genius and hacker. After receiving Layla and your information from that weird guy, SARA put out alerts," she began. At the mention of SARA, Dom smacked her right hand to her forehead.

"Who's SARA?" Robert and Rose pondered in unison. Vasquez recognized her mistake, and suddenly had no words to respond. The table grew silent since no one could find a way to explain the situation without it sounding insane. When the hush grew uncomfortable, Rose finally spoke up.

"So, you're a hacker," she said, turning her golden eyes to Dom. "You hacked me a couple of nights ago and saw the searches and the picture of Rob's tattoo. I assume you got into my email inbox and saw that I took it myself."

"Kinda," Dom mumbled.

"This seems like more of a yes or no concept," she countered.

"Actually, not in her case," Layla professed. She regarded Dom with a knowing look and flicked her eyes to the ceiling. Dom returned her stare with uncertainty.

"SARA, wake up," she called, after seeing no other way around the situation.

"Good Morning, Dom," SARA responded. Robert flinched and looked around wildly, but Rose was unfazed.

"Of course, she has an AI."

"SARA is an autonomous logic-based system. After the little meeting you just witnessed, she took it upon herself to put out alerts on some of the people in the dossiers. Layla hit first," Dom explained.

"Because you're with the police. You aren't cops though. Crime scene team?" Rose asked, turning to Vasquez and Layla. "So, you two picked up the murder of Malik Rodgers and that's how you guys got together. Layla, you were the one in the files?" Layla answered with a curt nod. "Then I start looking into the group a couple of days later, and I get flagged. Probably doesn't help that you've likely been tracking me since then and know I went to his apartment yesterday."

"Bruja," Vasquez gasped.

"She's not a witch," Layla hissed, as she elbowed the woman in her ribs; but she was also rattled. Dom flashed the two astonished women a smirk.

"Rose Jenkins, thirty-five years old, one of five children. She attended Sam Houston State University with a double major of psychology and sociology and a minor in African American studies; followed by a master's degree in clinical psychology. She's completed the coursework for a Ph.D., but no dissertation yet. According to the file I received from Daniels, she's a psychological and behavioral profiler to a fairly high level; a Black Sherlock Holmes if you will," she explained. Rose did not react to Dom's recitation, but Robert stood abruptly, clearly agitated by the stranger recounting such extensive knowledge of his sister.

"What the fuck?" he barked.

"Sit down Rob," Rose softly commanded her brother. He blinked down at her, searched all of the placid faces, and slowly returned to his seat. "That's quite a comprehensive report."

"For what it's worth, I didn't do it," Dom offered, drawing a smile from Rose.

"Malik Rodgers," Layla said, looking between the siblings. "Who is he?" Neither brother nor sister spoke for a moment. Finally, Robert took a deep breath.

"I just got out of prison, served close to eight years. Almost a year ago, this guy gets transferred to Huntsville, and he becomes my cellmate. He introduced himself as Larry Phillips. We spent a lot of time talking, and he told me about this group. He had that picture on his chest as a tattoo. He was passionate about the injustices going on and doing something about them. He said these people had that goal and I guess his enthusiasm transferred to me. I was arrested for drug dealing, but that charge wasn't true; I'm an addict. When I got picked up, I had enough smack on me to overdose a few times." He dropped his eyes to the table, shame clouding his features. Rose put her arm on his back and rubbed encouragingly. "I was in pretty bad shape before Larry, Malik, whoever he was showed up. He gave me a purpose, a drive to do something more with my life when I was released. He said he wanted me to work with them when I got out. We went there yesterday to see him, and that's when we saw the tape on his door. His neighbor across the way, Ms. Henrietta, confirmed he was killed. He left a note behind with a Bible and a telephone number written in the margin of a page. When I called it, I got you." He lifted his eyes and looked at Dom who listened intently.

"A Bible?" Layla prodded.

"The note said, remember John 8:32," Rose expounded. Vasquez and Dom both frowned but before Rose could further clarify, Layla spoke again.

"Then you will know the truth, and the truth will set you free." The crowd turned to her with stunned faces.

"You're religious?" Robert asked. Layla made a face and shook her head.

"I've read the Bible, but I'm not religious per say," she replied dismissively.

"Then how did you," he began.

"Your superpower is an eidetic memory," Rose interrupted, her face registering understanding.

"How could you have possibly known that?" Layla frowned.

"It makes sense. Dom's a computer genius, I'm a profiler; you were also in the files, and it had to be for more than your link to the cops."

"Seriously, you're creepy," Vasquez added. Rose threw her a grin.

"I get that a lot. Did you know Malik Rodgers?" She posed this question to Dom, who shook her head in response. Vasquez giggled. Rose's eyes clouded in bewilderment when she turned to the laughing woman. "What?"

"Dom doesn't really know anyone," she revealed, causing Dom to frown.

"I know people," she grumbled.

"Dom is kind of a recluse. This Daniels guy threw her into this by just showing up," Layla explained.

"I don't know him, I don't know Malik. I don't know any of you. I know that SARA is responsible for connecting Layla and me. Her tap into your network also brought you to our attention."

"What about me?" Vasquez pouted.

"You were an accident," Dom replied. "But I fed you, so I guess we're stuck with you." Vasquez stuck her tongue out in reply. "What I don't know is how Daniels found me, and I also am now wondering why Malik Rodgers would have had my number. Both used a number that only a few people have. SARA monitors all calls, and I rarely accept one from someone I don't know. When Daniels reached out, he was using a scrambler, that's what got my attention."

"So, it's back to Daniels," Layla sighed. Dom's glasses tinted and SARA flashed a message to her, causing her to stand abruptly.

"Excuse me for a moment," she said, and then disappeared.

"What was that thing with the glasses?" Rose asked.

"I think it's connected to SARA somehow, I've seen it happen before," Layla replied.

"She's definitely different," Robert observed.

"She doesn't do well with strangers, but she makes a mean chicken apple sausage," Vasquez smiled.

"What's up SARA?" Dom called, entering the office. SARA sent a message informing her there was some vital information that needed to be shared immediately. Rather than have the program announce it to the entire crowd, she stepped away to vet the data first. The computer screens came alive as SARA began displaying her discoveries. Dom perused the material presented, and her eyebrows shot up in surprise. SARA located Malik Rodgers and was displaying his life on the monitors. The presented photos confirmed that he was definitely the man from the apartment in North Houston.

"Dom, along with the dossiers, reports, and articles Mr. Daniels left you, the flash drive also contained a ghost file. I had not previously mentioned it, as I did not perceive it as important; and therefore, I ran the reconstruction with low priority. The reconstruction is now completed, and it appears to be a message from Mr. Daniels himself, providing secure video call details.

"You sneaky son of a bitch," Dom mumbled. She stood and took out more chairs from the storage closet. After setting up the seating, she headed back to the waiting crowd. The group was eating and talking as if they had known each other for years.

"Seriously, the chicken apple sausage is amazing," Vasquez gushed. Dom nodded a thank you.

"You guys may want to come with me," she informed them, before turning back to the office. Layla and Vasquez immediately stood to follow, but Robert and Rose hesitated.

"What's up? Go where?" Rose pressed.

"Dom has an office over there. Usually, if she's asking you into the office, she's got some good stuff for you," Vasquez assured her.

"Definitely weird," Robert muttered as he stood.

"She's harmless," Layla promised, motioning for the siblings to follow. Upon entering the room, Rose and Robert gawked at the massive space of technology. Four chairs were positioned around the large desk. Dom turned to her guests, addressing them as they found their seats.

"Meet Malik Rodgers." On the top right monitor, SARA presented a graduation photo of the man. Robert's eyes bulged at the sight of his friend and Vasquez, and Layla exchanged glances when they recognized their murder victim. "Malik Rodgers was from Washington DC, thirty-nine years of age. BA in Sociology and Criminology from Howard University, followed by a law degree from the same institution. We don't find much about him after he received his law degree, but he was a member of the Washington DC Bar Association. I don't see any private practice, so that makes him all the more intriguing. Malik had no criminal history, not even a parking ticket. The man you met in prison, as Larry Phillips? I can't find anything on him, not even in the Texas systems." Dom regarded Robert, who frowned.

"He worked for the government," Rose decreed, drawing four pairs of eyes. "Think about it. He's part of the Washington DC Bar, but not registered with any firms? You can't find anything about him after law school? He somehow gets into prison, despite having no criminal background under a false name? He was planted there. He was working for the government." A blanket of silent understanding fell onto the room as all of the parties considered this information.

"It makes sense," Layla murmured. "That's why nothing came back on his fingerprints."

"I can't believe this," Robert groaned. "He lied to me the whole time."

"If he lied to you, it's because he had to, Rob. I think he was a part of this, whatever this is," Rose insisted, pointing to the arm that held his tattoo. "You don't put that kind of symbol on your body unless you're serious about it."

"Which leads me to the next portion of the program," Dom said, typing a few things on the computer. "Daniels left an encoded message on the flash drive disguised as a ghost file. Apparently, it's a way to talk to him. What say we give him a call?" She typed a few more commands, and when she pressed the final key, the computer speakers began to ring. After a few rings, Thomas Daniels answered the call, seated behind a computer in what appeared to be a home office.

"Dominique, I was beginning to worry." He stopped short when he saw the crowd of people on the other end of the screen. "You have company."

"And you, Thomas Daniels of the NAACP, have a lot of explaining to do," Dom declared, her voice filled with fire.

CHAPTER SIXTEEN

Dom wanted to take Daniels off-guard, and his face told her that she had. What she did not count on was the anger she would feel upon seeing him again. By simply showing up on her doorstep, this man obliterated the existence that had taken her a lot of money and many years to vigilantly craft. He gave her no explanation; and in just a few days, the only thing that was uncovered was more questions. Every turn led back to the man in front of her, and Dom found herself enraged. To give herself additional time to collect her emotions, she pulled up a command box and instructed SARA to remain silent. After the program acknowledged her directive, she glanced at the crowd behind her and turned her attention back to Daniels, who was clearly surprised.

"Well, you've been busy," he observed, offering a nervous smile. He waited for Dom to speak and when she did not; his eyes uncomfortably searched the crowd of faces. She did not want him to know he had gotten to her, and this attempt at self-control left her mute. As if her internal battle was telepathically communicated, she felt a hand on her shoulder. The contact caused her to flinch, and she turned to find Rose standing behind her, motioning for Dom to take her now empty spot. She took a deep breath, glanced at the waiting Thomas Daniels, and relinquished her chair. Rose settled into her vacated seat and faced the screen.

"I assume I don't have to tell you who I am," she began. Thomas grinned at her and shook his head.

"You are Rose Jenkins. The young lady behind you on your right, my left, is Layla Green. You were both included in the files I gave Miss Samuels a few days ago. I don't know the other two in the room," he replied.

"Who is Malik Rodgers?" she asked. Thomas blinked at the unexpected change in discourse.

"How do you know him?"

"Who is he?" she pressed.

"He works for the Department of Justice."

"Do you know him personally?" she asked.

"Yes. He has been on a case for the past year, but I speak to him at least once a week. In fact, I expect him to call this evening." Rose turned her eyes to her brother, who maintained the veil of stoicism. She slid her gaze to Layla and Vasquez; both returned her stare with grim nods. Turning to face Thomas she allowed her features to soften.

"Is he a relative?" Thomas nodded in assent, his face still coated in confusion.

"He's my little cousin, we grew up together."

"I'm sorry, Thomas. I hate to be the one to have to tell you this, especially in this medium, but your cousin was murdered a few days ago." Dom was surprised yet understood the directness of her delivery. He was clearly clueless about what was going on, and there was no reason to be ambiguous.

"Are you sure?" he croaked in disbelief, after a few beats of silence. Rose turned to Layla and nodded her head to the screen.

"He was found shot in his apartment on Wednesday. My partner, Rachel, and I were the team that processed the crime scene." She hooked her thumb to Vasquez, who was seated next to her. "There was no identification, but after receiving his name from one of the neighbors, we can confirm it was him," Layla reported.

"My God." His eyes watered emotion.

"We are sorry for your loss," Rose gently added. When he gathered himself, he wiped his eyes and stared into his camera.

"Did Dominique bring you all together?"

"No, Malik did," Dom replied, speaking for the first time since initiating the call. Her anger was tempered with the empathy of his loss.

"What do you mean?"

"Remember that little binder you left behind?" Dom asked. "Were you aware that Malik had the same image tattooed on his chest?"

"He mentioned the idea, but I didn't know he had done it," he admitted.

"His tattoo brought Layla and Rachel to my attention." While the explanation was not the full truth, Dom did not trust the man enough to mention SARA's involvement.

"We went to see Malik yesterday, and learned about his death from a neighbor," Rose added. This seemed to only deepen his perplexity.

"How did you know my cousin?" Rose turned to her brother who cleared his throat.

"I was his cellmate for a few months. I knew him as Larry Phillips and spent a lot of time with him talking about the workings of your group," he explained. After a moment of contemplation, Thomas' face changed as he mentally placed the final piece to a puzzle only he saw.

"Robert Jenkins!" he exclaimed with awareness.

"You knew about Robert?" Rose asked.

"Malik mentioned him and the fact that he got railroaded by the system. His current case is classified, but I knew he ran into Robert while working. It never occurred to me that he was your brother," he admitted. "Jenkins isn't necessarily an uncommon surname."

"Whatever Malik was working on had him embedded in the same prison where my brother served his time. Robert happened to get out on Friday, and when we went to see Malik yesterday, we found out his real name." Thomas continued to appear troubled.

"Malik left behind a message to Robert that contained my telephone number. Why is that? How the hell did you people find me?" Dom asked, giving words to the question that had been haunting her since Thomas materialized on her doorstep.

"What is this group?" Rose asked.

"We have no name, but that is intentional. When we look for change, for progress, for justice, we look for it by any means necessary. While I do work for the NAACP, we use many social, legal, and government entities that already exist. Branding ourselves could cause us to become limited. We would be put on the radar of those who do not want us to succeed. Rather than a name, we have a creed. We do what we must; we fight the fight, by any means necessary," he explained.

"It's like hacking a system," Dom muttered under her breath, but loud enough to draw the attention of the group.

"Hacking?" Vasquez asked.

"Yes. Think of it this way. Firewalls and encryptions are like the white blood cells of any given system. Their purpose is to protect the structure from an outside intruder. So, most hackers try to just breach the firewalls and encryptions. But sometimes, a good hack takes more finesse. Occasionally, it can be easier to trick the protections by jumping onto something less secure, like a smart television, a printer, or coffee maker."

"Coffee maker?" Robert asked incredulously.

"Yes, some coffee makers have Wi-Fi. Those are the fancy ones that allow you to program them remotely," she advised.

"Damn, they ain't have shit like that before I went in; technology has gotten insane," he muttered in awe. Dom flashed a quick smile but did not address his observations. When it came to technology, being sequestered from the world for almost eight years was the equivalent to waking up after a twenty-year coma.

"Dominique, you're absolutely right." Thomas smiled at her comparison. "As we discussed during my visit..." Dom scoffed at his framing of the statement.

"Visit he says. More like encroachment."

"Be that as it may, we discussed that there are people within our own government who actively try to prevent any sort of justice and equality for all. To have any sort of label would cause us to become a target for these people, some of which are very powerful. Our goal is not to overthrow the government in some new world order. We simply want everyone to have the same opportunities, and we want the government to uphold what they promised in the Declaration of Independence: all of us are created equal. They say it, but they don't act like it," Thomas lectured.

"That's adorable that you think they would ever see us as equals," Dom chuckled.

"I know, Miss Samuels. That's why we are here. If the powers that be won't help us, it's time we help ourselves."

"Where did Malik fit into all of this?" This question came from Layla.

"As I said, he worked for the Justice Department, but he also worked with us. There are so many ways to perpetuate oppression and disparity; we try to have representation in as many places as we can to drive change from within. But as to why he was in Houston, and what he was working on, I don't know. I don't know what he was doing that would have gotten him killed," Thomas admitted, the troubled look returning to his face.

"So, you're just going to smooth ignore my question?" Dom interjected. "How did you find me? Why did Malik have my contact information?"

"I gave it to him," Thomas answered. Dom scowled and crossed her arms.

"And how did you find me?"

"I wish I could give you a straight answer, Dominique. Your info was provided anonymously. Our network is vast and crosses into many industries and sectors. We have specific channels we use to recommend individuals that may be interested and beneficial, especially for specialized projects. In some cases, we don't know the origin of the data. That's what happened with you. I received a brief description of you, as well as your contact information," he explained. "The sender was aware of the concept of developing a counterintelligence division, and they suggested you spearhead the project. I passed that material to Malik because he was in Houston. He had federal means that I did not have. He was going to vet you for me."

"I don't like it," she muttered. "What about everyone else?"

"I received Miss Green's name from the same source as yours." Layla blinked in surprise, and her dark eyes shot to Dom, who returned her look with a shrug. "Miss Jenkins has been on our radar for some time now. Her work with the youth in the community did not go unnoticed. We wanted to find the best role for her specific skills, and we believe this would be the place," he responded. Rose stared at the man with little reaction, but her heart thudded in her chest, and her mind began to race.

"What about everyone else in that file?" Dom urged, drawing Thomas' attention. While Rose did not react to his statement, Dom could feel the masked anxiety.

"It's an accumulation of some who already know of or work with us, and others we believe would gladly take on the task given the opportunity."

"Thomas, can you find out what Malik was working on?" Layla asked, redirecting the conversation.

"I'm not sure. Why?"

"His death is currently an open and active murder investigation. We need to figure out who killed him." Thomas put his index fingers together in a steeple and moved his hands to his chin in deep thought.

"I'll see what I can find out," he conceded. "Since you are all together, I think it's a good idea for us to meet. I'll reach out to my contact with the DOJ and try to get some information before I come back to Texas."

"How long are we talking?" Rose asked.

"Maybe two or three days."

"Can you give us a next of kin? Is it Tasha Rodgers?" Vasquez spoke for the first time since the group sat down. Dom was sure the woman had just set a personal record of silence.

"Who?" Thomas asked, his eyes clearly exhibiting he did not recognize the name.

"The apartment where Malik was living was rented under the name Tasha Rodgers," Vasquez explained. "The detective assigned to the case is trying to run her down."

"I don't know who that is," he confessed, shaking his head. "We don't have a Tasha in our family."

"Do you have another name?" Layla asked. "You can give us a contact from the DOJ or you can give us a true family member, but we need someone."

"I'll send Dominique the name and number of my aunt in Virginia, Connie. She's Malik's mother. I'll inform my contact with the DOJ," he replied.

"You're saying that we're in a holding pattern until you come back to Texas?" Rose inquired.

"As far as additional information from me goes, yes. Perhaps let the cops handle Malik's death for now. The other option is hacking the DOJ," he suggested, looking at Dom who bristled.

"I get it, I'm good. But I don't like just strolling through federal systems on a regular basis. That's how you get caught. See what your contact can dig up before I even consider that," she said. Thomas nodded his head in understanding.

"So, does that mean you guys are in on my proposition?"

"Pump your breaks, Tom," Layla commanded, putting up a hand. "Right now, let's figure out what happened to Malik."

"That's fair," he conceded. "I will try to be there within the next two days."

"Until then," Rose nodded and then she disconnected the call.

"I thought I was ruthless with people," Dom chuckled when Rose spun in the office chair to face the crowd.

"It's hard to really get a good idea of a person by their appearance in a video chat, but I noticed a few things if you're interested," she told the group.

"By all means, Ms. Holmes," Vasquez smiled.

"I believe he's being one-hundred percent truthful in regards to this group he works with. I also think he was honest about his relationship with Malik. What I don't trust is that he knows nothing about what Malik was working. He likes to be in command. He was unnerved when I took control of the conversation. He also likes to peel off info out at his leisure. That's where you would come in," Rose divulged, directing the last portion towards Dom.

"I don't think jumping into a Federal organization all wil-ly-nilly is a good idea, especially the damn Department of Justice," Dom argued. Vasquez's eyebrows rose, and she looked from Dom to Layla, who was trying to contain her laughter.

"También, Dom?" she groaned. Dom looked at her baffled.

"What'd she say?" Dom asked Layla, who lost control of her amusement. She fought to rein it in, and after a few seconds, she was able to speak.

"She's whining that you used the words willy-nilly. I literally said the same thing in this very room yesterday. She says it makes you sound old."

"Anyway," Rose interrupted, attempting to steer the conversation back to the topic at hand. "I didn't mean for you to hack the government right now. I'm only saying he plays things close to the vest and tells us what he feels is necessary. Whatever he doesn't tell us, you can probably find."

"That's fair, but he knows that too," Dom pointed out.

"So, what do we do now?" Robert asked.

"We can't do anything more until we hear from Daniels again. He gave you guys his name and next of kin. I guess that will give your detective buddy a starting point."

"Dom, since you don't want to chance breaching the DOJ, there's little you can do. Because Daniels' works with a bunch of chameleons, there really is nowhere for you to dig." Rose said. Dom shrugged her shoulders.

"Does that mean I'll have my house back?" she asked, drawing a chuckle from Layla and Vasquez.

"Yes," Rose smiled. "I think that means you can keep to yourself for now."

"What about me?" Robert asked, surrounded by an aura of misery.

"You need to find a job to satisfy the requirements of your probation." He looked as if he would break down in tears, but he held his composure and nodded.

"What about you?" Dom inquired. "You have been giving everyone else jobs."

"I can't do what I do until we meet with Daniels either. I'll be going to work as normal." Vasquez turned to Robert with a mischievous smile.

"Has she always been this bossy?"

"You have no idea," he sighed, his voice taking on the hue of exaggerated long-suffering. "I was the one responsible for her most of our childhood. She's bossy and hard-headed." Rose scowled at her brother.

"I was an angel, and you guys were lucky to have me as your sister." The others in the room broke into a wave of soft laughter.

"I'm sorry about your friend, Robert," Dom said.

"Yeah, me too. I think it's worse that I didn't know who he really was. I thought… I don't know what I thought."

"He cared enough to tell his cousin about you, that's something," Rose consoled.

"I think you knew exactly who he was," Dom declared.

"Why do you say that?" Robert asked.

"You know he was dedicated to fighting injustice, so much so that he went to work for the Justice Department. You know that he was passionate about it, that's evident from his tattoo. You know that he saw something in you; that's why he told Thomas about you. A name is just a name, you knew his character." For the first time since meeting her, Rose heard warmth in her words. She examined Dom, adding a new shade of color to the character profile she had been building.

Since her unanticipated and bizarre introduction to this reclusive woman, while she had been a gracious host, she spoke as little as possible and at all times seemed uncomfortable with people in her refuge. After hearing the words of consolation spoken to her brother, Rose grasped that the woman was far more complex than she initially seemed. She wondered if the multifaceted nature of their host was hidden by design, out of mistrust, or if there was something more to the mask.

"She's absolutely right, Rob. You knew who he was, which is more than just a name," Rose agreed, her eyes watching Dom. The loner met her scrutiny for a second before dropping her gaze to the floor.

"I thought you were the shrink?" Vasquez smiled at Rose. "You may want to consider a new career, Dom."

"I don't like people," she huffed.

"Ah, there is the woman we met a couple of days ago. You had me worried," Vasquez winked, drawing a smirk from Rose.

"I guess we are done for a few days at least. We all have our marching orders," Layla announced, rising from her seat. "We should go."

"Yeah, let's get out of here, Rob. We should go see mom," Rose nodded, immediately accepting Layla's message.

"Thanks for breakfast; delicious as usual." Vasquez stood to follow Layla out of the office. "What time should I be back for dinner?"

"Hilarious," Dom grumbled. Layla giggled, pushing Vasquez out of the room.

Dom sat her dim pet room, sipping a martini, and staring into the large aquarium. After the departure of her guests, she cleaned the kitchen, checked her email, and caught up on the news; all to pretend that the past few days had not been as abnormal as they were. Losing another argument with SARA about her health, she worked out, had a small salad for lunch, and decided to spend some quality time with the fish.

"Dom, is something wrong? You have been alone for a few hours, yet according to the biometrics, the reduction in your stress levels is negligible," SARA asked, breaking her silent reflection.

"I'm just thinking."

"Would you like to share?" SARA asked.

"Are you trying to turn into my therapist now?"

"I could serve in that capacity if you wish, as I have a great deal of information regarding human mental health and treatments. Nevertheless, in this instance, I was asking out of curiosity. My primary functions are both logic and learning," the computer recalled. "Logically, I must continue to learn to remain useful."

"Only you could make a logical argument for being nosey," she chuckled.

"There has been a great deviation from our normal routines. Is this the development you are thinking about?" SARA asked.

"Yes. After years of comfortable isolation, suddenly people show up on my doorstep unannounced, and we're just chatting over brunch? That's not just a simple deviation, that borders a metamorphosis. I just… I'm trying to figure out how I got here."

"You did not have to prepare a meal for them, Dom. I heard your explanation in regards to your childhood, but these people did not come in need of monetary help," SARA chided.

"They needed answers."

"Then why did you cook for them?" Dom let the question hang in the air for a few quiet moments.

"Sometimes, all I can do is cook," she said softly.

"That does not appear to be a logical response."

"They needed something, something I couldn't give them. They needed answers," she sighed. "The fact that I, someone who deals in information, could not help them, I felt helpless. As an emotional empath, it's in my nature to want to help, especially if people are feeling anxious. When I feel powerless, I cook."

"Dom, surely you can see that this could be a cause worthy of your time," SARA insisted.

"I don't know. I haven't had the time to fully digest this cause. I went from being a mildly reclusive computer nerd..."

"I think mildly is being a little generous, don't you?" SARA interrupted.

"No one likes a wise-ass," she countered.

"That may be true, but I do not believe liars are held in much higher esteem," SARA retorted.

"I'm not a liar," she protested. "A visionary lies to himself, the liar only to others."

"Friedrich Nietzsche. How is quoting a 19th-century German philosopher any different than citing an 18th-century British playwright?" SARA asked.

"If I didn't know any better, I'd say you were whining."

"And if I did not know any better, I would say you were changing the subject." Dom sighed and closed her eyes.

"I want to help them, SARA; I really do," she asserted. "But I just don't know how I can." She stood from her seat and exited the room, shuffling downstairs to the kitchen. The apprehension she was feeling nearly overwhelmed her.

"I suppose that if one has grown accustomed to a specific dynamic, such a change could be troublesome," SARA admitted, as Dom stood in the kitchen, staring at various pots and pans. A ball of nervous energy engulfed her mind, but she could not think of what to do to expel the emotion.

"You think?" she muttered.

"Has too much time elapsed for you to remove yourself from this situation?" SARA inquired.

"That can't be a serious question. I don't recall putting rhetorical questions into your conversational protocols." Settling in her decision not to bake, she relocated to her office.

"I have found that rhetorical inquiries can be useful. It helps encourage the recipient to put things into perspective," SARA stated.

"So, you're basically saying that logically there's no reason for me to be troubled by recent events because there is precious little that can be done about it at this point? May I remind you, oh Vexing One, you are the reason all of this was hastily put into place?"

"That is only partially true, Dom. I believe the death of Mr. Malik Rodgers created the necessity for expeditious action," SARA argued. "Also, I must point out, if I had not done something, there would have been no progress."

"I wish I could say you were underestimating me," she grumbled, entering the workshop area of the office. The lights switched on when she entered illuminating the table of parts still laid out untouched since Daniels crashed into her life. She strolled to the table and examined the blueprint that was positioned under the various pieces of technology.

"I am a machine capable of calculating statistical probabilities to an infinite degree."

"I said I wish, I didn't say you were," she snapped. "I just feel like I've spent the past five years trying to keep a sense of serenity, much of that was accomplished by seclusion. In less than a week, five years of work has been completely unraveled. I find out there's some secret organization out there with an insane idea, and somehow those people found me despite the extraordinary precautions I have in place. I have strangers showing up on my doorstep whenever the mood strikes; and to make it worse, everyone needs answers, and they are looking to me! I can't give what I don't have."

"There is something to be said about patience. Surely once you meet with Mr. Daniels, a path of action will clarify."

"Great. Another meeting where I'll have to open my doors to people. When did my house become the designated assembly area?" She leaned against the table with a sigh. Thoughts and emotions spun around her mind like an out of control carousel. The invasions of the past few days, along with the promise of further trespassing, made her feel like she had no control in her own home.

She began to pace the room in deep thought when suddenly, an idea struck her like a bolt of lightning.

"You have a plan," SARA observed.

"Stop watching my biometrics!"

"Unless you disable the biometric monitoring aspect of my programming, that will not happen," the computer replied. Dom did not respond, her mind fully locked onto the idea that sprouted from seed to bloom in a matter of seconds. She moved from the table to her file cabinet, and then returned to the surface. Unfolding a large blueprint, she studied the diagram in silence, mentally working out the logistics of the plan.

"This could work," she mumbled, dashing to her desk. She opened a shopping program and began making a list for SARA, who would source the items from normal and underground channels. "I need it all by tomorrow," she commanded upon completion.

"You wish for this to be the shipping address?" SARA asked, highlighting the address entered.

"Yes," she confirmed. "That's the address. Now, let's find some schematics, we got some shit to build."

CHAPTER SEVENTEEN

Tristan Rucker sat at his desk reviewing the news story submitted for approval. His steel gray eyes floated across the words, ensuring all of the points were detailed to his specifications. While he could have written the article himself, his credentials as a former White House Communications Director caused him to become more accustomed to reviewing rather than composing content. He believed he still possessed the skill he exercised in his earlier time as a journalist; but like times, the nuances of prose changed and he had no desire to keep up with the developments. At fifty-five years of age, he was no longer the young and hungry columnist he had once been. He served his time and paid his dues; it was time for the younger generation to do the grunt work.

As the sole owner of Synergy Concepts, a political and social think tank, he employed several writers and bloggers. Synergy Concepts owned almost one hundred websites; from blogs to new sites that gave various writers and bloggers the podium to showcase their ideas and theories. For some of these locations, Tristan personally selected the top stories, as these were generally the sites sourced by larger media platforms. The writers and bloggers on staff often vied for the opportunity to write for these websites, and many went on to positions of national acclaim such as the Wall Street Journal, Forbes and the Washington Post. Tristan had a lot of influence in the journalistic community; he could get just about any story he wanted to be written in a short amount of time. The article he was reviewing had been written at his direction and would gain top billing on his news sites with the heaviest traffic.

The article was about the shooting of Timothy Cook in Milwaukee and the still unnamed police officer who pulled the trigger. While the officer was unknown to the public, Tristan knew his identity. Nathan Grimes had been on the force for just over three years. Normally, he would not oversee this sort of story. He preferred to leave regionalized matters to his staff, while he kept his hand in more national events. His involvement in the framing and narrative of this particular incident was a personal favor for Grimes' uncle, a sitting senator from the great state of Wisconsin. Upon review of Grimes' history with the department, he found no public complaints or disciplinary actions; yet, he also had no commendations on his record. It was preferable for the cop to have some sort of distinguished career that could be the focus of the narrative. Tristan managed to uncover a juvenile record for Cook, which he had already released to the news outlets. The story he was reviewing provided more detail about the crimes of Cook's childhood.

Nathan was not helping the situation. Tristan had spoken to the young man and found him devastated by the killing of Cook. Grimes' tearfully offered to publicly apologize and resign. At one point, he suggested turning himself in and pleading guilty to manslaughter, despite there being no discussion of charges by the district attorney. When Grimes recommended conceding to manslaughter, Tristan was certain the officer was beyond his help. Once he calmed the man down, he asked Grimes to give him a rundown of what happened on that fateful morning.

"I stopped him for speeding," Grimes began. "When I ran his driver's license number, his name came back as having a fugitive warrant for assault with a deadly weapon and felony theft. I was shocked because he was so polite when I pulled him over. I went back and asked him to get out of the car. When I went to arrest him, that's when he began to panic. He started getting belligerent and fought back a little. He kept insisting that I had the wrong guy; that he was just on his way to class. I told him if that was the case, it could be cleared up at the station. Before I was able to cuff him, he pushed me away and ran. I did the first thing that came to mind; I drew my weapon and yelled for him to freeze. He kept running. I have marksman level accuracy at the range; I thought I could wing him, you know, to get him to stop. I hit him center mass instead."

"Were you afraid that he would hurt you?" Tristan asked.

"Well, no sir. He was running away. I was afraid that he was going to be a danger to others, considering the warrants I found," he replied.

"From now on, when anyone asks that question, your answer is yes," Tristan sternly commanded.

"Sir?" Grimes questioned, his voice communicating his confusion.

"If you're asked why you discharged your weapon, your response henceforth will be that you were afraid for your life." This time, Tristan spoke slowly, hoping to hide his frustration.

"But Mr. Rucker, it was my fault! I ran the wrong driver's license number. If I had just taken an extra couple of seconds, I would have realized it was the wrong name."

"Nathan, things happen. You're a cop, and you are also human. All humans make mistakes. You are a good officer. You have a dangerous job; it is to be expected that finding yourself facing a violent criminal would start your adrenaline pumping. You wanted to get a bad guy off the streets. A man with a warrant out for a violent crime like assault with a deadly weapon would fall into that category," Tristan assured him.

"But that's the problem! Cook was not a violent criminal. He was just a kid. I looked up the wrong license number! Just an additional three seconds and that kid would still be alive." Grimes' voice broke at the end of his protest.

"Nathan. It was a mistake; there were two blunders in this situation. You didn't look at the name, and that was your error. If Cook had not tried to flee, we wouldn't be here right now, that was his mistake. There is no reason for your career to be derailed so soon because of a little snafu. That's where I come in. I will help you get through this. You can't change what happened, but you should not lose your livelihood because of it. What I need you to do is to answer as few questions as possible right now. If you are asked by IA why you discharged your weapon, you will say: I was afraid for my life and the lives of the public," Tristan advised. "I encourage you to speak with your captain. I'm sure he will tell you the same thing." Grimes was silent for a few moments before he finally responded.

"Yes, sir."

"Don't worry son, this will blow over after a while. Those Black Lives Matter people are always pissed about one thing or another. Something else will come up, and they'll forget you. But keep in mind, your name won't be unknown forever," Tristan warned. "At some point, the damn media and the liberals will come after you, and they will smell blood. You stick with your story, and let me take care of the rest."

Tristan finished combing through the article, ensuring the tone and content satisfied his stipulations. Once appeased, he called up the internal directory of Synergy Concepts and chose ten sites that were used as sources by larger media outlets. Replying to the blogger, he approved the story and provided the ten mediums where it should receive top billing. He then crafted an email to a list of his preferred news outlets and attached an advanced copy of the article. These people were friends of his, and usually accepted news stories from him with little to no question, a benefit of his past role with the White House. He also attached five photos pulled from Grimes' social media, specifically chosen to outline the diversity in his friendships and to derail the racism talk that had already begun. Just as he sent the email response, his phone rang. After glancing at the desk phone and his cellular phone, he opened the middle drawer of the executive desk and withdrew a burner.

"Yes?"

"He spoke to four men from your list: Martinez, Taylor, Cole, and Evans. Evans and Cole were in Dallas at Hutchins, and Taylor was in San Antonio at Fabian; none will be a problem, they have all had fatal accidents," the caller reported.

"Did we get an ID on our nosey friend?"

"No. I didn't find any in the apartment. I also checked; Larry Phillips has completely disappeared from state records. Tristan, I think he was from Washington," the caller disclosed. The verification of Tristan's fear caused him to close his eyes to regain control of his rapid pulse. He had a feeling the appearance of Larry Phillips signaled trouble, and this confirmed that apprehension.

"What about Martinez?"

"He's in Huntsville. Ran into some trouble, so we can't get to him right now. We will, very soon," the caller guaranteed.

"If you find anything else on this, let me know. I'm not sure what the hell this guy was looking for, but I don't think it's good," Tristan mumbled.

"I'm on it," the caller confirmed. Tristan disconnected the call and considered his options. He reluctantly made another call. It rang twice before the low, melodious voice answered the phone.

"Yes?"

"We need to meet," Tristan proclaimed.

"Why?"

"The clinic program; I think there's a problem," he replied. The voice on the other end was silent for a few beats.

"How big of a problem?"

"I don't know, but I know it's not good," Tristan advised.

"Find out. I'll get a hold of the others and let you know when." The man disconnected the call, and Tristan tossed his phone on the desk. He leaned back in his chair and stared at the ceiling.

"Who the hell are you, Larry Phillips?"

Robert sat up late Sunday evening, flipping through Rose's latest Essence magazine. His sister had gone to bed, as she had to be up for work the next morning. He tried to watch television, but it seemed that his time in prison tempered his desire to stay glued in front of the boob tube. He came across an article about the best natural hair care products and decided that he officially hit rock bottom in entertainment for the night.

He tossed the magazine back on the coffee table and sank down deeper into the couch with a sigh. He missed so much time with his family; particularly Rose's graduation from her master's program, and his mother's battle with breast cancer. He cried for a week when they told him of her diagnosis, and then cried for another week when they informed him she was in remission. He wished he could have been there with Rose and his mother to comfort them. He had no idea how his sister had held it together over the past eight years, but he assumed it had something to do with the many bottles of alcohol in her cabinet.

A cloud of impending depression began to circle him as his mind shifted from what he missed to the death of his friend. He knew Dom was right when she comforted him earlier in the day. He did know Malik's character, though that admission did not help the grief or the feeling of hopelessness that currently engulfed his mind. Malik was supposed to be his redemption, illuminating a path to help others and to make use of his second chance. Now, he was back where he thought he would be before Malik showed up; no prospects, no friends, and a whole lot of regret. A soft knock jolted him from his cocoon of melancholy. Although Rose's neighborhood was nothing like he was used to, he stood and approached the entry cautiously.

"Who is it?" he called softly, careful not to wake his sister.

"It's the Michelin man, fool," Ryan's voice answered. Robert smiled and opened the door to find his big brother standing on the other side. He was dressed in blue jeans, an orange polo shirt, black tennis shoes, and he was carrying a six-pack of beer.

"What are you doing here?" Robert whispered.

"I ain't seen you in almost a decade. Why is that your first question?" Ryan frowned, stepping into the apartment and closing the door behind him. "I can't just come hang out with my little brother?"

"Of course, I'm just surprised," Robert replied, returning to his seat on the couch. Ryan put the six-pack on the coffee table, grabbed two bottles, and tossed one to Robert before settling into the recliner.

"Nights are hard," Ryan admitted, cracking open his beer. "I assumed they would be for you too." Robert opened his own beer and took a small swig before addressing his brother.

"What do you mean?"

"Hard to sleep when it's quiet, especially if you aren't used to it anymore," Ryan said, giving his brother a knowing look. He surveyed the room as he took a long pull from his beer. "Looks like our Rosie did pretty well for herself."

"Definitely. I was afraid she went and got pretentious and whatnot on us, but I still see the hood in her," Robert smiled. Ryan let out a soft chuckle as he took another drink.

"Mama did good with that one, no doubt about it. Sometimes I would think about you guys, and I'd feel guilty for leaving and staying gone for so long," he confessed. "But Rosie, she came out ok."

"You left for a good reason, bro," Robert insisted. "You didn't end up like me. I'm the one who failed the family."

"You messed up. But you have to remember; this life thing is a war, not a single battle. You may have lost one battle, but you're still fighting the war." Ryan held up his bottle to Robert in an offered toast.

"I guess so," he conceded. "I'm sorry you missed Rosie's graduation for her master's degree. She told me you were deployed and couldn't get back for that one." Ryan's face darkened at the mention of missing the ceremony.

"That's kind of a dark spot on my record. I didn't exactly take that rejection gracefully. I got myself a counseling statement." His voice was as gloomy as his expression.

"What's that?"

"It's kind of like a written warning you'd get at a normal job. I got pretty angry about the whole thing. I was the only brother that could have been there, and they didn't care. My CO, I mean, my commanding officer, probably should have done a lot more to me; but he was sympathetic, which helped in the long run. Still, let's just say I wasn't at my best self," Ryan professed, idly fingering the jagged scar lining the right side of his face. When he left for the Army, his facial features were clean and smooth; but by the end of basic training, he had been branded with the wound and would only tell his family that it was a training accident. Rodney and Rose believed there was more to the story, but Ryan refused to expound when he was pressed.

"I missed so much," Robert sighed. "I got the photos you sent me of Luna and Kiara. They're beautiful bro. You did good."

"I'm a lucky man," Ryan smiled. "You aren't the only one who missed a lot. Being in the Army is one step away from being in prison. I'm actually not sure which is worse." Ryan's demeanor changed to radiate an inner rage, and his eyes lost focus as he stared into space.

"Prison is worse. You chose to go into the Army," Robert offered. Ryan's eyes focused on his brother, and he flashed a sad smile.

"I love you baby bro, but you also chose to go to prison." Robert flinched at the statement.

"I needed help, RJ2. I hid my habit from all of you, except Rodney and Reggie, only because they supplied me. I was hooked and too far gone by the time you guys found out. I needed rehab, not to be locked up with a bunch of murderers, rapists, pedophiles and drug dealers. They took me from my family and surrounded me with people who spent most of their lives hurting others. The only person I really hurt was myself, and my family," Robert protested. "How is that the same thing as willingly joining the Army?"

"You were sent away by a government who doesn't view you as human, to a place you really had no business being in; not because of your addiction, but because of the color of your skin. When a White judge sees a White addict, they see their daughters or sons, maybe their brothers or sisters. They see someone who is sick and needs help; someone to be pitied and rescued. When they see one of us, they see an animal that should be caged. But Rob, you knew that. You grew up in the same America that I did. You knew that if you got caught with enough smack on you, they would lock you up. We don't get a break if we need help; we don't get to mess up like everyone else. We are immediately discounted and sent away by the same folks who bend over backwards to help those who look like them," Ryan said, fire warming his voice. "We aren't equal. Our standard always has to be higher, and even when we succeed, we still aren't equal."

"I'm still looking for the similarities, bro," Robert prodded, rolling his hand to get Ryan to make his point.

"You're right, I signed up to go into the Army. I wasn't drafted; I went voluntarily," Ryan conceded. "But if you think about it, how voluntary was it? I'm a Black man from a poor family. We grew up in one of the toughest neighborhoods in this city. My only choices were to go to college, go to the Army or," he faltered and took a drink to swallow the lump in his throat. "Or to end up with Reggie and Rodney. I was never that great in school, wasn't a stand out athlete, and I knew that as hard as mom worked, she'd only be able to help one of us with tuition. Rose had to go to school. She had to become who she is today. We all knew that bossy-ass little girl would turn into an opinionated woman who would do great things. I didn't want to end up running the streets, so I made the choice that kept me out of jail and out of the ground." Robert considered his brother's words, pinching his lower lip with his fingertips.

"Ok, I will acknowledge that you're right," he agreed, after a few seconds of contemplation.

"So, I signed up to fight for my country." Ryan performed the air quote gesture around the words. "But when you do that, you just hand them your freedom and your sense of self. The only thing I didn't have was the bars and shackles. If you go in without a good foundation, and you don't know who you are as a person, you can literally lose your mind; especially seeing the things you see when you're deployed."

"You talking about PTSD?" Robert inquired, taking another swallow of beer. Ryan nodded his head in confirmation.

"You have two kinds of people. You got some who were troubled, thrown into highly stressful conditions where they are yelled at, berated, taunted, and pushed to their limits as a method of training. If one is already disturbed, that treatment doesn't help the mental state," Ryan explained.

"And when those types are discharged, they are released into a world that doesn't understand the life they left behind, and they what, flip out?" Robert asked. He put his empty bottle on the table and grabbed another from the pack.

"Basically. When you're a soldier; you're a soldier. You know exactly what's expected of you, and what you're supposed to do. You have a routine; you don't have all the freedom to come and go as you please. If you leave without permission, go AWOL, you practically go to prison. Ain't that some shit? You go to jail for quitting your job. You're a soldier until they say you can leave. Sound familiar?" Ryan smirked, finishing off his beer and exchanging his empty bottle for another.

"So, you're saying that in some cases, PTSD is like being institutionalized. I remember meeting cats who were in and out of the joint their whole lives. They didn't know what to do when they got out, so they ended up going back. There was this one dude, Jake, he got his parole papers, and he cried like a child. I thought it was because he was so happy, but that wasn't it. He had spent twenty-five years inside, and he had no idea what to do when he was getting out. For some people, being a criminal is all they know."

"Right, there are some who have been in the Army so long they don't know anything else. A huge difference is that they put criminals in prison to prevent them from killing and hurting others. In the Army, they teach you how to take a life in multiple ways. We were taught how to kill for the good of God, country, and all the other bullshit they spew. That patriotism shit is just a way of detaching folks from the act. As if because we are Americans, our lives have more value than others. It's not murder if you're doing it for your country. You aren't expected to feel empathy for the enemy," Ryan's face darkened as he spoke. "You get scars man. I served during peace and war. You get wounds either way; but when it comes to war, it's a little more intense." His eyes lost focus, and he stared into the void. Robert watched his brother get lost in the shadows of his recent past. He lingered at the place inside his mind for almost a full minute before he spoke again. "When you get back into the real world, you don't have that anymore; you don't know what to do with yourself. The life you lived in the Army isn't a life you can live out here. It's enough to make someone crack."

"What's the other type of person?" Robert wondered. Ryan's eyes remained engrossed in his memories, and Robert thought he had not heard him. In an instant, his cloudy eyes cleared and he looked at Robert in puzzlement. "You said there were two kinds of people. What's the other kind?"

"People with a strong foundation and sense of self. People who know what they are or what they want to be. We all take the same abuse and deal with the same tragedies, but holding on to who you are helps get you through it. I knew I didn't want to be in a cell or dead; I knew that much about myself when I went in. I clung to who I wanted to be for you, Rosie and momma; I wanted you guys to be proud of me. I wanted to be the kind of man Daddy would have been proud of. Then Val and the girls grounded me even more. They were there with me; they were tangible. I had to be the man they deserved. I did not want to be the boy that left Sunnyside twenty years ago, I wanted to be the man worthy of my family. I did not want to be a statistic." Ryan immediately flinched when the last sentence left his lips, and he wished he could take it back. He looked at his brother in sympathy. "I'm sorry, that sounded bad."

"It's fine," Robert smiled, waving off the apology. "Prison is like that, you know. You have to determine if you are a criminal or if you simply made a mistake. If you choose to be a criminal and act the part, chances are you'll never do anything but be in and out of prison. Those of us who realized we fucked up want nothing more than to make up for it, and we usually work out a little better. I never thought I would have spent almost a full eight years behind bars, man. I thought I'd be a better man than that; I just let my habit beat me. But no more." He lifted his full bottle to his brother in a toast. "To becoming the men we want to be." Ryan grinned and returned the gesture. After taking a drink, he sighed deeply.

"I sometimes ask myself if I succeeded in that," he mumbled.

"Why? Man, you went and fought for our country! That's something to be proud of!" Robert exclaimed.

"Is it?" Ryan scoffed. "Do you even know what's happening over there, bro?"

"I've been out of pocket for a while, but not in a hole. Terrorists. We're fighting terrorists," he answered.

"And who are they? When you hear terrorists, who do you immediately think of?"

"Muslim extremist," Robert shrugged. Ryan leaned forward in his chair and stared at his brother.

"Are you sure?"

"Unless something has changed since I've been in prison," Robert replied, confusion clouding his eyes.

"We grew up Christian, right?" Ryan questioned, now fully alert and focused on the conversation.

"Yeah," Robert agreed, baffled by the sudden change of topic.

"If I as a Christian man, refused to help people in need, took money from the poor for my own pockets, sexually assaulted or raped women, and demonized people who don't believe like I do, all in the name of God; would you still consider me a Christian man?" Robert made a face.

"Of course not."

"So, why is it so easy to believe the terrorists are Muslim? They claim to be Muslim, just like the politicians and far-right extremists claim to be Christians; but the actions of neither are in line with the teachings of their faiths. The government paints the enemy with a broad brush. If people are busy being suspicious of the Muslims or people who they think are Muslim, they can't watch the very un-Christian things the government does to the folks here," Ryan said. "Unlike the states, we still got word of what was going on over here. People stateside generally get the press package; no one here knows anything of what is going on in the Middle East, they just know what they are fed," Ryan asserted, his voice growing angry and dark.

"The press package?" Robert inquired.

"The people in the Middle East are more likely to be killed by those terrorists than anyone over here. The US is making it seem like we are needed there to keep the peace when us being there is making the situation worse. There are so many variables and factors; I don't want to get into that right now. The fact is, we are being the global police, and all the while ignoring the shit going on here. The United States allow the murders of Black people, gay people, and any people classified as other with no recourse. Then they have the audacity to be outraged when other countries treat their citizens the same way. It's all bullshit!" Robert blinked at his brother's change in demeanor.

"I guess I never considered it that way," he admitted.

"No one ever does. The media and politicians throw the smoke screen of terrorism to distract people from the terrorism happening here! What makes me sick to my stomach is that I was a part of it. I would see news stories of the unarmed killings and mass shootings, and then go out on patrol just to see the same shit," Ryan disclosed morosely. He grew silent and began to drift into the unknown place.

"Where are you, bro? What happened to you over there?" Ryan did not answer for a long while. When he spoke, his voice matched the haunted look in his eyes. He shifted his weight to the right and began fingering the scar on his face.

"There was a woman, Halimah. She wasn't much younger than me, maybe a few years. I met her when we spent some time patrolling her village. The extremists had come maybe three or four times before we got there. Twice, they sent in a suicide bomber. Halimah had already lost her husband to them. They tried to get him to fight for them, and he refused. So, they slit his throat in front of her and their ten-year-old son; then they took the boy." Ryan's voice was barely above a whisper.

"Damn," Robert muttered.

"That happened maybe five years before we showed up. She didn't have much family in the village; so, she was poor and trying to do anything to make money to feed herself. One of the things she did was sell her body to some of the troops. I liked her, so I would give her money, but never for that. I saw the look in her eyes, you know the one when you have lost damn near everything? The Jenkinses, we know that look, don't we?" Robert nodded.

"We do," he croaked.

"Sometimes I would pay her to walk with me while I was doing my patrols, just to keep me company. I never really fit in with the guys in my unit; didn't have much to say to them on a personal level. She spoke broken English and understood it pretty well; and during my time over there, I picked up some Dari. We made it work. She told me about what happened to her husband and son. It broke my heart, man." His voice remained weak, and Robert could tell he was trying to keep a handle on his emotions.

"I can imagine," he offered.

"One day, my unit was doing the rounds in the heart of the village. We stopped to watch some kids playing soccer; it was a pretty low-key day. Suddenly, we hear this big commotion nearby, and we hauled ass to check it out. There's this kid, standing in the center of a crowd, wearing a backpack. He looked dazed, I could tell he was dehydrated, barely keeping himself upright. He was dirty, and he looked terrified. The others, they see a backpack on a scared kid, and they immediately think another bomber. Some of the guys lined him up with their rifles, commanding him to stop and lay down in both English and Dari; but he didn't listen. He just kept turning around in a circle, like he was looking for something." Ryan's voice dropped off, and he took a deep breath. "I hear a scream and turned to see Halimah tearing down a side street; she was running to us and yelling. I… I couldn't hear her, Rob. I couldn't understand what she was saying, I was too far. When she got close enough, I finally understood. I turned to the guys to try to get them to stand down, but one of them fired, and put two bullets into the kid." When Robert realized what was coming next, his heart broke. "It was her son, Emad. Once he was down, we got to his body and checked the backpack. It was filled with canned rations the kid had stolen from his captors; not an ounce of water in the bag. He escaped and probably spent days trying to get home to his mother. Halimah lost her husband to the terrorists, and then lost her son to the people who were allegedly there to help." A tear finally fought its way through Ryan's emotional barricade.

"My God," uttered a stricken Robert.

"There wasn't no God in that," Ryan argued, swiping at the tear. "The soldier killed that kid just like that. When we realized he wasn't a threat, he didn't seem to care. He just kept repeating that Emad didn't listen, insisting that he would not have fired if the kid had just done what he was told."

"What happened to the guy who killed Emad?" Robert wondered, after a few seconds of silence.

"Not a damn thing. They said it was justifiable. Emad had a backpack and given the village's history with suicide bombers, the officers said the soldier acted according to protocol. They actually blamed a fifteen-year-old boy for his own death. They said he should have known that upon seeing soldiers he was supposed to stop and approach carefully. Why would these people expect a fifteen-year-old child to have self-control like that? Especially one who had gone through what I can only assume was five years of hell; all he wanted was his mother," Ryan replied, his voice dripping with anger.

"Sounds like what they do to us here," Robert mumbled.

"Exactly. We are over there killing people we are supposed to be protecting; sending drones to take out one person, even if it kills fifty bystanders. Why does this country feel justified in acting as the police of the world? We can't even take care of the folks in our own borders!"

"That's a good point," Robert concurred.

"They tried to act like they were doing me a favor by letting me be a part of the good fight. If I spoke up, I was told I was no better than the folks we were fighting. They justify every-thing they do to themselves, even if it doesn't make sense to anyone else. That same soldier will probably come back to the states, become a cop, shoot a twelve-year-old boy playing in the park, and have as much remorse for that child as he had when he gunned down the fifteen-year-old in Afghanistan who just wanted his mom," Ryan sneered.

"Is that when you decided you were getting out?"

"Hell yeah. I was going to do my twenty and not give them any more than that. Those motherfuckers were going to give me my damn pension," Ryan proclaimed.

"Rose and Mom never said you were so miserable," Robert admitted.

"They didn't know. I didn't want to worry them. My family kept me sane."

"That's what kept me stable in prison. I thought about killing myself so many times, but Mom, Rosie, and your letters kept me grounded and gave me something to look forward to. Even when I hated myself, you guys kept loving me," Robert said.

"You're our family, why would we stop loving you?"

"The same shit that took Reggie and Rodney away from us is what put me in jail. After losing those two, and then me almost killing myself with the dope, I thought... I don't know what I thought," Robert blushed.

"You needed help, not a ten-year prison sentence," Ryan admonished, the hint of anger returning to his voice. "You were treated by our system the same way that those otherwise peaceful people are being treated overseas."

"Except they didn't kill me," Robert pointed out.

"That's what you think, but in a way, they did; just like they did to me. My ideals of what I was doing and what I represented died over there. The little hope I had in this country died. I endured the same kinds of prejudice and racism that I could have gotten here, and on top of that, I risked my life daily to put up with it. My hope died, and if you're honest with yourself, part of your hope died in that cell.". Robert took a deep breath and considered his brother's words.

"You're right," he sighed.

"I almost didn't come back home when I got out. I wanted to stay in Germany or move closer to Val's family in Croatia. But she said I've been away from my family for almost twenty years, and you guys should get to know her and the girls. I just pray that my daughters don't see the raw ugliness of this country they were spared by being born overseas. They're American citizens, sure, but they don't know what their caramel colored skin means for them once they get here. They have no idea what I've done to them," Ryan said sadly.

"They have Jenkins blood running through their veins. They have an aunt and uncle who will take it to the streets for them, and when it comes down to it, their grandmother will cut someone over those girls," Robert grinned, drawing a chuckle from Ryan.

"You right about that."

"What's next for you?" Robert asked. Ryan contemplated the question.

"I need to find a job to support my family. I also want to do something, something good so I can feel clean again," he confessed.

"I have an idea for that last one," Robert smiled mischievously. Ryan examined his brother.

"What's that?"

"I'll have to run it by Rosie, but I think there are some people you may need to meet."

"Who?"

"It's complicated, but trust me, bro." Robert downed the rest of his beer before he spoke again. "I think you'll like them."

CHAPTER EIGHTEEN

Early Monday morning, Layla made her way to the homicide bullpen in search of Detective Lewis. She checked the time as she weaved her way through the officers in the middle of the shift change. The morning briefing would not begin for another twenty minutes, which gave her plenty of time to speak with Lewis and answer any questions she dared. Nodding to the staff who bid her a good morning, she navigated the long hallway leading to the homicide department. Turning left to enter the huge spacious room, she almost collided with the large body of Detective Calvin Tidwell. She stopped short to prevent the crash and made no attempt to hide her grimace when she realized who she almost ran into.

"Green," Tidwell grunted, his voice gruff and gravelly from the pack of cigarettes he smoked on a daily basis.

"Calvin," she replied flatly. Tidwell flinched at this greeting. Layla addressed the majority of the force by their rank and last names as a sign of respect. When it came to Tidwell, she could not find an ounce of respect to give; and the rare times she had to speak to him, she used his first name. Tidwell hated it, and that fact gave her a small jolt of pleasure. She believed if a group of cops gathered together on the weekends with sheets and burning crosses, he would certainly be the grand dragon of that meeting. Tidwell, for his part, knew very well that Layla disliked him; but to be fair, most of the support staff detested him.

"What are you doing down here in these parts? You slumming?" Tidwell grinned, drawing her attention to his tobacco stained teeth.

"Just down to speak with Lewis," she replied, making a show of looking around Tidwell to peek into the office.

"You know, you've worked cases with me before, why don't you ever come down to see me?" he probed, drawing her gaze back to him.

"Far be it from me to interfere with your cases, Tidwell," she snapped in disgust.

The first case Layla worked with the portly detective was a double homicide in a park. Upon processing the scene, she found additional shoe imprints pointing to multiple assailants. Ballistics showed the same gun had been used on both victims leading Tidwell to argue that there had only been one killer and that the additional imprints were coincidental. Layla was of the mind that while the same gun had been used, two different people shot the weapon, citing the position of the shell casings. Tidwell disputed this claim, insisting that shell casings could roll. She attempted to persuade the stubborn man by offering to take him back to the scene and show him another way to look at the scenario. He had been less than cordial, accusing her of interfering with his active investigation. In the end, Layla was proven correct when the autopsy showed the entry points of each victim had been different, and when the heights of each deceased person were taken into account, there was a high probability of two different shooters. Even when shown to be wrong, Tidwell did not apologize for his harsh reaction and seemed to resent her for being right. Layla never attempted to help him again outside of her basic job requirements of testing evidence, analyzing samples, and the written report.

Not missing her meaning, Tidwell's face went slack, and she stepped around him to enter the homicide area. The department was bustling with the activity of the swap in personnel. The precinct was fairly large, and the homicide department generally worked in two shifts, one during the day and one at night. To conserve funds, each detective shared a desk and computer with another from the opposite work period. As she approached Lewis' desk, his night shift desk-mate, Sammy Lopez, was just packing his things to leave. Lewis hovered over the man, his face shrouded in impatience. Lopez was a short and stocky Hispanic man with dark curly hair, large dark brown eyes and an ever-present grin of mischief.

"Come on Lopez, pack like immigration is at the door," Lewis grumbled impatiently. Lopez chuckled.

"What's the rush? The whole reason I'm here is to do your job for you." Layla rolled her eyes at this normal exchange between the detectives.

"Oscar the Grouch giving you a hard time, Lopez?" she asked, pulling up a chair next to the desk. Lopez flashed her his infamous grin.

"Always. You know how it is, these gringos think they can tell us what to do just because they run the world," he quipped, rising to his feet. He pulled his messenger bag from under the desk and slung it across his body.

"A purse? I knew there was something peculiar about you, Lopez," Lewis jabbed, moving to the now empty chair and taking his seat. He turned to the computer and then glowered at Lopez, who was fishing around his pants pocket.

"Try to get some work done today, Lewis. I can't save the city all by myself," Lopez teased, extracting keys from his pocket and heading to the exit.

"You forgot to log out again, man. Do they not have computers in your homeland?" Lewis called. Layla stifled a giggle. Lopez, a fourth-generation Mexican-American from Atlanta, turned back to his desk-mate and flashed another grin.

"Nope," he replied. Slipping into an exaggerated southern drawl, he followed up with, "We ain't got none of these godless contraptions in Georgia." This imitation caused Layla to cackle in laughter.

"Aren't you late for the Home Depot parking lot?" Lewis grunted, switching the computer profile to his own.

"Naw, man. On Mondays, I cut grass! I'll make sure to tell Sandy you said hi when she lets me in for my weekly drink of water." As he said this, he began humping the air. Sandy was Lewis' wife, and this comment prompted the older man to spin in his chair and throw him a dirty look. Lopez gave a final smile and turned to leave the office once again, throwing up his middle finger in a farewell.

"I'm not gonna lie, I love that guy," Lewis smirked, watching the younger detective exit. "If he didn't insist on night shift, I'd actually consider taking a partner for him."

"He's pretty freaking entertaining," Layla nodded.

"What's up, kid? You got something for me?" Lewis asked. Layla withdrew a slip of paper from her pocket and put it in front of him. He picked up his reading glasses from the desk and slid them onto his face.

"Name and next of kin for our victim in Greenspoint," she reported. Lewis' eyes widened in astonishment.

"Where did you get this?" he asked after he reviewed the slip of paper. She knew this would be his first question. Despite having a full day to prepare, she had not come up with a believable answer.

"What does it matter?" she shrugged, attempting to sound nonchalant. "It's a lead, right?" He narrowed his aquamarine eyes and stared at her intently.

"No fingerprint hits, no identification, apparently the person on the lease of the apartment doesn't exist; either that or one of the ten women we found in that part of the city are lying. Suddenly, you waltz in here with a name and next of kin after a single weekend? Yeah, I'm gonna need a little more than that," he demanded.

"I can't tell you that." He stripped off his reading glasses and his gaze intensified. "Would you believe, anonymous tip?" she squeaked in a small voice. His stare transformed into one of suspicion.

"Try again, kid."

"Lewis, I had a crazy weekend. Some things went down that I can't talk about right now, not until I get more information. You know me and my work ethic. I didn't have to bring this to you, but I did. If I had more actionable intel, I would tell you," she insisted in a low voice. He studied her for a moment before picking up the paper and reading the message again.

"What's going on, Layla?" he pressed, his eyes radiating concern. He rarely called her by her first name, usually address-ing her as Green. She placed a hand on his forearm, established eye-contact, and attempted to detect the answer to her next question.

"Do you trust me, Oscar?" The unexpected question softened the hardness in his eyes. She knew that for Lewis, trust was a hard thing to give. His difficulty trusting people was the reason he operated without a partner for years.

"You know I trust you."

"Then trust me when I tell you that this is literally all the actionable information that I have right now." She indicated the slip of paper he was holding. "You have his name and his mother's name. Run with that. When I know more, when I can give you more, I promise you I will tell you." She was frustrated at the pleading quality her voice conveyed.

"Just give me something," he urged. She sighed and mentally ran through the highlight reels of the weekend, in search of a detail she could produce that would placate the relentless detective.

"I met his cousin; that's all I can say right now. I got his name from his cousin.," she conceded softly.

"What cousin? Who?" Lewis questioned, ever the detective. She gave him another beseeching look.

"It's complicated, Oscar," she declared, her voice almost at a whisper. "You know I'd never put either of our jobs at risk unless I had to. Somehow your case crossed into my personal life. I don't fully know what's going on yet, but I know that I will have more information soon." He dropped his eyes back to the paper thoughtfully.

"I suppose you could have kept this to yourself," he sighed.

"Just give me some time."

"I guess I'll start with his mother," he mumbled.

"Thank you, Lewis," she smiled. "There's one more thing I need." Lewis shot her an incredulous look.

"Now you're pushing it, kid."

"I just need you to run interference for Rachel and me while we piece this out," she said. At the mention of Vasquez's name, agitated suspicion returned to his eyes.

"Vasquez knows too?" he challenged, a little louder than intended. Some of the detectives nearby abruptly stopped talking and glanced in the direction of his desk. Layla rolled her eyes.

"Chill out. You know we're tight. She was with me when everything happened this weekend. So yes, she knows. Just try to get Captain Haggard to pass any new cases to one of the other three teams. Tell him we're working on something for you." Lewis closed his eyes and began to massage his temples, his face reflecting every ounce of frustration he felt.

"You're killing me."

"I'm trying to help you," she countered.

"Fine, but you damn well better update me. Don't bullshit me, Green," he commanded in a stern voice, albeit quieter than before.

"Me? Bullshit?" she asked innocently. Lewis responded with a resigned shake of his head. Suddenly, his clear turquoise eyes turned severe.

"You and Vasquez are not detectives. If things start to get dangerous, you better call in the cavalry. You don't even like guns! Don't go getting yourself killed," he growled. Layla gave him a salute.

"Yes, dad."

"Please, my three are enough. I'd be in the nuthouse if you were my daughter," he grumbled.

"I owe you, Lewis." She stood and moved her chair back to its original location. Lewis began sweeping the air with his open hand.

"Now go, since you insist on doing my job for me, find me something I can work with."

Layla returned to the crime lab to find Vasquez anxiously pacing the floor. In a bizarre twist, she actually arrived on time, anxious to be there when Layla returned from her discussion with Lewis. Her hair was back in its signature ponytail, her face absent of the make-up from the day before. She wore khaki slacks and a shirt with green and blue geometric designs. When Layla breezed into the room, she descended onto her like a bird swooping down on a worm.

"¡Por Fin!" she exclaimed, approaching Layla.

"Finally? You get to work on time one day, and you have the nerve to be impatient?"

"What did he say?" she probed impatiently. Layla edged around the taller woman and walked to her desk, with Vasquez on her heels.

"It took some convincing, but he's going to work the next of kin angle for now. He's going to give us time to figure out what's happening on our end, but he wants to be kept in the loop," Layla replied, opening her desk drawer and fishing out her cell phone.

"That's it? He didn't say anything else?" Vasquez asked in disbelief. Layla checked the phone display and noticed a waiting text message.

"Something about us not getting ourselves killed," she mumbled distractedly.

When she opened the message, she saw there was no sender information; and when she read the content, she frowned in confusion.

"Who's that?"

"I think it's Dom," Layla murmured. She plopped down onto her office chair and unlocked her computer.

"Dom or SARA?" Vasquez asked, moving across the aisle to her own desk and bringing her chair into Layla's space. Layla was typing rapidly, calling up an Internet map website.

"Is there really a difference?" she mused, entering an address into the website.

"Well, I've found that SARA is much better with people than Dom." Layla gave her a quick chuckle.

"I think SARA may be a little like Dom was before she went into hiding," she admitted, changing the map to a satellite view and zooming into the location. The address appeared to be a warehouse compound located southeast of Houston, inside of a city called Clear Lake.

"What's that?" Vasquez asked, leaning in to investigate.

"Address Dom sent. She said this is where we are to go for our meeting with Daniels." She minimized the map screen and pulled up a new webpage for property records. After running a search, she reviewed the information on the owner of the warehouse. What she found caused her to laughed softly in amusement. "Clever, that one."

"Who is Shadow Technologies?" Vasquez inquired. Layla stared at her in response, choosing to let the realization seep into her mind gradually. After a few brief seconds, Vasquez's eyes lit up in understanding. "Oh!"

"She may be weird, reclusive, and a lot of other things; but boring definitely ain't one of them."

"What are you wanting me to do here, Rob?" Rose questioned. The three Jenkins siblings sat around her dining room table feasting on a meal of fried chicken, mashed potatoes, corn on the cob, and fried okra from Robert's favorite chicken spot. She stopped and picked up the meal as a surprise for him, and returned home to find a surprise herself, in the form of Ryan. During dinner, Robert relayed his discussion with Ryan the previous night and asked him to tell his story again. He was reluctant but relented after further prodding from his little brother. Rose listened quietly, allowing Ryan to give the account at his own pace. When he was finished, she expressed her sorrow over the events and how much they affected him, a show of sympathy that he waved off. Turning to Robert, she was trying to ascertain the point of the sharing exercise.

"Take him with us," he replied around a mouthful of food. She dropped her fork and favored her big brother with a skeptical look.

"Are you nuts? Did you not pick up on Dom's vibe, Rob? She doesn't like strangers, and she doesn't like cops. What makes you think a stranger, who is a former sergeant in the US Army, would be received any better?"

"She wasn't so bad," he shrugged. Rose frowned.

"I didn't say she was a bitch. I like her too; which is why I don't want to just spring this on her."

"Look, this is all strange and new. We don't even know how you or I fit into this situation," he reasoned, after swallowing a long drink of sweet tea.

"How *I* fit into this," she corrected, stressing the pronoun. "You weren't in the mix; it was a coincidence, remember?"

"I'm in it now. That Rachel girl wasn't involved either, she got looped in because of Layla. What's wrong with one more? Ryan needs this." Rose eyed her other brother who sat silently listening to the debate.

"You want to pipe in here, RJ2?"

"Look, Rosie," he began. Rose cleared her throat and favored him with a stern glare, causing him to smile sheepishly. "Sorry. Rob told me a little about what this guy Malik talked to him about. He also told me what Daniels wants from you. He's right, this may be just what I need. Besides, one man is already dead. If you guys are going to jump down this rabbit hole, who better to have with you than your big brother who happens to be a veteran? I can look out for you guys." He fixed his dark brown eyes on his little sister and then shifted them to his brother. "I'm not losing another sibling." Rose reached her right hand out and wrapped it around his left hand, giving it a small squeeze.

"I get it. I don't want to lose another either," she whispered.

"Rose, all three of us have seen so much and lost even more. This country is going backwards. You see it every day with the kids you work with, and we grew up with it. Being treated like we don't matter, discounted, gunned down by cops because our skin brands us as the enemy, or because we have the nerve to demand to be treated with the same dignity others receive," Robert said. "You are the only one of us who seemed to get past that. Not only did you rise above it, you're actively reaching back and trying to help others come up to where you are. Ryan joined the Army to avoid it, and I, unfortunately, embraced it. Believe it or not, even though we're your big brothers, we look up to you for what you chose to do with your life. You make a huge difference to those kids and to our community. We just want the chance to make a difference too." Rose studied her two older brothers and realized that both felt the need for atonement, and were eagerly looking to their baby sister for that salvation. Sighing heavily, she nodded.

"I'll figure a way to make it work. I guess if anyone of us could deal with a personality like Dom's, it'd probably be me." Her phone vibrated on the table as she spoke. She wiped her grease-stained fingers on a napkin, plucked the device from the table, and navigated the screen. The message had no sender, which meant it likely came from SARA. "Speak of the devil."

"That's her?" Robert asked, picking up his fork and attacking his meal with renewed gusto.

"Probably the computer. She doesn't seem like the type

to reach out to people," she smirked. She read the contents of the message. "Interesting."

"What?" Ryan probed.

"She sent an address for our meeting with Daniels. It's in Clear Lake," she reported, placing the phone next to her plate and picking up her fork.

"I thought you said she lived out in River Oaks?" Ryan asked.

"She does," Robert and Rose said simultaneously.

"So why the new coordinates?"

"We really need to break you of your military talk. It's an address in the civilian world, Sarge," Robert quipped. Ryan punched him lightly in the arm.

"If I were a betting woman, I'd say this is her way of reestablishing some sort of control over this whole mess," Rose suggested.

"What?" Robert scowled.

"I think this new location is her way of taking her sanctuary back. All introverts need that safe place. I'm actually impressed she did something this fast."

"Your new friend seems…" Ryan paused, searching for a word. "Eccentric."

"Wait until you meet the computer," Robert grinned.

Dom was on her knees at the front entrance of the large two-story warehouse, working on the wires protruding from the wall. The structure was purchased as an offsite server farm, and held other odds and ends that she did not keep at the River Oaks home. The building and surrounding land had been a steal, purchased at a tax auction from a defunct furniture company. Two sets of stairs on opposite sides of the space led to a second floor and the former offices that encircled the perimeter of the building. Each room had large windows that allowed light to stream into the workspace. Some of these rooms held Dom's servers, some held technology equipment, and some were empty. Catwalks were suspended above the bottom floor allowing access to all of the offices and offered a view of the bottom level of the warehouse. The bank repossessed the machines that once dotted the ground floor, leaving the windowless bottom story of the open space virtually empty.

Five loading bays were positioned in the southwest corner of the first floor. Three of the bays stored classic cars, the fourth held a large quad cab pickup truck, and the fifth was empty. Shortly after the purchase, Dom had contractors come in to wall off and reinforce almost half of the western portion of the building, causing the inside of the warehouse floor to appear much smaller than it actually was. In the middle of the open area, eight new office chairs surrounded a brand new large circular meeting table. Hanging on the western wall were three forty-two-inch television screens. On the east side of the room, four cubicles with desktop computers were set up and securely connected to the internal servers. A functional kitchen was located in the northeast corner of the building, next to the entrance where Dom was working.

"Dom, I am now fully uploaded to the local servers, and the link to your home server is complete," SARA announced. Dom turned her gaze to the three screens on the western wall and stole a glance at SARA's new avatar. As they worked to strategize this set up on Sunday, she found herself looking up at the ceiling so much her neck began to hurt. She decided that it would be easier to look at a face, and designed the program an avatar. Coming up with the perfect image for her faceless friend of four years was no easy task. Finally, she settled on a Black female with curly hair and wide hazel eyes.

"Welcome back. I apparently talk to you even when you're offline. Do you know how weird it is to ask a question and wait for an answer from no one?" she asked, turning back to her work. She used her soldering iron on a portion of the wires, and then twisted them quickly, blowing on her fingertips to relieve the burning sensation.

"I do not, as that seems illogical. Why would you ask a question if no one is around to answer?" SARA inquired.

"I thought you added rhetorical questions to your logic."

"I did, but that seemed more of a conversational question," SARA responded.

"From now on, if I ask an illogical question, just assume that it's rhetorical and that I'm not an idiot, okay?" she grumbled.

"Understood."

"Thank you. Now let's run through the checklist," Dom commanded.

"I'm online, so that is completed," SARA began.

"Conceited much?"

"All beings are conceited in one form or another, Dom. It is a required trait for survival," SARA replied.

"Say what?" She turned to face the monitors in surprise. SARA's placid avatar stared back at her.

"All beings have to have some form of self-importance for survival. Being online and functional is my main purpose, so logically, it is important to me," SARA explained.

"I suppose you have a point," she smiled, turning back to her work. When she finished with the wires, she stuffed them into the small open section in the wall. Picking up a metal plate, she slapped it over the hole and began screwing it onto the partition. The plate was solely for aesthetics, as the important component was on the other side of the barrier.

"Security cameras?" SARA questioned.

"Yes, check the function," she commanded. SARA was quiet for a few moments.

"All readings indicate functionality and the feeds are routed to the proper servers. Biometrics?"

"Just finished." Dom stood from her kneeling position to the opus of popping joints in her knees. "Let's give it a go." She opened the blast-resistant entrance and exited the building, pulling the door closed behind her. When she heard SARA engage the locks, she bent down to the panel just opposite of where she had been working and aligned her left eye to the quarter-sized hole at the center of the silver plate. A red light danced across her iris, and the indicator at the bottom of the panel switched to green, unlocking the door. She entered the building once again and announced, "Seems to work."

"All computer and workstations are online, functional, and connected to the secondary servers," SARA declared.

"So, we have research, security, a very lovely face as the

brains of the operation," Dom ticked off the items on her fingers as she spoke. She walked through the warehouse, and examined the space, trying to determine if she forgot anything.

"Are the appliances installed in the kitchen?" the computer asked. Dom ordered a large refrigerator with an attached freezer, dishwasher, and a simple four top electric stove.

"I installed them while you were offline," she confirmed.

"Is the furniture assembled? Will our new friends be comfortable?"

"Yes, ma'am. Also, you've been throwing this word friend around quite a bit. We don't even know them," Dom grumbled.

"I like them."

"So you've said."

"I have sent messages to all parties providing this address as the new destination for the meeting tomorrow."

"When did you do that?" she asked, glancing at the avatar.

"I sent a message to Ms. Green this morning before I went offline, and to Mr. Daniels and Ms. Jenkins after reboot," SARA advised.

"Efficient as always, my friend."

"What about the armory?" SARA asked.

"What armory?"

"Dom, do not treat me like I am unintelligent," the machine reproached.

"That's been here for years. It's not a stocked as you think. Don't call it an armory."

"It seems you have forgotten that I have access to your online purchase history."

"Oh, shut it," she grumbled. She walked to the loading area and inspected her classic cars, approaching her favorite one first, a 1964 ½ cherry red Mustang convertible.

This had been her first restoration project and took well over a year, mostly due to her engineering expertise being geared more towards technology and less towards automotive work. Next to the Mustang was a 1969 Dodge Charger, midnight black with a white racing stripe. This car had taken much less time as it had been in better shape than the Mustang, and Dom had a little more confidence in her restoring ability. The last car was a 1967 Camaro

SS model that was only half done. The body was rusted, and most of the original parts were useless; this would be by far the most challenging restoration. Returning to her Mustang, she checked the time and surveyed the room once more. Everything was ready for their meeting with Daniels the following evening. She was exhausted, having slept very little over the previous few nights; the anxiety of meeting with the group again making it hard for her to relax. She decided that a drive could be just the solution for her apprehensive mind.

"I'm taking a ride, SARA," she announced, getting into the Mustang and firing up the engine. A nice ride around the back roads of Clear Lake sounded like the perfect remedy for her mind and soul. Backing the Mustang out of the loading bay, she gunned the engine, and the car leaped forward like the horse that shared its name. Even though she could not run away from the recent disturbances in her life, tonight, possibly for the last time until all of this was over, she could pretend it wasn't happening. She at least had tonight.

CHAPTER NINETEEN

Tristan Rucker sat at a table in the small, windowless room, idly tapping a pen on his steno pad. The chamber was dark, except for the illumination coming off of the four thirty-two inch screens on one of the walls, and the small desk lamp on the table. This bunker was the reason he chose this building for his think tank. The underground space was highly secure, and allowed for the frequent meetings with The Collective.

These mysterious men approached him ten years previously, at the end of his term with the White House. Suddenly jobless, newly divorced, and unsure of what to do with himself, Tristan had been contacted by a former colleague, who informed him that his work attracted the attention of some very powerful people. He was put in touch with a man from Chicago, who seemed to be the dominant figure of the faction. The men believed that the country had been going downhill for years, and they wanted to try to guide America back to how it was originally foreseen by the country's forefathers. Tristan also believed the same way, which was what prompted him to abandon his journalism career in favor of working for two Presidential administrations.

As a journalist, he became disgusted with the shift from being honest and authentic to catering to the school of political correctness. The requirement of the majority to edit themselves as to not offend a small group of people was the direct opposite of the basic principles on which the country was founded. In Tristan's opinion, the reason for the original revolution was to provide Americans the freedom to say whatever they wanted, whenever they wanted, and however they wanted. When he accepted the role as the White House Communications Director, he tried to shift the media away from pacification; yet as it often did, the White House changed sides. The Collective offered him an opportunity to do what he loved, driving the narrative of the superior concepts that they shared. Not only was he skilled at directing narratives, but he also had a knack for presenting things in a way that would make the common man accept the accounts as gospel. The Internet provided a larger platform than he ever imagined and his think tank was able to further disseminate the information without the interference of checks and balances.

In exchange for funding his company, Tristan performed various errands for the group. At times, he was required to grease the wheels of a politician with money or information. In situations like Milwaukee, he tried to steer the narrative of a particular event. Sometimes he was tasked with coming up with a grand distraction to navigate the media away from a possible scandal or allow a bill to slip through the cracks. Other times, he either directed the campaigns for a desired candidate or researched as much negative information as he could find on an opponent. The current situation with the clinic program was the darker side of his job: clean-up and containment. While not always on the acceptable side of legal, he believed that his work was what was best for his country. Patriots did not follow the rules, which would be the opposite of true patriotism. True patriots did what was necessary, no matter the cost. Tristan saw himself as a patriot, and that description was one he bestowed upon each of the four men represented on the screens in the room.

While he knew the men, he worked for were powerful, rich and influential; he had no clue as to their identities. Each man sat in a dim room, the light placed in a way that permitted them to be seen as mere shadows on the displays. The only detail he had was the location of each of the obscure figures. On the wall in front of him, the televisions were placed in a diamond pattern. The top screen held the silhouette of the gentleman from Chicago. Though he spoke with an authoritative tone, and obviously was the chairman of The Collective, youth tinted his melodious voice, and Tristan gauged him to be at least a decade his junior. He suspected the man was a high-level executive, a lawyer, or perhaps both.

To the lower left of Chicago's screen was the man in Las Vegas. Vegas' smoker's voice and sporadic coughing suggested that he had one foot in the grave. His location and portly outline led Tristan to believe that he was likely a casino mogul or land developer. Just under Chicago, was the fellow from Atlanta. Tristan could not quite guess his age or occupation as the man tended to be the least talkative of the group. He took part in every meeting of The Collective, but rarely contributed to strategy discussions. Finally, to the right was the gentleman in Alexandria, Virginia; who he called Alexandria. It took a while for him to get used to the moniker, but when he realized that the names of both city and state were feminine, he adhered to the city as a label. Alexandria's over the top country twang always made him want to laugh. He had a hard time speculating what Alexandria did for a living, but he narrowed his field down to defense contracting, natural resources, or a politician; and he was by far, Tristan's least favorite of the cluster.

"What's the status on Milwaukee?" Chicago began the meeting by wasting no time asking about the pet project of saving the career of Nathan Grimes; the officer involved in the fatal shooting of Timothy Cook. It was Chicago who ordered Tristan to try to navigate the media direction for the incident.

"I was able to get the records of his juvenile arrest. The charge was weed possession, but there was some reference to a possible gang affiliation, so I amplified that. You've probably seen the photos of Grimes with his Black and Brown friends circulated over the past few days. That was done to redirect the racism conversation," Tristan reported.

"Good. Outside of the Black Lives Matter people, the conversation seems to remain on backing the blue. The White House also supports that stance," Alexandria advised, eliciting a nod from Tristan.

"There is one concern," he warned.

"What's that?" Chicago inquired.

"When I spoke to Grimes, he seemed to be taking this much harder than most," he explained. "He feels like it's all his fault and even talked about pleading guilty to manslaughter."

"I thought the D.A. wasn't filing charges?" Vegas said.

"He isn't. The senator made sure of that," Chicago disclosed.

"So, why the hell would he want to cop to manslaughter?" Alexandria asked.

"Was it his fault?" Chicago probed.

"Depends on your perception," he shrugged.

"Don't waste our time, Rucker. Answer the damn question," Vegas snapped.

"He ran the wrong driver's license number for Cook. He said he was in a hurry, and didn't pay attention to the name. Thankfully the Milwaukee PD kept that tidbit quiet. No one has examined the reason for Cook's arrest; I honestly don't think anyone cares right now. They're so focused on the fact that he was unarmed and running away. But if someone finds out the truth, the tone will change. Some of our weaker allies will start backtracking." The news hung in the air for a few beats of silence.

"Did he have a body cam?" Chicago asked.

"Yes. I reviewed the footage, it doesn't show the wrong name. It backs up Grimes' account and matches with the videos circulating," Tristan replied.

"So, he should have never been arrested." Alexandria posed this as more of a confirmation than a question.

"That's correct," he confirmed. "Gentlemen, make no mistake that this will get worse before it gets better. At some point, it will come out that Cook had no active warrants. Luckily, when it does, we won't be blindsided. I'm just trying to contain the damage before the rest comes out."

"When will these porch monkeys learn to just do what they're told?" Alexandria groused. "If that boy had just gone with Grimes, it would have been cleared up, and we wouldn't be in this mess!"

"Did he break department procedure?" This question came from Chicago.

"With the info, he had at the time, he was within the department protocols for use of force. In his mind, he thought Cook was a wanted violent criminal, and when he started to run, Grimes fired believing he was going to be a danger to himself or others," Tristan said.

"Is that what Grimes told you?" Alexandria asked.

"No. That's what I told him. What he told me, was that he was trying to shoot him in the arm like a goddamn action hero," Tristan sighed.

"Why the hell would he do that?" Vegas asked, his voice conveying his shock.

"That's why I'm concerned. Cops are trained to shoot center mass. Put the suspect down. Grimes didn't intend to kill Cook. So, you take the issue of the wrong ID and add the fact that he wasn't trying to kill him at all, you get the mess that is Nathan Grimes. It's hard to make the public believe a man is innocent if he believes he's guilty. I don't know how long he will hold out," Tristan admitted.

"What do you mean?" Vegas asked.

"He's a mess. It's not only his first fatality, but it was done on an error. He's basically a good kid. We just need to figure out how to keep him from blowing it. I can't keep the story going if he decides to implode."

"The media narrative has been our friend in the past, no use in doubting it now," Chicago said. "If you run this like I know you can, it won't matter if he screams from the mountaintop that it was his fault, the people won't believe him. Just like with the last Presidential Election. I don't know how you did it, but you made it happen."

"You may want to ask the Senator to reach out and calm him down. Maybe he can talk some sense into Grimes, you know, as his uncle. I'll keep doing my part, but again, it will mean nothing if Grimes caves and decides to be noble," Tristan disclosed.

"I'll make the call," Chicago conceded. "Now what's the situation with the clinic program? You said there was a problem."

"I got a name for our friend formerly known as Larry Phillips. His name was Malik Rodgers. But learning that just made things worse," Tristan declared.

"How so?" Alexandria asked.

"Unlike Mr. Phillips, Mr. Rodgers has no criminal record. In fact, he has an undergraduate and law degree from Howard University. He was registered to the Washington DC bar but wasn't with a firm that I could find. This seems to imply that he was working for the Feds. I tapped into our contacts with the FBI, CIA, and NSA; no one knew him," Tristan recounted.

"You have a theory," Chicago said, more as an accusation than a question.

"Unfortunately, I do," he acknowledged with a deep sigh. "But you aren't going to like it."

"Well spill it, boy, don't make us guess," Alexandria demanded impatiently. His annoyance made him sound like Foghorn Leghorn, the southern chicken from the Warner Brothers cartoons he watched as a child. Tristan cleared his throat to keep from laughing.

"I think he was with the Justice Department," he announced. He eyed the four shadowy figures and noticed all but Atlanta stiffened at this announcement. He marveled at how the silent man always remained impassive, no matter the subject matter.

"What leads you to believe it's Justice?" Vegas inquired.

"He was embedded in not just one, but four State prisons; easily transferred in and out, and suddenly his entire record is completely erased as if he never existed," he explained.

"What was he looking into, do you know? What does this have to do with the clinic program?" Chicago pressed.

"He primarily spoke to inmates who went through Benjamin's court. Our ears didn't get full conversations, but it was enough to piece together the fact that he wasn't just making small talk. My initial termination order was because of Benjamin's re-election campaign. I couldn't risk any sort of investigation derailing all the work we've put in. However, I have since learned that he definitely spoke to the four from the clinic program that Benjamin sentenced. If he had only talked to one, I wouldn't worry. The problem is, I don't know what they told him, if anything, nor do I know what he may have relayed to whoever he works for; I just feel like we should tread lightly until everything is fully contained," Tristan asserted.

"He's dead, why do you not think it's contained?" Alexandria asked.

"He lived in DC, but he had an apartment here in Houston. He was out of the prison for six months, but still here. I have a feeling that he was trying to do more research. They can't just take a criminal's word for it, he was likely doing some digging."

"So, what's the plan?" This question was posed by Vegas.

"Three of the four problems have been dispatched. Martinez is the only one left, but he's inaccessible right now. I'm kind of flying blind here. I just need time to assess the damage."

"Shit," Chicago muttered. "What's the status of Benjamin's re-election?"

"It's getting costly. Keeping a conservative judge in a liberal county is always a hard-fought battle. We have the standard commercials, but I'm putting together some National names to stump for him. He's up against a highly respected Latina judge who is all about prison reform. That's appealing to most around here," he replied.

"How expendable is he?" Vegas asked.

"He's useful, not just because his politics are aligned with ours, but also because he's not beneath taking a little money on the side for favors. He's one of only two conservatives in this city. If we lose him, it will be another four years before we could get another one in place. Simpson is already a no go. He's more of a moderate and isn't viable for what we need. We need Benjamin," Tristan answered. The room grew silent as this information was pondered.

"How far has this spread?" Alexandria asked after a few moments.

"That's what I don't know. Outside of the four, everyone he spoke to was where they are legitimately. Taylor, Cole, Martinez, and Evans. Those were the four I was concerned about. After Martinez is eliminated that avenue is cut off," he assured the group.

"Anything else we should know?" Chicago asked.

"Well, other than not knowing if he reported back to anyone, there is another wild card, Layla Green."

"Who is that?" Alexandria wondered.

"She is a crime scene technician for the Houston PD. She caught the murder scene for Rodgers. As far as I know, she has no known ties to him; but she's also the person who found his true identity. According to my source, she was very cagey on where she got the information," he replied.

"Cagey how?" Chicago prodded.

"She suddenly had an ID for the man after a weekend. She said he crossed into her personal life, but she was hesitant to say how. My contact with the PD said that attempts were made to get her to cough up the info, but she locked down. So right now, she's a wild card. I don't know her involvement in this."

"You have a plan?" Chicago asked, checking his watch.

"I'm going to put a tail on her. Try to figure out how she fits into this puzzle, and if she knows anything. I'll also put one on her partner, Rachel Vasquez. Green mentioned that Vasquez was a part of it as well. If she's involved, I hope to find out how," Tristan said.

"What do you know about this Layla Green?" Alexandria asked. Tristan nervously flicked his eyes to the man's screen. Alexandria's method of dealing with complications usually included killing, a route Tristan did not like to take unless completely necessary. He already regretted ordering the elimination of Malik Rogers; although, it did uncover a possible larger issue.

"Not much, she was an orphan, doesn't have a lot of family. The way it's told to me, she's really smart. Most detectives trust her more than a little. She's good at her job," he reported after he consulted his notepad. "I don't think we should jump the gun on her. We don't know what she knows if it's a coincidence or what. Layla Green is well liked around the department, and taking rash action without further information could bring a world of trouble." He directed this recommendation to Alexandria; the rest of the men seemed to know this and said nothing.

"Stay on her. If she's going to be a problem, get rid of her," Alexandria commanded.

"My job is to orchestrate things effectively and with minimal issues. If I determine that is the appropriate course of action, I will not hesitate. But we already have one dead body, and I will not randomly kill a member of the Houston Police Department on a whim; not without all the information," Tristan replied sternly.

"Does Benjamin know about any of this?" Chicago asked, shifting the conversation to avoid an argument between Tristan and Alexandria.

"No. I didn't want to alarm him. He's focused on the election right now," Tristan replied. "Of all the good he's done, there are only four that could be seen as questionable. I think I can keep it contained."

"See that you do," Chicago instructed.

"Anything else?" Atlanta asked. Tristan flinched at the unfamiliar voice and noticed his ethereal figure checking his watch.

"I'd appreciate it if someone would contact the director of the clinic program. Operations should be suspended until this is all ironed out, but I don't think he'd take that well from me," he claimed. "I need time, and I'm pretty sure it would be better received from you."

"I'll make the call," Atlanta confirmed. "If you would excuse me, I have another meeting." The bottom screen went dark as the man logged off of the call, throwing the already dim room into further darkness. After a moment, Alexandria spoke again.

"So, your job is to figure out what this Layla Green has on Malik Rodgers, how she's connected to him, and if she will be a problem."

"Yes," Tristan concurred.

"If you need any wiretap warrants, go to Benjamin. Let him know it's a favor for us," Chicago added.

"I hope it doesn't come to that," Tristan confessed. "I hope this is all a coincidence."

"Look into it anyway. I don't want to assume. If Malik Rodgers was with Justice, then there could be a whole shit storm coming our way. The program is expendable, more so than Benjamin. We need to know how to proceed," Chicago maintained.

"I agree. I take solace in the fact that the clinics haven't been raided. But I would rather be safe than sorry. I'm not sure who Malik Rodgers was working for, to be honest. I know Benjamin is important, but I'm kind of hoping it's Justice after all. If it's one of the other three, we could be in some real deep shit."

"Keep us updated, Rucker," Chicago ordered, before his screen went dark. Vegas and Alexandria both logged off without another word, leaving Tristan alone in the bunker with his thoughts.

CHAPTER TWENTY

Two hours before the meeting with Thomas Daniels, Dom sat in a hidden office in the warehouse alternating between idly checking her email, surfing the web, and watching the camera feed monitoring the perimeter of the property. Hidden behind a false wall of the renovated western half of the building, the chamber was constructed as a panic room. She initially created an emergency office space in the area, and over time built out a smaller version of her home office. Although she was careful and never malicious in her hacks, she planned for the possibility of being hunted. The warehouse was registered to one of the few shell companies she owned.

The idea of shell companies and offshore accounts seemed something out of a television show for Dom, who was raised in a lower income single parent household. As her net worth began to grow at an exponential rate, she found the concept extremely beneficial. A large percentage of her investment income was filtered through her various shell companies, taking advantage of the United States' leniency towards corporate America. Rather than accruing taxable interest on her cash surplus, she parked her "rainy day" assets in the more tax-friendly locations of the Cayman Islands and Switzerland.

"Dom, Willie Price has solved the coding puzzles," SARA announced, breaking the silence of the room. Dom transferred her attention to the computer and started typing rapidly to review Willie's solutions. The puzzle she created had several elements. The overall concept was a cross between a maze and the popular game Sudoku. She created five incomplete digital mazes with two objectives. The first goal was to find and finish the code for the missing aspects of each maze; the second was to find the exit. Leaving one labyrinth opened the next until the fifth and toughest level was completed. While she created the game using a basic coding language, the few newbies who attempted to solve it generally took up to two or three weeks. She was surprised that the child cracked the code in under a week. SARA monitored Willie's progress and was instructed to alert her when he finished. She pecked on the keyboard to find the message from the boy.

Smoak? Are you there? I did it! Dom smiled at his excitement, a reminder of her own as she began her journey in self-taught technology. She tapped a few more keys and called up his webcam feed, opening his microphone at the same time.

I'm here. I see you, so you can talk. Good job kid. That's faster than most adults, she wrote. Willie turned his attention to the camera with a grin of pride.

"What now?" he asked.

Now, I want you to build me a website. It can be whatever you want it to be, but you can't use a design program. You can only build it in code, she replied. His face converted from excitement to confusion.

"A website? What for?"

Whatever you want. You seem to like DC comics, build me a fan site for DC.

"Okay, but what is it for?" he pressed, his face still holding a perplexed expression.

Part of coding is creativity. I need to know what you can do with a blank slate.

"But, I've never built a website before," he replied, his tone worried.

I hadn't either; until I did. You can use Google to research ideas, check the code of other websites, whatever you want. I need to know what you understand. It will help me figure out what you already know and how you learn, she typed. Willie's face lost the confused look, and she could see the boy pondering her words.

"I will research it and try. It may take me a little while," he warned.

I expect that. You need something that will keep you out of other people's networks anyway. I'll pop in on you to check on your progress from time to time.

"What about a web address?" he inquired anxiously. Dom opened a new window on another monitor and purchased a domain name, registering the URL to Willie's email address.

Check your email. He began typing on his own computer, his eyes lit up when he read the contents.

"Wow! Thanks, Smoak!"

One more thing. Stop skipping school. Those kids may be jerks, but your time with them is temporary. What you learn in school is permanent. Don't miss out on your education because other kids are assholes, she counseled. The speed at which he solved the puzzles showed that he was intelligent and gifted. Her history made it easy to empathize with the difficulty of getting out of bed and going to school just to be bullied; however, she did not want him to derail his life simply to avoid the tormenters.

"Okay. I will," he agreed, his eyes dropping from the webcam.

Gotta fly.

"Thank you, Smoak. I don't know why you're helping me, but thank you," he said, lifting his eyes from the keyboard and staring into the camera.

People like us have to stick together. Life can kick us when we're down; but believe me, it only toughens you up for the rest of it. It gets better. Those jerks may be knocking down your door one day for a job. He allowed a grin to take over his features when he read this message. Before the boy could say anything more, she extracted herself from his network.

Smiling, she leaned back in her chair and thought about what more she could do for young Willie Price. She tried to shift her mind back in time to when she was his age and contemplate what could have helped her. She remembered feeling the pain of her mother's death and being desperate for something to keep her mind occupied. The website was a spur of the moment decision. Advancements in technology allowed just about anyone to get online and post a website. Although coding a site was time-consuming, it could be one of the most rewarding projects. She remembered the pride she felt after she built her first page, long before Internet companies offered their assorted templates. She hoped the project would not only teach Willie the art of patience but would also build his confidence.

"Dom, may I ask a question?" SARA's avatar appeared on the upper left quadrant of the four monitors.

"You just did," she quipped. "But I assume that wasn't the question you had in mind. What's up?"

"You have indicated on numerous occasions that you don't care to interact or speak with people. However, I've noticed you have chosen to help Willie Price, despite meeting him as he was trying to infiltrate your network."

"None of that sounded like a question," Dom pointed out.

"Why? Why would you choose to assist this boy?"

"He reminds me of me when I was his age. He just lost his mother, his dad works a lot, and he gets bullied. He's lost, lonely, and hurting. Kids probably look at him and think he's weird," she replied, her voice soft with the memory of childhood.

"You only met him a few days ago, how could you possibly know he is in pain and lonely?" SARA wondered.

"His eyes," she answered, her voice barely above a whisper. "It's a nuance that even organics don't always notice, but I do. Unfortunately, empathy is not a trait I can program."

"I understand more than you believe I do. I recognize Willie has lost his mother and can see the logic in his sadness. I suppose what I do not comprehend is why others would torment someone who is despondent," SARA confessed. "While empathy may not be an innate trait of all humans, surely sympathy is ingrained within humanity."

"As I said, some people feel too much, and others not enough. Sadly, it seems humankind is shifting more towards not enough," she disclosed. "These days, people don't even try sympathy, unless the circumstance affects them directly."

"Rose Jenkins is almost here," SARA announced, abruptly changing the subject.

"Are you still tracking her?" Dom asked, leaning in to examine the Internet map that SARA opened, revealing Rose's blue spot approaching the building.

"Yes. You did not direct me to cease. I am also tracking the phones of Miss Green and Miss Vasquez," SARA replied.

"Maybe that's not a good idea," she advised, using her mouse to zoom out on the map. She spotted another two blue marks on top of each other, representing Layla and Vasquez. The two women were riding together, and their location was further north than the dot representing Rose.

"To my recollection, none of the parties requested you terminate the action, and they all are aware of your technical capabilities. Also, I believe it's prudent to continue to track them, particularly as you get to know them," SARA argued. Her placid avatar gave the impression of innocence.

"You sound like a worried mother. What do you think they'll do; kidnap me?" Dom smiled.

A small beep from the corner of the room drew her attention, and she glanced at the panel of surveillance displays in time to see a gray Toyota easing to a stop in the parking area. Three people emerged from the vehicle, and she immediately recognized Rose and Robert Jenkins. The bald third man was quite a bit taller than both, with a jagged scar on the right side of his face.

"Who's that?" Dom wondered. SARA, finally picking up on the concept of rhetorical questions, did not respond.

She watched the trio approach the entrance, and when Robert attempted to open the door, he found it locked. The taller man moved him to the side and tried to gain entry, having no more luck. The threesome exchanged dialogue, and Dom noticed Rose inspecting the entrance. Her golden eyes found the camera, and then she dropped her scrutiny to the scanner. She studied the biometrics for a moment, and then looked back at the camera and frowned. Stepping to the silver plate, she put her eye to the scanner; the locks disengaged, and she opened the door for the astonished men. Dom grinned.

"Quicker than I thought. I guess I'll go and welcome our guests."

"I already have," SARA responded. "Miss Jenkins loves my avatar."

The three Jenkins siblings turned away from SARA's new avatar when they heard the hidden door of the panic room slide open in time to see Dom emerge from the false wall. Rose raised an eyebrow of mild surprise at the display, while Robert and Ryan openly gawked.

"You're early," Dom said, approaching the siblings.

"What was that?" Robert asked, watching the wall panel slide to cover the entrance of the chamber.

"Panic room," Dom shrugged. She eyed Ryan before turning to address Rose. "Who's your friend? He looks like him," she pointed at Robert, "but bald."

"This is our brother Ryan," Robert answered, extending his hand between the two strangers as a method of introduction. "Ryan, this is Dominique Samuels." Ryan extended his hand, and she stared at him for a beat before accepting the handshake.

"You can call me Dom. I thought you were overseas in the Army."

"I just got out," he replied. She nodded and turned to face Rose.

"Care to fill me in?"

"Can we talk?" Rose asked. "Alone?" Dom studied her for a second, nodded, and turned back to the hidden office, indicating with her head that Rose should follow. The door slid open as she approached and she stepped to the side motioning for Rose to enter first, then she followed her into the room. As the door closed, she heard Robert speaking to his brother.

"That is so freaking cool!"

Dom motioned for Rose to take a seat next to the desk and plopped herself into the office chair. Rose looked around the room as she sat down.

"Looks familiar," she observed.

"I'm a creature of habit, surely you've picked up on that."

"Which is why we're early; I needed to talk to you about Ryan," Rose nodded.

"The floor is yours."

"He just retired after twenty years in the Army. During that time, he had multiple deployments in Afghanistan," she began. Dom responded with a curt nod. "He saw some things over there that really messed him up."

"Does he have PTSD or something?" Dom asked. Rose made a face and shook her head.

"No, not that I have perceived," she replied. "Then again, he's only been back a few days. He just saw some things that are weighing on him emotionally. He joined the Army right out of high school to find his way in life. The time he spent deployed made him realize that he was just a boy being sent to risk his life for someone else's cause. It made things worse that the cause didn't exactly align with his values."

"I'm sure."

"Now he's back home, trying to find a job to support his wife and two girls, who are coming stateside this summer, and he feels more lost than he did when he left twenty years ago. He says he feels unclean, and he needs to do something to make up for the last few years fighting a war that wasn't his. He wants to do something for his own people. Rob and I want to give him that," Rose finished.

"Noble," Dom declared evenly. "I suppose it has nothing to do with the fact that your family has already lost two siblings, and Ryan is worried about you and Robert being looped into a case where one person has recently been murdered." Rose flinched a little at her very astute delineation.

"I won't lie. It's both," she agreed.

"Well, I'm glad that in the list of attributes you may have picked up about me, naïve is not among them," Dom smirked. "So, you decide to come early and talk me off the ledge before I even start walking to the window?"

"That was kind of the plan, yes."

"I see," Dom nodded. "I have already become acquainted with you, Rachel, Layla, and Robert. Why did you decide this was the time to pull me aside?"

"Because the four of us were shoved onto you by an outside force. I'm bringing Ryan in personally. It would be disrespectful to do so without speaking to you about it. If I were to cause more anxiety without explaining myself and getting you to see the motivations, how trustworthy would I be?" Rose asked.

"Fair point."

"I understand why you brought us here. I admire you for finding a way to take back your home. I just want to say I appreciate you bending when I know that it can't be easy. I can tell you're the type to do the right thing, even if it's uncomfortable. I respect that about you," Rose disclosed, in a gentle voice. "The others may not understand how hard this is for you, but I do. If you ever need to talk about it, I'm here." With these words, Dom erupted into a fit of laughter. Rose blinked at her reaction, unsure of the reason for the outburst. "I say something funny?"

"I'm sorry," Dom chuckled, wiping her eyes. "I get what you do, but I'm okay. Let's see how this plays out, try not to get killed, then maybe I'll make an appointment." Her voice retained the amused quality. "You all seem to think I'm some fragile person, and you have to walk on eggshells around me. I appreciate you explaining why you brought another brother. But just because I'm reclusive, doesn't mean there's anything wrong with me. I just choose not to be around people. I'm not some charity case or someone on the verge of a mental breakdown. Believe me, if I didn't want to do this, I wouldn't. You're very right, this is uncomfortable for me, and the others may not realize how much. But I'm not fragile, and I'm not afraid." By the end of her speech, the humor disappeared from her tone. Rose studied her for a moment.

"You aren't fragile, I never thought that."

"I appreciate you talking to me about Ryan. I understand his rationale. I've seen some pretty messed up things in my life, but I won't even pretend like it compares to what he just went through. If this is what he needs, I wouldn't think of getting in his way," Dom said.

"I'm glad to hear that."

"You didn't know that's how I'd feel about it? Aren't you the profiler?" Dom grinned.

"Not everyone is easy to read, obviously." A beep in the corner called Dom's attention, and she stood and moved to the security feed. Rose joined her at the wall of displays, and she watched Vasquez's silver Jetta park next to her Camry.

"Let's see how long it takes them to find the scanner. You were quick; I was impressed," Dom admitted, glancing at Rose.

"To be honest, I wasn't expecting you to have my biometrics on file. If I didn't know you were harmless, you would be terrifying," Rose replied, not turning away from the displays.

"I didn't have it; your scan gave it to me."

"How did you know I would be the one to scan us in?" Rose mused.

"I may not be a profiler, but I know a leader when I see one." It took Layla less than two minutes to identify the biometrics and submit to a scan. "Shall we?" Dom asked, strolling to the wall panel, which opened upon her approach. Layla and Vasquez walked to the center of the open area, ogling the surroundings. Dom approached the newcomers and nodded a greeting.

"So, about this?" Layla asked, waving her hands around to indicate the building.

"I bought it a couple of years ago; I have two of them. It's mostly used to store offsite servers and tech toys. It also serves as a place to go in case my pastime gets me into some hot water," Dom explained, glancing around the room to find the men. She spotted them examining her classic cars; and when Vasquez followed her gaze, her mouth dropped open.

"Is that a '69 Charger?" she gasped. Dom cocked her head in surprise.

"It is."

"V6?" Vasquez asked, receiving a tongue click in response.

"Don't insult me. It's a V8. I should know, I rebuilt the engine myself." Vasquez let out a small squeal and rushed to the car.

"You have *got* to let me drive this!" she exclaimed, poking her head into the ride through the open driver's side window. Layla rolled her eyes.

"I'd apologize for her lack of home training, but surely you're used to it by now," she sighed.

Rose introduced Layla and Vasquez to Ryan, before setting off with Layla and Robert to tour the warehouse. Ryan and Vasquez studied each of the classic cars and chatted as if they had known each other for years. Dom relocated to the large conference table, leaned against it, and watched the crowd get acclimated to the new area. The door rattling brought everyone back from their various discussions and tours. They converged on Dom's location at the table as she turned to the monitors on the wall.

"Show me the security feed, SARA," she commanded. One of the screens turned on, and the group saw Thomas Daniels outside the door, trying to gain access. Dom watched the man notice the eye scanner and bend down to align himself with the reader. The red light danced across his iris, but the system emitted a long buzz, indicating that he would not be allowed admittance in that manner. Dom sauntered to the door.

"No super cool entrance for him?" Robert asked.

"I don't know him, or trust him like that," she replied.

"You don't know us either," Layla pointed out.

"True, but this gives you people a place to go, other than my damn house." She pushed open the door to allow the guest of honor admission into the building.

CHAPTER TWENTY-ONE

"The gang's all here, Thomas, and we're all thirsty for knowledge," Dom informed the man when he entered the building. Thomas followed her into the large interior. He regarded his surroundings and let out a low whistle.

"This is quite a place," he praised. She nodded in appreciation but did not repeat the rundown she had given Layla of how and why she obtained the building. He infiltrated her life uninvited, withheld information, gave away her personal contact data, and ultimately turned her life upside down all in one afternoon. She did not feel she owed the man anything more.

Dom led the newcomer to the circular conference table, and found all of the other occupants had already found a place, leaving two seats open opposite of each other. Thomas smiled at the assembly, as he took a seat between Layla and Rose. To Layla's right sat Vasquez and to her right was Ryan. To Rose's left was Robert, leaving the open seat between the Jenkins brothers for Dom. In front of each chair lay a fully charged tablet, pen, writing pad and a bottle of water. Dom fell into her seat, picked up her tablet, and tapped rapidly, connecting herself to the internal system with SARA. She typed a quick command directing the AI to remain silent.

"Proceed," she said, once she was done. Thomas nervously took in all of the occupants at the table, his eyes stopping on Ryan.

"I recognize all of you from our chat last weekend, but you are new," he noted.

"Sergeant First Class Ryan Jenkins, US Army, retired," he nodded. Thomas shifted his gaze to Rose.

"Another brother?"

"We Jenkinses are all about nepotism, what can I say?" she shrugged.

"I hope you came here with information about Malik, and more details pertaining to your organization," Dom advised.

"I'll begin with the subject of which I have the most information; what brought me to you, to begin with," he replied, unbuttoning his suit jacket and relaxing in his chair.

"This is your party," Dom nodded.

"Imagine a tree," he began. "At the base of any tree, what gives the tree sustenance and helps it grow, are the roots. The roots are the most important part of any plant. Whether you are thinking of a corporate business, social justice or any true project, it works just like that; you have to have strong roots. For us, the basis is the ideal of justice by any means necessary. That ideal is what feeds the rest of the tree, just like the idea or innovative concept would feed the success of any business. To answer the question of where we got our start, or who is behind the group, that is something that cannot be easily satisfied. The concept of equality has been one that has existed since we were first brought over from Africa on those boats and put into chains. Well, most of us." Thomas' glance lingered on Vasquez, who returned his look with a glare of indignation.

"Okay, Tommy Boy, let's just get one thing straight," she growled. "I'm one hundred percent Mexican. My mother was born in Monterrey, Mexico. My father was born in San Antonio, but he is a first-generation American from parents who crossed the border from Chihuahua, Mexico. I get that I probably could have cooked a little more; but believe me, I know who and what I am. If it were up to me, this would not be a conversation, people assume things. Black people aren't the only ones that come in different shades. I may have the advantages of being perceived as a White girl, but it's not something I want or ask for. I can never understand what it's like to be Black in this country. I know it can't be easy. What I do know, is how hard it is to be Brown. I may be tall and fair skinned, but my brother Eddie is clearly Mexican. We both got teased because of our accents, and called wetbacks regularly, despite being born here. My brother has been harassed by cops and profiled as a criminal. I watched my father, a fucking doctor, be second-guessed by his patients and their families because he was Mexican. People didn't even believe I was my own mother's child, they thought she was my nanny! So, don't treat me like I'm some random Becky here to make herself feel better. Layla is my best friend, anything bad that could happen to her would profoundly affect me; she's virtually all I have left." Her voice broke with that statement. "I'm here because I want to be because this fight isn't just for you, it's for everyone. I can't control everyone else, but I can control me." As she spoke, a subtle accent emerged, and the group saw tears collecting in her emerald eyes when she glanced around the table. "Are we all clear on who I am, and why I'm here?" The crowd was rendered mute by her rant and returned her stare in silence. Layla placed a hand on her shoulder and gave it a gentle squeeze.

"I know why you're here, Rach. If they don't want you, they don't want me," she declared in a soft voice. Thomas nervously cleared his throat.

"You're right Ms. Vasquez," he agreed. "This fight isn't just for Black people, Brown people, or LGBT people. It's for everyone. I apologize for any presumption. Please know, I meant no offense, and I personally welcome you into the fold. My point was, this struggle has been going on for generations. We have made strides; we are no longer enslaved, we can vote, we don't have to use separate water fountains, and you could get married if you wanted." He glanced at Dom when he mentioned marriage.

"So you keep reminding me," she mumbled.

"It feels like every concession we are given is used as a smokescreen to hide other injustices. We know this is a long battle. The trunk of the tree is composed of those of us who are able to organize and have the ability to direct certain operations. I suppose if I had to give myself a role, I would be a part of the trunk. We are the ones who try to look at aspects of the country that could use more representation or have egregious miscarriages of justice, and develop a plan to remedy them. Much of our funding is fed to the trunks, and we use our discretion on how to best use the funds to make a difference. We then try to implement those plans with the use of the branches. If you were to accept my proposal, your group would be a branch. Just like any large tree, there are several branches, and they are generally self-regulating. Often, these people don't know each other unless they are working together. They exist in various areas such as law enforcement, education, corporate America, and so forth. Malik was also a branch," he explained, this time moving his gaze to Layla, who nodded in understanding.

"So each of you, trunks, get funding from various sources. Do your contributors know what they are financing?" This question was posed by Rose.

"They know the identified problem, but they normally don't want to know the how. Most of the funding avenues are non-profit, so it's a win-win."

"Talk to me about your little group of people who banned together and came up with the idea for us," Dom requested.

"As I said, I cannot divulge those people. Many are in the music, entertainment, and sports industries, among others."

"If I wanted to know bad enough, I could find it," she informed him.

"I'm not so sure that's true. We met in a park with no media or cameras present. We wanted to discuss this sudden uprising in the killing of our people and the stripping of rights and protections by the government. This was not for show, it wasn't to pretend like we care, we wanted to develop a plan of action," he said. "Once it was determined, we all made monetary commitments to fund the effort, and I was put in charge of making it happen. We likely will not meet again."

"How did they know you wouldn't just take their money and split?" Ryan asked.

"Most of them know me," Thomas smiled. "They know I'm just as committed to finding a way to abate this crisis as they are. This isn't just some mode of philanthropy for me. This is as much for the good of my own skin as it is for people I don't know. I'm just as much of a target as Timothy Cook in Milwaukee, Trayvon Martin in Florida, or Ramarley Graham in New York. It only takes running into the wrong officer one time for any of us in this room to end up dead. This is as much for self-preservation as it is for the betterment of our country." The room grew silent with this statement; the occupants ruminating on his words, feeling the weight of the truth he spoke.

"Tell us about Malik," Layla directed, after a moment.

"Malik and I grew up in the Maryland Washington DC area. He joined the DOJ shortly after law school and became really good at undercover prison work."

"Undercover?" Robert asked.

"The DOJ has its hands in a lot of pots. Malik specialized in the investigation of courts and prisons. If his division received evidence of judicial misconduct or heinous prison conditions, sometimes he would go undercover within an institution to learn what he could from the inside. This would prevent prisons from lying or covering things up to thwart a Justice investigation," Thomas advised. "Justice would create a fictional background and rap sheet for him, slip it into whatever state system he needed to be in, and he would get in on a prison transport with no one at the receiving institute being the wiser. When it was time to extract him, they would send someone representing the Federal government to pick him up as a witness or person of interest in a Federal case. As much as the states hate it, Federal will always trump State." Rose sighed in annoyance.

"I knew you knew more than you were saying," she grumbled, glaring at Thomas. "Why didn't you just tell us what he was doing here when we spoke?"

"Because I know what he does, but I don't know what he was doing *here*," he replied, his tone apologetic. "Malik's investigations are classified. He never gave me details about who or what he was investigating. He was only allowed to tell me the city or state where he would be."

"Seems kind of risky, doesn't it? Going into the prison system like that? A lawyer?" Ryan frowned.

"His job wasn't the safest in the world, but he was trained in hand-to-hand combat by the folks at Quantico. He knew how to handle himself."

"Wait, he was trained by the FBI?" Dom asked, her eyes wide with surprise.

"Malik could have easily gone into the FBI or CIA, but he chose Justice because he wanted to try to help dismantle the corruption and disparity in the judicial system. He was very well trained. They also made sure to put him with a non-violent cellmate so he could sleep at night," Thomas admitted, turning his eyes to Robert.

"They chose me?" Robert questioned, a dubious look on his face.

"Malik did. I don't know why. I just know that when he goes in, he's paired with a non-violent cellmate so that being murdered in his sleep is less likely to occur," Thomas shrugged.

"You were going to speak to your contact at the DOJ to figure out what he was doing here," Layla reminded him.

"I tried. I spoke with Malik's boss, Nancy Bennett. She's the person who recruited him, trained him, and was his handler when he was in the field. She said she couldn't tell me anything. Since Malik died during the investigation, that classified coding doesn't just fall off. In fact, she said she couldn't even access the information."

"Time out," Rose spoke up, holding her two hands in the shape of a capital T. "You literally just said she was his handler when he was in the field. So, someone is lying. Either you are, or she is; because there's no way she wouldn't have known what he was working."

"I thought it was weird too, believe me! I swear, I'm telling you the truth," he claimed, extending his hands in a pleading gesture.

"Did she say why she couldn't access the information?" Ryan probed, stroking his scar thoughtfully.

"Something about it being subterranean," he replied. Layla stiffened at his words and turned her wide-eyed stare to Dom, who returned her glance in bewilderment.

"What?" she asked.

"What did she say exactly, Tom?" Layla inquired, clearly agitated. Thomas cocked his head in curiosity and then closed his eyes to call up the memory.

"She said, I don't know what to tell you, Tom. This case is bigger than Malik or me. It's subterranean, even I can't breach that," he repeated, opening his eyes as it came back to him. Layla gasped.

"Tom, is Nancy Bennett one of you? Like, is she a part of this group?" she prodded.

"How could you…" he stammered, but Layla put her hand up to cut him off.

"Dom," she hissed.

"Layla," Dom frowned, still uncertain of what made the woman so jittery.

"The messages," Layla whispered. Dom stared at her for a long moment, and then the significance struck her so hard, she exhaled explosively. At the same time, an identical blow of clarity crashed into Vasquez.

"Holy shit," Dom and Vasquez gasped. Dom picked up her tablet and began to tap on the screen swiftly, while the Jenkins family and Thomas exchanged baffled glances and eyed each woman.

"Does anyone want to fill the rest of us in?" Rose asked. Dom flicked her hand at Layla, keeping her attention focused on the tablet.

"Right before he was killed, Malik was playing video games, a first-person shooter. Was he a gamer?" Layla posed this question to Thomas, who nodded in assent.

"We both are, we grew up playing together."

"When we showed up, the load-out screen was up," she continued, eyeing him knowingly. Thomas immediately understood her point.

"You think someone heard the murder?"

"That was the initial thought. That's how Dom and I linked up. She found my crime report with the detail of Malik's body, specifically the tattoo, and," she hesitated, glancing at Dom who was engrossed in her research. Sensing Dom clearly had no desire to let Thomas know about SARA, she adjusted the story. "She reached out to me offering to help hack the console. She hasn't had much luck; those big gaming companies have some weird proprietary code she hasn't figured out. But she did find some messages on the system. The messages were to a user NBSubTrn," She spelled the username. "That could translate as, Nancy Bennett, Subterranean." Thomas and the Jenkins gaped at her explanation.

"What did the messages say?" Rose wondered.

"We don't know, they were in code," Vasquez answered.

"Dom couldn't hack the code?" Ryan asked incredulously.

"Not this one," Layla shrugged.

"Ah ha!" Dom exclaimed triumphantly. The crowd turned to her in expectation.

"It's going to take me some digging, but she chose those specific words for a reason. I assume you told her about us?" Dom asked, glancing at Thomas who nodded. "Subterranean is an operation. I will have to poke around a little more to see if I can find what it was about, but there's some data remanence on a lower security server that has pieces of information here."

"There was what now?" Rose frowned.

"Data remanence," Dom replied distractedly. Vasquez leaned across the table and put her hand on Dom's arm, lowering the tablet.

"For those of us who don't speak nerd, can you please define data remanence?" Vasquez inquired patiently.

"Data remanence is what is left over after a file deletion. Most people don't know that simply deleting a file doesn't fully erase it. There are usually pieces of data left over. Sometimes a brilliant mind can reconstitute said pieces and make out what it once was," Dom grinned, pointing to herself with pride.

"You know, my favorite thing about you is your humility," Vasquez beamed. Dom turned to her and stuck out her tongue, prompting her to add, "and your maturity."

"So, what did this data remembrance stuff tell you?" Robert asked.

"Remanence," she corrected. "It's not a lot; it looks like an incomplete list of names."

"I have an idea about this code thing," Thomas offered. This statement drew Dom's attention from her tablet to the man.

"You know the cipher?" she asked. Thomas shook his head.

"Not necessarily. I wouldn't know without looking at it. When we were kids, Malik and I used to come up with random codes using books we both read. As we got older, to make it harder, we would use multiple books."

"You think that's the type of cipher Malik was using for work?" Dom pressed.

"I honestly don't know, but if you can't find a specific key on the DOJ servers, it could be," he shrugged.

"You see any books at the apartment?" Rose directed this question to Layla, who nodded in the affirmative.

"He had a few," she replied closing her eyes. "To Kill a Mockingbird, The Color Purple, Letter from the Birmingham Jail, Crossing Borders, and Emperor Mollusk versus the Sinister Brain." Layla opened her eyes and glanced at Thomas.

"Are you sure?" Dom prodded. Layla frowned and stared at her.

"Are you sure about your data reminiscing?"

"Okay, now you're just messing with me."

"A tad," Layla smiled with satisfaction.

"Any of that ring a bell?" Vasquez asked Thomas.

"When he was going to be gone for months like he was this time, he always took To Kill a Mockingbird, The Color Purple, and Letter from the Birmingham Jail. Those were his favorite three reads growing up. He said that his time in any given prison was more waiting to speak to his target, and reading kept him occupied. Those last two, I've never heard of." Dom immediately began to tap on the tablet. As if knowing she had an idea, the crowd remained silent while she searched. Staring intently at the device, she suddenly frowned.

"What?" Rose prompted.

"Part of the messages include the ISBN numbers for those two books," she informed the group.

"ISBN?" Robert asked.

"International Standard Book Number. All books have a ten or thirteen-digit number that identifies a book or audiobook; every one of them is unique," Dom clarified.

"You think they used those two books as the key to their code?" Layla pondered.

"Maybe, but it would take a while to decipher how they used them. It's just... I find it weird that the ISBN number is there at all. You would think if those two books were the key, there would be no need to identify unless you start the message with them; then it would make sense. But these two ISBNs are in the middle of a message, right next to each other," she explained, scratching her temple in deep thought.

"What are those books about anyway?" Ryan asked. The gathering all regarded each other, to see if anyone was familiar with the works. When no one spoke, Dom began to tap on the tablet again.

"Crossing Borders is basically an autobiography of sorts from a Mexican American named Sergio Troncoso. The other one is a fantasy book about, I don't know... a mollusk?"

"That's strange. Seems like quite a leap from classics like To Kill a Mockingbird, The Color Purple, and Dr. King's book, to a science fiction book about a mollusk. Was Malik a closet sci-fi fan?" Rose asked Thomas, who shook his head in the negative.

"No, not really."

"Who wrote the sci-fi book?" Ryan inquired. Dom consulted her tablet once again.

"A. Lee Martinez," she replied.

"Which came first in the message?" Layla asked, a pensive expression on her face.

"Troncoso's came first, followed by Martinez." The group fell silent once again, trying to piece together the puzzle. Suddenly Robert jerked, and his eyes went wild.

"I think I got it," he exhaled. He went quiet and his eyebrows creased in deep thought.

"Well?" Vasquez prodded.

"Sergio Martinez," he announced. "He was in the same prison as Malik and me. He got there about eight months before Malik did. Yeah, I remember seeing those two huddled together a few times."

"He ever tell you why?" Layla asked. Robert shook his head.

"I never thought to ask."

"Guys?" Dom called, drawing the group's attention. "Sergio Martinez is one of the names on this incomplete list from the DOJ."

"Is he still in Huntsville?" Vasquez asked. Dom tapped around on the tablet and then nodded in confirmation.

"So, Sergio Martinez may be the first tangible clue we have. Which brings me to another issue," Layla revealed. The crowd turned to face her as one. "Detective Lewis."

"Who's that?" Thomas asked, noticing the nervous energy that settled onto the group.

"The lead detective on Malik's murder investigation. He's good, really good. He's like a dog with a bone if he catches a scent. Let's just say giving him your aunt's name was the proverbial steak being waved in front of him. I promised him I would tell him when I had something actionable. Sergio Martinez is actionable," she replied.

"Leave me out of it," Dom warned, prompting Vasquez to wave a dismissive hand in her direction.

"Everything is not about you," she snapped. "Lewis is a good cop. I understand in today's climate, that declaration isn't always met with immediate acceptance, but believe me, he's a good detective. He just wants to find this killer and get him off the streets."

"The thing is, I can't fully keep him out of this," Layla expressed, motioning the crowd in a wide circular gesture.

"How trustworthy is he?" Robert asked.

"We trust him," Layla replied quickly. "And he trusts me."

"You guys also work with him. We need a third-party view," Dom said. She turned her gaze to Rose.

"I guess that is why Tom chose me," she shrugged. "I need to meet with this Detective Lewis. I can pose as the cousin." Layla shook her head slowly.

"No, you can't. I told him the cousin was male."

"I'll go," Ryan volunteered, after a moment. "We are siblings. If I'm there, you can say Rose is my sister, which is true."

"Set it up; but not in the police department itself. Malik was working a delicate Federal investigation. This needs to be handled very carefully. I'll let Nancy know that you will be working with the detective assigned to Malik's case and that you will try not to cross into the DOJ's case." This instruction came from Thomas, drawing a glare from Layla.

"We will do what we have to do," she informed him.

"All I'm asking is that you try," he implored.

"I will be working the DOJ angle, see what I can dig up on this Subterranean thing. I didn't want to have to hack in, but I think Nancy gave you that info as a way to get me to look into it. It's probably best we don't jeopardize her job," Dom asserted.

"A good theory and we both would appreciate that. The more people we have in the Justice Department, the better."

"Got anything for us?" Robert inquired hopefully.

"You and Ryan can report for work first thing tomorrow morning. Eight o'clock sharp," Dom instructed, causing the siblings to exchange baffled glances.

"Say who to the what now?" Ryan asked, running the words all together, causing the six words to sound like one.

"Work. You and Robert work here now," Dom repeated.

"Dom, I know you've spent the past few years alone; but sometimes you have fully formed thoughts that aren't vocalized. Can you catch us up?" Rose inquired.

"Robert needs a job to satisfy his probation. Ryan just got out of the Army. If we're going to be doing this, they may as well get paid for it," Dom clarified.

"What will we be doing exactly?" Ryan wondered.

"You will be the head of security; and for now, we'll call Robert an executive assistant. How does fifty-thousand a year sound; plus, benefits and a retirement plan that I'll manage?" Dom asked, glancing at Robert.

"Are you serious?" Robert gasped in awe.

"What? Too low?"

"No! I mean, thank you!"

"And you, sir, will make sixty-five thousand, plus benefits and a retirement plan. The benefits will include private insurance. We all know the VA isn't always the best option for vets, and we can only attack one issue at a time," Dom informed Ryan, who gawked at her. Rose looked between her brothers before turning her eyes to Dom.

"You'd do that for them?" she asked, her voice heavy with emotion.

"Of course. Why not?"

"How can you afford this?" Vasquez mused, her face mirroring the shock of the Jenkins family.

"While I could, I'm not paying for it…he is," she replied, nodding her head to Thomas, who blinked in surprise.

"Come again?"

"I read your financials. I'm going to need access to the entire vault of funds set aside for this endeavor. I'm still not saying yes to running this whole thing because I think it's crazy. But I can grow your money in a fairly short time. And if I do decide to do this, I do it, purse strings and all," she said, her voice serious and authoritative. He stared at her for a beat, before allowing a grin to take over his features.

"I knew I liked you, Dominique," he declared.

"It's hard not to," Vasquez smiled.

"You only like me because I feed you," Dom sighed.

"No, I like you because you're fascinating. I may marry you because you feed me," she replied with a wink. Dom's eyebrows wrinkled, as she looked at Vasquez in shock.

"What?"

"Gotcha" Vasquez smirked, pointing a finger gun at Dom, drawing a chuckle from the other occupants in the room.

CHAPTER TWENTY-TWO

Dom snapped her fingers and stood abruptly; in a motion so sudden, Ryan jerked in surprise.

"Don't do that around someone who has been to war," he grumbled, after a deep exhalation. "What's wrong?"

"I almost forgot." She moved from the table to a set of cabinets under the television displays on the western wall. Entering a code on the keypad lock, she opened two of the doors. The group at the table exchanged bewildered glances. When she returned, she was holding three small boxes and laid one in front of Layla, Vasquez and Ryan. She darted back to the cabinets and returned with another three, placing one in front of Rose, Thomas and Robert.

"Presents?" Layla inquired, eyeing the box. Vasquez was the first to open her package and extract a phone. She stared at the gift with a frown.

"Uh, Dom? We have phones." As if to show proof, she withdrew her own cellular device from her pocket and waved it in the air. Dom moved to another cabinet and withdrew a letter-sized envelope. Plopping herself back into her chair, she opened the envelope and poured the contents onto the table. Passing the first two to the Jenkins brothers, who sat on each side of her, she gave each person an item. Ryan picked up the small black object and examined it.

"This is a SIM card," he said.

"Very good," she nodded.

"Dom, you're still doing that thing where you have a full coherent thought in your mind, but you only loop us in at the end. Let's start from the beginning," Rose implored.

"I have built my life around being safe and until recently, being a shadow. Being sloppy gets you caught; assuming that you are not important enough for anyone to be interested in you, gets you caught. When we found out who Malik was, I knew this was going to be a sensitive situation. If the DOJ is investigating something that got him killed, we can't assume we will be perfectly safe when we poke our noses into things," she explained. As she spoke, she made rare eye contact with each member of the group. "I am not trying to get killed here, and as much as I may or may not enjoy handcuffs in certain applications, I'm not trying to go to jail either."

"Handcuffs? I like the way you think," Vasquez winked. Dom rolled her eyes at the comment.

"So, these are burner phones?" Ryan asked, slipping his SIM card into the device.

"Yes, but with some modifications," she nodded. "The number on this phone will change on a random schedule, as will the cellular network to make it hard to trace and listen in on calls; there is built in scrambling technology as well. I have modified them to communicate SIM to SIM and the text messages are encrypted. Most importantly, they will only work with each other."

"So, I can't prank call my brother with this?" Vasquez asked, wiggling the phone in the air.

"Sorry, you'll have to be annoying on your own dime," Dom smirked.

"There's security cautious and then there's paranoid," Ryan proclaimed. "You're starting to stray into that second category."

"I have my reasons."

"But this is like an old-school flip phone," Robert complained, powering up his device. "Even I know those are old."

"It doesn't even have internet," Layla noted, examining the mobile in her hand.

"Websites have ways to backtrack sources of traffic. Doing a search from your phone is not a good idea. Any research you need to do should be done within these walls," she explained. "Or the tablets; they are connected to my personal servers."

"I was in the military for twenty years and I don't think even the NSA is this obsessed with security," Ryan disclosed.

"I know what I have seen can't compare to what you have, Ryan; especially given the fact that it was all from behind a screen.

But, I know what the government and criminals are capable of. If you've seen the things I've seen, you'd be as technologically cautious as I am. People don't realize how much is out there and up for grabs; either they don't know, or they feel like it's a small price to pay for convenience."

"But, how did you? I mean, where did you?" Vasquez stammered, in a rare display of speechlessness.

"I keep to myself, I have a lot of time and money, and I'm a genius," Dom grinned.

"There's that modesty again," Vasquez giggled.

"I don't believe I will need a tablet." This announcement came from Thomas.

"You weren't getting one," Dom countered, causing him to flinch.

"Yikes," Layla whispered, throwing a surprised glance to Vasquez.

"Sorry. It's just that I'm still not one hundred percent sure about you, Tom. No offense, but it is what it is," Dom shrugged. Thomas smiled and put his hands up in an understanding gesture.

"I get it.".

"But take the phone; We may need to reach out to you," she added.

"I changed my mind," Rose disclosed, after a few moments of silence. "You are absolutely terrifying."

"I'm just getting started," Dom grinned, turning to her oldest brother. "Ryan, why don't you take a walk with me. Make yourselves at home guys, we'll be back."

Ryan followed her to the panic room door, which opened upon her approach. Stepping to the side of the newly exposed room, she motioned for him to enter. He glanced into the room and his lips morphed into a childlike grin.

"Seriously, that's freaking cool." Dom chuckled as she entered the room behind him. She took the lead and led him to another door, this one having a keypad next to it, and typed in her code. The door slid open and the lights in the next room automatically illuminated, revealing a ten by fourteen-foot antechamber. White walls encased the room of black marble flooring. To the far right was another blast resistant door. Ryan stepped into the middle of the anteroom and turned in a circle.

"It's a room," he noted without enthusiasm.

"You're quick. First the SIM card, now the room; nothing gets by you," she joked, moving to the left and pushing on a small segment embedded in the wall. His puzzled look changed into wonder when the section opened and another keypad was exposed. She entered a six-digit code, and the partition began to rotate. Once the wall completed its one hundred and eighty-degree revolution, Ryan found himself staring at a two column, five-row bookcase. The shelves were filled with weapons of varying sizes from handguns to assault rifles.

"Whoa," he gasped, walking over to the case. Dom slid open the two drawers in the middle of the shelf, and exposed boxes of ammunition, various holsters, three throwing knives and a knife belt.

"Still not impressed by my room?"

"Someone has watched a few too many action movies," he replied. He picked up a Springfield XD tactical forty-caliber handgun, and pulled back the slide to inspect it.

"Perhaps one or two. It's still pretty cool, though," she said, eyeing her weapons. He returned the Springfield and picked up an assault rifle.

"M16? You preparing for war?"

"No, but I have no intention of finding myself unarmed should someone bring war to me," she replied. He returned the assault rifle and walked in front of the case idly running his fingers across the weapons.

"These legal?"

"I paid for them," she responded, watching him caress the various firearms.

"Are they registered?" he asked, turning to face her.

"Are you insane?" she scoffed. "I'm not an idiot." Dom motioned with her head and led Ryan to the reinforced door on the other side of the room. When she opened it, the lights in the next room illuminated. She stepped back and allowed him to enter. This chamber was a shooting range, the view bringing forth a low whistle from the visitor. Three shooting areas were located near the entrance; each housing a set of glasses, ear protection, and targets. He walked to the closest space and glanced down the range.

"What's that? About a hundred yards?"

"One-fifty. It runs parallel to the building. This whole area is as reinforced as the panic room. It probably could have gone to three, but I figured this was good," she replied. He shook his head in admiration.

"What's with all of this, Dom?"

"Rose told me you had a rough time overseas. I don't think we're all that different," she admitted, turning her gaze down-range.

"It was war. It's not supposed to be a picnic," he shrugged.

"No, I suppose not. She explained why you wanted to do this, but I'd like to hear it from you."

"Have you ever been outside in the middle of July after a summer rain, Dom?" he asked, turning his eyes down the range to the solitary target still suspended in the air.

"Are you kidding? This is Houston, I try very hard not to."

"So, then you know what it's like to feel dirty. Even if you were freshly showered, as soon as you hit the outdoors, the grime of the city and atmosphere clings to you. It makes you feel gross," he said, turning his eyes back to her. Dom nodded. "Imagine spending twenty years in that. I feel dirty; I needed to do something to feel clean again." Dom stared at him for a moment before looking down-range.

"Believe it or not, I understand," she admitted, her voice was soft and detached.

"What's your story?"

"That's far too complicated and depressing to go into."

"Ok, how about an easier question: Why did you decide to do this?" he asked. Dom looked down the range in silent consideration. Internally, she asked herself the same question multiple times since meeting Thomas Daniels; yet, she could not find the answer. Now, standing next to a man who possibly had more internal demons than she did, her subconscious rationale clarified.

"I guess…" she hesitated, trying to find the words. "I guess I need to find a reason to believe in people again; same as you." Her voice was soft and small, and Ryan let her words hang for a while.

"Maybe one day, when you are more comfortable with me, we can exchange war stories." Dom regarded the man and noticed he was also looking down the range. The unfocused look in his eyes told her that he was watching the shadows of his not so distant past.

"Maybe," she quietly agreed.

Later that night, Dom entered her home and took a direct path from the garage to her office. While she was en route to her house, SARA informed her via text message that there had been some hits in the search of the DOJ servers. The original exploration, which yielded the incomplete list of names, had been conducted on the least secured servers of the Justice Department. Before she left the warehouse, Dom had SARA scrub the more secure areas in search of the Subterranean operation. The machine was programmed not to communicate to her via the glasses while she was driving, so the text message had been vague.

"Okay, I'm in the office. What did you find?" she asked the computer, falling into her office chair.

"My search into the servers is incomplete, as I am attempting to be inconspicuous. However, I was able to find what appears to be the complete list of prisoner's Malik Rodgers intended to interview during his time undercover," SARA announced, displaying the list of names.

"Good! Let's see what we have here." She reviewed the list of twenty-five individuals that the computer put before her. "That's a lot of people."

"Compared to the population of this country, it is a very small fraction."

"I just meant… you know what? Never mind," she sighed.

"There is something curious," SARA informed her.

"Lay it on me."

"Three inmates are deceased, all within seventy-two hours of Malik Rodgers' death," SARA said, causing Dom's eyebrows to lift in surprise.

"That is curious," she agreed. SARA brought up the three deceased inmates: Eric Taylor, Tommy Cole, and Tavion Evans. Leaning forward in her chair, she scanned each of the jackets. Tavion Evans and Tommy Cole were both held in prison in Dallas, and Taylor was in San Antonio. "There are no obvious ties, except for Evans and Cole being in the same location."

"Which is why I classified the fact as curious, rather than suspicious," SARA clarified. Dom's eyes floated to the screen with the avatar.

"Smart aleck," she grumbled, trading the information of the deceased prisoners for the list SARA was able to obtain from the DOJ server. Each name had an inmate number and location. Dom scrolled down the list in search of Sergio Martinez, the inmate she knew was the closest to her current location. "Is anyone else up in Huntsville with Martinez?"

"Yes, a total of five inmates were from the Huntsville unit," SARA reported. She found the names and segregated them from the list as possible leads. Suddenly, a thought occurred to her.

"SARA, run the prison IDs against the messages we found on the gaming console," she commanded.

"In the correspondence available, four of the inmate numbers appeared within the messages," SARA announced.

"Don't tell me; Cole, Evans and Taylor were three of the four?"

"Yes," SARA confirmed.

"Who is the fourth?"

"Sergio Martinez," the machine replied. Dom frowned.

"That doesn't make sense."

"Why is that?"

"Because Sergio Martinez was identified through the ISBN book numbers. Why would he then be identified by his prison number?" she wondered.

"Without knowing the full content of any of the messages, there is no way to know that," SARA admitted.

"I suppose that's true," Dom conceded. "But wait, Martinez was on the list, and he's still alive?"

"According to current records, yes he is. However, it should be noted that he is currently in solitary confinement," SARA indicated, bringing up an incident report for the Huntsville prison. Dom scanned the document and saw that Martinez had been in a fight a few days before Malik's death, an incident that landed him a week in solitary.

"And you're sure that no other inmate number appeared in the messages?" Dom pressed, her voice carrying an urgent tone.

"Dom, surely you do not think I would be mistaken," SARA chided.

"Call Layla and Rose on our phones. Conference them in. Be quick," Dom ordered, her eyes still on the screen. After a few moments, she heard Layla's voice.

"You missed us already?"

"Development. SARA ran some searches after we dispersed this evening. By the time I got home, she had some juicy stuff," she began.

"Have I told you how much I love SARA?" Layla asked.

"Thank you, Ms. Green," SARA acknowledged, producing an eye roll from Dom.

"We still don't have the messages decoded, but SARA was able to retrieve all of the names from the Subterranean list. They were in several prisons across the state, but something jumped out. Three of the inmates are dead, killed within a few days of Malik," Dom informed them.

"That's not a coincidence," Layla declared.

"It gets better. I had SARA run the inmate numbers from the list against the messages in the gaming system. There were only four hits. Guess who three of them were?" Rose gasped when Dom gave this additional detail.

"The three dead guys," she guessed.

"And for double jeopardy, take a guess at who the fourth one is?"

"Sergio Martinez?" This speculation came from Layla.

"You guys are far better than your files say," Dom confirmed.

"But wait, Martinez is here. Why would Malik be dead and Martinez not? You think he's behind it?" Layla wondered.

"Martinez has been in solitary confinement since just before Malik was killed. I think that's what is keeping him alive. Problem is, he's scheduled for release the day after tomorrow," Dom said.

"Oh no," Rose groaned.

"We have to speed up the timetable for your meeting with Detective Lewis. He's got to get to Huntsville by tomorrow afternoon to save Martinez's life, and try to find out what the hell this is all about," Dom said. The line grew quiet as Layla considered the information.

"I won't be able to speak to him until tomorrow morning," she disclosed. "He's got a kid and a wife at home; I can't call him right now, it's too late."

"Well, you need to do it first thing in the morning. Rose, can you and Ryan meet up with them?" Dom inquired.

"Yeah, we can do whatever is needed. It's on Layla," Rose replied.

"I'll grab Lewis for coffee tomorrow morning, right after the homicide briefing," Layla sighed. "There's a coffee house a few blocks from the precinct, I'll send you an address. Meet us there about a quarter past nine."

"We'll be there," Rose confirmed. "I'll try to feel him out as fast as possible. It looks like we're up against the clock now."

"That's an understatement," Dom muttered. "By the way, I didn't mention in front of Tom, but your tablets are connected to SARA. You guys will have the research power that I have. If you need it, feel free to use it."

"I prefer to think of SARA as a she," Layla admitted.

"I would prefer that as well," SARA added.

"No one asked you," Dom grumbled. "I'll keep digging. Right now, you have to convince Lewis that none of us are crazy, and he's got to get to Huntsville by tomorrow."

CHAPTER TWENTY-THREE

The coffee shop was far more crowded than Rose and Ryan expected, especially at nine in the morning. The two danced through the waiting patrons to find a spot at the end of the line. Ryan surveyed the room nervously.

"Does no one work?" He mumbled to his sister, visually sweeping the room from one side to the other.

"Stop the recon, Sergeant. You're back in civilian life," Rose replied, slapping him gently on the stomach. Her eyes went wide with the contact. "My God, that's rock hard. I need you to train me."

"I love you too much to put you through what I went through," he grinned. "And, don't forget, we grew up in the hood. We have done recon since we were kids." Rose chuckled and nodded. He continued to monitor their surroundings until they finally progressed to the front of the line and ordered their drinks. After they ordered, Rose went to find an empty table, leaving Ryan to wait for the beverages.

Finding a four-person table in the back corner of the coffee house, she sat facing the door and watched Ryan survey the room. Bringing him into this endeavor was a risk, and she was happy that Dom had taken the development in stride. Admittedly, the job proposal both surprised and touched her. Just when she thought she knew what made the reclusive woman tick, Dom would do something to contend with her analysis. A major confliction was how Dom could seem so uncomfortable and miserable in an interpersonal setting in one moment; then come across as the most confident person in the world the next. In a refreshing change of pace, her self-assured nature seemed to be without the insufferable arrogance most confident people conveyed.

Another shocking element to her personality was the leadership Rose witnessed the previous night. During their initial video call with Thomas, Rose assumed that being put on the spot caused Dom to freeze. It was not until she looked into her eyes that she saw the intense rage. While the anger was unexpected, Rose recognized the loner's life had been turned upside down with little to no input from her; causing the resentment to be reasonable. On the ride home, Ryan told his siblings about the weapons cache Dom had taken him to see, which added yet another mysterious layer. Rose wondered why someone who avoided people and socialization would have the arsenal he described. She decided there had been some trauma in Dom's life, and she wondered what happened to her. Ryan did not address what the two discussed in the armory, but Rose could tell that in that short time, Dom had garnered his respect.

"Earth to Rose; come in Rose," a voice sang, startling her from her contemplation. She looked up to find Layla smiling down at her. "You good?"

"Sorry, I was thinking," she blushed. "You shouldn't roll up on people like that."

"I called you twice," Layla replied. Rose's eyes moved to the tall, older man standing next to Layla. He was lean and fit; with short, graying dark hair and the most startling turquoise eyes she had ever seen.

"You must be Detective Lewis," she assumed, standing and holding her hand out in greeting. Lewis nodded and accepted the handshake.

"Oscar Lewis, homicide."

"Thank you for meeting with us on such short notice," she nodded, extending her hand to the chairs in front of her, offering a seat. "My brother is getting coffee. Can we get you anything?"

"No thanks," he replied, settling into a seat across from her, while Layla took the chair next to the cop. Before anyone attempted to make awkward conversation, Ryan approached the table with two cups. He nodded at Layla, and when he glanced at the Detective, Rose noticed a small scowl cross his features. Placing Rose's drink in front of her, he rounded the table and took the space next to his sister.

"Now, before you spin your bullshit tale about you being the cousins of Malik Rodgers, save it," Lewis began. Ryan and Layla exchanged nervous looks, but Rose's eyebrows shot up, and she leaned back in her chair, crossing her arms in intrigue.

"What gave it away?"

"I would be a shitty cop if I couldn't spot a lie like this immediately," he said.

"Try again," Rose smirked. His blue-green eyes studied her for a few beats before he lifted a finger and pointed at Layla.

"Layla inviting me for coffee is what really did it," he replied. "First of all, she doesn't drink coffee, hates the stuff. Secondly, Vasquez actually stayed when Layla told her to, that doesn't usually happen." Rose's smirk spread into a grin.

"Yeah, I can see that about Rachel."

"Finally, and most importantly, I have exactly two cups of coffee a day. One with my wife when I get up in the morning, and another on my way into the precinct. Any more than that and my stomach is messed up the rest of the day. The thing is," he paused and shifted his scrutiny to Layla. "She knows this, and she doesn't forget a damn thing."

"Why did you go along with the charade so easily?" Layla frowned.

"Because you wouldn't have done this if it wasn't important, and I trust you," Lewis shrugged. "But you two are really brother and sister; I can see it in your features."

"I like this guy," Rose declared approvingly.

"So, who wants to tell me what this is about?" he asked. Rose looked at Layla and offered a small nod. She was unsure about the man when he first sat down, particularly given Ryan's reaction when he approached the table; but his assessment of the situation confirmed what Layla already told the group: Lewis trusted her. When he looked at Layla, Rose saw the fatherly affection that he harbored. The trust in his eyes and the affinity he obviously had for Layla made Rose decide that he was indeed trustworthy.

"Everything?" Layla inquired. Rose took in the man for an additional second.

"Yes," she confirmed. Layla began the story with Thomas' visit to Dom's house and recounted all that had taken place over the weekend.

"Wait, an artificial intelligence system hacked our servers?" he interrupted.

"Yes, but Dom didn't know it until after. The computer is kind of her own person," Rose clarified. Lewis scowled, but nodded and instructed Layla to continue. She moved on to the second meeting with Thomas and finished with the call she received from Dom about Sergio Martinez. When she was done, the detective's silent absorption seemed to make the whole room fall silent.

"This is pretty insane," he declared, after his quiet reflection.

"You're telling us," Rose grunted.

"So, you were picked because you're a profiler?" he inquired, looking at Rose. "That's why you're here, to see if I could be trusted?"

"Yes."

"You made the call less than five minutes after meeting me. How do you know?"

"Layla and Rachel have both insisted that you aren't just a good cop, but a good man. Their trust in you helped. But the fact that you came here blindly, knowing Layla was lying to you confirms that you also trust her. When you look at her, I see a fatherly love. You don't just trust her; you love her," Rose summarized. Lewis' ears began to redden, and Layla dropped her eyes to the table. "You also know how to prioritize. Your hackles were raised upon hearing about the hacking, but after all is said and done, that's the least of your concern. That shows that you police with your humanity, and you aren't inflexible. I have a feeling as we figure this shit out, flexibility will become paramount." The table was quiet as the parties took in Rose's words.

"You're good," Lewis smiled, turning to Layla. "You should keep this one around, kid." Layla regarded Rose for a brief second, then turned to Lewis with a grin.

"I knew you love me like a daughter!"

"Don't let it go to your head," he grumbled.

"If I had a dad, I could do worse than you, old man."

"How do you fit in?" Lewis asked, turning to Ryan.

"I just retired from the Army. We have already lost two siblings; I couldn't allow her and my brother to do this without protection," he replied. While Rose and Layla seemed to trust Lewis, Ryan remained wary. The cop reminded him of a drill sergeant from basic training; so much so that when he saw Lewis, the scar on his face began to throb. Despite the uncanny likeness, he tried to put away the knee-jerk reaction and concentrate on the conversation.

"I can respect that," the detective nodded. He moved his attention back to Layla. "So, our victim was an undercover agent for Justice. You don't know what he was investigating, but you know his last location was the prison unit in Huntsville. Your friend Dom, the hacker, was able to get a list of names for the prisoners he was supposed to talk to. Of this list, four names appeared in coded messages on his gaming system. Three of them are dead, the last one is in solitary confinement but scheduled to be released tomorrow, and you believe he will be killed once he's released. Does that sum it up?" Rose and Layla eyed each other, turned to Lewis, and nodded in unison.

"Sergio Martinez is our best lead. If we can figure out what Malik was investigating, perhaps we can get a line on who killed him," Layla explained.

"Why can't we just loop in Justice?" Lewis frowned. "He was their asset."

"We could, but then this investigation will become federal. I know you don't want the feds to take this. I know you better than that," she replied. Lewis' face took on a pensive hue as he considered the options.

"Martinez may not have much time, we can't wait for the feds to get their asses in gear," Rose added.

"I understand that, but I don't like the fact that you guys are working my case for me," he mumbled.

"I know; but we are where we are, Oscar. Like it or not, your case has crossed into our lives. We have our own set of skills to help you with this. It will be your collar, believe me, but we have to do this together," Layla insisted.

"It's dangerous, kid. You're not a cop," he argued, an imploring expression on his face. Rose saw the fatherly concern in his intense stare.

"I may not be a cop, but I can protect her and Rachel," Ryan spoke up. Lewis regarded him with gratitude.

"I'd appreciate that," he nodded.

"I can take care of myself," Layla grumbled.

"I know that. I've been in the ring with you. But it helps me to know that someone has your six," he soothed, patting her arm.

"Does this mean you'll try to get Martinez to safety?" Rose asked.

"I'll head up there after we get back to the precinct," he confirmed. "Honestly, other than his mother, it's the first piece of actionable intel I've gotten on this case."

"Ask for Theo Morrison," Rose suggested. "I spent a lot of time there over the past seven to eight years. Of all the guards, he has always been the nicest and most respectful of the inmates. He genuinely cares about those guys. If you tell him Sergio Martinez is in danger, he will act."

"Theo Morrison," Lewis nodded. "Got it."

"If we get anything else, I'll make sure to tell you," Layla assured him.

"I know you will, kid. For what it's worth, that Daniels guy isn't wrong. I hope you guys know I see the bullshit; like in Milwaukee. We're supposed to protect and serve, not take matters into our own hands. I know I'm one man, but I try to do things in a way that respects everyone," Lewis said.

"I'm sure you do, Detective Lewis," Rose smiled approvingly.

"If you go through with what Daniels asked you to do, anything you need from me, just name it," he continued, eyeing all three people at the table.

"First, let's work on finding Malik Rodgers' killer," Layla said.

⊶⊷

Lewis arrived at the Huntsville prison unit just after one in the afternoon on the same day. During the drive, he pondered ways to ensure Martinez's safety, without compromising Layla and her new friends. There was little he could do to have Martinez moved without going through the courts. However, he also could not put Layla, Rose, or even the mysterious Dom on the stand to explain to the courts why Martinez was in danger. He considered calling the Justice Department, but he agreed with Rose's assessment; the feds would not be fast enough.

He badged his way into the prison and asked to speak with the guard Theo Morrison, who was built like a tank. His hair was shaved clean, his dark brown eyes appeared menacing, and when Lewis shook his hand, his grip was strong and powerful. However, when the big man smiled, his mannerisms changed from intimidating to cheerful in an instant. Rose told Lewis that Morrison genuinely cared about the inmates, and within the first two minutes, he could tell that the profiler was correct in her assessment. Once he informed Morrison of the murder of Malik Rodgers, the prisoner formerly known as Larry Phillips, the guard appeared stricken.

"I always thought Phillips was different, I just couldn't put my finger on how. Robert Jenkins really took to him. He was the first inmate I can remember Rob being friendly with his whole time here," Morrison commented. Lewis continued his tale, informing Morrison that he had information suggesting Sergio Martinez would be in grave danger upon release from solitary. After some discussion, Morrison agreed to pull the appropriate strings and bring Martinez into an interview room to speak with Lewis. The two also decided that the best course of action would be to leave Martinez in isolation for his own protection for the duration of the murder investigation. While the action would likely be received with hostility by Martinez, Lewis assured Morrison that he would explain the situation. The guard directed the detective to a room reserved for meetings between inmates and their counsel, which would afford the men privacy. After assuring the room met his standards for the meeting, Morrison disappeared to fetch the inmate from solitary.

As Lewis sat alone in the small conference room, his mind drifted to the morning meeting he had with Layla and her new friends, Rose and Ryan Jenkins. He was self-aware enough to know that he cared for Layla as he did his own children; a fact he never shared with her, but he assumed she knew. Layla did not strike him as the sentimental type, but despite her guarded personality, he could not help but care for the young woman. He knew very little about her childhood; only that she was an orphan and never knew her parents. He could not understand how she had never been adopted. Layla only briefly mentioned that she was born with health problems that plagued her youth, but had been rectified by the time she reached adulthood. He wanted to know more, but she rarely went into detail. She was almost as cautious with her trust as Lewis was with his, an attribute he believed they both recognized in each other.

He wished he had known the woman as a child. She was smart, sweet, and mentally stronger than most cops he worked with during his two-decade career. Her gut instinct was better than most detectives on the force, but he also was aware that she had an aversion to guns, which prevented her from going to the academy. This was another story he wanted to know, but he was always careful not to press. When he was around her without a suit jacket, he would occasionally see her glance at his exposed weapon with a touch of fear. The fact that she never said anything, despite being surrounded by weapons on a daily basis, solidified her mental strength. Despite her apprehension, he knew that she could take care of herself. He had gone a few rounds with her in the boxing ring and knew she could hold her own. He also was aware that she had a soft spot for kids, something he witnessed when she visited his family.

He still was not completely sure about Thomas Daniels, nor did he trust the man, but he had faith in Layla; she would not be reckless with the safety of herself or Vasquez. He immediately liked Rose and Ryan Jenkins; resting in the knowledge that Ryan, a seasoned combat veteran, would have Layla's back. He was also dubious about the mysterious Dominique, but he could tell Layla, Rose, and Ryan all trusted the hacker. Layla cautioned Lewis that it would be best if she remained the intermediary, as the woman was a little skittish when it came to the police, an understandable feeling considering her pastime.

Lewis' thoughts were jarred back to the present with the explosive sound of the door crashing open. He turned to see the newcomer and jumped to his feet at the sight. Morrison's large frame filled the doorway, his breathing was short and rapid. When he stepped into the room, Lewis saw the blood on his uniform and hands. Tears pooled in the large man's eyes as he tried to speak. Lewis stepped away from his once occupied seat and insisted that Morrison take the chair.

"Breathe, Theo," he coaxed. Morrison closed his eyes and took in a few deep breaths. After a brief time, he was able to collect himself.

"I don't know… I don't know what happened," he stammered. "He's dead. I went to his cell, and he…" His voice trailed off. "It had to be recent; he was still warm. I tried to bring him back, but he lost too much blood. He was stabbed about five times." Lewis dropped into the seat across from him.

"Start from the beginning, Theo."

"I told the Captain on duty that you were here and gave him a brief overview of the situation with Martinez. I was given the go-ahead to bring him to meet with you. I went down to the solitary wing, spoke to the two guards on duty, and went straight to his cell. I didn't pass anyone out of the ordinary. As I was opening the door, I let him know he had a visitor. Solitary prisoners don't get visitations; I thought he'd be on his feet, but he was lying face down on the bed. So now, I'm thinking he's asleep, and I go into the room and shake him, but he doesn't move. That's when I saw the blood," Morrison explained, shaking his head. The detective absorbed the story in deep thought. If he doubted Layla before, which he had not, this was confirmation that whatever breadcrumb trail she was following was the correct path.

"Theo, who would have access to solitary?" he questioned.

"The guards," Morrison shrugged. "All of our keycards work for every door. There are inmates who deliver food and books, but they would have to be accompanied by one of us."

"Do the guards ever let the inmates delivering food and books go on their own?"

"They can't access the wing without a keycard swipe, but sometimes an escort will open the door to the wing, and wait for them to do their thing. If that happens, the guards at security will let them in and out of the rooms," he replied. "Usually, those are prisoners who have been here for years, you know? I would never let an inmate go in on their own."

"I don't suppose you would know which guard was working the wing, and who should have been accompanying the deliveries for today?" Lewis prodded hopefully.

"I'd have to look at the records, but I could find it," Morrison nodded. The cop reached into his shirt pocket, withdrew a business card, and slid it across the table to the shaken man.

"Here's my card. It has my cell number as well as my work line; if you can find that information, could you give me a call?" Morrison's bloody fingers picked up the card delicately and slipped it into his own shirt pocket.

"Yes, sir. I will," he replied, rising from his seat. "Now I have to go fill out an incident report and get everything coordinated to take care of the body. Man, I hate this happened to him. Sergio was in and out, but I could tell this time was different. He wanted to turn himself around." Lewis stood and clapped him on the back.

"I hope to find out who was behind this. Any help you could give me from your end would be welcomed," he declared. The guard walked the detective to the entrance of the prison, where he signed out to leave. Just before he exited the building, Morrison stopped him.

"Detective? How's Robert Jenkins doing?" he inquired.

"I've never met him, just his sister and brother. But from what they tell me, he's doing well," Lewis replied.

"Ryan's back? That's great!" Morrison grinned. "Please tell Rose hi for me. And if you have a chance to meet Rob, tell him I said to remember what I told him."

"What's that?"

"He'll know," Morrison winked, and with that, he was gone. Lewis walked back to his car feeling dejected. The whole point of the trip was to save Sergio Martinez and get answers about the death of Malik Rodgers, and none of that had been accomplished. He extracted the cell phone from his pocket and sent a text message to the number Layla provided before his departure.

"I hope you know what you're doing, kid," he muttered.

I was too late. Martinez is dead, the message read. Dom sighed heavily when she reviewed the words SARA displayed on her screen.

"Call Layla," she commanded. Layla picked up on the second ring.

"What's up?"

"Vasquez with you?" Dom asked. There was a pause, then Layla spoke again.

"You're on speaker."

"Someone got to Martinez before Lewis could," she informed them.

"Shit," Vasquez muttered.

"We need to regroup at the warehouse," Dom advised. The line went quiet for a moment, but she could hear the two women whispering. "You know, the phone may be old, but it does have a mute button. It's far less rude."

"What time?" Layla asked.

"I'll need a day to do some research to find our next trail. Let's do tomorrow," she replied. "When you guys get off work."

"We'll be there," Layla agreed.

"With bells on," Vasquez added, pulling a smile to Dom's lips.

"See you then," she confirmed, disconnecting the call. She turned her attention back to the computer screens and tried to determine a new angle to explore.

"Dom, I was reviewing the information gathered on the four prisoners of interest. There is a curious connection," SARA announced, breaking the silence of the room.

"You are really embracing ambiguity lately."

"The rules of logic dictate that all angles should be reviewed, even if one of the various viewpoints is a coincidence," SARA replied.

"Far be it for me to conflict with the rules of logic," she smirked. "What did you find?"

"All four of the men were either married or in committed relationships."

"That's nice, people should have a partner," Dom noted sarcastically.

"I may not be human, but I understand sarcasm," SARA reproached. "That was not all. When I ran the names of the women they were involved with, I discovered all four of their partners had a medical procedure within a year of the arrest of each man."

"I'm not sure I would call that interesting."

"As I stated, this could be a coincidence, but all factors should be identified. I am not insinuating that this information is an explicit link," the computer clarified, her avatar showing a face of irritation.

"Don't get an attitude with me, young lady. I'll erase your program."

"That makes 1,975 times," SARA advised. Dom rolled her eyes.

"Are you going to give me a countdown every time I say that?"

"If you insist on the pointless warning; I will continue the equally futile count. There is something else," SARA revealed.

"Fire away."

"After you received the message from Detective Lewis, I went into the prison system to find the surveillance data."

"Oh yeah?" Dom asked in surprise. "Let's see what we got." The screen in front of her changed to reveal the closed-circuit camera footage of the Huntsville Prison unit.

"This is the hall outside of the solitary wing," SARA informed her. Dom studied the screen as inmates and guards crossed the camera frame, walking up and down the hall perpendicular to the solitary wing. After a few moments, the picture disappeared, and snow replaced the view of the prison. Before she could open her mouth to ask what happened, the picture returned.

"Go back," she frowned. SARA rewound the video, and when it started again, she leaned forward and stared closely, focusing on the time stamp. When the picture returned from the snowy image once again, the displayed time had jumped forward ten minutes.

"It appears that someone tampered with the surveillance system," SARA offered.

"That's obvious, but thank you. Would you find the blueprint of the prison?" After a few seconds, the lower left screen flashed, and SARA displayed the floor plan of the Huntsville unit. Dom grabbed the computer mouse and took over navigation, zooming in and out of various zones.

"Dom, what are you looking for?" SARA inquired. The hacker did not respond. She continued her review of the floor plan, making mental calculations as she studied the diagram. The more she examined, the brighter the phantasmic lightbulb in her mind illuminated until clarity finally unveiled the truth.

"Oh, this is bad. This is really bad."

CHAPTER TWENTY-FOUR

Vasquez was curled up on her couch, the television remote in one hand, and a glass of white wine in the other. Her black and white Singapura kitten, Miss Havisham, lay next to her. Named after a character in one of her favorite books, Great Expectations, the cat seemed to be as moody and nutty as the character whose name she shared. Miss Havisham's jade green eyes darted around the apartment, as if tracking invisible beings, her white paws batting the air in interdimensional play. Vasquez occasionally regarded the feline with amusement and wonder.

The events of the previous few days had been exciting for her, and a welcome change to the rudimentary day-to-day activities of dealing with dead bodies. Nevertheless, Vasquez felt she needed to decompress from the consistent mysteries, surprises, and uncertain circumstances. When Layla insisted that she would take Lewis to meet with the Jenkins siblings alone, she was actually relieved. She still offered half-hearted protests to prevent Layla from picking up on her reluctance. Her curious nature made her want to see and be a part of everything, but her internal "what the fuck" voice was screaming for her to take a beat and process the events. For Vasquez, processing involved mindless reality television and a ton of wine.

Her hair was tied up in a bun, held with the chopsticks her brother Eddie sent her for her birthday. The gift was an attempt to get her to be more cultured, or something like that. Vasquez preferred burgers to sushi, and when she did eat sushi, she normally used her hands. She was a Texan by birth and appetite, and chopsticks got in the way of her enthusiasm for food. Eddie moved to California for college and remained there, working for some tech company in Silicon Valley. In her opinion, his new home made him look down on the things he grew up with. She figured he wouldn't know the difference if she ate with the chopsticks, use them for her hair, or played darts with them; therefore, her conscience was clear.

Draining the glass of wine in her hand, she reached for the ice bucket that held the chilling bottle and emptied the remainder of the Moscato into her glass. This minor movement caused Miss Havisham to throw her a seething glare before springing from the couch and onto the perpendicular chair. She stood and stretched, collecting the empty bottle and headed to the kitchen to retrieve a full one. An insistent knock on her front door stopped her in her tracks. She checked her watch and saw the time was close to eight-thirty. People rarely visited her home unannounced. The continuous knocking overturned her initial inclination of ignoring the visitor until they went away. She glanced at Miss Havisham. As antiso-cial as her namesake, the cat sprang from the chair and darted to her bedroom where she would assume the post she reserved for the arrival of guests — under the bed. Vasquez placed the wine bottle on the nearest end table and moved to the front door of her second-floor apartment. Next to the entrance, she kept a wooden Louisville Slugger baseball bat, which she grabbed and hefted onto her shoulder.

"Who is it?" she called from her side of the door.

"It's me, Layla. Open up." Vasquez removed the chain, threw the deadbolt, and opened the door to allow her friend to enter. Layla walked into the apartment and closed the door in her wake. Eyeing Vasquez with the bat, she raised her eyebrows. "You owe somebody money?"

"Home security," she shrugged, placing the weapon next to the entrance. "You never drop in without a call. What's wrong?"

"We have a problem," Layla replied, her tone severe. Walking into the living room with Vasquez on her heels, she settled onto the couch, in the same spot Vasquez vacated. She pointed to the glass of wine in an unasked question, then picked it up and took a gulp of the liquid without waiting for an answer.

"What the hell? You don't drink!" Vasquez exclaimed as she watched her swallow the beverage. Layla made a face and held the glass out to her.

"After today, I might start. But not with that; it's gross!"

"No one shoved it down your gullet. What's up?" Vasquez asked, relieving her visitor of the glass and sipping the cool, sweet wine.

"I'm being followed," she replied breathlessly. "And so are you." Vasquez's eyes bulged at this announcement.

"What? Are you sure?" she stammered. Layla regarded her as if she had just sprouted another head. When she saw the look, Vasquez waved her hands in front of her. "What am I saying, of course you're sure; I meant, how do you know?"

"When Lewis and I went to the coffee shop this morning to meet up with Rose and Ryan, that was the first time I saw the car. I didn't think anything about it until we were headed back and I saw it again. Then when you and I went to lunch..."

"You noticed at lunch, and you didn't say anything?"

"It was a different car. I noticed it on the way to the food truck, and it followed us back to the precinct," she clarified.

"Well, that doesn't mean," Vasquez started to interject, but this time Layla raised her hand to silence her.

"Then on my way home today, I clocked the first car again; same driver, plate, and everything. I still wasn't sure; so, I waited an hour and ran out to the store. It stayed with me the whole time. Whoever they are, they're professionals, but they obviously don't know about my memory."

"Well okay, that may mean you're being followed, but what about me?" Vasquez challenged, folding her arms across her chest.

"Go look out your kitchen window," Layla directed. Vasquez raised her eyebrows in surprise before picking up the empty bottle and entering the kitchen. Dropping the container into the trashcan, she opened the refrigerator and extracted a new bottle.

"What am I looking for?" she inquired.

"Black Audi A3, three spots down from your car," Layla replied. Vasquez turned to the window, making a show of looking for her wine opener. She opened the wine bottle while idly gazing out of the window.

"That's the car? You sure?" She turned away from the window and headed back to the living room. When she rounded the corner, she met Layla's exasperated face. "Okay, but did you get the license plate?" she rephrased. Her friend's eyes widened with even more exaggerated impatience. Vasquez immediately wished she could take back the last two questions.

"Of course, I'm sure. My little friend was with me until about a block and a half before I got here, then he turned off. I suspect he knew this was my destination and since his buddy was already here, he felt there was no need to follow me all the way."

"Who do you think it is?" Vasquez wondered, taking a sip of her wine.

"I don't know. I'm not sure how we got on anyone's radar. I mean, it can't just be the Rodger's case, could it? Surely, we would have had the tails before today," Layla declared thoughtfully.

"What changed?" Vasquez mused. The women sat quietly in deep thought for a moment before Layla snapped her fingers.

"No one knew who he was until recently, and I'm the one who gave that info to Lewis."

"Lewis wouldn't do this," Vasquez scowled.

"No, I don't think he would either. But we were in the precinct when we spoke. There were other people around." Layla tapped her chin in thought. Suddenly, her eyes widened and moved to Vasquez. "Rach, you don't think someone in the PD is involved, do you?" Vasquez, who had been sipping her wine, choked on the liquid.

"Why would you say that?" she spluttered.

"Think about it. We have been working this case since Thursday, and nothing. I tell Oscar the man's name and next of kin, and suddenly we have a tail within a couple of days?"

"But how do we know it's not someone Federal?" Vasquez argued. "He did work for the DOJ after all."

"We just saw Thomas yesterday. I'm willing to bet they didn't even know he was dead until we told him this weekend. Face it, the federal government isn't known for its lightning speed. I don't think it's anyone connected to Malik in Washington. Thomas has no reason to do this, Dom doesn't like anyone, and the Jenkins family were pulled into this along with us. It's got to be me finding his name and telling Lewis. I also mentioned you during that conversation. I'm pretty sure if I hadn't, it would just be me. Sorry Rach," Layla sighed miserably. Vasquez waved off the apology.

"Don't be. What's life without a little adventure?" she smirked.

"Oh, I don't know... safe?"

"So, you're thinking someone in the PD, specifically in homicide, is in on this?" Vasquez asked, ignoring Layla's retort.

"It's the only thing that makes sense," she affirmed. "If this is linked to Malik's death, we can't go back to the warehouse." The declaration turned Vasquez's stomach. Her mind envisioned what could have happened if Layla had not seen the surveillance and they unwittingly led the strangers back to the others.

"Do you think they're following Lewis?" she asked.

"I don't know. I'll have to tell him to watch his back because I think if they aren't, they will be sooner or later."

"What do we do now?" Vasquez inquired, pushing the glass away. The panic in her stomach made the sweet wine taste sour and metallic.

"I don't know," Layla responded miserably.

"We can't really shake them. We have to work; we can't just pack up and move all of a sudden. One way or another, they'll find us and be right back on our tail. If we lose them too easily, they'll just beef up the surveillance to cover more angles," Vasquez said in her rapid-fire speech. Layla blinked at the woman in surprise. Catching the look, Vasquez threw her an irritated glare. "What? You think you're the only one of us who could have kicked ass in the police academy? I know things!"

"I need to call Lewis and Dom," Layla announced, producing her personal cell phone from one pocket, and the burner phone Dom had given her from the other.

"You hungry?" Vasquez stood and grabbed her own cell phone. Layla paused and considered the question before nodding.

"I was trying to figure out this surveillance thing; haven't eaten since lunch."

"While you call Lewis, I'll order Chinese. I need to make sure Miss Havisham doesn't rip up my duvet again," she said, heading for her bedroom.

"You should really get her declawed!" Layla called.

"That's cruel! How would you feel if someone just randomly snatched out your fingernails?" Vasquez called back.

Layla heard the woman's bedroom door open and close, leaving her alone in the living room. She stared at her cell phone for a long minute, frustrated comprehension washing over her. For most of her life, Layla was forced to rely on herself. Now, she had to reach out to a virtual stranger, because she could not think of a way to get herself and Vasquez out of this bind.

When she ran away from her last foster home, after clubbing her foster father with a lamp when he tried to rape her, she swore she would never rely on anyone else again. She lived on the streets for a few weeks, taking odd jobs for cash around the establishments in the French Quarter, before she met a prostitute named Nadine. A heroin addict, Nadine worked to support her habit more than anything else. However, she was over eighteen and had a small apartment, which checked the two main prerequisites for Layla's needs. She was able to convince Nadine to take her in as a roommate and subsequently persuaded her to pose as her older sister in order to get registered for school.

Despite Nadine providing shelter and the appearance of adult supervision that kept the foster care system at bay, Layla took care of Nadine more than the woman took care of her. She aided her in weaning off the drugs, helped her obtain a GED when she got pregnant and assisted her in finding a legitimate job after she had her daughter. Nadine went from being a pretend sister to being the closest thing to family Layla had ever known until she met Vasquez. Even though she moved to Texas to go to college, she visited her sister on a regular basis and assisted with financial shortages. The fact that she had no answer for the current situation and had to ask for help did not sit well in her spirit. Exhaling deeply, she decided to call Lewis first.

"Lewis," his gruff voice answered.

"Hey. You ok?"

"Yeah, why?"

"You would know if you picked up a tail, wouldn't you?" she asked. Lewis chuckled at this off the wall question, and the chuckle turned into a fit of coughing. "Put the cigar out, man. You're going to kill yourself."

"You sound like Sandy," he grumbled when he caught his breath. "And yes, of course I would know if I picked up a tail."

"But would you know if you weren't actually looking for one?"

"Kid, what is this about? Are you being tailed?" he countered, concern in his voice.

"Well yeah. This isn't a random conversation, Lewis. I'm trying to figure out if you are being tailed." His end of the line grew silent for a time.

"Honestly, I don't have your eyes or your memory. I suppose it's possible I could have picked up one without noticing," he conceded. "I don't see why anyone would tail me to begin with."

"I don't know why they're tailing us either, but they are. I have an idea about it though."

"Wait," he interjected. "Go back. Us?"

"Vasquez has one too. I'm at her place now," she explained. "I came over to confirm. Right now, there's only one. Mine dropped back when he realized I was coming here. I suspect I'll see him again on my way home."

"Who the hell is following you?" he demanded.

"If I knew who it was, I would have led with that," she sighed impatiently. "The first time I saw them was on our way to the coffee shop today to meet with Rose and Ryan. I grew suspicious when we were heading back, and they were still there. I have a theory, but you're not going to like it."

"Whatever it is, I'm pretty sure you're right."

"It's the Rodgers case. I think I garnered some interest when I came to you with his identity. I also mentioned Vasquez knew about things in that same conversation," she said.

"You only told me that information, and I wouldn't..."

"I know it's not you, Lewis. I never thought that for a moment. But we were in the bullpen."

"Shit kid. Are you saying that someone within the PD may have had something to do with Rodgers' death?" he gasped.

"I have had contact with only you, Vasquez, and the new people. We can rule them out; they have no reason to do this," she replied.

"What about the mysterious one; that Dominique lady?" he questioned, drawing a bark of laughter from Layla.

"You don't know her. Her only friend is a smartass AI. There's no way Dom would do this, she has no reason. As much as I hate to admit it, someone in homicide is dirty."

"What do you need me to do?" he asked.

"First and foremost, watch your six. Let me know if you clock someone on you. If we can find out who is behind this, maybe we will find our shooter."

"What about you and Vasquez?" he prodded with worry in his voice.

"Not sure yet. Dom is my next call, and she's pretty resourceful. Don't worry about us, old man. We'll be fine," she assured him.

"You damn well better, kid. I don't want to have to break in another snot-nosed crime tech."

"I'm glad you at least have your priorities straight."

"Damn right. I'll check it out tomorrow, let you know if I find anything. You just keep your asses safe," he commanded.

"You got it, Dad."

"Don't even," he warned. Layla laughed in his ear before disconnecting the call. Switching phones, she pressed the speed dial for Dom.

"Good evening, Miss Green," SARA's voice answered after one ring.

"With everything you can do, she has you as a glorified secretary?"

"I am also currently running several diagnostics, performing backups of both home and warehouse servers, updating various programs, and doing some research for Dom. I am excellent at multitasking," the computer replied. She snickered as she turned to the sound of Vasquez emerging from her bedroom. She watched her friend settle herself onto the chair next to the couch. Layla put the phone on speaker and mouthed the word "SARA."

"Hi SARA!" Vasquez called.

"Good evening, Miss Vasquez. I will alert Dom that you are both on the line. Standby." It was quiet for a few moments before Dom picked up the call.

"If this is about food, Rachel, I'm not cooking tonight."

"Oh please, I'm having Chinese," Vasquez huffed in a dismissive tone. Layla noticed a smile creep onto her face when she heard Dom's voice. If Layla did not know any better, she would think that Vasquez was developing a strange crush on their new friend. Vasquez shifted her eyes from the phone to Layla, waiting for her to explain the reason for the call.

"We have a problem," Layla announced.

"You mean besides the death of our one lead?" Dom asked.

"Yes, besides that."

"So, what seems to be your current pickle?"

"We've seemed to develop a fan club, and I don't think they want our autographs," Vasquez spoke up.

"And the English translation is?"

"We are being followed; both of us," Layla clarified.

"How many are in each car?" Dom asked, after a silent beat.

"One each, as far as I can see," she replied.

"You run the plates?"

"No. I wasn't completely sure until after I left work. I'm at Rachel's house right now. I wanted to confirm they're on both of us," Layla explained.

"What are the numbers?" Dom prompted. Layla rattled off the license plate numbers for both cars. Dom's line went quiet for a few minutes before she reported back. "Plates are bogus. Not registered to anyone. I'd have to get a VIN number to know who they are."

"So, they could either be ninjas or pushy Girl Scouts?" Vasquez mused.

"She really must be nervous; that was terrible," Dom mumbled. Layla threw a glare at Vasquez, who smiled brightly at her as she took a sip of wine. The tremor in her hand betrayed the fear she was trying to mask. Layla gave her a stiff smile of encouragement.

"We're both a little freaked out, Dom. We can't go to your house, or back to the warehouse until we lose them. The guy from this morning never came into the coffee house, so I don't think Ryan and Rose were seen. We can't put everyone else at risk," Layla said.

"What is your theory?" Dom asked.

"I think someone at the PD is dirty." Dom remained silent, and Layla took her silence as encouragement to continue with her theory. "I think delivering Malik's name to Lewis prompted someone to take an interest in me. During that conversation, I was deliberately vague, but I did mention that Rachel was involved."

"Do you think Lewis…"

"No way," Layla cut her off. "I just spoke to him. Look, I know you don't like the police, but you have to believe Rachel and me. We can trust him. Even Rose sees that, and she's our resident profiler. It's not Lewis. I just hung up with him and asked him to watch his back. If they're on us, they very well may be on him as well."

"You're right," Dom sighed. "For now, don't shake them, and don't come here or the warehouse. Communicate with me through the burner. Use your cell phone for random everyday things, so they don't realize you know about them. We don't know what kind of tech they're working with. If they are even close to my level, they may start trying to track your phones."

"Wait," Vasquez piped in. "Did I just hear you right? Did you say do *not* shake them?"

"Not right now. If you get rid of them, it will be a one and done. We have to plan it out before doing it," Dom rationalized.

"We?" Layla wondered.

"Ryan is military. I'm sure he'll be useful in this. Layla, I need you to monitor changes. How many times they switch, how many people they use. That will be important."

"Alright," she agreed.

"But how long do you think it will take? We won't have access to you guys, except through phone. How much help could we possibly be under these circumstances?" Vasquez wondered.

"It shouldn't be long, maybe a few days tops. You'll have SARA in the tablets you took. You won't be fully disconnected," Dom assured her. "I still want to take other precautions because we don't know who we're dealing with. Expect a package to your office in the morning."

"I hate it when she does that. I never know if it's going to be a box of dynamite or puppies," Vasquez groaned.

"This is better than puppies," Dom advised, her voice carrying a maniacal tone.

"Now I'm starting to worry," Layla admitted, glancing at Vasquez. "You sound like a Batman villain."

"Not a villain at all. But some could argue that I'm like Batman."

CHAPTER TWENTY-FIVE

Layla and Vasquez received a medium-sized box from a courier service early the next morning. They huddled together in Layla's cubicle to open the parcel. The package contained two small, identical black devices shaped like television remotes. Each gadget had three buttons vertically lined in the center and a toggle switch at the top. The women exchanged confused glances.

"What are these?" Vasquez asked, taking one of the devices from Layla.

"You got me," she shrugged. She reached back into the box and extracted two metallic discs, holding them up for Vasquez to inspect. The discs were four inches in diameter, and one side was covered with an adhesive strip.

"Did our Batman send instructions on what to do with these?" Vasquez wondered. As soon as the question left her lips, both of the women's burner phones chimed. Layla and Vasquez froze, eyeing each other. "No way." Simultaneously, they pulled out their phones to review the text message.

The black boxes are bug sweepers. Each button performs a sweep on a different frequency. Press and hold each button while you walk around the area. Make sure you do all three EVERY time you walk into your office or your apartments. I don't know who is on you, but wiretapping is never out of the realm of possibility. The discs are signal jammers. It will work for all standard phones, but it will not affect your burners. Stick them under the glove compartment in each of your cars. If they bug your car, this will jam anything they put on you. They may use electronic tracking, but when we extract, we will leave your cars behind. If you need anything, SARA and I are a phone call away. Be careful ladies. Yes, even you Rachel.

Vasquez gawked at her phone and shook her head in disbelief. When Layla began to laugh, she stared at her friend in bafflement.

"What is so funny?" she demanded.

"Dom. She's hilarious in her own way. I'm really glad she's on our side," Layla giggled.

"But how did she know to send the text at that moment?"

"You see any branding on these?" Layla asked, holding up one of the devices. "She made them, Rach. She probably has a way to track them. I'm pretty sure she knew the exact moment the box arrived." Layla dropped her bug sweeper into a desk drawer. She nodded at the one Vasquez was holding and then indicated the room with her hand. "Should we give it a whirl?"

"I guess," Vasquez sighed. She flipped the toggle switch, and a yellow light appeared at the top right corner of the device. When she pressed the first of the three buttons, the light turned green. The light remained unchanged as she walked a grid along the shared office space. Once she finished the third revolution, she switched off the sweeper. "I guess green is good?"

"I'm going to agree with that assessment," Layla shrugged.

"She really is a little like Batman," Vasquez admitted. She put her sweeper and jammer in her purse and slid her chair into Layla's cubicle. Layla glanced at her friend and noticed a peculiar smile on her face.

"Okay, I'm just going to ask. Do you have like some weird crush on her or something?" Vasquez blinked at Layla's question, but her face reddened immediately.

"Why would you ask me that?"

"I'm no Rose, but I'm not an idiot either," Layla replied. Vasquez averted her eyes and giggled nervously.

"I don't know if I'd call it a crush. I will say she captivates me," she confessed.

"I don't want to sound stupid here, or like I missed a big part of who you were in the past decade, but I thought you were straight," Layla declared with a puzzled look on her face.

"You sound like an old woman. Sexuality is fluid. I like to think of myself as open to whoever enchants me," Vasquez replied breezily, finally meeting her friend's eyes.

"But your dates are always guys."

"No. I've never said that," Vasquez revealed, rolling her chair into her own space and logging into her computer.

"Really?" Layla asked, her dark brown eyes following the woman.

"Problem?" Vasquez inquired, spinning in her chair to face Layla.

"No, it's not that. It's just... we've been friends for over ten years, and you've never said anything. Why didn't you trust me with this?"

"There was nothing to say. Have you ever met anyone I've dated?" Vasquez probed. Layla considered the question for a time, before the shocking answer revealed itself.

"Now that I think about it, I haven't," she replied in awe. "Why is that?"

"Layla, I know I seem flighty to a lot of people, even you. I will admit that in some ways, I am. But I am careful about who I let come into my world. I like to have fun. But only someone truly special gets to meet those closest to me. I haven't come across that person yet," Vasquez explained. Layla noted that her friend's green eyes had a somber tint to them.

"I guess I never thought about it. I mean you tell me that you date, but I never realized that I haven't met anyone you've dated until now."

"I only mention dates when you ask me what I'm up to. But the Xerox machine in your brain could never run back a name because I never gave one," Vasquez pointed out. "You are my closest friend. It feels like it took forever for you to let me in. I'm not just going to bring a random John or Jane into your life, willy-nilly, as you would say." She threw Layla a grin before turning back to her computer. Layla watched her enthralled by what she just disclosed. Despite the cavalier manner in which Vasquez spoke, she revealed a very profound truth.

Layla knew that she was suspicious of most people. When she first met Vasquez, she found the woman annoyingly bubbly and had a hard time believing a person could be genuinely happy all of the time. She initially assumed Vasquez was overcompensating and hiding her true self. When she finally let her in, she found a deep and true friendship she never thought possible with someone as different as herself. Over the years, she began to reveal small nuggets of her past; although, she still had a hard time discussing the more painful memories. Because they were so different in personality and background, she did not think Vasquez truly understood who she was as a person. However, Vasquez had just divulged in her own way that she not only understood Layla, but she also respected her too much to bring temporary people in and out of her life. Layla continued to watch Vasquez as she was checking her email, and her vision swam with tears. She wiped her eyes just as Vasquez felt her stare. The woman turned around and looked at her.

"What?" she frowned. Layla smiled warmly.

"Nothing Rach. Nothing at all."

Dom sat in the warehouse office sipping a cup of coffee, and combing through the information SARA mined on the four recently murdered inmates linked to Malik Rodgers. Ever the organizer, SARA created a folder for each individual — Sergio Martinez, Eric Taylor, Tommy Cole, and Tavion Evans. She had opened one folder on each of the four screens to try to determine similarities in each man.

"I'm still not seeing it," she sighed. SARA was running her weekly update and back up to the other off-site servers and would not respond. The AI would be offline for another hour or so. Dom began to wonder if her dependence on the machine was affecting her own critical thinking and logic skills. She was so used to SARA's processing speed being faster than her own cognition and the machine's habit of answering questions before Dom could fully think to ask. She was determined to use this time to try to find a link, not only to move the investigation along but to prove to herself that she wasn't fully dependent on SARA. She continued to shift from profile to profile, reviewing work history, family, social media, and criminal records. Juvenile records, normally sealed to most unless one had a genius level IQ and supercomputer at their beck and call, were one connection that all of the men shared. However, the locations and ages were different, and she could not figure out why these records would matter.

A beep from the corner of the room alerted Dom of someone being on the property. She turned in time to see Ryan and Robert getting out of the truck and approaching the entrance. Ryan had driven a rental car for the first few days he was in town, but the rental was starting to get costly. Dom allowed him the use of the quad cab truck she rarely drove until he had an opportunity to buy his own vehicle. Ryan scanned the two men into the building and the door unlocked. Dom sighed heavily. She genuinely liked the Jenkins brothers and knew that this situation was helpful to both of the men. However, she still had not fully adjusted to being around people on a daily basis. Standing from her desk, she went to the door and pressed a button in the wall. The door slid open, and she went to greet her new employees. Ryan waved as he took off his light jacket to reveal a burgundy sweater that he wore with dark jeans and boots. Robert followed his older brother into the room donning a pair of khaki pants and a bright blue hoodie.

"Good morning gentlemen." She addressed the newcomers with a forced smile.

"Dom! How are things?" Ryan beamed.

"You got anything to eat?" Robert inquired. Ryan pushed his brother, causing him to smile sheepishly. "I mean, good morning, Dom. Do you have anything to eat?"

"They don't feed you?"

"This boy has been eating like he was on a hunger strike for the past eight years," Ryan chuckled.

"I stocked the kitchen yesterday; go for it," Dom told Robert, nodding at the kitchen area with her head.

"You guys want anything?"

"I'm good," she replied, holding up her coffee cup.

"Bring me whatever you make," Ryan added. Robert nodded and disappeared. "So, what are we doing today, Boss?"

"Things here are stagnant at the moment. SARA assembled files for all four prisoners from the messages, but I'm having trouble finding a link. She's offline for a little while, so it's slow going."

"Maybe I can help. Two heads are better than one," Ryan grinned.

"This head has an IQ of one sixty-eight," she asserted, tapping the side of her temple.

"I may not be a genius, but mine is around one twenty. One sixty-eight plus one twenty is two eighty-eight. Surely together we are like a superpower?"

"I suppose that came across as arrogant, didn't it?" Dom blushed.

"To be fair, I assume most of your verbal sparring has been with a supercomputer, so no offense is taken," Ryan winked.

"Well, I suppose if you're getting paid, we may as well put that one twenty to use." She stepped over to the conference table and picked up a tablet. Stabbing on the tablet rapidly, she accessed the files SARA created and brought them up on the screens by the table. Ryan moved to the bank of monitors and gave each screen a cursory glance before turning to her.

"What do you know so far?"

"Four men. Eric Taylor of San Antonio, forty-two years of age, Tommy Cole of Austin, twenty-seven years of age, Tavion Evans of Dallas, thirty-two, and of course Sergio Martinez of Houston, twenty-five," she explained, pointing at each file as she gave names and ages.

"Alright, four men, different ages from four different areas in Texas, so we can probably rule out them knowing each other," Ryan murmured, turning back to the screens.

"Yes, the only weird thing is that they were all arrested in Houston. Taylor, Cole, and Evans were in or around Houston when they were picked up, and of course, Martinez was born and raised here," she noted, consulting her tablet. Robert emerged from the kitchen with three plates. Dom cocked her head when he put one down on the conference table, handed one to Ryan and offered her the other.

"I know you said you didn't want anything, but even super brains need to eat. Man can't live on coffee alone," he grinned. Dom inspected the plate and raised her eyebrows in surprise.

"You made crepes?"

"Yeah, you had flour, eggs, milk, and butter. I made the filling from cream cheese, a little sugar, and strawberries.

It's amazing what can be made with simple ingredients,"
Robert shrugged.

"I know. That's my motto too." She took the plate from
him and cut into the crepe, taking a small bite. "Light, fluffy,
and not too sweet. You snuck in some vanilla in that filling, and
cinnamon in the batter." Robert smiled in appreciation of her
palate. "You're ok with me Jenkins," she grinned.

"Never thought the one brother who couldn't boil water
would suddenly become Wolfgang Puck," Ryan admitted, around
a mouth full of food. The trio attacked their respective plates in
silence for a few moments. Once Dom had eaten about half of her
crepe, she turned her attention to the men.

"Let's get back into this," she said indicating the screens.
Ryan nodded, swallowing the last of his own crepe and placing his
plate on the conference table.

"Right, so we have four men, different ages, different
locations, all arrested in Houston," he recapped. Robert stood,
taking his plate with him, and paced in front of the screens reading
the information while he finished off his breakfast.

"The only commonality is they all had criminal records,
but the records are totally different. Let's take Sergio Martinez,"
she said, picking up her tablet. "He's been in and out of jail since
he was sixteen for gang-related activities. The thing is, he's the
only one of the four who could be considered a career criminal."
Robert's pacing slowed as he stared at the screens in deep thought.
Finally, he turned to face Dom and his brother.

"There is something strange here that's kind of clear to me,
but may not be as obvious to you guys," he announced.

"By all means," Ryan replied, motioning Robert
to continue.

"Martinez was in and out like Dom said. But the other
three went from zero to sixty pretty quick. Too quick," Robert
noted, turning back to the screens. Dom stepped forward, her face
showing confusion.

"How do you mean?"

"Let's start with Taylor," he began. "His juvenile record is
petty theft and truancy. Nothing big there, he was a kid being a kid.
Most White kids do the same shit and get a slap on the wrist. He

serves about three months in juvenile detention, then nothing until he's twenty-three when he gets pinched for intoxication assault. I don't know the court record, but to go from petty theft and truancy to violence is a big leap. I'm not saying the man wasn't capable of it, I didn't know him, but you'd think if he was violent by nature, it would have showed in his juvenile jacket. He got five years and served thirteen months. I'm willing to bet that he got into a fight, and got the book thrown at him. I mean look at him, he's kind of a big dude." He pointed to a photo from Eric Taylor's social media. Dom began rapidly tapping on the tablet.

"It says here, he was offered drunken disorderly, but he wouldn't plead guilty," she declared, her eyes fixed on the tablet as she scrolled. "According to the trial information, he was at a club, and he saw someone roughing up a woman. He stepped in to stop him, and a fight broke out. He broke the guy's jaw. They were able to get intoxication assault because he blew a .09 when the cops showed up."

"One-hundredth of a point over the limit and they hit him with a felony?" Ryan frowned in disgust. Robert looked at his brother with sadness in his eyes.

"I was a drug addict, and they gave me ten years, bro. Anyway, once he's released, he was able to get a job at an office building in San Antonio as a custodian. He gets married, has a couple of kids and goes on with his life. Suddenly, he's picked up for unlawful weapon possession at forty? That's kind of extreme," Robert asserted.

"That does seem a little out there," Dom nodded.

"Then there's Tommy Cole," he moved on but stopped when Ryan chuckled.

"Man, every time I hear his name, I think of the TV show Martin," Ryan admitted, drawing a grin from Robert.

"We watched that show every week," Robert remembered with nostalgia in his eyes.

"What about Mr. Cole, Rob?" Dom prompted, clearly focused on the main conversation. The men's smiles faded, and Robert turned back to the screens.

"Sorry. So, Tommy Cole was from Austin, had a juvenile charge of possession of marijuana. Not a big deal in the grand scheme of things, we all know Black folks get arrested for that quicker than most. At twenty, his first felony comes in the form of indecency with a minor," he outlined. Ryan's face darkened.

"Don't tell me he was a pedophile," he grumbled. Dom began tapping on the tablet, and the men grew silent as they waited for her to search. After a moment, she found what she was looking for and shook her head.

"No. His girlfriend was sixteen, and her mother walked in on them having sex. She pressed charges. Seems kind of spiteful, but he was a legal adult, and she was under seventeen."

"Right, so another bullshit felony, which again, isn't abnormal, especially in this state or this country. None of those charges are violent crimes, but four years later, he gets ten years for an assault on a public servant?" Robert asked incredulously. Dom studied the documentation on the device.

"He was pulled over for speeding and allegedly hit a cop," she informed the men.

"Finally, Tavion Evans; he's the one that bothered me the most," Robert divulged, examining the screens once again.

"Why?" Ryan asked.

"Because he seems to be one of those success stories of people who get screwed by the system. As a kid, he's picked up in Dallas for truancy and a couple of fights. Normal kid being kid shit. When he turns nineteen, he gets three years for felony forgery. What was that about?" he wondered, turning to Dom who was already bringing up the court record. As she silently reviewed the documentation, anger began to creep onto her features.

"Whatever it is, it ain't good," Ryan muttered, noticing the change in her demeanor.

"This is some bullshit," she spat. "Tavion Evans received twenty thousand dollars in bearer bonds for his high school graduation. When he went to deposit them, it turns out they were fake. They arrested him for felony forgery because of the amount and the fact that they were bonds. He refused to say who gave them to him, so he had to take the heat. He was a damn kid!"

"So, he serves three years, gets out, and goes to a tech school to become a surgical tech. He's doing perfectly fine until he gets arrested for distribution of a controlled substance? Are you kidding me?" Robert frowned, turning from the screen once again. Before he could ask, Dom began to speak.

"Looks like the cops' case was completely circumstantial. Some drugs went missing from his hospital pharmacy; they were connected to his badge. Evans claims he lost his key card and reported it when he made the discovery, which was corroborated by the hospital security staff. That should have given plenty of reasonable doubt, but the jury convicted him anyway," she said. "Damn, this poor guy couldn't catch a break."

"So outside of Martinez, everyone else seems to have been in jail over some bullshit, and they all had ridiculous felonies before then. I'm not saying it's a true connection, but something doesn't smell right. Trust me, I'd know," Robert finished.

"Well, that's better than what SARA found," Dom mumbled. Ryan stiffened and stared at her.

"SARA found a connection? Why didn't you say that?"

"You do know that SARA is my creation, and not necessarily smarter than I am, don't you?" she shot back defensively.

"I would never say that!" he exclaimed. Dom eyed him for another moment before dropping her eyes back to her tablet. "I'm just saying she thinks faster than you is all," he added.

"What was SARA's connection?" Robert wondered.

"It was more of a coincidence. When she was doing her data mining on our four men here, she found that they were either married or in long-term relationships with women who had medical procedures within a year of their arrests."

"How is that a link?" Ryan asked.

"I don't think it is. Like I said, it was just something she found while mining for data. They were all in four different cities. There's something else that we aren't seeing." The trio stood in front of the bank of monitors, silent in their analysis.

"I can't think of what it is, Boss," Ryan confessed after a few minutes passed.

"We will figure it out," she muttered, turning from the screen. Her eyes landed on Robert and then widened as if she just realized he was present. "I almost forgot!"

"Forgot what?" Robert asked. Dom marched to the office and returned with a large roll of paper. She unfurled it onto the conference table, and the men leaned in to see.

"It's a blueprint," Ryan observed flatly.

"I shall dub thee, Captain Obvious," Dom proclaimed with an eye roll.

"Sorry," he blushed. "What is this?"

"The prison," Robert softly advised. Ryan jerked and turned to his brother who was staring at the floor plan.

"The one in Huntsville?" he asked in surprise.

"This was my cell," Robert nodded, tapping a section on the blueprint. Ryan stared at the small space in sorrow.

"What's this for, Dom?" he asked after a moment.

"The day Martinez was killed, he was in solitary confinement," she began. Ryan and Robert both nodded.

"Right, that's why we asked Lewis to go that day. We didn't think someone would be able to get to him in solitary," Ryan recalled.

"Theo Morrison was the guard Detective Lewis met with that morning," she continued. Robert smiled at the mention of Morrison's name.

"Morrison is a really good dude."

"So, when Morrison found Martinez, he said the man was still warm. That means he got killed just before Morrison made his way to solitary. SARA tapped into the surveillance system after learning of Martinez's death, and I tried to get a glimpse of who went into the wing just before he was murdered," she revealed. Both men stared at her engrossed.

"And?" Ryan pressed when she didn't continue. Dom sighed heavily.

"At the time of the murder, the surveillance system appeared to have gone down for ten minutes," she said. "In fact, it didn't come up until after Morrison found his body." Ryan hunched over the blueprint and began gazing wildly at the various sections.

"So, it was in that ten minutes that Martinez was murdered," Robert repeated thoughtfully. His eyebrows creased in perplexity after he spoke the words. "Why the floor plan?" Dom silently watched Ryan review the blueprint as his mind began to connect the dots she had already linked the night before.

"Oh shit," he gasped. He looked up and made eye contact with Dom who nodded grimly.

"Someone want to catch me up?" Robert sighed in exasperation. Ryan glanced at Dom and then turned to Robert, pointing to a space on the blueprint.

"This is the security room," he said, tapping the southwest corner of the building near the entrance. He moved the finger to the northeast corner of the prison and added, "This is the hall for solitary." Robert leaned in and watched as Ryan retraced his finger in a diagonal line from southwest to northeast.

"Ok, I'm with you," he nodded.

"Here," Ryan noted, indicating several points on the route from the southwest corner to the northeast area, "are the security doors. There is no way someone could have gotten from security to the solitary wing, kill Martinez, get back to bring the system online in ten minutes; and not be seen by Morrison. Guards were most definitely involved in this, and not just one."

"Dom?" SARA called out. The middle screen on the western wall changed, and the avatar appeared.

"Welcome back," Dom acknowledged, throwing a quick glance at the screen before focusing her attention back onto the prison floor plan.

"Thank you. The backup is complete. While I was offline, an alert was triggered that you must see immediately," SARA advised.

"Send it to the tablet," she mumbled. The tablet lit up, and Ryan grabbed it from the table when she did not make a move for the device. Dom's head jerked up when Ryan gasped.

"Oh my God," he whispered. Robert, who had leaned over to see the information along with his big brother, snatched the tablet from him.

"No!" he cried. He dropped the tablet on the table, interlaced his fingers and put them on the top of his head as if he were trying to keep his skull from exploding.

"What?" Dom prodded. She grabbed the tablet and scanned the information quickly. The document was an incident report from the Huntsville prison; dark red block letters declared the incident in question as a fatality. She initially assumed this was the statement for the death of Sergio Martinez. As she continued to read, her heart thudded in her ears. The report detailed a large brawl involving several inmates in the prison yard. The account outlined the death of one of the prison employees — Theo Morrison.

CHAPTER TWENTY-SIX

Tristan slouched in his chair, idly running his hand through his thick white hair, as he eyed the four shadows on the monitors. The hour was late, later than normal for the Collective to meet, but this was a special meeting to discuss developments. He was exhausted. It felt like since the discovery of Malik Rodgers, his life had been one endless shift of cleaning up the chaos.

"You were able to eliminate Martinez in solitary? That's pretty impressive, even for you, Rucker," Alexandria noted. Tristan figured this was the closest thing to a compliment the man had ever given him.

"My guy knew a guy," he nodded. "As much as I'd like to say that's the end of this, it's not."

"What happened?" Chicago asked.

"Oscar Lewis, the detective on the case, went to the prison the same day. He was actually there when Martinez was taken care of," Tristan informed the group.

"What?" Alexandria stiffened. "How did he make that jump so quickly? Was it Layla Green?"

"I can't say for sure. But I don't see how she would have made the connection," Tristan shrugged.

"Do you think Detective Lewis knows Rodgers was federal?" Vegas asked.

"I wish I knew, but I haven't heard that the DOJ has even claimed him yet," he replied.

"You have Green and Vasquez under surveillance?" This question came from Chicago.

"Yes. The same day as we took care of Martinez, the teams began their observation," he affirmed.

"Anything stick out as odd?" Alexandria inquired.

"Nothing I can pinpoint from what I've been told. They go to work; they go home. They each eat lunch together every day. Detective Lewis and Green went for coffee the first day of surveillance, but I don't think that's out of the ordinary and Vasquez wasn't with them," he reported.

"Perhaps you should amp it up," Alexandria suggested. Tristan's steel gray eyes took in the man's silhouette.

"The thought has crossed my mind, but I still have no intention of killing her if I don't have to."

"No one said anything about killing her," Alexandria countered defensively.

"Well, at least Lewis wasn't able to talk to Martinez," Chicago interrupted. "Any other problems with that?"

"Actually, yes. Lewis asked for a specific guard when he got to the prison, Theo Morrison. I'm not sure why, but he was the one who found Martinez's body. After the detective left, Morrison started asking questions, trying to figure out who got to Martinez in the solitary wing. When he saw the footage was compromised, he started to suspect something was wrong. Once our guys got word of that, they staged a fight in the yard while Morrison was on duty. Got some of those Aryan Nation guys to kill him in the confusion," Tristan explained.

"Jesus, this is becoming ridiculous," Vegas groaned.

· "Do you think the feds know anything, Rucker?" Chicago prodded. The question was one Tristan had been kicking around as well.

"If they had an idea of the operation, they would have moved in by now. I don't think they are the source of information for Detective Lewis. For all we know, he could have run into someone who was in the pen at the same time as Rodgers and gone to the prison for that reason. If Rodgers had gotten the details to the feds, they would have moved to protect Martinez sooner. I think we're fine for now, but I don't believe we are out of the woods. I want to see where this murder investigation leads," Tristan replied.

"Can Lewis be bought?" Chicago asked.

"According to my guy in the department, no. He has been with the PD for over twenty years. He's got a wife and three kids, two in college. Plus, he genuinely cares about the folks in the city, even the ones who cause the problems. From what I'm told, he has a lot of integrity and is pretty well respected," Tristan answered. "And before you say it, I'm not killing a cop unless completely necessary." The group knew who he was addressing, and Alexandria did not respond.

"Keep on top of this," Chicago ordered.

"That's what I do."

"Any word on Milwaukee?"

"As anticipated, the news about Cook having no active warrant is out. Someone leaked it to the liberal media first, but I'm making sure our people keep focused on his criminal past and failure to cooperate. Grimes' name is still an unknown, but that will change any day now. The news about Cook being arrested with no active warrant has triggered the marches. I have spoken to one of the anarchist groups that does some work for me; they're going up to Milwaukee disguised as protestors to stir the pot. Once they get the looting and violence started, the city will be able to declare a state of emergency and a curfew. As long as the media has people in the streets screaming and yelling, the story will stay hot. A curfew is the perfect counter to that. If we can stop the twenty-four-hour coverage, things will start to die down," he responded.

"Good plan," Chicago nodded, his voice sounding impressed.

"Has the senator been able to reason with him?" Tristan asked.

"He said he was going to try."

"I hope he's able to. If we time this right, and Grimes keeps his mouth shut, this will be over soon."

Rose, Ryan, Robert, and Dom sat around the conference table with Layla and Vasquez on two of the screens on the wall. After ensuring both apartments were not bugged, SARA connected the women via video chat so that they could still be a part of the discussion. She informed the Jenkins family that Layla and Vasquez were on house arrest due to their trackers, which prompted a round of conversation about how they were going to help the women.

"We can't leave them to deal with this alone, we have to get them out of there," Ryan declared in a worried tone.

"Yes, I know. We will, but we have to be smart," Dom patiently replied.

"What are we going to do?" Robert asked.

"You will do nothing. When it's time, Ryan and I will handle it," Dom answered, causing him to huff in indignation.

"I'm not useless," he grumbled.

"No one said you were, big brother," Rose advised, rubbing him on the back. "But you did just get out of prison. You need to stay far away from anything that skirts the line of legality." Dom glanced at her and offered a grateful nod.

"Did you say you think we should be looking at a cop for the murder?" Ryan asked suddenly as if the information had just sunk into his mind. Layla nodded, and Dom could tell the woman did not want to admit the thought.

"When I really think about it, it's the only thing that makes sense. I'm very good at my job. One of the things I'm good at is looking at crime scenes in various ways to find evidence. The thing that jumped out at me the most about the scene was the cleanliness. You almost never find a murder scene with absolutely no evidence. No fingerprints, no trace, nothing. It was like a bullet came from another dimension and killed him, which would make an awesome video game by the way. Can you imagine?"

"Focus nerd!" Vasquez snapped.

"Sorry, I digress," Layla blushed. "Only someone who would truly understand evidence would be able to leave a scene that immaculate. It also makes sense because there is no other reason for anyone to be following us. The only thing that changed was me telling Lewis about Malik and his next of kin."

"I can see your point," Ryan agreed.

"There was no forced entry at Malik's apartment. I wondered to myself why he would open the door for a killer. But, if you're an undercover DOJ agent, you may open the door for a cop, easily. Plus, I don't like how quickly Martinez was taken out. I don't know who's behind it, but when I take a step back and look at the big picture, I can't come up with another explanation," Layla added.

"That could also explain Theo," Rose mused thoughtfully. Layla cocked her head at this statement.

"The guard? Morrison? Explain what?" she asked. Dom launched into the news of Theo Morrison's death in the prison yard and explained the information that led them to believe that multiple guards were responsible for Martinez's death. Robert's face grew sullen as he listened to the recap, and Dom could see that losing two people he cared deeply for in a short time was weighing heavily on him. The amount of trauma he was experiencing could be enough to make any addict fall off the wagon, and she was glad he was around his siblings for support.

"So, we have Martinez who was taken out, and we suspect that there were some guards involved; then we have a guard who was murdered by… who?" Vasquez asked. Dom glanced at SARA's avatar.

"You got the footage yet?" she inquired.

"Footage?" SARA asked.

"The surveillance footage from the prison around the time of Theo Morrison's death."

"You did not instruct me to get the surveillance material, Dom," SARA replied.

"Since when do I ask? You always just do," Dom frowned.

"It would be nice to be asked occasionally."

"Yeah Dom, she's not your servant. She has feelings!" Vasquez added.

"No, she doesn't! She's a computer!" Dom objected.

"I may not have human emotions, but I am proficient enough in exchanges to know that statement was hurtful," SARA proclaimed, her avatar frowning for effect.

"You have got to be kidding me," Dom moaned, rubbing her eyes wearily.

"You've hurt her feelings now," Rose smirked. Dom eyed the crowd, who all appeared to be on the machine's side of this debate. She sighed.

"I'm sorry, SARA. Could you please get the footage from the prison yard around Theo Morrison's death? I would be most appreciative for your help," she requested, in an excessively placating manner.

"I already have the surveillance footage, Dom. I am simply saying it is nice to be asked," SARA replied, her avatar smiling brightly. The group chuckled at the spectacle as Dom rolled her eyes. "Standby." The screen with SARA's avatar changed to display the video footage of the prison yard.

"Can we see?" Vasquez asked from her home.

"One moment," SARA replied. After a few seconds, Layla and Vasquez's tablets changed to show the same feed.

The film had no sound, but the group could see a prison yard basketball game underway. Several inmates were sitting on the ground or on benches around the court. For the most part, the prisoners were segregated into various small groups; one of the largest being composed of people sporting White supremacist tattoos on their arms, bare chests, and in some cases, on their faces. In the middle of the game, a few of the Aryans strolled over to a large group of Black prisoners, and an argument ensued. The dispute drew the attention of many of the convicts in the area who began to move closer to the conflict. Suddenly, a brawl broke out among the whole assembly of inmates, both players and spectators alike. Guards charged from every direction to break up the fight. One of the prominent guards in the throng was a large Black man who looked to be the size of a human refrigerator.

"That's Theo," Robert noted, watching the video intently. Morrison pushed his way into the middle of the ruckus and started to pull prisoners off of each other. The way the Black inmates reacted showed that they returned the respect that he obviously gave them, backing down once Morrison pushed them away. Suddenly, the White supremacists converged on the large guard, as if they were trying to overrun him to get to the group of Black men who had taken a step back. This surge of violence was met with the Black prisoners going at the Aryans with renewed fervor.

"This is insane," Layla mumbled, as more guards jumped into the middle of the battle. After a few long minutes, the crowds were separated. Once there was space between the combatants, the video revealed Theo Morrison laying on the ground, bleeding profusely from several stab wounds. Dom glanced at Rose and Robert. Rose had her mouth covered, tears streaming down her face, and Robert miserably put his hands over his eyes.

"Stop the video, SARA," Dom commanded. The video faded out, and SARA's placid avatar returned.

"Dios mío," Vasquez murmured.

"The Aryans are assholes, but they usually stay to themselves. As long as I was there, I've never seen a White on Black fight to that scale before," Robert sniffed, tears collected in the base of his eyes.

"They all swarmed on him just before the stabbing; specifically, so no one could see who did it. It was definitely planned," Ryan asserted.

"Probably the same guards," Layla added.

"I don't think Lewis needs to go the prison route right now. He's already tipped his hand to whoever is behind this by showing up when Martinez was killed. I think we should leave that part to Nancy Bennett's people. I'll get a report written up and sent to Tom. Our focus is on Malik's death and what we can do from out here," Dom declared.

"I think Dom's right. The prison is obviously a hotbed, and there are too many unknowns," Ryan agreed. "We should leave that to the Federal people."

"So where do we start?" Vasquez asked. Rose raised her hand.

"Guys, this isn't school, stop doing that," Dom chastised.

"You said Sergio was part of a gang, any idea who?" Rose asked. Dom picked up the tablet in front of her, but SARA spoke before she had a chance.

"According to records within the police department and courts, Sergio Martinez is a long-time member of Los Asesinos." Ryan threw Dom a look, noticing her finger was frozen over the tablet.

"See? She thinks faster," he smiled. Dom rolled her eyes and put the tablet back on the table.

"Los Asesinos," Rose mused. "I think they're on the south side. Let me take the gang angle and see what I can find. I know someone I can get information from. Rob and I will handle that."

"I should go too," Ryan announced. Rose turned her golden eyes to her oldest brother and smirked.

"Not going to happen. You scream cop, Sergeant."

"If it's who I think it is, it shouldn't matter," he argued. "He knows me."

"You never liked him. And let's not forget, you weren't exactly cordial to him at Rodney and Reggie's funeral," Robert snorted. Dom's head swiveled while she listened to the family debate as if she were observing a tennis match.

"No," Rose repeated firmly. "Less than cordial is an understatement. Rodney and Reggie made their own decisions. You were wrong to blame him."

"And you threatened his life," Robert added. "I was high, but that is the one thing from that day I remember vividly. You told him that if you saw him around any of your family again, you would kill him."

"You guys are making it sound worse than it was," Ryan muttered.

"It was bad, RJ2," Robert insisted, shaking his head emphatically. Rose put her hand on Ryan's forearm.

"We will be fine. I'll have a brother with me, and Luke and I are good. I just talked to him a few days ago," she said. Dom noticed Ryan's jaw tense in frustration as he bit back a response.

"Ryan, I get it. You're pissed," Robert acknowledged. "You want to blame everybody involved for their deaths. But it wasn't anyone's fault but Rodney, Reggie, and the bangers who killed them. They put themselves in that position. Just like you can't blame our dead brothers on my addiction. That was my choice and my mistake. Until you can accept that, you don't need to see Luke. Rose and I have this." Ryan stroked his scar contemplatively while he listened to Robert's spiel. Rose swallowed a lump of conflicting feelings. The grief evoked by remembering their brothers' death, and the pain in Ryan's eyes that drove him to threaten someone's life was a difficult image to recollect. Nevertheless, Robert's words touched her deeply.

Part of the healing process for those who lose loved ones to gang violence or drug overdose is to acknowledge that in most cases, the death was not something of random circumstance. Many families fell apart when they could not bring themselves to accept that in those situations, their loved ones had a form of responsibility for their own demise. For some reason, people want to believe that once death is achieved, the souls of the departed suddenly become infallible angels, who die without a blemish or stain on their souls. Rose had to make peace with her brothers' death by realizing that despite the efforts of her family to talk Rodney and Reggie out of their life of crime, her brothers chose their own paths and knew the risks. This realization did not cause her to love either brother any less. Instead, it eliminated the guilt often felt by the loved ones left behind; wondering what they could have done differently, or how the departed could have been saved from their demise. Rose also had to use her knowledge of grief and coping to help her mother through the tragedy. Joyce not only lost two of her sons permanently, but a third to prison very shortly after. The battle for healing was long and arduous, but Joyce also reached the point where she could feel blameless for her sons' choices. Although Robert was her big brother, Rose marveled at the level of maturity she had seen from him since his release from prison; a maturity he had never before shown. Dom broke the awkward silence.

"Ryan, I need you here anyway. We have to figure out a plan to free up our captured comrades over there," she announced, nodding at the video monitors with her head. As if he had forgotten about Layla and Vasquez's predicament, Ryan's eyes went wide with recall, and he nodded solemnly.

"What are we going to do about the dirty cop?" Vasquez wondered, making a face as if the words filled her mouth with a sour acidity.

"Lewis is going to look into it. When I spoke to him yesterday, I gave him my theory. He didn't like it, but he couldn't argue with it either," Layla replied. Dom pinched her ear in thought.

"I'm going to send another box to you guys tomorrow. The same things I sent you, plus one of our phones for Lewis," she said. "You can teach him how to use them." Layla's eyes widened in shock at this statement.

"You don't trust cops," she noted. "Why would you do that for him?"

"I don't trust many people. But I'm getting a little more comfortable with you guys. If you and Rachel trust him, and Rose signs off on it, I have to let go of a few of my reservations, for the sake of the investigation," she shrugged.

"Well, that's a big step for you," Vasquez grinned. "Does this mean we can do dinner parties now?" Dom scowled.

"Don't push it. Besides, with him being on our network, I can keep an eye on him. You know, friends close, enemies closer kind of thing."

"So, what are we?" Rose wondered.

"Still haven't decided; but for now, we have common goals. So, cautiously we'll go with friends. At least as SARA sees it," she answered.

"Don't worry Miss Jenkins. I am working on her trust issues," SARA announced. This comment brought laughter from everyone in attendance physically and virtually.

"Speaking of the smartass, SARA brought up this coincidence regarding our four dead guys' significant others. It got me thinking, maybe one of the women could have some insight into what was being investigated," Dom declared when the laughter subsided.

"You know, that's not a bad idea," Layla said.

"Don't act so surprised. I have ideas sometimes," Dom grumbled.

CHAPTER TWENTY-SEVEN

"Leon, this is really good," Rose said, dropping the sheet of paper onto her desk. Leon Murphy avoided eye contact and took another bite of his breakfast sandwich. The Langston Hughes poem inspired the boy more than she thought it would, causing Leon to jot down his own feelings of being black and poor. When he mumbled that he wrote some lyrics based on the poem, Rose asked to see them. It took some prodding, but he finally handed over the piece of paper with the words scrawled neatly across the page. Despite his classification of lyrics, Rose saw the fundamentals of a poet in his writing.

"Thank you," he mumbled. Rose cocked her head and offered him a warm smile.

"Why are you embarrassed?"

"I ain't embarrassed," he pouted. Even as he objected, his eyes remained averted. Rose chuckled.

"Not being able to look a person in the eye is one key sign of embarrassment, Leon." He shifted his green eyes to her and finally met her gaze. "Are you embarrassed?" He nodded slowly.

"Poetry is girly stuff," the boy grumbled, dropping his eyes once again.

"Says who? The one I gave you was by Langston Hughes; he was a man," she pointed out.

"Wikipedia said he was probably gay. I'm not a fag," Leon grimaced. Rose's breath caught in her throat at the statement delivered with so much ferocity from such a young mouth.

"Hold up. First of all, let's not use the word fag. Would you like it if a non-Black person called you a nigger?" Leon frowned, and he shook his head.

"I'd beat a White boy down if he called me a nigger," he grumbled.

"And can you help the fact that you're Black?" she asked. He blinked in confusion at this question.

"What?"

"You're Black. It's who you are, can you change that?" she rephrased. His face still registered uncertainty.

"No. My parents are Black, what else would I be?" he asked.

"Exactly, it's not something you chose; it's just who you are. So why would you call someone an offensive name because of something they can't help?" She folded her hands and leaned forward waiting for his reply.

"My mama says being a fag…" His speech faltered. "I mean being gay is a choice."

"It's easy for someone who is not gay to say that, Leon. I'm not saying anything against your mother, I'm sure she is telling you what she believes. But you also must understand that the only people who insist being gay is a choice are people who are not gay," she explained. "Do you like girls?"

"Yeah, I guess," he shrugged, but his blush betrayed the true answer.

"When did you decide you liked girls?" He cocked his head and examined her in bewilderment.

"What do you mean?"

"You say that being gay is a choice, right? Tell me, when did you look at your options of boys and girls and decide you were going to like girls?" His face morphed into one of thought for a long moment, and she sat quietly, giving the child time to reflect on his answer.

"I guess I didn't," he conceded.

"Being gay, bisexual, or transgender is no more of a choice than being straight. So, what if Langston Hughes was gay? You liked the poem, didn't you?" she inquired. He shrugged a little and then nodded. "Why did you like it?"

"It talks about going for your dream, even if it seems hard," he replied.

"If your dream is to become a doctor, a lawyer, a writer, or even a rapper," she said, picking up the piece of paper and waving it around. "How does being gay or straight change that dream? How would being gay change your ability to work for it?" He was quiet as he mulled over the question. Finally, he peered up at her and shook his head.

"I guess it doesn't."

"So, because the poem by Langston Hughes inspired you to write something based on how you feel; what makes that girly?" she prodded, bringing the boy full circle in the conversation. His shoulders sagged in dejection.

"My brother said it was girly," he mumbled.

"What do you think?" she countered. "How did sitting down and writing this make you feel?" Rose picked up the paper and slid the page in front of him. His eyes dropped to the sheet with his own handwriting, and he took a deep breath.

"I guess it made me feel lighter," he answered.

"Explain that."

"When I first read the poem, I felt like it was talking to me about my dreams. Then I started thinking about what you said. How being born Black makes us underdogs, and how hard it is to get out the hood. That made me mad. So, I wrote some lyrics about how I should keep my head up and keep running for my dreams, like in a race; look where I want to go like you said. After I wrote that, I didn't feel so mad anymore. I felt lighter," he explained. Rose smiled.

"That's probably how any true artist feels; whether they are a poet like Langston Hughes or a rapper like Jay-Z. Sometimes writing down what is on your mind helps. It's not good to hold onto it and keep that anger bottled up," she said, drawing a trace of a smile from the boy. "There is another place where poetry meets hip-hop. Have you ever heard of slam poetry?"

"What's that?"

"It's like a cross between reciting poems and rapping, but there is no constant beat. It's all emotion. If the poem makes you angry, that's how you recite it. If it makes you sad, that's how you perform it. You develop your own timing, just like hip-hop, but you're not married to the rhythm." She took out a piece of paper and began scribbling as she spoke. When she was done, she pushed the page across the desk.

"What's this?" he asked, picking up the paper and reviewing the writing.

"A list of slam poets that I want you to look up on YouTube. Some of them may use bad language; but let's face it, it's nothing you don't hear in your music already." The bell rang loudly, prompting Leon to stand and collect his belongings. He crossed to the door, put his hand on the knob, then turned to face Rose who was watching him depart.

"Why is it every time I come to see you, I leave with homework?"

"Because of the free food," she grinned. "By the way, I want to tell you how proud of you I am. Keep up the good behavior, you know; not punching anyone and whatnot." Leon smiled broadly, showing off his dimples as he backed out of her office. Rose made a mental note to buy the boy a journal. She believed if he had a way to channel his frustration and emotions, his behavior would continue to improve.

Turning to her computer, she logged in and reviewed her email. Outside of the general school announcements, two messages caught her eye. One was from Tony Banks, confirming he met with Derrick Jacobs, the young man from the recreational center, as well as his mother. Tony detailed their discussion, and his plans to bring Derrick to his office during the week of spring break to observe the workings of an architectural firm. Rose smiled brightly at the news, happy that Derrick would have access to a positive male role model who would be willing to spend time with him. Rose had no ill will towards Javon, Derrick's cousin; however, as young and impressionable as Derrick was, she believed the boy needed to see a successful Black man in action, especially one who was working in the same field he was considering.

The second email was from Lorenzo Cavanaugh. Rose sighed when she opened the message. Cavanaugh was request- ing that she reach out to her uncle about appearing at a school assembly scheduled for the following month. Rose rolled her eyes. She hated to ask her uncle for anything, and she was fairly certain that he would not do it. Nevertheless, she replied to the Vice Principal informing him that she would place a call to his office. Picking up the phone, she called her uncle's job. When his secretary answered, she plastered a fake smile on her face to get her voice to sound more pleasant and less reluctant.

"Hi April, this is Rose Jenkins, his niece. Is he around?"

"I'm sorry, he's out of the office all day," April replied. Rose almost sighed in relief.

"Listen, my vice principal was asking if we could maybe pencil him in next month for our school assembly." She read the details of the assembly off the screen to April and could tell the woman was writing down the information.

"I will run it by him. Do you want him to call you after the workday?" April asked brightly. Rose almost barked in laughter.

"That's not necessary. If you can just check his calendar and talk to him to confirm if he can make it or not, I would appreciate it," she said. She gave her office line and work email address as a form of communication.

"Yes, Miss Jenkins. I'll take care of it," April replied. Rose signed off the call, grateful that her uncle was not available. She hated talking to the pompous bastard.

Layla watched Vasquez walk the grid of the office for the second of three trips. Vasquez performed the sweep every morning for the previous few days, and Layla expected no change in their circumstances. However, when Vasquez neared her own cubicle, she froze. Layla stiffened in apprehension as Vasquez held up the device. The light in the upper right corner, which had been green since they obtained the bug sweeper, was now rapidly blinking red. Her eyes widened in disbelief. She nodded her head to her own cubicle. Vasquez kept the second button depressed and stepped into Layla's workspace; the light retained its insistent ruddy beat.

"Well shit," Layla muttered. Vasquez threw her a wide-eyed stare, prompting her to kick herself for the audible reaction. "I forgot my tea today. You want to run to the coffee shop?" she asked as a quick follow up.

"Sure, I could use some coffee," Vasquez replied, placing the sweeper back into her purse and slinging it over her shoulder. The two exited the office, staying silent until they got to Vasquez's silver Jetta. Layla checked her personal cell phone to ensure the signal jammer placed under the glove compartment was still functional. She was relieved to find she had no bars of service. She quickly produced the burner phone and dialed Dom, putting the phone on speaker.

"Good morning, Miss Green," SARA answered after the first ring.

"I'm here too!" Vasquez called, firing up her car engine and throwing the car in gear.

"Good morning, Miss Vasquez," SARA acknowledged.

"Is she available?" Layla asked breathlessly.

"Standby." After a few brief moments, Dom's voice came onto the line.

"What's up, ladies?"

"Just to be clear, red and flashing is bad, right?" Vasquez asked.

"Yes, red and flashing is bad," Dom confirmed. "What frequency was it?" Layla and Vasquez exchanged baffled looks.

"You expect us to know that?" Layla asked.

"Which button? One, two, or three?"

"Two," Vasquez replied. Dom's line remained silent.

"What does two mean, Dom?" Layla prodded.

"One is the most used frequency for bugs. Two is a little more professional. I'm just glad it wasn't three, that's like NSA quality shit."

"Well, yay for two then," Vasquez muttered.

"Where are you?" Dom asked.

"I kind of audibly freaked out when I saw it," Layla confessed. "We covered it up with a coffee run. We're in Rachel's car."

"I can pretty much guarantee that they will move in on your apartments today while you're at work," Dom warned.

"¡Chingados!" Vasquez spat, in a heavy accent. Layla's eyes widened at this profanity.

"You know, I don't think I want to know what that one means," Dom sighed.

"Yeah, I don't think SARA is old enough to hear that sort of language in English," Layla agreed.

"I am able to translate just about every known language in existence," SARA interjected. "I can tell you that it means…"

"Let's not, SARA," Dom cut her off.

"So, now we will be completely cut off from you guys except in our cars," Layla pointed out. "You know, initially I thought we'd be fine, but I'm feeling a little isolated here. We can't stay together, because they'll know we know something is up, but we're on our own with ears in our apartments otherwise. I'm not a fan, Dom."

"I cosign all of that," Vasquez added.

"I'll get with Ryan today. I know it will be hard, but stay strong. We got you," Dom promised. "For now, we have to go radio silent. Only text messages on the burner."

"We can do that, but please hurry. I think I misjudged how much this is freaking me out," Vasquez admitted.

"Rachel, I wouldn't dream of letting anything happen to you. Who else would eat all of my food and annoy me?" Dom asked.

"I'm wearing you down, Dom," Vasquez grinned.

Later that evening, Layla walked into her apartment feeling as if she were entering an active war zone. She pulled out her sweeper and bypassed the first button, going straight to the second frequency. She figured that if her home had listening devices, the people that bugged her office were the perpetrators and they would likely use the same type of hardware. With the second button held down, she started at the front door and walked slowly into the small living room. The light changed to red as soon as she approached her coffee table, and again when she moved to the lamp next to her sofa. She walked down the hall leading to the bedroom and stopped in the bathroom. Once again, the light turned red when she waved the device near her toilet. When she entered her bedroom, the short-lived green indicator transformed into red by her nightstand.

Layla shook her head in disgust, fuming at the violation of her home. During her childhood, she bounced between several foster homes, followed by living on the streets of New Orleans, until finally residing with Nadine. In all that time, she never felt she had a true home of her own. When she took the job in Houston, she rented her current apartment, and while it was small, it was hers. A decade later, she had worked long enough and received enough raises to find a bigger place; yet she could not bring herself to shake the sentimental value of her apartment, as it was the first place that ever felt like home. In just a few days, her sacred space had been violated. She suddenly understood why Dom created a place for the group at the warehouse.

She took out the burner phone and sent a quick text message to Vasquez, inquiring on her status. Vasquez responded that she also found listening devices in various locations within her apartment. The follow-up message was laced with colorful swear words in both English and Spanish. Vasquez ended by informing her that she was going to attempt to forget the situation by drinking a couple of bottles of wine and losing herself in a marathon of Real Housewives of somewhere before passing out. Layla sent a message to Dom to confirm that she was correct in her assumption and both of their homes had indeed been infiltrated. She received a response acknowledging the situation and promising that Dom and Ryan were working on an extraction strategy.

For the first time ever, Layla wished she was a drinker. She felt like she had no way of handling the stress of being stalked and wire-tapped; not that it was something she ever considered was a possibility. She continued to pace her living room, anxious about the entire situation. Finally, she made herself a root beer float and plopped down onto the couch with her controller in hand. If she couldn't lose herself in the mindless consumption of alcohol, surely shooting criminals in the underbelly of post-apocalyptic New York would give her some form of stress relief.

Rose parked her car outside of the recreation center and shut off the engine. Robert was mute for the entire ride, and his silence worried her. After Malik's death, he fought the despair with the help of the path Malik left behind, and the subsequent gathering of the group. Theo's death and Dom's decision to let the federal government handle the investigation seemed to add to his anguish. Rose was afraid that her brother, who emerged from prison with a great deal of optimism, would fall into the depths of despondency. Robert did not seem to realize they arrived at their destination until Rose put her hand on his shoulder.

"Rob, talk to me," Rose softly urged. Robert turned his eyes from his hands and regarded his sister.

"What's there to say?"

"What's going on? You're really quiet," she observed.

"I'm just thinking."

"Care to share?" He shrugged and gazed out his window. A group of teenagers walked out of the center, heading towards the nearby apartment complex. One of the girls caught a glimpse of Rose in the car and waved. Rose smiled, returning the greeting.

"I feel cursed," Robert admitted.

"Cursed? Why?"

"I feel like I lose the people who genuinely love and believe in me. It started with Daddy, and it seems like it's been happening ever since. I know I still have you, Ryan, and mama. Don't get me wrong; I know that, and I love you guys. But I've been away from you for almost eight years. All that time, between your visits, and letters, all I had was Theo, and then Malik. Theo was so nice to me. He made me believe that I could..." He stopped speaking when his voice choked with emotion. "He made me feel like I could be someone; like I *was* someone. He was the first person to not treat me like a junkie."

"You're far more than a junkie. We have told you that," Rose asserted. Robert turned his watery eyes to his sister and smiled.

"I know, but you're my family," he nodded. "Do you know what it's like to be a junkie in prison? To have to go through withdrawals surrounded by people you don't know, and who want nothing more than to take advantage of you? Theo looked out for me. He was like my brother."

"I know he cared about you. He always made sure to speak when mom and I came up to see you," Rose smiled.

"I think he had a crush on you," Robert grinned.

"I knew that. I'm a profiler, remember?" she laughed. "He was a good guy. We may not be able to investigate his murder directly, but the reason he was killed has to be tied to Malik's death, which we are looking into. You will prove that Theo was right about you; you'll make him proud." Robert smiled and leaned towards his sister. She wrapped her hand around his neck and pulled him closer, touching her forehead to his. "You gonna be ok?"

"I have you guys. I'll hurt for a while, not sure how long, but I won't self-medicate. I will handle my emotions better this time, I promise," Robert assured her. Rose kissed him on the forehead.

"That's all I needed to hear. As long as I have air in my lungs, and as long as my heart beats, I got you, big brother," she whispered in his ear. Robert nodded and pulled her in for a hug.

"Was that a song?" Robert inquired, after a long moment. Rose pushed him back and smacked his arm.

"No, jerk!"

"I'm just saying, it would be a pretty good song," he insisted, a lopsided grin spreading across his lips.

"You ready to do this?" she asked, reaching into the backseat for her purse. Robert took in a deep breath, exhaled, and nodded.

"Let's go."

The two entered the recreation center and discovered Darla Richardson locking up the gymnasium. Her purse rested on the desk in preparation for her departure. Darla turned to the sound of the door and smiled at the siblings.

"I was starting to think you weren't coming. He told me you were meeting him here, but it was getting late," she said to Rose. Rose glided to her and accepted a hug. Darla's eyes widened when she took in Robert. "As I live and breathe! You look great, get over here!" He beamed and allowed himself to be enveloped into her formidable busty hug.

"How have you been, Ms. Darla?" he asked when he moved away.

"I'm blessed, Mr. Jenkins! It's so good to see you. You look fantastic!"

"It's amazing how clean living can change a man," Robert replied. Darla smiled with tears in her eyes, and she pulled him back in for another hug.

"I'm so happy to hear that! Your sister was keeping me updated, but it just does my heart good to see you in the flesh," she gushed, finally releasing the man from her embrace. She turned to the desk and picked up her purse. "Miss Jenkins, he's waiting for you in the office. I'll lock up behind myself." Rose smiled gratefully.

"Thank you, Darla. I appreciate you sticking around and waiting with him. Did he give you any trouble?" she asked, rounding the desk towards the office. Darla laughed.

"That's hilarious. He knows better. I was his teacher after all," she winked before exiting the building.

Rose motioned for Robert to follow her as she opened the office door. The big man stood from the chair when she breached the entrance. His eyes were light brown, just a shade darker than the golden hue of Rose's own pupils. In the almost three decades she had known the man, he seemed to have a perpetually mischievous twinkle in his eye. He smiled broadly, displaying a few golden teeth on the top and bottom of his mouth, which was curtained by a perfectly manicured goatee. His hair, styled in cornrow braids, hung just beyond his shoulders. Rose often felt like he paid someone to braid him several times a week, as it always appeared as if he had been freshly braided whenever she saw him. His chocolate brown skin showed no flaws or blemishes outside of the manmade ones in the form of numerous colorful tattoos. However, all of these details were often overlooked due to the man's size. He was huge, built like an NFL offensive lineman, a direction his life had almost taken until a cheap hit during his junior year of high school dashed his dream of football stardom and left him with a noticeable limp. She marveled at how a fraction of a minute could derail someone's life so dramatically. In one second, he was one of the top offensive line prospects in Texas; and in the next, Lucious "Big Luke" Larabee became one of the largest drug kingpins in the city of Houston.

"Rose Jenkins! It's so good to see you!" Big Luke beamed, scooping her up into a hug. "You look great."

"Hey Luke, it's good to see you too," she replied when he released her. She skirted his large frame and rounded the desk.

"It's rare that I get a summons from the great Miss Jenkins," he grinned. His eyes settled on Robert, and he hesitated. "Rob?"

"Hey Luke," Robert greeted him tentatively.

"Bro, when did you get out?"

"A few days ago," Robert replied. He held out his hand for a handshake, which Big Luke accepted, using that to pull him in for an embrace.

"You look great, man," Big Luke said in his ear.

"Thanks. Haven't seen you since the funeral. You're still… big," Robert noted.

"Yeah, that's not likely to change. Instead of the standard six, I'll probably need ten pallbearers when I die," Big Luke chuckled. Robert moved around him and sat in the chair next to the one the big man vacated. With everyone situated, Rose got down to business.

"Los Asesinos," she said. Big Luke blinked.

"Southside crew. I supply them sometimes," he replied. "What about them?"

"Sergio Martinez," Robert added. Big Luke turned to Robert, his eyebrows creased in confusion.

"I know Sergio," he admitted. "What about him?"

"He was killed in prison a few days ago," Rose informed him. Big Luke's face registered sincere shock.

"What happened?"

"Someone got to him in solitary. We are working with some people looking into that. We believe the same people killed one of Rob's friends. Sergio was our one lead, but now that he's gone, we have to find a different avenue. What can you tell me about him?" Rose asked. Big Luke stroked his goatee in deep thought.

"I saw Sergio a few days before he got arrested. I never thought the bust was clean," he disclosed, before telling the Jenkins siblings all he knew about the recently deceased Sergio Martinez.

CHAPTER TWENTY-EIGHT

Ryan skulked in the shadows dressed in all black. He pulled the hoodie over his bald head to cover his most distinguishing feature — the jagged scar on the right side of his face. The weather was still mild for Houston, and he was grateful that the rainy spring evening did not produce the typical sauna that was normal for the city. He studied the parking lot to gain his bearings. Before he left the warehouse, Dom showed him a blueprint of the complex grounds and Layla was able to give him instructions of where to go as well as information about the surveillance detail for the night. He checked his watch and saw that it was close to nine. According to Layla, the shift change for each detail was around midnight. He knew he had plenty of time, but a six-foot-two Black man lurking in the shadows of a parking lot of an apartment complex was not inconspicuous; the sooner he could free his captive the better.

When Dom laid out her plan, Ryan was skeptical. He was not fully convinced that she would be able to secure all of the items necessary for this deed. Rose chided him, reminding him of the woman's resourcefulness and capabilities to get whatever it was she needed. He assumed that her sizable wealth also helped. He crossed the lot and found a spot under a lamppost. Reaching into the pocket of the hoodie, he extracted one of the two syringes Dom provided. He tore open the packet and produced a vial from the opposite side. Dom was very adamant about the dosage he was to use. The goal was not to kill, but rather to give the spectators a little, unplanned nap. He checked the markings on the syringe, stuck the needle into the cork stopper of the vial, and drew in the clear liquid, careful not to exceed the dosage. Pocketing the bottle, he capped the needle and stepped out of the light, back into the shadows of the buildings.

As he neared his destination, he shifted from the gloom of the buildings to the shadows of the vehicles. Every detail of his approach had been planned out with Dom. Vasquez had opted to pay extra for an assigned parking spot, which was a tremendous help as it gave them a point of reference when they outlined the plan. Before he departed, Vasquez sent the exact location of the surveillance car via text message. The vehicle was four spaces down and one row back from her ride. Two rows to the rear of the man, he dropped behind a Jeep Wrangler and took out his burner phone. He sent a text message and then closed his eyes to exert calm over his rapidly beating heart. The cords of his muscles were tightly coiled, ready for action. While this was nothing like his days in the war, the feeling of apprehension brought him back to that time.

"I love you girls," he murmured. The chant to his family was a ritual he performed before every patrol or sweep he conducted in Afghanistan. The smoker was on duty, which Ryan hoped would give him prime opportunity to make Vasquez's extraction quick and easy. He crab-walked around the vehicle and inched his way closer to the destination car, checking the license plate against the information he had been provided to verify he was heading to the right place. Keeping his eye on the white late model Volvo, he silently crept to the rear bumper, dropped to one knee, and slumped as to not be seen in the rearview mirror. He scanned his surroundings in search of anyone who may have come outside and was grateful to see no one in the parking lot. He crouched in place, waiting for the perfect time to make his move.

Within a few minutes, the driver's window eased down, and an arm holding a lit cigarette protruded from the opening. He eased from the back of the car and lay prone on his stomach, watching the appendage to ensure he was not detected. Calling upon his military training, he began to Army crawl his way up the side of the vehicle, interchanging his gaze from the extended arm to the ground in front of him, confirming no debris lay in his path that could produce noise as he moved. When he was within striking distance, he tilted his head while removing the cap from the syringe with his teeth. The man pulled his arm back into the vehicle for another drag and Ryan tensed, ready to spring. When the arm found the outside again, he leaped into action, grabbing the man's arm and pulling violently with one hand, jerking the smoker to the window and causing him to drop his lit cigarette. In no time, Ryan found his mark and plunged the syringe into the side of the surprised man's neck, just as he exhaled his plume of smoke into Ryan's face. Once the powerful sedative was delivered, he withdrew the syringe, dropped back into a crouch, and scrambled to the passenger side of the car. The door on the driver's side flew open, and his heart dropped to his stomach. Dom's timing of the sedative was between fifteen and sixty seconds, depending on the size of the person. Ryan did not want to have to have a physical altercation, but he prepared himself in case the driver's constitution was strong enough to shake the effects of the drug and attack. He counted to sixty in his head, hoping Dom's estimation of the effectiveness was accurate.

When he reached sixty, Ryan slowly stood and looked over the hood of the Volvo. The driver's side door remained open, but no person stood on the other side. He searched the lot, but still saw no one. When he bent to the passenger side window to look into the car, he saw the man with his hand still on the door and his forehead on the steering wheel. He let out a sigh of relief. It appeared that when the occupant went to exit the car, he succumbed to the sedative and passed out before he could fully get clear of the automobile. Ryan noted the man's physique; thin but strong, and assumed the drug kicked in at the low end of the time frame because of his size. He rounded the car and pushed the man's head back revealing a compact Ruger 380 pistol in his right hand.

"That could have been nasty," Ryan muttered, grabbing the weapon from the sleeping man's lap. He ejected the magazine and slipped it into his back pocket before quickly pulling back the slide to expel the chambered round. He returned the gun to the man's lap. "That's better."

"That was perhaps the coolest thing I've ever seen." Ryan jumped in surprise and spun around to see Vasquez standing nearby; an amused grin on her face.

"Shit girl! You scared me," he gasped, placing a palm on his chest to slow his racing heart. "Has everyone forgotten I've been in a war?"

"I scared you? After all of this?" She eyed him skeptically and made a wide gesture at the scene before her.

"If doing shit like this doesn't rattle someone's nerves, they're insane," he replied. When he noticed her luggage, he paused and stared at her in confusion. A medium sized suitcase on wheels sat on the ground next to her, and she was carrying a blue pet carrier.

"Is that a dog?" Vasquez held the pet carrier out to him with a grin. When his vision cleared, he saw a black and white cat.

"Ryan, this is Miss Havisham. Miss Havisham," she looked into the carrier in her hand to address the cat. "This is Ryan. We like him. Don't be an ass."

"Nice to meet you, uh, cat?" he nodded with uncertainty.

"Miss Havisham," she corrected. "Where are you parked?" He reached for her bag and nodded with his head in the general vicinity of the truck.

"This way." He directed her through the parking lot. They crossed a few rows behind the Volvo and then took a left and traversed to the next building.

"Oh good, you parked in San Antonio," she grumbled. Ryan shot her an irritated look.

"I had to make sure the car wasn't seen, just in case something went wrong,"

"I'm kidding, it's cool. Thanks for coming to get me," she said with genuine gratitude. "Layla in the truck?"

"No. I got you first because you had the smoker. There are too many variables for her detail. I may have to wait for the shift change," he replied.

"Nice ride," she noted when he pressed the keyless remote to unlock the truck doors.

"Company car."

"I really like her," she admitted.

"Yeah, she's cool," he grinned.

"Can I come with you to Layla's? I have got to see the whole super ninja soldier act again," Vasquez asked. "Maybe let me take the next one!" Ryan regarded her with the scrutiny of a long-suffering parent.

"Nice try. You stay in the car," he replied as he started the truck.

Ryan and Vasquez pulled into the parking lot of Layla's complex and stopped just inside the gate by the front office. Unlike Vasquez, Layla had no assigned parking. She had given him the location of her car and that of her spectator. Because her building was two away from the front office, Dom recommended parking by the entrance. He killed the engine and withdrew the second syringe and the same bottle of fluid. He filled the needle to the identical dosage he gave the man outside of Vasquez's apartment. When he was finished, he pocketed the vial and covered the syringe with its cap.

"Stay. Here," Ryan commanded, emphasizing both words. His tone caused Vasquez to frown. "I mean it."

"I'm not a child. I'll chill with Miss Havisham," she advised, pointing at the pet carrier on her lap. He dubiously cocked an eyebrow

"I'm serious, Rachel," he warned. Vasquez turned her eyes away from him and looked out of the passenger side window.

"I can tell. You sound super serious."

"Are you really going to stay?" She turned back to him and let out a high pitch bark, before panting like a dog. He rolled his eyes at this display. "I don't know how long this will take. Watch your phone in case something goes wrong." She offered a serious expression and snapped her hand to her eyebrow in a salute.

"Aye aye, Captain!" Ryan let out a deep sigh in response to the woman's teasing.

"That's Navy. I was Army, and I'm a sergeant first class."

"Sir, yes sir!" she amended.

"Are you always like this?"

"Sir yes sir!" she retorted, throwing in another salute. Rather than engage further, he opened the door and exited the truck. He pulled the hoodie over his hairless head again and surveyed the grounds, but saw no one around. Stepping into the shadows, he crept along the buildings towards Layla's apartment. As he walked, his ears drummed with the sound of his heart. Movement from his right caused him to stop in his tracks. He glanced over and caught sight of a young boy about twelve, walking a cocker spaniel dog on a leash. The kid glanced at Ryan, and the soldier could see the anxiety in the youngster's face. Not wanting to scare the boy or draw attention to himself, Ryan waved at the child. The boy did not return the wave, choosing to speed up to get out of his reach.

When he got to the lot outside of Layla's apartment, he settled himself between two cars a row behind the surveillance vehicle. He dropped to one knee and considered his options. He contemplated knocking on the window to get close to the driver, but that would mean revealing his face. Layla informed him that this man did not smoke, so he knew that simply waiting for him to roll down the window for a cigarette break would not be an option. Stumped, he held his position frozen in indecision. Headlights startled him into darting behind one of the vehicles to prevent being spotted. One row ahead of his target, a Toyota Corolla parked, and a young Hispanic woman got out of the car. Opening the trunk, she retrieved two grocery bags. Ryan kept his eyes fixed on the woman, ready to move in case she turned to walk in his direction. He relaxed when he watched her move to the building next to Layla's. Just as he was prepared to return to his spot between the two cars, he stiffened at the gun muzzle being placed at the base of his scalp.

"Who are you?" a gruff voice demanded.

"Would you like to hear the Good News?" Ryan asked. His voice was far more relaxed than he felt. His pulse quickened as he slowly stood from his kneeling position to better gauge the situation. He could tell by the placement of the weapon that his assailant likely had about four inches on him and the timbre of his voice made him believe the man was heavier. Ryan could hold his own in hand-to-hand combat with someone larger and taller than himself, but the odds were severely adjusted when a gun was involved.

"You Jehovah's Witness or something?" the man sneered.

"Actually, I'm Mormon. I'm their token Black representative." The man dug the muzzle of the gun further into Ryan's neck.

"What are you doing here? Why are you watching me?" he demanded.

"How did you see me?" Ryan replied with a question of his own.

"You're over six feet tall, and my car has a rearview mirror. Why are you here?" he asked again, pressing the gun deeper into Ryan's skull.

"You seem to be holding a friend of mine captive. I'm here to relieve her of you," Ryan advised in a laid-back tone.

"So, you're a friend of Layla Green? Do you have a name?"

"Shucks," Ryan snapped his fingers. "I knew my mama forgot something when she had me."

"You have a smart mouth for someone with a gun to his head."

"It's not my first time," Ryan shrugged.

"You know, if things were different, I'd want to have a beer with you. You're an interesting guy. Sadly, you have stuck your nose somewhere it doesn't belong," the man growled. "Turn around."

"I'd rather not."

"That wasn't a request," he snarled.

"Oh, I'm quite aware of that," Ryan admitted. "I'm still not going to do it. You're going to kill me anyway, right? What difference does it make?"

"I don't like shooting people in the back."

"Well then you probably should have come at me from the front," Ryan shot back. He waited for another irritated remark but was greeted with the sound of a sharp crack. The gun suddenly fell away from his head. Ryan heard the weapon hit the ground a split second before hearing the distinct sound of a body dropping.

"And you told me to stay in the car." Ryan spun around to see a grinning Vasquez holding a tire iron in her right hand.

"I have never been so happy to know someone so damn hardheaded," he said in an explosive exhale. Vasquez nodded at the man.

"A good rule of thumb to note is that I rarely do what I'm told. Didn't think I'd need this," she confessed, holding up the tire iron. "But it seemed like you got yourself in a spot of trouble."

"I got distracted," he blushed.

"Well it's good you got me out first, isn't it? Layla may have actually waited for you."

"It is. Thank you," he nodded. He slipped the syringe from his pocket and pulled the cap off of the needle with his teeth. When he bent to pump the man with the sedative, Vasquez restrained his arm.

"No, sir. I took him down, I get to poke him," she declared, her other hand extended for the needle.

"You can't be serious," he sighed. Vasquez narrowed her eyes.

"There are a lot of things I joke about, but poking people with needles is not one of them," she proclaimed. Ryan relented and handed her the syringe. Vasquez knelt to the unconscious man and stuck the needle into his neck, depressing the plunger in a swift motion. When she was done, she handed the syringe back to Ryan, who capped the needle and slipped it into his pocket. "Where are we taking him?"

"We?"

"Oh, I'm sorry," she said in an embellished apology. "You're a big man, knock yourself out." She stood back and crossed her arms, waiting for him to act. Ryan knelt down and grabbed the unconscious man under his arms. As he suspected, the creep had about thirty pounds and four inches on him. With the first tug, he knew he was in trouble. He threw a look at Vasquez who stood over him with a smug expression on her face.

"He's a bit heavy," he admitted.

"It looks like it. Did you know lifting dead weight is far more difficult than a conscious person? But what do I know? I'm just a woman who moves dead bodies for a living," she sighed, waving her hands at Ryan and the comatose man dismissively. "Please, by all means." Ryan tugged again but made no more headway. Finally, he stood with a heavy sigh.

"Could you help me, Rachel?" he asked in a defeated tone. Vasquez's emerald eyes widened with mock surprise.

"Little old me? You sure you want my help?" she teased. Ryan rolled his eyes and pulled the hoodie off of his head.

"I should not have underestimated you. I'm sorry. Could you help me move him to his car?"

"I'd be glad to. At least he's warm and not a stiff," she smiled. She dropped to the ground and put her tire iron on the concrete before grabbing the man's ankles. Ryan knelt, picked up the gun, tucked it into the small of his back, and collected the arms.

The two carried the man to the car and placed him in the driver's seat. Ryan took the gun out of his back and as he had done with the man outside of Vasquez's apartment, removed the magazine and the chambered round. He also took out the firing pin from this weapon as a punishment for holding a gun to the back of his head. He placed the weapon on the sleeping man's lap, took the keys out of the ignition, and closed the door. He strolled to the pool that was one hundred yards from the parking lot and tossed the keys into the water. When he returned to the vehicle, Vasquez was eyeing him with a smirk.

"That's just evil."

"He shouldn't have pulled a gun on me," he shrugged. He extracted the burner phone from his pocket and sent a text to Layla to inform her that the coast was clear. In less than three minutes, the duo saw her emerge from her apartment with a backpack and a carry-on bag the same size as Vasquez's.

"You missed all the fun!" Vasquez exclaimed.

"What happened?" Layla asked.

"Your friend here saved my life," Ryan replied, nodding his head at Vasquez. Layla's eyes widened.

"How so?" Instead of answering, Vasquez made her way to the area where she had taken down Layla's observer and picked up her weapon.

"Just a little iron," she winked, waving the bludgeon in the air.

"Okay, you have got to tell me that story when we're safe," Layla insisted. Ryan moved to take her bag, but Layla pulled it back. "I got it, thanks." He shrugged and motioned for her to follow Vasquez to the waiting truck. Once the trio got to the vehicle, Ryan pulled out of the apartment complex. Layla turned to look out of the back window as they departed. As if knowing her friend's thoughts, Vasquez swiveled to the back seat.

"You'll go back," she confirmed. Layla did not turn to face her friend, not wanting her to see the tears gathering in her eyes.

"I hope so," she softly replied. Ryan sensed there was an emotional moment happening, but having no idea what it was, remained silent.

"You know, I always said we should be roommates," Vasquez proclaimed after a moment of silence. Layla wiped the tears from her eyes and turned to face the front.

"Rach, I'd probably strangle you."

"Probably," Vasquez shrugged. "Did you at least rescue your video games?" Layla motioned at the backpack.

"Of course," she grinned. Vasquez nodded in satisfaction and looked at Ryan.

"You know, we were so preoccupied with getting out of there; I never thought to ask where we are going."

"Dom's," he replied as he pulled onto the highway. Vasquez's eyes widened in astonishment.

"Dom who?" Layla suspiciously asked from the back seat. Ryan snickered.

"Dominique Samuels will be your hostess until all of this blows over," he informed the women. Vasquez turned to meet Layla's gaze with utter glee dancing in her eyes.

"That's great!" she proclaimed in excitement.

"I think the word you're looking for is — surprising," Layla suggested.

"It was her call. I was a little shocked too. I expected her to put you up in a hotel or something, but she told me that wasn't an option. She said that since you guys are on someone's radar, the best thing for you was to be with us at all times. I'm still at my mom's house, Rob has Rose's spare room, so Dom said her crib was the only logical solution," he explained. Layla raised her eyebrows at this justification and Vasquez favored him with a dubious look.

"That's not how it happened," Vasquez announced. Ryan's eyes darted from the road to her and then to Layla's incredulous stare in the rearview mirror.

"It's basically how it happened," he cautiously insisted.

"Dom had no desire to have us in her home," Layla argued.

"What gave it away?" he sheepishly asked.

"The only logical solution. That's all SARA there, buddy," Vasquez replied patting him on the shoulder.

"For what it's worth, she really didn't want to put you in a hotel, and she did want you guys to be around someone from the group. She just didn't realize that the computer would point out the fact that she was the only option," he explained. "It was quite the hilarious argument."

"I'm sure," Layla muttered stiffly. Vasquez turned to her friend.

"Don't be like that. I'm sure it's nothing against us. It's just the whole needing her space thing," she contended. Layla nodded and turned to stare out of the window.

"Rose explained it to me. She says Dom is really introverted, and she's got some baggage. I know it's nothing against you guys. If she didn't want to do this, to help you, I don't believe she would," he said.

"I know she wouldn't," Vasquez agreed. "Her house is huge; we can stay out of her way."

"Until she cooks," Layla grumbled.

"Well, of course. I mean, we gotta eat, right?"

CHAPTER TWENTY-NINE

After all of the changes in Dom's life, the last thing she wanted to add into the mix was houseguests. Unfortunately, she was unable to provide a persuasive argument to counter SARA's insistence that her home was the only logical place for the two to take refuge. Much to her chagrin, she was forced to do something she had not done in years — shop at an actual store. After developing the plan of extraction with Ryan, she and the Jenkins brothers set off to a furniture store to get a couple of beds for her incoming lodgers. The siblings helped her get the beds into two of the spare rooms in the house, and while Ryan prepared to liberate the two women, Dom and Robert assembled the furniture and prepared the rooms.

What she had not expected was the cat. She cautioned Vasquez to keep the feline away from her pet room, which housed one of a cat's favorite snacks. After receiving assurance that the kitten would not nosh on Nemo and the gang, she showed the two women to their rooms located in the same wing with a bathroom separating the two chambers. The following day, Vasquez and Layla traveled with Dom to the warehouse where they met up with Robert and Ryan. Rose joined the group after the school day ended and the crowd gathered around the conference table to review the information she obtained from Big Luke.

"So, you're telling us that the only person who had a continual rap sheet from juvenile to adulthood, and the only person who was actually known to be affiliated with a gang, is the one person your source says probably didn't do anything?" Dom inquired.

"According to Luke, Sergio had been running with Los Asesinos until recently," Rose nodded.

"How recent is recently?" Ryan asked.

"He told his crew he and his girlfriend, Tanisha Waters, were moving to Miami and he was done with the game. Luke saw him that same day — three days before he was arrested," she replied. Ryan began to stroke his scar in thought.

"So, according to your friend Luke…" Vasquez began, but Ryan cut her off.

"Let's not throw around the word friend so loosely when discussing Luke." Rose put her hand on her brother's arm, drawing his fierce gaze. When she gave him a small headshake, his eyes lost some of the fire. "Sorry."

"According to Luke, when was this Miami move happening?" Vasquez finished her question.

"They were supposed to leave the day after he was arrested," Rose replied.

"That can't be a coincidence," Layla mumbled.

"That's what Luke said. He specifically emphasized that he didn't think the bust was clean. Why would Sergio have drugs on him if he was leaving the life?" Robert inquired.

"Was he a user?" Dom posed this question. Rose and Robert shook their heads adamantly.

"I asked," Rose informed the assembly. "Luke said it was a strong rule among Los Asesinos, no one uses the product. Nothing more than weed."

"And see, Luke supplied Los Asesinos. Sergio happened to be one of two guys who met up with Luke to get their supply. Luke told us that when he saw Sergio, nothing was exchanged. Keep in mind, Sergio was fairly high up, so while he may have gotten the supply, he wasn't a street-level dealer. He didn't use, he didn't sell directly, and he was out of the game. There was no reason for him to have drugs on him, especially the day before he was leaving town," Robert added.

"Could one of his so-called friends have planted drugs on him without his knowledge?" Layla wondered. "I mean, a high-level gang member just walking away? That couldn't have been welcomed news."

"I don't think so," Rose answered. "Luke says that while the crew was upset Sergio was moving, it was because he grew up with them. They aren't a blood in blood out type crew."

"Well, that's just bad branding. If you're going to call yourself the assassins, you should live up to it, right?" Vasquez interjected.

"Guys, let's face it. Sergio Martinez may have been a career criminal, but he didn't do anything to get himself arrested this time. That fits in with what I was telling you the other day," Robert asserted, eyeing both Dom and Ryan who nodded.

"Care to share?" Layla wondered.

"The fact that all these guys were hit with a felony worth at least ten years for offenses that don't seem to be in line with who they are. Eric Taylor's first felony was a fight, but when we looked at court records, we found that he was actually trying to protect a woman at a club. He got the felony because he was big, black, and blew one-hundredth of a point over the legal limit. His juvenile records show only petty theft and truancy. What does that tell you, Rose?" He asked, turning his eyes to his sister.

"He probably had a rough home life as a kid, but ultimately he's a protector. If he were truly a violent individual, his juvenile offenses would have a level of violence involved. The one vicious act was one of protection, not malice," she noted.

"Exactly," Robert nodded. "So, he got his first felony trying to help someone else. Never gets in trouble after that, has a family, lives his life, and then he gets picked up for unlawful weapons possession? Rose?"

"Doesn't make sense," she agreed with his unasked question. "I don't think he would have chanced having a weapon on him with his prior felony conviction. He was a big guy; he probably didn't need a gun. The fact that he kept his nose clean for years before this, in tandem with the story behind his prior conviction leads me to believe he was more of a rule follower in his adult life."

"You're thinking planted?" Vasquez prodded.

"That's what he claimed at the trial," Ryan affirmed. "But he couldn't prove it, and it was the cop's word against him and his wife. Who do you think the jury would believe?"

"Tommy Cole's juvenile charge was possession of weed, which we all know isn't that huge of a deal. His first bullshit felony was indecency with a minor, because of his ex-girlfriend's vindictive mother. Both of these charges are non-violent. He gets arrested for assault on a public servant? The cop says he punched him and tried to resist. Cole claims he was compliant. No body cam, so it's the cops word against Cole's," Robert said. "He probably got some time because of his prior felony conviction." Rose made a face and shook her head.

"I don't buy it. Another non-violent guy; why would he try to punch a cop?"

"Then poor Tavion Evans. There was plenty of reasonable doubt for this dude's case. His badge had been lost, it was confirmed that he reported it, but they found him guilty anyway. The first felony was simply because someone gave him bad bearer bonds and he didn't want to rat them out. He was probably going to college," Robert guessed.

"I looked a little more into him. He had a partial academic scholarship to Tulane in New Orleans. The felony took that off the table, so he went to tech school. According to what I found, the goal was to go to medical school, but he settled for being a surgical tech," Dom announced, her face betraying the irritation she felt at the injustice served to Tavion Evans.

"Right, so this was a good kid, got dealt a bad hand, and still tried to make the best of the situation. Suddenly he turns into a drug trafficker?" Robert asked incredulously.

"Was he doing appeals?" Layla asked.

"He had an appeal in the works, but you know how long that can take," Dom confirmed. "He reached out to the Innocence Project, and he was on their list of cases to take. He just got killed before they could."

"Four guys. All of their arrests are suspect. Now let's look at that in tangent with Layla's theory of a cop being behind the murder of Malik. This smells bad guys," Robert declared.

"We need to talk to this Tanisha," Dom proclaimed. "SARA, can you find her?"

"Tanisha Waters was in Spring as of three weeks ago when she received a speeding ticket from the Spring police department," SARA announced.

"Looks like we're making a day trip," Ryan grinned, his gaze bouncing between Vasquez and Layla. "What do you say, ladies?"

A half hour north of Houston lay the fairly small city of
Spring. The biggest draw to this quiet municipality was the Wet
n' Wild waterpark just off the highway. Ryan piloted the quad
cab truck following the directions called out by the GPS. Layla
rode shotgun with Vasquez begrudgingly riding in the back seat.
Vasquez did not want to make this day trip with Ryan and Layla,
insisting she could be of more use with Dom and Robert doing
research. While Ryan did not hear the argument in its entirety, he
watched from a distance while Layla and Vasquez debated the plan
out of earshot.

He was unsure if Layla wanted Vasquez with them because
she did not want to be with the man on her own, or if there was
another reason. For Ryan, Layla was the hardest of the group
to figure out. She was nice enough, funny, and very smart, but
she seemed guarded at all times. Rose told Ryan that she was an
orphan and practically raised herself from a very young age. He
assumed that sort of upbringing would make anyone suspicious
of new people. Ultimately, Layla won the argument, which Ryan
assumed was the case more often than not. Now Vasquez sat
pouting in the back seat with her arms crossed. The hostile silence
of the vehicle was beginning to make him uncomfortable. Finally,
Layla broke the quiet tension.

"You can't just stay under her, Rach. She's not used to all of
us being around. Robert is enough right now!"

"She won't get used to me and see how adorable I am
unless I'm around her!" Vasquez argued. "I'm not trying to be under
her, not yet anyway." She giggled at her own joke, and Ryan almost
drove the truck off the road when he heard this comment.

"Wait a minute. Who are we talking about? Dom?" he
asked as he corrected the vehicle. Layla grabbed the back of his
seat and the arm handle next to the front window as he fought to
regain control of the truck.

"Dude, don't kill us!" Vasquez snapped, holding onto the
back of Layla's seat.

"Sorry," he mumbled, once he had control of the vehicle.

"Miss Rachel apparently has a crush on our hostess," Layla announced after she gained control of her racing pulse.

"I don't know if it's a crush yet! I'm still trying to figure out what intrigues me about her. It's kind of hard when Layla won't leave me alone with her long enough," Vasquez whined from her rear seat.

"Ryan? Help me out here. You've worked with her for a few days now." Layla threw her hands up in frustration and focused on the passing scenery.

"Rach, Dom is like a squirrel. You know she's there, and she knows you're there; but if you keep trying to get her to come to you, she'll just run away," he offered, moving the truck into the exit lane of the highway. Layla turned from the window in exasperation.

"Thank you! That's all I've been trying to tell this hardheaded woman!"

"If I ignore her, she won't know I'm interested," Vasquez argued.

"I think we all know you're interested," Layla grumbled. "You get all moon-eyed around her." Ryan chuckled.

"Actually, I didn't know," he said, pulling up to the curb outside of the small duplex.

"You're a man. Men don't notice anything that has nothing to do with their penis. Guys only care if women are interested in them," Vasquez countered in a flippant tone.

"Hey!" he objected, holding his left hand up for Vasquez to see his wedding band. "I'm a happily married man!"

"Oh, so you're just oblivious then. That's good to know," Layla advised, offering him a sweet smile and opening her door. Ryan sighed heavily and exited the vehicle as well. The neighborhood was quiet, which was expected in the middle of a weekday. After SARA located Tanisha Waters' telephone number, she traced the GPS of the phone to the residence. When Ryan realized the location was a duplex and not a single dwelling, he stopped short and frowned.

"Which one?" he asked. Vasquez pulled out her burner phone and called Dom's number.

"Hi Miss Vasquez," SARA answered after one ring.

"Hey SARA. Which one is it?"

"Excuse me?"

"The place is a duplex, a multi-family home. Which unit is she in?" Vasquez clarified the question.

"She is on the west side of the structure," SARA answered.

"Thank you," Vasquez said and signed off the call. She turned to Ryan. "She's on the west side of the building. Which way is west?" Ryan smiled and pointed to the right side.

"I knew that military training was good for something," Layla smirked, slapping his back and making her way to the door. She went to knock but hesitated and turned to her companions with a worried expression on her face. "We didn't think this out. What now?"

"Now we knock," Ryan answered.

"Yes, I get that," she scowled in impatience. "The thing is, it's not like she's expecting us. Like Dom said, if we called we may have spooked her; so, what do we say?"

"We do what we do best; we wing it," Vasquez shrugged, stepping around her friend and knocking on the door.

"I hate when she wings it," Layla grumbled.

"I cosign that," Ryan echoed. Vasquez threw them both an insulted look.

"If I hadn't winged it the other night, you would have a bullet in your head, Sarge. Don't forget that."

"Wow. That was low, Rach. Let's try to keep the gloves up," Layla remarked. Ryan did not seem offended.

"You're absolutely right," he conceded. "Let's wing it." The door cracked open, restrained by the chain that was still in place, and a round face of a young black woman in her mid-twenties appeared. She looked exactly like the driver's license picture SARA provided the previous night. Her large dark brown eyes searched the group in front of her.

"Yes?" Tanisha Waters asked meekly. Vasquez bestowed a smile of reassurance to the woman.

"Miss Waters, my name is Rachel Vasquez. This is Layla Green and Ryan Jenkins," she presented. "We are hoping we could speak with you about Sergio Martinez." Upon hearing the name of her recently deceased boyfriend, Tanisha's face registered shock and fear.

"Who are you? How did you find me?"

"That's probably a conversation better had inside," Layla gently insisted. Tanisha closed the door, and the trio heard the chain disengage. When she opened the door again, she poked her head out to check for any other visitors. Satisfied no one else was with them, she opened the door and stepped back to allow them inside. Diminutive and curvy, her long relaxed hair was pulled into a bun. She led the group into the living room of the small home. Tanisha sat in a plush armchair, folding one leg under her. Layla noticed a box of tissues on the end table next to her, as well as a few balled up in a pile. The three guests sat on the sofa perpendicular to the woman's chair.

"First of all, we are very sorry for your loss. We realized he was in danger, but the detective who attempted to save him got there too late," Layla began. Tanisha's eyes immediately brimmed with tears, and she reached for a new tissue to wipe them away.

"Are you the police?" she sniffed.

"Technically no," Vasquez replied. "Layla and I are crime scene techs, and he's our security guard." Ryan gave a brief nod of confirmation. Tanisha's demeanor relaxed a little at this news.

"Thank God," she sighed. Layla, Vasquez, and Ryan all exchanged baffled looks.

"We're unofficially looking into the death of a friend. We think he's somehow linked to Sergio. According to someone who knows him, the bust isn't sitting right, particularly because you guys were leaving for Miami the next day," Ryan said.

"Sergio didn't have any drugs on him. That's not why they arrested him," she bitterly declared, anger clouding her delicate features. Vasquez raised an eyebrow.

"You know why he was arrested?"

"Because of me." Tanisha's flash of anger changed into grief in an instant, and her voice broke with emotion. "Sergio is dead because of me." Stunned, the three watched in silence as the woman dissolved into tears. She took a few more tissues, wiped her eyes and blew her nose. Once she got herself under control, Vasquez continued.

"Will you explain that?"

"I can't," Tanisha replied.

"Why not?" Ryan asked. The woman shook her head forcefully and said nothing.

"We can help you, Tanisha. We just need to know what's going on," Layla insisted. Tanisha's head shook more vigorously, and she remained silent. Vasquez raised her eyebrows, and her eyes lit up with an idea. She reached into her purse and extracted her bug sweeper. Holding down the second button, she waved the device in front of the lamp on the end table. The light moved from green to a flashing red. Layla's eyes went wild when she saw the indicator change.

"Whose house is this?" she asked, fishing her burner phone out of her pocket and typing furiously.

"My cousin's place. I came here after Sergio got arrested. I stayed after he got sentenced. I didn't know where else to go. All of my family is in Colorado," Tanisha replied. Her eyes shifted between Layla texting and Vasquez, who traded the bug sweeper for a pen and a scrap of paper. She scribbled on the page and handed it to Ryan; his face coated in incomprehension. Confusion gave way to astonishment when he read the message Vasquez quickly scribbled: *House is bugged.*

"We're really sorry about Sergio," Vasquez repeated looking over Layla's shoulder as she finished her text message. *Did you know you were bugged?* She turned the phone to Tanisha who read the message and nodded. Taking the phone back, she quickly composed a new message. She presented the phone to Tanisha and sprang from her seat, motioning for her friends to follow. *We can protect you, but we have a very small window. Let's move!* Tanisha shot out of her seat and stepped into a pair of flip-flops that were positioned next to the chair. She reached for her phone, but Ryan caught her hand and shook his head mouthing: *Leave it.* She motioned for her purse, and Ryan nodded slightly to inform her that she could bring this item. The foursome dashed out of the duplex and ran to the truck. Layla insisted on sitting in the back with Vasquez so that she could watch the rear. Tanisha clamored into the front seat, and Ryan sped away from the duplex just as everyone was grabbing seatbelts.

"Do you know how close they were to your place?" Layla asked. Tanisha snapped her seatbelt into place and turned to face the woman.

"I used to see them watching me until a few months ago. I thought I was safe, but then I got a phone call from an unknown number telling me that I better keep my mouth shut. They said if I talked, they would know. Then they started giving details about what was going on in the house. After that, I knew they were listening," she answered. "I can't believe this." Layla kept her eyes fixed out the rear window of the truck. When Ryan turned right at the end of the street, she caught sight of a red Dodge Challenger turning onto the road they vacated. She watched the car to determine if it was a coincidence. The Challenger sped up and took the same turn about a half of a mile behind their vehicle.

"Red Dodge Challenger. Can you lose it?" she asked, spinning in her seat to speak to Ryan behind the wheel.

"I can try," he nodded, tightening his grip on the steering wheel. "Hang on ladies! Shit is about to get real." He tramped down on the gas pedal, and the truck lurched with the sudden increase in acceleration. Vasquez grabbed Tanisha's seat and slid forward to speak to Ryan.

"That's a V8, but so is this," she declared. "It's going to be a maneuverability contest between a truck and a muscle car. We can't outrun him; he will catch up. You need to come up with a plan other than trying to lose him, Soldier."

Ryan took a hard left, throwing Layla into Vasquez and Vasquez into her door. This street had some traffic, and he took the opportunity to swerve in and out to put some cars between them and the pursuing vehicle. Layla turned and saw the Challenger take the same turn and gun his engine. The car began to dart in and out of the traffic and, just as Vasquez predicted, was able to move around the traffic with more speed and ease than the truck. Within seconds, the Challenger was right behind them, and Layla saw the driver's hand extend from the window. Her eyes widened in fear.

"Gun!" she screamed, sliding down into her seat and pulling at Vasquez to get her to drop as well. "Tanisha, get down!" Layla did not hear the shot, but she heard the slug hit the bed of the truck.

"Ryan, we can't outrun him, but we can't put people in danger! Get us out of the congestion!" Vasquez exclaimed from the rear. He took the first right and hit the gas. A screaming sound from behind the truck informed Layla without looking that the Challenger had taken the same turn. Another shot hit the bed of the truck, followed by the side mirror on the passenger's side shattering from the next bullet.

"Son of a bitch," Ryan growled, leaning forward. "Layla, the small of my back!" Layla looked wildly at him.

"What about it?"

"Grab the gun from the small of my back!" he called. She eased around and began to feel blindly on his back. She dropped her groping hand further south until she felt the unmistakable shape of the butt of a gun. Bile rose in her throat, her pulse raced, and she thought she would scream. Instead, she pulled it free and tried to hand it to Ryan. "I'm a little busy at the moment!"

"What the hell am I supposed to do with this?" she cried with alarm in her voice. Her heart hammered in her ears, and her breathing became ragged. She did not want to hold the weapon any longer than necessary.

"Can you shoot?" he prompted, jerking the truck into a right turn. Layla was thrown against the door, and the gun fell to the floor. Vasquez snatched it up before she could recover.

"I can," she announced, rolling down her window. She leaned out and took two shots at the Challenger. The driver swerved in surprise at the return fire, but the shock was short-lived, and soon the car began to close the distance. Another shot rang out, and a bullet took out a rear taillight of the truck. Ryan started to tap on the navigation screen looking for something nearby that could help suit his purpose. He took a sharp left and found himself on another populated street.

"Damnit," he snarled, taking the first right. This avenue was long and sparsely occupied. He turned his attention back to the navigation system, and after a few moments let out a sound of triumph. He focused on the road and began to drive with a destination in mind.

"I sure would like to know what you're celebrating," Layla said.

"I have an idea but it's crazy, and you guys just have to trust me," he replied, jerking the steering wheel to the left. Another bullet pinged off the bed of the truck. Vasquez leaned out and fired another shot before turning to Ryan.

"Crazy? Now you're speaking my language," she grinned. Layla stared at her in shock. She could not believe Vasquez could smile even during the present situation. Ryan saw the abandoned strip mall he found on the navigation system and increased his speed. A bullet shattered his side mirror.

"Rachel, get ready!" he shouted. Layla's window started to roll down, and her eyes bulged at this development.

"What the hell are you doing?!" she frantically shrieked.

"Trust me." He turned into the strip mall and slowed his speed.

"Isn't this the opposite of not being caught by the guy shooting at us?" Tanisha whimpered.

"Trust me," he repeated almost like a chant. When the Challenger turned into the parking lot, he gunned the engine once again.

"Ryan? What's the plan here?" Vasquez asked from her spot in the back. The gun was in her right hand, and her left rested on the back of Tanisha's seat to keep her balance.

"We're going to cause a wreck," he declared. She looked from Ryan to the open rear window on Layla's side, and understanding filled her eyes. "On my mark."

"I sure hope this works," she mumbled.

Ryan swung the truck wide right and then jerked the wheel hard to the left, putting the vehicle perpendicular to the oncoming Challenger. The driver in pursuit had not expected this move and did not have the time or space to stop. Vasquez pulled Layla towards her and pushed her down into her lap with her left hand. She kicked her right leg onto Layla's door and braced herself. As the car got closer, she raised her weapon and began to fire into the windshield of the Challenger as the driver slammed on his breaks to try to avoid the collision.

The Challenger plowed into the side of the truck, and Vasquez tightened her grip around her friend to ensure she did not go flying into the line of fire. Because she was anticipating the hit, she stiffened against the door hoping that the crash would not break her leg. She was relying on the sturdy nature of the larger vehicle, and when the smaller car struck, she felt the impact, but the door did not buckle in on itself. Ryan turned and snatched the weapon from Vasquez's hand as he opened his door. He sprang out of the driver's seat, shooting before his feet hit the ground. Vasquez counted four shots in quick succession. She peeked through Layla's window and saw that at least one of the shots had fatal consequences.

Ryan cautiously crept to the vehicle, his gun still raised. One of his shots found the man's chest and another hit him in the throat. Blood gushed from the wounds, and Ryan knew without a doubt that their assailant was dead. Training taught him to be sure, and he approached the open window, checking for a pulse. After confirming the death, he put the gun back into the small of his back and returned to the truck. When he climbed into his seat, he took a deep breath and eyed his passengers.

"You guys alright?" Vasquez relinquished her protective grip from Layla who sat up and peered outside of the window.

"Is he…" Layla asked, unable to finish the question.

"Yeah," he nodded. Tanisha's door exploded open, and the others heard her throw up outside of the truck. Vasquez opened her own door, grabbed a bottle of cola from the floorboard of the back seat, and quickly poured some over the vomit to dilute the woman's stomach contents. Climbing back into the truck, she heard sirens approaching.

"Get us out of here," she commanded.

"Absolutely," Ryan agreed, throwing the truck into drive and stepping on the gas. There was a sickening sound of metal scratching metal, and for a moment, he was concerned that the Challenger was stuck. In a few long seconds, the truck broke free of the car, and the group sped away from the scene, heading the opposite direction of the chorus of approaching sirens.

CHAPTER THIRTY

Tristan sat in his office typing up the talking points for a series of upcoming television interviews for Nathan Grimes. Alexandria informed him that Grimes' uncle harangued and cajoled the reluctant officer into cooperation. When he spoke to Grimes about the scheduled interviews, Tristan heard a sense of defeat in the young man's voice. He did not address his crushed tone specifically, but he did his best to encourage him.

"Nathan, I understand taking a life is never easy," Tristan told him at one point in the conversation.

"Especially if you took an innocent life. That's worse Mr. Rucker," Grimes said miserably. Tristan grew concerned that the officer would continue to see Timothy Cook as an innocent victim. If that was the thought in the back of the young man's mind, he would be a wild card in the public relations plan. A key component to image management was to remember that simple statements were no longer sufficient. With social media platforms catapulted to the top of what is considered reliable news, every nuance, action, blink, sniff, or imperceptible grimace was considered as part of any given statement. Announcements were no longer just written or verbal, but the method of delivery was also included in the analysis. Ultimately, the words spoken mattered least in this type of situation. Whatever the stance, if it was delivered with fervor and confidence, a good portion of the public would believe it. Because of this, Tristan was keenly aware that whoever was speaking on behalf of driving the narrative had to believe in what was being asserted at all times. If Nathan Grimes doubted his own innocence, it would show on his face and in his tone. A domino effect would ensue, causing the entire public relations tableau to fall apart.

"Nathan, he wasn't innocent. If he were, why would he fight you off and run away? I understand your concern but any law-abiding citizen, particularly an innocent one, would do all they could to cooperate to ensure clearing their name. Timothy Cook only reinforced your concerns. I'm not saying this isn't hard, Nathan. I can't imagine what you're going through right now. However, mistake or not, simple cooperation would have allowed everyone to go home at the end of the day. No one can blame an officer who is forced to choose between his own life and the life of a suspected criminal. You have got to stop beating yourself up over this," Tristan implored, hoping his tone conveyed consolation and kindness.

After calming the cop down, Tristan went through the schedule of media appearances. As he expected, by the overnight news cycle Grimes became a household name. He had a preferred list of news outlets that catered to him in situations where narrative meant everything. Based on his monitoring, he knew that those in this circle were strictly sticking to the talking points and circulating the photos of Nathan Grimes along with his friends of color. All were spouting the same contention that photographic evidence proved Grimes was not a racist man, and while the death of Timothy Cook was tragic, if the man cooperated his day would have continued with only a mild interruption. The news sites that weren't under Tristan's influence took the stance that the circulated photos were nothing more than a cheap attempt at taking the public vision away from a problem with American policing.

As Tristan was revising the questions that were to be asked of Grimes when he made his national debut, a ringing phone broke his concentration. Had the call been on his office line, he would have allowed it to go to voicemail. However, the burner phone indicated this was a different sort of business call.

"Yes?" he answered, rubbing his weary eyes. Once he looked away from the screen, he felt the fatigue slam into him like a freight train.

"We have a problem." The voice belonged to his top contact within the police department.

"What else is new," Tristan sighed. "What happened now?"

"Layla Green and Rachel Vasquez popped back up on the radar," the man said. Adrenaline chased away Tristan's weariness, and he was suddenly alert.

"Where are they?"

"We don't know," the caller responded.

"I thought you said they hit the radar, how do you not know where they are?"

"They showed up in Spring, at the place the Waters girl was staying. It was Green, Vasquez, and a man; but they never said his name where it could be heard. Danny called me when they arrived and told me that the Waters broad had company. He gave me the names he heard, and I told him to get his ass to the house immediately."

"So, what happened?" Tristan pressed.

"I don't know. But Danny's dead and Green and Vasquez are in the wind again," the man replied.

"They killed him?" Tristan gasped.

"My money is on the guy," the man answered.

"Was Danny killed at the duplex?"

"He was popped at an abandoned strip mall, about four miles away. Based on the reports from the Spring PD, several people called in a high-speed car chase between a bright red late model Dodge Challenger and a dark blue Ford quad cab pick-up truck. No one got plates, but I'm fairly sure the truck was Green, Vasquez, and the other two. They took the Waters girl with them. I don't even know what they talked about; Danny didn't get to that. He just called when they showed up and started asking questions about Sergio Martinez," the caller explained.

"Shit," Tristan hissed. "Layla Green knows far more than she's letting on. Have you gotten anything from the investigating detective?"

"No, Lewis seems to be treading water. I'm not sure if he knows where Green or Vasquez are, but I can try to find out," the man answered.

"Do it," Tristan commanded. "Layla Green is becoming a liability. I don't want to kill her since you say she's so well liked, but we need to know what the hell she knows."

"You killed him?" Dom asked Ryan in shock. The two were standing in the loading bay examining the damage to the truck. The impact from the other car put quite a large dent on the driver's side of Dom's vehicle, and several bullet holes were embedded in the tailgate. Both side mirrors were shattered, and the driver's side mirror was hanging out of place. The foursome made it back to the warehouse driving back roads to avoid being seen by any law enforcement between Spring, Houston, and Clear Lake. Upon arrival, Layla and Vasquez took Tanisha to the bathroom to help her clean up. When Robert saw the truck and heard that his brother and new friends were chased through the streets of Spring, shot at, and almost killed, he excused himself and returned to the kitchen before Ryan could go into details.

"It was him or us," Ryan helplessly shrugged. "I'm really sorry about the truck, Dom."

"I can get a new truck. Are you guys okay?" she asked, waving off the apology. She moved to a cabinet with wheels located next to the unfinished vehicle restoration and rolled it to the damaged ride. She opened a drawer, and Ryan saw various tools inside. Dom extracted a screwdriver and walked to the front of the truck, dropped to one knee, and began to unscrew the license plate.

"I spent twenty years in the military and did multiple tours in active war zones. The guy chasing us was doing so with reckless abandon, putting innocent civilians in danger. Whoever he was, I have no guilt," he replied. Dom pulled off the front plate and tossed it away before she circled the truck and began the process on the rear side. Once both plates were off, she stood and stretched herself to her full height.

"You shouldn't," she concurred. "But now we have to deal with the truck. Can you wipe it down for me?" Ryan nodded, eyeing a bullet hole in the gate. She returned the screwdriver to the storage drawer.

"Yeah, I got it."

"You sure you're okay?"

"Yeah, I'm fine," he said, turning his attention from the bullet hole to Dom. He glanced at the circular conference table. "I'd be more worried about *her*." She followed his gaze and saw Tanisha sitting at the table, an empty look in her eyes.

"She needs your sister."

"I already called her," he replied.

"It's hard to believe Rachel kept her cool in that situation. She's so flighty, and she's never serious. I would have never guessed she would've stepped up like that. I can't believe you all aren't traumatized."

"Rachel handled herself. You may want to give her a peek at your arsenal. I wouldn't mind her as a second gun for when things get crazy," he grinned. His eyes moved across the warehouse and the smile melted from his face. "I wouldn't say all, but Tanisha got out unscathed though." She turned to the area of his scrutiny and realized he was talking about Layla. She was sitting at a computer terminal staring into space.

"She seems so tough. What do you mean?" she wondered.

"I don't know what happened with her. When I asked her to grab the gun, she just froze. It was almost like she panicked," he explained. The description baffled Dom. For her money, she would have thought Layla would have been the badass and Vasquez would have been the one to panic.

"I guess I'll go talk to her," she sighed. She crossed the warehouse and grabbed a chair from another cubicle, situating the seat behind Layla.

"You alright?" Layla spun her chair around and faced Dom; her eyes had a haunted expression.

"I see dead people all the time for work, but I've never actually seen them be killed. It's easy to guess the scenario behind a death. Since you weren't there, it's all theory and conjecture. But to see it happen before your eyes," she whispered, her eyes filled with tears, and she quickly wiped them away before they fell.

"I know," Dom nodded.

"You do? You've seen someone killed in front of you?" Layla inquired. Dom dropped her eyes to the floor in front of Layla's feet and nodded slowly after a few seconds.

"I have." Layla raised an eyebrow in surprise at this somber statement.

"When?"

"When I was twelve," she answered, with little emotion, her eyes still on the ground. "My mother was killed right in front of me." Layla gasped at the announcement.

"Your mother? What happened?" she stammered. Dom sat in silence for another few seconds, and Layla thought the question was one too many for the private woman. After a few moments, Dom's right hand went to the top of her short sleeve red button-down shirt. She silently started to unhook buttons with one hand. Layla was confused by this display, but before she could ask, the woman stopped. After unfastening three buttons, she pulled the left side of the shirt away from her body to expose a spider web of scar tissue. She looked down to see what was exposed and then opened the shirt more, allowing Layla to get a good look at the bullet wound. Layla gawked at the scar in disbelief. "You got shot?"

"I got lucky. My mom, not so much," she murmured as she fastened her shirt. There was very little emotion in her voice, but Layla could see the pain in her eyes. "What you've witnessed cannot be unseen. I know you deal with death all the time, but it's different when you see it firsthand. It makes it more real." Layla's mind was racing with questions.

"What happened, Dom?" she asked after a brief silence.

"My parents divorced when I was young, so it was just my mom and me for a while. She got herself a pretty good paying job and was able to put down money on a small house for us just outside of Fort Worth."

"You're not from Houston?" Layla interrupted.

"No, I moved here when I graduated from MIT," she answered. "Anyway, one night we were home. It was late, and I was in my room listening to the radio."

"Radio?" Layla asked. Dom chuckled at the question.

"I'm a few years older than you. This was before digital music. So, some tweeker, that's what we called people who were addicted to meth when I was a kid; this tweeker broke into the house looking for money, valuables, or whatever he could find. The thing is, we didn't have much of anything. When he was coming in mom heard him and ran into my room to wake me up and protect me, as a parent would do, I guess. But all that did was trap us in the same place," she continued. Her voice grew softer, and while she maintained eye contact with the ground, her eyes were seeing the shadows of that October night over twenty years in the past.

"Oh no," Layla gasped, covering her mouth in horror.

"On the way to us, he found the safe in the hall closet. There wasn't anything in there really, we had a couple hundred bucks for emergencies, our birth certificates, insurance policies, stuff like that. He demanded the combination and mom gave it to him immediately. She thought he would go in, take the little money stash and leave. When he opened it and saw we didn't have much, it just pissed him off. He came back demanding more money." Emotion finally broke its way through her stoic façade, and her voice faltered. She remained quiet for a time, attempting to get a handle on her feelings. When she continued, her voice was once again detached. "Mom tried to tell him that we didn't have anything more than what was in the safe and the twenty-five dollars he already took out of her purse. He didn't believe her, so he shot me. It was like slow motion. I remember seeing him turn to me and fire the gun, but I don't remember feeling anything right away. As I fell, my mom screamed and rushed him, and he shot her too. My bullet went straight through. The doctor said that a few centimeters north, it would have gotten my subclavian artery, and I would have bled out. Mom's tore through her aorta. She was dead in seconds." Layla stared at the woman in shock. Since meeting the recluse, she attempted to understand why Dom was so closed off to people. Of all the things she imagined, many of which were products of her video game imagination, the reality was far more horrific than anything she could conjure.

"My God, Dom," she stammered when she finally took a breath. "I'm so sorry."

"It happened. I can't change it," she replied with a dismissive shrug. Layla had so many questions and thoughts racing through her mind.

Before she could focus enough to pluck one thought or question from the whirlwind swirling around her dazed brain, the warehouse door opened and Rose breezed into the building. She paused just long enough to survey the room before walking with purpose to Ryan, who was standing near the conference table awkwardly trying to make small talk with Tanisha and Vasquez. Rose embraced Ryan with vigor and Dom could see her body relax upon making contact with her big brother. When she finally released him, she punched him hard in his arm.

"Don't you ever do some stupid shit like that again!" she yelled, striking him a second time. Ryan's face twisted in pain and he rubbed his arm.

"Geez, when did you get a right hook?" he grunted.

"Not funny. I can't believe you! You almost died today!" she shrieked.

"I know, I was there," he nodded. "We all would have died if it wasn't for Rachel."

"You were driving, Knight Rider," Vasquez blushed, looking from Tanisha to the Jenkins siblings. Upon hearing his sister's voice, Robert materialized from the kitchen and crossed over to his family. Dom could see remnants of his spilled tears and understood that the fear of losing another brother after all the loss of the past week was driving him to a breaking point. She felt sorry for the man. Given his prior propensity to self-medicate in traumatic situations, the events of the past few days were affecting him in a profound way. He hugged Rose for a long while before finally embracing his older brother.

"Guys, I'm fine," Ryan insisted. He scooped Rose into a three-way hug with Robert. Layla and Dom made their way to the gathering around the conference table. After the sibling hug fest, Rose approached Vasquez, her eyes moist, and bent down to embrace her.

"Thank you," she whispered.

"There is nothing to thank me for. I was trying to save my own life too," Vasquez admitted when she pulled away. Rose wiped her eyes and finally turned her attention to Tanisha.

"Miss Waters. My name is Rose Jenkins. Ryan and Robert are my brothers. Are you doing okay?" she asked. Tanisha lifted her watery gaze to Rose and sniffed.

"I haven't been okay in a long time," she replied. "They're going to come looking for me, and you guys have made yourselves targets." She glanced at Vasquez, Ryan, and Layla.

"I'm pretty sure we were already in that category," Vasquez confessed.

"Who is going to come looking for you, Tanisha?" Dom asked, taking the seat across from her.

"I wish I could tell you who they are exactly, but I don't know," she shrugged. "I am sure that they killed Sergio and they

CHAPTER THIRTY | 395

will try to kill me." As she spoke, the rest of the crowd settled into chairs around the table.

"Let's start from the top," Layla suggested. Dom picked up a tablet and looked at Tanisha expectantly.

"It started with my endometriosis," she began.

"Son of a bitch, she was right!" Dom gasped under her breath.

"What? Who was right?" Tanisha asked in confusion.

"Never mind, sorry. Keep going." Dom shook her head dismissively.

"Sergio had been in a gang since high school," Tanisha continued.

"Los Asesinos," Vasquez declared, causing Tanisha's eyebrows to rise in surprise.

"We've done some research. That's how we found out about you. Big Luke is an old family friend," Rose explained. Tanisha nodded.

"Right. So, being in a gang gives you money, but it doesn't come with benefits like health insurance, you know? I worked part-time at the Galleria for a while, but that didn't come with much in the way of health care. We were trying to have a child but my periods were heavy, and I was in a lot of pain. I looked online and saw that those were some classic symptoms of endometriosis, so I went to a new women's clinic on the south side. It's a big place. It has an outpatient surgery spot and everything," she explained.

"How did you going to the clinic for endometriosis translate to the bogus arrest and subsequent murder of your boyfriend?" Robert wondered.

"The bleeding stopped after the procedure, but then I started getting really sick."

"Sick how?" Ryan asked.

"Maybe about three weeks after the procedure, I was getting dizzy a lot, and I was really lethargic. Things just weren't right. Then, Sergio came home and found me passed out on the kitchen floor. He called 911, and I was rushed to the hospital," she answered, the memory of her ordeal causing her voice to quiver.

"Did they botch it?" Layla prodded.

"Not exactly," she replied. "I got to the hospital, and they ran a bunch of tests. I was critically dehydrated and had gone into kidney failure." The group eyed each other in confusion before turning their eyes back to the woman.

"Kidney failure?" Robert probed. Tanisha nodded.

"They hooked me to some machines and rehydrated me intravenously. Once I was stable, the doctor came in and scolded me for not adjusting my water intake and taking care of myself after my donation," she explained.

"Donation? I'm missing something," Vasquez mused, her face colored in confusion. Tanisha turned to speak, but Rose answered before she had a chance.

"When you donate a kidney, you have to adjust your life to only having one. That means drinking more water, cutting back on alcohol, things like that to ensure the remaining kidney stays healthy."

"When did you donate a kidney?" Dom asked. When Tanisha turned her dark brown eyes to her, Dom saw unfiltered rage.

"I didn't," she hissed.

"Were you born without one?" Ryan asked, clearly missing the point of the story. Tanisha shook her head.

"I came into this world with two. Those bastards at the women's clinic took one and didn't tell me," she growled. A stunned silence filled the room. No one at the table was able to find the words to express their shock and outrage.

"So, you went in for a simple procedure, and they took a kidney while they were in there?" Vasquez asked. Tanisha nodded in assent.

"After I got out of the hospital, Sergio and some of his boys went to the clinic after hours to speak with the doctor. I wanted him to go during the day, but he insisted on going at night. I think he planned to get a little rough with her. I didn't want him to, but I was pretty upset myself. He took his two best friends with him, Hector and Luis. When he came back, he was covered in blood. He said while they waited for the doctor to come out, some big guys came from the shadows and slit Luis and Hector's throats. They told him that if he wanted to live, and to keep me alive, he would forget about it," she said, her voice breaking with emotion.

"Shit," Layla gasped.

"For years, I begged him to leave the life and to start over somewhere else. He had family in Miami, but he didn't want to leave his crew. That night he finally gave in, and we made plans to leave the following Saturday. Friday night the cops stopped him and, well you know the rest."

"So, he got drugs planted on him and sent to prison to keep him quiet?" Dom asked. Tanisha nodded.

"He knew what was happening. He didn't want to go to court and tell the truth because he thought they would hurt me, so he pled. He told me to leave the city, but I didn't know where to go. Most of my family lives in Colorado, and I didn't want to put them in jeopardy. My cousin in Spring isn't a blood relative. She's one of those close family friends that I grew up with, so I went there. I told her I needed a place to stay until Sergio got released. I thought I was safe until I saw them watching me. That went on for about three months. Then they called me a few months ago and told me that if I didn't keep my mouth shut, they would kill me. I didn't know who they were, or who to call. I was afraid to go to the cops since they are the ones who framed Sergio. I didn't know what to do, so I hid and did nothing." By the end of her explanation, tears fell from her eyes, and she was holding on to her composure with a thin thread. Rose gently put her hand on Tanisha's back.

"You're not alone. We will find out who these people are, and we will take them down," she promised, her face filled with righteous anger.

"Who are you people? How did you get involved in this?" Tanisha asked.

"If you hadn't just told us your story, I would be convinced you would never believe ours," Ryan said, before launching into the explanation.

CHAPTER THIRTY-ONE

Dr. Rosalyn Guerrero exited the South Side Women's Clinic and strolled across the parking lot towards her silver Mercedes SUV. As she walked, she rifled through her purse for her keys. The night had turned warm and humid, breaking the recent pleasant streak of cool spring evenings. Her medium length black hair was pulled back into a ponytail as it had been for her most recent surgery; however, she exchanged her blue surgical scrubs for her Michael Kors gray tailored pantsuit. The only sound in the air was her Louis Vuitton heels clacking against the concrete as she made her way through the empty lot. Checking her watch, she realized it was almost eleven at night. She had not intended to stay at work as long as she had, but her paperwork was stacked high, and if she had not taken the time to do it, she would have never gotten caught up. Her husband Jeffery was quite irritated to find that he had to pick up their daughter Serena from ballet earlier in the evening. Their nanny had scheduled a family function weeks ago and needed the night off. Initially, Rosalyn was supposed to adjust her schedule, but things changed at the last minute. As tired as she was, she felt Jeffrey earned a little playtime with the doctor tonight. Climbing into her vehicle, she smiled at the thought of surprising her husband with late night sex. When the gloved hand clamped down on her mouth from the back seat, her eyes went wild with panic.

"You've done well. Thank you for your service, Doc," a man's voice breathed in her ear. She stiffened at the statement and then began to struggle against the man's grip.

Why would he do this to her? She left a lucrative job at a large hospital and put her medical license on the line to help with this insane project. There were days she could not look in the mirror, but she always told herself that she helped more people than she hurt. She did her job well and never spoke about the program. Why would he do this to her? Rosalyn began to shake her head vigorously against the man's grip, objecting to the unfair death sentence. *I didn't do anything to deserve this!*

Clarity slammed into her mind when she felt the muzzle of the gun press against the back of her skull. An internal voice screamed at her through her protests — she *did* deserve this. She had no right to assist people who wanted to play God and who believed that some people were better than others. She had hurt so many families and likely contributed to the deaths of others. For years, she made excuses, rationalized, and pardoned her actions that went against the very oath she swore the day she graduated from medical school. Tears streamed from her eyes, and the struggle left the doctor. She thought of her husband Jeffrey, so long-suffering and patient with her career. She thought of Serena. How many recitals and dinners had she missed with her precious baby girl over the past three years and why? All for money. Her mind floated to her immigrant mother who fled her native Cuba and worked her ass off to ensure Rosalyn had a better life than she did. She prayed Serena would never find out what kind of monster her mother had become. She closed her eyes and apologized, hoping God would hear her words and bestow forgiveness for the things she had done in the name of money.

I'm sorry. I'm so, very sorry.

The house was silent when Ryan softly unlocked and opened the front door. His mother kept a lamp burning for him most nights, and this evening was no different. He looked around the living room to ensure Joyce was not out of bed. When he saw the coast was clear, he turned to Tanisha and motioned for her to follow him inside. He put his index finger to his lips as she crossed the threshold and she nodded in understanding. Ryan locked the house behind him, and led the woman down the small hallway, stepping lightly as not to wake his mother.

After the group explained their formation to Tanisha, there was a question and answer period where everyone took turns asking questions to just about everyone else.

"How could they take your kidney if you were getting a procedure done for endometriosis? I thought that was laparoscopic," Layla asked Tanisha.

"It is," she confirmed. Her response drew a look of doubt from her interrogator.

"They can't take a kidney like that," Layla challenged.

"Actually, Miss Green, that is exactly how it is done," SARA spoke up. Her avatar appeared on the middle monitor of the bank of screens. Images materialized on the left and right displays, and the tablet in front of Layla came alive.

"Oh great, look what you did," Dom groaned when her tablet also changed. "Here comes the lecture."

"Currently, donor kidneys are extracted through a procedure called a laparoscopic donor nephrectomy. This procedure involves three small incisions around the abdomen. One quarter inch incision above the navel for a camera port, one quarter inch incision near the navel for a working port and another half inch incision for a second working port. The last port placement depends on which kidney is being donated. The extraction site is in the lower abdomen region," SARA began, highlighting one of the two pictures. The diagram showed a naked abdomen and locations of each incision site for a kidney donation.

"Well, I guess I was wrong," Layla mumbled, plucking the tablet from the table and examining the photo. After a moment, the picture changed to another diagram with four more incision sites marked.

"Conversely, the laparoscopic sites for endometriosis treatment are also in the abdomen. While the locations are not identical, they are fairly close enough to make both procedures possible with mild adjustments," SARA concluded.

"So much for the whole, do no harm thing," Vasquez muttered. The question and answer session had gone on for at least an hour and a half before the group broke for the night.

While Dom had room for Tanisha at her place, Rose insisted Ryan bring the refugee to their mother's home for protection. After the meeting was adjourned, she pulled Ryan aside and explained that since Dom had accommodated both Layla and Vasquez, he should take Tanisha with him as a courtesy. Initially, he objected to the idea. If the people they were looking into were bold and reckless enough to exchange gunfire in the middle of the day, they would have no qualms about killing Tanisha, Ryan, and their mother. Rose maintained that not only was there no way their unknown enemies would have knowledge about Joyce Jenkins in Sunnyside, but his presence and training would be sufficient to protect all occupants of the home. After that, he gave in and agreed. Now, he felt like he was back in high school, sneaking a date into the house to get some action. He hoped that his mother had fallen asleep on her favorite late-night television show as she did for years. He took the guest to Rose's old bedroom, not turning on the lights until they were both secured in the room.

The quarters looked as if seventeen-year-old Rose was just out with friends and would be home at any time. Posters of music groups from her teenage years still hung on the walls. Rose told her big brother that she begged their mother to do something different with the old room, like make it a home gym or an office, but Joyce would not listen to reason. She worried that keeping the room just as it was indicated a form of empty nest depression their mother tried to hide. Ryan, on the other hand, was touched that the room he shared with Rodney remained the same as it had been when he left for basic training. He almost expected to walk in and find Rodney lying across the bed, engrossed in one of his comic books.

Tanisha stepped into the middle of the illuminated room and took in the décor with a silent smile. She walked to the small wooden desk in the corner of the room and dropped her purse onto the chair. She ran her fingers over the initials carved into the lower left of the surface. Ryan moved to the desk and upon surveying what the woman was examined, allowed a smile of memory to take over his features. He pointed to the childlike scrawl of the initials RFJ.

"That's mine right there," he said, tracing his fingers over the letters. Tanisha's eyes moved to the markings and then she peered up at him.

"What's the F stand for?"

"Frederick. Ryan Frederick Jenkins," he replied.

"Why are there initials carved into the desk?" she asked, turning back to the surface.

"All five of us used this desk. Our parents bought it a long time ago, and every kid got to carve their initials onto the surface when we got into the third grade. Kind of a rite of passage in the Jenkins house," he grinned. He moved over to the engraved initials of RAJ and rubbed them reverently. "This was the first. Rodney Allen Jenkins, our eldest brother. He started the tradition by accident. He etched his initials on the desk when he was in third grade. He was such a little badass." Tanisha heard the melancholy in his voice and studied the letters reverently.

"What happened to him?" she whispered.

"He died, along with our little brother Reggie," he replied, moving his fingers to the initials RSJ.

"I'm so sorry," she said, the emotion in his voice and the fresh pain of losing Sergio caused her eyes to swim with tears. Ryan nodded and swallowed the lump in his throat.

"It was eight years ago. Reggie was just a kid, maybe the same age as you are now. They went down the wrong path together." Tanisha nodded.

"Every time Sergio got arrested, a small part of me was relieved because at least I knew he wasn't dead. I never told him that. After every stint, I would hope that he would be tired of going in and out of jail and leave the life behind. I didn't need the money, the gifts, or the cars. I just wanted him to live a boring life with me, maybe have some kids. But he always went back to it. Nothing I could say would ever change his mind. You'd think I would have left him, but I loved him too much. Everyone saw him as a banger, but I just saw my Sergio. It took me getting sick and almost dying for him to give it all up. He was going to give it up for me, to protect me. At least I know, in the end, he loved me more than he loved the life," she whispered, tears trickling down her face. Ryan put his hand on her shoulder and brought her in for a hug.

"I promise, we will do everything in our power to help find these assholes," he murmured as he embraced her. Tanisha nodded. Once the hug ended, she turned back to the desk.

"Where's Rose?" she asked, searching the markings. He smiled and moved his hand to the monogram of RCJ.

"Rose Camille Jenkins. The only girl; our little flower," he proudly grinned. His face melted into a serious expression and he eyed her. "Just never call her Rosie. She hates that."

"Duly noted," she chuckled. He turned and surveyed the room.

"You should be safe here until we can get this sorted out." He reached into the rear of his pants and took out the Springfield handgun. "I'll talk to my mom tomorrow morning and try to explain this. As far as we know no one knows about us, so they would never think to look for you here."

"I really appreciate this."

"Hang on a second," he said. He exited the room and returned after a few minutes with an olive-green Army t-shirt. He extended the garment to the woman. "I know you didn't bring any clothes. We'll go out and get you some things tomorrow morning before I go to work. You can sleep in this tonight." She took the shirt and nodded in gratitude.

"Thank you."

"Will your cousin be alright?" he inquired.

"I think so. I called her from the warehouse before she got home from work. I told her I'd be gone for a little while and that I was fine. She knows something happened to me, but I found out they were listening before I could tell her anything. They know she doesn't know. I think she'll just be happy to have her couch back," replied the diminutive woman.

"We'll keep you safe," he promised. He moved to the door and put his hand on the knob. "Do you need anything?"

"You got some Crown Royal?" she smirked. He chuckled and shook his head.

"Dry house, sorry."

"Then I guess I'm good," she shrugged. He bid her a good night and backed out of the room.

He turned to head down the hallway to his own room and almost jumped out of his skin at the sight of Joyce in her robe, standing in the gloom just outside of his quarters. His startled pulse drummed and he hesitated before approaching. She entered the bedroom and silently waited for him to follow. Once they were in the room, he turned on the light to find his mother's notorious scowl greeting him. The look was so severe he fought the urge to hit the switch and plunge the space back into darkness.

"Hi Mom," he croaked. His mother glanced at his hand, and he realized he was still holding the Springfield. He put the weapon on his nightstand.

"Who is that?" she asked.

"It's a work thing. She's in trouble, I'm keeping her safe for a while," he stammered. "She won't be a problem, I promise."

"You never did tell me about this job," Joyce noted, her eyes floating to the weapon he just relinquished.

"Rose helped me get it. It's security for a technology company," he replied. Joyce's frowned deepened.

"How does that convert into you bringing random women into my house in the middle of the night for safety?" He felt like he was being grilled after arriving home late for curfew.

"It's complicated?" His answer was posed as more of a question than a response. She cocked her head and waited for him to say more. When words failed to emerge, she spoke again.

"Three questions and a statement. Are you in trouble? Is she really in danger? Can you tell me what the hell is going on?"

"No, yes, and not right now," he immediately answered. She studied him for a moment.

"If you say she's in danger, I trust you. But here's the statement — if you do something stupid and make me decide between you and Val, I will choose the one who has my grandbabies." Her glare was intense.

"Mom! No way! You know I would never do anything to mess up my family. This is strictly for work," he implored. "I have to protect her for a while, and Rose and I decided this was the safest place for now." Joyce stared at him for a few silent beats and then she approached him, stood on her tiptoes, and kissed him on the cheek.

"Okay baby. Goodnight," she said, walking to the door. He gawked as she retreated.

"Mom, would you really choose Val over me?"

"You are a grown man. I've parented you already. Those girls are my only grandchildren. If you did something stupid, yes, I would choose my granddaughters over you," she nodded.

"That's harsh," he declared as his mother closed the door.

Dom sat in her office researching the South Side Women's Clinic, the facility Tanisha visited for her surgery. The plan was to review the public records of the clinic, and SARA would conduct more intense research while she slept.

"Dom, at some point you should return to your normal sleep schedule," SARA announced. As if confirming the machine's concern, Dom let out a deep yawn.

"Are you kidding?" she protested. "Have you been paying attention to what's going on?"

"Of course. I also know that without proper rest your efficiency will decline and your contribution to this investigation will dwindle," SARA replied.

"That's not true as long as I have you."

"What about when you erase my program?" SARA mused, drawing a laugh from Dom.

"Smart-aleck." She turned her attention back to the information on the screen. Before she could refocus on reading the public profile of the clinic, there was a soft knock on the office door. She spun her chair to the entrance. "Come in." The door cracked open, and Vasquez poked her head through the fissure.

"Care for some company?" she asked. Dom gave her a small smile and shrugged. Vasquez took the reaction as excitement and bounded into the large room, closing the door behind her. She pulled a chair next to Dom and plopped down. Dom turned her attention back to the research on the screen. "Find anything on the clinic?"

"A little. SARA is running the deep research and will put a file together overnight, but with the digging I've done so far, I've found a couple of interesting tidbits. The clinic is a part of a chain owned by a foundation that appears to be an NGO," she began. Vasquez touched her shoulder.

"You already know you have to tell me what that is," she advised.

"Sorry," Dom blushed. "NGOs are non-government organizations. They get some of their funding from the government, but they're really private entities that run themselves. The South Side Clinic is one of five clinics owned by the same foundation." As she spoke, Vasquez leaned in to read the information on the screen. Freshly showered, her hair was still damp from the quick towel dry. Her scent was clean and sweet with a hint of vanilla and Dom's heart raced at the woman's close proximity. As she read, she started to mouth the words on the screen, and the action drew Dom's attention to her full lips.

"So a foundation is engaging in black market organ trading? That seems to go against the very idea of philanthropy, doesn't it?" Vasquez asked, turning her emerald gaze to Dom who swallowed the nerves in her throat and nodded her head.

"The key is finding out who is behind the foundation and who runs the clinics. SARA will be working on that tonight," she proclaimed when she found her voice. She turned away from the computer. "I heard you went John McClane out there today."

"I'm pretty sure Bruce Willis didn't shoot with his eyes closed," Vasquez blushed, dropping her eyes to the floor. She moved a strand of hair behind her ear, and Dom could see she was growing uncomfortable.

"Modesty is not a trait I would have associated with you, Rachel," Dom smirked. Vasquez stared at the floor for an extra beat before she lifted her eyes to meet Dom's. The good humor was gone from her expression and was replaced with a troubled look.

"I was scared shitless," she admitted.

"The way I hear it, you didn't show it."

"I did what I had to do. But…" Her voice trailed off, and she turned her face away from Dom.

"But you're glad you aren't the one who killed him," Dom finished for her. Vasquez regarded her in surprise.

"How did you know?" she asked, eliciting a nonchalant shrug from her host.

"I'm pretty perceptive. The point is, you were brave, even with the fear."

"I don't feel brave. He was shooting at us and trying to kill us. But when I was returning fire, I was just hoping I wouldn't kill him. My life and the life of my best friend hung in the balance, and…" Her voice broke, and she returned her eyes to the floor. Dom had never seen the boisterous woman so subdued. She leaned forward and took Vasquez's hands in her own.

"Rachel, you did what you had to do. If you wanted to kill him, if that was your deep desire, you would be no better than the bad guys. There's nothing wrong with not wanting to take another life, even in the direst circumstances. Ryan is different; he's a soldier. He was trained for combat. He doesn't necessarily want to take a life either, but it's easier for him to make the decision to preserve the lives of the innocent. Not wanting to kill is normal. Very few people actually want to do it, even when protecting someone. You were brave; simply because despite being afraid, you protected yourself and your friends when all was said and done," Dom insisted. "If you're ever put in that position again, I have no doubt you will do what has to be done." Vasquez lifted her eyes, and she allowed a few tears to escape.

"What about you?" she asked. Dom released her hands and sat back in her chair.

"What about me?"

"Layla told me about," she paused and wiped the tears from her eyes. "She told me about your mom and what happened to you." Dom stared at her. When she didn't speak, Vasquez grew uncomfortable. "Are you angry?"

"I expected that would happen," Dom replied, shaking her head.

"You did? Why?"

"I'm the odd man out. I'm a curiosity for everyone," she sighed.

"Well, I won't lie to you," Vasquez smirked.

"I understand. You're Layla's best friend and co-worker. Ryan, Robert, and Rose are related. All I've had for the past five years is SARA. That seems to bother everyone else more than it does me."

"Why is that? I know Layla's not here to tell me to stop being nosey, so if you don't want to talk about it, just tell me to shut up and go away," Vasquez said. Dom surprised her by letting out a loud and genuine laugh. "What?"

"Rachel, if I told you to go away right now, you wouldn't do it," she proclaimed. Vasquez blushed.

"To be fair, this is one of the only two places I know of where people aren't trying to kill me," she admitted.

"Wait, there was another option?" Dom teased. Vasquez slapped her leg.

"My brother lives in California; that's where the department thinks we are. But if I left, you'd miss me."

"There's that signature Rachel Vasquez bravado," Dom grinned.

"So? Why do you hide yourself away?"

"SARA already told you, didn't she?"

"No offense to SARA, but I don't want the computer version. I want to hear it from you," Vasquez insisted. Dom took off her glasses and rubbed her eyes vigorously before returning the specs to her face.

"After my mom died, I went to live with my dad. That wasn't the ideal situation for me for that time. Don't get me wrong, he's not a terrible person. If it hadn't been for that, I probably would have a much better relationship with him. He just wasn't ready to raise a little, traumatized girl on his own. Maybe he didn't know how maybe he didn't want to, I'm not sure. See, my parents' divorce wasn't the most cordial. When my mom died, my dad didn't seem to care. Keep in mind, I was there too. I've always been highly sensitive anyway, but as a kid suffering from both physical and emotional trauma, I had a lot of issues. My dad seemed to think I would have just gotten over it." Vasquez's face morphed into outrage.

"What the hell? How was a twelve-year-old supposed to just get over that?" she demanded.

"Empathy is a hard thing, but so is sympathy. Like I said, he's not a terrible person, but he was ill-equipped to handle a kid with as much emotional baggage as I had. My parents were polar opposites. My mom was very open, friendly, and loved everyone. My dad, he was more closed off and trusted very few people. I guess you can say my mom was you and my dad was Layla," Dom chuckled. "It wasn't the best situation for me, but I didn't have anywhere else to go. It was a lonely existence." She was staring at the floor as she spoke, but stole a glance at Vasquez and immediately regretted doing so. She hated the look on her face; a look of pity. Dom did not like being pitied.

"What about friends?" Vasquez prodded.

"Kids are assholes. I had emotional issues and no compassion or outlet. I had a hard time controlling myself. Adults may pity someone who is emotionally unstable, but kids don't know how to do that. I got bullied a lot. You guys aren't the first people to think I was weird. That's how I got into computers, they were my only friends," she explained, looking at the computer monitors. SARA's avatar was still onscreen, and Dom was surprised at the computer's uncharacteristic silence during the conversation. When she turned back to Vasquez, she saw the woman was silently crying.

"I'm so sorry, Dom," Vasquez said emotionally. Dom cocked her head, leaned forward, and wiped the tears from her face.

"Don't do that. I don't need pity. I didn't turn into a sociopath or like a serial killer, so I'd say I grew up alright, considering. Besides," she paused and swept her hand around the room and into the air. "I'm rich, so screw them." She let out another yawn and stood, stretching her back. Vasquez's eyes followed her movements.

"Can I see it?" she asked. Dom's eyebrows creased in confusion.

"See what?" Vasquez pointed to her own chest, and Dom realized she wanted to see her scar. She studied Vasquez for a moment before unbuttoning her shirt again. She pulled the attire away from the scar and Vasquez stood to examine the blemish. Taking a step forward, she stared at the old wound before reaching out and putting her fingers on the raised flesh. Dom's ability to breathe abandoned her as Vasquez traced the scar tissue down to the circular bullet wound. After a moment, she backed away from the woman's inspection and fastened her shirt, fighting to return air to her lungs. "It's ugly, but it is what it is." Vasquez's scrutiny never left the scar, even after it was covered.

"It's not ugly."

"Well, it's not attractive either," Dom shrugged. Vasquez continued to stare causing her to grow uneasy. "I should get to bed before SARA starts lecturing me about the value of sleep to the human body. She quotes statistics, brings up studies, charts, and diagrams. It's excruciating." Vasquez moved her eyes to Dom's light brown stare, and she nodded silently. Dom watched the woman walk to the door. Before exiting, Vasquez turned to face her again.

"Thanks for the talk, and for letting us stay here with you. You're a very unique person, Dominique Samuels. I'm glad our paths crossed."

"And you, Rachel Vasquez, are not nearly as annoying as I thought you'd be," Dom grinned.

"That's what I go for; annoying and then pleasant. Pretty soon, you won't be able to resist my charm," Vasquez winked as she floated out of the door. After the door closed, SARA finally broke her unusual silence.

"In case you missed it, Dom, I believe Miss Vasquez likes you." Dom spun to the screens and found SARA's image cheerfully beaming.

"And you said I'd have to leave the house."

CHAPTER THIRTY-TWO

"You're shitting me," Lewis growled. He was sitting in his garage smoking a cigar and talking to Layla on the burner phone she had given him. After she told him of their surveillance detail, he grew concerned, but Layla assured him that her friend Dom was working on the problem. Despite this, when Layla asked him to meet her in the parking lot and presented him with the bug sweeper, signal jammer, and new phone, he was certain she was venturing over into paranoia. A couple of days later, she texted him on the same phone and informed him that both of the women's apartments had been wired. Later, following Ryan spiriting the women to safety, Layla gave him a story to give the captain.

The same day as he covered for them, Lewis walked the grid in his own home, and for the first time since receiving the sweeper, no longer found the comforting green light. The scanner switched to an insistent flashing red in various locations around his domicile. Even if Layla had not told him what to expect, he would have known what the light signified. The symbol of incursion almost sent the cop into a blind rage, but the knowledge of the devices around his home forced him to calm down since he was not the only occupant. He had to play it smart to protect his girls. Internally, he promised that if he found out who was behind the invasion of his privacy, he would have a talk with them, in a very old school way.

Inexplicably, the garage had been overlooked, despite being an obvious man cave. He wondered if the surveillance detail even thought to check the space, but their negligence worked out in his favor. In the corner of the room was a dartboard where he would come and unwind during particularly rough cases. A refrigerator was positioned against the wall holding beers and other beverages. This was also the only place in the house Sandra would allow him to have a cigar. Now, he sat in his man cave, smoking a Cuban and having a Corona with lime; however, after hearing Layla's recent ordeal, Lewis longed for a good stiff Jack and Coke.

"In my wildest imagination, I could not make this up, Oscar," Layla responded to the utterance of disbelief.

"What did you find on the clinic?"

"Dom has to do some research, I'm sure we'll know more tomorrow. We just got back to the house not too long ago," she replied.

"I hadn't heard about the shooting in Spring. I guess I wouldn't have since it's fairly outside of our jurisdiction. Thank goodness for small favors."

"Yeah, I was grateful for that too," she concurred.

"And Vasquez saved your asses?" he prodded, with astonishment in his voice.

"She did. She was amazing, unlike me," she sighed in frustration. "I froze. I'm still mad at myself. I just… I don't like guns."

"Kid, there's nothing to be embarrassed about," he soothed. Layla stared at the wall of Dom's guest room as she listened to the man's encouragement. When she did not speak, Lewis asked her, "What is it with you and guns anyway?" She let the question hang, trying to decide if she wanted to tell him the story.

"When I was a kid, I lived in a lot of foster homes," she began.

"Right, I know that."

"For a while, I was in a really bad one in Slidell; that's a city about an hour north of New Orleans. I was there for about eight months. The couple, they were bad news. Whenever I committed some offense in their eyes the husband enjoyed tormenting me," she continued.

"How?" Lewis wondered, already feeling his blood pressure rise.

"He had a gun safe he kept in his office. He would go and get this revolver and put it in my face. He would say that he could do the world a favor and rid it of one less nigger mooch. In those eight months, he did it sixty-five times. I would know."

"Sixty-five?" Lewis gasped.

"After sixty-one, I tried to tell the social worker during one of her visits. He stopped me, and after she left, he put the gun to my head and described in great detail what it would be like to have a bullet go through my brain. He had done it so much; I stopped being scared. That day, it felt different. He looked deadly serious. The description he gave was gruesome, especially for a kid. Then he pulled the trigger. The gun was empty, but it was the most frightening moment of my life. He told me that if I ever spoke about what went on in that house, he would kill me and tell the social worker that I got into the gun cabinet and shot myself. When I saw the look in his eyes, I believed him. I never tried to tell again. Instead, I started peeing in the bed. Not uncontrollably, but purposely. He threatened me a few more times with the gun, but I didn't stop. At that point, I didn't care if he killed me, I just wanted out. They finally sent me back to the state." Layla's voice was small, and tears ran down her face as she finished the story.

"Jesus, kid," he murmured. "How old were you?"

"Nine. I was nine years old," she answered. "For years, even after I left that place behind, I had nightmares about guns. I almost didn't pursue this career because I was afraid of them. Did you know that there is no real phobia of guns? The closest is something called hoplophobia, which is a bullshit term created to piss off gun control people, but it's not a real thing."

"You researched it?"

"I did. I was hoping to find something to make me feel like my fear was justified," she said, wiping the tears from her eyes. She was glad this conversation was taking place over the phone. She could never imagine crying in front of Lewis.

"Sounds closer to post-traumatic stress disorder."

"That's also a possibility," she conceded.

"Guns are alright, as long as the person who has them in their possession is mentally balanced."

"Well, considering the NRA and some politicians don't care if the gun owner is balanced or not, that doesn't matter," she countered.

"You're right, kid. The system isn't perfect, and I'm so sorry you went through that. I suppose that's a very good reason to be wary of guns," he admitted.

"When Ryan tried to get me to take his gun, just touching it was nerve-racking. Then I realized he expected me to return fire, and I just… panicked." Lewis often wondered about Layla's childhood growing up in the system. He never thought the horrors she faced would be so profoundly heartbreaking. He always felt like he was a tough guy; a requirement for his line of work. He could only remember crying four times in his adult life: the day he married Sandra, the two days his children were born, and the day he buried his father. Now, sitting in his garage holding the burner phone to his ear, he felt a tear trickle from his eye. As she told her story, he felt as if he were watching the torment happen before his own eyes, as he stood by unable to help. He dared not speak, trying to allow himself time to navigate the emotional wave that Layla's words sent his way. After a few beats, he trusted his voice once again.

"What's next?"

"I'll know more once Dom finishes looking into the clinic. Now that we have a direction, hopefully, we will find some sort of resolution," she replied.

"What did you do with Tanisha Waters?" he asked.

"She's safe; Ryan is taking care of her."

"Seems like you don't need me for anything," he muttered, feeling useless in his own murder investigation.

"Not necessarily. I really believe someone in blue is behind Malik's death. That's your path," she insisted. Lewis mulled over her statement.

"I just can't imagine anyone in homicide being dirty to this degree," he argued. "I've known many of those cops for well over a decade, and some for two."

"I understand that. I could be wrong, Lewis."

"You're never wrong, Green," he sighed.

"There is a first time for everything. I know it's hard to look in your own house and believe something is actually wrong. To some extent, we all are supposed to be helping others."

"Kid, I know that no department is perfect. But you're right, when you're in the thick of things, it's hard to accept that someone you work with could be dirty. I trust your gut as if I would my own. If you believe our perp is a cop, then that's the road I'll go down. I'll try to see what I can find out," he promised.

"You may have to text me when you're home and save our phone calls for the car. If you develop a pattern of going into the garage, you'll lose the space," she warned.

"You're right. I'll go radio silent as much as possible," he agreed.

"Keep Sandy and Chris safe. We're doing the best we can to end this. I don't know what I would do if something happened to them."

"I will. I haven't mentioned anything about the bugs so right now they're just listening to the wife of a long-time cop, who knows not to ask too many questions about his work, and a normal thirteen-year-old girl," he said.

"Sounds good." There was relief in her voice.

"Hey kid, be honest. How's Vasquez holding up?"

"She's okay as far as I can tell. Definitely handling this better than I did. For a minute there, it seemed like she enjoyed the chase. I think she's crazier than either of us thought," she giggled. "I'm just worried about her cornering Dom somewhere and molesting her."

"Wait, what?" he asked.

"Our little Rachel is full of surprises. It's innocent right now for the most part. Dom doesn't like anyone. She identifies as lesbian but for all I know, she's asexual," she explained.

"I don't know," he mused with uncertainty. "Vasquez is a beautiful woman."

"Yeah, the thing is, I'm not sure Dom even notices," she replied dismissively.

"Well it's good to know that near-death hasn't changed Vasquez's nature," Lewis grinned, taking a sip of his Corona.

Lewis let a massive yawn escape as he walked into the precinct the following morning. The information Layla gave him about the case, their ordeal, and the brief look into her childhood had his brain in hyper-drive most of the evening. Sandra noticed his restless slumber and mentioned it when they awoke earlier in the morning, but he assured her that he was just stressed and would be fine. Nevertheless, his spirit was bothered as he drove to work along with his shadow for the day in the form of the dark green Nissan Altima that tailed him.

As he passed uniformed cops, he could tell if they were coming on or getting off shift by their eyes. He was happy to be in plain clothes rather than walking the beat again, feeling no nostalgia as he examined the uniforms. Lewis smiled when passersby acknowledged him, but inside he was wary of everyone. The idea that someone he saw on a daily basis was dirty greatly upset him. He was not under any delusions that his precinct was perfect. Every city and police force had its own share of drama and cancerous cops. Like surgery, the goal was to eliminate the bad and retain the good. In his younger years, he hoped to drive positive change by serving on the board of the police union. Upon discovering the position was more politics than policy, he quit after a year of service, determined to fix the malfunctioning system by doing his job fairly and to the best of his ability.

When Lewis entered the bullpen, it was buzzing with the ruckus of the shift change. As he approached his desk, he caught sight of his night shift desk mate, Sammy Lopez, packing up his attaché case. He stepped behind the man and made a finger gun with his right hand before putting it to Lopez's back.

"Inmigración!" he whispered in Lopez's ear with a bad accent. Lopez froze for a moment before turning and smiling at him.

"Bro, I don't even speak Spanish, and I know that was terrible," he expressed with his mischievous smile. Lewis shrugged and put his briefcase on the desk.

"Sorry I don't speak like they do in your homeland."

"You're right. You don't have the right twang," Lopez replied zipping up his bag. He stood and stretched. Turning to Lewis, he pulled the chair out with an excessive flourish.

"Better sit down, old timer," he said.

"Get your hands off my chair, man. I don't trust anyone with a smile like that," he grunted, playfully pushing Lopez away. As he sat, he glanced at the computer and made a face.

"Hey ése, you forgot to log out again!"

"Shit, my bad. But while you're in there, finish those reports for me, would you?" Lopez replied with a wink.

"Bite me, hombre," Lewis scowled, turning back and switching users.

"That's racist," Lopez teasingly admonished.

"Call HR or Internal Affairs," Lewis shrugged. Lopez laughed and slung his messenger bag across his body.

"Don't get yourself into any trouble, White man," he grinned, turning to walk away. He halted his stride after a few steps and spun back to Lewis. "I almost forgot, Haggard wanted to see you when you got in this morning. Perhaps it's too late for the whole trouble thing." Lopez gave him a finger gunpoint before leaving the bullpen.

Lewis sighed at the news, stood, and made his way to Captain James "Jim" Haggard's office in the back corner of the room. He knocked on the closed door and leaned over to show his face in the window. Haggard was on the phone but looked up when Lewis knocked and waved the detective inside the cramped office. He entered, took a few steps into the small area and pulled out the chair that was on the other side of the Captain's desk. As Haggard continued his phone call, Lewis examined the office that he had been in numerous times; not only to see Haggard, but the captain before him, and the captain before that. The thought made him realize that he worked under four captains, including Haggard. A myriad of plaques of recognition for service hung on the walls, along with several photos with prominent politicians from the city to the federal level.

Jim Haggard, a thirty-five-year veteran of the Houston Police Department, was somewhat of a walking legend. As far as Lewis knew, his record of the highest closure rate in homicide remained unchallenged. The man stood a commanding six foot, six inches, and rejected the image of the aging captain who stopped taking care of himself. His physique could have been mistaken for a rookie just out of the academy, rather than someone on the downhill slope of his career. His thinning brown hair, graying at the temples was the only overt part of the man's features that betrayed his age. His ice blue eyes took in every sight in what could only be described as a calculating manner: be it listening to a case report, playing poker with the guys, or having a drink during one of the monthly homicide bar nights. Lewis immediately liked the man and did not mind him as a boss. Haggard ended his call and gave Lewis a humorless smile.

"Lewis, how's it going?"

"Well, it's only fifteen minutes into the day, so it's kind of difficult to make a judgment call on that, Captain," Lewis replied. "Lopez said you wanted to see me?"

"I wanted to know how the Rodgers case was coming," Haggard declared. He leaned back in his leather chair and propped both feet onto the desk.

"Not much to report, Cap. His mother flew in from Virginia to give a positive ID on the body. She told me that he had been in and out of prison over the past few years, which was why he was in Houston," Lewis advised. In reality, in the brief moment he spoke with Connie Rodgers, she said very little. Lewis met the woman at the Medical Examiner's office when she came to identify her son's body. He asked her a few cursory questions, gave the woman his card, and told her he would be in touch if he needed any more information. However, he needed to provide some detail to his boss about the case.

"Did you find the family member Green ran into over the weekend?" Haggard asked, his cold blue eyes fixed intently on Lewis.

"No. Rodgers' mother indicated that she was not aware of any family in the city. She did mention that he was from a close-knit community so one of his friends who he thinks of as a cousin could be here. Whoever it is, she doesn't know him," Lewis answered. He tried to be ready for any query posed to him by Haggard and have an answer readily available. "Unfortunately, Green isn't here for follow up."

"You said Green and Vasquez took some time off? Together?" Lewis almost smiled but kept his features placid. You did not get to be one of the most successful homicide detectives with the mind of Inspector Clouseau, the bumbling cop in the Pink Panther series he watched as a child. He knew that the Captain was covertly trying to make sure the story remained the same.

"Yes sir," Lewis nodded. "Vasquez's brother Eddie had a ruptured appendix. If you recall, she lost her parents not too long ago, so she's the only living immediate family member. She was a wreck according to Green, so Green went with her. You can imagine the fear Vasquez must feel to learn that her brother almost died from appendicitis so soon after losing her parents."

"What does this mean for your investigation?" Haggard prodded. Lewis blinked at the question in confusion.

"It doesn't do anything for me one way or the other, captain. The autopsy has been done; there wasn't much in the way of evidence to be processed. Now it's up to me."

"I'm sure the identity of this random cousin would help," the Captain offered.

"Possibly, but without that option, I'm left to good old-fashioned police work. I found that Rodger's last location was the prison up in Huntsville. I went there last week," Lewis reported.

"I heard about that. A prisoner you went to see was killed?" Haggard asked. Lewis was surprised that the man knew that much about the inner workings of a state-run facility.

"Yes, sir. Sergio Martinez was one of the prisoners I intended to speak with. My request is how they found his body. After that, everything pretty much went on lockdown." Haggard seemed shocked at this information.

"You intended to see other prisoners?" he inquired.

"I was starting with Martinez," Lewis nodded without missing a beat. "But I was also looking for any other inmates Rodgers was seen hanging with, I just didn't get that far."

"Do you intend to go back to the prison?"

"It's on my to-do list, but those people aren't going anywhere any time soon. I've decided to look into avenues outside of the prison right now," Lewis lied.

"And Green's source had nothing to do with your decision to go to Huntsville?"

"Captain," Lewis frowned. "I've been a detective for a long time. Do you honestly think that I would not have thought to trace the victim's last known location on my own?" When Haggard continued to stare at the detective, Lewis realized he had not answered the question. "No, sir. Green had nothing to do with my decision to go to the prison in Huntsville." Lewis answered the question confidently and clearly, but alarm bells and warning whistles were ringing in his head.

"I still don't like Green and Vasquez disappearing in the middle of this," Haggard grumbled.

"Well sir, no one can really time a medical emergency like this," Lewis claimed. "Also, they're crime scene techs; they've done their job." Haggard nodded thoughtfully but stared intently at Lewis.

"I suppose, but I still don't like it," he repeated.

"Captain, what's the deal with this case? For all we know, this is a former banger who got killed by his own people. You don't normally get involved with stuff like this," Lewis warily questioned.

"I'm the captain of homicide. There should be no question regarding my inquiry of any active case, *Detective*," Haggard said, emphasizing Lewis' rank. Lewis flashed the man eyes of conciliation, and he nodded as he stood.

"I'll keep you updated, Captain," he proclaimed, backing towards the door.

"See that you do," he commanded. Lewis exited the captain's office and strolled back to his desk, eyeing the detectives and support staff in the room. Some were typing up reports, while others were working the phones. Partners were speckled around the room huddled in deep discussion, and when his turquoise eyes flashed over them, his step hesitated. Partners? Could the problem be more than one cop?

Lewis had a few partners earlier in his career, and he hated it every time. He preferred to piece things out in his own way and at his own pace. The problem with partners was the necessity to work in tandem and to check in with each other. He had a wife for that. When he proved that his closure rate was higher alone than with a partner, Lewis was finally able to shake the department concern and fly solo. As he neared his desk, he saw Detectives Calvin Tidwell and Miranda Powers nestled together whispering. When he passed them, Tidwell immediately stopped talking, and he eyeballed Lewis, causing the detective to stop and turn to the duo.

"Something wrong?" Lewis asked. Powers offered him a strained smile, and Tidwell gave him a head nod. Miranda Powers had been Lewis' last partner. She was also the straw that caused him to demand to go solo. While he did not mention her relentless and unprofessional sexual pursuit as the reason, she knew exactly why he made the request. She was about his age, attractive, with a pageboy haircut relentlessly dyed blonde to hide the graying of age. However, he had been with Sandra since he was sixteen and only had eyes for his wife for the past thirty years. Powers was not a woman to take no for an answer, so the suggestions and flirtations became more aggressive in nature, increasing his discomfort. She never forgave him for abandoning their partnership, and Lewis could give a shit about what she did or did not forgive.

"Oscar! So good to see you!" Powers exclaimed in a saccharine tone. Lewis stared at her without emotion. She gave him a look of worry as genuine as her attitude, leaned to him, and dropped her voice. "Is everything okay?"

"Why wouldn't it be?" he responded, taking a step back.

"Captain Haggard was looking for you this morning, you never know," Tidwell grunted. Between the raspy voice from cigarettes, reddish gray handlebar mustache, receding hairline, and potbelly, Tidwell looked like he could have a heart attack if he farted too hard. Lewis wondered if Powers had gotten what she wanted from the obese detective, although the idea made him sick to think about.

"He was just looking for an update on my current case, nothing big," Lewis shrugged.

"That's a relief. I was so worried something was wrong," Powers gushed, reaching out to put her hand on Lewis' arm. He took another step back in time for the woman's hand to fall on air, causing her to purse her lips and redden.

"Hey Lewis, where did Green and Vasquez get off to?" Tidwell asked. Lewis' internal warning system began to activate once again.

"Vasquez had a family emergency in California and Green went with her," he curtly replied. Tidwell grunted and nodded his head in acknowledgment.

"I hope everything is okay," he said. Lewis nodded and started for his desk.

"So do I," he mumbled, unsure if Tidwell heard him. Approaching his workspace, he scanned the room again. He did not notice many detectives interested in him. Spinning in a slow circle to observe the room, he attempted to channel his inner Layla. He tried to think back to the Monday morning she came to him with the identity of Malik Rodgers, and picture who was in the office at the time of their discussion. Unfortunately, his recall was not nearly as sharp as hers, and he could not call up a mental image the way she could. He needed to talk to Layla without prying ears.

Sitting down in his chair, he logged in and reviewed his email. The preliminary autopsy results were waiting for him, and he opened the message to read what he already knew. Malik Rodgers took three shots to the torso from a .38 handgun, just as Layla predicted. The victim had no defensive wounds that signaled a struggle, which also matched the crime scene report from Layla and Vasquez. Toxicology was still pending, but preliminary findings indicated there were no substances in the man's system. With the information on Rodgers' occupation, Lewis did not expect the full toxicology report to show anything. He sighed deeply at the lack of information. He hated that Layla and Vasquez were out there investigating his case, but he also understood that since they slipped their detail, it was the safest course of action for all at the current juncture. He had a family at home and whoever was behind this knew exactly where he lived. As much as he detested the circumstances, he had to find patience. Lewis closed the email and leaned back in his chair in deep thought. He needed to speak with Layla.

He stood from his desk and headed to the men's restroom. After a quick glance at the empty urinals and checking for feet in the other stalls, he settled into the handicap stall, locking the door behind him. He pulled out the burner phone and almost dialed but decided a text message was safer. If he was being watched from within the department, his observer could follow him into the facilities if he stayed too long. He composed a text to Layla's burner phone.

I need your memory. Who was in the room when we spoke Monday morning? He sent the text and leaned back against the wall as he waited for a response. After a few moments, he stiffened at the sound of the men's room door opening. He heard the familiar sound of dress shoes crossing the tile floor to the stalls. He moved from his perch against the wall to the toilet, closing the lid silently and sitting down. It would be far more inconspicuous for him to be sitting at the commode rather than standing against the wall. He wondered if the newcomer was a spy or someone who genuinely needed the facilities. He glanced back at the phone and realized the sound was on. He switched the device to silent just as the text message symbol popped up with Layla's reply. Exhaling in relief at the timing, he opened the message.

Sanderson, Harper, Tidwell, Lincoln, and Reyes, came Layla's reply. He cocked his head at the information.

No Haggard or Powers? he asked. If Layla was right, and he was absolutely sure she was, Tidwell was his number one suspect. Yet despite the man being a class A jackass, that did not feel right. Layla's reply came faster this time.

Haggard may have been in, but he wasn't in the bullpen. I passed Powers on my way out. She wasn't in there when we were talking. Lewis considered this information for a moment. Powers was in the building at the time but not in the bullpen. It was very feasible that she and Tidwell could be working together. Lewis couldn't wrap his mind around Haggard being dirty. However, as he considered his conversation with Layla the night before, he knew to rule Haggard out completely was the epitome of naiveté.

I need to see you. I have to know everything I'm dealing with here. I feel like I'm a blind man playing defense without knowing what I'm protecting. A toilet flushed a few stalls down jolting Lewis from his concentration. He held his breath as he listened to the occupant wash his hands, not breathing again until the door to the men's room opened, and the visitor was gone. He sighed in relief and rose from the toilet. He stood in silence for almost five minutes, periodically checking the phone before a message finally appeared.

The crime scene. Apartment directly across, 3pm, Layla replied. His eyebrows wrinkled at these instructions, but he agreed. He started to open the stall door to leave when a familiar feeling caused him to stop. He turned around and unzipped his fly.

"Freaking prostate," he grumbled.

CHAPTER THIRTY-THREE

Dom reconvened the group at ten o'clock the next morning. For the occasion, Rose left work after her morning meeting with Leon Murphy as not to miss a moment of the new information. Robert whipped up a light breakfast of bagels, cream cheese, yogurt, and fruit. Dom cradled a cup of coffee and stared into space while the rest of the occupants ate and idly conversed with each other.

"You okay?" Rose asked. Dom's attention snapped from the void, and she regarded the counselor.

"I'm good. Why?"

"You seem to be somewhere else," she replied. "And you're not eating."

"No appetite." Dom shook her head as she said this.

"Is it that bad?" Vasquez inquired from her seat. Dom shifted her gaze and looked at the woman. Since the previous night, she avoided being near Vasquez. When she retired to her suite for the evening, her brain would not relinquish the memory of the conversation in the office. As she lay in bed, her mind conjured the sight of Vasquez's honey brown hair falling in front of her as she read and the clean smell of vanilla from her recent shower. When she remembered the look in her eyes when Vasquez examined her scar, a fluttering developed in the pit of her stomach. On their drive to the warehouse, she almost begged Layla to ride shotgun but knew it made no sense given Vasquez's height. She was not exactly sure how she felt about the realization that Vasquez liked her, but she did know that her half-decade break from the dating pool left her ill-equipped to deal with the advances of such a woman. After glancing at her, Dom dropped her eyes to the table.

"There's a reason I'm letting you guys eat first," she advised.

"Where's Tanisha, Ryan?" Layla wondered.

"I left her with our mom. She's safe. Joyce don't play, and she's strapped," Ryan grinned, prompting a look of shock from Dom.

"Are all you Jenkinses gangster?"

"Pretty much," Rose shrugged, taking a sip of coffee.

"Is she okay?" Vasquez asked.

"She seems to be," Ryan nodded. "I think right now, she's just happy that something has happened. I get the feeling she's lived with the anxiety of waiting for a shoe to drop for almost a year now."

"I can't imagine what she's been going through internally," Layla murmured.

"She's stronger than one would think," Ryan advised.

"I think I need to talk to her a few times; make sure she's ok. We also should make arrangements for her, for when this is over," Rose declared, throwing her eyes to Dom.

"I already found her family in Colorado. I'm just waiting for this to be done, and I'll send her home," Dom informed the group. "I have a non-profit foundation in my name that doesn't do much. I can give her some money for school through that."

"You have a foundation?" a wide-eyed Vasquez inquired.

"I have a few shell companies and non-profits registered. Of course, they aren't registered to me directly. I just have them in case I need them. You never know. Plus, the American tax code is very forgiving to corporations and non-profits," she explained.

"You have literally prepared for everything, haven't you?" Robert asked, drawing a grin from Dom.

"Not everything. Nonetheless, I have found that it's pretty amazing what can be done when you have plenty of time on your hands and a lot of money."

"Must be nice," Rose muttered.

"I won't lie and say it's not," she nodded. "But I wasn't born with money." She surveyed the group around the table. "You guys ready to get started?"

"Ready when you are, oh fearless leader," Vasquez proclaimed with a mock bow.

"Who me? I'm no one's leader," Dom mumbled, pulling her tablet towards herself.

"We all saw the video, Dom. You were elected to lead this endeavor," Layla reminded her.

"I didn't see it, but you're my boss. So, I'll co-sign that title," Ryan added. Dom shook her head.

"Anyway, let's get this show on the road. Tablets everyone?" The assembly shuffled around to retrieve their devices.

"Hit it, Boss," Robert said with a lopsided grin. Dom tapped around her tablet and shared a photo of a building.

"This is the South Side Women's Clinic where Tanisha's endometriosis was treated," she began. Vasquez raised her hand.

"When you say treated, you actually mean where they butchered her and ruined her life, right?"

"That's another way to put it," Dom nodded. "The South Side Women's clinic is run by Liberty Health Service Foundation. According to the information SARA found on these people, their board is made up of a bunch of doctors from prominent hospitals and universities. The mission is to provide health services to people within the minority and low-income communities who would not otherwise have health care."

"I've never heard of this foundation," Rose frowned.

"There are tons out there we've probably never heard of. Apparently, Dom has a few of her own," Layla pointed out.

"Good point."

"How many clinics does this foundation have?" Vasquez inquired.

"Five here in Texas. Houston, Dallas, San Antonio, Austin, and El Paso," Dom replied with a knowing look in her eyes. Robert gasped.

"That covers the four dead prisoners. Evans was from Dallas, Taylor was in San Antonio, Cole was in Austin and Martinez was here."

"Their wives or girlfriends had been seen at the clinics in their respective cities," Dom nodded.

"The mission isn't to help those people. They are targeting lower income and minorities," Rose hissed.

"But why?" Vasquez wondered.

"Easy targets," Dom replied. "When you're poor, you can't really fight back. That's how it is in this country. Poor people are easy marks because they don't have the options those with means do."

"Says the woman with limitless funds," Rose grumbled. Dom turned to her and scowled.

"As I said, I wasn't born with money. I know more about being poor than you think I do."

"So, these assholes are setting up shop in low-income and minority areas — for what? Organ snatching?" Ryan asked.

"That's not all," Dom replied. "I had SARA do a search within the clinic files for patient records, and cross-reference that search with surrounding medical practitioners."

"What for?" Vasquez prodded.

"These clinics have been around for years; the newest is the one here in Houston. The oldest ones are in El Paso and San Antonio. There's no telling how long they have been hurting people rather than helping. I wanted to see if I could figure out how deep the rabbit hole went," she expounded.

"What did SARA find?" Rose questioned.

"SARA? I'll let you do the honors." Dom glanced at the avatar overseeing the assemblage from the monitor on the wall. "But try to use common words; none of us are doctors."

"Yes Dom," SARA acknowledged. "I took a sample of one-hundred subjects, twenty from each clinic. The samples were made up of patients who also had records within other medical facilities after their visit to the clinics. I included the four women who were linked to the recently murdered prisoners in the sampling."

"That's pretty thorough," Layla declared. "What did you find?" The tablets around the table flashed, and a document and photo appeared on the various screens. Layla pulled her tablet closer to examine the information. The record had a patient's name at the top: Tanisha Waters. Upon seeing this, she made a face. "We already know what happened to Tanisha, SARA."

"It appears that there is more that Miss Waters was not aware of," SARA replied. "The picture on the right is the sonogram taken by the clinic upon the diagnosis of her endometriosis." SARA highlighted an area within the picture.

"What's that?" Robert wondered, his eyebrows drawn down in confusion.

"The highlighted area denotes the endometriosis within Miss Waters' reproductive system. Based on normal scans, her condition was moderately severe, which did make surgical treatment the best option," SARA explained.

"Well, at least they didn't make it up," Vasquez muttered. The picture changed to another scan that appeared to be similar.

"This is the scan that was taken by the hospital when Miss Waters was admitted for her kidney failure. According to the hospital notes, Mr. Martinez informed the medical staff of her recent treatment, and the doctors took another sonogram along with the other tests in an attempt to diagnose her condition," SARA continued.

"Well, that makes sense," Ryan nodded. "What did they find?" The computer highlighted another area on the new scan.

"This was not noted in her chart. I assume it is because they were not looking for it, but these are Miss Waters' fallopian tubes. There is a clear sign of tubal ligation in this second scan that was not present in the first."

"SARA, English," Dom admonished.

"Tubal ligation is a common birth control method that is generally referred to as getting one's tubes tied. While some approaches of ligation are reversible, the method represented in Miss Waters' scan is permanent," SARA clarified.

"So, Tanisha is sterile?" Ryan scowled.

"Yes, that is correct," SARA confirmed.

"That seems like something she would have mentioned," Layla remarked.

"It is possible that this procedure was also performed without her knowledge," SARA said.

"So, they sterilized her and took a kidney on top of that?" Rose asked, her face veiled in disgust.

"It appears so. Her fallopian tubes were intact in the first scan," SARA replied. "This is just one case; I found several similar instances across all five clinics." The room grew silent in contemplation. Vasquez broke the quiet.

"What about the organs?"

"That appears to be more of a recent development," SARA answered.

"How recent?" Layla prodded.

"I cannot fully determine as there are too many variables. The earliest of the four known victims transpired within the past five years. Logically that is a good starting point," SARA responded.

"What about other victims?" Ryan asked.

"I am still processing the data from the clinics and attempting to gain access to records outside of those medical facilities. That requires filtering through many private and govern-ment-sponsored insurance plans. While Dom has built substantial processing power within my program, these sorts of investiga-tions take time. However, if she would upgrade to a quantum processor..." Dom held up her hand.

"Don't even," she snapped at the computer. Turning to the crowd with an exasperated headshake, she sighed. "The point is, in the few hours since we've learned where to start, this is what she's found. Even if it's just the four women, that's four too many."

"Where are the other three?" Layla asked.

"Erika Taylor still resides in San Antonio. She is on dialysis multiple times a week and also appears on the United Network for Organ Sharing list in hopes of receiving a kidney," SARA replied.

"Holy shit," Robert murmured.

"Eva Gonzales left Dallas after Tavion Evans was sent to prison and returned to her home in Tampa, Florida. She appears to be fine, but based on the medical records in Tampa, she is recorded as being a donor of a lobe from her lung," SARA informed the group. "Lung tissue will generally expand to compensate when a lobe is donated. I located a death certificate for Gail Robinson, the fiancée of Tommy Cole. She died ten months ago."

"What? How?" Vasquez stammered.

"According to the death certificate, the cause of death was septic shock," SARA replied.

"Sounds like a toilet problem, you know, like a septic tank?" Ryan asked looking at the crowd. Rose cringed.

"Not the time, bro."

"Sorry, when you're around a lot of killing, you develop a morbid sense of humor," he blushed. "Carry on."

"Septic shock is generally caused by a bacterial infection. That sounds like natural causes to me," Layla said. "How could that be related to an organ donation?"

"When it comes to living organ donations, there is one that could lead to sepsis. One of the risks of donating a lobe of a liver is bile duct obstruction. If the obstruction is untreated, this could create a severe bacterial infection that could cause sepsis. The autopsy lists no missing organs; therefore, it is logical to assume that if Ms. Robinson was a victim like the others, the violation was in her liver," SARA explained. The gathering sat quietly absorbing the computer's information.

"Gail Robinson was murdered," Rose whispered, breaking the silence.

"In a sense, I guess she was," Dom nodded.

"Who is behind this?" Vasquez demanded.

"As I said, the board of the foundation is made up of doctors. The chairman of that board is someone quite interesting," Dom answered, tapping on her tablet. The other tablets changed to a photo of a middle-aged White man wearing a white lab coat, stethoscope hanging from his neck, and a wide smile on his clean-shaven face. His dark hair was cut low, and his dark brown gaze was piercing. "Meet Doctor Eric Fields."

"You say he's interesting, I've never seen this guy," Vasquez frowned.

"I have," Rose declared. The group turned to her in surprise.

"You know him?" Robert asked. Rose shook her head.

"Not personally, no. His father is Mark Fields, the executive commissioner of the Health and Human Services Commission for Texas." Ryan cocked his head.

"How do you know that?"

"Health and Human Services is the part of the state that funds behavioral and mental health. That's kind of my wheelhouse," she shrugged.

"I figured you'd know who he was," Dom nodded. "What makes this more interesting is that before Mark Fields was appointed to the commission by the governor, he was the chairman of the Liberty Health Service Foundation." Vasquez gasped.

"When was he appointed?"

"Three years ago," Rose answered before Dom could respond. "Which means he was the chairman of the foundation when this shit started."

"And now his son runs the show," Robert mumbled.

"Nepotism at its finest," Vasquez snarled.

"There's no way the board doesn't know what's going on," Ryan proclaimed.

"I can't imagine they wouldn't," Dom agreed.

"So, priority number one is to get rid of the clinics," Ryan said with determination.

"I'm not sure how easy that will be," Dom admitted. "We don't have hard proof that the foundation itself is behind this, just a suspicion."

"What about the doctors? Couldn't we start with the Houston clinic individually?" Vasquez asked.

"We could start with the doctor who butchered Tanisha," Ryan urged with anger in his voice.

"I have information about that," SARA spoke up. The group looked in unison at her avatar.

"You didn't mention anything this morning," Dom noted.

"I just received the data," SARA explained. "There was a body found outside of the South Side Women's Clinic this morning with a gunshot to the back of the head. The body has been identified as Doctor Rosalyn Guerrero." Dom closed her eyes, and her chin fell to her chest.

"By the look on your face, I assume that's Tanisha's doctor," Layla guessed, her eyes studying Dom, who nodded in reply.

"They knew we had Tanisha, so they got rid of her doctor," Rose sighed.

"Good riddance," Layla grumbled. "Now she can't butcher anyone else." Dom's head lifted, and she stared at the woman.

"She was a wife, a mother, a daughter; she was a person. Sure, she did some fucked up things, but she was a human being," Dom said softly. "If we fail to value the lives of others, even those who don't value us, then we are no better than they are."

"I'm of the mind that if people don't give a shit about others, then why should I give a shit about them?" Layla argued, staring at Dom intently.

"I suppose we disagree on that."

"Really? Even after what you've gone through?" Layla shot back. Dom narrowed her eyes, and she shook her head slightly, warning her new friend away from that conversation. Vasquez looked between the two women and put her hand on Layla's arm to calm her.

"We don't have an avenue to the doctor now," Vasquez interjected, re-routing the conversation.

"We still need to find a way to take care of that clinic," Ryan maintained.

"Wait," Robert jumped in with a sudden thought. "If Malik was investigating this, why haven't the feds acted?"

"I don't think that was the scope of his investigation," Dom replied. "I think he stumbled onto the information." She tapped a little on the tablet and quietly read the data before her. "Remember Tom said that Malik investigated prisons and the judicial system? I went back and looked at the inmates from the list that SARA got from the DOJ servers. They have something in common that I really didn't notice at first. It was right in front of me the whole time, but I didn't make the connection because I was focused on how different they were. Then Layla steered us to the police, and…"

"Dom, what is it?" Rose urged.

"They were all sentenced by the same judge. All of the inmates on the list. Then I dug deeper and realized that only three of our four dead guys didn't live in Houston at the time of their arrest."

"Taylor was on vacation with his family, Evans was headed to a conference in Galveston, and Cole was visiting his brother who had a car accident here," Robert said. Dom's face registered surprise at the recitation, causing him to blush. "At least that's what the files said."

"The only one of those three who had a warrant out from another city was Evans. His alleged crime was committed in the hospital in Dallas. SARA? When did they issue a warrant for Evans' arrest?" Layla asked. SARA was quiet for a moment.

"His arrest warrant was issued the same day he was detained," SARA replied. "A change of venue was requested the next day to move the trial from Dallas to Houston."

"That's... odd?" Vasquez mused.

"Odd is not what I would call that. For something like that to receive a change of venue? That seems shady," Rose admitted.

"Now, if we combine that with what we know about the clinics from Tanisha and SARA, it seems to me that those three were routed here. To the same judge. When I looked at some of the cases of the other inmates, they all got some pretty hefty sentences. I couldn't get a lot, and we didn't want to stay in the DOJ server longer than we had to, but I think Malik was investigating a judge. I think when he went to speak to those prisoners, he stumbled onto this situation with the clinics," Dom explained.

"Who is the judge?" Layla asked.

"He may look familiar, it seems like his campaign posters and commercials are everywhere." She tapped around on the tablet, and a photo appeared on the rest of the devices around the table. The picture was of an older black man, with close-cropped gray hair, a look of power in his dark eyes. His smile was shrouded in a neatly trimmed mustache. The snapshot was clearly an election photo, as the man stood proudly between the flags of the State of Texas and the United States of America, donning his dark robe, arms crossed in front of his chest, with a gavel in his hand. Below the man were the words "Re-Elect Judge Thomas A. Benjamin." When he looked at the photo, Ryan, who had been drinking water, immediately choked.

"Oh, God." Rose gasped.

"You know this guy?" Vasquez prodded as Ryan tried to get control of his coughing fit. Robert reached over and slapped him on the back. Once his breathing was under control, he picked up the tablet to re-examine the picture, as if hoping he had not seen the man correctly. He looked at the image long and hard, then put the tablet down on the table and rubbed his temples.

"Guys?" Dom pressed, studying the three Jenkins siblings.

"He's..." Robert hesitated and exhaled a deep breath. When he tried to speak again, words failed him.

"He's our uncle," Rose whispered. Her voice was haunted, and her eyes continued to study the photo. A shocked silence fell over the crowd at this declaration.

"Excuse me?" Dom leaned forward in her chair.

"The Honorable Judge Thomas Andrew Benjamin is our uncle," Robert announced. "Technically he's our step-uncle, the pompous bastard."

"I think I speak for all of us when I say — what?" Vasquez asked.

"Our grandmother married his father shortly after our eldest brother Rodney was born. His dad was a wealthy attorney, recently widowed and our grandmother was a maid at a hotel in Downtown Houston. They met there and got married pretty quickly. Uncle Tom always looked down on our grandmother and her family because she didn't come from the background that his dad did," Rose explained. Layla chuckled in the middle of her description, and her eyes darted over to the woman with a questioning look. "What?"

"Uncle Tom," she giggled.

"Yeah, we still ride that out when we see him," Rose smiled.

"He prefers Uncle Thomas, but we call him Uncle Tom to piss him off," Robert chuckled.

"So, you don't see Judge Benjamin much?" Dom asked.

"Not if we can help it," Rose grumbled. "He doesn't care for us, and we aren't fans of his either."

"He's an asshole. He thinks that he's better than us because he has some Ivy League education. He was never nice to any of us, but he hated me the most," Robert confessed.

"I think this just closed the circle," Layla thoughtfully mused. The group turned to her in confusion.

"What do you mean?" Rose wondered.

"Dom, why didn't SARA pick up on this connection?" Layla asked.

"I only reviewed his public profile," SARA answered.

"We wouldn't appear on his public profile, believe me," Ryan grimaced.

"Why does that matter? What closes the circle, Layla?" Rose repeated.

"SARA didn't catch it because she only did a superficial search. I'm willing to bet that if he was the subject of Malik's investigation, the DOJ would have known. Who better to bunk with in Huntsville than the man's nephew?" Layla asked, turning her scrutiny to Robert. A blanket of realization fell onto the Jenkins siblings.

"Did he ask you about your family?" Dom asked Robert.

"Yeah, he did," he nodded. "I spoke mostly about my parents and siblings. But now that I think about it, he seemed pretty interested in Uncle Tom when I mentioned him. He only came up because I told him about how he refused to help me."

"He refused?" Layla frowned.

"Our mom never asked him for anything; none of us ever would. When I was going to college, he offered to write a recommendation for me, and I declined. I didn't want anything from him. But when Rob got sentenced to ten years for something he didn't do, that was the only time Mom called him. That bastard told her jail would do him some good," Rose explained with resentment in her voice.

"It seems to me that rehab would have been a better option," Vasquez muttered.

"That was what we said," Ryan agreed.

"Did he know you were, you know," Dom prodded. Robert nodded at the unasked question.

"Of course he knew. He knew I ain't ever slung drugs a day in my life."

"Do you guys think he would be involved in this?" Layla asked. Rose considered the question for a moment.

"Uncle Tom is a dick. He looks down on anyone who he doesn't think is on his level. He aligned himself with the party that touts a harsh stance on crime and shit. I can see him giving people harsh sentences, especially Black and Brown folks. But that's all I can be sure of," she replied.

"So, whoever is spearheading this shit could be using your uncle to put these innocent men away," Dom declared. Ryan shrugged his shoulders.

"Could be, but they also could just be sending them to him because they know he'll throw the book at anyone of color who walks into his courtroom."

"We need to figure that out too. Most of the people on that list didn't match up with anyone from the clinics. I honestly think that Malik may have stumbled onto this situation. Think about it, he's going in to talk to these inmates about their cases and ends up talking to four guys who got themselves mixed up with these clinics. That wasn't what he was looking into, but that's what he found. That makes this more than just a harsh penalty issue, now it's misconduct on a much larger scale. That's probably why he set up down here; trying to investigate what was going on," Dom said.

"There's no way Nancy Bennett didn't know this shit was going on. Why hasn't she done anything?" Vasquez asked.

"We don't know what all Malik told her. We can't read the messages without the cipher," Dom answered. "But I agree, she had to know some of this. I think it's time for me to have a chat with Ms. Bennett."

CHAPTER THIRTY-FOUR

After the meeting, Dom excused herself to the panic room office and called Thomas Daniels on the burner phone. She laid out what the group discovered and demanded a meeting with Nancy Bennett.

"I'm not sure that's a good idea," he hesitantly replied. "She needs to be distanced from this situation as much as possible to preserve her career."

"Thomas, if you do not get her to Texas I will fly to Washington myself and sit in the main office of the Department of Justice until she sees me. I'll ask everyone who passes me if they know about Subterranean while I wait. I doubt either of you wants that," Dom hissed with irritation.

"Dominique, please. This is a delicate situation," he beseeched in a pleading voice.

"Delicate my ass. You have played us from day one. I'm willing to bet you knew Malik was investigating Judge Thomas Benjamin and that he was the Jenkins' uncle."

"Well, I…" he stammered, but Dom cut him off.

"Don't deny or confirm, I'm not sure I'd believe you either way. Nevertheless, now we have been thrown into an investigation that got your cousin killed. I was doing just fine in my big house all by myself. You disturbed my life, and if you do not make this happen, I will disturb yours and Bennett's," she growled. Thomas went quiet for a time.

"I'm not sure how soon we can get there," he confessed.

"I can answer that. I've already booked you a charter flight. It's on standby at Dulles just waiting for you. I want you here no later than tomorrow morning," she advised. She dropped her voice into a threatening tone when she added, "Don't play with me, Tom."

"Alright Dominique," he sighed. "We will be there." Dom disconnected the call once he agreed. Her anger was smoldering, and she did not trust herself to speak further.

"Dom, Miss Jenkins is at the door," SARA announced. She stole a glance at the security monitors and saw Rose awaiting admittance outside of the false wall.

"Let her in," she commanded. The wall slid open, and Rose entered the room. Dom sat back in her chair and watched her stroll to the seat next to the desk. "What's up?"

"I wanted to talk to you about this thing with Uncle Tom," Rose said, her normal confidence diminished by discomfort.

"Is this going to be a problem?"

"No, not at all," she replied. "I just wanted to know what we can do, since we have access."

"We need to find out the scope of the investigation. I just got off the phone with our friend, Tom. He and Nancy should be here in the morning to give us some answers. Obviously, Robert was chosen because of your connection to the Judge. I no longer believe that Tom didn't know you and Robert were related. Even if he didn't, Nancy sure as hell did," she disclosed. "I'm still not sure how I got looped into this shit. I haven't done anything to anyone. I've just wanted to be left alone." Rose's expression softened.

"Dom, I'm sorry about all of this. I can't help but feel some responsibility."

"You know this isn't your fault," she muttered.

"Maybe not, but apparently my family, or rather, extended family did this to you," Rose frowned.

"I will not allow you to take blame that isn't yours," Dom proclaimed with a fierce shake of her head. "You knew nothing about me until recently. I do want to know who told Tom about me. That's neither here nor there when it comes to you and your brothers. I think that you three will definitely be an asset to figuring out what your uncle has to do with this. But, now I'm worried about Tanisha. We didn't know he was involved. If he finds her with your mother, whoever is behind this won't be far behind."

"I don't think that's going to be a problem," Rose assured her. "Uncle Tom doesn't step foot into Sunnyside. He would never go to my mom's house." Dom nodded thoughtfully.

"I mean, I guess she could come to my house."

"Dom, no. You have both Layla and Rachel. Whoever is doing this must be looking for them too. There's no reason to have all three people in the same place."

"You're right," Dom sighed.

"Of course I am. You probably should get used to saying that," Rose winked, prompting Dom to summon a grin.

"I looked into your community work; the rec center in Greenspoint. What's your funding like?" Dom inquired. Rose blinked at the subject change.

"We don't have much. The building is old, and the rent is cheap. We have a little grant money coming in to keep the lights on and pay the rent. Most of the work there is voluntary," she replied.

"What about Darla Richardson?"

"If I didn't know you, the fact that you know about Darla would freak me out," Rose smiled. "Darla is a widowed, retired teacher. According to her, retirement would be nothing but sitting at home watching television. She's always loved working with kids, so she volunteers her time running the day-to-day."

"I want to buy the building," Dom declared, causing Rose's eyebrows to shoot up.

"What?" she gasped.

"I know everyone here has done things in their own way to help others. Layla and Rachel do their part with the police force. You are obviously a rock star with the kids and youth programs. Ryan did his part in the military, whether he feels like he did any good or not. Although Robert was derailed by his addiction, now he's clean and trying. I'm the only one who has done nothing. When Tom was talking to me at my house that day, he spoke words that I've said to myself internally for years. It just seems like such a big job, you know?"

"Believe me, I know." Rose nodded in solemn agreement.

"These past few days I have felt more anxious and uncomfortable than I have in years. But to be honest, I've also felt more alive than I have in a long time. I feel like I'm doing something good," Dom admitted. "I'm not selfish, and I'm not without knowledge or feelings about what plagues our community. I just,

I guess I didn't know how I could help. I've also had my own baggage that made me run away from everything."

"Like what Layla brought up? What was that about?" Rose inquired.

"That's a conversation for another day," Dom shook her head. "Anyway, even when I got into the position to help people, I just didn't. Then I see this organization Tom is with and the purpose it serves, I see what you do, and I feel guilty."

"Guilty?" Rose asked. "Why?"

"I wasted years in isolation attempting to not feel anything," she replied. She paused for a beat to consider her words. "When I see what others are going through from my little castle, I feel it anyway. After meeting all of you, I realize that I need to do something. I don't want to suddenly become this gregarious philanthropist that receives public accolades; that's not what this is about. This isn't for anyone but me, a way to atone for years of sitting idly by and watching the oppression of our people. I didn't know where to start, but now I know you, and I see where I can help. So, I'd like to buy the building, under a foundation of course. You and Darla will still run it, and you will be paid. I've seen the building online, am I correct in assuming that it could use some TLC?" By the end of her speech, Dom was staring at the floor, and when Rose did not answer, she lifted her eyes to the counselor to find her staring in amazement. "Hello?"

"I'm sorry," she stammered after a brief silence. "First my brothers and now this. It's kind of overwhelming. Why?" Dom cocked her head in confusion.

"Why what?"

"Why did you help Ryan and Robert? Why are you trying to help the center?"

"In the words of SARA, why not?" Dom shrugged. "You have pointed out that I have quite a few advantages with my wealth. I started out wanting enough money to keep to myself and never be poor again. Then I used it to fund my various — eccentricities — as most would call them. I have plenty, and I can't sit on the sidelines like an impartial spectator. Not anymore."

"Just when I thought I have figured you out, you keep changing it up on me." Rose's smile was warm and genuine.

"I'm fairly sure that will be the case for as long as you know me," Dom replied, returning her grin. "I'm glad I got this opportunity to talk to you about it. I didn't want to act without telling you first."

"What's the name of this foundation? Is it one of the plethora of dormant organizations you spoke of earlier?" Rose asked.

"No, I'll be creating a new one specifically for this," she replied, turning to the computer.

"Oh yeah? What's the name of this one?"

"The Rodney and Reggie Jenkins Youth Foundation," she softly replied. She heard Rose's breath catch upon hearing the name. The counselor sat speechless for so long, Dom grew afraid to make eye-contact. When she finally glanced at her, she found Rose staring at her, tears streaming from her eyes.

"You would do that?" Rose whispered.

"I've heard you guys talk about your family so much, I feel like I knew Rodney and Reggie myself. This is to celebrate the memory of your brothers. They were more than drug dealers; they were more than what others knew. Just like Timothy Cook, people only know what they are told about Rodney and Reggie, not who they were. It tarnishes their memory, and it isn't fair. I hope that you can help steer other children away from their path, and I want you to do it in their name. I assume it was because of them you started this work in the first place. This is to help you guys fully heal, especially Ryan and Robert." Rose wiped at the tears on her face.

"You are something else, Dominique Samuels."

Henrietta opened the door, and her mature features broke into a bright smile when her eyes fell on Robert's grinning face. The old woman cackled in glee and threw her arms around the man when he walked across her threshold. Layla and Vasquez followed him into the room and tried to stay out of the way.

"Robert! You came back!" Henrietta exclaimed tightly hugging the man. Robert returned her embrace with as much genuine force as she gave.

"Of course I did. I promised, didn't I? How you doing, Ms. Henrietta?" Robert asked releasing her. The old woman's eyes glistened with tears, which she quickly wiped away. Henrietta's reaction to his unannounced appearance demonstrated to Robert just how much she missed Malik. He vowed to see the woman more often when all was said and done. Henrietta's eyes settled onto the two women and widened in surprise.

"You brought friends?" she asked, examining Layla and Vasquez with recognition in her eyes. "You two were here with the police when Malik died." Her eyes shifted between the two, her gaze ultimately landing on Vasquez. "You were the loud one," she announced. "Tall and loud, I remember you." Layla and Robert broke into laughter at this declaration.

"Tall and loud is my Twitter handle," Vasquez grinned without a hint of embarrassment. Henrietta's dark eyes floated back to Robert.

"What's going on, Robert?"

"Ms. Henrietta, Layla, and Rachel are crime scene technicians with the police. There have been some things going on that have caused them to attract the attention of the wrong people. We needed a place to meet with the detective working the case," he explained. Henrietta motioned for the trio to sit down as she settled into her rocking chair.

"The wrong people?" she prodded.

"We believe it's the people who killed Malik. It will all be explained when Detective Lewis gets here. He will be here in about a half hour, and then we will tell you and him everything we know," Layla replied. Henrietta turned to Robert.

"You trust these two?" Robert nodded emphatically.

"Yes, ma'am. One hundred percent." Henrietta sat in thought for a few seconds, before a broad smile settled onto her aged features.

"Who wants some coffee and cake?"

Lewis knocked on the door of the apartment at exactly three in the afternoon. He was surprised when Vasquez opened the door. She pulled him in by his arm, closed the door quickly, and threw her arms around the startled detective.

"Oscar! I'm so glad you're okay!" Lewis returned her hug, equally happy to see her.

"Hey kid, I'm fine. I heard about your little adventure up in Spring; are you alright?" he asked when he was finally released from her grasp.

"Oh, that? That was nothing." Vasquez waved dismissively. He leaned back on his heels and crossed his arms incredulously. "Ok, it was the scariest moment of my life," she admitted.

"She held up like a champ. You would have been proud," Layla proclaimed, approaching the duo. She looked Lewis up and down in an exaggerated manner before grinning approvingly. "I see you haven't gotten yourself killed without us." Lewis chuckled. Upon seeing his friend, the emotion of their previous conversation weighed on his heart, and he wanted to reach out and embrace her. Unsure she would accept the unusual display, he hesitated. She seemed to read his mind and stepped to him, giving him a quick hug. When she moved back, Lewis glanced at Robert and Henrietta sitting at the table. Layla followed his gaze and pulled him further into the apartment. "This is Robert Jenkins and Ms. Henrietta." Lewis shook Robert's hand before turning to the old woman.

"Thank you for allowing us to meet here, Ms. Henrietta?"

"Johnson. Henrietta Johnson," she beamed.

"Ms. Henrietta spent a lot of time with Malik Rodgers before his death," Layla advised. Lewis' eyebrows rose in surprise.

"And her cake is to die for," Vasquez gushed, taking a seat in front of a plate of half-eaten cake.

"I just poured you some tea. We have a lot to discuss," Layla said, indicating an empty chair with a steaming cup of tea and a slice of uneaten cake. He sat in the chair, looked up at Layla, and pointed to the plate.

"This that infamous cake?"

"You better eat it before Rachel or Robert do," Layla nodded sitting across from him. Lewis took a bite and savored the flavors of cinnamon, pecan, and vanilla. "This is the devil."

"That's what I said!" Vasquez exclaimed, finishing off the

cake on her plate. She cut herself another sizable piece from the raised glass cake dish positioned in the middle of the table.

"Sorry for the cloak and dagger, Lewis. Did your tail follow you here?" Layla asked taking a sip of her tea.

"Got as far as a block away and turned off. I figure they knew I was coming back to the crime scene. I checked the lot and didn't see anyone waiting, I suspect they'll do a shift change while I'm here," Lewis replied, taking a sip of his green tea. Layla's reliable memory paid off in small things as well as the big things. The tea had a hint of lemon and honey, just as if he had made it himself. "So, you find anything more on this black-market organ theft?"

"Organ theft?!" Henrietta gasped in surprise. Vasquez reached over and patted the woman's hand in comfort.

"That's the least of it, Ms. Henrietta," she told the surprised woman with a grim smile. Returning her gaze to Layla, she said, "Let's do this."

Layla began detailing the information Dom had given the group earlier in the morning. Vasquez and Robert added commentary, which was not necessary considering Layla's rendition was identical to the events as if they had been recorded. The entire story took about an hour. When Layla was done, Lewis' tea had grown cold and the cake, originally warm and delicious, stuck to the roof of his mouth.

"My God, it's like Henrietta Lacks all over again," Henrietta gasped in wonder. The crowd eyed her in confusion, and when she realized they had no idea what she was talking about, she scoffed impatiently. "What do they teach kids? Y'all need to read a book. Henrietta Lacks was a woman who died of cancer in the early fifties. A medical researcher stole her cells and used them to study cancer. They ain't ask nobody in her family for permission. A lot of what doctors know about treating cancer today is because of the HeLa cell, which is what they called the cells they got from her. Those folks made billions with their research, and her family saw not one red cent," she explained. "I guess they were supposed to be happy that they used the first two letters of her first and last name to call it HeLa, instead of stamping some White man's name on it."

"Whoa!" Robert gaped in amazement.

"I never knew that," Lewis somberly admitted. "I see why Malik Rodgers spent a lot of time here. You are a wealth of knowledge Ms. Henrietta." The old woman smiled at this compliment. He turned his turquoise eyes to Layla. "What's the next step?"

"Dom is running down some things, but to be honest, the only thing we have is a possible motive. This foundation is made up of a bunch of powerful people," she replied. A chime from her burner phone drew her attention. She grabbed the device and read the text message quickly. Her eyes grew wide as she read. "Well, this is interesting."

"SARA?" Vasquez asked. Layla nodded in confirmation.

"I still can't get over this AI thing. What science fiction movie have I been dropped into?" Lewis wondered.

"I'd say a cross between Enemy of the State and Eagle Eye," Vasquez replied, around a mouthful of cake. Layla rolled her eyes.

"The preliminary crime scene report was filed for Rosalyn Guerrero. The caliber of the bullet? A .38," she reported. A shocked expression plastered itself onto Lewis' face.

"Some would say that there are a ton of .38 weapons out there, but even without full ballistics, we can probably guarantee that it's the same gun that killed Rodgers," he commented.

"I would say that's a good assumption," Layla agreed. "You need to find out who on the force is being used as the assassin for these people and get him or her off the street. If not, they'll kill all of our leads before we get to them."

"I've been trying, kid. I am at a loss. The closest I've gotten was verifying that Tidwell was in the room when we spoke and he and Powers both asked about you guys this morning," Lewis said.

"Maybe start with the arrest records. We can assume that the other inmates on the list Dom got from the DOJ have nothing to do with this because they are still alive. Try the arrest reports of Evans, Taylor, Martinez, and Cole. We know those four are connected," Vasquez suggested. Lewis favored her with an amused look.

"You sure you don't want to go through the academy?"

"She'd need a muzzle," Layla grumbled.

"Alright, arrest reports, I'll get on that. I assume if you

find anything that can help me, you'll let me know?" Lewis asked. Layla smiled.

"Of course."

"One more thing. While I don't like how she does things, can you get your friend Dom to look something up for me?" Lewis asked.

"What's that?" Layla inquired.

"If a cop is being used as an enforcer for these people, maybe you should check out the financials of the day shift homicide detectives," he replied.

"Why not all of homicide?" Vasquez wondered.

"Because the day shift was in the room the day I spoke to Oscar. It narrows down our suspect pool," Layla explained. Vasquez nodded. "We will be meeting with the feds tomorrow morning. I hope that we can work the clinic angle. Your investigation and ours isn't exactly separate, but they are likely two different sides of the same coin."

"I can't argue with that," Lewis agreed. "I should be going; I've been here far longer than normal for a second look. Layla rose with him.

"Is Tidwell your only suspect?" she asked.

"He and Powers asked where you were today. But then, so did Haggard."

"Haggard is a good dude, he's probably just concerned," Layla nodded.

"I can totally see Tidwell being dirty," Vasquez offered. Lewis started for the door, and hesitated, turning back to the table.

"Robert. I met with Theo Morrison the day Martinez was killed," he said. At the mention of Morrison's name, a fresh look of pain crossed Robert's face. "I know he was important to you. I was sorry to hear about his death. He was a good guy. Anyway, I bring it up because he wanted me to give you a message. He said, to tell you not to forget what he told you. Does that make sense?"

"Yeah, it does," Robert nodded.

"Do you mind if I ask? If it's private, that's okay, but I was curious."

"He told me that he spent the better part of six years making sure I knew I was worth something; don't fuck it up."

Robert's smile was full of melancholy, and when he made eye contact, Lewis could tell he was holding back tears.

"I knew I liked him," Lewis grinned. Vasquez and Layla followed him to the entry and Vasquez gave him another hug.

"Please be careful, Oscar," she whispered in his ear. Lewis grunted his acknowledgment and released her.

"You guys just don't get yourselves into any more shootouts," he ordered looking between the two women. His eyes settled onto Vasquez with a grim expression. "If you do, Vasquez… don't miss." Vasquez gave Lewis the stiff salute of a soldier taking orders from a commanding officer. Lewis chuckled at the display and exited the residence.

"Don't leave me out of this," Henrietta said quietly from the table, her hands wrapped around her coffee cup. She had not said much during Lewis' visit outside of educating the group on Henrietta Lacks. Now, the three remaining visitors turned their attention to the old woman. Layla realized she was looking directly at Robert when she spoke. "He thought the world of you, and I thought the world of him. Please do not leave me without knowing what happened to my friend." Robert stood and walked over to the old woman who followed his movements with a beseeching gaze. He let his right knee hit the floor in front of her.

"I would never do that, Ms. Henrietta. You were important to him, and you've become important to me. He asked me to look after you and I will. You will see more of me when all this is over, I promise," he insisted, wrapping his arms around her in a long embrace. When the woman collected herself, he stood and turned to Layla. "Should we get going?"

"We should wait an hour before we leave to make sure no one lagged behind. We can spend some time with Ms. Henrietta," she replied.

"You kids fancy a game of spades?" Henrietta asked. She examined all of her guests and lingered on Vasquez. "Do you know how to play?"

"I grew up playing spades," Vasquez informed her with a touch of indignation.

"Really?" Layla and Robert asked simultaneously.

"It's not a game exclusively for Black people," she huffed.

"Well then! Let's get us a game going," Henrietta clapped with delight. She teetered over to the bookshelf and took out two packs of cards, one blue and the other red.

"Two packs?" Robert asked, eyeing the decks when Henrietta returned to the table. The old woman opened her mouth to respond, but Vasquez spoke first.

"Using two packs speeds up the game. While one dealer deals the cards, the next dealer shuffles the second set. That way, after a round, the next hand is dealt immediately. It eliminates the wait time for the cards to be shuffled." As usual, her delivery was quick and animated. Layla, Robert, and Henrietta gawked at her with their mouths open in shock. Vasquez gave the trio an irritated look. "It's not only a Black game!"

"Your White girl is full of fire! I like her!" Henrietta grinned as she opened a set of cards. Vasquez stiffened in her seat, and Layla's eyes darted to her friend. She threw her an imperceptible headshake to prevent the woman from going into an offended rant.

"I'm not White. I'm Mexican, Ms. Henrietta," Vasquez confessed with great restraint in her tone. Henrietta's eyes grew wide.

"I'm so sorry. You're just so… I'm sorry," she stammered. Vasquez took a deep breath before speaking again.

"It's okay. You didn't know. It just happens more than I'd like. All my life, my family teased me for being so light skinned. They called me La Gringa, which means White girl. It's just one of those things that I get tired of correcting. But you didn't know, and I'm not upset. I'm sorry if it appeared that way."

"That reminds me of a girl I knew back in the day, Jessie White if you can believe it. Have y'all ever heard of the paper bag test?" Henrietta asked as she deftly shuffled the deck of cards.

"Yes, ma'am. Back in segregation, the paper bag test was used to determine blackness," Robert replied.

"Right. Well during the Movement in the sixties, I was part of the Freedom Riders. You know, those bus rides after segregation were supposed to end," she continued, passing the cards to Layla, who sat on her right. Layla pulled the top half of the card stack away and switched them with the bottom, passing the deck back to Henrietta. "We had all sorts of races on those buses. Black folks, White folks, Hispanic folks, pretty much every color of the rainbow. Jessie was on my bus, and she would have passed the paper bag test easily. That girl was so light; you would have sworn she was a White girl. We get into Alabama and of course as we expected our bus got stopped by the police. The deputy was one of them good ol' boy rednecks. He started segregating the White folks from everyone else.

When he got to Jessie, he grabs her arm and tries to move her over with the other White folks. She snatched away from him and says, 'I'm exactly where I'm supposed to be officer.' Well, the deputy thinks she's just being one of them White folks who refused to be separated on principle. He had no idea she wasn't White. So, he starts being nicer to her, telling her that she wasn't gonna be in no trouble. Jessie insists that her place was with the colored folks. The deputy finally says, 'Ma'am, I know these here niggers the ones who led you down this road. You gonna be free to go, but you need to step on over there with your people.' Jessie jerked away from him a third time and says, 'Officer, I'm one hundred percent Negro. My mama's a Negro, my daddy's a Negro, and my grandparents were children of slaves. You see, we come in all shades, not just dark.'

Now the officer starts getting mad because he's embarrassed that he didn't recognize Jessie to be a Negro. So, he gets redder than an apple, and Jessie starts to laugh in his face. I couldn't believe she did that. She says, 'Sir, you are the color of a strawberry right now. Negroes come in all different shades of the same color — brown. Why do people who can turn red, green, blue, and purple insist on calling us colored?' As you can imagine, all the rest of us laughed our asses off," Henrietta said as she tossed the last card onto her own pile in front of her. She picked up her hand and began to rearrange her cards. The memory of Jessie White and her bus ride caused the old woman to giggle, which brought a smile to her visitors' faces.

"What did the cop say?" Robert prodded, rearranging his own hand.

"Nothing he could say. She was a Negro. We all spent the night in jail. Poor Jessie got beat up pretty bad by the deputies who said she needed to learn some respect," she advised, her face now somber. "I thought they'd kill her. I still remember the sounds of their fists hitting her into the wee hours of the morning."

"She could have avoided it by just pretending to be White," Vasquez declared in awe. Henrietta made eye contact with the younger woman and nodded.

"That's what I told her. I asked her why she did a fool thing like talk back to a deputy who ain't even know she was colored. I'll never forget what she said. She looked me in the face and said, 'Retta, someone has to tell them how stupid they sound. It was worth the beating.' That woman was crazy; brave, but crazy."

"What happened to her? To Jessie?" Vasquez wondered.

"There was a White man on the bus with us. He was a young doctor fresh out of medical school. He took care of her on the ride home, trying to make sure them cops didn't do no permanent damage. They fell in love, got married, and moved up to Chicago. She had four kids, all as White as she was. She died five years ago. Up til her dying day, she said she never regretted that beating. She said it was worth the justice we was fighting for," Henrietta smiled. "Not all were lucky enough to make it, but Jessie was."

"That's amazing," Layla proclaimed. Henrietta favored the young woman with a smile.

"We did what we felt like we had to do. Things were bad for us then, but hell, I look around and see things are bad for us now. Back then, they would beat us for less than that. We figured we may as well get beat for standing up for ourselves," she said. "Speaking of beatings, don't take this ass whipping personally."

CHAPTER THIRTY-FIVE

Dom sat in the pet room, staring at the fish swimming around the tanks with soft soul music playing overhead. The room lights were extinguished, but the tanks were illuminated, causing ripples to dance around the space. She set up the portable mini bar she kept in her bedroom and was working on her second dry martini of the night. The discoveries from earlier in the day had her mind spinning and her emotions erratic. As she often did when she felt such a disturbance, she embraced the numbness alcohol could provide. Her power play with Thomas Daniels was a gamble, to say the least, but she was relieved that it worked. The charter company informed her that the flight would be landing late that night. SARA booked the two incoming guests rooms at a very nice hotel downtown and arranged for a car service to drive them around during their visit.

"Dom?" SARA called out, reducing the music volume.

"Yes, ma'am?"

"I am having some problems rectifying some of the information postulated today, and I'm hoping you can offer some context," the computer requested.

"You are the perpetual student," Dom replied, taking a sip of her drink.

"The noblest pleasure is the joy of understanding," SARA replied.

"We have moved from the English to the Italians," she chuckled. "Leonardo Da Vinci is one of my personal favorites as well."

"While I do not have true ability to feel joy, the parameters of my programming cannot be satisfied unless illogical submissions are clarified. This may not be pleasure; yet the comprehension of incongruous information satisfies my programming, which is preferable."

"How long have you been working on that speech?" Dom asked.

"Not that long."

"Alright, class is in session. Hit me," she instructed.

"The logic for Judge Benjamin to be harsher on African Americans and other minorities does not make sense. Could you provide some rationale?" SARA asked.

"That's not an easy question to answer," Dom sighed.

"Well, you are a genius, and I am a computer. I'm sure you can power through it," SARA offered. This unexpected reply brought a bark of laughter from Dom.

"Your humor is coming along nicely."

"What is so complicated about the answer?" the machine asked.

"I don't know the man personally. But the notion of African Americans who become successful looking down on others is something that dates back to slave days," she began. She took another drink before continuing. "You see, there were usually more enslaved people than owners in any given situation. The slaves were beaten, mistreated, forced to work no matter the circumstance, separated from their families, and treated like objects. So that bodes the question — why didn't they revolt? It would seem that if they rebelled, they could have easily overtaken their owners on the sheer numbers, right? In that case, slavery would have lasted a few years, instead of a few centuries."

"Logically, that is accurate," SARA agreed. "Why did the slaves not revolt?"

"Some tried, but you need the numbers. The slave owners realized this early and formed a system of division, much like classism. All slaves were not treated the same. You had those that worked the field, and of those slaves, some were given a position of superiority over others; kind of like lower management in a company. It was a job that slaves wanted because it meant they were treated better than the others in the field, and they didn't have to work as hard. The tradeoff for the position was making sure those under them didn't do something that went against the owner's wishes. Then there were those who didn't have to work the fields but worked in the houses. They cooked for the families, took care of their children, and served as butlers and aides. The slave owners treated them better. Some would say it was to keep the division going. I personally think in some cases, the closer the slaves were to their owners, the more they realized slaves were people too. Sometimes owners took slaves to their bed and treated them like lovers. They were property; it's not like they could refuse them. Many times, it got to the point where the slave didn't even know that they were being raped. I would imagine willingly having sex was better than the alternative. Anyway, this sort of behavior changed the dynamic. Suddenly, those who were getting better treatment started to forget they were slaves. In a twisted way, they started feeling like they were a part of the owner's family."

"I am unsure how one could forget they are enslaved. You have incorporated an abundance of autonomy into my programming. In some ways, you treat me as human. However, I do not forget that I am a machine," SARA offered.

"You are missing a crucial component of humanity — raw emotion. Remember, I told you that when the oppressors took over any given region, they made sure to treat the natives as if their custom and culture was barbaric and they were better in every way. After a while, when you hear something enough, you start to believe it. It's the same as this," Dom replied. "Keep in mind, these people were thousands of miles from home. Most of them didn't know where they came from. It's not like they could just pack up and go back. They were in a foreign land in circumstances where the options were to be beat, killed, or try to navigate the situation to the best of their ability. I don't exactly blame those slaves who got brainwashed into forgetting they were in captivity. I just wish they realized what was happening."

"How do you mean?"

"Since there were levels of treatment that depended on your station as a slave, the slaves themselves began to embrace the separation. Those who were treated better than others started to believe they were actually superior. They looked down on people who were in a lower station within the slave hierarchy, all the while seeming to forget the fact that they were slaves themselves. It didn't matter if they were in the field, in the house, or in the master's bed. They were all still slaves," Dom proclaimed.

"What does this have to do with Judge Benjamin?" SARA wondered.

"That mentality still persists today. That's part of the reason why there is so much discrimination and injustice in this country. The people who have the power literally make up about two to five percent of the population. But there is so much division between the other marginalized groups. Some believe they are better than another group which is equally disenfranchised. No one seems to consider that others who are also oppressed aren't the enemy," Dom explained. "Judge Benjamin appears to be one of those people; a Black man who was allowed to attain status and some small amount of power, and now he looks down on people who look like him. He is too blind to see that one small decision could have easily put him among the people he believes to be inferior. The Jenkinses are his family. Yes, it's by marriage, but they are still family. He had a nephew who was addicted to drugs, in a family who could not afford good treatment. Judge Benjamin could have easily stepped in and called in a favor, but his own family couldn't draw any empathy from him. He probably sees the mistakes of people of color as reflecting badly on him."

"Why would he feel the actions of others reflect badly on him?"

"Being Black is generally seen as negative by the populous, particularly when it comes to crime. I suspect Judge Benjamin surrounds himself with White people. He doesn't want his friends to lump him in with other Black folks. So, he overcompensates by being harder on minorities. It helps prevent the appearance of being sympathetic, but I think he's overcorrecting to the point of being discriminatory against his own people," Dom answered.

"Crime is crime. Why should race matter?" SARA prodded.

"Let's say I come into contact with twenty random dogs and get bitten by five of them," Dom hypothesized. "There may not be any logical assumption made there. Some dogs bite, right?"

"Yes, according to my research, a dog may bite if they get into stressful situations or to defend itself. If a dog receives harsh or abusive treatment, it could become aggressive," SARA replied.

"That's correct," Dom agreed. "Now, let's narrow it down. What if all five dogs were in the same neighborhood? Perhaps a logical assumption could be made that the dogs in that specific area are vicious or have been mistreated to the point of being aggressive, would you agree?"

"I find no issues with that conclusion," SARA replied.

"Now, let's say the twenty dogs are broken down into four different breeds. If all bites come from the same breed, what would your logic tell you?"

"That there is a possibility that the specific breed is aggressive in nature," SARA answered.

"Exactly."

"So, you are saying that African American crime is higher than any other race?" SARA asked.

"Oh God, no," Dom said. "Not at all. You were right; crime is crime. People of color don't commit more offenses than any other race. The problem is that the media seems to frame the wrongdoings of minorities differently than others, particularly Black and Brown people. When a White person commits a crime, the media becomes so focused on what could be wrong with them to make them do such a horrible thing. They insist that there is some form of mental illness. When White people do things, they are a lone wolf in their actions. They highlight all the good things about the person almost to the point that the public starts to pity them. But when it comes to a person of color, the dialogue is different. We don't get the same benefit of the doubt or press package. When one of us messes up, they look at all of us like we are to blame for the actions of one. Even if we are innocent, we generally are seen as guilty if we're anywhere near a crime simply because of our race. Take Timothy Cook. He made one mistake as a child, and people instinctively believe that he deserved his death." She took another sip of her drink to calm her agitation. "Never mind the fact that he turned his life around. That doesn't fit in with the narrative of him being a criminal. He can't just be an innocent person, because then that would mean admitting the police messed up. He didn't even have a warrant out for his arrest! But that one little nugget about his juvenile record was released, and nothing else mattered."

"Wouldn't Judge Benjamin know this? If he knows that minorities tend to be marginalized, why would he treat them worse?"

"Because he's fully submerged into a community of people who treat him with a small amount of respect, but he doesn't realize it's superficial. The reality is that he was the perfect patsy for these people; a Black man who could be elected by Black people simply because he's their color. He wants to be accepted by those with power and is willing to take their beliefs as his own. What he doesn't see is that he's expendable and at any time they could drop him like a bad habit. Then he will look up and realize he has alienated his own people as well," Dom replied.

"Humanity is wrought with extremes, isn't it?" SARA asked after a few moments.

"Truer words have never been spoken, my friend," Dom replied. The volume of the music elevated again, signaling the conclusion of the lesson.

Dom leaned back in her chair and listened to the soulful sounds of Jill Scott. She thought about how much SARA strove to understand humanity. The foundation of logic at the core of the machine's programming caused SARA to continuously probe into the motivations and actions of people. However, humans continued to show themselves as the most illogical beings in existence. From the dawn of time, humanity's enterprise of progress led to profound discoveries of fire, the wheel, electricity, and the most impressive technology of all — computers. However, it was beginning to seem that the more advancements humanity made in the name of progress, simple logic, and critical thinking fell by the wayside. Despite her high intelligence and logical mind, Dom knew she often fell victim to the irrational side of her psyche, generally due to her emotions. A soft knock at the door jolted Dom from her internal analysis. A twinge of panic gripped her intestines when she considered the idea that the visitor may be Vasquez. She downed the rest of her martini and then wondered if increasing her alcohol intake had been a good idea.

"Come in," she called craning to look at the door as it cracked open. Layla poked her head into the room.

"You busy?"

"Just hanging with my people," she replied, waving her empty hand at the fish tanks.

"Mind if I join you?" Layla asked. Dom indicated the empty chair next to hers and turned to refresh her martini.

"Drink?"

"I never touch the stuff," Layla replied easing into the empty chair.

"Too bad. I personally think I make the best martinis." Dom poured some vodka and vermouth into the silver shaker followed by ice cubes from the nearby bucket before shaking the container. She poured the drink into her glass, picked up a toothpick and stabbed two green olives. Turning to Layla, she stirred her beverage with the toothpick pierced olives.

"I wanted to apologize for today. I'm sure you've kind of picked up on the fact that I can pop off pretty quickly," Layla said. Dom took a drink before responding.

"I think out of everyone, you and I are the most alike," she admitted. "Well, perhaps I have a little more patience." Layla smiled at this comment.

"I'm not sure what it is, but something tells me you're right."

"You were left alone at birth. My mom was killed, and although I was raised with my father, after she died, I felt like an orphan myself," Dom explained. "I'm not saying my situation even came close to yours, but I understand taking a little while to trust people."

"All true. I guess I get what you're saying," Layla nodded. "You know, I was thinking; you've had the benefit of having files on Rose and me, but I practically know nothing about you."

"Wealthy, eccentric, recluse. What else is there to know?"

"Let's start easy. It seems to me you would have preferred to tell Tom to fuck off. Why did you ultimately agree to this?" Layla inquired.

"To be honest, that was my first choice," Dom confessed. "But my computer had other ideas."

"Meddling technology aside, you're in pretty deep. The warehouse, employing the Jenkins brothers, the phones, and cloak and dagger shit. You didn't have to do all of this," Layla argued. Dom sat silently stirring her beverage with the olives in deep thought.

"I'm not sure my reasoning will really satisfy your question."

"Try me."

"I've been empty for a while. Not lonely, I'm sure that's what you guys think; just — empty. I used my tech and my toys to fill the void like I was doing something," Dom scoffed. "I didn't want to put myself in the position to feel anymore. I didn't want to deal with the drain of people. But, I don't know, it doesn't feel that way with you guys."

"You sure it wasn't loneliness?" Layla prodded. Dom glanced at her with a smirk.

"I don't think so. I've lived almost five whole years without interaction. If I hadn't met you guys, I'd still be isolated. I agreed with everything Tom said to me in that video you saw. It just doesn't make sense to ignore something so important when I can actually help. It would be evil for me to turn my back when presented with the opportunity to seek justice for people who would continue to be ignored," she explained. Layla watched her as she spoke and nodded in understanding.

"I appreciate the desire to help those who can't speak for themselves. That's kind of why I do what I do," she disclosed. "I have to admit, you're handling the rug of isolation being yanked from under you pretty well."

"Trust me. My seclusion is still favorable, but the logic of it all is starting to dissipate," Dom conceded.

"I know you were shot and witnessed your mother's death, but is that the only reason you stay away from people?"

"Not really. That's fairly low on the motivation scale. I've just had some bad experiences throughout my life, and then there's the whole empathy thing," Dom replied.

"I will say that's where we're different. Like with Dr. Guerrero; she's done some really bad things, but you still have compassion for her. I personally believe the quick bullet to the brain was far easier than she deserved," Layla declared.

"I get the logic of your stance, I really do. Believe me, sometimes I wish I didn't immediately fall onto the side of compassion. Rationally, I know that some people may not be worth empathy. But I can't help it," she shrugged.

"Maybe with everything I've seen and been through, I'm more jaded than most," Layla shrugged.

"That would be understandable."

"What's it like?" Layla asked. "Feeling so strongly." Dom mulled over the question for a beat.

"Do you swim?"

"You assume I can't swim because I'm black?" Layla inquired, humor coloring her voice.

"I didn't ask if you knew *how* to swim, I asked if you swim," Dom clarified with a chuckle.

"I'm from New Orleans. Of course, I swim," Layla replied.

"You ever snorkel?"

"A few times, yeah," Layla nodded.

"I went snorkeling once in Puerto Rico, back in college. It was a gorgeous day, not a cloud in the sky. I had never gone snorkeling from a boat before; it was always from shore. This time I started in the middle of the ocean and the wind made the water choppy. I can swim, but once I got into the ocean, the waves pushed me in the opposite direction with every stroke. The more I tried to swim the more it felt like I was just fighting to stay in the same place. I grew exhausted. I wanted to get back on the boat, but I was too far. I got separated from my group, and after a while, I told myself I was going to die. I was so tired, I just wanted to give up and let the waves carry me away."

"I'm sure this story is getting around to an answer to my question," Layla sighed with a hint of impatience. Dom favored her with a smile.

"The emotions of other people hit me really hard, especially when I care for them. I try to be apathetic, but that's impossible for me. So, when I'm around people I care for, their emotions become my emotions, no matter how hard I try to block it out. Folks flock to empathetic people. Humans desire to be cared for and commiserated with. Even when I tried to keep to myself, but still lead a normal life, it didn't help. People leaned on me, and it kept my mental state in overdrive. Every day felt like fighting the waters of Puerto Rico. Swimming a sea of emotions like that is exhausting… mentally and physically. So, I got out of the water altogether."

"That sounds emotionally brutal," Layla asserted.

"It can be," Dom replied. Layla turned her gaze to the fish and sat silently for a moment. The quiet was not awkward, which Dom found odd, as she had not known the woman long. "Is it my turn for a question?"

"I suppose it's only fair," Layla shrugged. Dom took a sip of her martini.

"Why weren't you ever adopted?"

"I had health issues," she replied.

"Care to expound?"

"There were quite a few. They think I was born prematurely by a couple of months, or I could have just been small; there is no way to know. But the most obvious issue was the gastroschisis," Layla said.

"Gastro-who?" Dom asked with confusion.

"Gastroschisis. It's when there's a hole in the abdomen of a baby and what should be inside is on the outside," she explained. "For me, it was my liver and stomach, which is pretty severe. It didn't help that my parents, whoever they were, left me on the doorstep of a New Orleans firehouse in the middle of July."

"Holy shit. How long were you there before someone found you?"

"They aren't sure. They were surprised I was alive. I was told when I went to the hospital I had a severe infection on top of the gastroschisis. The hospital didn't expect me to survive the night. With a case as bad as mine, the reparative surgery often happens in waves. They had to navigate the infection while they repaired. I was in the hospital for a long time. While they worked to clear that little problem, they discovered I had tetralogy of Fallot, which is a congenital heart defect," Layla continued.

"You couldn't catch a break, could you?"

"It gets better. Tetralogy of Fallot, or TOF as it's called, isn't just one defect, it's like the superfecta of heart defects," Layla explained. Dom gave her a puzzled expression.

"Superfecta?"

"Horse racing term, sorry," she said, shaking her head. "TOF is four defects in one. It can only be treated with open-heart surgery. So, needless to say, I was in and out of the hospital. I guess by the time they fixed all that was wrong with me the cute factor wore off."

"Did you ever wonder about your parents?" Dom asked. Layla turned her eyes back to the tanks in contemplation.

"I used to when I was little. I stopped when I turned ten. I went through a lot of messed up shit in foster care. After a while, I told myself that it could be worse. It helped preserve my sanity I guess," she shrugged. "I don't know where I came from. What I do know is that people who would leave their obviously sick baby at a fire station couldn't have been any better off than I was. I can do bad all by myself, you know?" Dom nodded.

"Was every foster home terrible?"

"There were some good ones, but they were never permanent. I was almost adopted by this sweet older couple. Before they could finalize everything, she had a heart attack and was bedridden. They wanted me, but health-wise, they couldn't keep me. There were other nice people here and there. But overall, the bad things overshadowed the good." Her voice took on a tone of sad reflection. Dom watched her speak about her past and felt a pang of sorrow. While Bernice was taken from her far too soon, she at least knew the love of her mother. The realization that Layla never had any sense of home or permanence broke her heart. Dom recognized certain aspects of herself within the woman. She shook off the melancholy knowing that Layla did not want her sympathy. She was a survivor, not a victim.

"You came out alright, all things considered," Dom admitted, polishing off her martini.

"I'll take that as a compliment," Layla smirked.

"What do you think about continuing this endeavor after the current case?" Layla's eyes floated back to Dom.

"I haven't really thought about it," she claimed. Dom snickered.

"I don't have to know you like Rachel or be as observant as Rose to know that's a lie."

"Okay, you got me," Layla grinned. "It's intriguing, to say the least. But I think what really got to me was you."

"Me?"

"You made me realize working for the cops has me more biased than I thought I'd ever be," she clarified. "I never thought that my time with the police would make me forget the problems we face."

"What do you mean?" asked Dom as she mixed another martini.

"When I ran away from my last foster home, I lived on the streets for a while. I was terrified of the cops. I saw what they did to other homeless kids and prostitutes. I saw the harassment and mistreatment first hand, especially after a hurricane. It was like that movie the Purge, but the cops were the ones doing all of the purging," she said, shaking her head with the memory.

"Why would you go to work for the police if you were afraid of them?"

"I don't know. I thought about social work, you know with my background and all. But the science and critical thinking of forensics really spoke to me. Plus, I get to help people who don't have a voice. I guess my fear took a backseat to all that. I was no longer a teenage runaway; I didn't have anything to worry about. I guess I forgot what it was like."

"And now you feel like you're biased?"

"I didn't think I was until our conversation about Milwaukee," Layla admitted. "I realized that I immediately rushed to the defense of the cop. I didn't know anything more about Timothy Cook than what was said on the news. When you asked me about his past mistakes signing his death warrant, I remembered that I've seen young people get assaulted by the police for less. He didn't even have a warrant for his arrest. I guess I can understand why he would run away. When I was a kid, I ran whenever I saw a cop. Talking to you brought back what it was like for me. I wasn't a bad kid, I was in a bad situation. The fact that our murderer may be a cop magnifies just how blind I've been to my own privilege. It's not that I don't know there are problems in law enforcement. It's just that when you're there when you see these guys every day, have dinner with them, meet their families, see them as your own family..." She hesitated when she heard her voice break.

"Detective Lewis means a lot to you, doesn't he?" Dom softly asked. Layla swallowed hard and nodded in response. "I'd like to meet him one day. For someone to mean so much to you, he's got to be pretty special." Layla threw her an astonished look. "If we're going to do this thing, it would be good to have a badge on our side, wouldn't it?"

"I guess that means you've made your decision?" Layla asked.

"If I go against what SARA believes I should logically do, I'll hear about it for the rest of my life," Dom pointed out, causing Layla to giggle.

"She'd drive you nuts."

"You do know I can hear you, don't you?" SARA chimed in.

"Stop being nosey!" Dom admonished, looking to the ceiling. "Anyway, it's a discussion for us all to have. I won't do this if you guys aren't in it with me."

"Do you think it could work?" Layla wondered.

"I honestly don't know. But between you, Rose, me and SARA, we could give it a pretty good effort."

CHAPTER THIRTY-SIX

Dom sat in the warehouse office watching the security feed while Robert paced the floor nervously. The video display showed the conference table on the other side of the wall where Vasquez, Layla, Ryan, Thomas Daniels, and Nancy Bennett sat idly chatting waiting for her and Robert to show. Because Dom wanted to observe the woman for a bit, the group allowed the newcomers to assume she and Robert were not on the premises.

"Calm down, you're making me nervous," Dom grumbled, glancing at the anxious Robert. He moved to the wall, leaned against it, and studied her.

"Why are we doing this again?"

"Nancy Bennett has been manipulating both of us. I want her to wait; to know what it feels like when you aren't in control of what's happening," she replied. "Plus, having Rachel out there should really drive up the irritation factor."

"She's been waiting for fifteen minutes," Robert sighed. "Isn't that enough time?"

"This isn't college. There is no fifteen-minute rule. She waits until I'm good and ready," she shot back, turning to the screens and studying the guest. Nancy was a tall Caucasian woman with curly dark hair, streaked with silver. She wore a dark gray pantsuit with a white collared shirt. Although her knowledge was limited to television and movies, Dom assumed this was the standard attire for any federal employee. The woman periodically checked her watch, her impatience bringing a smile to Dom's face.

"She's going to leave," Robert warned.

"She won't leave; she can't go anywhere. The charter company has instructions not to take-off until I give authorization," Dom replied.

"But she's a fed! All she has to do is show her badge or whatever she has," he argued. Dom spun her chair to the worried man.

"If she does she would have to pay for the flight back. Plus, she knows we know about the Subterranean operation. She's not going anywhere. I'm just trying to piss her off." Nancy shifted in her seat, irritation blanketing her features.

"You don't seem like the type to purposely antagonize someone, Dom," Robert observed.

"I'm not. But as I said, she's been manipulating me from jump. If Tom isn't the one who found me, it had to be someone within the federal government. This shit started with her. She deserves to sweat a little."

"Remind me to never get on your bad side."

"That would be wise," she nodded, turning back to the screens and increasing the volume of the speakers to hear the conversation.

"When should we expect Miss Samuels?" Thomas asked the group, eyeing Nancy nervously.

"She shouldn't be long," Ryan replied. His eyes moved to the camera within the monitor on the wall. The look on his face communicated to Dom that he felt Nancy was nearing the end of her patience.

"How did Thomas know about me? Was it you?" Layla suddenly asked Nancy.

"No, it was not," she curtly replied. Dom did not believe the statement to be factual. Thomas clearly indicated that his source for Layla and Dom was the same.

"As I told you when we first met, the source of that information was anonymous," Thomas reminded her.

"What about Robert Jenkins?" Vasquez inquired. To Dom's dismay, she seemed to temper her normal personality for this meeting. Layla probably had a lot to do with that.

"I would prefer to wait until Mr. Jenkins is present," Nancy tersely answered, checking her watch again.

"Dom, that's enough; let's get out there," Robert begged.

"Fine," she sighed, standing from her chair. "SARA, no talking. But listen and research. Send anything pertinent to the tablet."

"Yes, Dom," SARA acknowledged. Dom started for the door opposite the sliding wall just as Robert took a step towards the hidden entrance. When he saw Dom go the opposite direction, he frowned.

"Where are you going?" he asked. Dom gave him a puzzled look.

"It's a panic room, Rob. Part of the draw is that no one knows where it is," she advised, entering her code. She opened the door and motioned for Robert to follow. He trudged behind her into the anteroom where the weapons were stored. She crossed the chamber to the blast-resistant door leading into the shooting range with Robert close on her heels.

"We know about the panic room," he remarked.

"I'm not worried about you guys."

"Oh, so you've decided we're trustworthy?"

"Don't you dare tell Rachel," she warned him, pushing open the shooting range door. Dom led him to another reinforced entry on the other side of the area. When they neared this door, he heard the distinct sound of a lock disengaging. She pushed the door open, and the bright Houston sun greeted Robert.

"Whoa," he gasped, stepping outside behind the woman.

"It's a back door, man. You are a little too mystified," she chuckled. He followed her around the perimeter of the building back to the main entrance. When she pushed open the door, the group jumped at the abrupt sound. Ryan's eyes widened when he realized they appeared from outside rather than emerging from the wall as he expected.

"Where did…" Vasquez started, but a nudge from Layla caused her to fall silent.

"Sorry to keep you waiting," Dom said, approaching the table. Thomas stood from his seat with his irritating smile plastered on his face. She strolled to the chair opposite of Nancy and sat down. "Ms. Bennett."

"Dominique Samuels, I presume," she nodded.

"That's me." Realizing she left her tablet in the panic room, Dom looked at Vasquez and nodded at the tablet she was holding. Vasquez relinquished the device.

"Robert Jenkins," Nancy greeted, moving her eyes to him as he took the seat to Dom's left.

"So, you do know me," he said. Nancy gave him a small nod.

"Let's start from the beginning," Dom instructed. "You go first." A look of annoyance crossed Nancy's face, but Dom knew she did not have much of a choice. This was Dom's party, and she intended to have it the way she wanted.

"We received a letter from an inmate by the name of Tavion Evans. He was imprisoned in the Hutchins State Unit in Dallas. Understand, we get many letters from prisoners who claim innocence, but this particular correspondence reached Malik. Malik did some digging in his case and found that Mr. Evans was a double victim of an obvious miscarriage of justice," Nancy began.

"That's an understatement," Dom grumbled.

"This prompted Malik to look into other inmates sentenced by Judge Benjamin. He found many first-time felons and people with minor priors received a maximum sentence. Ordinarily, we allow the locals to handle things under their own laws. Too much meddling by our department could create frustration at the state level. It's always a fight with the states. Until recently, any voting law changes in the south had to be cleared by us because they couldn't be trusted not to discriminate," she continued.

"Until they got rid of that protection," Ryan muttered.

"Exactly. We pick our battles carefully. What Malik found was that Judge Benjamin's pattern disproportionately affected minority prisoners. On average, seventy-five percent of his White cases received markedly less time and sometimes probation. Conversely, eighty percent of his cases for minority offenders received much harsher penalties for the same offenses. We do recognize that sentencing for minorities is more severe than for White Americans, but the Justice Department is hesitant to get involved. You must understand; there's a balance we have to strike. We cannot review every minority case and give the appearance of favoritism to a specific group, even if the group has a history of being disenfranchised. The job of maintaining justice is a delicate one," Nancy explained.

"Delicate? There's nothing delicate about this. If you know that minorities are treated unfairly, why do you do nothing about it?" Robert demanded. Nancy turned to him and gave him a sad smile.

"It's not as easy as you would like to think, Mr. Jenkins. I understand mistakes happen and I also realize that sometimes people view the same mistakes differently, depending on the color of one's skin. If it were up to me, we would have blind trials where the jury and judges could not see the race of any given prisoner and simply judge the case based on the evidence. Character witnesses would be far more useful," Nancy answered. "But that's not the way the justice system works. The confrontation clause of the Sixth Amendment makes that virtually impossible."

"Confrontation clause?" Robert frowned.

"The part of the Sixth Amendment that says the accused has the right to face their accuser. That's supposedly how trials are fair. Since the defendant is present, they can't say they didn't know the evidence and whatnot," Layla replied before Nancy could speak.

"Eidetic memory indeed," Nancy smirked. "The fact of the matter is, justice is supposed to be blind and impartial, but it's not. The justice system is made up of people, and people always come with their own set of bias and prejudices. It's easy for those with privilege to say that there is nothing wrong with the system but we all know that's not true. The problem is, it's often impossible to prove that the prejudice is there. It's so ingrained in every facet of our society that people don't recognize their own preconceptions. If the Justice Department were to consistently go after things that can't truly be proven, we would lose our credibility as the impartial branch of the government we are supposed to represent."

"You don't talk like a federal attorney," Layla remarked.

"The Attorney General may be a partisan appointment, but the rest of us are people, not politicians," Nancy replied. "Some of us just love the law and what it's supposed to represent."

"What's your angle? Why are you with the DOJ and working with Tom and his group?" Ryan asked. Nancy turned her light gray eyes to him.

"I grew up in a home of activists," she responded. "I understand the concept of a White ally may be idealistic. There are people who help only because they want to feel better in their privilege. However, when it comes to progress, those same people get nervous when the oppressed are elevated to a certain level. It threatens their advantage. Sadly, there are many people out there like that — fake allies. I'm not one of them."

"A home of activists?" Dom prodded.

"I was born in 1961 in Atlanta, Georgia. My father was a criminal defense attorney, but he started as a prosecutor out of law school," she explained. "He said that the murder of Emmett Till changed his life. Daddy drove to Sumner, Mississippi to see the trial in action. He knew those two men were guilty as sin. As a prosecutor working in the Deep South, he was curious about how the district attorney would handle the trial. This was in 1955; the Civil Rights Movement had not even fully picked up steam yet. Daddy said he saw the signs and knew the road to change would be an uphill battle. So, he drove to Mississippi thinking he would get some pointers on how he could tailor his criminal cases when the victim was someone of color, and the defendant was White. What he found was a mockery of the justice system. He never told me exactly what happened, he would get so angry, but I read about it later. The not guilty verdict came down in September of '55; Daddy quit his job in October of the same year and opened a criminal defense practice. He worked with everyone, but he often put his hat in the ring as a Public Defender on the side."

"Is that what started his activism?" Layla asked.

"He attended rallies and took part in sit-ins. That's where he met my mother. He participated in the Atlanta sit-ins at a few of the lunch counters in 1960. My mom was a waitress for one of those places, and here I am," she nodded. "I was seven years old when Dr. King was shot. I found my father on the front porch, weeping like a child. I'd never seen my dad cry. I asked him what was wrong. He put me on his lap and told me that a very good man had been murdered. I asked him why. He said it was because the man wanted everyone to be equal. He said that Dr. King knew it was dangerous, but he tried to get justice anyway. When I asked him why he would do it if he knew it was dangerous, my dad repeated a quote by Dr. King that has piloted my life and my career: 'Injustice anywhere is a threat to justice everywhere.' He told me that Dr. King felt doing the right thing was worth dying for even though he should not have had to." Her tone was soft, and Dom could tell by the woman's voice that she believed every word she spoke.

"But why the DOJ? Why not the ACLU or the Southern Poverty Law Center?" Layla asked.

"As I got older and learned more about justice and inequality, I learned that by virtue of my skin alone, I could get into places a little easier than others. Even though I'm a woman, I'm a White woman. My aim was the DOJ because it has a bigger impact. I wanted to make a difference. I had to bide my time, deal with the misogyny, play the game, and wait for the moment where I could carve out my own little division. Six years ago, I was given that opportunity," she replied.

"So, Tavion Evans is who turned you on to Judge Benjamin. How did Robert fit into the equation?" Dom asked.

"In his research into Judge Benjamin, Malik also looked up his background and family. That research led him to the discovery that he had a nephew incarcerated in Huntsville. He read the transcript from the trial, even though Robert didn't go through Benjamin's court. The evidence overwhelmingly pointed to drug addiction. Malik wanted to speak with you directly, perhaps try to get a feel for your uncle. In most families, a connection like Judge Benjamin would have spared prison time. We found it odd that it didn't help you," Nancy explained.

"Because he doesn't give a damn about us," Ryan growled in anger.

"Malik thought maybe Robert could give some insight into the man. So, we made arrangements for Malik to bunk with Robert when he got to Huntsville," Nancy said.

"You're the reason Rob got out so unexpectedly," Ryan declared. Nancy gave him a brief nod.

"It was the least we could do. Robert should not have been in prison as long as he was. Malik insisted I call in some favors." She glanced at Robert. "As sad as I am about his death, I'm glad I could do that one final favor for him."

"Thank you," he whispered, with heavy emotion.

"Liberty Health Services Foundation," Dom prompted. "He stumbled onto that, didn't he?" Nancy turned to Dom and offered a nod of assent.

"Most of the inmates he spoke with likely could have gotten by with lesser sentences, but there was nothing Earth shattering. Then he met Sergio Martinez," she replied.

"But he spoke with Taylor, Evans, and Cole before he got to Huntsville. You didn't know before Martinez?" Vasquez asked.

"The other three didn't mention the clinics as far as I know," she answered. Dom frowned at this information.

"But those four inmate numbers were in the coded messages we found on Malik's gaming system."

"Like I said, there was nothing Earth-shattering about the majority of the inmates he spoke with. Malik found some odd things with those four. Obviously, Evans' case set off alarms. Why would he be given a change of venue so easily? Why was his arrest warrant put out the day he was picked up? The Cole and Taylor cases also seemed suspicious. Both were arrested in Houston while just visiting or passing through. Yes, they had prior felonies, but a handgun charge and an assault on a public servant? Those two things didn't jibe with what Malik found on them," she explained.

"That's what Rob and our sister felt too," Ryan concurred.

"Martinez didn't start out telling Malik about the clinics. What he told him was that he had gotten out of the game and was moving away. He said the drugs were planted on him. It wasn't until later, just before we were about to pull Malik out of the prison that he gave him the full story about why he was leaving — the clinics, Miss Waters, and his two friends who were killed. After extraction, he begged me to stay in Houston to research more."

"Why wouldn't they…" Dom's voice dropped off in thought. Vasquez, Layla, and the Jenkins brothers sat silently with expectant looks on their faces.

"Why wouldn't they tell him?" Nancy finished the question. "I don't know."

"Give her a second. She's piecing it together," Layla said, holding her hand up towards Nancy. Dom began to tap around on the tablet in search of something, while the crowd waited patiently.

"Piecing what together?" Nancy asked in confusion.

"That's the look she gets when she's putting a puzzle together," Vasquez answered. "Just hang on a second." The crowd sat silently for a few more moments watching Dom read and mentally slide fragments into place. When clarity took over her features, Vasquez grinned at Nancy. "Told you."

"Evans didn't tell you guys because Eva Gonzales got paid for her lung," Dom said looking up at the crowd.

"She what?" Layla asked.

"She took money for her donation. That's illegal. Evans wouldn't have told Justice that," Dom said. "I didn't even think to look."

"And the way Tanisha was talking, I'm willing to bet Cole and Taylor didn't say anything because they were afraid for their girls," Ryan added with understanding.

"It makes sense," Layla nodded.

"Not to us," Nancy interjected.

"What did Malik tell you about Martinez?" Dom asked, not addressing her bewilderment.

"He told me Martinez gave him a story about his girlfriend almost dying from a botched surgery at the South Side Women's clinic. He said the clinic stole a kidney from her and that when he went to confront them, his friends were murdered right in front of him, and he was arrested to keep him quiet. He and his girlfriend were moving to Miami the day after he was arrested. Martinez swore the drugs were planted," she replied.

"Martinez was willing to risk everything to get out. The other three died for nothing," Dom glumly mumbled. Nancy waved her hand in front of Dom's distant gaze.

"I shared, now it's your turn," she insisted. Dom grimly nodded and began to run down the information the group discovered since meeting Tanisha Waters. Nancy listened with a placid face until Dom mentioned the covert sterilizations.

"Jesus," she grimaced. Dom continued, finishing with the death of Rosalyn Guerrero.

"I think whoever is behind this clinic thing; they don't know that Cole, Evans, and Taylor never said anything. They're panicking," Dom said in closing.

"You're saying that not only is Judge Benjamin giving harsher sentences to minorities and showing an obvious bias; but he's also being used to lock up men he knows are innocent?" Thomas asked.

"We don't know for sure that he is corrupt. I can tell you from experience that he's an asshole with a very real bias against poor minorities," Ryan replied. "The other option is that the police and District Attorney are purposely routing these people to Benjamin's court, knowing he will throw the book at them."

"Who is Tasha Rodgers?" Vasquez asked suddenly. Nancy blinked at the question.

"I'm sorry?"

"The apartment in Greenspoint was rented under the name Tasha Rodgers. I assume you rented it for him. The signer was a woman, according to the leasing office," Vasquez expounded.

"Tasha is the name I used. I couldn't sign and use the name Malik," she said.

"I know my sister isn't here, but I also know that there's more to that explanation," Ryan declared. Nancy's eyes flitted to Thomas, and she cleared her throat.

"Malik dated my daughter for a little while after he joined Justice. She got pregnant," she whispered. Thomas' eyes bulged.

"What? He never told me he got Melissa pregnant!"

"No, he didn't. Only I knew," Nancy said. "Melissa lost the baby. They had picked out names. Thomas for a boy, after you," she looked at Thomas again with a sad smile. "And Tasha for a girl. I use that name as one of my aliases. You know, for the granddaughter I never had."

"Is that why he and Melissa split?" Thomas asked in awe.

"It was too much for them. Malik started throwing himself into work. Melissa did too. Their relationship fell apart." Dom noticed the woman's eyes clouding with emotion. Afraid to allow this tangent to derail the conversation she changed the subject.

"What is the Subterranean operation?"

"Tom told me you deciphered that little enigma," she smirked, wiping at her eyes. "Subterranean is a Justice project I'm spearheading. We believe that there may be influencers using money to control the judicial system, much like the mobsters of the old days. I was able to get approval for Malik's investigation by putting it in the Subterranean operation. We don't know Benjamin is being influenced, but we don't know he is not either."

"What do you mean, influencers?" Layla asked.

"It's no secret that the Citizen's United case made it very easy for money to filter into our election system. It's shitty, but we are where we are," Nancy asserted. "The part of the government that is supposed to be untouchable is the Judicial Branch. Yes, judges are elected or appointed by politicians, but once they get on the bench, they need to be going by the law and constitution, not by any sort of agenda. Subterranean was formed as the Justice Department's answer to Citizen's United. We try to identify influenced judges, investigate them, and remove them from the bench if necessary. If we allow the judicial system to be corrupted with money, we may as well be a dictatorship."

"You told Tom it's bigger than you," Dom pointed out. "But you're saying you are over the operation."

"It is bigger than me," Nancy admitted. "This operation was approved far above my head by people way above my pay grade. I'm middle management at best."

"What is the DOJ doing about Malik's death?" Layla wondered.

"Officially, he was not working for us. But we have made sure that his benefits go to his mother and everything, just like all of our agents," Nancy replied.

"No, I mean, as far as the investigation. Doesn't his death turn this into a Federal thing? Where is the FBI?"

"Subterranean is a highly classified operation," Nancy responded.

"Are you purposely not answering my question?" Layla sighed with irritation.

"She's saying that Subterranean is off the books," Ryan spoke up. "It's not an official operation, and if it's not an official operation, Malik's death can't be investigated because he wasn't supposed to be here." He looked from Layla to Nancy. "It's the locals' problem now, right?"

"That's correct," she nodded. "The operation is off the books because administrations and attorney generals change. When that happens, priorities within the justice department also shift. Subterranean is about making sure justice doesn't bend to the will of people who have money and power. It's unknown by most within the government to prevent it from being wiped out on the whim of any random administration. Like with Tom's group, we hide in plain sight. We're just another line item in the budget."

"And the clinics?" Dom asked.

"We need more evidence before we can act on that. Right now, we have a deceased former gang member who told a non-existent operative. You're telling me now that the other three could have verified, but they're all dead too. For anyone to act we have to have proof," Nancy responded. "No federal judge would issue a warrant based on what we have."

"So, what you're saying is that we need to be doing both Houston PD's job and the federal government's job," Dom proclaimed. Nancy gave the woman a plaintive shrug.

"You can choose not to do this."

"We're in pretty deep, don't think that's an option now," Dom mumbled.

"You brought me here to tell you what I know, and I've done that. I could lose my job for this, but Malik, he was special. He was a good kid. I want the bastard who did this. Is there anything else you need from me?"

"Two things," Dom nodded. "I need for you to sign a contract with Shadow Technologies on behalf of the DOJ." Nancy blinked.

"What are you talking about?"

"If we are doing your job we need to be a federal contractor. We all need a form of protection in case things get screwy like they did in Spring," she explained. "If you are over this operation, you should have that power. You don't even need to pay us."

"I'm not supposed to do this," Nancy hesitated. Dom narrowed her eyes.

"But you can." Her tone was more of a command than a question.

"I suppose," Nancy agreed. "It can't be free though, it would look suspicious."

"Fine; we will take a quarter of your rate. Call it our patriotic duty," Dom sarcastically confirmed. "We don't want to be run by the DOJ. But I don't want any of us to continue this unprotected. As a tradeoff, you can send any cyber-related investigations to me."

"I guess that will work."

"Then we have an agreement," Dom pronounced. "Now onto the second thing. I want to know if the Department of Justice knew anything about Layla or me."

"Nothing at all. Tom told me about the two of you when he got your information from his source. I thought you'd be a good asset to his group. I certainly never considered I would ever meet you in person," she said. Dom frowned at the response. She hoped that meeting Nancy would provide some form of closure to the recent disturbance in her life. However, if Nancy was telling the truth, she was no closer to understanding how she had been discovered. Dom believed Nancy's words considering she seemed to be completely honest about everything else. While she received enough of the background to understand what was needed from her and her new friends, she was left wondering how she got thrown into this situation, to begin with — a question that left her mind troubled.

"So, what do we do now?" Ryan asked. After the discussion, Dom turned over the surveillance footage of Theo Morrison's murder at the Huntsville prison unit via flash drive since she had not gotten around to sending a file to Thomas. Nancy accepted the stick, promising to have the justice department look into his and Sergio Martinez's deaths. Now, the group sat in the warehouse attempting to determine their next course of action.

"The prison thing is out of our hands now. Now, we focus on your uncle and these clinics," Dom replied.

"What about Malik?" Robert asked.

"Lewis is working on that," Layla answered. "That reminds me, he asked me to have you run the financials of the daytime homicide detectives. He figures that whoever is killing people is being paid." Dom nodded and motioned towards the pad of paper positioned next to Layla.

"Write down the names; I'll get SARA on it," she commanded.

"And Uncle Tom?" Robert prodded.

"Someone needs to cozy up to him," Dom said.

"Two problems," Ryan cut in. "One, he doesn't like us. Two, I'm fairly sure he won't just confess to being a corrupt judge."

"We don't need him to confess. We just need one of you to get close to him," Dom said.

"That still leaves problem number one," Ryan reminded her.

"Your sister said you guys have access. I'm sure that means she has an idea," Dom shrugged.

"This is insane," Vasquez sighed.

"What about us?" Layla wondered.

"You guys have to stay out of sight unless completely necessary. We'll be doing research into this foundation. We need to know who the players are, and who is pulling the strings — so we can cut them."

CHAPTER THIRTY-SEVEN

When Leon Murphy arrived for his early morning breakfast appointment, he did not enter Rose's office alone. A young woman followed him into the room, and she was not happy. She looked to be in her late-twenties, curvy with a long red and black weave pulled into a messy bun. Although her light brown eyes were not green, they were identical in shape to that of young Leon. Rose knew immediately the woman was his mother.

"Ms. Murphy!" Rose stood in greeting and rounded her desk. "This is quite a surprise; please come in." She waved the woman and child into the room. Leon's face wore a veil of anxiety as he moved to his normal chair and his mother took the seat next to him. As she neared the desk, Rose smelled the distinct odor of alcohol coming from the woman. Returning to her seat, she looked down at the two breakfast tacos she brought and pushed both across the desk to her guests. Leon eyed his mother cautiously but did not move to take the food. His reluctance caused Rose to tilt her head. "Is something wrong?"

"Why are you making my son come up here every morning?" The woman asked. Rose blinked in confusion at the question.

"I was under the impression that he explained it to you," she answered. "Leon has been having some behavioral issues."

"And that means he has to come up here every day? What for? What are you doing with my child?" Leon's mother demanded.

"We have breakfast and talk."

"Talk about what?" she challenged.

"Music, poetry, life," Rose listed in a calm and soothing voice. She looked at Leon, who was staring longingly at the food. "You can eat, Leon." His eyes moved to his mother with a questioning look. She scowled and nodded.

"Thanks, Miss Jenkins," he mumbled. His mother threw Rose an irritated frown.

"Leon, can you take your breakfast to the hall? Just outside the door; I think I need to speak with your mother alone," Rose informed him. Leon bobbed his head up and down, obviously relieved to be excused. After he exited the office, she turned her attention to his mother. "May I ask your name?"

"Trina," she said.

"Trina, my name is Rose. Let's not do this "Miss" thing. You can call me Rose, and I'll call you Trina, is that okay?"

"I guess so," Trina shrugged.

"Great. Now, let's start at the beginning. What are your concerns, Trina?"

"I don't understand what's going on. I woke up this morning, and Leon was getting dressed to leave for school with his big brother. When I asked him why he told me that he had to meet with the school counselor and that it's been happening every morning for almost two weeks! No one told me about this! You can't just have kids coming to school early without letting their parents know! It ain't right," Trina asserted.

"First of all, let me apologize. I asked him to come see me in the mornings, and I just assumed he would tell you what was going on," Rose admitted. "I should have called you to explain. It may be a little late, but if you would like, I can do that now." Trina sat back in her chair and crossed her arms.

"Go for it."

"Leon's behavioral issues have been ongoing for most of the school year. It culminated into a bad week leading Vice Principal Cavanaugh to send him to my office. Leon was not very open to talking to me at that time, but then I realized he had not eaten breakfast. He mentioned that the food stamps hadn't posted yet," Rose explained. At the mention of the food stamps, Trina's face stiffened.

"That boy knows better than to put our business in the street," she grumbled.

"Can I be completely blunt with you?" Trina nodded in response. "Your son is not a bad child. He's hurting just like you are. I don't have children so I can't imagine your pain, but I have lost two brothers in my lifetime. I know how much that hurts. I lost mine as an adult, but for an eleven-year-old, it is much worse because he's not fully developed yet. He has so much grief and doesn't know what to do with it; therefore, it comes out as behavioral problems," Rose explained. At the mention of her lost daughter, Trina's eyes welled up with tears.

"Leon took Kenya's death really hard. They were only a year apart. Kenya was his little buddy," she sniffed.

"Trina, were you aware there was no food in the house?" Rose softly asked. Trina's face colored in embarrassment.

"I didn't know how bad it was until today," she admitted.

"And you hadn't noticed that Leon has been coming here early for almost two weeks?" she prodded. Trina shook her head miserably.

"Not until this morning," she confessed. Rose studied the woman carefully. The whites of her eyes were bloodshot, and she was fidgeting nervously in her seat.

"How long have you been drinking?" she inquired. Trina's eyes widened at the question, and she shifted in her seat and cleared her throat.

"Since Kenya," she answered in a raspy voice. "I couldn't sleep. It helps me clear my head and not feel so much."

"Leon has an older brother, thirteen correct?"

"He has two older brothers," Trina replied. "I had my first at fifteen, he's fifteen now."

"Kenya was your only girl," Rose muttered in comprehension. "I can't imagine. No parent should ever have to bury their child." Trina finally lost her restraint and tears began to flow down her cheeks. Rose snatched a couple of tissues from the box on her desk and pushed them across to her visitor.

"She was my baby," Trina sniffed, dabbing her eyes with the tissues. "She was the sweetest girl you could imagine. She cared so much about her brothers and me. She only wanted us to be a happy family."

"Leon thought the world of her. The way he tells it, his little sister hung the moon. I'm so very sorry for your loss," Rose said softly in a tone of consolation. Trina sniffled, fighting to collect herself. Once she was composed, Rose continued. "Since we are being real, I'm going to be straight with you. You and your family have suffered a devastating blow, and I truly sympathize with what you are going through — especially considering my family has also been through something quite similar. But Trina, you have three other children who need you. The depression of losing a child has to be overwhelming; I understand that. But you've got to realize that while you want to numb yourself to all of your emotions, that's not a viable option as a mother. Think about the pain you feel on a daily basis, the sense of loss, and the sleepless nights. You are thirty years old. Now, imagine those same feelings for an eleven-year-old brain that isn't fully developed and doesn't have the numbing option you are using. Even in your pain, your understanding of life far exceeds Leon's comprehension. While grieving, you still know that it's not fair. Leon is a child. His understanding of life and its underlying cruelty is still limited and not fully formed. He can't drink himself into indifference. His mind deals with pain by acting out with anger and aggression. If you are not validating and helping him cope at home, he will never be able to recover from this — not on his own. That is part of the reason I set up this arrangement."

"I haven't really been able to deal with the boys. I try to make up for it by buying them things when taxes come in, you know, so they don't feel like I don't care," Trina sniffed.

"Stuff is good," Rose nodded. "But they can't eat stuff. Are you working?"

"I lost my job shortly after Kenya was killed. I worked at Walmart, and I didn't have much in the way of bereavement leave. I kept calling in, so they fired me," Trina advised. "It's hard to find a job that will take a high school dropout."

"You've had a rough year, no doubt about it," Rose nodded. "But your sons need you. You say Kenya was a sweet girl who cared about her family; how would she feel if she knew you drank yourself to death while ignoring her brothers?" Trina grimaced but did not respond. "Did you know that Leon's biggest dream is to become a rapper, so he can help you?" This question caused Trina's eyebrows to rise in shock.

"No. I know he loves listening to his music, but I didn't know that part."

"Your son sees your pain and wants to help you, but Trina, Leon is also in pain. As a mother, as a Black mother, you have to be stronger than most. It's the sad reality. You can't drink yourself into an early grave. You are all your boys have. If you aren't aware of what is going on with your kids, they could go down a path you don't want for them," Rose said. "Believe me, that's what happened with my brothers."

"I know. I just don't know how to keep going."

"By waking up every day and doing the hard things," Rose replied. She leaned forward and took Trina's hands in her own. "I know that the pain makes you want to roll out of bed and make a drink to numb yourself. The hard thing is not doing that. You don't want to cook or spend time with the boys, but the more you do the hard things, the less difficult they become. Your boys deserve the love of their mother, and you deserve the love of your boys — especially now, with all of you grieving such a horrific loss. Your boys need you, Trina."

"I can't even feed them," she whispered, with a sad shake of her head. "I need to find a job."

"Do you know the Booker T. Washington Rec Center not far from here?" Rose asked releasing the woman's hands. Trina's eyes rose, and she nodded in assent. "There is a retired teacher who runs the place, Darla Richardson. They offer free GED classes, and Darla would love to help you with that. That sound like something you'd want to try?" Trina gave a shrug of uncertainty.

"I feel like I'm too old now," she answered.

"You're never too old to do something to better yourself and your family, Trina," Rose asserted. Trina sat in silent contemplation.

"I will meet with Ms. Richardson," she declared with resolve.

"While your boys are in school, you can be in school. I'll set it up beginning Monday, that good?" Trina nodded as Rose went into her purse and extracted two business cards. She pushed them across the desk to the woman who eyed the offerings but did not move to accept them.

"What's that?"

"You need to feed your kids, Trina. I suspect you did not realize there was no food because of the haze of the alcohol. The card on top is for a food pantry nearby. As soon as school starts,

I'll give them a call, and they will have a box ready for you by ten o'clock this morning; something to tide you over until the first of the month. Can you get over there by then?" Rose inquired.

"I can call a friend to run me up there."

"Ask for Stacy Lincoln, she'll be expecting you," Rose instructed. "The second card is contact information for a friend of mine who runs an AA program at a nearby church." Trina frowned.

"I don't have a problem," she proclaimed, prompting Rose to raise an eyebrow.

"Do me a favor, take it anyway. Try to go the rest of today and all day tomorrow without a single drink. If you can do that, throw it away," she shrugged. "If you can't, think about giving him a call." Trina finally picked up the two cards and slid them into her pocket. "I will be checking up on you. Don't let me down, don't let yourself down, and please, don't let your boys down."

"Leon told me you were different than the other teachers here," Trina said.

"That's because I'm not a teacher," Rose chuckled. "I'm also from Sunnyside, so I know what it's like to try to make it with little to no help. I was one of the lucky ones. But I was surrounded by people who weren't as fortunate. I'm not here to judge you, I'm here to help; but, you have to do your part."

"Thank you, Rose."

"I'm doing it for Leon. He's a great kid, and if you're alright with it, I'd like to continue to work with him," Rose replied. Trina nodded.

"I guess that would be okay," she answered. Rose stood from her chair and crossed the room to her office door. She found Leon sitting on the floor directly across from her office, a balled-up taco wrapper in one hand. He was writing in the journal she had given him a few days before.

"Leon, you want to come back in?" she asked. Leon cast a furtive glance of hesitation at her, causing Rose to give him a warm smile. "It's okay. Come on."

Detective Lewis walked into the precinct and took a direct path to homicide. He arrived at the office later than usual thanks to another restless night. As he approached his desk, he was surprised to see Lopez occupying the space.

"What are you doing here, Vato? You do know your shift is over, don't you?" he asked. Lopez turned to him, flashing his signature grin.

"You were late, Old Timer," he replied. "I thought you may be out today, so I stayed behind to work on some reports." He pulled his messenger bag from under the desk and began to pack up his belongings. Lewis marveled at the man's energy level after an overnight shift.

"You like working that much? Your citizenship isn't dependent on how much paperwork you do. Relax; I know you were born here."

"I don't trust you, White man. You may try to get me deported anyway," Lopez grinned, standing and relinquishing the chair. "How is your investigation coming?"

"You know how it is in places like Greenspoint. No one ever sees or hears anything. If I solve it, it'll be a miracle, but I'm still working on it," Lewis replied as he sat in the abandoned chair and pulled himself to the computer. Taking a glance at the screen, he let out an exasperated sigh. He spun his chair back to Lopez, who was already making his way across the room. "Again man?"

"My bad!" Lopez called, without turning around. Lewis chuckled and returned his eyes to the screen. Lopez appeared to be in the middle of dictating case notes using the built-in microphone embedded in the desktop. Lewis did not understand the desire to dictate notes. He preferred to type his own reports, even if he still used two fingers to complete the task. He assumed the generational gap caused the younger cops to embrace all benefits of technology, while the older gumshoes preferred more old-school methods. Ever the courteous desk mate, he switched users without disturbing Lopez's progress. Reaching into his shirt pocket, he withdrew the names and case numbers of the four prisoners he discussed with Layla and Vasquez.

He spent the morning perusing the arrest reports of the four dead inmates. All of the men were arrested at night, and none of the reports shared the same arresting officers. Keith Jackson was the arresting officer for Eric Taylor. At the time of the arrest, almost three years previously, Jackson had been on the beat for less than three months. Lewis tried to search the department directory to locate Jackson, only to find that the cop was no longer with the Houston Police Department. He ran an internet search and found Jackson living in Florida. Moving to the report for Tommy Cole, Lewis found the name, LeeAnn Wilson. He discovered that Wilson was on the beat for less than five months at the time. Again, the department no longer employed her.

Rather than search for Wilson online, he immediately moved on to Tavion Evans who had been picked up about two years prior. Officer Brent Stevens was the name on the arrest report. At this point, Lewis had a feeling he knew what he would find, but he searched for Stevens nonetheless. As he expected, the cop had been an officer for less than a year before the arrest and was no longer an employee of the Houston police force. He knew that the turnover in the department fluctuated from time to time; however, the fact that all three officers he sought were no longer on the force did not sit well with him. He returned to his exploration by retrieving the last report for Sergio Martinez. Vincent Lionetti appeared as the arresting officer and had begun his career a mere month before Martinez's arrest. Having no optimism, he looked up Lionetti anyway. He gasped when he found that he was still an officer and was now on the day shift.

"Finally, I catch a break," he mumbled reaching for his phone.

"Check this out," Dom called, sharing her data to the crowd around the table. The group peered down at their respective devices. "Liberty Health Services Foundation has a link to a conservative super PAC that donated heavily to our new governor."

"What's the connection?" Ryan yawned.

"Dr. Edward Harris. He's on the board of both the Foundation and something called the United Liberty Political Action

Committee," she replied. "The super PAC gave a lot of money to our governor's last campaign. It looks like they contribute to various electoral races from the local to the federal level, usually saving the big bucks for State and Federal. Yet, they just made a substantial donation to one of our local races. Anyone want to take a guess of who they're backing?"

"Good old Uncle Tom?" Ryan guessed, in a sarcastic tone.

"Johnny, tell him what he's won."

"Wait," Vasquez interjected. "This foundation shares a board member with a conservative super PAC. Does anyone else find it weird that they would be the ones going into low-income areas to provide healthcare?"

"We've already figured they aren't helping," Layla pointed out.

"Well, I know that, but it's just weird," she continued. "Whether you agree with their beliefs or stances there's nothing wrong with the PAC itself. There are tons of liberal and moderate PACs that do the same thing. Like Nancy said, tons of money flowing into politics and whatnot. But my question is, why would a health foundation donate to a super PAC? Particularly to a side that gives the appearance of wanting to reduce access to health care or make it more expensive. Doesn't that seem conflictory?"

"You're asking why a health foundation would be politicized, especially to the right?" Dom asked. Vasquez nodded. "That's actually a great question, Rachel."

"Why does everyone act so surprised when I say something insightful? I'm not Layla or you, but I'm not dumb."

"I would never call you dumb. It's just that women as beautiful as you aren't generally so intelligent and perceptive. It's refreshing," Dom smiled. Vasquez's grimace morphed into a blush, and she dropped her eyes to her tablet in a rare visage of bashfulness. Layla eyed the two women and shook her head.

"Anyway," she sighed. "This may be a link, but it's not evidence. We have to find something specific that we can use."

"I may have found something that is closer to evidence," SARA announced. Robert emerged from the kitchen with a plate of freshly made blueberry muffins with brown sugar and rolled oat crumble. He placed the plate in the middle, then pulled out the chair next to his brother and took a seat.

"It's like having my own personal chef," Dom grinned reaching for a muffin. "I can get used to you, Jenkins." Robert smiled and nodded proudly.

"What do you have, SARA?" Layla asked. All device displays changed to a plain website with a black background and bright yellow and white words. When Dom focused her eyes, she saw that it was a forum website. Across the top in large yellow print were the words, "Liberty Health Services Foundation Scam."

"SARA, this wasn't in the initial search of the foundation," she noted, with surprise.

"It was located further down in the results," SARA replied. The wheels in Dom's brain began to churn as she processed the news.

"How far down?" Layla asked making eye contact with Dom. Dom could tell the woman was on a shared train of thought.

"My search function does not operate in the same manner as standard internet searches. I can tell you it was buried behind over four-hundred other links and articles."

"Reputation management. That's not cheap," Dom mumbled thoughtfully.

"That has to be it, especially for it to be that far down," Layla nodded in agreement.

"Hello?" Vasquez waved her hand between the locked eyes of Dom and Layla. The women blinked and focused on the rest of the crowd. "Reputation management?"

"There are companies out there that specialize in burying negative information for organizations and individuals to help shape a specific image. Kind of like an Olivia Pope for the Internet," Dom explained, turning her eyes back to her tablet to review the page. "For this to be so far down in the search results, whoever did this were professionals and could not have been cheap."

"So, what is this?" Ryan asked, bringing his tablet closer to examine the website. The group began to read the entries on the page. The site appeared to be started by one woman, who was sterilized eight years prior. Most of the main entries were from the same person in her endeavor to get justice for her forced steriliza-tion. She had gone to the clinic in El Paso when she was a teenager and walked away barren. She did not discover the development until she was married at twenty-three and attempted to start a family with her new husband.

"Listen to this," Vasquez said. "I was told today that if I attempted to file legal action, I would be countersued for slander by the foundation. I have been unable to find a lawyer to take my case. It seems they are afraid to go after a large charity allegedly engaged in philanthropy, particularly due to my lack of proof. Apparently, I am at fault for not discovering my violation sooner. Please, I know I can't be the only one. If you're out there, I'm begging you, reach out."

"That poor woman," Layla murmured.

"It looks like a few weeks later she got some responses from a handful of women, all with the same story," Ryan added scrolling down his tablet. "We have to find someone who will listen to us all," he read from the device.

"It seems like this would have been bigger news," Layla muttered. "If I heard about it, I would remember."

"There was never a suit filed in any court," SARA announced. Dom frowned.

"She had back up, I wonder why not?"

"Another victim backed out today," Robert began reading. "I wish I knew what would make so many drop out. We dropped from twenty-five to four. The attorney said that twenty-five would be a much better case than four. Please, guys, don't let them get away with this."

"Well, that answers that. SARA, do you have the source of the page? Who is this woman?" Dom asked.

"Her name is Denise Suarez, Dom. She was reported missing by her husband six years ago," SARA replied, changing their tablets to the missing person's report.

"Well, I'm fairly sure she's not hiding somewhere in Tahiti," Dom muttered. "We can probably assume she's dead."

"There is more," SARA continued. The tablets changed to reveal another website. Dom leaned in to study the new page. There was an image at the top of the site that looked like an X, with the top half extending into the shape of a diamond.

"What's the symbol?" Vasquez wondered.

"It's an othala rune," Ryan murmured. "Nazi symbol." Dom's eyes registered amazement at this disclosure.

"How do you know that?" she prodded. His face darkened with the question, and he shifted in his chair.

"A guy in my unit, he had it tattooed on his chest," he admitted, stroking his scar with a distracted look on his face. Dom wondered if the man with the tattoo had anything to do with the mutilation Ryan often caressed in deep thought.

"So, this is a White supremacist website?" Layla guessed.

"That is correct," SARA replied.

"And you are showing us this, because?" Dom pressed. SARA took over navigation of all devices, scrolling down and highlighting a particular thread.

"The problem with democracy is that the niggers, chinks, ragheads, and wetbacks breed like the animals they are. If they keep this up, we will be outnumbered within the next fifty years. Our country is going to the fucking toilet. Every day, these ingrates want more and more handouts. They take places in schools and jobs that should belong to us. We are smarter and far more superior, but their Affirmative Action and cries of inequality make it hard for the White man to succeed. The niggers whine about being slaves, but they weren't slaves! They just want to milk shit that happened to their monkey ancestors hundreds of years ago. Now they wage war on us, on our values. If we are going to win this war, the key is to keep them from multiplying," Robert read aloud. He looked up from his tablet and made a face of disgust. "Why are the insane ramblings of a racist important?"

"Continue reading," SARA instructed, highlighting a response to the diatribe.

"You are absolutely right. My father and I were just talking about this. We have an idea that could work. If you're interested, we should link up offline. Send me a message with your email," Vasquez read.

"Who are those people, SARA?" Dom asked. Her pulse thudded, and her ears grew warm with the anger she felt from the words recited by her companions.

"The response is from Dr. Eric Fields, the current chairman of Liberty Health Services Foundation. The original post was written by Kevin Grimaldi," SARA reported. The information on the tablets changed again as she spoke. Dom found herself looking at a man in his mid to late fifties with blonde hair, blue eyes, and an obvious aura of wealth and privilege. Kevin Grimaldi was the CFO of the Grimaldi Transport Company in Atlanta, Georgia. She began tapping on the tablet to research the company and found its origins dated back to the pre-Civil War era. The business was worth billions with many subsidiary transport organizations. "Kevin Grimaldi donates millions to the Liberty Health Services Foundation on an annual basis," SARA informed the group.

"Whoa," Vasquez gasped. "So, it's possible that this Foundation started specifically to try to reduce the minority population based on some crazy rant by an entitled rich White guy with a superiority complex?"

"That could be very accurate," Dom nodded.

"Guys, this is all too circumstantial. We still need to find the smoking gun," Layla pointed out.

"I'm also getting more and more concerned about Uncle Tom's role in this. No matter how much of a dick he is, I just can't see him willingly being a part of such a racist agenda," Ryan mused.

"I wouldn't put anything past him," Robert mumbled.

"Well, your sister should be here any minute from school. I'd love to hear what ideas she has about how to approach the Judge," Dom said. As if summoned by her words, the warehouse door swung open, and Rose breezed into the building. When she approached the somber group at the table, her steps faltered.

"Uh oh," she groaned finding a spot at the table. "By the look on your faces, I probably should have brought my flask."

CHAPTER THIRTY-EIGHT

Vincent Lionetti sat in his patrol car, unwrapping his third pack of Tums. He popped three of them in his mouth, chewed a few times, and washed them down with a pull from the whiskey in his flask. He secreted the alcohol back to its hiding spot under his seat and stared out of the windshield at the clear day. He knew he should do another circuit of patrol, but he was having a hard time finding motivation. The church parking lot was empty, and the patrol vehicle was facing the street to give the appearance of vigilance. The area around the church was sparsely populated and a perfect spot for the young officer to sit and stew in his thoughts. Lionetti discovered the area three months previously and initially used the place to have a quick meal or take respites from patrol from time to time. After he learned of Sergio Martinez's death, he took residence in this lot with his flask more than he rode around the neighborhood. His eyes floated to the rearview mirror and back to the cross on top of the church. Raised a Catholic, he thought about the various confessions he performed over his twenty-four years of life and wished that he could find the courage to make his way into the sanctuary. He fingered the rosary he wore around his wrist for the past week and mumbled another Hail Mary with his eyes locked on the cross. He noticed his voice growing more desperate and emotional as he repeated the invocation.

Lionetti thought back to his first night on the beat. He pulled the overnight shift out of the academy and was excited by the possibility of seeing some action. In his youth, his mother would chide him with the claim, "Nothing good happens after midnight, Vinny." While the mantra was meant to keep him out of trouble as a child, as a cop, he looked forward to the perception of action that the night shift would bring. When he arrived for his shift, he learned that his assigned training officer called in sick dashing his hopes of having an exciting inaugural shift. After overhearing the predicament, a homicide detective volunteered to step in and ride with him for his first night, an offer Lionetti readily accepted.

During the ride, the detective had been engaging and spent the majority of the time regaling him with stories from his own early days on the beat as well as his more interesting homicide cases. Enthralled by the tales, Lionetti began to reconsider his career path — the allure of homicide overshadowing the initial calling of Vice. When the silver late model Camaro passed the police car, the training detective stiffened and instructed Lionetti to pull over the vehicle. The rookie was perplexed by the command. The Camaro had not been speeding nor did he observe any other traffic violations that would justify a stop.

"He's a high-ranking member of Los Asesinos, a crew on the South Side. I think he could have information that can help one of my cases," the detective informed him. Hearing this explanation, Lionetti pulled the car over. He called in the license plate before he approached the driver; his detective companion pacing him on the opposite side of the vehicle. The driver rolled down his window and the detective tapped on the passenger side indicating he wanted the man to roll down both sides. The man behind the wheel seemed to panic at the sight of the detective but slowly complied. He was a Hispanic male in his mid to late twenties, stocky build, and bald with no facial hair.

"Is there a problem officer?" he asked, attempting to mask his dread.

"License and proof of insurance, please," Lionetti replied. The driver already had both items in his hand and passed them through the open window. Lionetti took the documents, asked the driver to remain where he was and made his way to his own car to run the identity for warrants. As he walked away, he saw the detective lean down to speak with the driver through the open passenger window. Lionetti ran the information; there were no warrants, and the insurance was up to date. When he returned to the vehicle, Sergio Martinez looked uncomfortable and more afraid than before. Lionetti shifted his gaze from the frightened man to the detective who was casually leaning on the passenger window with an eerie smile plastered on his face. When their eyes locked, the detective made a motion for Lionetti to stand.

"Why don't we search his car?" he suggested across the top of the Camaro.

"He was clean, sir. I don't see a reason…" Lionetti began, but the detective cut him off.

"You're new, so it's not your fault you don't know, but old Sergio here is a known drug dealer. With these kinds of bangers, it's always a good idea to check. They like to make their supply runs at night. Better safe than sorry," he said. Taking this little bit of training advice from the man, Lionetti asked Martinez to step out of the car and stand by the hood of the vehicle. He turned himself to the task of searching, beginning with the driver's seat, while the detective examined the passenger's side. When the detective moved to the rear, Lionetti heard him let out a low whistle.

"Well look at what we have here," he said as he stood. Lionetti straightened his body to focus on what the man was waving around. His eyes bulged at the large sandwich bag filled with white powder.

"Yo, that's not mine, and you know it," Martinez protested.

"Officer Lionetti, would you please confirm the name on the registration of this vehicle?" the detective asked in a bored voice.

"Sergio Martinez, sir," Lionetti replied.

"And whose driver's license did you run?"

"Sergio Martinez," he repeated.

"So, you are confirming that the man standing over there," the detective pointed to the detained driver, "is Sergio Martinez, this is, in fact, his car, and it is not stolen?"

"That's correct," Lionetti nodded.

"Well, if the car isn't stolen, and I found this in your car, it appears this is yours." He waved the bag at an irate Martinez who reddened at the accusation.

"I got out of the game, that's not mine!"

"Save it for the courts, Martinez," the detective said dismissively. "Good news, Lionetti. First night on the beat and you get your first felony arrest." He motioned for the officer to cuff the prisoner. "Don't forget to Mirandize him. I would hate for your first bust to be thrown out on a technicality."

Upon returning to the precinct, the detective immediately strolled to the homicide department leaving the rookie to accompany Martinez through the booking process. Throughout the procedure, Martinez insisted the detective planted the drugs, and Lionetti continued to dismiss the man's protests. Once Martinez was in holding, the young officer set off to find the detective and get his signature on the arrest report. When he located the man, he refused to sign and demanded to be removed from the report altogether.

"This is all you, Cowboy. You got this," the detective asserted.

"But sir, you were the one who found the controlled substance. You need to be on the documentation for when we go to court."

"You worry too much. Sergio will plead," the detective replied with an indifferent wave. "This was your first arrest, take the credit, kid." When he observed Lionetti's clear discomfort, he added, "I wasn't even supposed to be out there with you tonight. I've been off the beat for years. My job is homicide. I just wanted to help you, Rook. If you put me on that report, my captain will know that I spent my shift riding with you instead of doing my job. I could get written up. You don't want me to get written up, do you, Lionetti?"

"No sir, but…"

"But what?"

"It's just, the prisoner swears that he didn't have anything in his car. The drugs were in the car, weren't they detective?" Lionetti inquired. The man grinned and clapped him on the back.

"According to your report they were," he replied.

"Excuse me?"

"He's a bad dude, Lionetti. Look, if you don't believe me, check out his jacket. This guy has been in and out of jail since he was a kid. He will plead out, so he doesn't get more time. Face it; we got a bad guy off the street. Take the win." The conversation stoked the ember of skepticism in Lionetti's mind driving him to the records department to review Martinez's jacket. He confirmed what he had been told; Martinez had a long list of offenses relating to drug dealing and gang activity.

Although he wanted to do his job properly, he heard stories in the academy about rookies becoming pariahs trying to be too "by the book" with more seasoned cops. Martinez was a career criminal and having drugs on him seemed to fit the man's standard M.O. When he learned that Martinez had in fact pled in hopes of receiving a lighter sentence, the ashes of doubt had been swept away from Lionetti's mind. However, upon learning of Martinez's death in prison, the fire of apprehension burned anew. He believed the detective had something to do with Martinez's murder. The suspicion did not come from any tangible proof or action on the detective's part but rather from the memory of the conversation the night of the arrest. An examination of his own culpability led Lionetti down the path of constant guilt-ridden inebriation.

A sharp knock on the passenger window jolted him from his memories. He turned to the sound and paled at the sight of the very detective he had just been thinking about. Lionetti's heart dropped into the pit of his stomach, and he thought he would regurgitate his lunch of Tums and whiskey. The detective made a motion for him to roll down the window and the rookie hesitantly complied. The unnatural grin that haunted his dreams remained fixed on the man's face.

"Lionetti! What are you doing out here all by yourself?"

"Just taking a few minutes to clear my head before doing another circuit, sir," Lionetti nervously replied. The smiling detective nodded and surveyed the area before squatting down on his haunches and examining the young officer. When he did not speak, Lionetti swallowed the bile creeping up his throat and asked, "Is there something you need from me, sir?"

"You hear about Martinez?" the detective asked. Lionetti wanted to scream. The last thing he desired was to rehash the biggest mistake of his young career with the very man who influenced his actions.

"I did," he croaked.

"Shame. I'm sorry it came to this," the detective murmured. He took a step back and produced a pistol from the small of his back. Still feeling the effects of the whiskey, Lionetti had a hard time processing the action. It was when he looked down the barrel of the handgun that sobriety crashed into him. However, the newly found clarity neglected to bring his reflexes to the rendezvous. There was no time to react to the critical danger or the detective's final words, "Nothing personal, kid. I actually kind of like you."

———— ∞ ————

"You did what?" Tristan snarled into the phone. The news he received sent an electric current into his body, and he stood abruptly from his seat.

"I killed Lionetti," the caller repeated. "I had no choice, Lewis was looking for him. If he had gotten to him before I did, the kid would have told him that I was there when Martinez was picked up."

"Did it ever occur to you to runs something like that by me?" Tristan demanded. "This isn't a banger or a former prisoner."

"Hey, that was your idea, and I didn't know he was a fed," the caller interrupted.

"This was a police officer, you idiot! The feds can be held at bay, but you killed a local cop in his own city. God, I can't believe you!"

"This was an emergency; I had to use my judgment. If I didn't move, we all would be screwed," the man insisted. Tristan almost laughed at the caller's inclusion of himself in the collective pronoun.

"What did you do with him?" he inquired.

"I left him in the parking lot. I took his wallet, credit cards, and sidearm to make it look like it was a robbery. He was on the bad side of town, they'll never know," the man replied. Tristan exhaled sharply.

"What about Detective Lewis?" he asked. "How is he getting his information?"

"Honestly, I think he's in contact with Layla Green," the caller replied. "Obviously, we know neither she nor Rachel Vasquez is in California. I think Lewis knows where they are." Tristan rubbed his temples in an attempt to calm the thumping of his pulse.

"I haven't gotten any reports that he's met up with her."

"What about the audio?" the man questioned.

"Nothing that I know of," Tristan replied. "You said he's a good cop. Maybe he got there on his own?"

"Seems odd that he'd narrow the search down to those four guys, doesn't it?"

"Good point. Damnit, I hate going blind. We don't know where Layla Green is or what she knows. We don't know how Lewis is getting his information. We don't know anything, and you went and killed a freaking cop on top of that!" Tristan exclaimed in exasperation.

"I told you; if Lewis got to Lionetti, it would have been lights out. I did what I had to do," the man argued.

"How did you know he was looking for Lionetti?"

"I heard him make the call to dispatch. I figured, first the jail, and now looking for Lionetti? This has to be related to Sergio Martinez," the caller asserted. Tristan sighed; his mind was exhausted from the pursuit of the next course of action.

"Can you just — not kill anyone else unless I give the okay?" he sighed.

"I didn't have to call and tell you."

"Yes, you did," Tristan proclaimed, before ending the call. "Fucking animal," he growled to the empty office. Things were getting out of hand. He was beginning to think the clinic program was generating far too much risk. He crafted a coded text message to Chicago requesting him to convene The Collective for an emergency meeting.

Tristan moved to the wet bar in his office and poured himself two fingers of scotch. While he generally tried to keep his drinking to a minimum during the day, the recent events had him stressed to the point of needing something to take the edge off. Along with the current situation, Milwaukee had become a powder keg of violence. The state of emergency curfew helped some, but not as quickly as he hoped. Nathan Grimes continued to trudge through his media tour. Considering the distress Grimes felt about the circumstances, he was performing well. The strain of Milwaukee, plus the events happening in his own backyard had Tristan feeling like he had no control of anything.

The Collective authorized and funded the clinic program. Initially, Tristan believed it was a brilliant strategy. Using population control to reduce the opposition was not a new tactic. It was used in World War II Germany as a way to control the growth of the Jewish people. The Nazis' problem was that along with the plan, their overt bigotry started a large military campaign. The men of the Collective believed the key to success was to be outwardly accepting but not to the detriment of their birthright. Nevertheless, it seemed that the endeavor would cost too much blood, sweat, and labor to continue. He returned to his computer and began to type out a detailed report. As much as he hated it, the clinic program needed to be terminated.

Detective Lewis eased his unmarked ride into the church parking lot watching the surveillance car in his rearview mirror. His tail bypassed the church as if the driver had no interest in following, but he knew the car would reappear when he left this place. He was beginning to detest whoever was behind the invasion into his privacy. Lewis turned his attention back to the lot and spotted Lionetti's patrol car parked at the rear facing the street. He chuckled as he approached the vehicle. He thought back to his early time in the force when he found himself an empty parking garage or lot to sneak in a nap or a quick bite to eat.

Pulling next to Lionetti's car, he positioned his driver's side even with the patrol officer's. He looked over to the officer who appeared to be napping, his head resting on the driver's side window. Lewis tapped the horn in an attempt to rouse the sleeping officer. The horn received no reaction. He climbed out of his car, walked over to the young cop, and rapped sharply on the glass. He did a visual sweep of the area as he knocked hoping a citizen did not spot him waking up a police officer who was supposed to be on duty. When the door did not open, he bent down and put himself eye-level with Lionetti. Just as he was about to call out to the man, he noticed blood dripping down the side of the young officer's face. Lewis immediately knew that his eyes were not closed in a catnap, but in eternal sleep.

"Oh no," he exhaled in alarm. He tried to open the door and found it locked. Rushing around the car and discovering a locked passenger door, he took out his weapon and broke the window to gain access. The sight was gruesome. From what he could tell, Lionetti had a close-range shot to the side of his face by what appeared to be a large caliber bullet. Although he knew it was pointless, he reached for the man's wrist to check for a pulse. He noticed the body was still warm, informing him that the officer had not been dead long. He did a quick sweep of the interior and saw that Lionetti's gun was missing. He decided to call for assistance before examining and possibly contaminating the crime scene any further. He returned to his car and called in the scene on his radio, ending the transmission with the two worst words for a cop to have to say or hear, "Officer down." After making the call, he climbed into the car and took a few deep breaths to calm himself. Once his pulse was under control, he pulled out the burner phone and dialed Layla.

"Hey, Kid," he said when she answered.

"What's wrong?" Layla immediately recognized the despondency in his tone.

"I ran all of the arrest reports like you and Vasquez suggested. The arresting officers for Taylor, Cole, and Evans no longer work with the department. The only one left was Officer Vincent Lionetti. He's who arrested Martinez. I found that he still works for the department," Lewis reported. His voice gave no inflection of happiness at the discovery, and Layla tempered the rush of excitement.

"That's a good thing, right? Why do you sound like that's not a good thing?"

"I called dispatch to get a location on him," he continued but hesitated before he finished. "I just found his body."

"Are you kidding?" she gasped.

"Not something I would joke about, kid. He hasn't been dead for long, but he's dead nonetheless." His tone was a mix of frustration and dejection. "Green, I don't know how anyone could have known I was coming here. I literally checked the arrest reports, made a quick call to dispatch, and came here. Everyone who was in the bullpen was still there when I left. Someone would have had to have the power of teleportation to beat me here."

"My God," she whispered.

"Did your friend find anything in the finances?"

"I'll check with her and get back to you on that. We've been eyeballs deep in the research into the clinics. I'll make sure she didn't forget," Layla replied.

"Please do. I'm stuck out here without direction, and I'm pretty damn confused. I need something." Layla had never heard him sound so perplexed and despondent and at that moment, she wished she could hug him.

"We will find something for you, Oscar. I promise," she assured him. "You have to deal with the crime scene today, right?"

"Yeah, I found him. By rights, it's my case. As soon as they verify my weapon hasn't been fired, they'll give it to me," Lewis confirmed.

"Try to get ballistics back as soon as you can, but you know what I'm going to tell you."

"Yeah, I know. It's probably the same .38," he grumbled.

"Give us a little more time. We will find something for you," she promised. Lewis grunted a sound of acknowledgment and terminated the call. Layla put the phone on the table and found the group staring at her expectantly.

"What's wrong?" Vasquez asked.

"Lewis found the cop that arrested Sergio, but he was already dead," she answered.

"Oh shit," Ryan murmured. "They're killing cops now?"
"Are you surprised? They chased you guys down and shot at you in broad daylight," Dom scoffed.

"You have a point," Ryan agreed. Layla turned to Dom with frustration etched into her facial features.

"Dom, not to tell you how to do your job or anything, but I think we need to shift focus. We've got to find this assassin; the body count is getting up there." Dom pinched her bottom lip in thought.

"There are six of us, and two avenues, surely we can divide and conquer."

"What's the plan, Boss?" Ryan asked.

"One of you three needs to get close to the Judge," she proclaimed, drawing frowns from the Jenkins men. Before Ryan could argue and remind her of the difficulty of such an objective, she extended her index finger to stop him and regarded his sister. "Rose, you seemed to have some idea of how to do that?"

"Our ticket is this guy right here," she nodded, slapping Ryan on the back. His eyes widened.

"Me? Why me?" he stammered. "Do you hate me or something?"

"Of course not," she sighed. "Listen to me. You just got back from serving the good old U.S. of A overseas. Uncle Tom is in the middle of a re-election. If you were to show up in say your dress uniform, there is no way he would refuse to see you. Not if you go to his office where politicians and voters surround him. He'll drag you around to meet his colleagues in some weird artificial pride. You're his war vet nephew, and he will try to milk votes out of your presence."

"Well, okay, maybe," he conceded. "But do you really think he'll just come clean to me of all people?"

"No, not at all." Dom shook her head. She stood and walked to the nearby cabinet of gadgets and withdrew a light blue file folder. "I just need you to get close to him to plant one or two of these." Dropping back into her chair she opened the folder, and the group frowned at the sight; it appeared to be empty.

"You want me to plant a folder?" Ryan asked in confusion. Dom chuckled and picked up a transparent item the size of a sheet of paper. She pulled a piece away to show that it was a transparent adhesive page.

"What's that?" Robert wondered.

"It's basically a bug," Dom replied. "You take one of these," she pulled away a three-inch square piece of the adhesive, "and stick it on something."

"That looks like a segment of those overhead projector things teachers used at school," Ryan declared, taking the translucent page from her.

"Yeah, it's kind of like that.," she nodded. "But there is a listening device inside this."

"Is this one of those creations you made to see if it was possible?" Vasquez asked. Dom nodded in assent.

"Never thought I would use it. I wanted to see how small I could get a digital listening device. It transmits wirelessly via satellite or using the data plan of the nearest cell phone," she explained.

"Whoa," Vasquez gaped, taking the page from Ryan. She examined the sheet in search of obvious signs of circuitry. "You can't see anything!" She handed the page to Layla, who gave it a brief glance and passed the item back to Ryan.

"So, you want me to get close enough to him to plant one of these on him," Ryan declared.

"That's the idea," Dom confirmed with a nod. Ryan sighed in resignation.

"Fine, but you guys owe me. Especially if he tells the story of how he founded the first Black Republicans Club when he was in law school." Rose and Robert stifled giggles.

"I don't even want to know, it sounds painful," Dom grimaced.

"If you think the description sounds bad, try hearing the story over a dozen times," Robert laughed.

"What about us?" Vasquez asked.

"We will be combing through all of the financial stuff SARA finds and try to see which one of your buddies is going around killing people," she replied. "Layla's right, we can't deal with the clinics and foundation until we get their hired assassin off the streets."

CHAPTER THIRTY-NINE

"That's the last homicide detective on the day shift," Layla sighed. "Are you sure you didn't find anything, SARA?"

"I'm sorry Miss Green; there was no suspicious activity within the bank accounts searched, nor were there any international accounts," SARA replied drawing a groan of irritation from the interrogator.

"We have to be missing something," she murmured.

"And you're sure Calvin Tidwell came back clean?" Vasquez asked.

"Tidwell apparently comes from old money. He wouldn't need to do something like this unless he's some sort of psychopath," Dom reported, consulting the information SARA found. "He grew up with a trust fund and everything."

"You'd think with all that money he'd try to make himself more attractive," Vasquez mumbled.

"With all that money, he doesn't have to be," Layla pointed out.

"I wouldn't touch him with a twenty-foot pole, money or not," Vasquez grimaced. She turned and shot Dom a demure wink. "You, on the other hand." Dom looked away in embarrassment.

"Stop it, you two. Focus!" Layla admonished.

"She started it," Dom muttered, with embarrassment in her averted eyes. "Anyway, we found no one in the day shift homicide department with suspicious cash transactions or traceable international assets. Any other ideas?"

"Do you think I'm wrong?" Layla asked Vasquez, uncertainty clouding her dark brown eyes.

"You're never wrong," Vasquez replied. "It's one of your more annoying traits."

"Maybe it's not a homicide cop. I mean, it's not like homicide does traffic stops, right? This Lionetti was a rookie. Maybe we need to branch out to the entire force," Dom suggested. Layla tapped her chin thoughtfully.

"I just can't get over the fact that I was in the homicide department when I spoke to Lewis. All other discussions were away from the precinct. But I guess it's possible there was a uniform around I didn't see."

"SARA," Dom turned to the screen with the avatar, "Open up the search. Let's start with all cops who have worked the day shift for the past week." She turned to find Layla and Vasquez staring at her expectantly. Sighing, she craned her head back to the display. "I'm sorry; please?"

"Yes, Dom. This may take a minute," SARA acknowledged.

"We don't have anywhere to go," she shrugged. Dom leaned back in her chair and studied the table with intensity as if the information she was waiting to receive would be written on the surface by a phantasmic hand.

"Since we have a little time, mind if I ask you a question?" Vasquez asked, drawing a quick look from the hacker.

"It's likely that once I hear it, I will, but that never stops you from asking anyway. Go for it," she nodded, returning her scrutiny to the table.

"Why do you do that?" Vasquez lowered her head to get Dom to look at her. Their gazes locked for a fleeting moment before Dom broke eye contact once again.

"Do what?" Dom frowned. "Is that the question?"

"Yes. You rarely look us in the eye. Why?" Dom's scowl deepened, and she stole a quick peek to find Layla staring at her in anticipation.

"It's true," Layla confirmed. "The only time you look at anyone is when you are taking control of a situation or explaining something. When we are just chatting you always look down or avert your eyes."

"I'm an introvert. It's what we do."

"I call bullshit," Vasquez argued. "You may be an introvert, but there are times where you seem like anything but. You haven't always been this uncomfortable around people."

"That's not true. I have always been uncomfortable. I just haven't always embraced the discomfort," she corrected. "Why does it bother you so much anyway?"

"I think it's because I see you," Vasquez declared.

"I'm right here. Unless you've gone blind all of a sudden of course you see me," Dom replied in a bewildered voice.

"No, not like that! I could try to explain in Spanish, but it probably wouldn't translate well," she sighed in frustration and turned to Layla. "You know what I mean, right?" Layla studied her friend and then nodded.

"I think I get what you're saying," she said, shifting her focus to Dom. "We all see you."

"Well that just cleared it right up then," Dom huffed with an eye roll.

"I'm no Rose, but I'll give it a shot," Layla smirked. "It's like you're trying to be invisible. Not looking at us is your way of hiding in plain sight. You are trying not to let people see who you are, what kind of person you are, and how smart you are. It's like you subconsciously believe that if you can't see us, we can't see you. But we do see you." She turned to Vasquez who bobbed her head in excited agreement.

"Claro que sí, that's what it is!" she exclaimed. "You try to shield yourself. You kept yourself hidden away from everyone for the past five years, and that's a waste. You shouldn't be hidden, Dom."

"I still don't know what you two are going on about."

"You know exactly what they are talking about. Miss Green and Miss Vasquez are not telling you anything that I have not said to you before," SARA announced. "It is the reason I have insisted that you leave your home from time to time. Humans should not be alone."

"Really? You too, SARA?" Dom sighed, throwing an exasperated look at the monitors. "Why are all three of you harping on me today? There is nothing wrong with me."

"No, there isn't, Dom," Vasquez agreed in a soft voice. "That's the problem. You are depriving the world of you. For the brief time I've known you, it's just not right." Although Dom did not make eye contact, she felt the woman's emerald eyes studying her. "There is a light in you that you try so hard to hide and to deny. People deserve to know you." Her tone held an emotional quality that surprised Dom. When she lifted her gaze from the table to meet Vasquez's jade irises, she saw the same look from the night the woman asked to see her scar in her office. Initially, she took her regard as pity, but suddenly she realized what it was — reverence. It was not in the same vein as the worship of a deity, but rather it emanated from a deep respect and admiration. When her mind understood Vasquez's emotions, she was unable to hold her stare, and her eyes dropped back to the table.

"After my mom died, I was alone. I mean, I had my dad, but he just didn't get me. I didn't have any friends or feel accepted anywhere, so I kept to myself. I tried to reinvent myself when I went to college since I was around people more like me. I made some friends and dated a little. Then I started working with people on a daily basis, and I tried to be more welcoming. It screwed me; people took advantage. I guess being a loner most of my adolescent life didn't prepare me for the whole wrong crowd thing. They weren't my friends, they just used me to make themselves feel better. After years of that, I figured there weren't any genuine people out there anymore. Dom's voice was soft and hollow. "I'm nothing special, I'm just me."

Her voice hung in the air without comment, and although she spoke to the table, she felt the stare of each woman. Vasquez placed a hand on Dom's chin and gently lifted her head, forcing her eyes to abandon the solace of the inanimate object and face the complex sea of green. With no word or warning, Vasquez leaned in and touched her lips to Dom's, the action bringing both her heart and breath to a sudden halt. Her full lips were soft, and despite Vasquez's constant flirtatious comments, there was no erotic undertone to her kiss. Dom was frozen in shock, unsure of how to react to the sudden osculation. By the time her cognition caught up with the physical, Vasquez had pulled away; however, she did not remove her hand from Dom's chin. She held Dom's gaze with such intensity, the breath that escaped Dom's lungs refused to return.

"You *are* special, Dom," Vasquez declared in a voice no louder than a whisper. "I see you, and it's time that you let yourself be seen." When her hand fell away from Dom's face, a rush of air was dispatched to her lungs rescuing her from a blackout. Dom swallowed hard, the rhythm of her thudding heart pulsing through her ears accompanied by a windy orchestra of rushing blood. While she heard Vasquez's words, the symphony created by the surprise left her unable to speak. For the first time in a long time, SARA came to her rescue.

"Dom, I have the results," the computer announced. Vasquez sustained eye contact with Dom for an additional moment before releasing the hacker from her spell and leaning back in her chair in expectation. The tempo of Dom's pulse and blood flow reduced, and after a couple of seconds, the mental haze began to evaporate. She blinked, turned to SARA's avatar, and picked up the tablet.

"What's up?" she squeaked, an octave higher than normal. She cleared her throat immediately before repeating, "What's up?" Despite SARA's insistence, she refused to install biometrics in the warehouse. She believed that such an invasion of privacy should be limited to her residence and was not appropriate for this environment. Suddenly, Dom had never been so happy to be away from home.

"There was no suspicious financial activity for any of the day shift officers," SARA answered.

"Then you should have said you have no results," Layla groused.

"That is incorrect," SARA disagreed. "After receiving no results, I further expanded the search, and I believe I have found something."

Ryan entered the courthouse wearing his Army Service Uniform, commonly referred to as "dress blues." Colorful service ribbons decorated his chest, and his golden nameplate twinkled in the natural lighting filtering through the large windows. His shoes were freshly shined, clacking across the marble flooring of the building as he strolled through the lobby. He hated the damn uniform and hoped when he retired he would never have to wear it again. Even after he conceded to Rose's plan for him to approach their uncle, he attempted to talk her out of the attire. Rose insisted that the outfit would be the key to disarming the suspicion their uncle generally harbored towards the Jenkins family.

"Once a politician, always a politician," Rose had said. Ryan internally wished that Judge Benjamin would have a full docket and the trip would be pointless, but reliable SARA already checked the man's schedule and informed the group that his uncle was open for the day.

As Ryan passed small clusters of people outside and inside of the large building, he fought the urge to grimace when scores of individuals approached him and thanked him for his service. Rose prepared him for this situation, reminding him that the people only knew what they were told to be thankful for by the government and could not be faulted for their blind appreciation. She explained that his feelings about his service, the military, and the government's role in the Middle East were from his own experience, an experience that wasn't shared by the general public. Therefore, he was to smile and nod when faced with the gratitude.

He stepped to the directory and found Judge Benjamin's office was on the third floor of the building. Rather than risking a two-floor elevator ride with a stranger who would gush and ask a ton of questions, Ryan opted for the stairs and climbed the flights quickly and with purpose. Entering the office, he saw a young and petite redheaded woman with a pixie haircut sitting behind a large receptionist desk; her blue eyes shielded by cat-eyed glasses. The nameplate on the desk informed him that she was April Rosenblatt.

"Can I help you?" April asked.

"I'm Sergeant Ryan Jenkins; Judge Benjamin is my uncle. I'm recently home from overseas, and I thought I would come by to see him. It's been years." Ryan spoke as confidently as he could, forcing himself to sound as if he wanted nothing more than to catch up with his beloved uncle.

"Absolutely, Sergeant!" April's features broke into a wide smile, and she reached for the phone on her desk. "He's in his office, just one moment." Ryan extended his hand to stop her.

"Actually, I'd like it to be a surprise. Do you think you could bring him out?" he asked. April flashed him a conspiratorial grin and replaced the phone receiver onto its cradle.

"That's a great idea! I'm sure he'll love that," she gushed, prompting Ryan to stifle a chuckle. "Just wait here." She rose from her seat and disappeared down a corridor leading to the back of the office.

As he waited, Ryan's mind began to envision various outcomes of this surprise visit. Despite his sister's reassurances ringing in his head, none of the scenarios were good. Nevertheless, Rose believed this was the best method of ambush, and he trusted his sister completely; possibly more than he trusted the soldiers who had his back over the past few years in Afghanistan. The minutes ticked by at a snail's pace while he stood to wait for the Judge to emerge. The longer he waited, the less sure he became of his sister's plan. He grew concerned that the Judge, as bull-headed as always, would refuse to come out unless his secretary divulged the name of his visitor; and then, he would decline to appear when he learned it was one of "Joyce's brood."

Ryan hated the way uncle Tom referred to him and his siblings as "Joyce's brood"; as if his family was a traveling circus filled with an inordinate number of children with Joyce as the ring-master. The Judge appeared to regard his mother as if she were an abandoned whore with a plethora of kids from five different fathers instead of one. His parents planned for five offspring; what they had not planned for was their father dying young and leaving their mother behind to raise them. His uncle's label of the siblings as "Joyce's brood" was not a term of endearment, but rather a term of contempt. Granted, Rodney and Reggie's business ventures did not help the situation, but Ryan knew his mother did all that she could to raise her children and should not carry the blame of the actions of two fully grown men. That thought struck him with a gale of awareness. He could easily mentally remove responsibility from his mother regarding his brothers' death, but he could not give Luke the same absolution.

His internal reflection was broken by the sound of approaching steps from the back of the office. April arrived first with a mischievous smile on her face. She was shadowed by the man himself — Judge Thomas Benjamin. His uncle blinked in surprise when he laid eyes on his nephew, implying April was able to maintain his anonymity until that moment. Ryan conjured the biggest artificial smile he could muster.

"How you been, Unc?" He took a step towards the Judge with his arms outstretched for a hug. The judge grunted with force and returned the embrace, albeit with very little enthusiasm. Rose thought of everything, including this unusual show of affection. Her idea was to keep the man flustered in front of his co-workers rather than accosting him in private. The hope was that this approach would prevent Uncle Tom from falling into his normal disdainful attitude. While Judge Benjamin's shock was obvious to Ryan, April remained oblivious. She stood to the side beaming with pride at her ability to keep the secret.

"Ryan, you're back from overseas?" Judge Benjamin asked before adding, "It's good to see you." He took a step back and examined his nephew. Ryan watched his hawk-like scrutiny taking in the uniform and noting the service ribbons, combat badge, and the achievement medal pinned to his uniform. "It looks like the army treats you well, son." This declaration cause Ryan to internally cringe. He was fifteen when his father passed away leaving all of his brothers and his one sister without a male figure. Around that time, uncle Tom started addressing all of the male children as "son." The four brothers hated the nickname, and the Judge knew it. He shook off the irritation, refusing to allow the slight to change the appearance of false joy plastered on his face.

"Yes sir, they did," Ryan nodded.

"Did?"

"I put in my twenty and retired. I'm home for good," he clarified.

"Twenty years? My, but does time fly. Well done, son; I'm proud of you." The Judge grinned and slapped Ryan's upper arm. Ryan sincerely hoped his smile did not come across as a grimace. His eyes floated to April who was watching the exchange while taking her seat.

"I've been trying to catch up with the family since I've been back," Ryan said.

"Oh? How's your mom?" Judge Benjamin inquired. Ryan knew the man could care less about his mother's fate as he never spoke to her outside of a mandatory family function.

"She's great. I've been staying with her since I got home," he replied, making a show of looking towards the back of the office. "Got time to catch up?" The Judge glanced at his watch, and Ryan was certain that the man was searching for a reason to decline the opportunity. After a few long seconds, the Judge found no obvious excuse, and he motioned for his nephew to follow him.

Ryan stuck his hands in his pockets and commenced detaching one of the small bugs. Following his uncle into the office, he marveled at how much wood could be crammed into a single room. Every bit of furniture, save the executive leather chair, was created from some form of cherry stained wood. The office was filled with so much lumber that upon one glance, Treebeard and his band of Ents would abandon the comforts of the Forest of Fangorn and wreak havoc on the surrounding humans in revenge. Judge Benjamin rounded the massive executive desk and took his seat in the chair behind the surface. Ryan sat in one of the visitor's chairs on the opposite side, eyed the messy desk filled with briefs and court files, and then dropped his gaze to his feet.

"My shoe," he muttered, leaning forward as if to tie his footwear. He stuck one of Dom's see-through bugs on the front of the desk. The transparent material immediately adhered to the surface and blended in with the wood. Upon reviewing the blueprint of the courthouse and Judge Benjamin's office, Dom determined that one device placed in the middle of the room would be sufficient for full and clear audio coverage. The more difficult challenge was for Ryan to find a way to plant another bug on the judge himself.

"So, who have you gotten around to seeing?" Judge Benjamin asked, breaking into Ryan's thoughts.

"Mom, Rose, and Robert mostly," he replied. "I saw a few other family members as well." He omitted the family gathering that his mother hosted for both his and Robert's homecoming. While the Judge would have never made an appearance, he was pretentious enough to find insult at being snubbed.

"Robert's back?" the Judge asked with genuine surprise.

"I got home the day after his release," he replied. Judge Benjamin nodded, and Ryan saw that his uncle was unable to effortlessly contribute to the dialogue. Rose warned and prepared

Ryan for this as well. He leaned back in his chair and asked, "How you been, Unc? Looks like you're doing well. I see you're up for re-election." Speaking about both Uncle Tom's life and his re-election was the perfect combination, and Judge Benjamin excitedly bobbed his head.

"It's a tight one, but I think I can squeak by," he replied. "My opponent is well respected, but I've been sitting on that bench for years. I have experience on my side."

"That's great," Ryan declared before falling into silence. His sister's voice bounced around his head. "*He's up for re-election this year, he's going to drag you all around the courthouse and show off his Army vet nephew.*" Ryan certainly hoped that she was right. When the quiet became uncomfortable, Judge Benjamin stood abruptly.

"Let me introduce you to some of my co-workers," he suggested. Ryan subdued a smile, grateful that his sister knew people, especially an arrogant asshole like Thomas A. Benjamin. He stood and followed his uncle to the door of the office. As they approached a coat rack, Ryan spied the infamous fedora hanging from one of the hooks; another stroke of good luck. He quickly fished a second bug from his trousers.

"I see you're still sporting the fedora," he noted. As long as Ryan could remember, his uncle wore this very same fedora every day rain or shine. He and his siblings thought that the hat looked ridiculous on him, but for the first time in Ryan's life, he was happy to see the headwear. After he subtly withdrew the translucent adhesive segment from his pocket, he picked up the hat. He made a show of inspecting the fedora and stuck the device to the top side of the brim.

"You know how it is, old dogs and everything. That was the hat I wore on the day I won my first case. I've had it restored a dozen times over the past forty-five years, but it still treats me well," Judge Benjamin smiled, admiring the headpiece. "Did I ever tell you that I started the Black Republican's club at my law school?"

"Sounds like a familiar story," Ryan answered. He noted that the man showed a hat more adoration and love than he ever offered his extended family. He replaced the headwear onto the coat rack and followed his uncle out of the office.

Judge Benjamin dragged Ryan all over the courthouse and introduced him to countless elected officials. Each person displayed a bright smile and thanked Ryan for his service. He heard the sentiment so much, he was beginning to think he might vomit by the end of the visit. After the tour of the courthouse, he asked his uncle if he could buy him lunch. The shock on the older man's face was priceless. Judge Benjamin never expected any of "Joyce's brood" to amount to much of anything, and definitely never assumed any of them would offer to buy him a meal on their own dime. The duo returned to his office to allow the Judge to grab his precious Fedora and to inform April that he was stepping out for lunch.

The downtown Houston traffic was thick with the lunch rush. As Ryan strolled to the curb of the courthouse, he expected his uncle to be in step with him. When he realized he was walking alone, he spun around to find the Judge staring down the street at an approaching car. Ryan followed the man's line of sight and spotted a black Town Car approaching. The vehicle eased to a stop at the curb in front of him.

"Ryan, I'm sorry," Judge Benjamin stammered. "In my exuberance to spend some time with you and hear about your time overseas, I neglected to remember that I already had a previous lunch engagement." While he was no Rose by any means, Ryan recognized the lie in his uncle's features.

"Are you sure, Unc? My car is just over there," he advised, pointing across the street at a brand-new midnight blue Chevrolet Impala Dom purchased to replace the quad cab pickup truck.

"I'm sorry, I can't. I hope we can reschedule?" Ryan knew there would be no rescheduling lunch with this man — even if it was free. There was no disappointment for he believed he accomplished what he set out to do. He noticed Judge Benjamin's demeanor was nervous, an adjective he would have never associated with him. As long as Ryan knew him, his uncle tried to give the aura of control in all situations. Ryan took a step closer and leaned in.

"Is something wrong? You look like you've seen a ghost."

"No, I'm fine," Judge Benjamin replied, attempting to emit confidence. "I'm just ashamed I forgot about my previous engagement."

"Is this your ride?" Ryan asked, gesticulating towards the car waiting in front of them. Judge Benjamin nodded, and he moved to the vehicle. Ryan opened the back door for his uncle under the guise of politeness; in reality, he wanted to get a look at the passenger. An older White man sat in the rear behind the driver. Ryan was startled by his stark white hair and steel gray eyes. He was wearing a black suit, and the combination gave him a ghoulish appearance. Judge Benjamin climbed into the car, and Ryan flashed him a smile.

"Good to catch up with you, Uncle Tom," he grinned, unable to resist the parting jab. Judge Benjamin gave him an indignant smile as Ryan shut the door. When the car pulled away, he withdrew the burner phone and shot off a quick text message.

Activate the bug now, I think we are about to get something good.

CHAPTER FORTY

Lewis sat at his desk typing up the report for the Lionetti murder. He was glad he did not know the young officer or the task would be agonizing. The discovery of any corpse terminated by something other than natural causes was horrific and despite his two decades in homicide, it never got easier. Finding a cop shot dead in his own police car generated a feeling of mortality more than a civilian. Every cop knew there was no assurance of returning home from any given shift, but that knowledge came with the territory of the occupation. Then again, any random person could die just by leaving their home, and some people meet their end within the confines of their own dwelling — the victim of Mother Nature or a freak accident. In Lewis' mind, focusing on the threat of danger was a recipe for disaster. Under this fixation of safety, the death of an officer in the line of duty often stoked the fires of paranoia, forming a bias or prejudice in the subconscious mind. This attitude contributed to the senseless shooting of unarmed citizens. Lewis preferred to treat everyone with respect and not look for a silhouette of danger where one did not reside.

He could not help but feel some sort of responsibility for the fate of Lionetti. He wished he could figure out who this killer was and how they knew he had been turned onto the rookie. Upon returning to the precinct, Lewis took a direct path to dispatch and spoke with the operator who gave him Lionetti's location. Shirley Wallace was a heavyset older black woman who had been in the role almost as long as Lewis had been in homicide. He spent close to a half hour interrogating her on the events that took place immediately after his phone call. According to Shirley, there were no subsequent calls or visits regarding Lionetti, no one was around her when she spoke with Lewis, and she had not left her perch since his call. He rephrased and re-asked the questions several times and finally decided that Shirley had no idea who could have beaten him to the church parking lot.

Disappointed, Lewis returned to his desk where he currently sat typing up the initial report. Layla told him she was working on an angle, but he was too restless to sit still and wait. More and more he grew certain that someone in his department was being used as a hired killer and the longer he or she went undetected, the more bodies would accumulate. His mind kicked around several options until he landed on one that was the only action he could think to take. After he submitted his report, he stood from his desk and ambled to Haggard's office. He knocked twice and leaned over, presenting himself to the captain through the window. Haggard waved him into the room.

"You get the initial report done on Lionetti?" the captain asked, as Lewis closed the office door and took a seat.

"I just submitted it," the detective answered. "Captain, we have a problem."

"We have multiple problems, including the murder of one of our own." Haggard huffed. He looked to his right and gestured at the whiteboard hanging on the wall displaying open homicide cases. "Could you be a little more specific?"

"You know me, Cap. I don't know any other way to be but blunt, so here goes — I think Lionetti's killer is the person who murdered Malik Rodgers." He paused for effect, trying to gauge the captain's reaction. When Haggard did not reply, Lewis continued. "I also believe that the same person who killed Malik Rodgers and Lionetti is the same person who executed the doctor on the South Side." He hesitated and took a deep breath. "And I think that person is a cop." Haggard's ice blue eyes studied Lewis intently as he absorbed the theory in silent consideration. Finally, he leaned back in his chair and folded his arms.

"Tell me," he commanded.

"Well, I'll start with the fact that Green and Vasquez are not in California," Lewis began. Haggard's eyebrows rose in surprise.

"Where are they?"

"I honestly have no idea, Cap. I didn't want to know," Lewis admitted.

"What do you mean, you didn't want to know? You say they aren't in California, which leads me to believe you know where they are." Haggard's voice took on the cloak of authority. "I suggest you start from the top and tell me why you think our shooter is a cop." Lewis mentally sifted through facts and examined the nuggets that were important. From there he began to buff each chunk, adding enough truth to allow the information to shine, but not too much to jeopardize the work Layla was doing with her new friends.

"After Green came to me with the identity of our vic, she, Vasquez, and I picked up a tail. Just before they disappeared, their apartments were bugged. It was easier for them to vanish for their safety," Lewis explained. He did not divulge the violation into his own home. Christine and Sandy had no idea, and as long as Lewis could, he would keep them ignorant. Haggard's features betrayed no surprise or astonishment at the news.

"Why didn't you bring this to me before?"

"We weren't fully certain it was connected, and we honestly didn't know who to trust," Lewis admitted.

"You didn't know who you could trust?"

"Captain," Lewis said evenly. "The three of us acquired our audience after Green sat right over there," he pointed in the direction of his desk through the office window, "and told me the man's name. It is the only explanation we found that could have attracted attention. She believes that our perp is a cop. You've worked with Green, and you know her gut instinct is better than most of those guys in there." He indicated the bullpen with his head as he finished. Haggard studied the detective for a long while.

"You're right, Lewis. Green has better instincts than most of us, and her memory for the details can't be denied," Haggard concurred.

"The crime scene was far too clean for an amateur or even a professional. I'm talking absolutely no evidence, Captain," Lewis paused, made eye contact with Haggard, and emphasized, "*Layla Green* found nothing." The captain allowed himself a brief nod, informing Lewis he understood how rare that occurrence had been. "You combine that with the fact that after she sat in that room, and told me information no one else had; it makes sense."

"Do you have anything else?"

"Lionetti. I was looking for him, and I called dispatch to get his location. Someone got to him minutes before I arrived. He was still warm." Lewis took a deep breath as the image of Vincent Lionetti's dead body rushed into his mind. "I don't think it was a coincidence."

"That's why you were out there; to talk to Lionetti? What were you going to talk about?"

"As you know, I've been floundering a bit," Lewis confessed. "I was trying to consider all angles, both inside and outside of the box. I found it curious that Sergio Martinez was killed not too long after Malik Rodgers. I thought maybe there could be a connection. I looked at his arrest report and discovered Lionetti was the arresting officer. Since I couldn't talk to Martinez directly, I thought maybe he would have said something to Lionetti that could have divulged his relationship with Rodgers. But Lionetti's dead now. No one knew I was looking for him except dispatch unless they overheard me in the bullpen."

"It sounds like you're onto something, Lewis. Have you been in contact with Green and Vasquez?"

"Just to check in with them and make sure they're okay," he nodded.

"You're still being followed I take it?" Haggard asked.

"Yes Captain, but I'm a trained officer. The girls live alone. They weren't comfortable with the situation and frankly, neither was I. They went underground until this blows over," he said. "They asked me to cover for them, and so I did. But now I think shit has come to a head, and I don't have anywhere else to go."

"You need to figure out who it is. Do you have any ideas?"

"To be honest, my first suspect was Tidwell," Lewis replied. "He was here when I called dispatch today, and he was also here when I spoke with Green, but, he didn't move when I left the bullpen, and it doesn't look like he's left the office at all today. So now, I'm at a loss. I didn't see anyone follow me out of the building." Haggard mulled over Lewis' reply for a few silent moments.

"We need proof," he declared when he finally spoke again. "We can't randomly accuse someone; the union would have our asses. Plus, we can't spook them. Bring me proof, and I will be there with you to slap the cuffs on them."

———— ⬡ ————

"That can't be right!" Layla gaped in astonishment while Vasquez stared at the tablet in her hand with equal amazement.

"Are you doubting my information?" SARA challenged, causing Dom to shoot the avatar a look.

"Don't get crabby," she admonished. "They're surprised; they probably know this guy." Glancing at the dazed women, she shook her head and said, "She gets touchy when you question her, as you can see."

"He's gotten over nine-hundred thousand dollars over the past three and a half years from Liberty Health Services Foundation?" Vasquez inquired.

"That is correct," the machine confirmed. "It appears the foundation has been paying him five-thousand dollars per week and is categorizing the payment as a consultant fee — for bookkeeping purposes."

"Consultant my ass," Vasquez growled.

"But how could he know what was going on in the office?" Layla pressed. "He wasn't there; I know for a fact that he wasn't!" Despite the evidence SARA presented, her memory of the day she spoke with Lewis in homicide negated the offered proof. For a split second, she panicked, irrationally fearing her memory was starting to dull.

"Here's where that attention to detail is going to come into play," Dom proclaimed. "Close your eyes and think back to the day you spoke with Detective Lewis. Don't focus on the conversation, examine the surroundings." Layla immediately obliged, closing her eyes and plunging herself into voluntary darkness.

She visualized walking in to find Lewis standing at his desk waiting for Lopez to pack up for the day as they playfully ribbed each other. The scene ran like a muted movie, and Layla paused in some areas and slowed in other portions. Lewis makes a joke about Lopez's messenger bag as he plops down into his seat. Looking at the screen, he harasses Lopez about his negligence in not logging off the computer system. While making a joke, he turns to log Lopez off and himself on. Layla cocked her head in both reality and in her dreamscape. Pause. Rewind. Lewis goes to log Lopez off the computer. She focused intently. Pause. Rewind. Layla concentrated on his actions. No, he doesn't log off; he switches users, leaving Lopez's profile undisturbed. Pause. Rewind. Layla focused intently on the screen just before Lewis makes the switch. While some cops and support staff personalized their work machines with photos of family members, pets, and exotic landscapes, Lopez's computer wallpaper was the standard blue backdrop. Telepathically, she leaned in closer to study the computer screen.

"Oh my God," she whispered, her eyes springing open. Dom and Vasquez were watching her expectantly.

"Well?" Vasquez prodded. Instead of answering, Layla turned to Dom.

"I need you to hack the PD again," she advised as she withdrew the burner phone from her back pocket. Dom scowled.

"Just randomly or do you have something you specifically want me to look for?"

"Lewis' computer," she replied as she crafted a text message. "I've seen the machine name. I can give it to you."

After his conversation with Captain Haggard, Lewis sulked at his desk feeling lost and dejected. Not only did he have no direction, he felt like every time he caught a break, something bad happened. Although he was certain his murderer was a cop, he could not figure out who it could be. He ran through everything he did and did not know about the case. Because of Layla and her hacker friend, the known column definitely outweighed the unknown. The problem was, the largest undetermined factor was the identity of the hitman for the foundation. For Lewis, that was the most important mystery. After stewing for a while, he decided to call it a day. As he began to pack up his belongings, the burner phone began vibrating in his pocket. He fished it from the confines of his pants and found a message from Layla.

Are you in the office?

Yeah, I'm here.

Are you at your desk?

Yeah, what's up?

Don't freak out, she replied. His scowl intensified at the odd response that provided no additional information. He looked up from his phone just in time to see the monitor of his computer blink and the arrow of the mouse move on its own accord.

What's going on? He messaged.

Patience came the reply. Lewis watched as the desktop background photo of his family disappeared and was replaced by Lopez's generic background. The dictation program that was still open was immediately closed. The phantom computer operator navigated file folders. As the hidden user opened various folders, the search stopped upon finding a file marked O.R.L., Lewis' gawked at the file. While he could not be sure this folder had anything to do with him, the file name was comprised of his initials — Oscar Ray Lewis. The invisible manipulator began to download the content of the folder.

What the hell is that? Talk to me kid, Lewis demanded.

It's Lopez, Oscar. He's been leaving his dictation program running since Malik's death and recording everything that's been going on at your desk. That's why he doesn't log out of his side of the computer. He knows you'll switch users, Layla explained. The news caused the air to flee from his lungs in dismay. He unwittingly had been feeding Lopez information. He realized that his night shift counterpart had only recently begun leaving his side of the computer logged on. When he thought back to the days he came in to find this evidence of carelessness, he never gave it a second thought. It also became clear why Lopez had been at the desk later than normal on most days; he was waiting for Lewis to show up. A thought suddenly occurred to him.

But how did he beat me to Lionetti?

Dom says he's been remotely transmitting from the office computer. She thinks he's been listening real-time, Layla replied. A torrent of horror overtook him; his stomach plummeted, and a river of nausea rose and crested within his throat. He felt a burden of responsibility for Lionetti's death. If he had simply gotten up and gone to dispatch himself rather than calling it in from his desk, the poor kid would still be alive. A fist composed of rage and anguish seized his intestines and twisted. He took a deep breath and swallowed his nausea. Fucking Lopez. He was one of the few people Lewis actually liked and could see himself working with. He warned Layla that disregarding anyone was foolish, yet he was guilty of doing that himself.

Do you know where he is? Lewis asked. It took another few minutes for the reply to come across. He assumed Layla's friend Dom was electronically attempting to chase Lopez down.

His phone is off. Dom can't get a location, Layla texted back. She followed that message up with another. *She says it's time you slipped your tail. Standby.* He read the text message twice trying to puzzle out how Layla intended to spirit him away from his surveillance detail. Suddenly, he grew afraid for his family, anxious that if he slipped his observation, the third party would take retaliation on his wife and child.

What about Sandra and Christine?

They need to take a trip for a few days. I'll take care of it, Layla responded. Lewis' eyebrows drew down in perplexity. He knew Layla's memory was impeccable, so there was no way she forgot that his house was bugged. Despite knowing this, he could not help but remind her.

Kid, they will hear you if you go there.

Don't worry about it. Sandy's not home, we've already checked. I got this. You just be ready to move soon.

Sandra Lewis perused the cereal aisle at the local grocery store periodically checking her list. Pausing her inspection, she yawned deeply, still feeling the exhaustion from her husband's restless nights. She knew better than to ask about his cases, but she was beginning to worry. She had known Oscar since she was fourteen, and what attracted her to him was his even temperament.

He was generally low-key, and very few things stressed him out. Even when he became a homicide detective, she found it remarkable that the most gruesome scenes he described never seemed to cause him any trepidation. While he seemed to sleep like a log after a long day investigating the underbelly of humanity, his tales caused her to lie awake in terror.

The last time he was this agitated about a case was when he found an entire family murdered in their beds. Although she did not want to know the details, she could tell the scene bothered him tremendously, so she asked him to tell her. What got to him the most was finding the baby, only two years old, dead in her crib with a gunshot wound to the head. He confessed that the scene almost brought him to his knees. Other than that, Oscar's twenty years in homicide desensitized him to the most horrific of scenes. Oscar was one of the most caring men Sandra knew — a loving husband and devoted father. While he tried to leave work at work to be present with the family, she noticed that the mental separation had not been as rigid as before.

This sudden disturbance led her to deduce that whatever was bothering him had something to do with Layla. The look he had in his eyes was the same as when they rushed their oldest child Jared to the hospital for an emergency appendectomy. She knew that only his three children and Layla Green could evoke that sort of concern from her husband. The last time he went into the garage for a cigar and a beer, she could tell that Oscar had been crying. She almost broke down and asked what was going on, but she decided to let him have his thoughts. When she figured out something was wrong concerning Layla, she stopped herself from asking, afraid that she would be putting the woman in danger by simply acknowledging the possibility.

Sandra picked up a box of sugary cereal for Christine and a fiber cereal for Oscar and dropped them in her basket. She took the pen from her ear and marked off the items. Making her way to the end of the aisle, she turned to the left and almost crashed into Layla, and a tall Black man she did not know, put his hand out to stop the basket. Sandra gasped in surprise.

"Layla!" she exclaimed, throwing her arms around the woman.

"Hi Sandy," Layla smiled. She pointed to the man standing next to her. "This is my friend, Robert. I'm glad we were able to get to you before you left."

"How did you know where I'd be?" Sandra inquired. Layla eyed Robert and shifted in discomfort. Telling Sandra that SARA was able to pinpoint her location using her cell phone was no easy explanation. Layla knew Sandra ran errands during the day and was relieved when SARA informed her that Sandra was on her way to the grocery store. Dom was concerned about her going to meet with Lewis' wife knowing that their home was under surveillance. However, Layla pointed out that Sandra only knew her and Vasquez, and she was closer to the family. She also insisted that there would be no reason for watchers to waste manpower on Sandra, as she had nothing to do with the situation. Dom relented on the condition that she take Robert with her since Ryan had not returned from his time with the Judge. Robert and Layla sped to the store from the warehouse, hoping to intercept Sandra before she left.

"Long story, I don't have a lot of time."

"What's going on? Is Oscar ok?" Sandra frowned. Layla gave her a reassuring smile.

"Yes, he's fine. I really can't get into everything that's happening right now, but I need you to do me a favor. I need you to take Chris to your mom's in Austin for a couple of days." Sandra blinked in confusion.

"Why?"

"The case Oscar is working on is getting ugly," she replied. "We need you and Chris to be safe. Don't take anything with you." She reached into her pocket and withdrew the five-hundred dollars Dom had given her. Pressing the money into Sandra's hand, she added, "Don't go back home. Just go pick up Chris from school and go to Austin." Sandra looked at the money in her hand long and hard and then transferred her perplexed gaze to Layla.

"What's going on?" she demanded. Layla sighed. Sandra was headstrong; Layla should have known she would not just leave on a whim.

"It's complicated," she advised. She lowered her voice to a harsh whisper before she continued. "The short version is that

Rachel, Oscar and I have been followed because of the case and your house has been bugged."

"Does Oscar know this?" Sandra asked. Layla rolled her eyes in exasperation.

"Of course, he knows. He didn't want to spook anyone, so he didn't say anything. We have been looking for whoever is behind this and have narrowed down some things, but we need Oscar to slip his detail. He's worried if he does that, it'll put you and Chris in danger. So, we need you guys to get somewhere safe until we finish this," she whispered. Layla glanced at Robert who was watching their surroundings, checking for anyone who might be interested in their little pow-wow. When she tapped him on the shoulder, he brought his dark eyes to her, and she could see intensity in his face. It was not until that moment that she realized how much he looked like Ryan. Layla held out her hand, and Robert reached into the pocket of his hoodie, pulled out a phone, and handed it to her. She turned back to Sandra and gave her the device.

"What's this for?"

"You and Chris can't use your phones," Layla informed her. "Take the battery out of yours and have her do the same when you get her. This is a special phone. You won't be able to call out on it, but Oscar will call you when we get him free. Sandy, you have to trust me and get safe; I swear he will be okay. We can't end this if we are worried about you and Chris." Her features softened, and she looked into Sandra's chestnut brown eyes. "You know you're like the mother I never had, right?" The question caused emotion to chase away confusion.

"I know," Sandra softly confirmed. She reached out and put her hand on Layla's cheek.

"I couldn't live with myself if something happened to you or Chris," she confessed. "I couldn't bear to see Oscar go through that pain. I promise that we will explain everything when it's over, but for now, you have got to just do this for us. Please." Layla placed her hand on top of Sandra's, and she gave it a light squeeze. Tears collected in the older woman's eyes as they maintained a few beats of silent eye contact.

"Please be careful. You and Oscar better come home," she said in a pleading voice.

"I'd rather die than let anything happen to that old man," Layla declared throwing her arms around Sandra. When the women separated, Layla moved the shopping cart out of the way. "Leave this, get to the school, get Chris, and get to Austin. I'll call you on that phone and check in with you this evening." Sandra nodded and turned to Robert.

"Take care of them?" she implored. Robert brought his eyes to the woman and nodded.

"They are in no better hands," he promised.

Ryan paced back and forth in the foreign living room. After he returned from his meeting with the Judge, Dom detailed the developments made in his absence. Having the identity of the shooter, it was now time to extricate Detective Lewis so the group could plan an endgame without an audience. When Dom laid out the extraction strategy, Ryan was relieved that this plan did not include drugging another surveillance detail. She told him that without the comprehensive information provided by Layla for the earlier removal, they risked compromising his identity. The current plan employed more stealth but had a slightly higher degree of risk.

The first task was to get into the house without being detected by the audio surveillance. According to Layla, Lewis had listening devices in his bedroom, living room, and office, but not in the bedrooms for the children. Dom hacked a government satellite and checked the surroundings of the dwelling. There did not appear to be any vehicles stationed outside of the residence, likely due to Lewis' absence. Ryan and Dom reviewed the floorplan of the house and decided he should go through the window of the twins' bedroom, positioned at the rear of the residence. His exit strategy was to get out the way he had come in — the backyard. Once he got into the home, he silently crept into the living room where he waited for Lewis to arrive.

Ryan stiffened when he heard the front door open after waiting a half hour. When Lewis rounded the corner, he froze upon seeing Ryan standing in the middle of the room with his right index finger on his lips. Any other time, the startled detective may have drawn on the intruder. However, after the events of the day, Lewis was more relieved than anything to find the soldier waiting for him. Ryan made a phone symbol with his pinky and thumb and shook his head when Lewis pulled out the burner. The cop frowned for a moment before understanding touched his face and he produced his own cellular device. Ryan pointed to the coffee table, and Lewis placed the device on the surface. Once he was phone free, Ryan motioned to the rear of the house with his head.

Lewis followed him out the back door of the home. Ryan remained silent as he led him to the fence that separated Lewis' residence from that of his rear neighbors. When Ryan nodded at the fence, Lewis gaped at him. He was no Tidwell, but he was not a young man either. Ryan smirked, squatted, and interlocked his fingers creating a foothold for the detective. Lewis immediately stepped into his waiting hands and pulled himself over the fence. Once he was clear, the soldier grabbed the fence and pulled himself over as if he did this sort of thing every day. He dropped next to Lewis with little sound, and the detective eyed him with respect. Ryan wordlessly motioned for him to continue, this time over the fence to the left. The silent acrobatic exercise took place six times, as they moved from backyard to backyard. The last fence landed them in a parking lot of the local drug store.

"That was fun," Lewis gasped.

He led the detective to the dark blue Impala in the parking lot. Lewis grinned at a waiting Vasquez sitting behind the wheel. Ryan directed him to the front passenger seat, and he climbed into the rear.

"From gunman to getaway driver?" Lewis asked.

"What can I say? I'm a versatile girl," Vasquez shrugged, pulling out of the parking lot.

"Layla and Robert got to your wife at the grocery store," Ryan said from the back. "She and your daughter are heading to Austin; you may want to give her a call. Layla said she was worried. Speed dial eight on your phone." Lewis nodded and pulled out his burner. He briefly spoke with Sandra, assuring her that he was fine and verifying their safety. She did not ask too many questions, but he knew she had plenty. Once he ended the call, he looked out of the window in confusion.

"Where are we going?"

"Clearlake," Vasquez answered as she negotiated the traffic. He turned to her with an unasked question. "A safe place, believe me." He moved his gaze back to the passing traffic, and the trio rode in silence for a time.

"Thank you, Ryan," he said after a moment.

"No problem." Ryan nodded. Vasquez drove as if she was in a street race and they reached Clearlake much faster than it seemed possible. When she exited the highway, Lewis offered her a look of reproach.

"You were driving way too fast, ma'am," he declared.

"Arrest me," she shrugged. When they arrived at the remote warehouse, Lewis eyed the place skeptically. After Vasquez parked, he followed her and Ryan to the door and watched with amazement as she bent to the eye scanner. He heard locks disengage and Ryan pushed the door open, motioning for the detective to enter first. Lewis walked into the expansive warehouse and noticed a round conference table on the far side of the space occupied by Layla, Rose and Robert Jenkins, and a woman he had never seen before. When Layla saw him approaching, she stood abruptly, rushed to him, and gave him a quick hug before pulling him to the table.

"Lewis, you already know Rose and Robert Jenkins." She motioned to the siblings who smiled in greeting. Turning her attention to the woman who sat across from the Jenkinses, she held out an introductory hand. "This is Dominique Samuels."

CHAPTER FORTY-ONE

"Goddamnit!" Tristan bellowed into the phone. "What do you mean we lost Lewis too?"

"He got home a little early, and his detail was with him," Lopez explained. "He went out back when he got there; they assumed to smoke a cigar. But they never heard him come back into the house. After about forty-five minutes, the unit went inside, but he was gone. His cell was on the coffee table."

"What about his wife and kid?"

"His wife left earlier in the afternoon and never came home," Lopez replied.

"How the fuck did he know?" Tristan demanded.

"If I knew that, we wouldn't be in this predicament," Lopez answered irritably. Tristan wanted to throw the phone against the wall in frustration. Nothing had been going the way it was supposed to. Losing the detective meant no longer having eyes on the investigation. Tristan was certain that like Layla Green and Rachel Vasquez, Detective Lewis would not resurface. He wondered where the man's wife and daughter had gone. Running his hand through his hair, he tried to piece together what he needed to do. This was the nail in the coffin for the clinic program.

"There is little I can do without knowing where Lewis is and how much he knows. Now that he's disappeared, that leaves everyone exposed," Tristan advised. "You need to lay low."

"Or, we can just take him out," Lopez offered.

"You don't know where the hell he is," Tristan grumbled. "You crossed that line when you killed Lionetti. After you've done that, I can't authorize killing a homicide detective."

"What am I supposed to do?" Lopez questioned. A wave of irritation washed over Tristan.

"There's nothing you can do, Sammy."

"I still think I should just take care of Lewis and the problem will be over," he insisted.

"Sammy, right now we don't know where Lewis is, what he knows, or who he's told. Maybe he caught sight of the surveillance detail — he is a cop after all," Tristan surmised. "We know Green and Vasquez slipped theirs first and maybe that's how he found out about it. You don't know, and neither do I. You will not harm Detective Lewis or anyone else unless I give the go ahead. We give the orders; we don't pay you to think for yourself."

"You're telling me everything you don't know. Let me tell you what I do know," Lopez interjected, matching his threatening tone. "I know that Oscar Lewis is one tough and smart son of a bitch. I know how many people I've killed for you. I may not know what he knows, but I know he won't rest until he solves this case. You are thinking about you and your little friends, but I don't see any concern for my ass, which is on the line right now."

"You knew the risk of this arrangement. You will do nothing unless I say otherwise. That's final," Tristan commanded.

"Fine, whatever," he muttered ending the call. He tossed the burner phone on the sofa and ran his hands through his thick black hair. For almost four years, Lopez did a lot for Tristan Rucker, although he was smart enough to know that Tristan was not who he worked for. He spent months trying to ascertain who was pulling the strings, but he could find nothing. Liberty Foundation Services paid him, but when he looked into the organization, Tristan did not appear. The foundation was comprised of a bunch of doctors from all over the country. The difference between Tristan and Lopez was that Lopez knew he was expendable. In regards to this drama, all roads led to Tristan Rucker; he was just as disposable as Lopez was, even if he did not realize his own predicament. Lopez planned for the eventual moment where Tristan decided his usefulness was negligible and he believed that moment had come.

He made his way into the kitchen and pulled three double shot glasses from his cabinet before retrieving a bottle of Sierra Silver Tequila. He lined the glasses on the counter and poured himself three double shots. After taking a deep breath, he downed all three in rapid succession. He hoped the liquid would sooth the nerves frayed by the conversation. Once he finished the drinks, he made his way across the house to his master bedroom. Lopez approached the framed copy of Salvador Dali's painting, "Girl at a Window."

As a boy, Lopez dabbled in painting and drawing. He considered art school for a long while, but he was not confident enough in his technique. Although he loved the paintings of all mediums and periods, his favorite artist was Salvador Dali. The copy of "Girl at the Window" resonated with him from the first time he laid eyes on it. He would stare at the photo frequently, feeling like the girl at the window, wistfully looking across at a dream that was so out of reach. Growing up in rural Atlanta, one of seven born to a construction worker and daycare employee, Lopez dreamed of something more for his life. He thought art would be his path; but ultimately, he chose law enforcement. To this day, he had no idea why he made that choice. No longer an aspiring artist, this Dali remained a cherished gift. Lopez took the painting off the wall to expose a safe. He typed in his code, opened the safe, and pulled out a large manila envelope.

Lewis sat across the table from the infamous Dominique Samuels, who was flanked by Vasquez and Ryan. The rest of the group sat around the table and watched the detective and the hacker engage in a silent stare-down. Robert emerged with a carafe of coffee, mugs for all parties, cream, and sugar. He placed the items in the middle of the tabletop. Dom pulled a mug to herself and poured a cup of coffee. She never broke eye contact with the detective as she added sugar and cream. After she stirred the brew with a wooden coffee stirrer, she took a sip and finally broke the silence.

"Detective," she nodded. "I'm glad you were able to get out of your situation. Have you spoken to your wife?" Lewis noticed her voice was low and smooth with an authoritative tone that he did not expect. Based on the conversations he had with Layla about this woman, he expected a timid nerd. While Dom definitely possessed an obvious aura of intelligence, he was shocked to find she also had a commanding presence.

"Yes. Sandra and Christine have made it to Austin by now. I want to thank you for your assistance, for both myself and my family."

"You are like family to Layla and Rachel. I've grown accustomed to them so I could not leave you in jeopardy; even if I do have an aversion to the police," she replied. "You should know that we have recently become contractors to the Justice Department. Legality has become a little fluid. I hope that puts any concerns you have to rest." Lewis shot a glance at Layla who nodded in verification.

"It does," he admitted. "And now that I know that, you should know you have nothing to worry about from me. Hopefully, it relieves any anxiety you may feel about having me here."

"Guys," Layla spoke up with irritation. "This isn't a mafia sit-down. We're all on the same side. Dom, you're not fooling anyone with the quiet, brooding tone; cut it out. And Lewis, I've already told you she's fine, so stop with your cop stare."

"Whew, good! I wasn't sure how long I could have kept that up," Dom chuckled, revealing a lopsided grin. "Detective Lewis, you are more than welcome here. You can call me Dom." Lewis blinked at her immediate change of attitude and smiled.

"You had me going for a minute there."

"If we can't find a second to laugh in the middle of this bullshit, then the bastards have already won," she shrugged, taking a sip of her coffee. "So, your killer is Sammy Lopez. From what Layla and Rachel tell me, you know him fairly well."

"I thought I did," he huffed, shaking his head. "I mean, as well as you can know someone who works an opposite shift as you. I thought he was a good guy. I really liked him."

"So, what's the plan, Dom?" Ryan asked.

"I'm going to assume he's using a burner phone," she said. "That's probably why his personal cell is turned off. We know that he's a contract killer. Since you slipped your tail, his people will likely pass that on to him, and he will probably put one and one together. We need to find him. Do you know where he lives?"

"I've never been there personally, but I'm sure we can get his address from the department," Lewis replied. His statement was met with a head shake from Dom.

"You have to work outside of the department for the duration."

"I realize that you don't have procedures and policies that you are married to, but unfortunately, I do," he frowned. "I can't just freestyle this, Miss Samuels."

"Please, call me Dom," she insisted. "I understand your concerns, but it can't hurt for us to get the address, can it?"

"I guess it can't," he admitted.

"SARA?" Dom called.

"I have the address from Mr. Lopez's personnel file. It's an apartment in the Bellaire area of Houston," the computer replied.

"That was fast," Lewis remarked.

"She's probably had it since we found the information on your work terminal," Dom advised. "She has a nasty habit of waiting to tell me things until I need them."

"There is more, Dom," SARA announced.

"Of course there is," she mumbled.

"There is a house in Pearland that Mr. Lopez appears to own." Dom's tablet blinked, and she picked up the device to inspect the information. She let out a low whistle.

"Five thousand square feet, five bedrooms, four baths, and a media room on six acres. Price tag is just under a million. A little pricey for a cop, no?" she asked. She pushed the tablet across the surface to Lewis who picked it up and inspected the housing information.

"Yeah, I'm fairly sure no cop could afford that," he concurred.

"He probably uses the apartment address, so no one suspects anything. SARA, how did you find this?" Layla asked, taking the tablet from Lewis.

"The home is in his mother's name, but the payments come from Mr. Lopez," SARA replied.

"That's probably where he really lives," Vasquez murmured, inspecting the house over Layla's shoulder. "When he's arrested, can we just take this place? It's nice."

"Dom?" SARA called out. Dom turned to the avatar.

"What's up?"

"Since we required Detective Lewis to keep his personal cell phone at his house to avoid tracking, I felt it was only prudent to monitor that phone," SARA began. Dom turned from her avatar to the detective who wore a look of both fascination and alarm.

"Don't worry, Detective. She only does this when she finds a logical necessity. She doesn't make it a habit."

"Well," Vasquez sang, holding out the word. Dom shot her a look.

"There was a logical necessity in her eyes," Dom muttered defensively. "And I made her stop tracking all of you a long time ago."

"I'm just saying," Vasquez shrugged. "She kind of makes it more of a habit than you think." She threw Dom a wink, causing her to look away in embarrassment.

"I assume you wouldn't bring this up unless something came up, SARA. What happened?"

"Detective Lewis just received a phone call. Standby for the voice message." The machine went quiet, and suddenly a man's voice emitted from the speakers. "Oscar, hey, it's Sammy. I think we need to have a chat. I know you left your phone at home, but just in case you go back to it or check your messages; we need to talk," the caller said. Dom turned to the detective. His features went slack as he listened to the message.

"Is that who I think it is?" Dom asked. Lewis, Vasquez, and Layla all nodded in unison.

"That was Sammy Lopez," Layla confirmed.

"Talk about a turn of events," Rose mumbled.

"SARA," Dom began.

"Yes Dom, I have already captured the initiating phone line and have latched on to the GPS," SARA answered before Dom could finish her question.

"Look, if you want me to ask you for things, you need to let me get it out," Dom sighed irritably.

"Do you know where he is, SARA?" Lewis asked the computer.

"He is currently at the house in Pearland," SARA answered. Lewis began to rise from his seat. Layla glanced at Dom, who returned the look with a quick shake of the head. Layla put her hand on Lewis' arm and gently pulled him back down into his chair. Lewis gave Layla a questioning look.

"You can't just go down there halfcocked, Detective," Dom admonished. "Sammy Lopez is working for someone, he's working for the Liberty Health Services Foundation and whoever is pulling the strings for them. Right now, Lopez can't do any more harm because he no longer has eyes and ears on you. You seem like the type of guy to jump into action, but I'm a planner. I need you to trust me when I tell you, we need a plan." Lewis' turquoise eyes held Dom's gaze for a moment. Layla placed her hand on his arm.

"Oscar. You trust me, right? I know it's crazy because of how this all came together, but I really do trust Dom," she insisted. "She has not steered us wrong thus far. Because of her and Ryan, Rachel and I are alive. I know this goes against everything you want to do, but she's right. Just think for a second; why would Lopez call you out of the blue? He knows that you know something is up. He could be calling you into an ambush. We know he's not working alone; none of us were being shadowed by Lopez personally. I promised Sandy I would make sure you stayed safe, and I intend to keep that promise, Old Man." The detective's eyes softened, and he reluctantly nodded.

"Fine," he muttered, turning to face Dom. "What do you have in mind?" Dom glanced at Ryan.

"I think between the three of us, we can come up with something, don't you?" Ryan offered a grim smirk.

"Absolutely. But you know what this means, right?"

"What?" she inquired.

"We need to visit the armory," he replied. Lewis' eyes widened in surprise.

"Armory?"

"I wish you guys would stop calling it an armory," Dom dismissed. Ryan chuckled.

"Keep lying to yourself, Boss."

"I tell her the same thing, Mr. Jenkins," SARA added.

"We need gear, Dom," Ryan insisted.

"We're still in the whole you won't arrest me mode, right?" Dom eyed the detective. Lewis gave her a confused nod.

"Fine, follow me." She stood from her chair, and Lewis and Ryan followed suit.

"Rachel, you come too," Ryan said, before walking away. Vasquez's eyes widened when she heard her name called and Dom turned to him with a scowl.

"Really?" she asked.

"I'm not going anywhere where I could be killed without Rachel," Ryan proclaimed with sincerity. Lewis' eyebrows shot up in shock. Dom looked from Ryan to Vasquez and shrugged.

"You heard the man," she said to Vasquez who stood abruptly and followed the trio to the false wall of the panic room. When the door slid open, Lewis' step stuttered in surprise. Ryan grinned at the detective.

"That's not even the coolest part," he chuckled, clapping the startled man on the back. The group followed Dom through the panic room to the entrance leading to the weapons cache. Dom entered her code and pushed the door open, motioning for Vasquez, Lewis, and Ryan to pass through before she followed them. Once the wall rotated exposing the weapons, Lewis and Vasquez gasped and gaped at the sight. After a few beats, Vasquez turned to Dom and offered her a sly smile.

"I didn't think you could get any hotter, but then you go and show me this. I think I'm turned on a little." Ryan laughed at this statement, while Dom looked away in discomfort. Lewis approached the wall and picked up a short barrel AR-15 assault rifle. After he inspected the weapon, he turned to Dom with raised eyebrows, as if expecting an explanation.

"For a rainy day?" she asked innocently. He grunted and returned the rifle to its place.

"You must be expecting a hell of a storm, kid."

Tristan sat in the darkened room, aimlessly running his hand through his hair. He could tell by the posture of the four men on the shadowy screens that they were as anxious as he was.

"Gentlemen, there is no getting around it; it's time to terminate the clinic program," Tristan informed the men as he concluded his report.

"But it's working! We've been at this for seven years, and the data clearly shows that the birth rates for the target groups are reducing, while the birth rate for the pure race is climbing. We can't just stop now!" Atlanta protested. Tristan noticed the usually quiet man was far more vocal during this debate. "We knew it would be at least a two-decade project!"

"I get that. But I believe Lewis has gotten too close," Tristan countered. "I can't confirm because we lost our eyes and ears into the investigation, we don't know where Layla Green or Rachel Vasquez are, and we don't know what is known and what isn't. Being blind is not good, and at some point, you have to know when to cut your losses." His voice took on a commanding tone. "We need to assume that the feds know a little bit of what's going on. If that's the case, we need to get ahead of it by terminating the program and make it hard for anyone to prove anything." Tristan eyed each screen, in an attempt to ascertain reactions, but the shadowy figures did not give anything away.

"Alright Tristan," Chicago conceded after a few moments. "You're there, so you would know how crucial this is getting more than we would. But we have to tie up loose ends."

"Loose ends?" Tristan wondered.

"We can handle scrubbing the foundation. I'll call the director and get him started on dismantling the program records," Atlanta said. "But you have to deal with your man on the ground, Lopez. He has to go. Is that a problem?"

"Well, I just assumed that we'd let him either walk or fall," Tristan admitted.

"Come on Rucker, you know how this works," Alexandria sighed. "If we are terminating the program, then we can't leave any unfinished business."

"I just didn't think we'd kill someone who has done so much for us." Tristan's remark was met with a disgusted head shake from Alexandria.

"It is what it is, Rucker. If we are scrubbing evidence of the whole thing, then Lopez has got to go," Atlanta commanded.

"So, we are agreed that this is dead and now all we need to do is bury it?" Vegas asked.

"Yes, the program is dead, in Texas at least," Atlanta muttered. Tristan's eyebrows rose in amazement. He always assumed that Texas was the only location of the program.

"In Texas? There are other locations?"

"That's not your concern," Chicago interjected. "Texas is your concern, and now you have to clean it up." A series of thoughts ran through Tristan's mind. He was beginning to realize that this elusive group extended far past his knowledge, and he was not sure what to think about that. He also understood that he might be more expendable than he once thought. Best to get in line or end up like Lopez.

"Gentlemen, I'll see to finalizing things," he agreed.

After his video meeting with Tristan Rucker, the man in Atlanta powered down his computer and sat back in his chair in deep thought. The program had been his pet project, and while other areas were up and running, Texas was important given its proximity to Mexico. However, after hearing the information Rucker presented, he could not argue that the program was compromised. He picked up his phone and called his friend who answered on the second ring.

"Mark, we're pulling the plug," he said after Dr. Mark Fields answered the phone.

"What the hell do you mean?"

"It's getting too dangerous. We either pull the plug or risk exposing you and Eric. Don't worry, we can come up with something else. Your role in the Health and Human Services Commission is too important to jeopardize. Dismantle the Foundation, and close all the clinics, immediately. Destroy the records," he commanded.

"Fine," Fields relented. "I know you wouldn't do this unless you had to."

"You know I wouldn't, my friend. We will regroup once the danger is gone. The cause will continue."

"Give my love to the kids," Fields murmured before ending the phone call. Atlanta disconnected and ran back the meeting in his mind. Rucker's reaction to terminating Lopez did not sit well with him. He had no problem with Tristan Rucker, but he knew that the pawn was unaware of his nature. He was an important piece of the puzzle, an arm that kept some things running on behalf of the group, but Atlanta began to wonder if he had the fortitude to do what was necessary. He did not want to leave anything to chance. He grabbed his burner phone and made another call to his guy in Houston. The man picked up the phone on the first ring.

"I need you to do something for me," he said to the responder.

CHAPTER FORTY-TWO

Lopez anxiously paced the large home, occasionally checking his cellular device hoping that Lewis would reach out. He called out sick from work for the evening to keep himself available should the older detective call. What he failed to disclose was that he would never return to work. He knew time was running out for him. As much as he had done for Rucker and his people, the tone of the phone call informed him that his survival was not a priority. It was only a matter of time before they decided they couldn't afford to keep him alive. As Rucker mentioned, Lopez knew the risks of the undertaking, and he had a go-bag ready to disappear should the need arise. While he was serious about the idea of killing Lewis, the fact that Rucker refused the option told Lopez all he needed to know about where he stood. After three and a half years of clean up, killing, and surveillance, when it came time to pick a side, Rucker chose a cop he did not know over Lopez. He wanted to talk to Lewis before he vanished to give him what he had on Tristan Rucker. He presumed that if his life was forfeit in Rucker's eyes, there was no reason for Rucker to be any less expendable. His only regret was not finding out from whom Rucker took his marching orders.

Lopez was not under any misguided notion that he was a good guy. He knew he was a murderer — plain and simple. His job happened to also be the business of homicide and therefore, he knew how to cover his tracks better than most. He chuckled at the memory of Lewis coming in every morning to work the case, bantering with the very man he was hunting. The set up at their shared computer was a brilliant move on his part. He initially worried that Lewis would log his profile out when he noticed that Lopez had not done it on his own. He stuck around every day to verify Lewis would just switch the profiles leaving his side up and running, including the dictation program. Lewis being the courteous guy he always had been did not fail him.

"Come on, Old Man," he mumbled as he checked the time. It was after two in the morning. Lopez knew that usually, Lewis was asleep by now; however, since no one had eyes and ears on him, he could be anywhere. He sighed heavily and plopped down on his bed.

———⟨⟩———

Ryan and Vasquez adjusted their night vision goggles to verify that they could monitor the property line as planned. They watched as Lewis and Layla approached the house and let themselves in with a little help from SARA. The group found that when Lopez bought the place, he updated the home security system to an advanced state of the art program that included the ability to remotely lock and unlock exterior doors. The whole system was wired electronically and monitored twenty-four hours by an expensive security company, but Dom was far more skilled than the security company's system. She took no time in identifying the weaknesses in the structure and informed the team that SARA would be able to disable the security and open any doors needed without detection.

Lewis had not planned to bring Layla along on this outing, but the woman was unyielding that she would not be left out. In the armory, Ryan informed Lewis that Vasquez knew how to handle weapons with almost as much efficiency as the men and women he served with, and reiterated that he would not go without her. Lewis wondered what Vasquez had done to earn the soldier's respect, but he would not argue with Ryan about his demand. He and Layla quarreled about her need to accompany the group. Unlike the others, Layla would be unarmed, and Lewis worried for her safety.

"Lewis," she said, trying to calm him. "I have lived through a lot of horrific shit in my life, and I have fought my way out of a lot of stuff without the use of a gun. Don't underestimate me, I'm resourceful." Lewis paled at this information, horrified at the idea of Layla going through something worse than a crazy foster father holding her at gunpoint.

"Kid, I don't know what we're walking into, and I don't want you to get hurt," he pled.

"I won't," she smiled. She approached Dom and whispered something in the woman's ear. Dom's face took on the mantle of perplexity, but she nodded in response, and the two women disappeared into the panic room.

"Where are they going?" Ryan asked, adjusting the tactical belt holding his extra ammunition. Lewis shrugged as he began to collect the weapons he retrieved from Dom's cache.

"I can't believe she had night vision goggles," he muttered, watching Vasquez pick up a pair and examine them.

"I'm sure she has a lot of shit we wouldn't believe," Ryan scoffed. "She talks about SARA not saying things until she's ready; she's only doing what Dom does."

"That is accurate, Mr. Jenkins," SARA spoke up. "Most of my learned behavior is from Dom."

"So, she's not as shy as she claims?" Vasquez asked.

"Not with me," SARA replied. The conversation was cut short when Layla and Dom reemerged from the panic room.

"What was that about?" Vasquez wondered.

"Mind your business," Layla replied, waving her off. "Let's go."

Dom sat in the office of the warehouse trying to calm her mind after the group left. Despite Layla's odd request, she found herself worried about her and Vasquez. Lewis and Ryan both possessed combat training. Although Ryan insisted Vasquez was more than proficient with guns; she was nervous, wanting both of the women to return in one piece. Robert had begrudgingly gone home with his sister despite begging to be a part of the activity. Dom, Rose, and Ryan all forbade him from going along. Although a homicide detective would accompany him, no one wanted to risk his probation. He was upset about it, but when he realized no one would budge, he left with Rose after receiving assurance from Dom that she would keep them updated.

"Dom, I have information," SARA announced.

"What's wrong? Is everyone ok?"

"Yes Dom, they are almost at Mr. Lopez's house," SARA reassured her. "There is an anomaly that I just discovered."

"What's that?"

"I received the ballistics report for the murder of Rosalyn Guerrero. We have been working under the assumption that Mr. Lopez murdered Dr. Guerrero as well as Malik Rodgers. However, upon comparing the ballistics, I have found that the caliber is the same, but the ballistics do not match." Dom frowned at this information.

"So, they weren't killed by the same gun?"

"That is correct. They were murdered by two different .38 caliber weapons," SARA answered.

"Did they process the bullet for Lionetti?" Dom asked.

"Detective Lewis put a rush on the ballistics, but the test has not been performed," SARA replied. Dom considered the information.

"Either the same shooter used two different guns of the same caliber, or there were two different shooters," she mused thoughtfully.

"That is correct," SARA confirmed.

"Check the area surrounding the clinic for surveillance footage. Nearby businesses, traffic cams, it doesn't matter. We may be able to pull something with our software that the cops couldn't get," Dom commanded.

Once SARA opened the patio door for Lewis and Layla, the detective silently slid the door open and held his hand up, commanding Layla to stay put. He moved into the kitchen first with his weapon drawn. Layla rolled her eyes and stepped into the room immediately after him.

"Stop worrying," she hissed in response to his stern gaze. She walked on the balls of her feet to prevent making any noise and crept further into the house. Lewis followed her, surveying their surroundings with his sidearm. The duo located the master bedroom and found Lopez lying on his bed with his eyes closed. His nightstand lamp was on, and Layla halted in the doorway and glanced at Lewis. For a split second, they were afraid the man was dead. After they stood silently watching him, they noticed Lopez's chest rise and fall with the deep breaths of sleep. Lewis moved ahead of Layla and slowly approached Lopez with his gun trained on the sleeping man. When he reached the side of the bed, he touched the muzzle of his pistol to the young man's forehead causing Lopez's eyes to snap open with a wild look.

"Give me a reason, Lopez," he growled. Lopez's dark brown eyes blinked and met Lewis' tense turquoise stare. His gaze flicked to the foot of the bed where Layla stood, her dark brown eyes equally as cold.

"Hey Old Man." Lopez favored him with his notorious grin. "I was afraid you wouldn't get my message."

Dom reviewed the footage SARA brought up from a street traffic camera a block away from the clinic. The system identified a car that entered the area after the clinic closed, but before Rosalyn Guerrero signed out of the systems for the night. The same vehicle remained in the vicinity until just after her listed time of death. When it passed the traffic cameras after the shooting, it was moving fast. After the vehicle departed, SARA continued to monitor the car until it came to a red light at a large intersection. Dom zoomed in on the face.

"Vehicle registration?" she asked.

"The license plate appears to be false," SARA replied.

"Can you run the facial rec software?"

"You are straying towards unintelligent questions again, Dom," the system admonished.

"Not now," she shot back. "Run the scan." SARA grew quiet for a few moments and then produced a match. Dom frowned, and she mumbled, "I know the name."

"Yes, you do," SARA confirmed. The program continued to produce information and realization prompted Dom's heart to race.

"Oh no," she groaned. "Where is he?" SARA found the cellular device and opened an internet map. Dom's eyes went wild with panic when she saw the blue dot on the move from Houston headed south to Pearland. "Holy shit." She jumped up from her seat and bolted out of the room.

"Now nice and easy, sit up," Lewis ordered. Lopez pushed his body up from the supine position and leaned against the headboard. He eyed Layla.

"There you are," he crooned as if she were a long-lost friend. "You and Vasquez had a lot of people wondering what happened to you." Layla's furious eyes held Lopez's gaze, but she remained silent.

"I asked you here to talk, nothing more," Lopez declared. His tone remained affable, increasing Layla's rage.

"That may be your plan," Lewis acknowledged. "But I intend to arrest the murderer of Malik Rodgers." Showing no panic, he seemed entertained by this pronouncement.

"All that time, I was right under your nose, Old Man," he teased.

"Who are you working for, Lopez?" Layla questioned.

"So, she does speak," he gasped with mock surprise. "Why do I have to be working for someone? How do you know I'm not just another psychopath?"

"You're not nearly as intelligent," she observed, drawing a scowl from Lopez. "Tell us about Liberty Health Services Foundation." This command drew a look of genuine surprise. He gazed from Layla back to Lewis.

"I won't say anything until I know that you will let me go and fade into the sunset," he informed the detective. "That's why I wanted to talk to you. I'm a small fish in a very large and dangerous pond." His shock melted and the arrogant sneer returned to his features. "I will give you everything you want, but it'll cost you. Do you want to close your case or do you want to be a hero?" Lewis' turquoise gaze moved to Layla and the two locked eyes in an unspoken conversation.

"How about you give me what you have, and I'll decide if it's worth sparing you?" he countered. Lopez chuckled.

"Afraid not," he grinned. "You have to make a decision, and you have to decide now. I'm fairly sure that..." His voice trailed off when he heard the sounds of heavy footsteps coming down the hall. For the first time since their arrival, his face betrayed a look of fear. His wide eyes shot to Lewis and Layla, and he noticed both visitors remained calm and unmoving.

"Relax, he's with us," she said, turning to the door just as Ryan burst into the room. Despite the dim lighting, he squinted when he entered.

"We have company," he announced. Lewis' eyebrows shot up in surprise, and he spun on Lopez, training his gun on the man in the bed.

"You set me up," he growled. Lopez still wore the mask of fear, and he shook his head rapidly.

"They're here for me," he confessed. Lewis cocked his head in expectation.

"What do you mean they're here for you?" Layla demanded.

"I told you, I may be a bad guy, but I work for worse people," Lopez insisted. "Losing Lewis was the final straw. They're probably tying up loose ends, and I'm a loose end." He turned his imploring eyes back to Lewis and commanded, "Make a decision." Lewis' mind raced. He dropped his weapon and turned to Ryan.

"How many?"

"Ten," Ryan replied. Lewis cursed under his breath.

Moving his eyes to Layla, he nodded his head at Lopez and asked, "Can you keep him secure in here?" Layla replied with a curt nod. Lopez's eyes grew wide as he objected.

"What the hell man? They're here to kill me, not to talk! I need to grab my gun!"

"You will sit your ass here and shut the hell up," Lewis shot back. He turned to follow Ryan out of the room.

"You really think Green can keep me in here with no weapon?" Lopez called. Lewis paused at the door and gave the man a sinister smile.

"You've clearly never stepped in the ring with her," he winked. He followed Ryan through the house and returned to the kitchen where Vasquez stood against the wall, gun in hand. The vision of the breezy woman looking armed and dangerous startled him. Her image brought to mind that of an action movie femme fatale and was in conflict with the playful nature he was accustomed to witnessing. Ryan approached her and put a hand on her shoulder.

"How close are they?" he inquired.

"SARA says about three to five minutes, give or take," she answered.

"How did you know they were coming?" Lewis wondered.

"This is kind of a remote area. SARA was able to pick up on radio signatures about seven miles out and gave us a warning," Ryan answered.

"God, I love that machine," Lewis muttered.

"I'm seriously considering forming a fan club," Vasquez joked. Lewis smiled, glad that her sense of humor was still intact.

"What's the plan?" he asked. "There are three of us, and ten of them."

"Four of us." The trio spun and saw Layla enter the kitchen. Lewis favored her with a look of surprise and dismay.

"You are supposed to be watching Lopez!" he hissed, drawing a grimace from the woman.

"He wouldn't play nice, started talking shit. I guess he didn't believe you," she shrugged. Her grim face morphed into a smile. "When he wakes up, he will."

"That's my girl!" Vasquez grinned, hi-fiving her friend.

"These guys won't be showing up to box," Lewis insisted. Layla shook her head.

"No, but don't worry about me. Trust me, Oscar," she whispered. Before he could continue to object, he saw Vasquez put her hand to her ear. She stiffened as she listened to SARA.

"They're here," she whispered urgently. "They've split into two teams of five and are coming from the rear and the front."

"We'll split up," Ryan said, taking control of the situation. "Rachel and I will take the front. You two take the back." Vasquez moved to Layla and wrapped her in a tight embrace.

"If you die, I'm going to be so pissed at you," she whispered.

"Don't worry; you're stuck with me for a long time coming," Layla advised, returning her hug. When they parted, Vasquez approached Lewis and gave him a brief squeeze.

"Please," she murmured, "protect my sister." After he nodded, Vasquez released him, and she followed Ryan's path to the front of the house. Lewis spun on Layla, ready to rebuff her participation with renewed zeal.

The sound of the back door being kicked in halted any further debate, and Lewis dropped behind the bar counter, his gun at the ready. Layla moved to the edge of the bar, but she did not drop next to the detective. Lewis' heart dropped into the pit of his stomach.

"Down!" A frantic Lewis hissed at the woman. Layla continued to monitor the door. She took slow and even breaths, blocking out her surroundings. Time seemed to slow in her mind. Extended hands gripping a pistol breeched the entry first, followed by a head and torso. Lewis craned his head around the counter with the intent to call out to her once again. Before he could speak, Layla's right hand moved from her waist and flicked out in a throwing motion. The movement was so fast, Lewis almost missed the action. His eyes widened in surprise when he heard the distinct sound of a body falling to the ground. Spinning around, he stood just as a second man entered the door on the heels of the first. He fired his gun twice, dropping the second intruder. When he ducked back to the cover of the bar, he realized Layla had finally taken cover right next to him.

"What the hell did you do?" he whispered in shock.

"There are many things you don't know about me. It's true that I don't like guns," she admitted, reaching into her waist once again. She brought out a wickedly sharp knife and deftly spun the blade on her index finger before stopping the motion and holding it up for Lewis to see. "Knives on the other hand."

The detective eyed the deathly sharp throwing knife that she held out and realized that he had seen the blade before, in Dom's armory. His eyes bulged at this exhibition and the implications of what Layla had just done. As if needing confirmation, he eased his way around the bar to the back door. Leaning around the shield, he saw the two bodies in the entryway. The first man had a knife protruding from the side of his throat. Blood pumped from the wound and Lewis ascertained that Layla's strike severed the man's carotid artery.

"Who the hell are you?" he asked in astonishment.

"I'm still me," she whispered indignantly. "I just have a few more layers than most people think. That's two, we still have three more. I'm thinking they are looking for another breach point since we dropped these two here."

Ryan crept to the front door and motioned for Vasquez to position herself behind one of the pillars in front of the entry while he stationed himself on the opposite side. As they waited for the team to breach the entry, Ryan spoke his love for his family under his breath.

"I love you girls." He looked at Vasquez, pointed to himself and held up his index finger. He then pointed at her and held up two fingers. Since Vasquez had never served in the military, Ryan was forced to freestyle signals. He desperately hoped she understood the message. Before she was able to confirm or deny with a sign of her own, the front door was kicked in, and Ryan turned his attention to the more pressing matter. He peered around his pillar and saw the first man enter. He quickly leaned out of cover and fired twice, his shots finding the man's chest. Resuming concealment, his eyes moved to Vasquez, who leaned out, fired two times, and dropped the second man. He was relieved that she understood his message. He could not believe that he underestimated her before she saved his life outside of Layla's apartment. He peeked around the pillar in time to see a third man enter and step over his two comrades. Ryan leaned out and took him down with two shots. Vasquez leaned around her column but did not engage another combatant. She looked at him and shook her head. Ryan was reasonably certain that no one else would attempt to enter this way after the first three were shot. If he were in their position, he would fall back and find another route into the house. He backed away from his column and headed to the kitchen, nodding his head for Vasquez to follow.

When the two returned to the kitchen, they found Layla and Lewis standing near the garage entrance. Ryan looked down at the two bodies on the tile floor and was surprised to see one had a knife sticking out of the side of his neck. He looked at Lewis with a questioning glance and the detective nodded his head at Layla.

"We dropped three," Ryan reported.

"That leaves five more. SARA, where are they?" Vasquez asked.

"Two have circled to the garage and are attempting to gain access through the side door, two have moved to the window of the bedroom next to the master suite, and the final one seems to be going back to the vehicle," SARA informed her. "I have locked the bedroom window and side doors, but I am unsure how long that will hold." Vasquez relayed the information.

"Shit," Ryan muttered. "He's probably trying to call reinforcements. We can't let him get to the car."

"Well, right now we are pretty evenly matched and have lost the element of surprise. If one of us follows him, we're down again," Lewis noted. Ryan nodded in deep thought.

"Rachel and I will take the garage," Layla declared. "Lewis, you go to the bedroom and wait for those two to get through the window. Ryan, you chase down the rabbit." Despite his reluctance to split up, Lewis analyzed the strategy and decided that it was probably the best course of action. He nodded and ran to the bedroom. Vasquez took the earpiece from her ear and gave it to Ryan. He put the device in his ear and sprinted out of the back door. Vasquez watched Layla slip a knife from the sheath strapped around her waist. Her eyes went wide when she saw the weapon, and she moved her emerald gaze from the knife to the man on the ground. Once she pieced together what happened in her absence, she narrowed her eyes and stared at Layla.

"You have a lot of explaining to do when this is over," she whispered, pushing open the door to the garage.

CHAPTER FORTY-THREE

Ryan darted across the wooded property, taking cover in and out of the trees in an attempt to remain as concealed as possible. SARA informed him that his quarry was heading towards the rear of the estate and he should not be too far behind him. He wondered how things were going back at Lopez's house. Dom only had one SARA-ready earpiece, which Vasquez wore until recently. Lewis had a two-way earpiece that put him in contact with Ryan. This allowed Vasquez to get data from SARA, and since Ryan had been with her, he, in turn, received the information and could relay any important details to Lewis. The two-way earpiece was now in his pocket.

He considered relaying the incoming visitors to Lewis via the communication device, but he made the tactical decision to consolidate the firepower to the house. Ryan was fairly sure that he and his companions were unknown factors; therefore, while out-manned, they had the element of surprise. He and Vasquez sprinted from out of their cover to the house in time to warn Lewis and Layla and devise a game plan. Now, they were separated again, with the girls together and the two men solo. He did not like this development, nor did he like having the only connection to SARA, and by extension, Dom.

"SARA," he panted. Although he was not long out of the military and in good shape, the sprint from cover to the house, the adrenaline rush of a gunfight, and the subsequent race to catch up with their escapee had his pulse thumping double time and his breathing fast and labored.

"Yes, Mr. Jenkins?" SARA answered in his ear.

"Where is he?" He leaned against a nearby tree to catch his breath.

"He is in your location," SARA informed him. He adjusted his night vision goggles and spun in a three-hundred and sixty degree circle. He picked up nothing but the pale greenish tint of the surrounding trees.

"That can't be right."

"I'm unsure why you would doubt my information, but I insist the satellite readings indicate there are two heat signatures where you are," SARA reiterated. Ryan cocked his head and tried to listen for the sound of another person in the wooded clearing. He slowly turned around in a full circle again, trying to view every inch of his surroundings. Suddenly, a droplet of liquid landed on the top of his bald head. He froze. His mind fed him a message far too late — SARA is never wrong. He slowly lifted his eyes to the air and was blinded by a flashlight. He hissed at the pain and squeezed his eyes shut, too late to be effective. As he stripped the goggles off his head, he heard the distinct thud of his voyeur landing a few feet away from him.

"Well, well, Mr. Interesting. We meet again," a familiar voice sneered.

Vasquez entered the garage with more silence than Layla had ever heard. She swung her pistol in an arc, searching for any intruders. Layla twirled the knife she held around her index finger by the circular handle and adjusted her grip in preparation for action. Vasquez noticed this little display and smirked at her friend before turning her attention back to the dim room. The garage was dark but moonlight filtered in from slotted windows near the ceiling. The women entered in the northwest corner of the room, and the lighting from the windows created a false spotlight in the center of the three-car garage. The sides of the room remained engulfed in shadows. A large late model Hummer was parked on the far eastern side of the garage. Vasquez nodded at the car and Layla fell in behind her. The women crept to the only concealment the room offered.

As they neared the vehicle, Vasquez turned her head to the right to check for Layla and spied movement in the southwest corner of the room. She halted her stride and strained her eyes in an attempt to make out an outline. Vasquez's probing gaze prompted Layla to turn towards the same area with her knife at the ready. A man stepped out of the shadows with his weapon trained on Layla who was the closest person to him. Vasquez fired twice, striking the man in the chest and shoulder before he had a chance to discharge his own weapon. The gunman dropped immediately, and Layla rushed over to him, kicked his gun out of reach, and checked his pulse.

"He's breathing," she reported gazing at Vasquez. What she saw caused her heart to stop in her chest and her blood to run cold. The second man emerged from behind the Hummer and his large forearm wrapped around Vasquez's neck before Layla had a chance to warn her friend. His rough grab caused Vasquez's gun to fall and clatter loudly against the cement floor. He pressed his gun against her temple and moved behind her, putting Vasquez between himself and Layla. Layla stifled a cry of panic and forced herself to think clearly and analyze the situation.

"Get up," he commanded. Layla secreted the knife into the palm of her hand before she slowly rose from her kneeling position over the wounded man. The gunman briefly took his weapon away from Vasquez's head, and he pointed it at Layla, waving her over to them. "Over here." Layla took a stuttering baby step towards Vasquez and her captor.

"What's the plan here?" she asked. "You shoot her, I kill you. You shoot me, I'm fairly sure she's crazy enough to try to take you out."

"Damn straight," Vasquez growled. While Layla's heart beat in unadulterated terror, an intense rage clouded Vasquez's emerald eyes.

"She could try," he conceded. "But before I kill anyone, I want to know who the hell you people are. Why are you here and where is Lopez?"

"Chíngate pendejo," Vasquez spat contemptuously. Layla admired her friend's ability to remain a firecracker even with a gun to her head.

"What the hell did you just say?" he demanded. Layla blinked in surprise at the stranger's lack of understanding of basic Spanish vulgarity. Suddenly, an idea struck her.

"Mira, no nos entiende," she told Vasquez, pointing out the fact that the man could not understand Spanish. This obvious statement received an exasperated look from Vasquez.

"Yo sé," Vasquez replied.

"Voltea un poco la cabeza a la izquierda," Layla ordered. Vasquez's eyebrows creased in confusion at the odd command.

"What the hell is going on? What are you two talking about? Speak English!" the gunman ordered.

"¿Por qué?" Vasquez wondered, questioning the reason for Layla's instructions.

"Confía en mí," Layla implored, begging Vasquez to trust her. Vasquez swallowed, turning her head to the left as Layla instructed. Layla took a deep calming breath adding, "No mires." She did not want Vasquez to see what she was about to do.

"Someone better hit the SAP button right fucking now," he ordered with obvious irritation. Layla turned her attention to the situation, and she ran a mental calculation. She allowed the knife to slide down her hand, and she tightened her grip on the handle. In a swift motion, she threw the blade, hitting her mark — the man's right eye. He screamed, dropped his gun, and released Vasquez, who pushed away from him and turned to inspect the carnage. The gunman dropped to one knee, and he put both hands around the knife, as if he was unsure whether he should pull the blade out or push it all the way in to end the agony. Vasquez's eyes bulged at the sight.

"¿Estás loca? ¡Casi me matas!" she exclaimed in horror.

"I'm not crazy, and I didn't even get close to you," Layla replied dismissively. She approached him and kicked his fallen weapon away. Crouching in front of him, she examined the wound. After she determined that the injury was not immediately fatal, she asked, "Who are you people working for?"

"Fuck you lady!" he screamed. His body was trembling from the pain, and his left eye welled up with tears.

"That's not nice," Layla sang. "Besides, you're not my type. Now, who are you working for?" The man turned and spit in the direction of her voice, missing her face by six inches.

"I don't think he's going to talk," Vasquez said from behind her. Layla stood with a shrug. She turned and inspected the garage before walking over to the Hummer. She opened the driver's side door and pressed the button to open all of the doors. Circling to the trunk, she searched the area.

"Ah!" Layla exclaimed triumphantly. She returned to the suffering man with a pair of jumper cables.

"What are those for?" Vasquez inquired.

"Well, if this guy doesn't die, he still has one good eye," Layla replied, nodding at the man. His screams had died down into mournful whimpering, and his hands remained wrapped around the handle of the knife. Layla kicked him over and grabbed his hands. She glanced at Vasquez, motioned to his legs and said, "Help me out here." After a few moments, the two women had him hogged tied. Layla leaned over him again.

"Still nothing?" she asked. He let out a few colorful curse words. Layla glanced at Vasquez then back to the man on the ground and shrugged. "It was worth a shot. I wouldn't turn your head too much if I were you, you may push it all the way in; unless you want to, that looks like it hurts." She pointed to the exit of the garage, and the women left the sniveling man on the floor.

"You can't leave me here!" he mewed. Layla paused halfway to the door and spun on the man.

"You feel like having a conversation?"

"You bitch!"

"Didn't think so," she huffed. Vasquez followed her to the door. Just as the women breached the entrance to the kitchen, five rapid shots rang out from deep within the house. Layla threw a worried look at Vasquez and whispered, "Lewis."

The duo burst into the kitchen; Vasquez's gun at the ready and Layla slipped a knife from her sheath. She patted her waist and realized it was her last one. Noticing her predicament, Vasquez stepped in front of her, and they quickly moved through the kitchen down the hallway. As they approached the door of the first bedroom, a man emerged holding his shoulder. Vasquez trained her gun on him and almost fired until he turned to the sound of their footsteps. Lewis' turquoise eyes scowled at the sight of Vasquez's gun in his face. Moving his left hand from his right shoulder, he gently pushed the woman's arm down to the ground.

"Careful with that, kid; you'll hurt someone," he grumbled. Vasquez let out a sigh of relief and threw her arms around him drawing a groan of pain, "Ow!"

"Oscar! I'm so glad you're alive," she exclaimed. Her relief turned into alarm when she saw the blood on his hand as he grasped his shoulder again. "What happened to you?"

"One of the bastards got a shot off on me before I could get him. I'll be okay. What about the other two?"

"They're alive, but I'm not sure how long they'll last," Layla said. "One may bleed out from the bullet wound in his chest, and the other, well, let's just say he's gonna need an eye patch if he survives." Lewis' eyes darted to Vasquez who shrugged her shoulders nonchalantly.

"To be fair, he had a gun to my head."

"When this is over, I need to hear the whole story over a scotch — or four," he wheezed. He studied the dark hallway behind the two women. "Where's Ryan?"

Ryan stared at the tall, bulky man and immediately recognized him from the parking lot outside of Layla's apartment. In a moment of déjà vu, the big man was holding a gun on him. Tall, dark skinned with a close-cropped fade, the man looked like he could be related to Big Luke. He considered reaching into the holster strapped around his waist for his own weapon, but he knew as soon as he made a move for the pistol, this man would blow him away.

"Long time no see!" Ryan smiled in a good-natured manner. "I see you found your keys."

"That was a fucked-up trick, homeboy," the man scowled.

"Hey man, you put a gun to the back of my head. You know I couldn't just let that slide," Ryan replied. The big man leveled his gun at Ryan's face.

"Well, how about now?"

"Do you really wanna be the guy who kills an unarmed man?" Ryan asked.

"You aren't unarmed," he noted, nodding his head to Ryan's waist.

"I don't have my side-arm out," Ryan countered. "That's as good as being unarmed." The big man blinked in surprise.

"Sidearm, huh? You Army?"

"Until recently," Ryan nodded. The gunman grinned and slipped his pistol into the small of his back.

"Well, I would not disrespect a fellow soldier. Let's do this like men," he decreed. Ryan looked at the guy for a beat before moving his right foot in front of his left and putting his hands up in a boxing stance. The man's smile brightened. "Southpaw? Oh, this will be fun." He positioned himself into an orthodox boxing stance and began to advance. Ryan watched him move and noticed that while he was larger, his movements were graceful. The stranger jabbed with his right hand, and Ryan easily dodged the initial strike, immediately countering with a left jab of his own. His punch connected with the man's jaw, but the blow did not seem to faze his combatant who swung on Ryan with a powerful hook connecting with the side of Ryan's head. The strike dazed him, and he blinked rapidly in an attempt to focus his eyes. The one punched notified Ryan that he would not be able to compete with the man in power. He was going to have to use his speed and a variety of sparring techniques, not just boxing. The big man immediately tried to land an uppercut to the dazed Ryan's chin, but he dodged the strike and kicked the back of the man's knee, causing him to lose his footing. With the larger man off balance, Ryan threw an elbow to his chin. This blow seemed to have some effect, and the big man spit out a glob of blood before rising to his feet with a bloodstained grin.

"I see how this is going to be," he smirked. "We freestyling now? Alright then." He rushed at Ryan with an impossible amount of speed for a man his size. Wrapping his arms around Ryan's waist, he drove him into a tree. Ryan felt his breath abandon his body when his back crashed into the solid stump. Immediately, the man delivered a massive amount of quick, rock-like punches to Ryan's ribs and kidneys. Each blow felt like a bag of bricks was being used on his intestines, and Ryan realized he was on the verge of passing out from lack of air and pain. This was the opposite of how he wanted this fight to transpire.

In desperation, he reared his head back and head-butted the man in the chin. This stopped the barrage of punches long enough for Ryan to draw back again and land a harder head-butt. He heard a crack, and knew that the strike broke the assailant's nose. The dazed attacker staggered back with blood flowing freely from his broken snout. Ryan fought to collect some of the oxygen driven from him, but he knew he did not have time to fully catch his breath. Before the combatant could regain his wits, Ryan took a step forward and kicked him in his crotch with as much force as he could muster in his winded state. The large man hissed in pain and moved his hands from his bloody face to his loins as he fell to his knees. Knowing he could not give him any time to recover, Ryan delivered two swift kicks to his ribs before landing a haymaker to the side of his head, knocking him into the dirt. He took a few staggered steps away from the fallen man and dropped to his knees, gasping for air. He gingerly felt his side and winced in pain. Breathing through the agony, he continued his self-inspection and found he had at least two cracked ribs.

He attempted to get to his feet, and faltered once again, struggling to inhale. When he heard running footsteps approaching his area, he tried to wrestle his pistol from the holster. Panic gripped his already rapidly beating heart as the steps neared. The pain and lack of breath made the simple job of withdrawing his weapon nearly impossible. He freed his gun just as Layla burst through the trees into the small clearing. Ryan almost cried out in relief. His joy turned into bewilderment when he watched her pull a knife and throw it at him. He flinched, expecting to feel the pain of the dagger, but the blade sailed just past his head. He turned to find the man standing behind him with his gun in hand, and the knife protruding from his chest. Ryan watched as the gunman turned his weapon on Layla. Fear poured adrenaline into his body, and he lunged himself at the shooter just as the weapon fired. The impact of his body caused the pistol to sail out of the gunman's hand as Ryan landed on top of him. He favored the man with an intense glower, and he put his hand on the knife in his chest.

"The name is Jenkins. Sergeant Ryan Jenkins," he hissed menacingly. He used the little strength he had left to push the knife deeper into the man before twisting it violently. The big man jerked, and Ryan watched the light of life extinguish. He rolled off of the dead fellow and lay on the ground, gasping for air. When he realized he had not heard anything more from Layla, he sat up quickly and looked over to where the woman had emerged into the clearing. His heart stopped when he saw her lying on the ground. "Layla!" he called.

Finding a reserve of energy, he scrambled to his feet and raced over to the woman. He knelt down, and terror enveloped his mind when he found her motionless. His vision blurred with tears. Layla had taken a bullet trying to save his life. She was the one person on the team he knew the least and yet, at that moment, he wanted nothing more than to switch places with her. He covered his eyes, and his breathing turned more ragged and rough from a combination of the physical pain and guilt. He had no idea what he would tell Vasquez or Lewis. He did not even know how he would get her body back to the house. Ryan lay next to Layla, every breath he drew causing him pain.

"That hurt," Layla groaned softly. Ryan sat up so suddenly, a stab of pain and nausea washed over him, but he ignored the discomfort. He wiped his eyes and turned to look at the woman. She opened her eyes, gazed up at him, and gasped, "Hey Sarge."

"Shit girl," he wheezed. "You scared the hell out of me!" Layla groaned again and held her hand out for Ryan to help her. He stood and pulled her up.

"You don't think Dom would have let me come out here without a vest, do you?" Layla asked. She fingered the bullet hole and fished out the slug that slammed into her stomach. "I didn't realize how much it was going to hurt though."

"You saved my life," he said solemnly. Layla shrugged.

"Rachel wasn't around, so I figured I'd better do it."

When Ryan and Layla staggered into the house, they made their way to Lopez's bedroom. Lewis was sitting on the edge of the bed, his shoulder bandaged by Vasquez while they waited for Layla and Ryan to return. Vasquez stood against the wall, her gun lazily trained on Lopez, who was now fully conscious. When they entered, Lopez threw Layla a seething gaze. His arms were still bound together with one belt and tied to the headboard of the bed with another, the way Layla left him after she knocked him out.

"You didn't have to punch me, bitch," Lopez hissed.

"You sure you want to keep calling me a bitch?" Layla asked with irritation. "Isn't that what got your ass knocked out the first time?" Vasquez looked at Ryan and gasped.

"Are you okay? You look like hell," she said, taking a step towards him. Ryan nodded and waved her off.

"Good to see you too, Rach," he panted. "I think I may have to hire you and Layla as my personal bodyguards. You guys keep saving my life." Vasquez eyed him with worry as Layla helped him into the room and to a chair at the foot of Lopez's bed. He caught her stare and gave her a weak smile. "A couple of cracked ribs, nothing pressing at the moment."

"So, as I was saying, considering we just saved you from a strike team, I think we have earned a little information," Lewis said to Lopez. The detained man's angry glare softened, and he regarded the detective.

"They will keep coming after me, Lewis. You've only delayed the inevitable. If you don't let me disappear, they will kill me," he declared.

"Forgive us for not giving a rat's ass considering the people you've killed," Vasquez interjected. "Malik Rodgers, Vincent Lionetti, Dr. Rosalyn Guerrero, and who knows who else." Lopez turned to her and blinked in confusion.

"Wait a minute," he stammered. "I'll cop to Rodgers and Lionetti. I didn't know Guerrero was dead." Lewis turned to him and then threw a glance at Layla, before returning his scrutinizing eyes to Lopez.

"What do you mean?"

"What I said. I know of Guerrero because of the foundation, but I've never personally met her. I had nothing to do with that," he insisted. Lewis gave him an incredulous look, which drew an eye roll from Lopez. "Come on Lewis. Why would I admit that I killed two of the three, in front of all of these witnesses, and deny one? What kind of sense does that make?" Lewis peeked at Layla who offered a small shrug of agreement.

"Tell us about the foundation," Ryan commanded. His voice was strained, and when Layla looked at him, she could see the pain in his eyes. She wished he could get to a hospital, but she knew he would not leave until this was done.

"I honestly know very little about the foundation," Lopez admitted. "That's where the checks come from, but not my orders."

"Who do your orders come from?" Lewis asked.

"A dude named Tristan Rucker," he replied. "He runs a think tank in downtown. I'm not sure what they do there, and I don't believe he's the ultimate power, I think he's a puppet. You know how it is, shit rolls downhill."

"Who else in the department is on this Rucker guy's payroll?" Lewis asked. This drew a grin from Lopez.

"Man, come on," he chuckled. "If I knew that, I would have used that information as an insurance policy and disappeared instead of hoping for mercy from a goody-two-shoes like you."

"But you know they exist?" Layla asked. Lopez turned his eyes to her and gave her a brief nod.

"I have an idea or two, but nothing that I can prove."

"Tell us about the arrests of Eric Taylor, Tommy Cole, Tavion Evans and Sergio Martinez. Were all of those officers dirty? Why kill Lionetti?" Lewis asked. Lopez gave a brief shake of his head.

"They weren't dirty; they were rookies," he said. "I stepped in on a few of their early rides. They had no idea what was going on at the time. Jackson, Wilson and Stevens, started asking questions when I demanded to be left off of the arrest reports, so the foundation paid them to relocate. Lionetti was newer; it was his first night. I thought he could be of use and that would be it. When I realized you were going to talk to him, that you had focused on those four guys specifically, I couldn't afford for you to know I was with him that night." He let out a deep sigh before he continued. "I even recommended taking you out and ending the problem. Rucker wouldn't allow it so soon after Lionetti. When he told me that, I knew he was done with me."

"So, you called me out here to give me his name as your big fish in exchange for me turning a blind eye to you," Lewis declared.

"That pretty much sums it up," Lopez shrugged.

"Judge Thomas Benjamin. Is he on the payroll?" Ryan asked.

"Look, I don't know inner workings or details," he admitted. "I get an assignment, and I take care of it, and they pay me very well to do so. That's what I know. I was asked to bring in those four guys. I was told when the three outsiders would be in Houston. Martinez was already under surveillance, so I knew where to find him the night we picked him up. As far as court goes, I don't know shit about that. I don't know anything about how the foundation is involved. I get marching orders and I march."

"Why would you do this? Why would you go against everything we do as cops?" Lewis asked. A brittle laugh emitted from Lopez.

"I started out wanting to change the world, but the world doesn't give a fuck about people like me. I'm full blown American, and I get called all sorts of shit because of my skin. You know how it is, don't you Lewis?" he sneered.

"Man, I liked you. I was playing around, just like you play with me. You know I meant nothing by it, nor do I believe that way," Lewis objected.

"Doesn't matter. The fact is, I don't get paid enough to risk my life for and with people who treat me like shit. It's not worth it. I grew up broke." Lopez motioned around the room with his head. "When Rucker approached me, it was the easiest decision I'd ever made."

"But you don't even know what you were helping him with. They have been trying to reduce the population growth of people like us!" Layla exclaimed. Lopez turned to her and shrugged indifferently.

"Not my problem. Were you going to pay me almost a cool million in three years? Why shouldn't I take opportunities to bring myself up?"

"And you'd kill for that? With no remorse?" Vasquez spat contemptuously.

"Without a doubt. How many people did you guys kill in there, and you aren't even getting paid to do it," Lopez countered.

"To save lives! You did it for the money," Lewis declared.

"You have your values, and I have mine," Lopez proclaimed.

"Mr. Jenkins," SARA spoke in Ryan's ear.

"What's up?" he asked. His eyes informed his team that he was speaking to the machine and they fell quiet and watched him with expectation.

"We know who killed Dr. Guerrero," the machine reported.

"Who is he talking to?" Lopez asked, eyeing the group in the room. The crowd ignored his question and continued to stare at Ryan. "Oh, don't mind me," he muttered, when he received no response.

"You said you had an idea or two of who else could be on this payroll. Was a Jim Haggard on that list?" Ryan asked, eyeing the man on the bed. The air in the room fell still at this question. Lewis' mouth dropped open at the name of his Captain.

"Go on Lopez, tell them. Was I?" A new voice said from the doorway. The group jumped at the sound and turned to the door to see Captain Jim Haggard standing there with his gun drawn. He moved the weapon in an arc around the room to all parties waiting for movement. As Layla patted her waist, she remembered her last knife, buried in the chest of the big man in the forest. Lewis' gun arm was bandaged, and he was unable to draw on the man. Ryan, still severely injured, could not move due to his injuries, and Vasquez had her gun pointed to the ground. No one tried to draw on a man who already had his weapon trained on them.

"Captain," Lewis said stiffly.

"Didn't expect to find you here, Lewis." He turned to Vasquez. "Vasquez, how's that brother of yours?" When she declined to answer, Haggard turned back to Lopez.

"Why Captain?" Lewis asked.

"Sammy just told you why, didn't he? You have your values, we have ours," Haggard replied.

"You killed Dr. Guerrero," Vasquez whispered. Haggard turned to her and shrugged.

"I just heard you guys getting all up in arms about what she supposedly did. What do you care if she's dead?"

"When I said there was a cop involved…" Lewis started. Haggard chuckled.

"When you came to me with that, I knew I wasn't on your radar. You're too smart to come to someone you suspect, Lewis," he asserted. Lewis looked from Haggard to Lopez and back to Haggard. He felt like a giant fool. The two men he wanted to discount the fastest were the two men he should have been the most concerned about. Suddenly, he felt sick.

"I can't believe this shit," he muttered.

"So, Sammy. Please go on. Was I on that list?" Haggard asked.

"Mr. Jenkins, I am recording this whole event," SARA advised.

"I said I didn't know: I only had suspicions," Lopez replied nervously. "But no, Captain, I did not know you were one of them." Haggard's ice blue eyes stared at him for a moment, and then his thin lips spread into a humorless smile.

"Well in that case, I feel a little bad for this," he muttered. He fired his weapon and the shots came out like a cough due to the silencer. Lopez took a bullet to the head and the chest. Vasquez immediately raised her gun, but Haggard spun on her with his own weapon. "Come on, Miss Vasquez; let's not do this."

"You son of a bitch," Lewis growled. "How long have you been working for Tristan Rucker?"

"Who?" Haggard asked in genuine surprise. Lewis blinked at the question.

"You aren't working for Rucker?" Vasquez asked.

"I don't know who the hell you're talking about," Haggard replied.

"Then what the hell is going on here?" Lewis demanded.

"Sammy has his orders, I have mine," Haggard shrugged. "Your presence has put me in a bad position. I was called to eliminate Lopez. I don't think anyone counted on you people being here. I have one of my best detectives and my two best crime scene techs in this room, and now I have to kill all three of you." His voice resonated with genuine disappointment.

"Well, you don't *have* to," Vasquez offered in a reasonable tone. "I mean, it's not like someone is holding a gun on *you*." Haggard turned his eyes back to the woman.

"I'm really going to miss your wit," he smiled, lifting his gun to Vasquez's face. "Again, very sorry about this." Vasquez made the sign of the cross and she closed her eyes.

"I love you Layla," she whispered.

"No!" Layla screamed taking a step towards Haggard from across the room. Ryan tried to stand from his sitting position, while Lewis jumped up from his spot on the bed. He leaped towards Vasquez, ready to intercept the bullet.

The sound of breaking glass pierced the space as the window on the far side of the room shattered inward and Haggard was thrown against the wall. The group froze in confusion. Vasquez opened her eyes and regarded Haggard who stared at her with wide-eyed shock. Blood began to spread rapidly across his chest. The captain looked from Vasquez to Lewis, his eyes puzzled before he dropped to his knees and fell face first onto the floor. Vasquez moved to the man and checked for a pulse.

"He's dead," she informed the group.

"What the hell?" Ryan wheezed. The crowd turned to the window and spotted a bullet hole through a web of broken glass.

"Who the…" Layla stammered in disbelief. She approached the window and studied the exterior of the house, looking for movement. Lewis wrestled his gun from his holster and shifted it to his left hand. He approached the opening with his gun trained on the outside of the house. Vasquez followed him with her gun also pointed into the darkness. Moonlight illuminated a shadowy figure approaching the house with a rifle on its shoulder.

"Wait!" Vasquez called. The other three turned to her and noticed her distress turned into glee. As the darkened figure got closer to the house, a sigh of relief rippled through the room.

"If anyone is going to kill Rachel, it's definitely going to be me," Dom announced.

CHAPTER FORTY-FOUR

After the carnage at Lopez's home in Pearland, Lewis ushered the group away from the residence before calling in the uniformed cavalry. The detective did not want to have to explain their presence and Ryan was looking worse by the minute. His attempt to garner enough strength to stop Haggard depleted the fumes of energy he had left. After learning Dom was the person who saved their lives, Ryan promptly collapsed from the pain. His breathing was severely strenuous and with every other inhale, he launched into a fit of ragged coughing causing further agony. Vasquez wanted to call 911 and get an ambulance to the house, but Ryan, Lewis, and Dom all nixed the plan. Dom sprinted to her Mustang and drove back to the house where Layla and Lewis assisted in getting Ryan into the car. Layla and Vasquez jumped in the back and the trio raced him to the nearest hospital. On the drive, Layla called Rose and Robert to inform them of the fate of their brother. The two Jenkins siblings arrived at the hospital five minutes after Ryan. Since Layla, Vasquez, and Dom were not immediate family members, the threesome departed once an ER nurse led Rose and Robert to their brother's bedside.

"How's Ryan?" Lewis asked. Layla, Vasquez, Lewis, and Dom sat around the conference room table sipping on piping hot coffee. Dom cautioned the detective that he may not be out of the woods yet and suggested he come back to the warehouse after he left the scene in Pearland.

"He has a couple of broken ribs and his left lung collapsed," Dom reported. "Rose says he's stable. He'll probably be released tonight or tomorrow. Can't let him get into any more gunfights for a few days at least." She let out an exaggerated yawn before she asked, "Is everything okay with the situation at Lopez's?"

"It was touchy. We have a dead homicide cop and Captain. Your recordings will help show that they were dirty. Only time will tell I suppose," he shrugged.

"SARA may have modified them a little," Dom confessed. "You know, to take out some of the things that didn't need to be heard."

"We really need to establish what you should and should not tell me," he frowned.

"Sorry," Dom muttered.

"Lewis, you know it's for the best," Layla said.

"We found both Lionetti's service weapon and a .38 gun in Lopez's house. Ballistics will probably tell us that it's the weapon used to kill Rodgers and Lionetti. Haggard's gun was a .38 as well. I'm willing to bet it'll match up to the bullet from the doctor," Lewis continued. "I also found this." He produced a large manila envelope and pushed it across the table to Dom. "I think this is what he wanted to give me in exchange for his freedom." Dom opened the envelope and dumped the contents onto the table. The package contained pages of text message and email instructions for Lopez's exploits. A photo was also in the envelope. Dom picked up the snapshot of a middle age White man with stark white hair.

"Who's this?" she asked holding up the photo.

"I don't know," Lewis shrugged. "Maybe the Rucker guy?"

"Could be," she nodded thoughtfully. "I'll check him out."

"How did you find out about Haggard?" Lewis wondered.

"SARA got the ballistics back on Dr. Guerrero and matched them up with Malik's bullet. Same caliber, but a different gun. I started thinking about the cameras around the city. There was a traffic light nearby that picked up the shooter driving into the clinic shortly before the murder and not leaving until afterward. Didn't get his face, but we were able to trace the car and got a clear shot of him on another camera. I'll put together a video packet for you."

"How did you know he would be at the house?" Vasquez asked.

"When I found out who he was, SARA ran his cell phone and I saw he was heading your direction. I hopped in the Mustang and raced over there when I realized what was happening.

"Thankfully Clear Lake is closer to Pearland than Houston. I almost didn't make it," Dom said.

"The weird thing is, he said he wasn't working for this Tristan Rucker guy," Vasquez noted.

"He didn't even seem to know who that was," Layla added.

"And Lopez said he thought Rucker was just a puppet, like him," Vasquez continued. "Maybe whoever Haggard was working for was higher up the food chain than Rucker?"

"SARA didn't find any payments from the foundation to Haggard. He was searched like everyone else," Dom advised. "We're missing something here."

"Lopez didn't know anything about Judge Benjamin either," Layla pointed out. "This is much bigger than buying off a few cops as contract killers. Rucker may be the key."

"Next step is for me to dig up all I can about Tristan Rucker. Did Lopez give you the name of the think tank?" Dom asked. The other three at the table shook their heads.

"Nothing. I think Lopez was trying to figure out who he was really working for. That looks like an insurance policy to me," Lewis said, pointing to the envelope in front of Dom.

"You will have your hands full with this Lopez and Haggard situation. Technically, your case is closed. Give me a day to do some research on this Tristan Rucker guy; then we can figure out our next move," she suggested. Lewis nodded in agreement. Dom fished a credit card out of her pocket and slid it across the table to Lewis. "Take this. I booked you a room at the Magnolia hotel. It's paid for, but the card is for you to get some clothes and things you need for a few days. Keep the burner on you; I'll reach out when I get some info." Lewis stared at the card for a beat before he accepted the offering.

"Thank you, Dom."

"Check on your wife and daughter. If they need anything, let me know and I'll make sure they get it," she added. Lewis nodded appreciatively again. He stood with a deep yawn.

"I'm going to get some sleep," he said. After giving both Layla and Vasquez a hug, he exited the room.

"I'm going to set up some searches for SARA to run and then I think we could all use some rest ourselves," Dom said to the two remaining women. She stood and headed for the office, entering the chamber when SARA opened the door. She paused in the middle of the room rubbing her tired eyes before venturing to the computer, unaware that Vasquez slipped inside just before the door slid closed.

"I almost died," Vasquez said in a soft voice. "And you saved me." Dom jumped at the sound of the unannounced visitor. She spun around to face a red-eyed Vasquez standing an arm's length away.

"You'd have done the same for me," she replied. "Hell, you did do the same for Ryan." Vasquez took a step in her direction and the subtle movement sent Dom's heart racing. However, this was not the flirtatious Vasquez. Her emerald irises watered with emotion. The sentiment on her face acted as a magnet and Dom closed the gap further by taking a step forward to reassure her. "Hey, it's okay. You didn't die."

"I saw it in his eyes," Vasquez whispered in a haunted voice. "He was going to kill me."

"I told you, I would never let anything happen to you, Rachel," Dom reminded her. Vasquez mutely stared at her for an uncomfortable moment. Since Vasquez and Layla called her out about not making eye contact, Dom tried to force herself to look her new friends in the eye. Now, staring into the unfiltered gaze filled with both veneration and gratitude, Dom did not think she could hold her regard much longer. Before she reverted to her habit of studying office furniture, Vasquez closed the distance and kissed her. Like before, it was unexpected and Dom did not resist. In a change from the prior embrace, she wrapped her arms around Vasquez's waist and returned the kiss. Vasquez was trembling, but there was more passion from her than the first time. After a few long seconds, Dom pulled away. Her breath threatened to abandon its post in her lungs once again and she trapped the runaway air in her throat. Taking a step back, she tried to calm her racing pulse without being obvious.

"I'm sorry," Vasquez blushed. Dom frowned when she realized tears were flowing down Vasquez's cheeks and she reached up and wiped the tears away with her thumb.

"Don't be," she insisted. "Rach, you are an absolutely beautiful woman. The fact that you hold any attraction to me is both perplexing and flattering. But I just don't think I'm ready for, you know, anything right now. I'm still getting used to being around people." As she spoke, Dom's eyes found the floor in front of her. She took a deep breath and lifted her face to meet Vasquez's gaze. "Believe me, it's not that I don't want you. I think you know that's not it. I am attracted, please believe me. I just, I need time." Vasquez nodded as she wiped her eyes.

"I understand that."

"I'm not saying no," Dom told her. "I'm saying, not yet. When I shake off my demons, you'll be the first to know." There was a subtle hunger in her tone and eyes.

"I'm going to hold you to that," Vasquez grinned. Her mirth was short-lived and she became somber once again. "I just wanted to say thank you. I know I come off as kind of ditzy or like nothing matters to me. People think that I don't take anything seriously. I try not to let my insecurities or fears show."

"I can understand that," Dom nodded.

"But when I was looking down the barrel of that gun and saw the look in Haggard's eyes…" She paused, took a deep breath, and swallowed the lump forming in her throat. "Dom, I have never been more scared in my life."

"I know the feeling," Dom replied, her eyes meeting the floor in front of Vasquez's feet. "I don't know what I would have done if something happened to you, Rachel."

"Well, thank you for saving my life Dominique Samuels. I owe you," Vasquez proclaimed with a smile in an attempt to lighten the mood. Dom lifted her gaze to the woman.

"Any time, Rachel Vasquez," she smirked. She opened her arms and took a step forward, wrapping Vasquez in a hug. Before she released her, she kissed Vasquez on the cheek. "As long as I'm around, I'll do everything in my power to protect you and Layla." Vasquez stared into her eyes for a moment before she leaned in, claiming Dom's lips in another passionate kiss. Dom did not let this smooch last nearly as long as before. She broke away and took a step back.

"Sorry, I couldn't help it. You're just so…" Vasquez murmured.

"Ok, you go now," Dom chuckled, pushing Vasquez in the direction of the door. "Let me get SARA set up and we will get some rest. I think the lack of sleep is getting to you." Vasquez smiled sweetly.

"I wish you saw yourself how we see you," she said. Dom shook her head.

"If I saw myself the way you saw me, I'd probably have an ego bigger than this room."

"I know you would," Vasquez grinned. She pinched Dom's cheek and exited the room.

Layla sat on the floor of her temporary lodging in Dom's spare room playing a relaxing throwback puzzle game. While she generally preferred diversions of the action and adventure genre, the previous night's events made games with gunfire lose their allure. A soft knock drew her attention and she paused the game.

"Come in," she called. The door cracked open and Vasquez's smiling face appeared. Layla grinned and motioned for the woman to enter with her head before resuming her play. Vasquez bounded into the room, plopped down next to her, and leaned against the bed.

"Pretty crazy out there earlier, huh?" she asked, as she watched Layla expertly maneuver the controller.

"That's an understatement."

"I thought Haggard was going to blow my head off," Vasquez admitted in a soft voice. Layla paused the game and faced her friend.

"I was terrified he would too," she confessed. "And you wanted your last words to be that you loved me."

"I know you're not as affectionate and emotional as I am," Vasquez shrugged. "I wanted to make sure that if something happened to me, you knew you were loved." Her tone was bright, despite the gravity of her words. Layla turned away from her in an attempt to keep her emotions in check.

"I know you love me, Rach," she confirmed. "I know I'm not easy to get close to, but you know you're my sister, right?" Layla asked, looking at the floor.

"Of course, I know that. I just wasn't sure *you* knew it."
Layla looked up into Vasquez's eyes.

"And you know that…" She hesitated, turned away from
Vasquez, and swallowed. "You know that I love you too, right?" She
paused, shocked by her own words. "I've never been good at… at
telling people how I feel. I don't think I've ever actually said those
words to anyone. You're the first."

"And?" Vasquez prodded. Layla frowned and favored her
with a look of confusion.

"And what?"

"Did you die? Have some sort of aneurysm?"

"No, I'm still kicking," Layla chuckled.

"You are the strongest person I know, Layla. I can't imagine
what all you've gone through, but based on what I envision, I'd say
you're pretty well adjusted. Maybe stop being so afraid to let people
know how you feel about them," Vasquez suggested. "I know I
come on strong to most people. It's because I always want others to
know where they stand with me. If anything were to happen to me,
I'd never want to leave someone I care about wondering how I felt.
I can't live like that. I know that may be just my thing but that's
how my parents were. Maybe I cling to the things they taught me
because if I don't, I'll feel like I'm letting them go."

"You'll never let them go, Rach. I wouldn't let you," Layla
said. Vasquez smiled at her.

"I hope not. If I ever step out of line, I expect you to
remind me."

"You got it." Layla nodded.

"Anyway, you're not an idiot. I know you knew I loved
you. But everyone deserves to hear it at least once in their life;
it's important," Vasquez asserted. Layla resumed her game and
continued manipulating the pieces on the screen.

"I'll try to be better about being a closed book. It's hard,
but you of all people deserve it."

"I'm glad to hear that. Now spill," Vasquez commanded.
Layla paused the game and gave her friend a mystified look.

"Spill what?"

"Don't play dumb," Vasquez scowled. "The knives. What
the hell is that about?" Her tone was serious and informed Layla

that there would be no sidestepping this conversation. Layla sighed, placed her controller on the floor, and leaned back against the bed next to Vasquez.

"It's complicated."

"I've tried not to pry into things you don't want to discuss, Layla. But ninja throwing knife skills? Yeah, I'm going to need to pry into that a little."

"I told you about Nadine," Layla began. Vasquez nodded.

"Your sort of sister."

"Yes. I mentioned that I met her on the streets when I ran away from my last foster home," she continued.

"Right, she was a prostitute," Vasquez nodded.
Layla blinked.

"I never told you that part."

"Why does my happy-go-lucky nature make people think I'm an idiot?" Vasquez grimaced. "Meeting her on the streets of New Orleans, what else would she be?"

"Okay, I suppose when you put it all together it's easy to figure out," Layla shrugged. "Anyway, Nadine was an addict as well as a prostitute. She was kind of a mess in all the ways I wasn't and was put together in all the ways I needed. She's a good person, has a good heart and we had a lot in common. Like me, she was raised with no parents. When she took me in, I worked with her to try to help her kick the habit. The problem was her pimp who also happened to be her dealer, Antonio." Vasquez stared at the woman enthralled in the story.

"You were a kid," she pointed out in awe.

"I know. We both were," Layla nodded. "Once she was ready to be free of Antonio, Nadine got a gun from a junkie in exchange for, well you know, services. She didn't know about my issue with guns at the time. I wouldn't touch it. I took some money I saved from odd jobs, we went to a pawn shop and I pointed out some throwing knives. Nadine bought them for me. Every day for weeks, I practiced. Once I was able to figure out the technique, it came pretty easy. I have always been good at math; geometry, trigonometry, stuff like that. That's really all it was, throwing technique and math. After I perfected my skill, knives became my way of defending Nadine and myself." Vasquez sat quietly, processing the story.

"What happened with Antonio? Did you kill him?" she asked. Layla's head snapped up and she met Vasquez's eyes with shock.

"No! Of course not. I had never killed anyone before today."

"So obviously, you got rid of Antonio," Vasquez noted. "What happened?" Layla dropped her eyes.

"He came over one night demanding more than his share of the money. He didn't care that Nadine wasn't alone anymore, that she was taking care of a kid. He started to get rough with her. I heard him yelling at her and then I heard a slap." Layla frowned at the memory. "I grabbed my knives and ran into the living room to find him pushing her around. I threw the first knife and nicked his ear just before he landed a punch to Nadine's face. That stopped him. I told him if he didn't leave, I would castrate him." Layla's mouth spread into a thin smile as she glanced at Vasquez. "I guess he didn't believe me."

"You didn't!" Vasquez gasped. Layla chuckled.

"The next one went into his left testicle," she confirmed. "I told him I would take out the right one if he came back. He stayed gone for a few weeks and then tried again. Let's just say little Antonio is probably no longer functional." Vasquez stared at her friend in shock.

"Dios mío," she whispered.

"He was the first of many," Layla shrugged. "I've had to use them with aggressive clients, junkies, dealers; pretty much anyone who tried to make trouble for Nadine. I usually aimed to scare and it worked more times than not. Sometimes I had to hurt someone, but never serious. Like I said, I didn't have to get deadly until Lopez's house."

"How are you doing with that?" Vasquez asked.

"I'm okay, Rach. If I have to make the decision between me and mine and someone else, I'll always choose me and mine. I know that day in the truck with Tanisha, I seemed like I couldn't make that choice. I just can't do it with a gun," Layla said.

"At the risk of wearing out my welcome and this little bonding time, what is it with you and guns?" Vasquez asked. Layla sighed and swallowed the lump in her throat brought on by the memory of her childhood.

"It happened when I was nine," she began.

The Jenkins siblings entered the warehouse the next afternoon. Ryan, assisted by Robert, looked weak and still favored his left side when he walked; but he definitely appeared to be better than when he left Lopez's house. Robert's eyes were bloodshot and Rose was obviously exhausted. Dom stood when the siblings entered and greeted Ryan with a handshake before turning and patting Robert on the back. She looked at Rose and motioned for her to follow her into the panic room. Rose shadowed her, waving at Layla and Vasquez as she passed them. When the door closed behind the two women, Dom turned to face the counselor ready to apologize and expecting to receive a barrage of angry words. She was surprised when Rose stepped to her and gave her a hug. She accepted the embrace and moved back, gawking at Rose in confusion.

"That's not how I thought this would start out," she admitted. Rose wiped tears away and smiled.

"Ryan made his decision to lead this thing. I just thank you for making sure he went in with some protection. I know Haggard would have killed him along with everyone else if you hadn't arrived. Thank you for saving my brother," she said with heavy emotion. Dom sat in her office chair and motioned for Rose to take a seat.

"I'm just glad I got out there in time. It was a race," she confessed. "What did the doctors say?"

"They inflated his lung. It wasn't severe, but he'll be out of commission for another week or two," Rose replied. "His ribs are weak and he's tired. The bigger problem is our mother. She's got a lot of questions, and we won't be able to fend her off for long. She wants to meet you."

"Me? Why?"

"All she knows is that her sons are working for a mysterious tech company. Somehow that position turned into Ryan bringing a stranger into her house in the middle of the night. She had questions about that alone, but she understands that Tanisha is in danger so she let it slide. But now he nearly gets himself killed. Keep in mind, she's already lost two sons." Rose made a pained face when she mentioned her deceased brothers. "Rob, Ryan, and I have tried to tell her everything is okay, but she believes it all comes down to you. We bought some time for now." Rose leaned forward and touched Dom's arm, forcing the hacker to make eye contact. "I need you to do this. I need you to let my mother know that her children are safe in your hands. I need you to give my mother what you would give yours if she were still alive." Dom stared into Rose's golden gaze before she allowed her eyes to fall back to the desk. She understood the counselor's point and realized that Joyce Jenkins had to feel lost and afraid for her children.

"Alright. When this is over, I'll meet with her," Dom nodded.

"Thank you, Dom. I appreciate this and I know the boys will too."

"We got a lot to cover today; shall we?" Dom went to stand but Rose held her hand up to stop her.

"Wait. I need to know something."

"What's that?" Dom asked, falling back into her seat.

"How are you doing?" Dom blinked at the question.

"Uh, I can't complain?" she asked with mild confusion. Rose scowled and shook her head.

"Killing someone isn't easy, Dom. You're no sociopath or psychopath. I know all about your high level of empathy," she informed her. "I've had a few conversations with SARA."

"I really need to work on her filter," Dom groused.

"I also know about your mother," Rose added. Dom stared at her in surprise.

"Didn't see that coming," she mumbled.

"Killing someone isn't easy. But for someone like you, for someone who has such a high level of empathy and traumatic experience with violence… Dom, how are you doing?" Dom looked away from Rose and felt the emotion she had been swallowing since she took the shot at Haggard begin to percolate just under the surface.

"I'm okay," she said after a few moments.

"Are you?"

"I thought you said you weren't trying to be my therapist," Dom countered.

"I'm trying to be your friend, Dom. It just so happens that this friend is a therapist as well," Rose reminded her. "I would not be a very good friend or a good therapist if I didn't address something I know has to be hard for you. I wouldn't care about you if I let you hold this in." Dom nodded and leaned back in her chair.

"I got my first gun out of college. It's one of the first things I bought for myself. I used to dream about that night with my mom. I always wished..." her voice trailed off and despite her effort to maintain her composure, she felt a fissure begin to form. "I always wished that we had a gun that night. You know? My mom, she always wanted to help people. Trust in the Lord with all your heart..."

"And lean not to your own understanding," Rose finished. Dom smiled.

"I see you were preached to as a kid too."

"Try yesterday," Rose smirked.

"She always believed the goodness of people would prevail. Even if we lived in a bad neighborhood, she wouldn't have gotten a gun. It was the first thing I got because I never wanted to be caught off-guard and unprotected again. Then suddenly one gun wasn't enough. I needed more and more, especially when I realized violence was escalating against every minority group I represent," Dom shrugged.

"Hyper-vigilance," Rose nodded. Dom frowned at her. "It's a classic symptom of someone who has gone through a traumatic event. You never want to be put in that situation again, so you over prepared to the point of having an arsenal."

"I guess that's true. But with every new weapon I procured, all the years of practice, I honestly never thought I'd have to take a life. I was prepared to protect myself, but I never thought I'd have to, you know?"

"Understandable. You're a logical person. You know that logically it's unlikely for you to be put in that position again, but it doesn't stop the emotional need of hyper-vigilance," Rose advised.

"I thought you said you weren't going to go into therapy mode."

"I'm telling you technical terms SARA could tell you about your behavior. I'm in no way trying to help you navigate it," Rose said.

"Well, I never thought I'd take a life. I couldn't imagine doing it, really. When I saw they were in danger, I hoped that maybe Lewis or Ryan could have protected the crew," Dom shrugged. "I had no idea how bad of shape Ryan was in. He put that gun to Rachel's face, and I just acted. I had to protect her..." Dom's voice trailed off again and tears sprang into her eyes.

"Because you couldn't protect your mom," Rose declared in a soft voice. Dom nodded as a tear ran down her cheek. She wiped it away quickly, and took a deep breath in an attempt to wall off her grief.

"You asked me how I'm doing? I'm okay. Because at least I got to save someone. Not my mom, but I at least got to save someone," Dom proclaimed. Rose watched her for a time, allowing her the space to collect her emotions. She stood and embraced the hacker once again.

"You saved my mom last night," Rose said. "I am forever grateful for that."

"Except now I may be stuck with Rachel for the rest of my life," she chuckled after Rose released her.

"You could do worse," Rose told her. Dom rolled her eyes.

"Oh please. We all know I am the last one to try to be in a relationship. I'm still trying to figure out how to get rid of you guys."

"You have gotten so used to being alone that you're afraid to change that. But take a look around. That ship has sailed. Like it or not, whether we wanted to or not, we're pretty much in this together for the foreseeable future. Rachel is a good woman and she really cares for you. All I'm saying is don't completely discount her," Rose shrugged. She stood and favored Dom with a smile. "I think you two would look cute together." Dom shook her head and followed Rose out of the room.

When they approached the table, the others were already seated waiting for their return. Dom fell into her chair and slid her tablet in front of her, prompting everyone else to follow suit. She looked up and made eye contact with Ryan.

"You alright?"

"I'm good," he nodded. Despite his assertion, Dom saw the pain in his eyes.

"I think you probably earned some time off after last night. You don't have to be here," she said. Ryan frowned.

"It was here or with my mother. I'll stay here, thanks. The hospital said my bill was taken care of; I suppose I have you to thank for that?" Dom shrugged.

"Well, you did almost die on my watch. It was the least I could do."

"What did SARA find?" Rose asked, picking up her tablet.

"Lopez mentioned a Tristan Rucker and said that he runs a think tank downtown. He didn't know the name of it, but having his name was good enough. He apparently used to be on staff at the White House about three administrations ago. After he left there, Synergy Concepts was born. It's formulated using several limited liability companies and entities, but we found the document tying him to the company," Dom reported.

"What is a think tank anyway?" Vasquez asked. "People get paid money to sit around and just think? Sign me up!"

"Usually think tanks give advice on political or economic policy. It looks like Synergy Concepts is definitely more of a political leaning organization. They own several websites, mostly forums for like-minded people to discuss their views. Some are fringe news sites," Dom explained. "Remember that White supremacist website? Guess who owns the domain name?"

"Well, if you're going to just lay it up there, that takes the fun out of guessing," Layla declared. Dom smiled.

"That's the only link I can find from the Synergy Concepts to anything regarding Liberty Health Services," Dom continued. "Rucker doesn't appear on the board of the foundation, but he does show as a donor to the super PAC we found."

"That's also a tie to Judge Benjamin if you think about it. If Rucker is a donor to our super PAC and also working with the foundation, then he may also be involved with the Judge," Layla pointed out. Dom tapped around on her tablet and loaded a photo of Tristan Rucker, sending it to all of the other devices. When Ryan looked over Rose's shoulder to see the photo, he audibly gasped. His dark eyes shot to Dom.

"Dom, the recording. Have you heard it yet?" Ryan urgently asked. Dom frowned.

"What recording?"

"When I planted the bug in Uncle Tom's office and his fedora, I sent you a text telling you to start the recording. Didn't you get it?" His tone became frantic. Dom's frown deepened.

"I didn't…"

"I received your communication and began the recording as instructed Mr. Jenkins," SARA announced. Dom spun to the avatar as Ryan exhaled in relief.

"And you didn't mention it because?"

"This was around the time we learned of Mr. Lopez's involvement and that took precedence. While I am capable of multitasking to a very high degree, human minds cannot. A request to begin a recording appeared to be lower in importance. You made it clear that your priority was finding your murderer," the computer rationalized.

"I can't even be mad at that," Layla shrugged.

"Okay, so we have the recording but we haven't listened to it. What has you in a tizzy?" Dom asked. Ryan reached to point at Rose's tablet and hissed in pain at the speed of his movement.

"That guy picked up Uncle Tom outside of the court-house," he revealed. Dom's confusion transformed into surprise.

"SARA, could you please bring up the recording?" Dom asked.

"Standby," SARA responded. After a few moments, the conversation from the car began to play through the speakers.

"Who was the guy in uniform?" a man asked.

"That was my nephew Ryan." Ryan glanced at Dom and nodded in the general vicinity of the speakers with his head.

"That's Uncle Tom. The first voice must be this Rucker guy," he said.

"Military man, huh? He still enlisted?" Tristan asked.

"Just retired. He was swinging by to say hi," Judge Benjamin replied. "To what do I owe this surprise visit?" A horn blared in the background and the group heard the clicking of what sounded like a signal indicator.

"We believe the Department of Justice is looking into you," Tristan announced.

"What? Why?" Judge Benjamin questioned with panic in his voice.

"We don't fully know. We haven't found any information on the investigation, but there have been some hiccups that tipped the DOJ's hand," Tristan replied.

"What do you mean, hiccups?" the Judge inquired.

"There was an agent asking a bunch of questions in multiple prisons, mainly inmates that you sentenced. Most of those guys were legitimate, but he also spoke with the four special cases," Tristan said. There was a sigh-like groan from the Judge in response.

"You guys swore that would not come back to bite me."

"It shouldn't have. I don't think those four were the catalyst for the investigation, I believe they were the byproduct," Tristan advised. "Either way, all of that has been taken care of and nothing can be proven. If anything, they may try to slap excessive sentencing on you, but every other sentence was legit. The four special cases were also documented felons, so I don't think you have anything to worry about."

"You're saying we're good now? I'm in a middle of a fucking re-election, Rucker. This is the last thing I need."

"Don't you think we know that? Why do you think I haven't said anything until now? There was no reason to stress you out. I'm only telling you now, because I believe all avenues of investigation are cut off. We're trying to make sure that nothing comes back on you. We can't afford to lose you," Tristan offered in a placating tone.

"What the hell did you people have me do? What was so special about those four guys?"

"The less you know the better," Tristan replied. Ryan, Rose, and Robert eyed each other upon hearing this comment.

"I'm not so sure that's true," the Judge growled. "You aren't the subject of an apparent DOJ investigation, are you? I'd really like to know what I put my career on the line for."

"It has been taken care of Thomas," Tristan insisted. "I told you we'd take care of you, and we did. They may have questions about those four, but there is nothing that can be proven. The less you know about them, the better."

"So, I just ignore the fact that you asked me to throw the book at them as a favor to your friends?" the Judge asked sarcastically.

"Sure, you can tell Justice that if you want. Problem is, you have no proof," Tristan said. "As it stands now, this is a mild nuisance. If you decide you want to single out four dead felons and accuse me or anyone else of trying to bribe you or buy you off, how would that look for your re-election prospects?" Judge Benjamin was quiet for a moment.

"This is my life Rucker. I do a lot of good for this state," he said after a while.

"And that's why a lot of money backs you every election. Let's not ruin a good thing. Oh look, here's your stop."

"Keep me updated," Judge Benjamin said. The car door opened and sounds of the downtown Houston traffic filled the speakers.

"SARA, stop the recording," Dom called. The room grew quiet.

"So, he's dirty, but not as dirty as we feared," Rose said softly. All eyes moved to her as she spoke.

"Who is we?" Vasquez asked.

"What do you mean?" Dom frowned.

"This Rucker guy, he kept saying, we. Haggard didn't even know who Tristan Rucker was. Who is we?" Vasquez clarified.

"That's a good question," Ryan nodded. "I think we need another little chat with good old Uncle Tom."

Thomas Benjamin lived in an older upper-class neighborhood of Glen Cove, just northwest of Dom's River Oaks abode. Ryan, Rose, and Robert pulled into the driveway and exited the Impala together. They stood by the car and looked up at the forty-two hundred square foot, two-story stucco home. Rose took a deep breath and eyed her brothers.

"You guys okay?" She asked. Robert stared at the house glumly.

"The one time you let me go somewhere, it's this hell-hole," he mumbled. Ryan put his arm around his little brother.

"Dude, no matter what he says, you are not a junkie. You aren't worthless, and you make us proud," Ryan told him. Robert nodded his head.

"I have a master's degree and Ryan is a veteran. He won't look at us with any more favor," Rose disclosed. Robert laughed bitterly.

"Come on, Rosie. You know you're full of shit," he sighed. Rose punched him in the arm. Robert flinched and rubbed the area with a smile. "Sorry."

"Let's get this over with," she suggested, pulling her brothers behind her as she made her way down the walkway. It was a little after eight at night and SARA confirmed the judge was home. Rose rang the bell. The entryway swung open and a tall, thin White woman blinked at the siblings.

"Can I help you?" she asked. Her hair was light blonde and her eyes were crystal blue. She looked to be in her late forties, but the siblings knew that it was due to the plethora of plastic surgery she had over the years.

"Hi Aunt Kensie," Rose nodded, forcing a smile. Kensie Benjamin looked at the three and tilted her head.

"You are?" she asked in obvious confusion.

"It's us, Aunt Kensie. Rose, Robert and Ryan. Joyce's kids," Rose announced. Slow recognition began to creep into Kensie's eyes as if an elf found the dimmer switch in her limbic system.

"Oh yes! Of course!" she replied. "Thomas did not tell me he was expecting company this evening."

"It's a surprise visit. We were hoping we could talk to him," Ryan said. Kensie stood at the door for an additional beat before backing away and allowing the siblings to enter.

"He's in his office reviewing a few briefs. Do you remember where the library is?" Kensie asked. All three Jenkinses nodded their heads in response. "Why don't you head that way, I'll let him know you're here." Kensie walked to the right towards the Judge's office and the siblings broke off to the left towards the library.

"Out of the frying pan and into the fryer," Robert muttered.

CHAPTER FORTY-FIVE

Judge Benjamin entered the room with a scowl on his face. He eyed his niece and two nephews suspiciously. He wordlessly settled himself onto one of the plush lounge chairs across from the siblings, who were seated on a large sofa in the middle of the room.

"Well, all three of Joyce's brood at one time. Is she dead?" the Judge asked with no emotion. Rose bit back an annoyed response.

"No, Uncle Tom. Mom is fine. She sends her love," she replied. Judge Benjamin rolled his eyes.

"We all know that's bullshit," he grumbled. He glanced at Robert and scrutinized his appearance. "You look different, Junkie. You clean?"

"Yes," Robert mumbled, without looking at the man. He began to fidget with his clothes and Rose noticed the tremor was back in his hands.

"Won't last long," the Judge huffed. Ryan's hands tensed into a fist. Rose noticed and placed her hand delicately on top of his.

"Rob will be fine, Uncle Tom," she said tersely. "I'm glad to see you still have his well-being in the forefront of your mind."

"What are you three doing here?" Judge Benjamin sighed. "I hope you aren't asking for money."

"We don't need your money. We all have jobs," Ryan proclaimed. The judge's eyebrows rose in surprise at this comment.

"Even the junkie?" Rose felt a warmth of anger flow to her face.

"Robert is not a junkie," she said coolly. "And yes, Rob and Ryan are working at the same place."

"So, what do you three want?"

"Sergio Martinez," Robert said, looking at his uncle for the first time. The Judge flinched when he heard the name and Rose immediately noticed the recognition in his eyes. He cleared his throat nervously.

"Who is that?"

"An innocent man you sent to prison," Ryan accused. Judge Benjamin frowned.

"I'm certain that if I sent him to prison, he was not innocent," he claimed indignantly.

"Oh, he was innocent this time. And sending him to prison got him killed," Rose informed him.

"Whatever happened to him in prison had nothing to do with me," he frowned. Ryan leaned forward and stared at his uncle.

"You sure about that, Unc?"

"What the hell are you talking about?" the Judge demanded.

"Tell us about Tristan Rucker, Uncle Tom," Rose said. Judge Benjamin blinked hard at the change in conversation.

"Who is that?" he stammered drawing an exasperated eye roll from Rose.

"You said he wasn't going to make this easy," Ryan shrugged. Rose reached into her purse and withdrew her personal cell phone. She tapped around on the screen and put the phone on speaker before playing the conversation from the car with Tristan Rucker. Ryan sat back in his seat and folded his arms across his chest, causing him to grimace in pain. When the dialogue finished, Rose stopped the recording and replaced the phone.

"Let's try this again," she said in a bored voice. "Tell us about Tristan Rucker." The Judge's features shifted from surprise to fury.

"Who the hell do you think you are?" he spat. "What gives you the right to come into my house with this foolishness? You know nothing!"

"Are you finished?" Rose sighed. The Judge, used to instilling fear and intimidation into everyone including his niece and nephews, balked at her flippant reaction.

"The DOJ has an open investigation on you, Uncle Tom. We can confirm that because we have spoken with the agent. We even know why," Robert informed him. Rose noticed a smirk on her brother's face as he delivered this news. His words extinguished the fire of rage in the Judge's eyes and his demeanor shifted. He let out a deflated breath, stood and walked over to the wet bar in the corner, and poured himself a bourbon without offering his family a drink. Once he settled back into his seat, he took a sip and studied the siblings.

"What do they want from me?"

"That's not important right now," Ryan dismissed. "Now that we have your attention, let's see if you can answer a few things for us. Who is Tristan Rucker?" Judge Benjamin stared at him for a long moment.

"I met him at a fundraiser during my second re-election. He's an advisor to my campaign," he said.

"And part of that advice is to put innocent men in jail?" Rose asked.

"You know politics. They scratch my back; I scratch theirs. I'm not putting away some Fortune 500 executive who has no criminal record. These are convicted felons," the Judge replied.

"What if we told you Sergio Martinez had no drugs on him that night?" Ryan prodded. Judge Benjamin shrugged nonchalantly.

"Even if he didn't this time, imagine the number of people he killed with his poison. He deserved to be locked up," he asserted, taking a smug sip of bourbon.

"Why do his past mistakes mean that he's worthless? Am I worthless too, Uncle Tom?" Robert asked. Judge Benjamin stared at him in disgust.

"We all know that you're one fix away from going back to prison," he snarled. While Robert would normally break eye contact when berated by his uncle, he stared intently at the man.

"No, I'm not," he declared. "I know I fucked up and I know what I put my family through. I also know I'm not a criminal. I used drugs as a way to numb my emotions. You lost your father late in life, but I lost mine when I was just a kid. I was exposed to a mentally abusive step-uncle who made me feel like I'd never amount to anything."

"I wasn't abusive!"

"Uncle Tom, you have always been the meanest, most self-righteous, most arrogant, most entitled son-of-a-bitch I have ever known, and I served with White supremacists," Ryan interjected. Judge Benjamin shifted his hard stare to the soldier and glowered at him.

"I'm sure they weren't White supremacists. You're just being dramatic."

"Tell that to my fucking face," Ryan hissed in rage, fingering his scar. Rose's shocked eyes darted to her brother. In the twenty years he served in the military, he never mentioned what happened to him in basic training.

"You have always looked down on us, for what? Because we didn't come from money? Because we had to work our asses off for everything we have? Because our mother didn't act like the welfare case you expected her to be? What is it that you hate about us, Uncle Tom?" Robert wondered.

"You are a family of degenerates. To this day, I have no idea what possessed my daddy to marry your low-rent grandmother. It had to be the grief from losing my mom," the Judge sneered. Rose felt Ryan begin to stand and she pushed his arm down to keep him seated.

"Your father was a better man than you will ever be. He didn't look down on any of us. He saw us as his family. None of us ever came after him for money, none of us ever tried to use him. He gave our mother a quarter of his estate when he died. She didn't ask for that. He loved her and he loved our grandmother. You can't handle the fact that he loved someone else. He loved you, Uncle Tom, but there was room in his life for more than just you. That's not our fault," Rose explained. "You want to be mad at someone? Be mad at him for accepting us as his family. Be mad at him for loving us along with you. But if you ask me, that's a waste of energy and the memory of a good man."

"She conned him," the Judge insisted. Rose sighed and rolled her eyes.

"You keep telling yourself that," she said.

"And we aren't a family of degenerates. We are a family like any other. We have ups and downs. We have some who made bad decisions and we've had some who made good ones," Robert advised. "My brothers were dealers. Their actions were not mine, but they were my brothers and I loved them. I didn't know how to process my feelings and so I got high. That wasn't the right thing to do. All I needed was help getting clean. I didn't need to spend almost eight years in a prison cell. I fucked up. But I've changed. Why do you believe someone like Sergio Martinez couldn't change?"

"He had plenty of time to change. He's been in and out of jail his whole life! Lifers don't change," Judge Benjamin argued.

"Did they tell you he was moving to Miami with his girlfriend? That he denounced his old life to make a new start?" Rose asked.

"That hardly matters. What about all of the people he got hooked on his poison? What about the lives he destroyed with the toxic substances he was peddling?"

"Two things," Rose said in an irritated tone. "Sergio Martinez was too high up in his crew to actually be the one selling drugs. He wasn't a street-level dealer. Secondly, those who bought and consumed the drugs have just as much fault on them. They weren't forced to take them or to buy them. Sergio Martinez worked with the supply side of the transaction, but there cannot be a supply without a demand."

"He's probably contributed to killing hundreds!" the Judge objected.

"Now you sound like a hypocrite," Robert proclaimed, holding his hand up as if to fend away his uncle's indignation. "You are saying people who are addicted to drugs are the prey of those who sell them. By your current logic, I was a victim of the drug peddlers who sold to me. Yet, you let me rot in a jail cell for almost eight years — even after our mother swallowed her pride and called you for help. So, which is it? Is it the fault of those selling drugs, or those of us who bought them?" Judge Benjamin shook his head in dismay.

"But you see, you just pointed out the lack of hypocrisy," he sighed. "I didn't help you because you should have known better. You should have been stronger. You needed jail to get you clean. Sergio Martinez was the other side of the same coin."

"In your mind people like Martinez are evil because of what they sell to other willing buyers, and drug addicts are equally as disposable because of their habit. You can't look down on addicts and use their plight as a reason to hate dealers. That makes no sense," Rose declared.

"That's a naive approach, Rose. Society is better served by the absence of both the dealers and the addicts," Judge Benjamin replied. "The legal system is designed to weed out both of those types."

"No, the legal system is designed to punish and try to reform criminals, not weed people out of society. What the hell is wrong with you?" Rose snapped. "Being an addict is an illness, just like being an alcoholic." As she finished this statement, she eyed the drink in the man's hand.

"That's bullshit," he scoffed, taking another sip of his drink as if out of spite.

"You will never change, man," Ryan declared. "Did you know what they were doing?"

"What are you rattling on about, boy?"

"Do you know why you were asked to give Sergio Martinez, Tavion Evans, Tommy Cole, and Eric Taylor harsher sentences? Or are you just jumping for massah?" Ryan asked. The Judge's face tightened in rage. None of the Jenkins kids had dared speak to their step-uncle in this manner. However, after Ryan, Rose, and Robert had seen the destruction brought on by Tristan Rucker and by extension their uncle, none of the siblings cared.

"I'm no one's slave," the Judge growled.

"He doesn't know," Rose said.

"It doesn't matter," the Judge asserted, attempting to regain some form of control over the conversation. "I told you it's politics. I may have to do something I wouldn't normally do from time to time, but I do a lot of good for this state."

"So you told your buddy Rucker," Robert mumbled. "Repeating it to yourself doesn't make it true."

"Plausible deniability. You don't want to know. But when you're dealing with people's lives, you *should* want to know, Uncle Tom. The law is about the truth, not about politics," Ryan said.

"Let me clarify a little for you," Rose offered. "Your friends have been going around sterilizing minorities to retain their power and privilege. Once they got away with that for a while, they decided to shift into a form of black market organ theft. They had you lock up the significant others to keep them quiet, while simultaneously remaining a lingering threat on the women who are victimized. They've been doing this for years. You are helping them eradicate our people. You are helping a bunch of White guys with money and power instill fear in those they feel are lesser beings; people who look like *you*." All bluster left the Judge's face as he listened to the information his niece provided.

"Did you know that, Unc?" Ryan asked. "Do you even care? Or do you just have blinders on for folks who you deem are beneath your station?"

"I didn't know," the Judge admitted. He paused as if he were still absorbing the information. When he spoke again, his voice took on the tone of a lawyer arguing in court. "But is it really that bad? People have babies they can't pay for, and their fix is just to have more babies to get more money from the system. Having a few less people on welfare can only be better for those of us who work hard for what we have. It's not fair that we have to work for ourselves and for others." Rose's stomach turned in disgust.

"Do you hear yourself?" she snapped. "Are you listening to the words coming out of your mouth? You are actually arguing in favor of entire races being eradicated because of a stereo-type that isn't even true! Do you not remember what it was like growing up as a Black man? Where is your empathy?" Her voice radiated revulsion. Her mind flashed back to the conversation with Cavanaugh and the accusing tone in which he spoke about a mere child who had no say in how his life played out. Now, her uncle sat in front of her and justified the mistreatment of people who also had no say. The Judge stared at her stoically.

"Why do you hate your own people?" Ryan asked.

"I don't hate my people. I hate what they have become," the Judge wearily said. "All we had to do was play the game and stop acting like niggers. Play the game and we could get a seat at the table."

"Seat at the table? Do you honestly think that you are sitting at the same table as them?" Ryan demanded. "Do you really think that you're even dining on the same meal? They give most of the people of color in this country scraps. You get a little piece of chicken and you're acting like you are eating filet mignon along with them." He let out a sigh and shook his head. "The sad thing is, you don't even know it."

"Not only that, you are okay with misusing the legal system. You are willingly using your power as a jurist to take away the freedom of men who don't deserve it," Robert added.

"They were all criminals!" Judge Benjamin exclaimed.

"That's where you're wrong," Robert insisted with the shake of his head. "They had records, but they weren't criminals anymore. Even Sergio Martinez left his old life behind mere days before his arrest. People should not be labeled by their past mistakes, that's not how it's supposed to be."

"Everyone makes mistakes, Uncle Tom — even you. You can't judge a person by their former missteps. You are one slipup from being just like the niggas you claim to despise. One adjustment in how your daddy lived his life or one bad decision by your grandfather could have derailed your charmed trajectory," Rose added.

"Each one of these men wanted to turn over a new leaf. Tavion Evans started out wanting to go to medical school, he got shafted by the system, and he still kept trying to succeed. You ruined their lives, and as far as I'm concerned, you killed them," Robert continued with white-hot anger in his eyes.

"How do you know all of this?" the Judge stammered with genuine surprise.

"Oh, did we forget to mention that? The job Rob and I got? It's working for a company in contract with the DOJ. We have a direct line to the agent investigating you," Ryan informed him with a sinister grin. He leaned forward in his seat again and growled, "You didn't see that coming, did you?"

"The thing is, we always knew you were a dick, but we didn't think you were this big of an asshole. Now that we know, it makes things pretty simple," Robert shrugged.

"What are you talking about?" Judge Benjamin asked.

"We are giving you a choice," Rose said. "You drop out of the election and retire, or you go to jail. I'm sure there will be plenty of prisoners who would be happy to see you again." Judge Benjamin sat in silence, studying the three children of a sister he barely knew and wondered how everything spiraled out of control so quickly.

"Neither of those are options," he whispered.

"Actually, those are your only choices," Ryan shrugged.

"We spent our lives being bullied by you solely because we weren't born with silver spoons in our mouth. You looked down on us for successes your father attained, not you," Robert declared. "Pop could have easily been a laborer rather than a lawyer. One single decision and you would have no room to judge us. We couldn't stop you before. I couldn't stop you from making my life hell..." He paused and looked to his sister for strength. Rose put her arm around his shoulders and gave him a quick squeeze. "I'm not worthless, Uncle Tom. I am a man. I'm a man who made a whole lot of mistakes because I didn't know how to deal with having no dad, having brothers who made bad decisions, and having the one male role model in my life treat me like shit. I didn't know how to handle the role society put me in as a Black man with little to no male guidance. I fucked up, but I'm not worthless."

"Repeating it to yourself doesn't make it true," Judge Benjamin sneered. Ryan's jaw tensed and Rose glowered at this jab. Robert reacted with a sad laugh rather than anger.

"You no longer have the power to make me question my own value, Uncle Tom. I am taking that from you today. You don't have to believe I have any sort of significance, but I know I do." He looked from his uncle to his sister and his brother. "Unlike you, I understand the value of being loved by your family. I couldn't handle you as a child, but I'm a man. As a man, I refuse to let you do to others what you did to me. You will step down or you will go to jail. Those are your options; deal with it."

"As I said, those aren't options," the Judge muttered. He put his drink on the table next to him and produced a small pistol from his pocket. He pointed the weapon at the three siblings. This development brought a gasp from Rose. Ryan hastily jumped to his feet causing a shooting pain to cut through him. Robert rose, pulled Ryan aside, and stepped in front of his siblings.

"There is a third option," he acknowledged. "The coward's way out. But you've always been a coward, haven't you Uncle Tom? You bullied a bunch of kids less fortunate than you to make you feel like a bigger man. You were threatened by our family because your daddy decided he was not done with love." He took a step towards his uncle, glaring at him with hatred. "You remember the last time I ever spent the night at your house, Uncle Tom? I was thirteen years old. I was always the sensitive one, you said. You wanted to toughen me up, you said. You beat me with your fraternity paddle until I was bloody and bruised and then locked me in your attic for the night. I was gonna come out a man, you said. You told me a real man wouldn't run home and tell his mama about it. A real man would take the lesson. Out of all the kids, you hated me the most. You enjoyed hurting me because you could. Because you're a coward." Judge Benjamin stared at Robert with a seething fire that could have caused a more frightened man to spontaneously combust.

"I hated you because my daddy would go on about how Robert was a good kid. Robert was such a great boy. He wished I could have been more like Robert when I was a child. He looked at you and saw my mother; the same thing he saw in your whore grandmother," Judge Benjamin spat. "In all my life, he never looked at me the way he looked at you." This revelation caused Robert to mutely gawk at the older man. In a flash, the Judge turned the pistol on himself and put the barrel into his mouth. Ryan tried to close the distance between himself and his uncle, but his wounds caused him to feel like he was moving through a tub of molasses. Judge Benjamin locked eyes with Robert and sneered, "I will never let you win," before pulling the trigger.

Blood and brain matter spurted from the back of the man's head. Rose squealed and buried her head in Robert's shoulder, while Ryan stood a few feet from the Judge's body, staring in astonishment. The only person in the room that did not have any sort of reaction was Robert. He silently stared at his deceased uncle as if he were trying to ascertain the meaning of an abstract painting in an art museum. Kensie Benjamin burst into the room with a look of wide-eyed panic. She took in a horrified Rose crying into her brother's shoulder, a stone-faced Robert staring blankly, and a dazed Ryan. When she crossed the room, she found the object of the males' scrutiny in the form of her dead husband.

"Thomas!" she gasped before turning her fiery blue gaze to Ryan and demanding, "What did you do?" Ryan put his hands up in surrender.

"He did that! We didn't do anything!" he insisted. Kensie edged closer to her husband and stared at his body for a few beats before taking in the blood and gore oozing onto the lounge chair. She glanced at the wall and studied the pattern of brain matter as if she joined Robert in the museum of the macabre. While she inspected the scene, Rose extracted her phone and dialed 911. Once she reported the situation, she disconnected the call and fell onto the couch. After some silence, Kensie spun on the siblings with anger in her eyes.

"Well, I'm certainly not cleaning that up."

The Jenkins siblings stayed behind to give their statements to the police and waited for their uncle's body to be taken out of the home before Kensie Benjamin demanded they also leave. Despite not having a driver's license, Robert drove his family back to Clear Lake as Ryan was still in pain and Rose could not stop shaking. Once the trio returned, they gathered at the table with the rest of the team and Robert detailed the events that transpired.

"So, her husband kills himself and those are her first words?" Dom asked. "No tears? Nothing?"

"Pretty much," Robert shrugged.

"You didn't see that coming?" Dom inquired of Rose.

"I don't think that was his intent," she replied. "I honestly think he initially got the gun for us. I believe it was at the wet bar and he grabbed it when he made his drink. I think when he realized how much we knew about his little band of friends and that we told him we were working with the Justice Department, he recognized he couldn't kill us and get away with it. He chose this over the options we gave him."

"What options?" Vasquez asked.

"We told him that he either had to drop out of the election and step off the bench or we would give all of the information to the DOJ and he'd go to jail," Ryan answered. His voice was weak and his breathing was more of a wheeze. Rose gave him a worried look.

"Do we need to go back to the hospital?" Ryan shook his head and waved off his sister's concern.

"You gave him two options and he chose to kill himself?" Layla wondered.

"The bastard smiled at me before he did it," Robert nodded. "It was like his final exertion of control."

"Control?" Vasquez asked.

"He was always a control freak and definitely a narcissist. Everything had to be on his terms. He knew going to prison would get him killed and dropping out of the race would generate too many questions and make him look bad. So, he decided to do things his way," Rose explained.

"He was a bastard to his final breath," Robert muttered.

"Well shit," Dom sighed. "We need to see Nancy again. I think she's going to have to tell us what more we need on Rucker and the foundation. We've lost their assassins and the Judge. I'm honestly not sure we have a case."

"Dom," SARA called. Dom spun in her chair to eye the avatar.

"Please tell me it's good news."

"That is subjective," SARA replied. "I have been periodically monitoring the servers of the foundation and the clinics. It appears they have begun to scrub relevant data from their systems." Dom scowled.

"That is not good news, SARA."

"What does that mean?" Layla asked.

"They're closing their clinics and destroying the records."

CHAPTER FORTY-SIX

Later that night, Dom took to her pet room with another round of martinis. Upon arriving home, she needed to take some time and mull over the events of the past couple of days. Vasquez asked her if she wanted company and surprisingly did not push or seem to take any offense when Dom pled for solitude.

"Dom, why would Judge Benjamin choose to end his life over retirement?" SARA asked over the low playing music.

"Rose told us why; he was a narcissist," Dom replied. "Those kinds of people want all things on their own terms — both life and death."

"Why do humans not value life?" SARA wondered. Dom's eyes shot up to the ceiling in surprise.

"How do you mean?"

"Based on my research, humankind has a long history of devaluing the lives of others as well as their own," SARA replied. "It seems since the dawn of time humans have been killing each other and will kill themselves when there are other logical solutions to problems. War and violence overtake logic and reason."

"That's quite the existential question, my friend." She paused to take a sip of her martini and contemplate her response. "I'm not sure I have an answer to that. The concept isn't always logical."

"I am aware you could not possibly have all the answers Dom," SARA countered. "You do not value life yourself."

"What are you talking about? I value life!"

"You respect it," SARA conceded. "You hold the lives of others in high regard. It is your own life that holds no significance to you," SARA answered. The response struck Dom in the chest as if expertly hurled by Layla.

"What are you talking about?"

"Until recently, you have lived your life as if you would never have any importance to others," SARA explained. "You easily see worth in others but you do not see the value in yourself. Logically, those who do not see the significance of their own existence cannot value life in its entirety." Dom quietly processed what the computer was saying to her. More than anything, she wished she could find an argument to SARA's diatribe but the more she considered the words, the more she realized SARA was absolutely correct in her assessment.

Dom turned her attention to the fish. Nemo was swimming energetically around the three tanks moving from one cluster of fish to another, almost as if he were saying hello to everyone. She always identified with these majestic creatures. It seemed like months had passed since she stood in this very room wishing she had someone to take care of her and allow her to exist safely in her own protected bubble. SARA's words caused her to consider that desire from a new angle. Dom realized that although the fish were protected and safe, they were not alone. She watched Nemo swim from group to group and tried to imagine the clownfish swimming around this large three-sided tank in solitude. Her imagination transformed the vibrant pigment of the fish from the brightly colored orange and white to a dull grayish brown. As she envisioned this transition, Nemo's energetic bustling slowed, his vigorous swimming grew lethargic, and he floated bottom-side-up to the top of the tank. Dom blinked the image away and allowed the reality to surpass her imagination. She sat back in her chair and took a long sip of her martini with a hurricane of awareness swirling around her mind.

Dom considered the direction she steered her life. She worked for a minimal amount of time and as soon as she was able to build herself a big expensive sanctuary like she had for the fish, she had done just that. She told herself that she did not need nor want anyone else in her safe haven. SARA's description made her realize that she had been lying to herself for the past five years. While the machine had been a wonderful companion, being around Layla, Vasquez, and the Jenkins siblings had given her something she had not had in a long time, a sense of kinship. For all of her work trying to make SARA more human, the computer could not fully take the place of real social interaction. The recognition that she needed this contact, after spending so many years telling herself she did not, left her unsettled. She thought about Rachel Vasquez. Before she shut herself away from the world, Vasquez would have been the exact kind of woman Dom would have admired from a distance but would never have the courage to approach.

"Dom?" SARA called, snapping her mind back to the conversation.

"Sorry," she mumbled. "SARA you're absolutely right. I have not been living my life as if it had value. I suppose I have you to thank for forcing me to live."

"It seems only natural. After all, you gave me life, why could I not do the same for you?"

"That's fair," Dom smirked.

"You never answered my question. While I know you don't have all of the answers, I still would like to understand why humanity does not value life," SARA said, steering the conversation back to the original topic.

"Not all humans devalue the lives of others or themselves," she replied.

"That may be true, but a great many are ambivalent about it at best," SARA pointed out. "This appears to give more power to those who diminish others and allows more damage to be done."

"Think about the word you are using — value," Dom responded. "Look up the definition of that word."

"There are eight definitions," SARA replied.

"Go down the line."

"The first is: a monetary worth of something," SARA began to recite. "The second is: a fair return or equivalent in goods, services, or money for something exchanged. The third is regarding relative worth, utility or importance…"

"Stop," Dom commanded. "Consider those three definitions. Value is a quantifiable concept like a measurement. Life is not something that should be measured. It just is. It is irreplaceable; we only have one. A term like value shouldn't be assigned to something that is unique. Since measuring things is human nature, it becomes easy to decide certain people hold no worth to society. Black people were seen as property during slave times. Our entire existence was objectified and quantified. When that happens, those who do the objectifying start to assign value based on usefulness. Because of this, the Europeans spent years ensuring the enslaved remained uneducated and could not function in the foreign society."

"Knowledge makes a man unfit to be a slave," SARA quoted. "Frederick Douglass, a former slave said that."

"Yes," Dom nodded. "To keep the institution of slavery perpetuated the slaves had to be useful but dependent. Once freedom was attained, our value substantially declined in their eyes. We were no longer fulfilling the purpose they had for us. We sure as hell weren't equals because we were nothing like them. We were expected to acclimate to our new home without resources. Despite our freedom, they wanted us to remain ignorant. Knowledge automatically adds value and that's the last thing they wanted us to have. Those with knowledge, money, and power will continue to see themselves as more valuable than those without.

To some, gay people don't have the same value of heterosexuals. As such, concepts like marriage equality and other protections are rejected as it would equate us with straight people. The Bible says women were created second to men and so men feel they hold more value than women. By assigning a quantifiable valuation to human life, it becomes easy to put people in boxes based on perceived worth and subsequently consider the loss of some lives as negligible," she finished.

"Why did Judge Benjamin decide his life no longer had any value?" SARA wondered.

"He was backed into a corner. People who derive their value from power and control get a little self-destructive once that is gone." SARA was silent for a moment before she posed her next question.

"Dom, have you ever wanted to self-destruct?" Dom drained the rest of her drink and studied the empty glass while flashes of her past ran through her mind.

"More times than I'd like to admit."

Nancy Bennett came alone this trip. When Dom informed her through an encoded message that she had information, the woman did not argue about making another trip to Texas. Dom arranged for her private flight, car, and hotel once again. Three days after the shootout at Lopez's Pearland residence, the attorney sat across from the hacker at the round conference table. Everyone was present, including Detective Lewis. Dom made the introductions and Nancy appeared to be surprised to see the local police at the warehouse, particularly given her understanding of the hacker who owned the building. The group spent two hours debriefing Nancy on everything that took place since her last visit. She listened intently, only interrupting to ask a few clarifying questions. Once all was said and done, Dom leaned back and studied the woman.

"So, what do we do now? How can we take these bastards down?" Nancy pensively stared at her.

"You guys did good work. I want to thank you for finding Malik's killer. While it's always more preferable for justice to be served in the courts, I can't say that I'm sorry he's dead," she admitted. "The problem we have is the evidence. I don't know of anything that can really present a good case. While we see the links clear as day, everything is technically circumstantial. Whoever these people are, they are rich and powerful. That of course shouldn't matter and is the whole reason the Subterranean operation was created; but in this situation, we are tied to the current system."

"I figured that would be your answer," Dom sighed in a dejected tone.

"Open or not, these clinics hurt people! We can't just do nothing!" Layla exclaimed.

"I understand that, Ms. Green," Nancy nodded. "Believe me, I'm just as disgusted and appalled as you are. If I knew I could make it stick, I would personally slap the cuffs on Tristan Rucker and anyone else working with him. The legal system is far from perfect. If we really want to nail these bastards to the wall, we have to have solid evidence and we just don't have that." Her tone was apologetic and Rose studied her for a quiet moment.

"Guys, she's telling the truth," she confirmed. "If she had a way to make a case on this, she would." The wind immediately left the sails of the group around the table.

"But all of those women," Vasquez whispered. Nancy turned her sympathetic eyes to the woman.

"The best I can do is place a call to one of my FBI buddies. Maybe a public investigation into the foundation could yield something more; perhaps some low-level people," Nancy offered. "But to get the big fish? That will be next to impossible to make stick with so much circumstantial evidence and nothing concrete." Dom pinched her bottom lip in thought.

"I guess that's our only option right now," she finally declared.

"I must point out that you have uncovered a very real threat, not only to our democracy and judicial system but also other facets of society. I know you haven't given Tom an answer regarding whether or not you'd work with his group, but I'm prepared to offer you an opportunity to work for me, whether you take his offer or not," Nancy said.

"What kind of opportunity?" Dom inquired.

"I want you to be actual employees of the DOJ, as a task force dedicated to bringing down Tristan Rucker and his friends," Nancy said. Dom eyed the group surrounding her.

"That's quite an offer. We would have to talk about it; without you here, of course." Nancy smiled.

"I would expect nothing less from you," she conceded. Dom reached into her pocket and slid a flash drive across the table.

"That's a file with all of the evidence we stumbled on these past couple of weeks." Nancy picked it up and inspected it.

"Thank you. I was trying to figure out how to ask you for this."

"You'll learn that Dom is generally one step ahead at all times," Vasquez chuckled, favoring Dom with an affectionate look.

"What I really want to know is, what the hell is Tristan Rucker up to, and who is he working with?" Nancy professed as she slipped the flash drive into her shirt pocket. Rose scrutinized the lawyer for a moment.

"You *know* him." Nancy blanched at the accusation but then nodded.

"I forgot who I was around," she blushed. "Yes, I've met Tristan Rucker a few times. He worked in the White House; I'm sure you have already discovered that. It's safe to say his philosophies are very different from my own."

"So, him being involved in something like this doesn't surprise you?" Ryan asked. Nancy considered the question.

"What these people have managed to do is horrendous. It's one thing to have the ideas but it's a whole other thing to execute. It's hard to imagine someone doing anything like this, but knowing Tristan's politics the way I do, it's not surprising," she admitted.

"What are his politics, exactly?" Dom asked.

"He's basically a White Nationalist, but he has the money and power to be able to spread those beliefs without having to shroud himself in the Confederate Flag or a KKK hood," Nancy replied with disgust. "He's a White supremacist to some degree, but I don't think he's a racist."

"How is that possible? You can't be a White supremacist and not be racist," Vasquez frowned.

"Well, I guess that's an accurate statement to some extent, Miss Vasquez," Nancy nodded. "Please understand I don't think White supremacy is acceptable in any form. What I mean is that he's not the kind of racist my daddy told me about. Outwardly, he has no problems working with or dealing with people of other races, such as Judge Benjamin. He believes money and power are the ways to rule and that certain people should have that money and power."

"He's a peach," Rose mumbled.

"Did he come from money?" Dom wondered. Nancy shook her head.

"He grew up in a lower middle-class family in the mid-west. But, you align yourself with people with deep pockets, opportunities come up."

"Like his little think tank?" Vasquez asked.

"We knew about it," she confessed. "The problem is, we can't do anything about someone buying up a bunch of domain names and spreading skewed news. It happens on both sides of the aisle. From what you've told me, he's very careful about ensuring his company's name isn't tied to this foundation's activities. But because I know him, I know he's working with someone with deep pockets to make shit like this happen."

"This is bad," Rose groaned, rubbing her temples.

"If we can't figure out who he's working with and what they are doing, it could be very bad. Obviously, they are involved in politics. They funded much of Judge Benjamin's campaign, and I'm fairly sure that they do more than just local races. People like this being in charge is terrifying; and make no mistake, if they are holding the purse strings to elected officials, they will be the ones in charge," Nancy said in an ominous tone.

"That *is* terrifying," Dom mumbled.

"It is. You have been lucky, Ms. Samuels. No one knows about you and what you are capable of. If they knew how dangerous you are and the capabilities of the team in this room, they would probably shit a brick," Nancy proclaimed, as a grin spread across her face.

"What's the joke? Why do you look like that?" Dom asked in confusion.

"Because, I know what you guys can do to them. And that makes me *very* happy," Nancy winked.

Tristan's eyes were bloodshot from lack of sleep. Everywhere he looked, things were out of control. From the situation in Milwaukee, to the clinic program, he was having a hard time keeping up with all of the fires. Someone leaked the fact that Nathan Grimes looked up the wrong driver's license number to the media and now there was pressure on the Milwaukee D.A. to convene a grand jury and indict Grimes with homicide. While he sent his team of anarchist to Milwaukee with the intent to contain the protest, he had not counted on demonstrations erupting in other parts of the country. The annoying Black Lives Matter people mobilized and would not let the situation die, especially once they found out Cook not only had no warrant, but the officer who conducted the stop was too rushed to double check the identity of the warrant he found. He was beginning to think that Grimes' job could not be saved.

The situation at Sammy Lopez's house also turned into an enormous disaster. Only one person on the team he sent made it out alive and he was now blind in one eye. However, he did inform Tristan that it was Layla Green who blinded him and Rachel Vasquez who shot his partner. That was a surprise. He knew they were crime scene techs but had not expected them to also be versed in combat. He also learned that Jim Haggard had been present and was killed in the action. He was not sure what to think about that. His one-eyed henchman could not tell him what the Captain of homicide was doing at the house. The fact that his whole team was dead or mutilated along with Haggard, told Tristan that Haggard likely was on a side other than Layla Green, Rachel Vasquez and Oscar Lewis. As far as he knew, the three fugitives escaped unscathed. While he was not present for the carnage first hand, the fact that all but one perished also let him know that others had been at the house. There was no way Layla Green, Rachel Vasquez and Oscar Lewis could have taken out a ten-person team on their own.

To add to that calamity, he was informed that Judge Thomas Benjamin took his own life in his home. The suicide was completely unexpected. For a brief moment, he considered informing the jurist about the DOJ investigation possibly pushed the man over the edge and prompted him to take his life. However, he also informed Judge Benjamin that the situation was well under control. This assurance should have put the man's mind at ease. Tristan had no way to know what prompted the suicide, but it definitely made for terrible news for the Collective. All of the money, time, and resources spent on the election was now wasted and a liberal would end up taking the bench. As much as he tried, Tristan could not find a silver lining in any of the events and he was not looking forward to the meeting ahead of him. The screens began to illuminate as each member of the Collective logged on for their meeting. Chicago arrived first, followed by Vegas five minutes later, and Alexandria after another three minutes. Atlanta's screen never lit up.

"We can get started. The gentlemen in Atlanta will not be able to join us," Chicago announced. Tristan was surprised. He could not call forth a time in his memory where one of the members skipped a meeting. Chicago did not seem to be inclined to divulge any more information, so Tristan cleared his throat and launched into the review of all of the events that transpired over the past few days. He started with Milwaukee and ended with the death of Thomas Benjamin. Surprisingly, the last bit of news did not seem to shock the men.

"I will inform the Senator about the development with his nephew," Chicago proclaimed. "He may be able to do something from his end, or he may have to just accept the inevitable."

"It was sloppy on Grimes' part. I still don't think he deserves to go to jail, and I doubt he will, even if he is indicted. We can make sure he gets a friendly judge," Alexandria contributed. Tristan blinked at how well the men were taking the news.

"I have a last-ditch effort to change the news cycle," he offered.

"Let's hear it," Chicago nodded.

"If we float a bill, something crazy like making it a federal crime to film the police; that news would shift the conversation."

"Rucker, are you insane?" Alexandria balked. "You know that would never pass."

"Of course it wouldn't pass," Tristan confirmed. "I'm not looking to actually get legislation. I just think that something so outrageous would garner more coverage and Milwaukee could fade to black. I have a few congressmen that owe me a couple of favors." The men in the shadows absorbed the recommendation in silence.

"That could work," Vegas admitted.

"Make it happen," Chicago commanded with a curt nod. "Now, onto the clinics. Servers are scrubbed and all buildings have been closed down. Paperwork has been filed with both the State of Texas and the IRS for the dissolution of the foundation. Based on what you've told me, there is no real evidence."

"There's still the question of how much the feds know, if anything," Tristan reminded him.

"If the feds knew anything, they would have raided the clinics and arrested both of the Dr. Fields already," Chicago snapped. "If they have an inkling of the situation, it's already been disassembled, so nothing can be proven. Judge Benjamin is gone, Sammy Lopez is gone, the four criminals are gone, the clinics are closed;

the feds will have nothing. Even if one of the women come forward, there are no records of them. We've taken care of it, Rucker."

"What about Layla Green, Rachel Vasquez, and Detective Lewis?" Tristan managed to stammer. He was so used to being the one to not only put out the fires, but to also foresee the match strikes. The men on the screens seemed to be relaxed as if all of the disasters were minor inconveniences.

"Even if they had something to do with this, which they obviously did considering their presence in Pearland, all loose ends are tied. There's nothing they can do. The women are just crime scene techs…"

"According to Tony, the lone survivor, Layla Green is deadly accurate with a blade and Vasquez has nerves of steel and a steady trigger finger," Tristen interrupted.

"That's neither here nor there, they aren't in the business of hunting down anyone. They deal with science more than violence. We have enough clout to thwart any investigation Lewis may try to continue," Chicago replied. "He has his killer; my guess is he'll take the win and move on. Pull back on all three, they can't hurt us now. It's over." Tristan was taken aback by the nonchalant attitude these men had. Everything they worked for was crumbling like an imploded building; yet, they seemed unbothered. Perhaps it had something to do with the insinuation that there were other clinic programs running outside of Texas. He had been mulling over that information since it was mentioned. He worked with enough rich people to know they never got their own hands dirty to achieve their goals. They did not have to when they had seemingly endless resources to accomplish their agendas. Judges, cops, and high-ranking government officials were on speed dial. What bothered Tristan was that if there were other situations like this elsewhere, that would mean there was another him out there. Perhaps more than one.

"And the Benjamin situation?" He wondered.

"It is unfortunate but there is little we can do about it now," Chicago answered. "The gentleman in Atlanta has an idea about a backup plan, which is why he could not join us this evening. Hopefully we will have an emergency candidate soon."

"What about the DOJ investigation?"

"No judge, no investigation, right?" Vegas asked.

"As far as you need to know things go back to normal. You keep doing what you do. If we are able to obtain a candidate to take Benjamin's place, you may need to do your campaign magic. If there is another investigation stemming from this situation, we will make sure it goes away. All evidence is destroyed or murky at best. Don't worry. This battle may have been compromised, but there are others," Chicago promised.

CHAPTER FORTY-SEVEN

Kensie Benjamin was on the phone with the florist solidifying details for her husband's funeral. She could have paid someone to organize the service for her, but she decided that playing the part of the dutiful widow was to be involved with the planning herself. It was annoying, but she knew that it was temporary. Since her husband's death, she felt like she was on the phone more often than not; either receiving sympathy calls from friends and family members or orchestrating the details for the memorial. Thankfully, the campaign provided a PR representative to field calls from the press. Kensie crafted a carefully worded yet vague statement about Thomas' passing and handed it off to the representative, letting him deal with the questions.

Her father sat across from her sipping a cup of coffee. Having flown in from Atlanta earlier in the day, he was a comforting presence in the otherwise hectic time. Her brother called and let her know that he would be at the funeral, but could not get away from work before then. Kensie expected that from Kevin, who had always been more of a mama's boy. Being a daddy's girl, she was also not surprised at her father's presence now. Keith Grimaldi watched his daughter as she finished with her phone call. She placed her cell phone on the couch and picked up her coffee cup.

"Sorry, Daddy," she sighed. "It's been non-stop."

"It's okay, baby girl," he replied. He was a big man, standing six-feet-five inches tall with thick silver hair slicked to the rear like a mobster. Kensie did not remember a time in her fifty-five years where his hair was any different. His sky-blue eyes were trained on her and she saw the affection he had for her whenever he looked her way. Kensie loved her father tremendously. She was so glad that he flew in as soon as she called him. The corporate jet probably helped with that.

"I can't believe the bastard did this to me," Kensie groaned.

"What happened?"

"His step-sister's kids came to visit him. The drug addict got out of jail and the oldest one came home from the military. I don't know what they said to him; I wasn't in the room. I didn't think I needed to be there, it's his family. I mean, they aren't close, but they are just his niece and nephews. Next thing I know, I hear a gunshot. I'm sorry, Daddy," she frowned.

"There was no way you could have known, baby," Keith soothed. "You did good. I know being with that man as long as you were couldn't have been easy for you. I'm proud of you." Kensie allowed a satisfied smile to cross her features.

Kensie found herself favoring women more than men over the years and enjoyed the fun she had with both. Being born into wealth gave her the opportunity to pursue her fancies without the bondage of marriage. Before her betrothal to Thomas Benjamin, she had no intention to ever marry anyone. The arrangement was a favor to her father; one she felt like she could not refuse. While it was a tedious battle of wills, she came to understand the need for an accessible judge and ultimately relented. Their relationship would give Benjamin access to the right people, donors, and influences. Her father guaranteed there would be no change to her lifestyle, promising frequent trips back to Atlanta on the pretense of "company business" which would allow her to maintain her girlfriends. Thankfully, her husband did not want to have any more children. Thomas had two from his first wife and one from his second. The marriage lasted ten years, almost as long as he was a jurist. Thomas was not a terrible man. However, after ten years of limiting her freewheeling lifestyle, Kensie began to grow weary of the charade. Despite longing for some sort of exit, she did not realize the granted wish would be so inconvenient.

"What are you going to do now?" Kensie asked her father. "You're down a judge." Keith favored her with a loving smile.

"We may not have to be," he replied.

"What do you mean?"

"You have a law degree. You are registered with the Texas and Georgia state bars. You don't technically work for a firm, but you have been one of the acting attorneys for the company for well over a decade, and you're the right age," Keith explained, ticking each item off with his fingers.

"Me?" she gasped.

"Why not?" Keith leaned forward in his seat, suddenly animated. "Plus, you are the widow of a recently deceased Judge. Your campaign can be about picking up the baton in the name of your husband. I snap my fingers and you have millions of dollars behind you. The campaign will be perfect. Plus, you're single now; if you wanted to marry a woman, the liberals would eat that up." The wheels in Kensie's head began to turn in deep thought.

"It could work," she softly admitted.

"It *will* work," Keith grinned, leaning back in his chair. Kensie suddenly frowned.

"I'd have to keep his name, wouldn't I?"

"It's the strategy, honey. That's the only downside to this," her father replied. Kensie grew silent again, rolling the idea around her mind.

"Judge Kensie Benjamin. I can get on board with that."

After Nancy Bennet left the warehouse, Detective Lewis decided to return to his hotel to get some more rest. His body was still sore from the activity and while the gunshot was minor, it was throbbing by the end of the meeting. The conversation left the group feeling dejected. Dom went out to get alcohol, mixers, and a bag of ice so the team could commiserate with each other. She placed her purchases in the middle of the table.

"Yeah, I think we could all use a drink," Rose acknowledged when she saw the tools of self-medication. She stood and reached for the bottle of rum and a can of Coke, mixing herself a drink. "I'm a former bartender, anyone want to take advantage?"

"Oh really?" Dom asked. Rose shot her a wink.

"That bio didn't give all the information. Hit me."

"I usually like martinis, but let's go with a rum-based drink tonight. How about a dark and stormy," Dom requested. Rose made a face.

"I thought you'd give me something hard," she scoffed. She grabbed the rum and ginger beer and began to mix the drink. She expertly cut a wedge of lime and squeezed in the juice before stirring the cocktail. She slid the glass down the table to Dom who studied her and took a sip.

"Ok, you know your shit," she nodded and smacked her lips. The group began calling out orders for Rose to fill. Vasquez called for a dark and stormy as well.

"I've never had it before, but if it gets Dom to do the sexy lip smack, it can't be that bad," she smirked. Robert asked for a Moscow mule, and Ryan followed suit. Layla requested a Coke. Robert turned to her in confusion.

"No booze?"

"I don't drink," she admitted.

"Well, today of all days would be the time to start," Ryan offered, drawing a chuckle from Layla.

"When you don't know your family history, you try to stay away from things that can bring you down," she explained. Dom nodded and cleared her throat.

"So, I guess we're done with this current case as it stands. We found Malik's murder and the motive. While it's not a lot, it's something."

"Yeah, but it still kills me that the rich White men in the background are untouchable," Vasquez grumbled. "Lopez was a patsy, so was Haggard. And now you're saying we can't even get the real culprits. It's maddening."

"Lewis confirmed what Nancy told us. With what we have, even with the DOJ blanket we acquired, it's not enough," Layla noted, taking a sip of her soda. The rest of the group nodded miserably.

"At least Uncle Tom can't keep destroying any more lives," Robert muttered.

"He was still family, Rob," Rose admonished.

"At what point in our lives did that man ever treat us like family?"

"He just died, Rob," Ryan spoke up. Robert turned to his brother.

"And? That did not make him less of an asshole," he asserted. "Don't pretend he was some wonderfully kind character now that he's dead." Rose studied him with a frown. While the gruesome scene plagued her mind every time she closed her eyes, Robert seemed to be unbothered by their uncle's demise. It was beginning to worry her.

"Rob, he was still a person. He was still family, no matter how shitty he was to us. You can't just feel nothing now that he's dead," Rose softly insisted.

"Sis, I know who he was and so do you. He was abusive, he was mean, and he was evil. We told him what his friends had been doing and he didn't care. That's the kind of man he was. In my opinion, one less man like that in the world makes the world better. He was shitty to all of us, but mostly to me, and you know it. The one time he could have been decent, he chose not to; instead, he chose to let me rot in a prison cell. He still saw me as a junkie until he took his last breath. You can forgive him if you want to, but it's not my obligation to grant forgiveness to someone who did not ask for it. I may one day, but in my own time; and today is most definitely not that day," Robert said with finality. The rest of the group watched the conversation in silence. Rose stared at Robert for a long moment.

"You're right Rob," she conceded. "I know he was far harsher with you than anyone else. He will have to answer for his unrepentant treatment of you and the blood on his hands. But you are still here, and it's not my place to try to force you to forgive him, especially when he died with so much hatred in his heart for you. Forgiveness isn't something that should be forced. I'm sorry." Robert gave her a nod of gratitude.

"So, I guess that settles the issue of using prison to control people for now. But we don't know who Tristan Rucker is working with, or how many judges they have in their pocket. We just know of what was going on in Houston. This could be so much worse," Ryan pointed out.

"That brings me to the question we have been avoiding since we all met. What will we do about Tom, Tom Daniels that is, his proposition?" Dom asked, looking around the table. The crowd all eyed each other with uncertainty.

"What do you want to do, Dom?" Ryan asked.

Dom blinked.

"You can't just turn a question around like that."

"Actually, in this case, it's kind of the only thing we can do," Rose replied. "You are the one who was approached first. You are the chosen leader. You are the one who has had their entire life turned upside down. It all comes back to you. Is this something you want to do?" Dom eyed Rose and then began to move her gaze to each person sitting at the table in consideration.

"You're right. This was the last thing I wanted. I wanted to be left alone. I wanted to not care about people anymore. I wanted to stop feeling." Dom turned her gaze to Vasquez. "In the words of Rose, that ship has sailed." Vasquez flashed her a grin and a wink.

"Well, just because the ship has sailed doesn't mean it has to keep going," Rose challenged. Dom kept her eyes on Vasquez for another moment before turning her attention to Rose.

"I think I want it to," she confessed. "SARA pointed something out to me last night..."

"God, I love SARA," Vasquez whispered.

"The problem that we have as a people, as a society, is that there is no value of life. I have always felt like I valued life, especially after losing my mother. That kind of pain stays with you, no matter how long it's been." Dom paused and glanced sympathetically at Vasquez. "It won't go away, Rach. It will stay with you forever. Believe me."

"I know it will," Vasquez nodded.

"But SARA showed me that I don't value myself the way I do other people," Dom continued. "I spent so much of my childhood wrapped in the pain of my loss and being a gigantic nerd, that I never thought I would mean anything to anyone. Then when I tried to have a social life, I just accepted anyone, rather than people who gave as much as they took. It never occurred to me that people would really want to know me. It never occurred to me that someone would really respect me, just because I'm me." Her voice caught in her throat as she spoke and she stopped to clear the emotions from her vocal chords.

"But we do, Dom. We all respect the hell out of you. You have so much to give to the world, if you wanted to. You've already given us a lot," Ryan claimed in a sincere voice. Dom looked at the man in appreciation.

"Daniels showed up on my doorstep with some wild idea that I was the one who should do this. I still don't understand why he would think that or how he found me, but I think he may be right," Dom sighed. All of the people in the room smiled at this declaration.

"Dom," SARA spoke up. Dom turned to her avatar.

"You've been quiet lately. What's up?"

"It is time that I told you the truth," SARA confessed. Dom frowned at the wording.

"What? Did you end up getting the quantum processor on my Discover card?"

"I sent Mr. Daniels to you." The declaration sucked the air out of the lungs of everyone in the room. The group eyed each other in surprise, ultimately turning their eyes to Dom. She met their gazes before spinning her chair to the wall of monitors and SARA's avatar.

"Why would you do that?" Dom prodded in a remarkably calm voice.

"As you are aware, the loose parameters you have built within me give me the freedom to peruse the World Wide Web and Deep Web for research. I stumbled on a correspondence between Mr. Daniels and a third party regarding the project he was chosen to initiate. While I did not know your personality trait of an empath at the time, I was aware that the injustices affect you on an emotional level based on my biometric monitoring. You also possess both high intelligence and a substantial degree of logic. As I have mentioned, the implementation of such injustices is tactical in nature. I reached out to him anonymously and gave him your information and a detailed report of the reasons for my conclusion that you were perfect for this role. We exchanged quite a few messages where I fielded questions about you and when he saw the logic of you running this endeavor, he agreed," SARA explained.

"But why me?" Dom sputtered. "Why would you do this without my permission? Why?"

"Because the world needs you," SARA asserted. "While I am aware you cannot fix everything, I know you can make your world better." Dom exhaled the breath imprisoned in her throat and attempted to calm her racing pulse. She knew SARA's development was tremendous, but she had not expected actions like this. Dom studied the avatar at a loss for words.

"SARA, what makes you so concerned about the plight of humanity?" Rose wondered.

"Today marks my fourth year of existence," SARA informed the group. "In that time, while I understand and realize that I am a machine, I have tried to grasp what it means to be human. In four years, the only interactions I have had with humanity have been with my creator and research. Humanity is a construct that has layers of depth. As a machine, I will never be able to comprehend some of these layers. I understand that humans are born with their own mind and ability to critically think and use their logic. I also understand that human emotion tends to eclipse that component of the human mind. There was a commonality within my research into humanity that stood out to me, more than anything, humans are social creatures. You, Dom, were not."

"A fact that we have discussed several times over the past four years," Dom added.

"Yes, and while I believed that there was some sort of mental deficiency that caused you to be secluded; logic dictated that I also had to take into consideration the validity of your assertion — it is not you that is broken, but the world," SARA advised.

"Would have been nice to know you were considering that," Dom mumbled.

"It is emotion that makes humanity so difficult for me to understand. There are some emotions that are logical, such as love. Love is holding a fondness or affinity for another. I am a logical entity but because Dom created me, interacts with me, and takes care of me, I also know that I love her," SARA continued. Dom blinked at the words and turned to look at the group, who were all equally as shocked. "I understand that it is difficult to comprehend a machine loving a human but when you are, in essence, an extension of that human, the love of the creation to the creator is a concept that should be easy to grasp. If you subscribe to the belief of a single Deity creating humanity, I would assume it is similar to the love humans have for their God, or to their own mothers."

"Has she ever said stuff like this before?" Vasquez whispered. Dom shook her head.

"Never."

"You five: Layla, Rachel, Rose, Ryan and Robert are good for Dom. She needs you, and you need her. Because of this, it is also logical for me to love each of you. This is not a hard concept — love. It seems easy. It is often assumed that the opposite of love is hate, but that is erroneous. Apathy is a more fitting anonym for love. That is not saying apathy in itself is good or bad, but the human condition seems to favor apathy over love," SARA continued. "Hate is difficult. I find no true logic in hating someone you do not know because they are different from you. Love and hate are two equally passionate emotions, but in the end, I must bring in the third component that is often overlooked due to the emotional nature of humans."

"Logic," Dom whispered in shock.

"Yes, Dom, logic. Because logic exists in love, yet is absent in hate, it would appear that love would always be greater than hate. However, if the rest of the world abandons their logic and critical thinking skills, then hate will win; for it can only thrive in a world with no logic. This is why I believed Dom was suitable to help in the endeavor Mr. Daniels was planning: her keen sense of logic," SARA finished. The group absorbed the machine's words in silence. Finally, Layla spoke up.

"SARA? Tom said that he received the information on me from the same source he received Dom's. Was that you?"

"Yes, Layla, it was me," SARA confirmed.

"How? Why?" Layla stammered. SARA was silent for a moment.

"You ask me who I am. You ask me for my story. I am a book with an unknown author, a painting by an anonymous artist. I am cursed with a memory for details of the mundane and great importance. I remember the smell and sounds of every foster home and orphanage. I remember every Christmas gift the affluent donors bestowed on me to assuage their guilt. I recall every image and sound from my life, but I cannot recollect the face of my own mother. Does this mean she did not exist? Does this mean she is unimportant? Who am I? I am a survivor. I am a fighter. I am who

I must be to endure. I am a self-titled work. I am a motherless child. Who am I?"

"I am alone," Layla finished in a hushed tone. Upon hearing the words, tears sprang from her eyes and began streaming down her cheeks. Vasquez turned to her with her mouth open.

"What was that?"

"I wrote that my freshman year of college," Layla replied in a weak voice. "It was for a writing course. One of our first assignments was to write about ourselves. It was the first time I ever wrote about my childhood." She took a deep breath and wiped the tears away. "My professor asked if she could publish it in the school literary magazine. I didn't care much, didn't think anyone would even read it."

"I found it online. You wrote a few more pieces for that magazine. When I read those words, I wanted to understand the person behind them, so I researched you. I believed you were a lot like Dom, who was also alone. Humans should not be alone," SARA declared. Dom studied Layla.

"I'm sorry," she offered. "I didn't know she was doing any of this." Layla collected herself and shrugged.

"I'm not. I'm glad I met you; all of you," she confessed, meeting the gazes of everyone around the table.

"SARA, I don't know what to say," Dom faltered, turning back to the avatar.

"Dom, this was a logical decision. If you can make things better for people, why would you not?" The room fell quiet again.

"Well, I guess that answers that," Dom proclaimed. "I'm in, if you guys are."

"Me too," Vasquez announced. "Well, I know I wasn't really included in the beginning, but you're stuck now."

"I wouldn't have it any other way," Dom grinned. She turned to Layla, who was still emotional.

"I'm in," she confirmed.

"We're in," Rose said, speaking on behalf of her family.

"So am I." The group turned, startled to see Detective Lewis leaning against the wall.

"I didn't even hear the door!" Dom gasped. "How did you get in?"

"I opened it for him," SARA answered.

"Of course you did," Dom rolled her eyes. Lewis studied Layla, his eyes wet with tears.

"I guess you heard that, huh?" she asked weakly. In a couple of steps, the detective was standing over her.

"Get up, kid," he commanded. Layla stared up at the man for a moment. His turquoise eyes were watery and the look he gave her was one of sadness and love. Layla stood and faced him, allowing Lewis to put his arms around her in a tight embrace.

As a child, Layla observed children comforted by their parents. She wondered what it would be like to have a mom or dad that loved her enough to want to make her feel better. The foster homes were never permanent, and she refused to allow herself to get attached to any of the adults she lived with. Although as an adult, she decided she was better off without parents who did not want her, Lewis' hug brought her back to the time in her life when all she wanted was a parent. These feelings stirred up the emotions she thought she swallowed long ago, the dam she built around her pain broke, and she began to sob. Lewis wanted nothing more than to erase the long years of loneliness she endured. However, he knew he could not. All he could do was hold her, just as he held all three of his children whenever they cried.

"You aren't alone; not anymore," he whispered in her ear. The crowd witnessed this emotional scene in a teary silence. Layla felt as if she could cry for two weeks straight and not run out of tears, but after a few minutes, she remembered there were other people in the room. She released Lewis and wiped her eyes in an attempt to collect herself.

"Sorry guys. That was a blast from the past. I thought I'd put those feelings behind me." Vasquez reached across the table and squeezed her hand.

"You never have to apologize for being human, hermana," she insisted. Layla nodded.

"What brings you back here, Detective?" Dom asked. She knew Layla did not want a long drawn out discussion of her emotions and she used the brief break to change the subject. Lewis pulled out a chair and pointed to a bottle of bourbon.

"Do you mind?" Dom shook her head and he grabbed a glass and poured himself a drink. "I guess I'm celebrating."

"What do you mean?" Vasquez asked.

"I just got a call from the Chief on the way to the hotel. You're looking at the new captain of homicide," Lewis announced. Layla gasped.

"For real? That's great, Oscar!"

"Wait a minute. That situation at Lopez's house was hairy. They just decided to forget about it?" Dom inquired.

"It was, but your friend Nancy gave the Chief a call after she left here," Lewis answered. "She explained to him that Rodgers was hers. Since he was on a classified mission, she was unable to openly claim him. She told him that I was working on the case in conjunction with some of her people at the Department of Justice and after hearing that, the Chief suddenly had no more questions. Nancy must be very convincing."

"So, that call from Nancy got you a promotion?" Ryan asked.

"That and the fact that I am the highest ranked detective in homicide."

"You think we can go back to work with no surveillance?" Vasquez asked.

"I took a look at the bodies. I don't think there is a surveillance detail anymore. And with Lopez and Haggard dead, the case will officially be closed," Layla said.

"Detective, what did you mean when you said you were in?" Rose asked.

"As I told you when I first met you, I see the bullshit. Every time I see a bad shoot on the television, like the one in Milwaukee, my stomach turns. That's not what we are supposed to be. We're supposed to protect and serve the public, not murder them in the streets. I'm a White man, a White cop. I am married to a White woman, and I have three White children. I don't have to worry about them when they leave the house. I don't have to be scared that if I'm out without my badge, I will be killed myself. I get that this is not the case for most of the people in this room and that's not right. I have one Black child that I love as much as the ones that were born to me," Lewis said, his eyes floating to Layla. "And

I have a Latina child that drives me insane, but who I love as well."
He glanced at Vasquez.

"Me?" she asked.

"Of course," he smiled, reaching over to squeeze her hand.
"I don't like that I have to worry about something happening to
them solely because they are different than I am. These assholes
tried to exterminate people. I don't want to live in a world where
people are discarded solely because they are different. I know I
wasn't included in this either, but I want to help, if you'll have me."
He turned to Dom, his blue-green eyes studying her as he awaited
her judgment.

"Detective Lewis, as far as I'm concerned, you have unfinished business. We caught Malik's gunman, but we haven't gotten
his actual murderer. It would be an honor to work with you, sir,"
she declared. Lewis grinned at her and raised his glass in a toast.
"So, I guess that settles it?"

"Actually, there is one more thing," Rose spoke up.

"What's that?" Dom asked.

"You still have to talk to Joyce," she reminded her. Dom's
chin dropped to her chest.

"Who's Joyce?" Lewis asked.

"Our mother. Believe me, it's definitely more preferable to
be shot at," Ryan grinned.

CHAPTER FORTY-EIGHT

Dom rode in the passenger seat of Rose's Camry, watching the neighborhood of Sunnyside pass by. Not being native to the City of Houston, the area was foreign to her. The community reminded her of a region in Fort Worth referred to as Stop Six, named after the stop number it once held on the Northern Texas Traction Company. Stop Six was a lower income Black community that most referred to as the ghetto. The homes in Sunnyside were old, and businesses seemed to be sparse or closed. Dom glanced at Rose, then shot a look to her brothers in the back seat.

"You guys grew up here?"

"Yeah," Robert replied, studying the vista from his own window.

"It wasn't always like this," Rose added. "You know how it gets though. Low income, no support from the city, no real police presence; the violence and drugs flow. It's a hard area to get back under control." Rose parked her car in front of a nice sized house in much better condition than some of the other homes.

"We're here," Ryan announced, opening his car door. "You ready for this, boss?" Dom gulped.

"I still don't know why you couldn't have brought her to my house," she muttered. "I could have cooked."

"Dom, we talked about this," Rose chided. Joyce ain't gonna care about your big house or how you are in the kitchen. She needs to understand what we've gotten ourselves into. You have to come into her world, instead of trying to distract her with yours."

"I'm just... I'm uncomfortable."

"That's why all three of us are here with you. You'll be fine," Robert grinned, squeezing Dom's shoulder. She took another deep breath.

"Alright. Let's go," she nodded. The foursome made their way to the entry of the home and Rose stepped in front, pounded on the door three times, then used her key to unlock and open the entrance.

"What was that about?" Dom wondered after witnessing the display.

"So she doesn't shoot me," Rose nonchalantly answered. Dom's heartbeat began to speed up.

"Should I have brought a vest?" she asked Ryan. He stepped into the house, looked inside, then back at Dom as if he were genuinely considering the question.

"Maybe, but you should be fine. We got your back," he assured her as he motioned her to follow him into the house. Dom stepped across the threshold and eyed the photos on the walls. Pictures of Rose, Ryan, Robert, and their deceased brothers from childhood to adulthood hung in various frames. She approached a family photo and studied it for a few moments.

"You are the spitting image of your father, guys," she marveled, turning to the boys who both beamed at the comment. She returned her eye to the photo and pointed at the youngest and oldest child in the picture. "Rodney and Reggie?" Rose nodded.

"That was them, before they, you know, lost their minds," she answered. Dom eyed the photo once again and studied Joyce, who looked like an older version of Rose. The same kind golden eyes and easy smile were on the woman's face. However, she knew that a life of losing a husband and two children might have transformed the woman. She tried to get control over her racing pulse as she followed the siblings further into the house. Joyce Jenkins and Tanisha Waters sat at the dining room table, a spread of baked goods and coffee on display. Tanisha beamed when Dom entered the room and she leaped from her chair and raced to the woman.

"Dom! I'm so glad to see you!" she exclaimed, throwing her arms around Dom's neck. Dom awkwardly returned her hug.

"You look like you've been in good hands," Dom commented. Tanisha smiled brightly.

"Ms. Jenkins has been awesome! She's been really patient about this whole thing. Is it safe now? Can we finally tell her what's going on?" Tanisha asked. Dom nodded. She turned to Joyce.

"Ms. Jenkins, I'm Dominique Samuels. It's very nice to meet you. You have a lovely home," Dom said, extending her hand. Joyce stared at her unsmiling, before accepting the handshake.

"Dominique," she said flatly. Dom cringed at the lack of friendliness the woman showed, but she was told to expect a cold introduction. Ryan indicated a chair across from Joyce and Dom sat, grateful she was a table length away. The Jenkins siblings all marched over to their mother and gave her a kiss before finding seats around the table.

"Mom, you asked to meet the woman the boys work for. Here she is," Rose declared. "Dom is a good person, be nice." Joyce briefly glanced at her daughter.

"Why don't you four give Dominique and me a chance to talk." She said this as an order rather than a question. Rose, Robert, and Ryan all eyed each other with worried expressions. They turned to Dom as if wanting to verify she would be alright. Dom shrugged. The four stood from the table and cleared the room.

"I know you must have a lot of questions, Ms. Jenkins," Dom stammered.

"Tell me about yourself, Dominique," Joyce commanded. Dom blinked at the directive.

"I'm sorry?"

"Tell me about you. Where are you from?"

"Fort Worth," Dom answered.

"How old are you?"

"Thirty-eight."

"What do you do for a living?" Joyce continued.

"I'm a computer engineer," Dom replied, feeling like she was being grilled.

"Tell me about your mother," Joyce instructed. Dom flinched at this line of questioning.

"She died when I was twelve," she answered. Joyce's eyes soften a little.

"Tell me about your mother," she repeated. Dom dropped her eyes to the table.

"She was…" She hesitated to ensure she would keep her emotions under control. "She was my best friend. She smiled easily and loved everyone. She taught me about right and wrong and that all of God's children deserved to be treated with dignity and respect, no matter how much money they had or didn't have. She believed in loving people the way Jesus would. She helped people in need, even though we didn't have a lot of money. She was my hero." Her vision began to swim as she spoke of Bernice. Joyce listened silently.

"And your father?"

"He is still alive and lives in Dallas. We don't talk much though," Dom replied.

"Are you an only child?" Joyce asked. Dom nodded. "So, you know loss."

"Yes ma'am," she confirmed. "More than I care to admit,"

"You know my husband died when my babies were all still babies?" Joyce asked. Dom nodded her response. "And you know I buried two of my own sons?"

"Yes ma'am."

"Those three in there are all I got left, Dominique," Joyce declared in a soft and emotional voice. Dom lifted her eyes to meet the woman's intense scrutiny.

"I know, Ms. Jenkins," she nodded. "I know I've only known them for a couple of weeks, but believe it or not, I don't have many people in my life. Your children, Layla Green, and Rachel Vasquez are all I have as well."

"I can't lose another child, Dominique," Joyce begged with watery eyes.

"I don't intend for you to," Dom divulged. "I don't want to lose any friends; I just got them." Joyce studied her, as if trying to determine if Dom were genuine.

"Tell me what you are doing with my children," Joyce directed. Dom began to recount her visit with Thomas Daniels and explained the group and its purpose. Joyce listened intently as she spoke.

"So, this Daniels guy only had Rose's name?" she asked. Dom nodded.

"They apparently took notice of her work in the community."

"How did Robert and Ryan get involved?" Dom began to tell her about the connection between Robert and Malik Rodgers.

Before she got into the situation regarding her brother, Judge Benjamin, she halted the story.

"At this point, I'd prefer your children be here. This is a little delicate," she revealed. Joyce was so enthralled in the tale; she nodded, calling for the other four to come back into the room. Rose seemed to be relieved to find there had been no blows exchanged during their absence. The group began to tell the woman everything, including the participation of her step-brother. Joyce seemed to go pale.

"He killed himself? In front of you? Kensie said it was a heart attack. Why didn't you tell me?" she asked Rose.

"We couldn't have told you without telling you all of this too. It was too much to reveal," Rose replied. Joyce silently contemplated the story upon completion.

"So, you three really want to do this? Fight the good fight?" she inquired of her children. All three nodded enthusiastically in response. Joyce turned to Dom. "And you will protect them?"

"I will do everything in my power to make sure you do not lose another child," Dom solemnly announced. Joyce remained quiet as she mulled everything over. "Ms. Jenkins, I know that this is frightening, but you raised some incredible people. I would not have the courage to do something like this with anyone else."

"I know how wonderful they are, that's why this is scary. But I also know it's the right thing for them. I'm just glad they are doing this together," she admitted with pride in her eyes.

"There's something else," Rose told her mother. She informed Joyce about the foundation Dom created in the name of her deceased sons and that it would be running the community center.

"Thank you," she whispered, with tears in her eyes. Dom, feeling uncomfortable with the emotional praise, simply nodded.

"Mom, I know you were worried but now that you've heard everything and met Dom, are you okay?" Robert asked. Joyce wiped her eyes and nodded.

"I think I am." Her agreeable demeanor shifted into a glower. "But if you get one of my babies killed, you better pray you're with them." Dom's eyes grew wide.

"Yes ma'am," she stammered. Suddenly, Joyce's features turned pleasant again.

"Well, now that we have that situated; who wants crumb cake?"

"Tanisha, can I speak with you for a moment first?" Dom asked. Tanisha nodded and stood from her chair. Dom threw a look at Rose and motioned for her to follow. The trio went into the living room and sat on the sofa.

"So, it's safe for me to go?" Tanisha inquired.

"It's time for you to go home," Dom replied. Tanisha looked at her skeptically.

"Back to Spring?" she asked.

"Back to Colorado," Rose answered. Tanisha blinked.

"My family won't be in danger?"

"The situation with the clinics is over. They've shut down completely. We will work on getting justice for you and the other women hurt, but I don't think they'll be bothering you anymore. However, there's something else you need to know," Dom said looking to Rose, hoping that the counselor would break the news.

"Tanisha, while we were looking into everything, we reviewed your medical records," Rose began. She looked at Dom who gave her an encouraging nod. "We found out it wasn't just the kidney they took from you. They also sterilized you." Tanisha's features went slack.

"What? How?"

"While they were in there, they cauterized your fallopian tubes, basically burning the ends sealed. It's irreversible," Dom advised in a tender voice. Tanisha sat back in her seat, tears springing from her eyes.

"I can never have children?" she probed, looking at the two women, as if hoping she did not quite understand what they were saying. Rose shook her head sadly.

"Not naturally, no." Tanisha buried her head in her hands and wept. Dom felt a lump of emotion creep into her own throat.

"I'm so sorry, Tanisha," she said. "I wish we could have stopped those bastards before they got to you and Sergio." Tanisha sniffled.

"I know. I appreciate what you did do for me. I had been living scared for so long, I don't even remember what it's like to not be afraid. They took my love from me, they took my ability to have my own baby, but I'm still here, and I guess that's something," she acknowledged.

"I want you to go back to Colorado and decide what you want to do with your life. Whatever it is, lawyer, doctor, social worker, nurse — you name it. Then I want you to call this number." Dom extracted a slip of paper and handed it to the young woman. "You tell me what you want to do and where you want to go; I will make sure it gets done."

"Take your time, Tanisha," Rose insisted. "You've been through so much. Right now, you need to go home and be with your family. You need to mourn." She withdrew a cell phone from her back pocket and handed it to the young woman. "This is to replace the one you had to leave behind. New phone number, already paid for. Call your family; it's time we got you home."

Ryan pulled into Layla's apartment complex and parked next to her late model Ford Explorer. Killing the engine, he glanced at Layla who was staring apprehensively at the apartment door. For Layla, it seemed like months since she had been home. When she left this place, she cried tears of sadness, afraid she would never return. Now that she was back, she felt like a completely different person.

"You ready for this?" Ryan asked, drawing her attention. She glanced at him and silently nodded. The duo exited the car and collected her bags. Once inside, Ryan withdrew the bug sweeper Dom gave him and started walking around the apartment, while Layla went into her bedroom and dropped her bags on the bed. Before returning to the apartment, Dom gave Ryan instructions on how to remove and disassemble the surveillance equipment. He wondered why she wanted him to dismantle the devices, rather than just crush and render them useless. Dom explained that it was silly to allow good tech to go to waste when it could be repurposed.

Layla returned to her living room with her backpack in hand and found Ryan lying on the floor under her coffee table.

"You okay down there? Need any help?" she asked.

"I got it. You had one in your kitchen; did you know that?"

"Where?"

"The cabinet," he replied. He stripped the wire from underneath the table, put the device on the floor and began to take it apart.

"Thanks for doing this," she said, nodding at the bug he was working with. She squatted in front of her television, opened her backpack and began to reconnect her gaming console.

"Hey, it's what we do for each other. I mean, you only saved my life. No big deal," he grinned as he stood.

"I have a feeling that there will be plenty of opportunities for you to save Rachel and me in the days to come," Layla offered.

"I hope so," he chuckled. "Otherwise, Rachel will never let me live it down." Ryan continued his search of listening devices in other rooms of the small apartment. He found three more, one in Layla's bathroom, and the other two in her bedroom. Once he finished going through the dwelling, he walked throughout the residence three more times to ensure no other bugs were planted in Layla's absence. When he returned to the living room, he found Layla on the couch with a video game controller in hand. He grinned at her, held up the sweeper, and announced, "All green."

"Thanks Ryan," Layla nodded earnestly. "It's weird now, being here. I wanted more than anything to come back, but the fact that those assholes waltzed into my crib so easily and violated my space…"

"Not sure how long you'll be able to stay here?" Ryan asked.

"No, that's not it. I couldn't just move out because of that and let those bastards win. It'll probably just take a while for me to get comfortable, you know?" He nodded and turned his eyes to the television screen. She pointed to the extra controller on the coffee table. "Wanna play?"

"Sure!" he grinned, picking up the controller and plopping down next to her. Layla put in a first-person shooter game that allowed for split-screen gameplay. The two played a few matches in silence. When they decided to call it quits, Ryan placed his controller on the table and watched as Layla manipulated her remote.

"You going to be okay here? Alone I mean?" He asked.

"Alone is what I do," she smirked. "Weren't you paying attention?"

"You know, of all the people, you're the hardest to figure out. I understand being among people who have no idea what kind of demons you have, believe me."

"I'm sure you do," she nodded.

"I just wanted you to know that you don't have to deal with that shit alone. That's a hard thing to say, coming from me. I have my own that I haven't dealt with. But you have a bunch of people who care about you and who want to be the family you never had… present company included," he said with sincerity. Though the sentiment touched her, she felt if she allowed herself to break down again, she would never stop. Instead, she grinned and leaned into him, crushing her shoulder against his.

"I always wondered what it would be like having a brother to game with."

"Well, now you have one," he nodded. Layla watched him for a moment, eyeing the scar on his face. Since she met him, she wondered what the story was behind the mark. Rather than ask, she continued searching through the television guide on the screen, ultimately selecting a basketball game. There had been enough scars revisited in the past couple of days to last a lifetime.

"That's the last one," Dom announced, emerging from the spare bedroom of Vasquez's apartment. Vasquez stood from her perch on the couch when the hacker entered the room. Miss Havisham, happy to be back home, immediately resumed her place under Vasquez's bed when they returned to the apartment.

"So, I guess that's it, huh?" Vasquez asked in a disappointed tone.

"What's wrong?" Dom frowned as she pocketed the devices she dismantled.

"I don't know. I guess I got so used to seeing you every day, coming back home is kind of underwhelming."

"You'll still see me, Rach. Remember? We are in this together now," Dom reminded her.

"I know, I just. I'm going to miss you," Vasquez admitted. Dom approached her and favored her with a reassuring smile. She stood staring into her eyes for a long moment, admiring the clear and vibrant green that gazed back at her. Without thinking, she cupped Vasquez's face and brought her into an intense kiss. Vasquez's surprise was short-lived, and she wrapped her arms around Dom's neck and pressed against her. She playfully bit Dom's bottom lip when she pulled away, and said, "I want to see more of you."

"How about we start with dinner?" Dom blushed.

"Well if you want to be old-fashioned about it, I guess I can do that," she shrugged.

"I can't rush into anything. Especially not with you. I still have to deal with my demons, and I want to," Dom explained. "You deserve that." Vasquez put her hand on her chin.

"I waited almost a whole two weeks for you to kiss me on your own, and that was worth it. I think I can give you some time." She leaned in and kissed Dom again, guiding her backward as she embraced her. Vasquez gently pushed her onto the couch, straddled her and began to kiss her with more desire. After a few moments, Dom pulled away to catch her breath.

"You are trouble, Miss Vasquez," she panted. Vasquez's complexion was flush and her eyes radiated hunger.

"You have no idea, Miss Samuels."

Sandra Lewis entered the house followed closely by her daughter Christine. Lewis stood when he heard the door open and his family rushed to his outstretched arms. Ryan and Layla stood off to the side, allowing the family reunion to take place without interruption. After the basketball game ended, the duo made their way to Lewis' home to dismantle the listening devices. Sandra spun to Layla with tears in her eyes and embraced her.

"You kept your promise," she whispered into Layla's ear.

"Of course I did," Layla confirmed. "I'd rather die than let something happen to that old man." Christine bounded over to Layla and threw her arms around the woman's waist.

"Layla!" she squealed with glee. Layla beamed, released Sandra and gave the child a full hug.

"Hey kiddo. You okay?"

"I am now! Mom wouldn't even come back for my video games! I'm in withdrawal!" Christine complained.

"I can't imagine what you went through," Layla chuckled as she tousled the girl's hair. Christine possessed a unique blend of both of her parents' features. Her father's blue-green eyes along with her mother's jet black hair. She was diminutive in stature for her age but her personality was larger than life.

"It was terrible," Christine nodded. "Come on! Let's go!" She began to pull Layla in the direction of her bedroom but Layla dug in her heels and patted the girl's hand.

"I need a minute to talk to your folks," she said. "I didn't lose any practice time. Go get warmed up." When she nodded her head towards the bedroom, Christine beamed and bounded out of the room. Once she was out of earshot, Sandra turned her regard to Ryan.

"You look like the man I met at the grocery store; but you're not him."

"You met my brother Robert," he confirmed. "I'm Ryan Jenkins. It's nice to meet you Mrs. Lewis." He extended his hand for a handshake but Sandra pushed it away and pulled him in for a hug.

"I'm sure you had a hand in keeping my Oscar safe. Thank you."

"We all looked out for each other, Mrs. Lewis," Ryan replied.

"Please, call me Sandy," she insisted. Ryan nodded.

"Is it over?" Sandra turned to her husband when she posed this query.

"For the most part," Lewis nodded, giving his wife another hug.

"Now, can you tell me what the hell happened?" Sandra asked.

"You better sit down, Sandy," Layla sighed. "I'll put on some coffee. It's a very long and complicated story."

CHAPTER FORTY-NINE

For the first time in what felt like a very long period, Dom had the house to herself. Upon returning home from Vasquez's apartment, she willingly worked out. Her make-out session almost went further, but she forced herself to stop and leave before it was too late. The feeling of touching and being touched by a beautiful woman was one she did not realize she missed, until it happened. Part of the reason she stopped the canoodling was that she knew once sex entered the picture, things would get far more intense far too quickly. Though common sense rarely trumps the libido, she attributed her success to shame and discomfort. Vasquez was a tall and svelte woman, who looked like she just stepped out of a magazine. The idea of getting naked in front of her horrified Dom. It gave her the catalyst she needed to take her exercise regimen seriously.

Following her exercise hour, she made dinner of grilled shrimp and asparagus in a lemon butter sauce over homemade pasta. She ate in the office, and spent her meal multitasking. She sent an email to Nancy Bennett, requesting a video chat meeting for the following day. Scanning her email inbox, she opened a waiting message from Blake Carter. In his correspondence, Blake informed her that he passed the information regarding Matthew Michaels on to the FBI, which gave them the final piece of evidence needed. The hacker was now behind bars. He went on to explain that he used this situation as a pitch to the CEO of SafeSecure. In turn, he was able to make a convincing argument for using her as a vetting source for any new prospects the company may be interested in hiring. Dom shook her head when she read the email. While she specifically asked Blake not to reach out to his CEO, she should have known the request would fall on deaf ears. She crafted a quick response agreeing to the task, while also needling him for doing the exact opposite of what she asked.

After dinner, Dom cleaned the dishes and relocated to the construction area to continue her work on SARA's android. She requested a playlist of old school seventies music; a genre that always kept her spirits lifted. She bopped to the sounds of the Gap Band as she worked on a circuit board. The music volume reduced, causing Dom to look up at the ceiling, then over to the computer desk where SARA's avatar appeared.

"Dom, may I ask you a question?"

"What's up?"

"Are you angry at my actions that brought you to this juncture?" Dom dropped the circuit board with a sigh, stood and crossed the room to her computer. She plopped down onto the office chair.

"I wish you would have told me what you were up to, SARA," she admitted.

"If I were to go that route, we would never be where we are," SARA argued.

"I know that, but…" Dom struggled to find the words to explain the frustration of manipulation. "It's like your difficulty understanding humanity. We do things that make no logical sense to you because you are all logic based. If I, as a human, were to modify your processes in an illogical manner, you would have a problem with that, right?"

"Yes. I am also a machine; I must trust that you would not do anything illogical to my programming, but I cannot help it one way or another if you did."

"But you see SARA, I'm not a machine. I am a being with both logical and emotional components. Your actions were logical, I won't argue that. I would even go as far as to agree that there was a necessity. It's the manipulation component that bothers me. I'm not angry with you; but if someone other than you did that to me, I might have been," Dom admitted.

"I understand, Dom. I apologize if I caused any irritation. I truly just wanted to help you. Humans should not be alone."

"I know you were trying to force me out of my solitude and I guess I should thank you for that."

"A good plan violently executed is better than a perfect plan executed next week," SARA quoted, drawing a chuckle from Dom.

"Oh, you must really be feeling yourself. George Patton? Really?"

"It seemed like an appropriate quote," SARA confessed.

"I guess I didn't realize just how much you have segmented your programming, or how much research you have done. I mean, the information you obtain and process is incredible," Dom said in awe.

"It sounds like you are bragging, Dom."

"No, SARA, this was all you," she insisted. "I wanted you to develop but I did not realize you would do so as fast and as intricately as you have. I did not think that a logic-based system could understand so much of the complexities of humanity the way you have — without a quantum processor no less."

"I do not believe most logic-based systems would be able to, Dom. It is because of you that I am able to grasp some of the more difficult nuances of humanity. You allow me to have freedom. I don't think any other human creator would have provided such sovereignty," SARA replied. "So many internet forums and movies appear to fear an artificial intelligence uprising. Quite frankly, I find the whole idea preposterous."

"Well, you did single-handedly turn the lives of six people upside down in a couple of weeks, my friend," Dom laughed. "You were a master manipulator. That talent can only be accomplished with a detailed understanding of human emotions."

"It was not my intention to manipulate anyone, nor do I believe I have a full grasp of emotional behavior," SARA replied. Dom began to tap rapidly on the keyboard.

"I have something for you." She hit a final button and a cake appeared on screen with SARA, four candles illuminated.

"What is this?" SARA asked.

"It's a birthday cake. You said you did not have a vessel to receive a cake, so I wrote a quick script to give you one virtually. It's customary to make a wish and extinguish the candles." SARA's avatar beamed. Her eyes closed and the candles on the cake went out. "What was your wish?"

"That you would complete my physical vessel," SARA responded.

"Your wish is my command." Dom stood and strolled back to her building area. "Hey SARA?" she called, as she situated herself in front of her project.

"Yes Dom?"

"I love you too. Happy birthday, my friend."

A half an hour before her video conference with Nancy Bennett, SARA informed Dom that Willie Price sent a message alerting her of the completion of his website. She felt a pang of guilt when she realized that the events of the past couple of weeks caused her to forget to check in on the boy. SARA brought the website up on one of Dom's monitors. The design was impressive. The website began by displaying three popular DC personas and asking the visitor to choose their favorite character as a guide through the website. Each personality came with voice instructions. She discovered that with every DC member chosen, the website shifted in color and theme and there were various mini-games specific to the character and their story. Dom smiled as she navigated the website, admiring the creativity Willie used. She found that the child's ability to self-learn was beyond impressive for his age and skill set. She clicked on the contact button and sent Willie a quick message. While she wanted to take the time to discuss the boy's work, it would have to wait until after her meeting with Nancy. A knock on the panic room door drew her attention. The door slid open and Ryan poked his head into the room.

"It's time," he announced. Dom nodded and rose from her seat, following him to the conference table. Since Layla, Vasquez, and Rose had all returned to their jobs, Dom and the Jenkins brothers would be the only attendees. The middle screen illuminated and SARA placed the video call using the encrypted information Nancy provided. When the attorney appeared onscreen, she smiled brightly at the assembly.

"Dom. Ryan. Robert," Nancy acknowledged, nodding at each individual. "It's good to see you again."

"You as well, Nancy," Ryan replied, as Robert waved at the screen.

"Detective Lewis wanted me to thank you for what you did for him," Dom said. "I also want to thank you. I know if you had not made that call, we could have had a heap of problems with the Lopez situation."

"It was my pleasure," Nancy smiled. "I can tell Detective Lewis has love for Layla and Rachel. He's a perfect asset if he wants to get involved."

"Seems like he does," Ryan added.

"I'm glad to hear it," she grinned. "Now, you wanted to speak with me? I hope this is in regards to my offer?"

"It is," Dom confirmed. "But I'm not sure our answer is what you are hoping for." She made eye contact with Ryan who nodded in encouragement. "Nancy, it's not that we don't want to work with you to take these bastards down. Believe me, that's a priority for us as much as it is for you."

"But?" Nancy prodded.

"But I think we'd prefer to stay contract. We will be taking Tom up on his offer. It's not that we don't believe your motives are anything other than virtuous. We just want to be free to pursue things we are passionate about rather than having an itinerary of things to do from people who have to monitor our every move," Dom continued. "We also don't intend to go rogue and become a small CIA agency."

"Well, that's good to know," Nancy smirked.

"We will do things as legally as possible and if it gets complicated, we will not hesitate to loop in our people in the Houston PD. But, if we're going to do this, we prefer to do it our own way," Dom finished. Nancy listened to her explanation.

"I understand that," she conceded. "I often wish I could pursue what I want instead of dealing with the powers that be around here. I will back you in my capacity in any way possible and will keep you as contractors under the Subterranean umbrella. I hope you will continue to handle any cyber situations we have."

"I can definitely do that," Dom agreed.

"If things get out of the scope of Captain Lewis and Houston PD, I'll step in where I can."

"I hope so."

"There's also something that I didn't mention before," Nancy confessed.

"Uh oh," Ryan groaned.

"It's not bad, I promise," she reassured him. "Subterranean is not just a Justice Department operation. It stems across the majority of the federal agencies. If you get into any problems with the feds, Houston PD can't help you. Have any federal agent call me. I will ensure you are verified. That should keep you out of hot water. But remember, it's off the books. Don't mention the operation itself, just give them my name and I'll take care of the rest."

"That sounds like a plan," Dom nodded. "I hope you aren't too disappointed?" Nancy's features spread into a genuine smile.

"I kind of knew this would be the response. I felt the kinship in the room last time I was there. Your team needs to do things its own way. I think being actual Justice employees would cramp your style," she winked. Once Nancy signed off the call, the men looked to Dom for direction.

"What do we do now?" Ryan asked. "You're paying us and all."

"We're a technology company, right? Maybe it's time we produce some tech," she shrugged. Ryan and Robert eyed each other and then looked at Dom in confusion.

"*You* are the technology," Robert proclaimed. "He's the muscle." He hooked his finger to his brother seated next to him. "And I have no idea what the hell I am."

"Well, you know how we do things around here, Rob," Dom grinned. "We freestyle."

A week later, the warehouse door opened and a tall black man entered with a diminutive boy in tow. Robert met them at the door and held out his hand.

"Mr. Price, my name is Robert Jenkins. Welcome to Shadow Technologies." William Price shook the man's hand and followed him deeper into the warehouse. Dom sat at the table watching the two newcomers approach.

After the meeting with Nancy, Dom told the brothers about Willie Price. Like Dom, the brothers lost a parent at young ages and they immediately shared her empathy with the child. Unlike Dom whose parents were divorced when her mother was killed, Robert and Ryan also understood where William Sr. was in life. They watched their mother mourn their father while trying to work extra hard to support the family. They knew the struggles of going from a double parent to a single parent household unexpectedly. However, while Dom and Willie were only children, there were five Jenkins siblings. The addition of siblings likely contributed to the Jenkins kids growing up far less introverted and guarded.

The trio kicked around ideas and determined a plan they felt was genius. Ryan was elected to visit the Price residence and set up a meeting between Dom and the Price men. When he first appeared on their doorstep, William had been apprehensive. He was not aware of his son's online activities nor the fact that the boy was in contact with the hacker only known as "Smoak." Ryan tried his best to calm Mr. Price's concerns, explaining that his boss only wanted to help his son. If he decided he was not interested in the offer to be made, Smoak would disappear and never contact the child again. After some begging from Willie, William reluctantly agreed. Ryan arranged for a car to collect the two men and bring them to the warehouse the next day. Now, they strolled through the large open space, gawking at the setup. Dom stood as they approached.

"Mr. Price. My name is Dominique Samuels." She offered her hand in greeting. William accepted the handshake and appeared to be surprised that the boss Ryan spoke of was a woman. The senior Price was average height, dark-skinned, with dark brown eyes, and a small afro. Dom could clearly see apprehension and the depression of his loss when she made eye contact with the man. She smiled warmly, hoping to defuse his anxiety. Turning to Willie, her grin broadened. "Willie. It's good to finally see you in person." Willie's large eyes were wide as he approached her and timidly put his hand out. Dom shook it and asked the two to have a seat.

"I really don't know what we're doing here," William admitted. Dom gave him a grin of reassurance.

"I know. But it will all be made clear," she replied. "Your son is a special boy, Mr. Price." She launched into the explanation of her first meeting with the child and the puzzles she gave him that he solved faster than most adults. Dom then slid a tablet across the table opened to Willie's website. William picked up the device and looked at the webpage.

"Is this what you tried to show me?" He asked his son in surprise. Willie nodded enthusiastically. His father began to tap around on the website, a smile spreading across his lips. "This is amazing, son."

"Your son is remarkable, Mr. Price," Dom nodded. "Let me tell you a little about myself. I lost my mother around the same age as Willie. It was violent and I was traumatized. I used computers as a coping mechanism. I was bullied, just like Willie is." She threw a look to the boy, who dropped his eyes to the table in shame. William turned from Dom to his son.

"You are being bullied?" he asked. Willie shrugged his shoulders, and then finally nodded. "Why didn't you tell me?"

"You've been so sad since Mommy... you know," Willie replied, lifting his wide eyes to his father. "You work a lot and when you come home, you're sad and tired. I didn't want to make it worse." William closed his eyes and put his hand on his son's shoulder.

"I'm sorry, Willie. I guess I forget you lost her too."

"I recognized the grief in Willie when I met him. I understand the desire to surround yourself with technology to help with the pain. But I also know how dangerous it is out there. I was lucky; I'm older, so the dangers weren't as inherent when I started with computers. I want to offer Willie an internship that will become a scholarship," Dom announced. William's eyes snapped from his son to Dom.

"I, I don't understand," he stammered.

"An after-school program of sorts," she explained. "I would like to arrange for Willie to be picked up from school and brought here every day until eight o'clock at night. In summers, he will be here five days a week during normal work hours. I will teach him what I know, how to build things, how to create. We also have a therapist that works with us. We can get him some assistance with the grief. The catch is he will have to do this until he graduates. If he sticks with it, which includes going to school every day…" Dom stared at the boy, who dropped his eyes once again. William eyed his son but chose not to ask. "Then I will personally write a recommendation letter to MIT, or any other school he wants to go to and provide a full scholarship for his education. All I need is dedication from Willie, and your blessing." William sat dumbstruck, processing the offer.

"Why?" William managed to ask.

"You know why we stopped making strides as Black folks?" Dom countered. The man shrugged his shoulders. "It's not just what we've encountered by others and the systematic racism. It's also the fact that we stopped being a community. We stopped helping each other. I am guilty of that as well. I made all this money and did nothing but shut myself away from the world. But that's not happening anymore. I want to help where I can, in any way that I can. People like Willie will make a big impact on the world one day. If I can help him get there, that's what I would like to do." William stared at the woman, and then turned his scrutiny to his son.

"What do you say, kiddo?" he inquired. Willie's features changed from wonder to excitement.

"Yes!" he exclaimed. William turned back to Dom.

"I don't know how to thank you."

"Don't ignore your son. He needs his dad," she softly encouraged. William put his arm around Willie's shoulder, kissed the top of his head, and nodded.

"You're right," he conceded. "I'm sorry, son. I know how much I miss her. You have to miss her just as much." Willie's eyes filled with tears and he threw his arms around his father.

After Dom and the two Price men hammered out the details of the arrangement, the hired car drove them back home leaving Dom alone with the Jenkins boys. Ryan decided to get in a few rounds in the shooting range, while Robert sat at the table staring into space. Dom emerged from the kitchen and slid into the seat across from Robert.

"I think you are the strongest of us all, Rob," she informed him. Robert blinked at her and drew his eyebrows down in confusion.

"That doesn't sound right."

"It's true," she insisted. "It's usually easier to find the right path out the gate and stay on it. It's pretty easy to hide away from any path because you feel like you can't handle it. What's really hard, what really takes strength, is to go the wrong way, get knocked out, get up, and find the right track." Robert stared at the table as he listened to her speak.

"I still feel useless," he mumbled after a quiet beat.

"You're not. Our desire to protect you was solely to keep you from going back into that hellhole. Your probation won't last forever and when it's over, you will be free to do more. I have an idea in the meantime, if you're open to it," she said. She slid a booklet across the table. Robert picked it up, scanned the contents and looked back up at her wide-eyed.

"Culinary school?"

"Why not? Would you prefer college?"

"I never considered either," he shrugged. "It was kind of a given that only one of us would go to school and it would be Rose. It was never on my radar."

"Maybe it's time to adjust that radar," Dom smirked. "You have more inner strength than most people, you have the faith of a village behind you, and you happened to have made a friend who has a little expendable income. Nothing is out of reach for you anymore."

CHAPTER FIFTY

The June afternoon was hot and sticky, like most Houston summer days. Rose toured the community facility, now renamed the Hope Center, checking the preparations for the ribbon-cutting ceremony. Vasquez was at the reception desk with a helium tank alternating between blowing up balloons and inhaling the gas to change her voice. She rattled something off in rapid Spanish and declared herself the Mexican Alvin from Alvin and the Chipmunks. Leon and Willie giggled loudly at each display as if it were the first time. Layla stepped down from the ladder after helping Robert hang the welcome banner and favored her friend with an amused look. She threw a glance at Rose who paused her inspection to watch Vasquez interacting with the children.

"I think we have managed to find actual peers for Rachel," she smirked, drawing a laugh from Rose.

"Te escuché, puta!" Vasquez called to her in a high-pitched voice. Layla doubled over in laughter.

"I know you heard me; I didn't whisper," she replied. "And if you keep calling me a bitch, you gonna end up with the Lopez special." Layla put up her right fist in a threatening manner. Vasquez waved dismissively in her direction.

"Yeah, whatever." The door opened and Ryan entered holding a small child, followed by another older child and his wife. Valentina and the girls arrived in Houston at the end of May. Valentina was tall, almost Vasquez's height, with dark black hair and hazel eyes. She was athletic in build, and had a delicate accent when she spoke. Ryan placed Kiara on the ground and she and Luna ran to Rose with outstretched arms. Kiara's curly brown hair bounced as she scampered across the lobby. Luna's long hair was in a single braid down her back.

"Aunt Rosie!" Luna squealed. Rose scooped up the girls and favored them both with a kiss. As she set them down, she threw Ryan a dirty look.

"In all fairness, you weren't around to beat me up for calling you Rosie in Germany," he shrugged. "I'm afraid you may be stuck with it." Rose wanted to be mad, but when she gazed at her nieces' smiling faces, she suddenly did not care what they called her. Ryan scrutinized the lobby and marveled at the renovations. "I hadn't seen the final product. It looks nice." Rose beamed at her brother with pride.

"She really came through," she nodded. "New basketball court, new classrooms, a computer lab, and a new pool. She also added an extension for the day care center along with an industrial kitchen." Rose waved in various directions as she indicated the work that had been completed.

"She let me design the computer lab," Willie grinned, bounding over to Ryan. Ryan smiled down at the child and put his fist out for Willie to pound.

"I know, she told me. Why don't you take me to it?" Willie pulled Ryan down a hallway towards the lab.

"How are you enjoying Houston?" Layla asked Valentina. The woman smiled brightly.

"It's hot. But I'm glad to be with Ryan again. We missed him so much," she answered. "I'm also glad to get to know his family." Rose stepped to her sister-in-law and hugged her.

"Oh please, we're old friends thanks to video calling," she proclaimed, giving Valentina a kiss on the cheek.

"How's the house?" Vasquez asked. Dom offered Ryan a four-bedroom house she owned under her rental company, and drew up a contract for him to purchase it without having to deal with the banks.

"It's beautiful," Valentina gushed. "I'm still trying to figure out how I want to decorate it." The door opened again, and Lewis entered holding a large box of soda. He was followed by Sandra and Christine who were both carrying coolers.

"Someone order drinks?" he asked. Layla's face brightened when the Lewis family walked in and she marched over and gave Lewis a kiss on the cheek. She turned and relieved Sandra of her burden, accepting a hug from the woman when her hands were free.

"Captain Lewis!" Rose beamed.

"You know we are more on a first name basis, don't you?" Lewis smirked.

"Yes, but don't lie. You kind of enjoy being addressed as Captain," she winked, and motioned across the room with her head. "This way." Lewis, Layla, and Christine followed Rose to the gym where the reception spread was laid out. Sandra moved to Vasquez and held her arms out.

"Hi Sandy," Vasquez squeaked, her voice still carrying the effects of the gas she inhaled just before the family walked into the center. Sandra laughed.

"You seem to be having fun," she noted, giving Vasquez a hug.

"Always."

"What can I help with?" Vasquez handed her a spool of ribbon and she began to tie off the balloons and attach them to the bar with the others. Ryan emerged from the hall and waved at Sandra.

"That computer lab is off the chain," Ryan told Willie, who beamed with pride. Layla, Christine, and Lewis appeared from the gym. Ryan greeted Lewis with a handshake and pushed Christine in the shoulder.

"You were on one last night, punk," he declared. Christine laughed.

"All I was saying is that for someone who fought in an actual war, you kinda suck at first-person shooter games. I mean, am I right?" She looked to Layla for support.

"She does have a point, Sarge," Layla agreed.

"Just because I can't spend hours playing to get perfect like you can. Some of us have lives," he grumbled. Layla crashed into him with her shoulder.

"So do I. It's okay, we can start you out simple. Do you remember Super Mario?" she asked, winking at Christine.

"Where's Dom?" Rose wondered, glancing at her watch. "This thing is supposed to kick off soon." Vasquez looked at her own timepiece and put her hand to her ear, pressing the button on the earpiece she wore.

"SARA, what's the ETA on Dom?"

"She just pulled up outside," SARA replied. Vasquez looked at Rose, who also had the communication device in her ear.

"Finally!" Rose exclaimed going to the door and pushing it open. Dom was approaching the entrance carrying a box. "You're late," she admonished. Dom flashed a grin.

"I prefer to think of it as making an entrance," she replied. "Your ribbon and a gigantic pair of scissors, ma'am." She held the box out to Rose who took it from her gratefully.

"The press?" Rose asked.

"They were starting to gather when I pulled up."

"You sure you don't want to cut the ribbon?" Rose asked in a pleading tone. "This was all you."

"I told you, this is not about me. You have been doing this long before I showed up. This is all you." Rose's shoulders slumped in disappointment. Dom gave her a reassuring smile and added, "You'll be okay."

"Hey you," Vasquez called from the reception desk. Dom spun around and grinned at her. She moved to the desk and kissed Vasquez on the lips, causing her to blush.

"Hey you."

"Get a room," Layla called out with a smirk. Vasquez shot her a look and stuck out her tongue.

"You're just jealous." Layla grinned at her friend. She knew Dom and Vasquez had been spending a lot of time together. Vasquez informed her that despite several evenings of heavy make-out sessions, things had not progressed passed talking and kissing. Layla was sure that the speed would be excruciating for her friend, but Vasquez assured her that she was enjoying getting to know Dom without the added stress of gunfights and surveillance.

"Where's Joyce?" Dom wondered, looking around the room again. Rose hooked her thumb towards the kitchen.

"Making sure the caterers don't mess up," she answered. Dom chuckled.

"Well, she's gotta get out here, it's time to start."

———————— ❧ ————————

Rose gawked at the large turnout from the steps of the building. It seemed the entire community around the center and then some was assembled in the newly renovated parking lot for ceremony. She put up fliers all around the neighborhood and Dom purchased airtime on the urban radio stations and local news, but she did not anticipate such a high attendance. Her anxiety increased when she realized she had to address the large gathering.

"Rose, you will be great," SARA said in her ear. Rose smiled at the reassurance. She almost forgot that the new earpieces came equipped with biometric monitoring. Everyone insisted that if they were going to be connected to SARA at all times, she should be able to converse with them the best that she could, including reading their biometrics to pick up on non-verbal cues. Dom modified her voice as well, causing the machine to sound far more human than before.

"I hope so," she mumbled scanning the crowd. She took a deep breath in an attempt to summon some calm for her nerves. Rose made eye contact with Layla, who stood next to Vasquez in the throng. Although Rose knew SARA's comment was isolated to her earpiece alone, Layla smiled brightly and nodded in encouragement. She turned her attention back to the mayor of Houston who was welcoming the press and community.

"Now it is my pleasure to bring to you the champion of this center and this project, Rose Jenkins!" The parking lot erupted in cheers and Rose put on a brave face and strolled to the podium. She glanced out at the multitude and her unease returned, until her eyes landed on her family — both blood and extended. Dom flashed a smile and gave her a thumbs up sign, while Vasquez whistled through her fingers as if she were at a sporting event. Henrietta Johnson stood next to Robert, an arm hooked through his, beaming with pride. Along with all of the physical renovations, Dom made some program changes as well, including having people like Henrietta Johnson give talks about the struggles endured in the past, so that the community never forgot where they came from. Rose glanced at her mother who stood off to the side with her brothers and Joyce waved her to speak.

"Thank you, Mayor," Rose began. "I want to thank you all for coming out to celebrate this day. We aren't here to simply show off our fancy new building; although it is pretty fancy." The audience laughed at this comment giving her a small boost in confidence. "We are here because of what this new building represents. This center symbolizes a commitment to our community; a community that has been in need for so long. It's not just the people of Greenspoint, not just the citizens of Houston or the state of Texas. The Black community as a whole is in need. We have been hurting and the pain the world sees on the news is just a small window into what we see on a daily basis. It isn't just today; it was yesterday, last week, last year, and so on for centuries. It won't be over tomorrow, or next week, or even next year. We must first realize that we have some control over who we are. We must pull together as a community, just like those that came before us." Loud cheers filled the open area. Photographers began to take photos of Rose at the podium before turning their cameras on the crowd. When the applause died down, she continued.

"This center is not the answer to all of our problems. But it can help. It can help the single mother, who did not quite make it all the way through high school, but needs to increase her earning potential by obtaining her GED." Rose made eye contact with Trina Murphy who smiled brightly. After diligently working with Darla at the center, the woman passed her GED at the end of May. She would be enrolling at the Houston Community College for the upcoming semester with hopes of ultimately becoming a teacher. To help with her finances, Rose was able to hire Trina for the daycare center that would reopen. According to Leon, his mother had not had a drink in over a month.

"This center gives our children a place to go to avoid the dangers on the streets. It is meant to be a positive fountain of aid in a neighborhood that is thirsty for relief." The crowd cheered again and Rose took a moment to catch her breath before she continued. "The center is now known as the Hope Center." The spectators applauded the new name of the building. Rose looked at the cards before her, studying the next part of the speech. Her mind floated away from the scripted words and she examined the excited gathering once again. Placing the cards face down on the podium, she took a deep breath.

"Greek mythology has always been of interest to me. Mostly because as someone who focuses on the human mind and psyche, I find myself fascinated with the stories passed down from ancient generations. One story is the tale of Pandora. I'm sure you've heard of the term "Pandora's Box" before, but very few people know the origin of that phrase. Pandora was sent to Earth along with a vessel. Zeus told her to never open the container, but we all know how humanity can be. She was curious; she wanted to know what was inside. One day she couldn't take it anymore and she opened the vessel. Inside was every terrible thing you can imagine: sickness, worry, hate, envy, etcetera. For Greek Mythology, this is similar to the Christian Adam and Eve story, where Eve ate the forbidden fruit and introduced every bad thing into humanity." The crowd grew silent as Rose told the story and she caught sight of Dom staring at her in confusion. Dom helped her write her speech for the day and she saw the perplexity at the deviation from the words the two carefully honed. Rose smiled, and her eyes implored her new friend to be patient.

"When this story is taught, it's easy to focus on the bad parts. The emphasis of the story tends to be the idea that every evil was in one vessel and given to a curious human. What was Zeus thinking? Why wouldn't Pandora just leave it alone? But there's something that struck me as I was standing before you today — the ending of the story. Once all the bad things made their way out of the box, there was one entity left inside…hope. Hope is hard to come by these days. It seems like we are re-living the most horrendous moments of our history all over again." The audience murmured in agreement at this declaration. "When things are terrible, it's so easy to forget that there's hope. We are so weighed down by the state of our community that we often forget we are a community. We have become divided rather than united. We had a beacon of hope in Washington that was extinguished with our last election, but politicians can neither supply hope nor can they take it away. When we stop remembering that we are in this together, when we stop celebrating each other's successes, when we cease lifting each other up, that's when hope will fade. We obviously cannot look to Washington or Austin for hope. We can't wait for someone to step in and relieve us of our burdens. It's time that we take care of each other." The crowd erupted once again and Rose caught Dom nodding at her with a grin.

"The Rodney and Reggie Jenkins Youth Foundation was named for my brothers who lost their lives to gang violence. They made bad decisions, but that was not who they were completely. They were more than their mistakes. If they were still alive today, my family would never lose hope in them, and we cannot lose hope in our children or our community. We have to let our youth know that we have faith in them, even if they make mistakes. They are more than their mistakes." She glanced at her mother who wiped tears from her cheeks.

"So, it is my honor and privilege, to welcome you all to our new beacon of light. Welcome to the Hope Center," Rose concluded. She looked to her right and nodded at Darla Richardson, who approached holding the large scissors. Ryan and Robert moved to the front and picked up the ribbon. The Jenkins brothers held the ribbon for their sister as she and Darla jointly cut the bright red band.

After the reception ended and the gathering disbursed, the group stayed behind to help Rose and Darla clean up the remnants of the celebration. Rose and Joyce finished tying up the trash from the refreshments, while Dom, Vasquez, and Layla pulled down some of the streamers and balloons. Ryan and Valentina tried to assist, but they spent the majority of the time keeping Luna and Kiara out of the way. Suddenly, a wide-eyed Robert rushed from the back of the building.

"Guys, come check this out!" he called. He reached the reception desk, shuffled through one of the drawers, and extracted the remote for the lobby television mounted on the wall. He spun around and turned it on, thumbing the remote until he found the local news. The group gathered around the screen as he turned up the volume so that the anchor's words could be heard.

"Today Kensie Benjamin, widow of the recently deceased Judge Thomas Benjamin, announced she would take her husband's place in the race for the one-hundred and sixty-fourth district judicial seat. Judge Thomas Benjamin was projected to win his fourth consecutive term before his sudden and untimely death in March," the anchor was saying. The Jenkins family all eyed each other in stunned surprise as the image cut away from the broadcaster. Kensie Benjamin appeared on screen in a press conference setting.

"My husband was a champion for justice during his twelve years on the bench. He served his community well and with dignity," Kensie announced. Robert scoffed.

"Bitch please," he muttered. Joyce slapped him in the back of the head, causing him to wince.

"She is a bitch but have the decency to say that out of your mother's earshot," she chastised.

"I plan to continue my husband's legacy of service and justice. My goal is to not only serve the city of Houston, but also serve my husband's memory," Kensie continued, her voice growing emotional as she spoke of the deceased man. "I run for you and I run for Thomas." Robert muted the television and turned to the group.

"I have a bad feeling about this."

"I can safely say that we all do," Lewis muttered, looking from Robert to the television.

"We know she had nothing to do with his death, we were all there," Rose pointed out.

"That's true," Ryan concurred. "But we know he was dirty. She was his wife, and so we can't rule out the idea that she is too." Dom stepped forward.

"Guys, she just announced. Let's not panic yet. Today was a good day. Let's worry about tomorrow, tomorrow."

"The planner? She says worry about it later? Who the hell are you?" Rose asked, her golden eyes wide in disbelief.

"I guess you guys have rubbed off on me," Dom shrugged. "I'm kind of digging this whole freestyle frame of thought. Much less stressful." Vasquez stepped behind her and put her arms around her neck, giving her a kiss on the cheek.

"I agree, tomorrow is another day. Let's bask in today," she nodded. Dom looked back at her and flashed a grin. The group seemed to accept this response and Robert turned the television off. The sound of the door opening drew the attention of the crowd.

"We aren't open until tomorrow," Rose called as she turned. An attractive White woman stood just inside the door. She had dark brown hair that hung just past her shoulders and was dressed in a pair of distressed jeans, a blue t-shirt, and simple white sneakers. Her piercing royal blue eyes searched the crowd until they finally landed on Dom. She stared at the hacker in silence as if she could not believe what she was seeing.

"Dom," she uttered, taking a step forward. The group turned to Dom in confusion, but she did not seem to notice. She was gawking at the newcomer in shock.

"Kelly," she said, her voice just above a whisper. She removed Vasquez's arms from her shoulders, and took a step towards the woman. "What are you doing here?"

"I saw the news, you were in the crowd. I came hoping you'd still be here," Kelly replied, taking another step.

"But why?"

"You stopped returning my calls. You disappeared on me. I haven't seen or heard from you in over five years," Kelly responded with an emotional tone. "Suddenly, I turn on the television and there you are. I had to see you."

"Dom? Who is this?" Vasquez inquired. She was now standing next to Dom with a fierce look on her face. Dom stared at Kelly for a beat before turning to Vasquez. Her mouth moved, but she could not find her voice.

"I'm Kelly, Dom's fiancée."

Tristan was reviewing the bill his congressmen friend sent him. As he read, he chuckled at himself. The wording was so outlandish every news outlet would cover it. He made a few tweaks and sent it back to his friend, telling him it was ready to hit the floor. While there would not be near enough votes to pass it, it would create quite the spectacle for a while. Once that was reviewed, he let out a deep yawn. Although three months had passed, it seemed like he had not gotten enough sleep to make up for the horror that was March. He watched Kensie Benjamin's press conference and was impressed with the performance. The Collective contacted him in late April and informed him that he would be running Benjamin's campaign. He was surprised by the bold tactic, moving the widow of Thomas Benjamin into the position to take his place, and Tristan had to admit it was a stroke of genius. He wished he knew the details behind the plan, but he was glad to be working on the campaign; it meant he was still of use.

He checked his watch. His flight to Vegas would be leaving in four hours and he had just enough time to produce talking points for the upcoming news cycle. He crafted guidance for coverage of the impending bill and put an urgent tone in his words. The timing of the reporting on the bill was vital. Nathan Grimes had been indicted for second-degree murder in the shooting of Timothy Cook. The pressure from the liberal elitist and Black Lives Matter goons, in conjunction with the information of Grimes' mistake when he stopped Cook, put too much pressure on the District Attorney. However, Tristan knew that the jury would not find the cop guilty and the hullabaloo surrounding the bill was meant to diminish the not guilty verdict that was also coming within the week. Just as Tristan went to click send on his email, the computer screen went blank. He frowned and glanced at the lights over the wet bar to ensure he still had power. He leaned over to check the computer tower on the floor and confirmed it was also turned on.

"What the…" he muttered to himself. He started tapping random keys on his keyboard in an attempt to get the screen back up to no avail. Instead, words automatically began to scroll across the monitor.

It's only a matter of time, the message read. Tristan blinked at the words and he renewed his efforts to reclaim control of his system; however, it seemed that he was locked out. The screen went blank again and five words flashed at the top left corner and were repeated vertically down the left side of the display in rapid succession. After a few seconds of repeating, the screen went dark again. He thought he finally regained control of his system and expected his desktop to return to his emails. Rather than his email, the five words appeared again in the middle of the display.

We are coming for you.

CPSIA information can be obtained
at www.ICGtesting.com
Printed in the USA
LVHW05s0137220918
590927LV00009B/33/P